Science Fiction Masterpieces

Isaac Asimov

Science Fiction Masterpieces

Galahad Books   New York

Published in 1993 by

Galahad Books
A division of Budget Book Service, Inc.
386 Park Avenue South
New York, NY 10016

Galahad Books is a registered trademark of
Budget Book Service, Inc.

Published by arrangement with Davis Publications, Inc.

Library of Congress Catalog Card Number: 86-81057
ISBN: 0-88365-713-9

Printed in the United States of America.

ACKNOWLEDGMENTS

The editor makes grateful acknowledgment to the following authors and author's representatives for giving permission to reprint the material in this volume:

E. Amalia Andujar for *Softly Touch the Stranger's Mind* by E. Amalia Andujar, © 1978 by Davis Publications, Inc.

Isaac Asimov for Editorial: *Escape to Reality?* by Isaac Asimov, © 1980 by Davis Publications, Inc.; for *Good Taste* by Isaac Asimov, © 1976 by Isaac Asimov; for *How It Happened* by Isaac Asimov, © 1978 by Davis Publications, Inc.; for *The Missing Item* by Isaac Asimov, © 1977 by Davis Publications, Inc.; and for *Nothing for Nothing* by Isaac Asimov, © 1979 by Davis Publications, Inc.

Michael A. Banks for *Horseless Carriage* by Michael A. Banks, © 1978 by Davis Publications, Inc.

Michael A. Banks and George Wagner for *Lost and Found* by Michael A. Banks and George Wagner, © 1978 by Davis Publications, Inc.

Blackstone Literary Agency for *Keepersmith* by Randall Garrett and Vicki Ann Heydron, © 1978 by Davis Publications, Inc.; for *The Napoli Express* by Randall Garrett, © 1979 by Davis Publications, Inc.; and for *Polly Plus* by Randall Garrett, © 1978 by Davis Publications, Inc.

Herb Boehm for *Air Raid* by Herb Boehm, © 1976 by Herb Boehm.

F. M. Busby for *Backspace* by F. M. Busby, © 1977 by Davis Publications, Inc.

Jack Chalker for *Dance Band on the Titanic* by Jack Chalker, © 1978 by Davis Publications, Inc.

Jo Clayton for *A Bait of Dreams* by Jo Clayton, © 1979 by Davis Publications, Inc.

Conway Conley for *On the Way* by Conway Conley, © 1978 by Davis Publications, Inc.

Sharon N. Farber for *Born Again* by Sharon N. Farber, © 1978 by Davis Publications, Inc.

John M. Ford for *On the Q167 File* by John M. Ford, © 1978 by Davis Publications, Inc.

Alan Dean Foster for *Bystander* by Alan Dean Foster, © 1978 by Davis Publications, Inc.

David Gerrold for *Hellhole* by David Gerrold, © 1979 by David Gerrold.

Stephen Goldin for *When There's No Man Around* by Stephen Goldin, © 1977 by Davis Publications, Inc.

Jack C. Haldeman II for *Home Team Advantage* by Jack C. Haldeman II, © 1977 by Davis Publications, Inc.; for *Longshot* by Jack C. Haldeman II, © 1978 by Davis Publications, Inc.; and for *Louisville Slugger* by Jack C. Haldeman II, © 1977 by Davis Publications, Inc.

Robert Lee Hawkins for *A Simple Outside Job* by Robert Lee Hawkins, © 1977 by Davis Publications, Inc.

Linda Isaacs for *A Many Splendored Thing* by Linda Isaacs, © 1977 by Davis Publications, Inc.

Virginia Kidd, Literary Agent for *Against a Crooked Stile* by Nancy Kress, © 1979 by Davis Publications, Inc.

Nancy Kress for *A Delicate Shade of Kipney* by Nancy Kress, © 1977 by Davis Publications, Inc.

Anne Lear for *The Adventure of the Global Traveler* by Anne Lear, © 1978 by Davis Publications, Inc.

Frederick Longbeard for *A Time for Terror* by Frederick Longbeard, © 1979 by Davis Publications, Inc.

Barry B. Longyear for *Proud Rider* by Barry B. Longyear, © 1979 by Davis Publications, Inc.

6 ACKNOWLEDGMENTS

Frederick S. Lord, Jr. for *But Do They Ride Dolphins?* by Frederick S. Lord, Jr., © 1978 by Davis Publications, Inc.

Gary D. McClellan for *Darkside* by Gary D. McClellan, © 1978 by Davis Publications, Inc.

Dean McLaughlin for *Omit Flowers* by Dean McLaughlin, © 1977 by Davis Publications, Inc.

Drew Mendelson for *Star Train* by Drew Mendelson, © 1978 by Davis Publications, Inc.

Scott Meredith Literary Agency, Inc. for *Joelle* by Poul Anderson, © 1977 by Davis Publications, Inc.; for *Pièce de Résistance* by Jesse Bone, © 1978 by Davis Publications, Inc.; for *No Room in the Stable* by A. Bertram Chandler, © 1977 by Davis Publications, Inc.; and for *Quarantine* by Arthur C. Clarke, © 1976 by Davis Publications, Inc.

Melisa Michaels for *In the Country of the Blind, No One Can See* by Melisa Michaels, © 1978 by Davis Publications, Inc.

Robert P. Mills, Ltd. for *Guilt* by James Gunn, © 1978 by Davis Publications, Inc.; and for *Cautionary Tales* by Larry Niven, © 1978 by Davis Publications, Inc.

Keith Minnion for *Ghosts* by Keith Minnion, © 1979 by Davis Publications, Inc.

Henry Morrison, Inc. for *The Last Defender of Camelot* by Roger Zelazny, © 1979 Davis Publications, Inc.

Patricia Nurse for *One Rejection Too Many* by Patricia Nurse, © 1978 by Davis Publications, Inc.

Kevin O'Donnell, Jr. for *Low Grade Ore* by Kevin O'Donnell, Jr., © 1977 by Davis Publications, Inc.

Garry R. Osgood for *To Sin against Systems* by Garry R. Osgood, © 1977 by Davis Publications, Inc.

Diana L. Paxson for *Message to Myself* by Diana L. Paxson, © 1978 by Davis Publications, Inc.

Jesse Peel for *Heal the Sick, Raise the Dead* by Jesse Peel, © 1978 by Davis Publications, Inc.

Ted Reynolds for *Boarder Incident* by Ted Reynolds, © 1977 by Davis Publications, Inc.

Michael Schimmel for *The Man Who Took the Fifth* by Michael Schimmel, © 1978 by Davis Publications, Inc.

Sally Sellers for *Perchance to Dream* by Sally A. Sellers, © 1976 by Davis Publications, Inc.

Paula Smith for *African Blues* by Paula Smith, © 1977 by Davis Publications, Inc.

Southmoor Serendipity, Ltd. for *The Small Stones of Tu Fu* by Brian Aldiss, © 1978 by Davis Publications, Inc.

Sherwood Springer for *Lorelei at Storyville West* by Sherwood Springer, © 1977 by Davis Publications, Inc.

Steven Utley for *Time and Hagakure* by Steven Utley, © 1977 by Davis Publications, Inc.

John Varley for *Good-Bye, Robinson Crusoe* by John Varley, © 1976 by Davis Publications, Inc.

William Jon Watkins for *Coming of Age in Henson's Tube* by William Jon Watkins, © 1977 by Davis Publications, Inc.

F. Paul Wilson for *Lipidleggin'* by F. Paul Wilson, © 1978 by Davis Publications, Inc.; and for *To Fill the Sea and Air* by F. Paul Wilson, © 1979 by Davis Publications, Inc.

CONTENTS

Science Fiction Masterpieces

ISAAC ASIMOV

Editorial: Escape to Reality?

For some twenty years I've liked to say that science fiction is an "escape to reality." I have done this, for one thing, because in my younger days science fiction was labeled "escape literature" and, in this way, dismissed in contempt.

This has offended one fellow who read the quote in *Time* and who wrote me a very angry letter in consequence. In essence, he complained that if science fiction were an escape to reality, why is it called science *fiction*? What, he demanded, is there in science fiction that is real?

Was I trying to say that sword-and-sorcery is reality; that somewhere out there in the future are mighty-thewed barbarians fighting evil, dark-hued magicians? What else, then? Faster-than-light travel? Multi-dimensions? Intelligent beings on every planet? Galactic Empires? Time travel?

In short, he demanded that I explain to him where and how science fiction represents an escape to reality.

The reader is a perfectly sensible person, but he has revved himself up into indignation and flame-breathing fury over a phrase taken out of context. Had he read the statement as part of an essay he would have had no trouble with it. So let me explain again.

I have always maintained that the prophetic element in science fiction, while present, is small and not very significant. To be sure, we talked about flights to the Moon, for instance, and atomic power and television and robots and overpopulation and artificial brains and a great many other things that have come true in general.

We have even made specific remarks that have been successfully predictive. For instance, I described popular resistance to space exploration back in 1939, long before there was any space exploration to arouse the resistance.

I described pocket computers in 1950 some 15 years before they existed. I described space-walks in 1952, several years before the first one was taken, and apparently I had described the sensations accurately.

If we look elsewhere, we find that Robert Heinlein described the nuclear stalemate in 1941 before there were any nuclear bombs over which to be stalemated; and Arthur Clarke described communications satellites (not in an actual fiction piece, however) in 1945, long before they came to pass.

None of that is important, however. If we weigh these predictions against the vast mass of science fictional incidents and events and societies and discoveries and theories—none of which are likely ever to come true and many of which couldn't possibly come true—then we see that the kind of predictions I have described do not suffice to make science fiction an escape to reality.

In particular, what are we to say of the kind of science fiction we feature in this anthology, where the accent is on action and adventure and where science is de-emphasized so that anything goes provided it isn't actually *bad* science?   Perhaps science fiction would appear to be an escape to reality least of all in a collection such as this, as far as my letter-writer was concerned.

Yet even so, science fiction *is* an escape to reality; even in here.

Consider—

All the important social and economic changes in the history of humanity have been the result of advances in science and technology.   If you doubt this and wish to mention other change-causing events, just remember you're going to have to match the changes introduced by such things as fire, the wheel, agriculture, met-allurgy, the magnetic compass, printing and paper, the steam engine, the internal-combustion engine, television, and the computer.

Advances in science and technology, and the changes they produced, were in-credibly slow at first; but they were cumulative.   The more science and technology advanced, the more likely it became that further advances would be made.   The result is that the rate of change in science and technology has been increasing steadily over human history.

With those factors in mind, you can see that through most of history the rate of advance of science and technology has been too slow to be apparent in a period of time as short as a single lifetime.   That meant that the social and economic situation seemed static to a given individual.

That, in turn, meant that through most of history, people have taken it for granted that "there is nothing new under the sun" and that nothing changes.   In fact, if anything did happen to change noticeably, people tended to be offended and horrified and considered it a degeneration and would speak wistfully of "the good old days."

But as one passes along the course of the centuries, the rate of change increased steadily; and eventually there had to come a time when change became apparent and unmistakable even in the course of a single lifetime.

To my way of thinking, the turning point came with the Industrial Revolution. After a few decades in which the steam engine came to be used as a way of mechanizing the textile industry and then as a way of powering ships, it became obvious to people living in societies that were undergoing such industrialization (notably in Great Britain and in the United States) that things *were* changing.

Indeed, science fiction came into being in the early 19th century as a direct consequence of this new realization.   After all, the coming of visible change produced a brand-new curiosity: "What will things be like after I die?"

Science fiction tried to answer that question, but not necessarily prophetically. It was sufficient to excite, to astonish, to amuse, and that could be done even without true prophecy.

But very few people read science fiction.   Even fewer read it with sufficient intention and thought to see what it is saying.   The result is that despite the evidence of change everywhere, and the evidence of faster and faster change at that, most people insist on clinging to the age-old belief that things do not change and that any sign of change that forces itself on them is an offensive and horrible sign of degeneration.

By now, though, the rate of change has become whirlwind.   In one generation there have been television, jetplanes, microcomputers, the disappearance of colonies, the rise of terrorism, the rise of the United States to world domination *and* its fall to near-impotence, and the shift of the world to oil as its major energy source *and* the dwindling of that energy source.

Under such conditions, imperviousness to change is virtual suicide.

For instance, in ten short years, the United States has gone from energy self-sufficiency to dangerous energy-dependency.

Can the United States take wise measures to prevent disaster?   Not as long as most Americans insist on believing that no change has taken place, that the oil isn't really running out, that the United States isn't really energy-dependent.

And the whole world pursues "national security" and "war-readiness" as though it were still 1938 and there were no nuclear weapons anywhere.

What is the greatest and most important reality in the world today?—The fact of change and the inevitability of further change!

What is the greatest and most important danger in the world today?—The refusal of most people to admit the existence of change.

What is the only activity in the world today that has always been predicated on the existence of change and on the inevitability of change?—Science fiction.

It doesn't matter whether the details of a science fiction story can ever come true.   It doesn't matter if the science fiction world of 2080 in a particular story features time-travel, faster-than-light travel, and intelligent monsters from an interstellar gas cloud.

The point is that it tells us that 2080 will be completely different from 1980, and that is *true*.   That is the great reality that people will not accept!

It is for this reason that people who leave the everyday humdrum world in order to read science fiction, leave the world of dangerous ignorance and falsehood that tells them everything will always be the same, and enter a world that tells them the reality that everything will inevitably change.

It is that which makes science fiction an escape to reality; and I hope that my letter-writer, having snatched the phrase from *Time,* does a little serious reading now and then, and that he picks up this anthology and reads this essay.   He may then even agree with me.

MELISA MICHAELS

In the Country of the Blind,
No One Can See

Allyson Hunter lay nestled in her protective foam, listening to the howling storm outside. She looked like a fragile china doll packed for shipping. The fragility was deceptive. Pale, perfect skin; wide, sky-blue eyes shaded by wary lashes; pink-tinged, high-boned cheeks—but under the china perfection was something sterner and stronger than china dolls. Her eyes glittered like ice. Her mouth was set in lines of habitual determination. Even the casual elegance of her posture was as dangerous as a coiled spring. She waited.

She couldn't see past the foam to tell how her sisters were, and there was nothing she could do till it melted but wait and listen. At least there was no fire; the pilot must have jettisoned the fuel pods in time. Otherwise the foam would have melted within seconds of impact, to give survivors the best chance of escape. In the absence of fire it took several minutes, to ensure an adequate, enforced rest period and decrease the chances of severe traumatic shock.

Old as the skimmer was, it was still a good craft. There'd been no guarantees either way. If they hadn't gone off-course, if the sandstorm hadn't come up . . . She shivered, listening to the screaming wind. Outside the skimmer's hull the fine red Martian dust raged against metal. Allyson had seen junk craft brought in after a sandstorm. The skimmer would look newly polished, scoured of all paint and identifying markings. Like a huge, winged mirror.

At least it would help the search craft find them. Assuming any pilots dared bring search craft out over the high desert after them. Against the threat of sandstorms, they might not.

The skimmer had been doing fine—the pilot called back to say the radio was out, and to ask if Allyson or her sisters had personal coms that might be affecting the directional finders—but they'd been floating soft and easy in the terraformed Martian atmosphere like a beautiful big blue bird. And then the sandstorm hit.

It must have come out of the east, behind them. One moment they were gliding silently over the Martian plains, and Allyson was just about to ask Kim if it didn't look a lot like high desert down there; maybe they were more off course than the pilots realized. . . .

Then the skimmer bucked and dived and she had time for nothing but strapping in, hanging on, and hoping. One of the pilots shouted a warning, but his words were lost in the screaming wind. The pilots fought it as best they could, but they hadn't a chance.   Even in a modern craft they couldn't have bucked those winds. One last stomach-churning dive . . . the wrenching sound of metal against rocks . . . a brief ear-shattering wail as the skimmer's starboard wing ripped off . . . a tumble of red and metal and breaking . . . and the silent, soft crash foam spilled out and built up around Allyson, enveloping her before the skimmer was still.

Since then, only the sound of the wind, and waiting.   At first she called to her sisters, but neither they nor the pilots answered.   There was nothing more she could do.   The skimmer was canted at a weird, impossible angle and it shook now and then with the fury of the winds, but seemed overall steady.   They must have landed on rocky ground, but at least not hanging over the edge of a crater or chasm. The pilots were good; if they had any choice in landing places, they'd have taken the best available.   But they probably hadn't been able to see through the sand.

If only they or her sisters had answered her calls!   She was afraid to call again, now.   Her sisters should be protected by the same crash foam that saved her.   If it had failed . . . she didn't want to think about that.   Safer to think of the pilots, strapped into their cockpit seats.   There were a dozen reasons why they might not have answered; they might not have heard her.   Or they might be injured.   Or it might not have occurred to them that their silence would frighten her.

They thought of her and her sisters more as furniture than people.   Cargo. They'd even said that, and then stared at each other with their dark shadowed eyes, and one of them had smiled and said with polite indifference, "Excuse me.   I mean clones."   Because they knew she was listening.   So they knew she had some feelings, anyway.   But they still might not think of her now.

"Don't ever forget what you are, no one else will."   That was one of the earliest lessons of her childhood.   "Nobody else is going to forget for a second, so always be one jump ahead of them.   If you're ever to be accepted as people, you'll have to act twice as human as natural-borns; and that only in the ways they respect.   No human frailties.   Just strengths."

She could almost hear Barbara saying that.   And she remembered the first time she'd heard it.   Allyson, Kim, and Rebecca were very young; they came in crying from some encounter with the local natural-borns, and listened patiently to that lecture from Barbara.   Rebecca had cried, "We can't *do* that!   You don't know . . ."

But Barbara interrupted, with that soft, sad smile that looked like a mirror of them thirty years from now, and said, "Rebecca.   I know exactly what you can do, and what you can't do.   And I know how hard it is."

None of them understood, then, how true that was.   But later, when they understood genetics, they began to guess.   And later still, they knew how much of it was more determination than truth.   But they had inherited Barbara's determination, and it stood them in good stead.

It was only by accident of nature, or lab procedure, or some unknown that they had been allowed to live at all.   When they were scheduled for cerebral death, their EEGs were automatically checked, and they showed the strange, doubled pattern of potential espers.

Even clone espers were needed to guide and communicate with the starships on their long voyages, so they were spared.   The process was not yet then sophisticated enough to determine how strong their latent talent was, or they still would have been destroyed; since as it turned out the talent was weak at best.

But they lived.   Clones with the same level of talent were now automatically murdered.   The testing equipment had been considerably refined.   But Allyson and her sisters lived.   And Barbara, their donor-sister, the woman whose genes they carried and who had fought for the right to raise them as her children once their right to live had been established, had instilled in them her own fierce horror of the entire cloning industry as it was used today.

Because it led to questions like: why bother protecting endangered species?   Just clone some extras.   And why not indulge in dangerous, deadly pastimes?   Sun-jamming and high-diving and race-driving and all the other risk-filled enterprises man's sensation-hungry mind could conjure.   It was no more risk than driving a car was a century earlier.   If you got mangled, your clones would supply new body parts.   If you died, you died.   And if you were lucky, you were one whose brain could be transplanted into the body of one of your clones and you'd be immortal!

But your clone wouldn't.   He never had a chance.   And nobody thought twice about it; they were only clones, after all.   Destroy one, make another.   No problem.   It wasn't as if they were real people, after all.

So Allyson and her sisters spent their lives trying to be real people; what they among themselves called natural-borns.   And they were reminded, every day in a dozen little ways, that they weren't real people.   Everything about them was stamped "clone."   Their IDs, their credit cards, even their bodies.   At least that was on the soles of their feet, where people couldn't see it all the time.   But it was there.   And it was like being a carbon copy of a real person; a copy okay for certain functions but not nearly as good as the original.

She should have expected Frank and Todd Lewis's reaction when the three of them came into the little flight office with their request that the brothers fly them and their skimmer to Viking's Rest.   Three identical, carbon-copy women; their sky-blue eyes identically wary; their faces identically tense; even their clothing and sun-burned hair identical—they didn't have to show their IDs to be known for what they were when they travelled together.

They dressed alike as a gesture almost of defiance.   Natural-borns never noticed the freckles on Kim's nose; or the way Rebecca's hair stuck up in a little cowlick in back; or that Allyson was always the one who took charge.   They just saw three identical women, and called them clones.   All interactions were governed by that. If the three of them dressed alike, it was like a shout of pride.   They made no effort to conceal what they were; and they expected the reactions they got.

But when Allyson first saw Frank and Todd Lewis she thought, just for a moment, that they were clones, too.   Heart in her throat, she stared with wild unexpected hope at their identical faces—and immediately realized she was wrong.   They were too comfortable, too confident, too secure.   Nothing stamped "clone" could be so self-assured.   So proud.

She knew at once why their shadowed eyes went narrow with unease when they saw her and her sisters.   Still, it hurt.   She said, before they could, "You're twins!   How fascinating; I've never met identical twins before."

One of them lifted an eyebrow and both of them smiled.   It wasn't a friendly smile.   If she'd thought she could alleviate their dislike by recognizing its cause, she was mistaken.   They were no more pleased she could tell they weren't clones than they would have been if the skimmer could, and no more concerned for her feelings.   She wasn't a person.   She was just a clone.

She sighed and shifted in the crash foam, trying to get free of a particularly binding safety belt.   The wind was definitely abating now, and the foam was receding.   In a few moments she would be free to see how the others had fared in the crash.

She was working her way out of the safety harness when the door from the cockpit opened and one of the pilots stepped through.   He towered over her seat next to the doorway, his long frame bent a little to keep from bumping his head. There was something wild and terrible in his eyes as he surveyed the cargo hold, but his voice when he spoke was casual and steady.   "You all right?" he asked.

"I am," she said.   He could see past the foam to where her sisters were strapped in their seats.   She kept her voice steady and met his eyes as she asked, "Are my sisters alive?"

He glanced at her and then past her, over the foam.   "One is," he said.   His voice was unexpectedly gentle.   There was something like fear or terrible pain in his eyes.   "I can't tell about the other.   Here, let me help you out of your harness. Then you can check on them.   I've got to get my brother out; he's hurt."   He bent over the foam to release Allyson's straps, touching her body as indifferently as he would a box of cargo.   In that moment she hated him.   But it showed only in the darkening of her eyes.

"There's a medikit in the compartment in front," she said.

"I found it," he said.   When her straps were loose he stood back, surveying the odd angle of the deck and the melting foam.   "What a mess," he muttered, more to himself than to her.

She was disentangling herself from the straps, trying to stand up, and she spoke without thinking.   "You've been in worse," she said.

Those implacable brown eyes returned to her face, impaling her.   She stared, oddly frightened.   "How would you know?" he asked.

She managed a shrug and a tentative smile.   People reacted even worse to espers than to clones.   Any sign of talent was always taken for full telepathy.   "A guess," she said.   "You're a pilot with quite a reputation.   You don't get that without a few mishaps along the way."

He watched her a moment longer before he answered.   "Yeah," he said, and suddenly all interest in her was gone.   "You're right.   See to your, um, sisters, okay?   If you need the medikit, let me know.   I'll be in front; the storm's just about over, and I want to see if we can get out of here and get some signal out for the search planes.   I don't suppose this crate has an ADS?"

"Autodirection sender?   No, I don't think so."

"It figures." He turned away, but on impulse she caught his arm to stop him.

The words were harder to phrase than she'd expected. But she'd wanted all her life to say them to someone else; and his indifference angered her enough to say them: "Which one are you? I can't tell you apart." She could, but he had no way of knowing that.

The sardonic twist of his lips showed he knew exactly why she asked. But he said simply, "Todd," and turned away. So he was better at insults than she. Because he didn't bother to ask which one she was. He didn't care.

"Allyson?" With a guilty start, she let Todd go and turned toward the opposite wall where her sisters sat in the melting foam. Rebecca was awake and watching her, her eyes puzzled. "Allyson, are you all right?"

Todd disappeared into the cockpit and Allyson slipped and slid across the foamy floor to Rebecca's side. Near Rebecca, Kim sprawled limp and lifeless in her harness. The side of her head was covered with blood. Half her face was ruined. The other half was still a perfect replica of Allyson's and Rebecca's to the last delicate detail. The one remaining china-blue eye stared in blind consternation at the opposite window, sanded to frosty luminescence by the storm outside.

Allyson set her teeth and forced herself to lift one of the limp white wrists to check for a pulse, but there was really no question. Still, she checked the carotid artery before turning away, blinking back tears. Rebecca watched without comprehension.

"I'm okay, Rebecca," Allyson said. "Are you?" Her voice was thin and wavery, like a child's. And her throat hurt.

Rebecca put one hand to her head. "I think so," she said. And then, with sudden realization, "Kim? . . ."

"She's dead," said Allyson. Rebecca closed her eyes, her face pale. Allyson silently released her safety straps. Rebecca was always quicker to tears than Allyson. Her chin trembled. Allyson pushed the straps aside and put her arms around her sister.

"Those damn pilots," said Rebecca.

"It wasn't their fault, Rebecca," said Allyson. "Now, come on. One of them is hurt; we ought to see if we can help."

Rebecca sighed and wiped her eyes. "You're right," she said, rising. She didn't look at Kim. "Okay," she said, steadying herself against a projecting security bar. "I'm ready; let's go."

They tried the cargo bay first, but that was blocked with dust or some other obstruction, and wouldn't budge. They would have to get out through the cockpit.

Todd and Frank were still inside. Todd had awkwardly covered an abrasion on Frank's temple with spray bandages. They were working on the outside door, which appeared to be drifted shut. They pushed it open an inch or so, and a thin trickle of red dust filled the bottom of the crack.

"Need help?" asked Allyson.

Todd glanced up, startled. The gaunt lines of his face seemed hollowed and pale. The dark eyes searched her, and for a moment she thought she saw something questioning, something pleading in his gaze; then it snicked shut like a door closing and suddenly he was a person and she was furniture again. He shrugged. "Why not?" he said.

Together the four of them wrenched the door open and climbed out over the drift that blocked it. While the others stared in dazed surprise and growing horror at their surroundings, Frank stood by the door, waiting. He kept turning his head from side to side with nervous little gestures like a fox in a cage, his face white, the skin drawn taut over the bones of his cheeks. He didn't say anything, but Allyson realized with a start of unexpected sympathy that he was now blind.

Beside him, Todd stood with one hand still on the door as if for support, and said slowly, "It's a crater, Frank. We're inside the damn thing."

"Inside?" Frank moved his eyes as if he could see, but they were flat and lifeless. "Is it deep? Narrow?"

"Not deep," said Todd, "but too damn narrow. I don't know how visible we are, but I'd say not very. And even if we had an ADS, the signal would bounce off the walls and never get out."

"Oh." Frank thought about it for a moment. "Well, you'd better get busy," he said. "Show the clones how to build solar stills; and we'll need shelter. If you bring me whatever electronic equipment you can find, including that damn radio, maybe I can build us some communication equipment."

"We already know how to build stills, Mr Lewis," Allyson said. "We're Martians, too, you know. Look, why don't you sit down and let my sister have a look at that head wound while your brother and I get the supplies out of the skimmer."

"I'm all right," said Frank.

"My sister's a doctor," said Allyson. "I think you should let her take a look at your injury. Maybe she can't do much, with the equipment at hand, but please let her try." She ignored Todd's startled eyes. Why the hell were people always so surprised Rebecca was a doctor? Todd and Frank were identical twins; surely they wouldn't believe, as so many people did, that because they looked alike the clones were interchangeable.

"Your sister's a doctor?" said Frank. He turned his head again, searching his private darkness, perhaps looking for hope.

"That's right," said Rebecca, "I am. Here, let me help you find a place to sit; I'd really like to take a look at that wound, if you'll let me."

Sunlight glittered off the sanded hull of the skimmer. The air smelled like hot dust and herbs bioformed from Earth varieties for the Martian desert. Allyson reluctantly met Todd's eyes and waited.

He shook himself and glanced from her to Frank and back again. "Sure, let her look at it, Frank," he said. Hope burned like fire in his eyes; Allyson realized with odd disappointment that he wasn't going to comment on the clones' differences. He was wrestling with some personal demon and didn't care about the clones. They were cargo. In a crash, you make use of whatever cargo turns out to be handy.

Even the usual stupid questions would have been better than indifference, she thought, and wondered why it mattered.

"You," Todd said, "could help me get the supplies."

"I have a name," she said, and immediately wished she hadn't.

"Most of us do," he said. Those sardonic eyes raked her again and she blushed.

"Let's go," she said stiffly.

He smiled; a thin, unexpectedly bitter smile; and led her back into the skimmer. While he disconnected the radio and collected what other electronic gear he could find, she sorted through the supplies in the cockpit, piling undamaged goods on an emergency blanket and tossing the useless things aside. They worked in silence, and she was careful to avoid his eyes.

"There's more food and water in back," she said at last. She hesitated, thinking of Kim. She didn't want to face that awful apparition again; but they might be here for days. They couldn't leave her where she was. "And my sister," she said with difficulty. "We'll have to," she swallowed, "bury her."

"I can do that," he said.

She looked up, startled, and met his eyes. They were unexpectedly kind; but there was still a cold, determined barrier there. He held himself apart from her with a fierce, blind rejection that was like a physical pain.

"That's kind of you," she said, "but I can manage."

He shrugged. "Whatever," he said, and his expression went flat again; distant and reserved, as if a fog obscured him from her.

She wanted to say, *Clones aren't any different from identical twins, damn you!* But she bit back the words and swallowed a painful lump in her throat. Because they were different. Identical twins were natural-borns. They were identical to each other, but carbon copies of nobody. And they'd never been thought of as organ banks. There was nothing to protect. You could recognize them as people and still not be a murderer; because none of them were slaughtered to provide organ replacement for others.

The tattoo on her foot had branded her soul, but she knew why it had to be there. The first use of clones had been for replacement parts; it was still their main function. Those few who were permitted to live, their cerebrums intact, could not be considered human. Because what would that say about all those thousands whose cerebrums were destroyed?

So it made no difference how many scientific facts people knew; or how much genetics. Every high school student knew that on a genetic basis there was no difference between clones and identical twins. If anything, the twins were stranger; it was perfectly well-known what formed clones. You take the nucleus from a cell, put it in an egg from which the nucleus has been removed, and presto! you have the equivalent of a fertilized egg; a diploid cell or zygote, ready to grow and divide and form an embryo.

But it still wasn't known why identical twins sometimes occurred. You take two haploid cells, put them together and they're a fertilized egg or zygote; but why do the two cells of its first division sometimes separate from one another and develop into two independent embryos? Nobody knew, and it wasn't really important. Because they were natural-borns, and nobody questioned their right to live.

But clones—people created in the lab, by artificial means—that was different. They were replacement parts.   They'd been created for replacement parts, and the first ones permitted to live had been so grateful for the gift of life they'd set the stage for all the discrimination to follow.   Of course they didn't demand their rights as people; that would be saying their benefactors were murdering a person every time they destroyed the cerebrum of a cloned embryo.

Allyson smiled thinly, as she always did when she reached that point in her philosophical fury.   Maybe it wasn't really much different from abortion.   The only real difference was that the cloned embryos were created intentionally for "abortion."   And the real question was, would it make any difference to the social attitude if the sex act were somehow involved in the creation of clones?

"What's funny?"

She came back to the present with a start, to find herself staring into Todd's dark, watchful eyes.   His face was pale, and there were hard lines of tension around his mouth and eyes.

"Oh, nothing," she said.   "I was just thinking."   For a moment her face, usually rigidly guarded, retained a look of vulnerability or of terrible sorrow; then, as she focused on Todd's hooded gaze, the lines of her expression slowly tautened. The straight, stern set of her lips returned; and the startling intensity of her eyes. "Are you all right, Todd?" she asked.   "You look pale."

His own expression hardened.   "I'm fine," he said.   Their words hung between them like a glittering facade on a broken building; the tone and content bore no relation to their expressions.   It was as if four people sat there; two friends speaking, and two wary strangers watching.   "While you're in the back," he added in the same friendly tone, "why don't you see if you can find some clear plastic sheeting for the solar stills?   I'm gonna get this stuff outside and see what Frank can do with it."

She hesitated.   "He may not be able to," she began.

"It'll give him something to do," he said without meeting her eyes.   It was quite a concession; he'd explained a behavior, as if she were a normal person with some stake in what happened.   But before she could respond he added impatiently, "Go on and find some plastic.   We're gonna need all the water we can get."

"Okay," she said.   "Hand me the pliers; I'll need them to get into the emergency supplies."   Her eyes were as cold and gray as a winter sky.

He kept his hard-shadowed gaze on her as he reached out with the pliers, holding them flat on his palm so she could pick them up without touching him.   But she had to look down at his hand to find them, and paused with her hand half-extended, staring.

It wasn't quite a surprise, but it was a shock.   She had guessed something was wrong.   She hadn't guessed how wrong.

When she didn't accept the pliers he glanced down at them, then looked back at her face, his eyes widened with surprise and something like fear.   "Oh," he said, and glanced at his hand again, then drew it back.   He made an ineffectual effort to wipe the sticky red stain from their handles, but it was too late.   "It's just a scratch," he said, "a little cut.   It bled a lot. . . ."   He paused, watching her. His face was shiny with sweat. But it was early morning, and still chilly outside.

She waited. Her eyes revealed nothing. He offered her the pliers again. "I'm all right," he said. "There's nothing to worry about."

"So you're a hero," she said. The words were as cold as her eyes.

He shrugged. "Think whatever you want to," he said. "Just get some plastic from the back, okay?"

"The only human left, so you have to stay in charge, right?" She took the pliers and turned away. "For God's sake don't trust a clone; they're not real people."

"Whatever," he said. "If you need help later with your sister back there, let me know."

She whirled on him in a fit of fury. "You won't *touch* her," she said. "Do you hear me? You won't so much as *look* at her! I can handle it by myself, or with Rebecca, and I don't want your filthy natural-born hands on her; she can be spared at least that!"

He stared. "Fine," he said mildly. The sardonic, mocking smile was still in his eyes, but fogged or faded as if by a sheet of scratched acrylic between his face and hers. She turned away from him with a bitter feeling of defeat.

When she got outside with the plastic and the rest of the emergency supplies, Frank was settled happily in the shade of a large rock, fiddling with the electronic equipment Todd brought him. Todd and Rebecca were working on the other side of the skimmer, draping parachutes from the wing and weighting them against wind with rocks and soil. If another sandstorm came up, they'd have to get back in the ruined skimmer; otherwise, the wing would make a good shelter. With a fire under it, they might even manage to stay warm at night.

Todd and Rebecca were doing well enough by themselves. Allyson deposited the plastic and supplies in a heap near the skimmer's door and climbed back into the cockpit. Just in case another sandstorm did come up, it would be a good idea to have Kim's body somewhere else. And in spite of what she'd said in anger to Todd, she didn't think Rebecca would be much help with that task. She'd be fine if it were a stranger's body. But not Kim's. Not her sister, with half her face caved in.

Allyson had always been the strongest of them, both physically and emotionally. But even her strength didn't quite match her task. The three of them had always been very close. They had to be; they had no one else. And they were almost identical. So what Allyson had to move was not just the body of her sister, but also the image of herself discolored and distorted by death.

She set about the task reluctantly, but it had to be done. By the time she had Kim's body out the cockpit door tears streaked her cheeks and she was shaking uncontrollably. But she resolutely grasped Kim's wrists and dragged her as far from the skimmer as she could. Only when she was out of sight beyond a low ridge of jutting rocks did she sit down with her head in her hands to cry.

At least, she thought as she piled rocks over the broken body, Kim was free now. She died too far from civilization to be whisked into hospital, taken apart like a mechanical thing, and moved piece by piece to an organ bank or other people's bodies.

Oh, true, the same thing would happen to anybody who did die within civilization's reach. It wasn't only clones who were viewed as spare parts of the moment of death. Especially on sparsely populated Mars, nobody was "wasted." And that was as it should be. Still, for a clone, the idea of being used as spare parts any time held a peculiar horror.

It seemed oddly fitting that Kim should, instead, have a lonely burial under the rocks and sand of the desert, with only another clone to bid her goodbye. Allyson pushed the last rock into place with a sad satisfaction and settled back on her heels to rest.

Her hands and face were dusty and streaked with tears and sweat. The red dust was everywhere. She could even taste it, along with the sticky salt taste of tears. She wiped her cheeks with the back of her hand and sat for a long time beside her sister's shallow grave, staring with unseeing eyes at the hard red rim of the crater around her. The desert air smelled of dust and pungent herbs. And there was silence, as far as forever. It was a good place to be buried. It might even be a good place to die.

When Allyson returned to the skimmer there was a peculiar light of defiance in her eyes. She set silently about digging holes for solar stills, and when Rebecca and Todd joined her she barely glanced at them.

"I buried Kim," she said.

"We built a shelter," said Todd, as if it were of equal significance. Perhaps it was.

"How's Frank?" she asked without much interest.

He was sitting within hearing distance, but too engrossed in his electronic puzzle to hear what they said. He seemed oddly unconcerned by blindness. Most people in his place would have fought it. He accepted it, and was learning already how to work within its boundaries.

"I'm worried about him," Rebecca said quietly. "The optic nerve is under pressure, obviously. If we don't get him to medical facilities in time, it may atrophy—"

"He'll be all right," said Todd.

Allyson looked at Rebecca. " 'Fight when you can win,' " she said. " 'Accept the inevitable when it is.' " She smiled, a sad little smile that twisted her lips and barely touched her glass-blue eyes.

"What's that?" asked Todd. "Sounded like a quote." He had paused in his work and settled back on his heels, watching her. His eyes were sunken, shadowed places in a hollow face. She was startled at the hopelessness there.

"Just something Barbara used to say," she said. "Are you all right?"

"Barbara? Who's that?" he asked.

"Our original sister," said Rebecca. "The one we're copies of." She frowned at him. "You do look pale," she said. "You could be in shock; you should rest."

He shook his head. "I'm okay," he said.

"He's a hero," said Allyson. Her voice was harsh, her eyes cold. But she caught him when he fell. And was surprised at the answering note of tenderness she felt when he stared up at her with pleading eyes.

"Allyson," he said, and she was so startled she barely heard the rest of what he said. *He knew all along! He could tell them apart!* "For God's sake, tell Frank I'm all right," he whispered before those splendid, pain-wracked, frightened eyes slid shut.

And then she understood. She stared at Rebecca, her own eyes dark like storm clouds. "He *is* a hero," she said. Her voice broke. "Oh, please," she whispered, "will he be all right?"

They carried him to the shelter he had built with Rebecca, and put him on a blanket in the shade. It took them a moment to find the injury; he'd bound it clumsily with spray bandages to slow the bleeding. It was an awful, deadly puncture just below his ribs. Rebecca sent Allyson to get the medikit and water while she tried to make him comfortable and examine the wound.

Allyson knew very little about medicine and, as a rule, cared not at all. She brought the water and kit and sat down beside Todd, but her fear was so distracting, Rebecca sent her away again. So she wandered out to the rock Frank sat beside with his electronics.

The sun was beginning to encroach on his little island of shade. He heard her coming and lifted his head, blind eyes as private and shadowed as Todd's. "It's Allyson, Frank," she said. "How're you doing?"

"I'm fine," he said. "I always said I could put one of these things together blindfolded. Now I've had a chance to prove it. And I think it's gonna work! It's almost done."

"Then we can call Umbra Landing!"

"If we can get the signal outside this crater," he said. He turned back to his work, his fingers moving among the wires as confidently as if he could see. "How's Todd?" he asked casually.

She stared. "He's," she said, and paused. Frank waited, his shoulders hunched a little against whatever news she might bring him. He knew something was wrong. Todd thought he could keep knowledge of his injury from Frank, but Frank probably knew from the start. All Todd succeeded in doing was keeping it from the clones, who could have helped him. "He'll be all right now," she said. "Rebecca's taking care of him." And heard in memory her own terror whispering, *Please, will he be all right?*

They sat in silence for a moment while Frank's busy fingers traced patterns among the wires. "He didn't want to scare me," Frank said. It wasn't a question, but she answered it anyway.

"No."

Another silence. Then, "D'you do that? It's just like being identical twins, isn't it? D'you find yourself doing stupid things to protect the others?"

She nodded, forgetting he couldn't see her. "Sometimes from dangers that aren't even real," she said.

"Yeah." He put his tools down and rested his hands on the radio. "You know," he said slowly, "identical twins are really clones.   Accidents of nature, but one of us is a clone of the other.   I remember wondering in high school why they were so careful not to use that word when they described the genetic process that caused us."

"For the same reason they're so careful always to use it with us," she said. The sun was very hot on her back.   She thought about getting up to move into the shade, but it was too much trouble.

"I know that now," he said.   "I guess we're just lucky the first identical twins happened a long time before they knew how to do organ transplants."

She picked a branch from a shrub beside her and twisted its leaves in her fingers till the sharp odor of its sap filled the shimmering air.   "What will they do," she said, "when they figure it out?"

He turned a sardonic smile to her, so similar to Todd's it wrenched her heart. "They've figured it out, a long time ago," he said.   "They don't know what to do."

She sighed.   "Is the radio fixed?"

"I think so," he said.   "You'll have to take it up on the rim, to get a signal out.   Is it climbable?   Its got to be line-of-sight, so if you can't get it high enough we'll have to wait for a search craft."

"To fly right over us," she said.   "I can take it up on the rim.   How does it work?"

"Push this," he said, "and pray.   Here's the microphone."

She took the awkward bundle in her hands and paused, watching him.   "You'll be all right?"   The lines of his face were different from Todd's.   Not as sharp and distinct.

"I'm fine," he said.

Still she hesitated.   "We're all heroes," she said.   "We keep protecting each other from our own demons, so half the time we don't even see each other's."

"And if we do," he said, "we still can't touch them."

"No," she said, and closed her eyes.   "No, we can't touch them."   Abruptly she jumped up, clutching the radio, and ran.   He couldn't see her tears, but she wouldn't cry in front of him anyway.   She had never in her adult life cried in front of anyone; she wasn't going to start now.

She returned empty-handed through the shimmering heat of the afternoon.   The skimmer lay like a broken mirror at the base of the rim.   There was no sign of life.   Rebecca and the twins must have taken refuge beneath the shade of the wing. Allyson sat down to rest on the rocks just above the skimmer, and stared for a long while at the emergency blankets guarding the little shelter under the wing, before heat and thirst finally drove her down the slope.

Her face was streaked with dust, her hands and knees scraped and bloody from the rocks.   But in the shade of the shelter, only her glittering eyes were visible. "The radio worked," she said.   "The forecast's okay, so there should be a rescue craft here by nightfall."

Rebecca handed her a cup of water.   Frank lay beside the skimmer next to his brother.   None of them spoke.   Her eyes still blind from the sun, Allyson couldn't tell if the twins were awake.   She accepted the water with trembling hands, squatted just inside the shelter as if prepared for flight, and drank sparingly, watching the darkness where the twins lay.

She was afraid to speak.   She rested the cup on her knees and held herself still with a terrible effort.   The silence was like a living thing around her.   Out in the desert sun, that had seemed like a blessing.   Here it kept her poised, tense, listening. If he were dead they would say it, surely.   *Oh, please, will he be all right?*

A pebble scraped in the darkness.   Her eyes, dark, burning pits in her sunburned face, were beginning to adjust to the shadows.   She waited, staring with a frightened and frightening intensity at the darker shadow that was the twins.   Beside her, Rebecca took the forgotten cup from her and sipped from it, looking over its rim at the twins.

Just when Allyson had decided it never would, the shadow moved, separated, became two people.   One of them lying with his bandaged head on a folded blanket; the other pushing himself up on one elbow to smile his sardonic, guarded smile at her.

It's one thing to make the decision never to cry in front of anyone.   It's quite another to stick to it.   She didn't know how she got across the little shelter and into Todd's arms.   She was just there.   And it was where she belonged.

"So," he said softly.   "You're a hero, too."

RANDALL GARRETT & VICKI ANN HEYDRON

Keepersmith

Earthbird Class: *Small (96m) destroyers of tremendous power, with hulls having a full 2 mm of endurium plating, and manned primarily with fighting personnel, these ships were designed, not for space warfare, as the larger craft were, but to board and destroy the Snal-things in their hidden deep-space nests wherever they were found.*

Keepersmith stood in the doorway of Keepershome and faced the three people who had come through the chilly morning at his command.

He was a big Man, with wide shoulders and a tough-muscled body that had been hardened by the same heat and pressure that forged raw steel into Smithswords.

"I am leaving," he said quietly.

Only Hollister, eldest of the three, understood.

The aged Macson, whose eyes reflected craftiness but little wisdom, said, "Of course you're leaving! The thaw has begun and your Ironhunt was due several days ago. I was just saying to Yarma—"

"Never mind, Macson," said Yarma. Almost as tall as Keepersmith, Yarma's brawn had slipped and puddled around his waist, but his brain was active and he sensed some little of what Keepersmith meant. "When will you be back, Keepersmith?"

"Before the first snow," Keepersmith answered in his deep voice. "I will return when I can."

And then they all understood.

Keepersmith was clothed as usual for an Ironhunt, in a fur garment which covered his torso but left his arms and legs free, and fur boots thong-wrapped to his knees. At his left side hung his own great sword, the finest ever forged. At his right, in its own holster, was Ironblaster, the legacy of the *Hawk*.

All that was normal: the sword for his own protection, and Ironblaster, which only the Keepersmith could use, which he held in trust for the future when the *Hawk* would return for his people, and which was the only instrument that could draw iron from stone.

But the heavy pack was not normal. Strapped to his back, it was usually empty when he left and full of iron when he returned, but now it was obviously already loaded with supplies.

"Where are you going?" asked Hollister.

"South," said Keepersmith tersely.

Macson blinked.   "For how long?"

"For as long as it takes."

"But—you can't do that!"   Macson's voice seemed to break, but he cringed back as Keepersmith's dark gaze flashed to his face.   "I—I mean, you have duties here!"

"Joom will remain," said Keepersmith evenly.   "He is skilled and has iron enough.   He will serve you well.   And as for duty, it is my duty to go."

After a moment's silence, Hollister said, "Something has happened."

Keepersmith's hard face softened as he looked at the old woman.   To Hollister would fall the great burden of leadership once he had gone.   Macson and Yarma were useful as leaders only if she led them.

"Perhaps.   I cannot say for sure.   That is why I must go.   To be sure.   Joom knows the Reading, and I have left Writing with him which tells why I must go. If I have not returned by snowfall, he will read the Writing in your presence."

"And then?"   Hollister looked at him steadily with her wise old eyes.

"Then Joom will be Keepersmith, and another decision must be made."

Yarma looked troubled.   "Leave Ironblaster."   His voice quavered a bit under Keepersmith's gaze, but he continued.   "If there is a chance you won't return, you *must* leave it."

"No.   If I leave it, there is less chance I will return.   I am Keeper until my death."   Without another look, he walked away from the home he had known since he was apprenticed to the last Keepersmith at only ten summers.

Half a day from the village, Keepersmith was still walking steadily through the slowly warming foothills.   The air was fresh and slightly chill, and the ground laced with small furious rivulets from the melting snow that came from the mountains behind him, but already there were loudbirds and a touch of budding green in the branches of the hedgelike vecca trees that covered these lower hillsides.

At noon he rested briefly and ate.   He drank from one of the icy streams and was on his way again, moving steadily south.   The ground grew more level, and the rivulets of water more scarce.   When he paused at dusk, he filled a skin with water, and ate sparingly.

The night was clear, and well-lit by Gemni, the double moon, and this was still familiar land, land he had travelled often.

Near midnight he saw a flickering light ahead.   He moved quietly to the edge of a stand of tall thran trees and looked out into a small clearing.   A last rocky ridge extended here from the mountain range, and under an overhanging cliff some four meters high a small campfire was burning.

Beyond the fire, with his back to the stone wall, sat a scaled creature with four Man-like limbs.   He sat motionless, staring with shining eyes which protruded from a delicately boned, chinless face.   Firelight reflected from the webwork of scales that was his skin, sending up a sheen that made his skin look wet.

How he likes the fire, Keepersmith thought.   *I believe that it was good to teach them about fire. But should we give them the secret of* forced *fire? Could we trust even Liss with that power?*

Deliberately, he stepped out from the trees, and the eyes of the creature lifted from the fire directly to him. "Sssmith." The soft voice blended with the fire noises.

Keepersmith walked to the fire, squatted down beside it, and put aside his pack. "Where is it, Liss?" he asked.

The Razoi picked up a bundle from the ground near him and reached into it with a long-fingered hand. The object he handed Keepersmith gleamed in the firelight.

It was a handweapon much like Ironblaster but smaller, and the control knobs along the side were not the same.

The Razoi, unfamiliar with both weapons, could not see the differences. "It *iss* the ssame, Sssmith," said Liss, looking across the fire. "The ssame metal as Ironblasster."

"Yes," agreed Keepersmith, "much the same."

"You ssaid that two dayss ago," Liss reminded him. "Why did you ssend me away sso ssoon?"

"Don't be offended, friend. I could not explain then. I cannot explain yet, but—" Keepersmith turned the thing in his hands so that the firelight highlighted the Writing on the controls:

Kill—Stun.

And across the butt:

I. S. S. Hawk.

"This is not for everyone to see. It is important and I must understand it before I tell anyone else about it."

"Tell *me* about it, Sssmith."

Keepersmith looked up from the shiny thing in his hand and considered the being across the fire. He was a Razoi, one of the oldest of a long-lived race, a member of the tall northern tribe which had for many Man generations lived across the high mountains from the valley where the Men lived.

Keepersmith had met Liss when he was a boy, walking for pleasure in the hills above the Smithy. The Razoi had appeared from behind a group of boulders and had called to him. The boy, frightened because he had heard so much evil of this kind of creature, nonetheless had stood his ground—but the Razoi had only talked to him. In halting Man language he had spoken of friendship, of learning, of sharing.

"You will be leader," Liss had said, and the boy knew then that the Razoi had lain in wait not for *any* Man, but only himself. And it impressed him, as not even learning the Writing had done, that he would one day have to lead the Men on this world.

"You will learn," said Liss. "Teach uss. Teach *me* and I will teach them. We will not fight you."

Then Liss had come down from the hillside to stand in front of him. They had been of a size, the gangly, already muscular thirteen-summer boy and the slim and ageless Razoi.   Liss had raised his weapon, a wooden staff with a stone axe at one end and the other sharpened to a point, and had laid it down at the feet of the boy.

"I will khome again.   Remember."

Then Liss had walked into the brushy hillside and the boy had stared after him, still speechless.

Liss had come again ten summers later, as the new Keepersmith walked those same hills in wordless grief, struggling to accept not only the loss of a man who had been a father to him, but what that loss meant—the heavy responsibility fallen now to his own shoulders.   Keepersmith had accepted the Razoi's friendship then and had not yet regretted it.

The village did not approve when this one Razoi left the guarded trading compound to visit Keepersmith outside—always *outside*—the Smithy.   They suspected, but couldn't forbid, that Liss sometimes went along on ironhunts, and had watched while Ironblaster melted into a mountainside.   But they did not know that Liss asked only for what Keepersmith could give, and in turn gave him something the lonely boy and the solemn man could never know otherwise—the companionship of an equal.

Another ten summers had passed, and, in all that time, Keepersmith had never spoken to Liss of the *Hawk* or the heritage of Men.   He had sensed that it was this knowledge Liss really wanted, but would not ask for fear of offending Keepersmith.   The Razoi had been the enemies of Man in the past, and though Keepersmith trusted Liss, they were too different.   They would never truly understand one another.   And the secrets of the *Hawk* had been guarded by Keepersmiths for generations.   Could he be the one to reveal them to a Razoi?

If it weren't for Liss, I'd never have seen this. . . .

Suddenly he lifted Ironblaster from its place at his belt and set both things beside the fire.

Ironblaster was much larger than the other object, but it was obvious that they belonged together.   Their shapes were roughly similar and the bright glow of the fire lit up the matching inscriptions: *I. S. S. Hawk.*

"Ssee, Sssmith, it iss sso like Ironblasster.   But it is ssilent, while Ironblasster roarss.   What doess it mean?"

"It is a message from the *Hawk*," Keepersmith answered.   "A message I do not understand.   Liss, what do you know of how Men came to be here?"

"Only that one day they were here.   They ran up from the ssouth, purssued by dussteaterss.   And they sslew my people, and we fought to live.   They drove uss out of our valley and tookh it for themsselvess."

Keepersmith could not conceal his surprise, and Liss smiled grimly.   "Ssome things do not need Writing to be remembered."

"Those Men had no choice, Liss.   They had a duty—to the *Hawk*."

"And what iss the *H-hawk?*" asked Liss, hesitating over the unfamiliar word.

"Not all Men agree about that, Liss.   Some believe that the *Hawk* is a god, a mighty being who cast us out of the sky to punish us for something we did.   Others say that such talk is only superstition, and the *Hawk* does not exist at all."

"And you, Sssmith? What do you ssay?"

"I know the truth, Liss, or as much as the Writing can tell me. This world is only one of many—there are hundreds of others, surrounded by something called space, where there is no air to breathe. The *Hawk* is a ship which could travel between those worlds. It brought my ancestors to this world. . . .

"And then left them here."

"Why?"

"Not even those who made the Writing knew that. But they were sure of one thing—the *Hawk* would return for them. The first Keepersmith, who spoke for the *Hawk,* said that we must keep all the knowledge we had, so that when the *Hawk* did return we would be ready."

"Ready?" asked Liss.

"To leave," answered Keepersmith, so lost in his own musing that he did not see the spasm which crossed Liss's face. "The *Hawk* will take us all away from your world, Liss. It will be yours once again."

Keepersmith reached over and picked up the small object. "This may be the signal we have been waiting for. Or it may not. I must know for certain; I must go to where it was found."

"*I* found it on the belt of one of the ssouthern—" He used a word in his own language, and the contempt in his voice was unmistakable. "Before he died, he told me where he found it."

"Can you take me there?"

"Yess."

Keepersmith put the small thing in his pack and holstered Ironblaster. Then he stretched out beside the fire.

The Razoi stretched out too, as near the fire as he could get without scorching himself. They lay there in silence for a few moments, and then Keepersmith spoke.

"Are your people bitter, Liss?"

"Ssome of them. But we have akhssepted it. Our livess are better for your potss and your cloth. And now for your fire. My tribe iss ssettled now in *our* valley—we would not wissh to move again."

"Why do the southern tribes raid and kill?"

"There iss only one ssouthern tribe left. They fight and sslay bekhausse—" the closest the Razoi could come to the Man's "k" sound was a throat-clearing noise, "they have always done it. They are sstupid. They are our enemiess too."

"If we must go now, Liss—will you be glad to have us gone?"

The other was quiet for so long that Keepersmith was afraid he had already fallen into the odd open-eyed sleep of his kind. But at last the soft voice came sibilantly across the fire.

"No. You and I, Sssmith, we have made our own beginning. You are teaching me and I will teach my people. We will both be sstronger for it.

"And I would misss you, Sssmith."

That dawn and the many that followed found them moving, Liss in the lead and setting a steady, moderate pace. The passing of time and the changing character of the land made the terrain greener, but less inviting than Keepersmith's mountain valley.

For here, where there was plenty of game and adequate water and little effort needed to grow half-wild crops, there was also continual danger. Pockets of Men had drifted down from the mountains and settled here in a territory that was still claimed by the Razoi as their own.

In places where a single Man village lived in uneasy truce with its nearest Razoi neighbors, both were in constant fear of the southern tribe. Thought to be desert-based and so called "dusteaters" by the Razoi, they were shorter than the northern breed and of slightly different coloring, but they were broad-shouldered, heavily muscled, and ferocious fighters. They struck northward in small bands and then retreated to the safety of the southern desert. They were raiders and bandits, hated by everyone.

Yet the common enemy was not enough to unite the plains peoples into the kind of peace that Keepersmith and Liss shared. The raids only made the Men more suspicious of their neighbors, regardless of their different appearance. A Man travelling with a Razoi was not only unusual—he might be viewed as traitorous.

So Liss and Keepersmith avoided any settlements as they moved southward. They camped one evening beside a clear placid stream lined almost down to the water with broad-leaved fera trees. Keepersmith picked one of its fruits, but the orange hue and crisp skin of the small ellipsoid told him that it was still in its second phase and would be poisonous to a Man. So he rested against the thick trunk of the tree and ate some dried meat while Liss put aside his pack and staffaxe and dived soundlessly into the stream.

Keepersmith watched the shiny green forehead bobbing up every few seconds until it disappeared around an upstream bend. Then he bent over and took the small thing Liss had brought to him out of his pack. He reflected, as he did so, on the importance of the material from which the pack had been made.

The alth was a large carnivore which was hunted for food by the northern Razoi. Its thick skin, virtually indestructible once shaped and properly cured, had been the first basis of trade between Liss's people and the shivering human refugees who had fled northward.

The southward tribes could not stand the cold, but alth skins made the climate livable for Liss's people. They covered cave mouths and the doors of earthern huts, and made warm sleeping nests for the families. They lasted so well that the Razoi had more than they needed, and the Men needed them badly.

But the Men had nothing to trade.

Had it not been summer when the Men reached their valley, they would not have survived. For it took weeks of experimenting and failing before they struck the right mixture and the right process to manufacture a tradable item—a glazed jug which would store water, so necessary to the Razoi through winter and drought.

But trade began in time, and by winter the Men had cured enough alth skins to clothe themselves and make their primitive shelters bearable. And one Man had carefully split squares of the thick hide into supple, thin layers. She had rebound them with a hide thong and begun the Writing.

The Writing was knowledge, and it was the very heart of Keepersmith's life. It contained all the knowledge the *Hawk* had left with them, and all the things they had learned on their own. The pottery formula. All the useless designs and the one successful one for a loom to weave the fibery grainflowers into coarse cloth. The secret of forced fire and the agonizing story of how they tried and failed, that first winter, to forge steel.

And the Writing told of that next summer's hardship, when only Ironblaster saved them from being overrun by wave after wave of southerners returning to fight in the warmer weather. A passage from that section had special meaning for Keepersmith as he held the metal thing.

All the guns are gone now, broken by stone axes or clubs or, bless them, by dying men who would not have them reach the three-fingered hands of our enemies.

The Blaster is all we have left now of the *Hawk*'s equipment, but its explosive effect makes it useless at short range. We have weapons, but they are not much better than the Razoi's, and we are only learning to use them. The Razoi are skilled and strong and savage, and we are all weak and hungry.

Winter will be here soon, and we will have some rest from attack. We have managed to store some food—dried meats and some wild grain. Some of us will survive this second winter, but we will all die next summer if we don't have some kind of short-range weapon more effective than the ones the Razoi carry.

I see only one choice for us. I must take the Blaster with me now, before winter sets in, and hunt out some iron deposits. Then, through the winter, I will try again to forge a workable steel weapon—a sword. That will give us longer reach, and a cutting edge. It may be enough of an advantage.

I am leaving secretly, because I know there are those among us who would see only that I am leaving the settlement undefended. They would not understand, as I do, that if I don't go we have only one bleak winter ahead of us. If I do go, and I am successful, we may live to see the *Hawk* return.

I pray that it may be so.

There was no doubt in Keepersmith's mind that the object he held was one of the "guns" the Writing referred to. It said little about them, except that they operated on the same principle as Ironblaster, and Ironblaster was described and diagrammed in detail.

He heard a splashing sound, and looked up to see Liss climbing out of the water some twenty meters downstream, carrying three large fish. He twisted the head off each one and placed the heads carefully on the bank. Then he squatted down and began to eat the fish in small, delicate bites, thoroughly chewing all the bones except the backbone. He would be a long time at his meal.

Keepersmith looked back at the gun in his hand. Now was the time.

A sharp twist removed half of the butt and revealed a latch which, when pressed, lifted off another section. Keepersmith examined the interior of the gun, comparing it to his knowledge of Ironblaster.

Similar, but far from identical. The Bending Converter was much smaller.

The Converter used a process which Keepersmith did not entirely understand.   He knew that it took common water and converted it into helium and oxygen.   But he was not certain why it created the power which, focussed through the barrel of Ironblaster, created enough heat to melt mountains.

He knew what the energy of Ironblaster could do.   Fired at a living thing, tree or Razoi or . . . Man, the water in the target turned instantly to high-temperature steam, causing a tremendous explosion.   Ironblaster was not a weapon that could be used at close range.

But in the gun which Liss had brought, there was a different sort of apparatus. The power created by the Bending Converter was apparently channelled electrically through a vibrator which changed the tremendous electrical energy into ultra-sonic vibrations and focussed it down the short barrel of the gun.

That much he knew from the Writings.

He frowned in concentration, trying to remember the Writings about Ironblaster.

The reserve energy cell broke water down into hydrogen and oxygen.   The oxygen was discharged as a waste product, and the hydrogen converted into helium in the Bending Converter.   Ironblaster's reservoir held a good mouthful of water, but there was no reservoir in the smaller weapon.   But the Bending Converter was obviously there, and so far as Keepersmith knew, its fuel was—*had to be*—water. Where, then, did the water come from?

Again he searched his memory.   The little vents in the rear of the barrel told him they took in air and condensed the water from the air.

And then he suddenly knew what this weapon was.   It was something that Ironblaster had never been designed for.   It required only the power it could draw from the moisture in the air, and it could kill enemies at close range.

He looked again at the switch on the side.

Kill.   Stun.

It was not even necessarily designed to kill.   Again his probing eyes looked at the mechanism in the open butt.   This weapon should, like Ironblaster, be self-fueling and self-operating.   Then why wasn't it?   There were stains on the butt which indicated the gun had been used as a club—surely even a southern Razoi would have figured out how to use it properly if it were still working.

Carefully, reverently, he drew Ironblaster from the holster at the right side of his belt and opened it in the way that only he knew how.   Yes, they were similar. Not identical, but similar.   He traced the thin lines of Ironblaster's circuits and compared them with the smaller, thinner lines of the strange weapon.

It took time, but finally he saw the break.   A tiny black scratch across the engraved circuit.

He knew how that could be healed, but would it restore the gun to full efficiency? Without the tools and equipment at hand, there was no way to find out.

His concentration was broken by a scream.

He dropped the gun and sprang away from the tree, looking downstream to where Liss had made his meal.   He saw that the Razoi had finished and, according to his habit, had been burying the fish remnants, head and backbone, each at the base of a tree.   The scream had come from the creature which had dropped out of the tree above him and clubbed him as the bodies met.

Keepersmith now saw the attacker stand up and whirl to face the unconscious Razoi.   It lifted something in both arms above its head, and he could see the gleam of steel. . . .

"No!" he shouted, and ran down the bank, drawing his sword.   The figure jerked around, the sword still held high.   It was a woman, dressed in a cloth tunic and wearing a sword harness.   Her face was an ugly mask of hatred.

"A Man," she said.   Her voice was barely a whisper, but it carried infinite menace.   "A Man defending this filth.   *Defend yourself then!"*

She was barely ten centimeters shorter than he, and fast, strong and skilled.   He saw that the moment her strong right wrist whipped her Smithsword up for a direct slash downward.   It was all he could do to parry the blow without killing her.

Her steel rang against his, slid toward his wrist, and he flipped it off the quillions. He had barely time to recover before her slash came in toward his waist.

His parry was almost too late, because she snapped her sword in mid-swing toward his legs.   He fended off the slash, but rather than counterattack, he leaped backward.

"Peace!" he called.   "We are not enemies!"

But he could tell from the fighting glaze in her dark eyes that she did not even hear him.   He had to leap back again as her sword came up in a swoop toward his crotch.

As it passed him he leaped in and swung up his own sword with the flat turned, slapping her hand against the grip.   Her weapon spun crazily away and half-buried itself in the soft turf near the river.

She faced him defiantly, shaking her injured hand, ready for the deathblow. When it didn't come at once, she glanced at where her sword lay.

"Don't think of it," Keepersmith said.   "Sit down and keep still."

She did, and he saw her clearly for the first time.   Her face and limbs were dirty and scratched, her long black hair a filthy, matted mane, her sandals badly worn.   But there was still spirit in the eyes that watched him as he moved sideways, his sword still drawn, to where Liss was trying to sit up.

"Are you all right, Liss?"

"Mosstly," said the Razoi, rubbing the back of his head and watching the woman.

"Why did you try to kill my friend?" Keepersmith asked the woman.

"Your *friend?*   What kind of Man calls a Razoi his *friend?"*

"I do," he answered, quiet power in his voice.   "I am called Keepersmith."

All the hatred drained from her face, and amazement took its place.   "Keepersmith!"   She looked at him, and he could tell that she was comparing the Man before her to everything she had heard about him.   He wondered if she would challenge him, but evidently there were few Men on the plains of his stature. There was sullen respect in her voice, as she asked, "What are you doing this far south and—"   She glanced at Liss.   "—in such company?"

"It is not for me to answer you," he said sternly, and she dropped her eyes. "I ask you again, why did you attack my friend?"

"He is Razoi."

"That is no answer."

She raised her eyes to his face.   "It is answer enough for me."

"But *not* for me!"

For a moment more she hesitated. Then she shrugged her shoulders and seemed to shrink as her defiance faded and weariness washed over her.

"A band of Razoi raided my village," she told them. "I was in the fields, planting. Hilam, my husband, was working on the house—the rains were heavy last winter, and he wanted to build a new roof all made of wood.

"Hilam had insisted that I take the sword to the fields. He said the village was well enough defended, but . . . he was wrong. I heard the alarm and rushed back—but they were already gone. I found Hilam. . . ." Her voice broke, and Keepersmith did not urge her. After a moment she went on.

"I found my husband dead in the doorway of our house. And beside him . . . our son. Six summers only, and Thim had his wooden training sword in his hand. . . ."

She straightened up, and looked at Keepersmith. "I swore vengeance for the death of my family, and for days I have been on their trail. Last night I got this far. They watered here, but I was too tired to go further. I slept in that tree, and when I woke and saw a Razoi here, it seemed he had to be one of them. . . ."

Suddenly Liss spoke up, his voice angrier than Keepersmith had ever heard it. "You thought I was a ssouthern dussteater?" He stood up, but Keepersmith forestalled whatever he had planned to do.

"Liss—be still, please, she does not understand." Then to the woman, "The southern Razoi are his enemies, too. In my mountains there is peace between Men and Razoi. And this is Liss, *my friend.*"

They both looked at Liss, whose usually unreadable face was working heavily as he struggled to conquer his resentment. "I have never killed a Man," he said at last. "And I *would not* kill a child." He turned away, finished burying the fish remnants, and dived into the stream.

The two Men watched him go, then the woman stood up and faced Keepersmith.

"Help me," she said.

"I have my own path to follow."

"But you are Keepersmith, the Voice of the *Hawk,* who watches over us." The reverence in her voice told him what she believed about the *Hawk.* "Give me back my sword and help me destroy the scum who killed my family!"

"No," he said. Her sorrow touched him, but he could not yield to her pleading. He was not, he reminded himself, an ordinary Man. "The *Hawk* has another duty for me.

"But take your sword, in any case." He picked it up off the ground, and held it by the blunted lower third of the blade. As he offered her the hilt, he said, "I do not approve, but if vengeance will be some comfort for your loss, I will not forbid it."

She gripped the handle of the sword, but still he held it. Her eyes questioned him.

"I want your promise that you will not use this against Liss."

She looked startled, as though she wondered if Keepersmith had read her mind. "He is truly your . . . friend?"

"I have said it."

"Then . . . I will not harm him.   I swear it."

He released the sword, and she sheathed it with trembling hands.

"How long since you have eaten?" he asked.

She shrugged.   "A day.   Two."

He gestured toward the stream.   "Bathe and rest for this day.   I can spare you some food."

She hesitated.   "The stream—" she began.   "The Razoi is there."   When he said nothing, she continued heatedly, "*I* swore not to harm *him*—I have heard no answering promise!"

"Liss!" Keepersmith called.   The Razoi appeared from the stream almost at the woman's feet.   She stepped aside as he came ashore.

"I heard," he said.   He faced the woman, standing closer to her than she obviously liked.   "You need not fear me.   Sssmith is my friend, and your enemiess are mine alsso.   If it will easse your mind, I will sstay out of the sstream while you bathe."

Keepersmith and Liss walked back to their camp in silence.   Keepersmith was digging in his pack for the food when a sharp cry of pain from the Razoi made him whirl around.

"What did you learn?" Liss asked, holding out the fragments of the small gun.   "What did you learn by breakhing it?"

"I did not break it, Liss.   It was already broken inside.   *That* is what I learned."   He took the pieces and snapped them back together, then offered the gun to Liss.   He accepted it, balancing it in his hand.

"You give me only what iss worthlesss, ass ussual," he said.   The bitterness in his voice surprised Keepersmith.

"Liss . . ."

"I have never ssaid it, Sssmith.   Not before thiss.   But that one—" He jerked his head downstream.   "—to her I am no better than the dussteaters who sslew her people.

"You have ssaid I am your friend.   Yet you do not trusst me either.   You are the ssame."

"No, Liss!"   But the words stung.

"Then why did you give me fire, but none of the ssecret wayss Man can usse it?   Why may I watch Ironblasster workh, but never be sshown *how* it workhss?

"Sssmith, do you believe I would usse Ironblasster againsst *you?*"

Keepersmith felt a tightness in his stomach.   How would he have felt in Liss's place?   He could not speak; he shook his head.

"Then sstop giving me only what we khannot usse.   Teach uss how to makhe potss and sswordss.   How to kheep that knowledge and give it to our children.   Teach uss the Writing!"

Liss was holding the gun out toward Keepersmith, clutching it desperately.   His whole body was tense, his voice pleading.   "Sssmith you ssay thiss thing may mean you and your people will leave.   We have sshared our world with you— sshare your learning with uss.   Sssmith, do *not* leave uss ass you found uss!"

Keepersmith laid down the food and went over to his friend.   In all their long acquaintance they had never touched except by accident but now, deliberately, he placed his hands on the Razoi's shoulders.   They were cool and still damp from the stream.

"How often have I said that I cannot speak for only myself in these matters? The fate of all Men rests with me.

"But I swear this to you, Liss.   If Men are to leave your world at last, I will do everything in my power to see that the Razoi are taught all our knowledge before we leave."

"And if there iss no messaage in thiss metal thing?   Will it sstill be as it wass? Dribbless of nothingss for the Rassoi?"

Liss's anguish crystallized the decision Keepersmith had been delaying for twenty summers.

"Then I will try to persuade the others that you can be trusted with more fire knowledge.   Please understand, Liss, that is our most important secret; in that I would have to obey their wishes.

"But I *will* teach you Writing.   I give you my promise.   *Whatever* happens, I *will* teach you Writing."

The scaled face turned up toward Keepersmith.

"You know I have wanted thiss."

"Yes.   You have been very patient.   And you have been a good friend."

He released Liss, picked up the food, and walked downstream to where the woman was dressed again and sitting on the bank.   They sat silently together while she ate.   When she had finished, she said, "I will come with you."

"What?"   Keepersmith had been staring thoughtfully at the stream, planning how to keep his promise to Liss.

"I said I will come with you."

"Why?"

"They have too long a start.   And there is nothing to go back to."

"But you don't know where we are going."

"It doesn't matter.   You said it is an errand in the service of the *Hawk*—perhaps this was all . . . arranged by the *Hawk* himself so that I would be willing to help you."

"The *Hawk*," Keepersmith said quietly, "takes no responsibility for the actions of Razoi.   You are here by accident,"—but for a brief moment he wondered— "and if you wish to come with me, it is your free choice and no fate decreed by the *Hawk*."

"Then by my free choice," she said, looking directly at him from a face made younger for being clean, "I will go with you."

Keepersmith looked back at the camp, where Liss was stretched out in the last patch of sunlight.

"He travels with us."

She followed his gaze.

"I have sworn not to harm him."

"It is not enough.   You must trust him."

She hesitated only a moment before answering, "It is you I trust. But since you speak for him, then I trust him also."

Keepersmith nodded, and stood up to return to the campsite. "We move on at first light."

They travelled faster now, each in a separate silence. Liss led the little column and Marna brought up the rear, and both were glad of the great wall of Keepersmith between them.

Keepersmith's packed food was soon running low, and they had to pause, sometimes for a day at a time, to hunt and to gather the ferafruit that was already ripe in the warmer southern climate. They were never far from a river or stream, so that Liss was well fed. They might have asked him to catch more fish than he needed so that they could share his meal, but they respected his horrified aversion to cooked fish. So the Men snared small game and grazed the edible plants.

It was near dusk of a day so long that Keepersmith knew midsummer was very close when Liss halted abruptly. The tense attitude of his body warned them as no word could do, and Keepersmith and Marna melted into the brush at either side of the rough trail. Liss moved cautiously forward and inspected something on the ground, half-concealed by a bed of fork-leaved creepers. Then he straightened up and waved them forward.

When they stood beside him they saw what he had seen—a brownish-green hand covered with dried and flaking scales.

They dragged the body out into the clear. It was a southern Razoi. His angular face had shrunk to fit the skull, and the finely scaled body was totally dehydrated.

"How long has he been dead?" Keepersmith asked Liss.

"It iss hard to tell," answered the Razoi. "One of my people would lookh likhe thiss only a few hourss after death. But thesse ssouthern dussteaterss need lesss water. He hass been dead for many dayss."

"Then they are far enough ahead of us," said Keepersmith.

"For a time," said Liss.

"What does that mean?" demanded Marna. "This is one of the raiders who attacked my village." She touched one of the emaciated legs with her sandalled foot. "I recognize his two-toed track. Are we following them, after all?"

"Not following," said Liss. "But we are going to the ssame plasse they are."

"Why?"

"On the *Hawk's* business," stated Keepersmith, "and I'm impatient to get it done. Liss," he gestured toward the ugly body, "do you want to bury him?"

"A *dussteater?*"

"Then there is no need to linger."

He started off down the partially cleared, winding track they had been following for some days, leaving Liss and Marna to come after him at their own speed.

The demanding march had dulled the edge of Marna's suspicion and Liss's resentment, so that they walked now barely a meter apart in comfortable silence.

"Why don't you want to bury him?" Marna asked suddenly.

"Why sshould I?" came the answer over Liss's shoulder.

"But your people bury their dead. I have seen it. . . ." She stopped abruptly as Liss whirled around to face her.

"He is a *dussteater,*" he hissed. "He is *not* one of my people. Do you sstill not see the differensse between uss?"

Startled by the sudden confrontation, Marna held back the sharp words that came so readily to her tongue. Instead she said awkwardly, "I—I am trying to learn, Liss. I have promised Keepersmith to trust you, and I—" to her surprise, she meant it, "I do. But it's hard to trust someone you don't know."

There was a long silence as Liss's bright, wet-looking eyes stared at her steadily. Then he said, "I know what it iss to be denied knowledge. Assk what you will— I will try to answwer. But let us sstay with Sssmith."

They walked on together, hurrying for a time to make up the few moments lost. When they could see Keepersmith's broad back a few meters ahead of them once again, they slowed their pace.

"About the burying . . ." began Marna.

"Yess. We bury dead things to bring them to life again."

"You mean like the fish, to—uh—"

"Fertilisse the ssoil?" He smiled at her look of surprise, revealing the double ridge of serrated bone that served him as teeth. "It is only the term that I learned from Sssmith. We have alwayss known that buried dead flessh feedss the living thingss near it.

"But we do it for another reasson—to free the sspirit of the dead thing to return again."

Marna frowned in concentration. "How does burying the body of a thing—?"

"It is all one. When the flessh returnss to new growth, the sspirit returnss too. But if the flessh is abandoned, the sspirit is trapped in the dead flessh and it diess."

"But if you believe that—"

"Yess?"

"Leaving that one unburied is a horrible revenge—worse than even I would ask."

The scaled shoulders shrugged. "It iss their own khusstom. It iss one markh of their ssavagery. And it iss why they have dwindled while my people have grown."

"But you did not abandon him out of respect for his custom?"

"No," Liss answered. "I *wanted* hiss sspirit to die. I would desstroy them all if I khould."

"I know *my* reasons, Liss. But why do *you* hate them so?"

"I hate them because they are sskhavengers, and live on the workh of otherss, and never give anything to the earth.

"I hate them bekhause they have been our enemiess ssince before the first Men khame here.

"I hate them," he turned to look at her, "bekhause they made *you* hate *me.*"

He increased his pace and moved ahead of her until he was halfway between her and Keepersmith.

She watched the iridescent scales on his back as they moved with his sinuous walk, and said softly, "I don't, Liss. Not now."

A few nights later, they had camped beside a stream, and on Liss's advice had foregone their fire. They had lost the tracks of the southerners, and could not be sure where they were.

Keepersmith sat on a log at the edge of the water, chewing the last of their ferafruit. Something splashed nearby and he looked up to see Marna climbing out of the river. A softer splash upstream drew his attention, and in the bright silver light of the full moons, he saw Liss's shiny head appear and sink again.

"You're not afraid to swim with him now," he said, as the woman pulled her light woven tunic over her head.

"No," she answered, sitting beside him and leaning over to wring the water from her long black hair. "But I don't understand him, either. Or you."

"Me?"

"You are Keepersmith, our leader. And here you are further south than Men have gone for generations. Can't you tell me at least where we are going?"

"I gave you the chance to go your own way," he reminded her.

"And I reject it now as then," she answered hotly. Then more calmly, "But I am walking totally blind. Liss knows more than I do."

"And you resent that?"

She started to speak, paused, and began again. "A season ago I would have given you good and valid reasons why I did *not* resent it."

"And now?"

"Now I am free to admit that I do."

Suddenly Keepersmith laughed. His rich voice rumbled out over the water, bringing Liss to the surface nearby.

"Sssss!" At the quiet sound the laughter stopped instantly. "You are ssometimess a *fool,* Sssmith!"

Keepersmith's voice was choked and hardly above a whisper. "You are right, my friend. But it has been so long since I laughed." He cleared his throat. "Marna has asked me why we are here, Liss."

"Then tell her," came the crisp answer. "Ssoftly." He ducked back under the water and was gone.

A moment later, Keepersmith handed Marna the small gun. She accepted it gingerly, astonished at the lightness and the cool touch of the metal.

"What is it?" she asked

"Call it—a small Ironblaster. But it doesn't work."

She lifted her eyes to his face with sudden understanding. "The Words say that Ironblaster was the gift of the *Hawk.* This . . .?"

"I don't know," he said grimly. He turned the gun in her hands so that the bright moonlight shone down on the inscription.

"This writing is the mark of the *Hawk,* but—"

She interrupted him, growing more excited as the implications struck her. "Has He . . . Is it time . . . oh, Keepersmith!"

"I have said it. *I don't know what it means!*"

He took the gun from her, gripped it tightly as doubt washed across her face.

"But—you are Keepersmith! The Ironfinder! You taught my village Smith the Words, but you alone knew the Writings! You *speak* for the *Hawk!* If you don't know—"

"Then who does?" he finished for her. "No one does. But I am supposed to. It could mean whatever I say it means. But this time I cannot lie."

"Lie?"

He stood up and walked a few steps along the bank. "I have shocked you. Yes, I lie.

"When a Man asks a question, he needs an answer. Two Men each claim that this varipig is his, or that newborn boychild isn't. Someone must decide for them.

"When is it best to plant—this day or that? Which fields should lie fallow? How many pots should we have for next season's trading?

"An answer. A judgment. I have always offered *my* best judgment, but they— Macson, Yarma, Hollister, the others who have been leaders in the seasons since I became Keepersmith—they believe that the *Hawk* speaks *through me.*"

He turned toward where she sat motionless. The fluid reflections from the river water danced across their faces. Keepersmith's was grim with strain.

"I have never spoken of this before, but I say it now: If the *Hawk* speaks through me, *I cannot tell it.* I have borne this burden *alone.*

"If this," he raised the hand with the gun in it, "is a signal of the *Hawk's* return, then I *welcome it!* For it will mean the end of—"

His head turned sharply at the splashing sound, but not before three-fingered hands had grabbed the ankle and thigh of the leg nearer the river, and unbalanced him. He toppled awkwardly sideways, and slapped loudly into the river.

The water churned furiously, and Keepersmith heaved himself out of the water. He stood on the floor of the river bed and tried to shake off the small yellow-green Razoi clinging to his shoulders and pinning his arms.

At the first sound, Marna had leaped across the small clearing to where she had left her sword when she went to bathe. Two Razoi rushed out from the forest and blocked her before she could reach it. She spun around and fled into the trees across the clearing.

It was dark under the vine-woven trees. The Razoi who followed her could see better than she, but she was bigger and faster. She swung up to the lowest limb of the nearest tree, waited until they had passed beneath, then dropped to the ground and ran back to the clearing.

Keepersmith was half on the bank. His arms and shoulders were bleeding badly, but his right arm was free and his sword in his hand.

She caught up her sword and whirled to face the two who had followed her. They were shorter than Liss, but wider. Their shoulders bulged with muscles, and they knew how to use their staffaxes. They rushed at her simultaneously, bringing down the axeheads in vicious overhead strokes.

She blocked the one on her right, accepting all the power of the blow on the blunted edge of her sword near the hilt.   At the same time she twisted to the right. The second axehead struck harmlessly in the grass, but swept up in a wide horizontal swing aimed at her waist.   She turned her wrist to let the first wooden staff slide off the tip of her sword, and jumped backward just in time.

Then she realized she had done exactly what they wanted her to do.   Keepersmith's back was unguarded!

The Razoi in the river were struggling to pull him into the water again, where they had at least some advantage.   Three yellow-green bodies were floating downstream, already almost totally submerged.   But three more still clung to Keepersmith, one of them pinning his left arm in such a way that Keepersmith couldn't strike at him effectively without injuring himself.

The two Razoi Marna had been fighting turned as one and ran for Keepersmith, staffaxes raised and already moving downward.

Marna charged after them, drawing from her body every ounce of speed it held. Too far!

With a last lunge she threw herself under the feet of one of them.   He stumbled and went down, and the axe flew away from his hand.   He surged to his knees and launched himself bare-handed at her.   The weight of his compact body struck her and pinned her to the ground before she could stop rolling and get her sword free.

Through her own desperate struggle, she saw that the second Razoi had reached Keepersmith, and the deathblow was even then on its way down. . . .

A streak of green flashed between Keepersmith and the southern Razoi, and suddenly Liss was there, his staff braced and blocking that powerful blow.   The sight brought her new strength as she fought the scaly creature who was trying to fasten his ridged jaws in her throat.

She brought her elbow up under the chinless, snouted face, and pushed.   For a straining few seconds he resisted, then his clutching grip was broken and he was propelled off her.

As he staggered backward, her sword came up from the ground in a clean arc and sliced through his neck.

Liss had forced the smaller Razoi toward the trees.   She whirled around to see him back into the broad trunk of a fera.   In that brief instant of surprise, Liss turned his staff from its cross-brace and jabbed the sharpened point downward. The southerner cried out once and sank dead to the ground.

Keepersmith had killed another of the attackers.   The last two knew they were beaten, and as Liss and Marna ran toward Keepersmith, they released him and dived for the deep water in the middle of the river.

Marna halted at the shore and helped an exhausted and bleeding Keepersmith to pull himself all the way out of the water.

Liss dropped his staff and dived after the fleeing Razoi.   In a few moments one of them floated to the surface a few meters downstream.   Liss returned with the other one and half-dragged him out of the water.   He threw the southerner down on the bank with a hissing curse.

"Why did they attack us?" asked Keepersmith.

"You are Men, and we are nearing their sstronghold.   That alone would be enough reasson."

"You say that as if it is not the only one," said Marna.

"They know who you are, Sssmith," Liss said.   "They know that the Men would be eassier prey without you.   And they wanted your sswordss."

"They know me?   How?"

"Bekhausse they know me, and there iss only one Man who would be with me." He turned to his prisoner, cutting off their questions.   "None of the otherss ess-khaped.   But this one will lead uss where we musst go."

Keepersmith looked at him in surprise.   "You told me *you* knew where it was."

"No," Liss corrected him.   "I do know *where* it iss—in a valley in the ssouthern mountainss.   But there is only one entransse to the valley, and it iss well hidden. I ssaid that I khould lead you there."

"And if you hadn't captured a dusteater to find the entrance for you?   How had you planned to lead us through the hidden entrance?"

"I planned," Liss answered steadily, "to khapture a dussteater to find the en-transse."

And now it was Marna who laughed, a clear mellow sound, and Keepersmith joined her.

Soon after that the ground began to rise sharply.   They marched faster, stopping only briefly.   The southern Razoi maintained a surly silence except when Liss addressed him directly.   Then he answered with fear and grudging respect in his ugly scaled face.

Keepersmith and Marna had dressed their wounds with mud and herb poultices, which dried and cracked off within two days, leaving only faint red lines in their skin.

As soon as the land left the level, the ground began to dry out and it wasn't long before they were trudging through a rising, stone-littered desert.   Keepersmith had never been this far south, and he asked Liss about the terrain.

"Thesse mountainss are the ssame as ourss.   They run from our valleyss far to the wesst, then turn back ssouthward.   The wind bringss the rainfall from the ssouth and easst, and the mountainss sstop it here.   Beyond the mountainss iss dessert.   No Rassoi hass ever khrossed it."

Besides being much drier, these mountains were higher and more forbidding than Keepersmith's.   The little party was climbing steadily toward one great sheer cliff which stood out above a group of smaller hills.

At last Liss paused, stopping their prisoner with a sharp word.

"The entransse to their valley iss here ssomewhere," he told them.

"Then let's rest before we go in," suggested Marna.   "We have been running on little food, and you need some water, Liss."

The Razoi did indeed look uncomfortable.   The dry dusty heat had made the Men sweat profusely, but it was not the heat but the dusty air that affected Liss.

His skin was dried out until the tiny scales looked separate and brittle, and he was breathing raspily.

But he said, "No. I thankh you, Marna, but there must be water in the valley if even thiss," he gestured toward their prisoner and used the Razoi word Keepersmith had heard before, "khan survive."

When he heard that word applied to him, the southern Razoi cried out and threw himself at Liss, his clawed hands reaching for the taller one's throat.

Liss was ready for him. He stepped aside and grabbed one of the arms, spinning the southerner off balance. Then he whipped his other arm around the stocky yellowish neck and applied pressure. He grabbed up his staff and flipped it around so that its point was aimed at one of the creature's eyes. He hissed something in his own language, barely loudly enough for his captive to hear it. After a moment the snouted head nodded very slightly.

Liss released him and let him fall to the ground.

"He needed more perssuassion," said Liss. "He will lead uss now."

The southerner stood up, rubbing his throat, and led the way off to the left. For several minutes he wound in and out of the rocks. Then suddenly he darted away.

Liss was right after him, and the two Razoi disappeared into the maze of rocks. The Men could hear clattering stones and the sounds of a struggle, but could not be sure of their direction.

Then they heard a high-pitched cry, and in a few moments Liss appeared, panting heavily. "Thiss way."

They followed him, and paused for a moment beside the dead body of the Razoi prisoner.

"He tried to get through and warn the otherss," Liss said. "I give him honor for that." He looked at Marna. "When it iss over, I will bury thiss one."

Behind them was a narrow crack in what seemed to be an otherwise solid wall of stone. Liss's slim body slipped through it easily, but the two Men had to literally scrape themselves through the rough-edged opening. Beyond it was a space large enough for Keepersmith and Marna to walk upright, a short corridor which ended in sunlight. They looked out into the valley.

It was an awesome place.

It was roughly triangular, and it stretched before them for several hundred meters. At its far end loomed the mountain that had been their landmark. It towered over the valley a kilometer high, and it seemed perfectly smooth along the top half of its face. The valley widened and sloped sharply upward to meet the mountain until it seemed, crazily, that it was the valley which braced up and supported that vast ominous cliff.

Fed by the little rainfall the cliff drained off the passing clouds, and by underground springs which carried the melting snow from the high regions further west, the floor of the valley was green. But the growth was wild, untended.

Keepersmith's practiced eye could see that the valley could support no more than three hundred Razoi, and even that number would require an unusually large stock of fish in the one surface river. It ran the length of the valley and fed into an opening in the mountainside, not twenty meters from where they stood.

They did not expect to find sentries—the concealed entry was protection enough for the valley. Still they moved cautiously toward the river, and Marna and Keepersmith stood watch while Liss dived gratefully into the water. When he climbed out again a few moments later, his skin was already returning to its natural luminous green.

"Now, Liss," asked Keepersmith. "We are here. Where is the metal room?"

Marna started, but did not interrupt. Soon enough she would have answers.

Liss pointed toward the cliff.

"You ssee where the valley rissess and khlimbss the fasse of the mountain?" Keepersmith nodded. "The dussteaters live in holess along that lowesst ridge. Above their holess the way iss ssteeper but sstill possible. Below the khrest of that nekhsst ridge—" They followed his directing arm, tracking the way with their eyes. "You ssee that darkh sspot? It iss the mouth of a khave. Insside iss where he found the ssmall Ironblasster-like thing."

"In the metal room."

"Yess."

They moved off along the edge of the valley. They had worked their way almost to the foot of the slope when a whistling sound cut through them. Marna made an odd noise and slumped to the ground.

Suddenly twenty southern Razoi came pouring down from the ridge. Above them, protected by the edge of the ridge, others were shouting and swinging strips of hide which cast stones at them.

"Back up the side of the slope!" shouted Keepersmith as he drew his sword . . . and Ironblaster. Liss did not hesitate, but bent down to the ground and with surprising strength lifted Marna in his arms and went scrambling back up the rocky hillside they had just left.

Rocks from the slings rained around them, but his route was fast and erratic, and he made it to the shelter of a group of tall rocks.

There he left Marna. With a word of apology, he took her sword and slid back down to Keepersmith.

The rain of rocks stopped near Keepersmith, for the southerners did not want to disable their own fighters. But he was hard pressed in personal combat, surrounded by waist-high, snarling Razoi and their deadly axes. He needed all his skill merely to defend himself, and even so his living attackers already had to step over dead ones to get at him.

Liss burst into the fray like a whirlwind. Even in that turbulent moment, Keepersmith gained a new understanding. For the sword Liss held was no more strange to him than his own staffaxe. He used it everywhere to its greatest advantage. How long had he been studying it, waiting to own his first sword?

Taken aback by the suddenness and unexpected nature of Liss's attack, the southerners fell back momentarily.

"Break it off, Liss," called Keepersmith. "There are too many of them."

"Then you musst usse Ironblasster!" Liss shouted in return. "Go! I will hold them!"

There was no time for Keepersmith to argue his friend's sacrifice. Keepersmith turned and ran down the center of the valley, luring some of the southern Razoi after him. His long legs easily outdistanced them, and as he ran, he pulled a pair of goggles out of their pocket near Ironblaster's holster, and put them on. The lenses had come with Ironblaster from the *Hawk*.

Wearing them, he turned and raised Ironblaster, and the pursuing Razoi stumbled to a panicked stop.

Even at this range, Keepersmith could not use Ironblaster on the Razoi themselves. The explosion of the water in their bodies, turned instantly into superheated steam by Ironblaster's tremendous power, would consume him.

Through the goggle lenses, Keepersmith saw the valley exactly as it had been. But the sun . . . the sun high overhead was a molten black disc.

He glanced quickly at the mountain towering over him. Along the third and final ridge, the coloring of the rock was different, and all his experience told him that the formation was unstable. If he could disturb it enough to jar loose a landslide . . .

Sick at heart for what he was doing, sorry for the death he would cause but seeing no other way out, and knowing full well that he might be destroying the very answers he sought, Keepersmith aimed Ironblaster at the middle of that third rise of land, some twenty meters below the dark opening which Liss had told him was the entrance to the metal room.

"*NOW*, Liss!" he warned, and Liss dived away from the southern fighters, who had been startled motionless by the giant voice echoing through the valley. He ran for the shelter of rocks where he had left Marna. He knelt beside her and pressed his face into the rock, covering his head with his arms.

Marna stirred, and moaned. Liss hissed urgently. "Your eyess! Khover your eyess!"

She sat up and looked out into the valley. She saw Keepersmith standing in the clear, aiming Ironblaster upward. . . .

With a cry of terror, she copied Liss.

And Ironblaster roared.

The valley shook with the thunder of it, and Keepersmith could not hear the cries of pain. Every southern Razoi in the valley went instantly blind as Ironblaster's lightning reached up to drag down the mountain.

To Keepersmith it was a clean, straight black line that stretched upward to the face of the mountain. Where it struck, a small black sun bloomed, and moved across the ridge at Keepersmith's command.

To Marna, who raised her head to look in brief, careful glimpses out into the valley, that black line was a searing bolt of light. She did not know, as Keepersmith did, that Ironblaster had been designed primarily for use at great distance in airless space, not to waste a part of its terrible energies heating atmosphere to blinding incandescence. She only knew that the passing filled her mind with fire, and she did not dare to look to where it struck the rock.

The black sun crept along the mountainside, melting a shallow groove in its wake. Then it died.

Keepersmith lowered Ironblaster and removed his goggles.

But the thunder still rang in the valley, rumbled in the stone itself, beneath their feet, all around . . . above . . .

"Liss!" Keepersmith shouted. "Marna! Run this way!"

The two figures scrambled down to the valley floor and ran desperately away from the shaking wall which towered above them. They reached Keepersmith. He turned and ran with them.

For Ironblaster had indeed disturbed the balance of the mountain. Along the narrow groove, vertical cracks were snaking downward, shaking the lower ridge and breaking off great monoliths which toppled outward and skidded down the hillside, dragging loose surface shale with it.

The three ran to the end of the valley, then they turned to watch as the massive weight of the second ridge sagged downward with a thunder not even Ironblaster could match, crushing and collapsing the tiny caves where the southerners had lived.

As the ground slipped away below the gaping, smoking wound, the ridge above it slowly shattered. Great crumbs of rock caromed wildly downward, setting off new landslides until the entire surface of the newly formed, unstable slope was in motion again.

Of this the watchers could only guess from the deafening, ground-shaking noise. For the tortured mountainside had vomited a great cloud of dust to shield its dying.

The sound diminished slowly, and at last there was utter silence. Taking its own time, a gentle breeze blew the dust clouds away.

And when the dust had cleared,the three of them could only stare for long minutes.

Up there, in the mountainside, above where Keepersmith had made his cut with Ironblaster, the thousands of tons of rock had slid away to reveal a vast metal wall curving outward from the cliff face. Its silver-gray, dusty surface gleamed dully in the sunlight, stretching nearly a hundred meters along the rocky face, and standing over a third as high.

There was one small, doorlike opening in it.

At last Keepersmith turned to Liss. "That is not the metal room the southerner spoke of."

"No," answered Liss. "He ssaid that it wass ssmall, barely ass tall ass you and very sshallow. That—"

There was so much awe in his voice that he could not continue.

"That," echoed Keepersmith, "must be the answer I have been sent here to find."

"Sshall we go with you?" asked Liss, his eagerness so plain that Keepersmith turned a face full of pain to him.

"Not this time, Liss. It is a secret I must understand alone—at least for now."

There were many things he wanted to say to these people who had shared his food and his peril for a long, wild summer. But he merely turned away and began to climb toward the giant shining secret that waited above him.

Liss and Marna watched as his huge figure grew smaller. They suffered helplessly as Keepersmith toiled his way up to the first ridge and then to the second, often falling, always getting up again.

At last the toy Man stood beside the dark opening in the metal wall. He stepped into it, and disappeared. For several minutes they watched anxiously, but when nothing happened, they relaxed their vigil and rested on the ground beside the mud-choked river.

A lud metallic sound rang through the valley, and Marna leaped to her feet, screaming.

"The opening is gone, Liss! I can't even tell where it was! Liss—the thing has swallowed Keepersmith!"

Liss, too, was disturbed. But he had known this Man longer than the woman had. So he calmed her as best he could. "He knowss what he iss doing, your Kheepersssmith. He will be backh. And he ssaid it—it iss a thing he musst do alone. We khan't help him now. We musst wait."

"Wait?" She realized that it was indeed their only choice. "Of course, we must wait for him, Liss. Wait and watch."

Just after the sun rose on the third day, the door in the small metal wall opened and Keepersmith stepped out. The door closed again behind him.

He walked back to them out of the dawn, carrying a black box and a small gray metal container. His powerful frame had thinned and his face was drawn and weary, but in his eyes there was a new wisdom.

"We are going back," he said.

Liss and Marna stared at him.

"Tell uss," said Liss. "Pleasse tell uss."

Keepersmith opened his mouth, but hesitated. Liss turned bitterly away.

"It iss the ssame," he said. "I am a Rassoi!"

"No, Liss." Marna reached out and touched Liss's arm lightly. "I am a Man, and the secrets of the *Hawk* are not for me either. Only the Keepersmith can know them."

Suddenly Keepersmith spoke in a voice barely above a whisper. "No more." They waited.

"All Men must know what I have learned here. We have lived in the shadow of error for centuries.

"The *Hawk* is not a god, Marna. It is only a machine which carried Men through the space between planets—" His eyes looked through them and they knew he was seeing something in his mind, a memory carried out of the place of secrets. "—between stars.

"The *Hawk* brought our people here; that much is true. But it will never return. Because it never left.

"*That*—" he said, gesturing toward the great metal wall shimmering in the new sunlight, "*That is the* Hawk!"

"I don't understand," wailed Marna. "Why—?"

"They didn't understand either, Marna. Our ancestors were warriors. Ironblaster found its true destiny here, for it was built for killing!   The *Hawk* landed, and some of the Men took Ironblaster and went out into this world searching for their enemies.   They came back—and the *Hawk* was gone.''

Liss gestured with one three-fingered hand toward the distant metal wall.   ''But you jusst ssaid . . .''

''That was the error.   It didn't leave.   It was just that our people could not find it when they returned.

''It must have happened suddenly.   One Man was still in the air lock—that was the small metal room, Liss.   The door leading into the ship was closed and locked. The outer door was open.

''And then the whole mountainside, disturbed perhaps by the shock of the *Hawk*'s landing, at last gave way and slid down to bury the *Hawk* from the sight of Men. There may have been others outside.   If so, they have been buried under that rock for centuries.

''There were only two on the ship itself, the Man in the airlock and one other, sealed helplessly inside.   This Man was hurt, and she died soon after—but she has left us this.''   He held up the metal cylinder.   ''It is a kind of Writing.   A speech Writing.   It tells much, and there is even more to learn.''

He did not mention the two long racks of Ironblasters that he had seen within the ship; that was knowledge that could be held until later.

''And our ancestors were the fighting Men who had been sent away from the *Hawk?*''

''Yes, and they too left a Writing.   The one that we have lived by.   They believed that their ship had flown off for some reason, but would return when it could.   They wanted us to be ready when it came back.   We have been waiting for centuries,'' his voice tightened, ''for a machine that has been buried at our feet!''

Out of the silence that followed came Marna's voice.   ''What—what will you do?''

''I will tell them the truth.   Whatever fate brought me here, I *have* learned the lesson of the *Hawk*.''

''And what iss that, Sssmith?''

''That the waiting is truly at an end.   In a sense, the *Hawk has* returned, and now we must save ourselves.   We must stop merely surviving and begin to grow.'' Again he held up the black box and the cylinder.   ''With these we can start to learn all the lost knowledge of the *Hawk*.''

He looked deliberately at Liss.

''We will *all* learn.''

''Your people,'' whispered Liss.   ''Will they agree?''

''They will,'' said the big man as he stepped between his friends and led the way out of the Valley of the Hawk.

''I am still Keepersmith.''

ISAAC ASIMOV

Good Taste

It was quite clear that it would not have happened—the family would not have been disgraced and the world of Gammer would not have been stunned and horrified—if Chawker Minor had not made the Grand Tour.

It wasn't exactly illegal to make the Grand Tour but, on Gammer at least, it was not really socially acceptable. Elder Chawker had been against it from the start, to do him justice, but then Lady Chawker took the side of her minor and mothers are, at times, not to be withstood. Chawker was her second child (both of them sons, as it happened) and she would have no more, of course, so it was not surprising that she doted on him.

Her younger son had wanted to see the Other-Worlds of the Orbit and had promised to stay away no longer than a year. She had wept and worried and gone into a tragic decline and then, finally, had dried her eyes and spoken stiffly to Elder Chawker—and Chawker Minor had gone.

Now he was back, one year to the day (he was always a young man to keep his word, and besides which the Elder's support would have ceased the day after, never fear) and the family made holiday.

Elder wore a new black glossy shirt but would not permit the prim lines of his face to relax, nor would he stoop to ask for details. He had no interest—no interest *whatever*—in the Other-Worlds with their strange ways and with their primitive browsing (no better than the ways on Earth of which Gammerpeople *never* spoke). He said, "Your complexion is dirtied and spoiled, Chawker Minor." (The use of the full name showed his displeasure.)

Chawker laughed and the clear skin of his rather thin face crinkled. "I stayed out of the sun as much as I could, Elder-mine, but the Other-Worlders would not always have it so."

Lady Chawker would have none of that either. She said warmly, "It isn't dirtied at all, Elder. It breathes a warmth."

"Of the Sun," grumbled Elder, "and it would be next that he would be grubbing in the filth they have there."

"No farming for me, Elder. That's hard work. I visited the fungus vats at times, though."

Chawker Major, older than Minor by three years, wider of face, heavier of body, but otherwise of close resemblance, was torn between envy at his younger brother's having seen different worlds of the Orbit and revulsion at the thought of it.   He said, "Did you eat their Prime, Minor?"

"I had to eat something," said Chawker Minor.   "Of course, there were your packages, Lady-mine.   Lifesavers, sometimes."

"I suppose," said Elder Chawker with distaste, "the Prime was inedible there. Who can tell the filth that found its way into it."

"Come now, Elder-mine."   Chawker paused, as though attempting to choose words, then shrugged.   "Well, it held body and soul together.   One got used to it.   I won't say more than that.   —But Elder-Lady-mine, I am so glad to be home. The lights are so warm and gentle."

"You've enough of the Sun, I take it," said Elder.   "But you *would* go.   Well, welcome back to the inner world with light and warmth under our control locked away from the patch and blaze of sunshine.   Welcome back to the womb of the people, as the saying goes."

"Yet I'm glad I went," said Chawker Minor.   "Eight different worlds, you know.   It gives you a view you don't have otherwise."

"And would be better off not having," said Elder.

"I'm not sure about that," said Chawker Minor, and his right upper eyelid trembled just slightly as he looked at Major.   Chawker Major's lips compressed but he said nothing.

It was a feast.   Anyone would have had to admit that, and in the end it was Chawker Minor himself, first to push away.   He had no choice; Lady would else have kept on supplying him with samples out of what seemed to be a bottomless larder.

"Lady-mine," he said, affectionately, "my tongue wearies.   I can no longer taste anything."

"*You* not taste?" said Lady.   "What kind of nithling-story is that?   You have the skill of the Grand-Elder himself.   At the age of six, you were already a Gustator; we had endless proofs of that.   There was not an additive you could not detect even when you could not pronounce them right."

"Taste-buds blunt when not used," said Elder Chawker, darkly, "and jogging the Other-Worlds can utterly spoil a man."

"Yes?   Well, let us see," said Lady.   "Minor-mine, tell your doubting Elder what you have eaten."

"In order?" said Chawker Minor.

"Yes.   Show him you remember."

Chawker Minor closed his eyes.   "It's scarcely a fair test," he said.   "I so relished the taste I did not pause to analyze it; and it's been so long."

"He has excuses.   See, Lady?" said Elder.

"But I will try," Chawker Minor said hastily.   "In the first place, the Prime base for all of them is from the fungus vats of the East Section and the 13th corridor within it, I believe, unless great changes have been made in my absence."

"No, you are right," said Lady, with satisfaction.

"And it was expensive," said Elder.

"The prodigal returns," said Chawker Major, just a bit acidly, "and we must have the fatted fungus, as the saying goes. —Get the additives, Minor, if you can."

"Well," said Chawker Minor, "the first dab was strongly Spring Morning with added Leaves A-Freshened, and a touch, not more than a touch, of Spara-Sprig."

"Perfectly right," said Lady, smiling happily.

Chawker Minor went on with the list, his eyes still closed, his taste-memory rolling backward and forward luxuriously over the tang and consistency of the samplings. He skipped the eighth and came back to it.

"That one," he said, "puzzles me."

Chawker Major grinned. "Didn't you get any of it?"

"Of course I did. I got most of it. There was Frisking Lamb—not Leaping Lamb, either, Frisking, even though it leaned just a little toward Leaping."

"Come on, don't try to make it hard. That's easy," said Chawker Major. "What else?"

"Green-Mint, with just a touch of Sour-Mint—*both*—and a dusting of Sparkle-Blood. —But there was something else I couldn't identify."

"Was it good?" asked Chawker Major.

"Good? This isn't the day to ask me that. Everything is good. Everything is succulent. And what I can't identify seems very succulent. It's close to Hedge-Bloom, but better."

"Better?" said Chawker Major, delightedly. "It's mine!"

"What do you mean yours?" said Chawker Minor.

Elder said, with stiff approval, "My stay-at-home son has done well while you were gone. He devised a computer-program that has designed and produced three new life-compatible flavor-molecules of considerable promise. Grand-Elder Tomasz himself has given one of Major's constructions tongue-room, the very one you just tested, Flyaway-Minor-mine, and has given it his approval."

Chawker Major said, "He didn't actually say anything, Elder-mine."

Lady said, "His expression needed no words."

"It *is* good," said Chawker Minor, rather dashed at having the play taken away from him. "Will you be entering for the Awards?"

"It has been in my mind," said Chawker Major, with an attempt at indifference. "Not with this one—I call it Purple-Light, by the way—but I believe I will have something else, more worthy of the competition."

Chawker Minor frowned. "I had thought that—"

"Yes?"

"—that I am ready to stretch out and think of nothing. Come, half a dab more of Major's construction, Lady-mine, and let's see what I can deduce concerning the chemical structure of his Purple-Light."

For a week, the holiday atmosphere in the Chawker household continued. Elder Chawker was well known in Gammer and it seemed that half the inhabitants of the world must have passed through his Section before all had had their curiosity sated and could see with their own eyes that Chawker Minor had returned unscathed.

Most remarked on his complexion, and more than one young woman asked if she might touch his cheek, as though the light tan were a layer that could be felt.

Chawker Minor allowed the touch with lordly complacence, though Lady disapproved of these forward requests and said so.

Grand-Elder Tomasz himself came down from his aerie, as plump as a Gammerman ever permits himself to be and with no sign that age or white hair had blunted his talents. He was a Master-Gustator such as Gammer might never have seen before despite the tales of Grand-Elder Faron of half a century ago. There was nothing that Tomasz tongued that did not open itself in detail to him.

Chawker Minor, who had no great tendency to underrate his own talent, felt no shame in admitting that what he himself had, innately, could not yet come anywhere near the old man's weight of experience.

The Grand Elder who, for nearly twenty years now, had governed the annual Awards festival by force of his skill, asked closely after the Other-Worlds which, of course, he himself had never visited.

He was indulgent, though, and smiled at Lady Chawker. "No need to fret, Lady," he said. "Young people these days are curious. In my time we were content to attend to our own cylinder of worth, as the saying goes, but these are new times and many are making what they call the Grand Tour. Good, perhaps. To see the Other-Worlds—frivolous, Sundrenched, browsive, non-gustational, without a taste-bud to content themselves with—makes one appreciate the eldest brother, as the saying goes."

Grand-Elder Tomasz was the only Gammerman whom Chawker Minor had ever heard actually speak of Gammer as "the eldest brother" although you could find it often enough in the video-cassettes. It had been the third colony to be founded in the Moon's orbit back in the pioneering years of the twenty-first century; but the first two, Alfer and Bayter, had never become ecologically viable. Gammer had.

Chawker Minor said, with tactful caution, "The Other-World people never tired of telling me how much the experience of Gammer meant to all the worlds that were founded afterward. All had learned, they said, from Gammer."

Tomasz beamed. "Certainly. Certainly. Well said."

Chawker Minor said, with even greater caution, "And yet such is self-love, you understand, Grand-Elder, that a few thought they had improved on Gammer."

Grand-Elder Tomasz puffed his breath out through his nose (never breathe through your mouth any more than you can help, he would say over and over again, for that blunts the Gustator's tongue) and fixed Chawker with his deep blue eyes that looked the bluer for the snow-white eyebrows that curved above them.

"Improved in what way? Did they suggest a specific improvement?"

Chawker Minor, skating over the thin ice and aware of Elder Chawker's awful frown, said softly, "In matters that they value, I gather. I am not a proper judge of such things, perhaps."

"In matters that *they* value. Did you find a world that knows more about food chemistry than we do?"

"No! Certainly not, Grand-Elder. None concern themselves with that, as far as I could see. They all rely on our findings. They admit it openly."

Grand-Elder Tomasz grunted. "They can rely on us to know the effects and side-effects of a hundred thousand molecules, and each year to study, define and analyze the effects of a thousand more. They rely on us to work out the dietary needs of elements and vitamins to the last syllable. Most of all, they rely on us to work out the art of taste to the final, most subtly convoluted touch. They do so, do they not?"

"They admit all this, without hesitation."

"And where do you find computers more reliable and more complex than ours?"

"As far as our field is concerned, nowhere."

"And what Prime did they serve?" With heavy humor, he added, "Or did they expect a young Gammerman to browse."

"No, Grand-Elder, they had Prime. On all the worlds I visited they had Prime; and on all those I did not visit, I was told, there was also Prime. Even on the world where Prime was considered fit chiefly for the lower classes—"

Tomasz reddened. "Idiots!" he muttered.

"Different worlds, different ways," said Chawker Minor rather hurriedly. "But even then, Grand-Elder, Prime was popular when something was needed that was convenient, inexpensive, and nourishing. And they got their Prime from us. All of them had a fungal strain brought originally from Gammer."

"Which strain?"

"Strain A-5," said Chawker Minor, apologetically. "It's the sturdiest, they said, and the most energy-sparing."

"And the coarsest," said Tomasz, in satisfaction. "And what flavor-additives?"

"Very few," said Chawker Minor. He thought a moment, then said, "There was, on Kapper, a place where they had an additive that was popular with the Kapperpeople and that had—possibilities. Those were not properly developed, however, and when I distributed tastes of what Lady-mine had sent me they were forced to admit that it was to theirs as Gammer is to a space-pebble."

"You had not told me that," said Lady Chawker who, till then, had not ventured to interpose in a conversation that had the Grand-Elder as one of its participants. "The Other-Worlders liked my preparations, did they?"

"I didn't often hand it out," said Chawker Minor. "I was too selfish to do it; but when I did, they liked it a great deal, Lady-mine."

It was several days before the two brothers managed to find a way of being alone together.

Major said, "Weren't you on Kee at all?"

Chawker Minor lowered his voice. "I was. Just a couple of days. It was too expensive to stay long."

"I have no doubt Elder would not have liked even the two days."

"I don't intend telling him. Do you?"

"A witless remark.   Tell me about it."

Chawker Minor did, in semi-embarrassed detail, and said, finally, "The point is, Major, it doesn't seem wrong to them.   They don't think anything of it.   It made me think that perhaps there is no real right and wrong.   What you're used to, that's right.   What you're not used to, that's wrong."

"Try telling that to Elder."

"What he thinks is right, and what he is used to, are precisely the same.   You'll have to admit that."

"What difference does it make what *I* admit?   Elder thinks that all rights and wrongs were written down by the makers of Gammer and that it's all in a book of which there is only one copy and we have it, so that all the Other-Worlds are wrong forever.—I'm speaking metaphorically, or course."

"I believe that, too, Major—metaphorically.   But it shook me up to see how calmly those Other-World people took it.   I could—watch them browse."

A spasm of distaste crossed Major's face.   "Animals, you mean?"

"It doesn't look like animals when they browse on it.   That's the point."

"You watched them kill, and dissect that—that—"

"No."   Hastily.   "I just saw it when it was all finished.   What they ate looked like some kinds of Prime and it smelled like some kinds of Prime.   I imagine it tasted—"

Chawker Major twisted his expression into one of extreme revulsion, and Chawker Minor said, defensively, "But browsing came first, you know.   On Earth, I mean. And it could be that when Prime was first developed on Gammer it was designed to imitate the taste of browse-food."

"I prefer not to believe that," said Chawker Major.

"What you prefer doesn't matter."

"Listen," said Chawker Major.   "I don't care what they browse.   If they ever got the chance to eat real Prime—not Strain A-5, but the fatted fungus, as the saying goes—and if they had the sophisticated additives and not whatever primitive trash they use, they would eat forever and never dream of browsing.   If they could eat what *I* have constructed, and will yet construct—"

Chawker Minor said, wistfully, "Are you really going to try for the Award, Major?"

Chawker Major thought for a moment, then said, "I think I will, Minor.   I really will.   Even if I don't win, I eventually will.   This program I've got is different."   He grew excited.   "It's not like any computer program I've ever seen or heard of; and it works.   It's all in the—"   But he pulled himself up sharply and said uneasily, "I hope, Minor, you don't mind if I *don't* tell you about it?   I haven't told anyone."

Chawker Minor shrugged.   "It would be foolish to tell anyone.   If you really have a good program, you can make your fortune; you know that.   Look at Grand-Elder Tomasz.   It must be thirty-five years since he developed Corridor-Song and he still hasn't published his path."

Chawker Major said, "Yes, but there's a pretty good guess as to how he got to it.   And it's not really, in my opinion,—" He shook his head doubtfully, in preference to saying anything that might smack of *lèse-majesté*.

Chawker Minor said, "The reason I asked if you were going to try for the Award—"

"Well?"

"Is that I was rather thinking of entering myself."

"You?   You're scarcely old enough."

"I'm twenty-two.   But would you mind?"

"You don't know enough, Minor.   When have you ever handled a computer?"

"What's the difference?   A computer isn't the answer."

"No?   What is?"

"The taste-buds."

"Hit-and-miss-and-tastebuds-all-the-way.   We all know that sound and I will jump through the zero-axis in a bound, too, as the saying goes."

"But I'm serious, Major.   A computer is only the starting point, isn't it?   It all ends with the tongue no matter where you start."

"And, of course, a Master-Gustator like Minor-lad-here can do it."

Chawker Minor was not too tanned to flush.   "Maybe not a Master-Gustator, but a Gustator anyway, and you know it.   The point is that being away from home for a year, I've gotten to appreciating good Prime and what might be done with it. I've learned enough—Look, Major, my tongue is all I've got, and I'd like to make back the money that Elder and Lady spent on me.   Do you object to my entering? Do you fear the competition?"

Chawker Major stiffened.   He was taller and heavier than Chawker Minor and he didn't look friendly.   "There is no competition to fear.   If you want to enter, do so, Minor-child.   But don't come whimpering to me when you're ashamed. And I tell you, Elder won't like your making a no-taste-batch of yourself, as the saying goes."

"Nobody has to win right away.   Even if I don't win, I eventually will, as *your* saying goes," and Chawker Minor turned and left.   He was feeling a little huffy himself.

Matters trailed off eventually.   Everyone seemed to have had enough of the tales of the Other-Worlds.   Chawker Minor had described the living animals he had seen for the fiftieth time and denied he had seen any of them killed for the hundredth.   He had painted word-pictures of the grain fields and tried to explain what sunshine looked like when it glinted off men and women and buildings and fields, through air that turned a little blue and hazy in the distance.   He explained for the two-hundredth time that no, it was not at all like the sunshine effect in the outer viewing-rooms of Gammer (which hardly anyone visited anyway).

And now that it was all over, he rather missed not being stopped in the corridors. He disliked no longer being a celebrity.   He felt a little at a loss as he spun the book-film he had grown tired of viewing and tried not to be annoyed with Lady.

He said, "What's the matter, Lady-mine?   You haven't smiled all day."

His mother looked up at him, thoughtfully.   "It's distressing to see dissension between major and minor."

"Oh, come."   Chawker Minor rose irritably and walked over to the air-vent. It was jasmine-day and he loved the odor and, as always, automatically wondered how he could make it better.   It was very faint, of course, since everyone knew that strong floral odors blunted the tongue.

"There's nothing wrong, Lady," he said, "with my trying for the Award.   It's the free right of every Gammerperson over twenty-one."

"But it isn't in good taste to be competing with your brother."

"Good taste!   Why not?   I'm competing with everyone.   So's he.   It's just a detail that we're competing with each other.   Why don't you take the attitude that he's competing with me?"

"He's three years older than you, Minor-mine."

"And perhaps he'll win, Lady-mine.   He's got the computer.   Has Major asked you to get me to drop out?"

"No, he did not.   Don't think that of your brother."   Lady spoke earnestly, but she avoided his eyes.

Chawker Minor said, "Well, then, he's gone moping after you and you've learned to tell what he wants without his having to say it.   And all because I qualified in the opening round and he didn't think I would."

"Anyone can qualify," came Chawker Major's voice from the doorway.

Chawker Minor whirled.   "Is that the way it is?   Then why does it upset you? And why did a hundred people fail to qualify?"

Chawker Major said, "What some small-taste-nitherlings decide means very little, Minor.   Wait till it comes to the board."

"Since you qualified, too, Major, there's no need to tell me how little importance there is to some small-taste-nitherlings—"

"Young-mine," said Lady, rather sharply.   "Stop it!   Perhaps we can remember that it is very unusual for both Major and Minor of a single unit to qualify."

Neither ventured to break the silence in Lady's presence for a while thereafter—but their scowls remained eloquent.

As the days passed, Chawker Minor found himself more and more involved in preparing the ultimate sample of flavored Prime that, his own taste-buds and olfactory area would tell him, were to be nothing like anything that had ever rolled across a Gammer tongue before.

He took it upon himself to visit the Prime vats themselves, where the delectably bland fungi grew out of malodorous wastes and multiplied themselves at extraordinary speed, under carefully idealized conditions, into three dozen basic strains, each in its varieties.

(The Master-Gustator, tasting unflavored Prime itself—the fungal unalterate, as the saying went—could be relied upon to pin its source down to the section and corridor.   Grand-Elder Tomasz had more than once stated, publicly, that he could tell the very vat itself and, at times, the portion of the vat, though no one had ever quite put him to the full test.)

Chawker Minor did not pretend to the expertise of Tomasz, but he lipped and tongued and smacked and nipped till he had decided on the exact strain and variety he wanted, the one which would best blend with the ingredients he was mixing in his mind. A good Gustator, said Grand-Elder Tomasz, could combine ingredients mentally and taste the mixture in pure imagination. With Tomasz, it might, for all one knew, be merely a statement, but Chawker Minor took it seriously and was sure he could do it.

He had rented out space in the kitchens (another expense for poor Elder, although Chawker Minor was making do with less than Major had demanded).

Chawker Minor did not repine at having less, for, since he was eschewing computers, he didn't require much. Mincers, mixers, heaters, strainers, and the rest of the cookery tools took up little room. And at least he had an excellent hood for the masking and removal of all odors. (Everyone knew the horror-tales of the Gustators who had been given away by a single sniff of odor and then found that some creative mixture was in the common domain before they could bring it before the board. To steal someone else's product might not be, as Lady would say, in good taste, but it was done and there was no legal recourse.)

The signal-light flashed, in a code sufficiently well-known. It was Elder Chawker. Chawker Minor felt the thrill of guilt he had felt as a child when he had pilfered dabs of Prime reserved for guests.

"One moment, Elder-mine," he sang out, and, in a flurry of activity, set the hood on high, closed the partition, swept his ingredients off the table-top and into the bins, then stepped out and closed the door quickly behind him.

"I'm sorry, Elder-mine," he said, with an attempt at lightness, "but Gustatorship is paramount."

"I understand," said Elder, stiffly, though his nostrils had flared momentarily as though he would have been glad to catch that fugitive whiff, "but you've scarcely been at home lately, scarcely more so than when you were at your space-folly, and I must come here to speak to you."

"No problem, Elder, we'll go to the lounge."

The lounge was not far away and, fortunately, it was empty. Elder's sharp glances this way and that made the emptiness seem fortunate for him and Chawker Minor sighed inaudibly. He would be lectured, he knew.

Elder said, at last, "Minor, you are my son, and I will do my duty toward you. My duty does not consist, however, of more than paying your expenses and seeing to it that you have a fair start in life. There is also the matter of reproval in good time. Who wishes fair Prime must not stint on foul waste, as the saying goes."

Chawker's eyes dropped. He, along with his brother, had been among the thirty who had now qualified for the final Awarding to be held but a week in the future, and, the unofficial rumor had it, Chawker Minor had done so with a somewhat higher score than Chawker Major had.

"Elder," said Chawker Minor, "would you ask me to do less than my best for my brother's sake?"

Elder Chawker's eyes blinked in a moment of puzzlement and Chawker Minor clamped his mouth shut. He had clearly jumped in the wrong direction.

Elder said, "I do not ask you to do less than your best, but rather more than you are doing. Bethink you of the shaming you have inflicted on us in your little onset with Stens Major last week."

Chawker Minor had, for a moment, difficulty remembering what this could apply to. He had done nothing with Stens Major at all—a silly young woman with whom he was perfectly content to confine himself to mere talk, and not very much of that.

"Stens Major? Shaming? How?"

"Do not say you do not remember what you said to her. Stens Major repeated it to her elder and lady, good friends of our family, and it is now common talk in the Section. What possessed you, Minor, to assault the traditions of Gammer?"

"I did not do such a thing. She asked me about my Grand Tour and I told her no more than I have told three hundred others."

"Didn't you tell her that women should be allowed to go on the Grand Tour?"

"Oh."

"Yes. Oh."

"But, Elder, what I said was that if she would take the Grand Tour herself there would be no need to ask questions, and when she pretended to be shocked at such a suggestion, I told her that, in my opinion, the more Gammerpeople saw of the Other-Worlds, the better it would be for all of us. We are too closed a society in my opinion, and Elder, I am not the first to say so."

"Yes, I have heard of radicals who have said so, but not in our Section and certainly not in our family. We have endured longer than the other worlds; we have a stabler and fitter society; we do not have their problems. Is there crime among us? Is there corruption among us?"

"But Elder, it is at the price of immobility and living death. We're all so tied in, so enclosed."

"What can they teach us, these Other-Worlds? Were you not yourself glad to come back to the enclosed and comfortable Sections of Gammer with their corridors lit in the golden light of our own energy?"

"Yes—but, you know, I'm spoiled, too. There are many things on the Other-Worlds that I would have very much liked to have made myself accustomed to."

"And just exactly what, Minor-madman-mine?"

Chawker Minor bit back the words. After a pause, he said, "Why simply make assertions? When I can *prove* that this particular Other-World way or that, is superior to Gammerfashion, I will produce the proof. Till then, what is the use of just talking?"

"You have already been talking idly without end, Minor, and it has done you so little good that we can call what it has done you harm outright. —Minor, if you have any respect left for me after your Grand Tour, which Lady-yours wheedled out of me against my will, Gammer knows or if you have any regard for the fact that I still deny you nothing that my credit can obtain for you, you will keep your mouth shut, henceforward. Think not that I will halt at sending you away if you shame us. You may then continue on your Grand Tour for as long as the Orbit lasts—and be no son of mine thereafter.''

Chawker Minor said in a low voice. ''As you say, Elder. From this moment on, unless I have evidence, I will say nothing.''

''Since you will never have evidence,'' said Elder grimly, ''I will be satisfied if you keep your word.''

The annual Finals was the greatest holiday occasion, the greatest social event, the greatest excitement of any sort in the course of the year. Each one of thirty dishes of elegantly-flavored Prime had been prepared. Each one of the thirty judges would taste each dish at intervals long enough to restore the tongue. It would take all day.

In all honesty, Gammerpeople had to admit that the nearly one hundred winners that had taken their prize and acclaim in Gammer history had not all turned out dishes that had entered the Great Menu as classics. Some were forgotten and some were now considered ordinary. On the other hand, at least two of Gammer's all-time favorites, combinations that had been best-sellers in restaurants and homes for two decades, had been also-rans in the years in which they had entered the contest. ''Black Velvet,'' whose odd combination of chocolate-warm and cherry-blossom had made it the standard sweet, did not even make it to the Finals.

Chawker Minor had no doubt of the outcome. He was so confident that he found himself in continual danger of being bored. He kept watching the faces of the individual judges as every once in a while one of them would scoop up a trifle from one of the dishes and place it on his tongue. There was a careful blankness to the expression, a heavy-liddedness to the eye. No true judge could possibly allow a look of surprise or a sigh of satisfaction to escape him—certainly not a quiver of disdain. They merely recorded their ratings on the little computer cards they carried.

Chawker Minor wondered if they could possibly restrain their satisfaction, when they tasted *his*. In the last week, his mixture had grown perfect, had reached a pinnacle of taste-glory that could not be improved on, could *not*—

''Counting your winnings?'' said Chawker Major in his ear.

Chawker Minor started, and turned quickly. Chawker Major was dressed entirely in platon and gleamed beautifully.

Chawker Minor said, ''Come, Major-mine, I wish you the best. I really do. I want you to place as high as possible.''

''Second place if you win, right?''

''Would you refuse second place if I win?''

''You can't win. I've checked somewhat. I know your strain of Prime; I know your ingredients—''

''Have you spent any time on your own work, all this time you've been playing detective?''

"Don't worry about me. It didn't take long to learn that there is no way you can combine your ingredients into anything of value."

"You checked that with the computer, I suppose?"

"I did."

"Then how did I get into the Finals, I wonder? Perhaps you don't know all there is to know about my ingredients. Look, Major, the number of effective combinations of even a few ingredients is astronomical if we consider the various possible proportions and the possible treatments before and after mixing, and the order of mixing and the—"

"I don't need your lecture, Minor."

"Then you know that no computer in existence has been programmed into the complexity of a clever tongue. Listen, you can add some ingredients in amounts so small as to be undetectable even by tongue and yet add a cast of flavor that represents a marked change."

"They teach you that in the Outer-Worlds, youngling?"

"I learned that for myself." And Chawker Minor walked away before he could be goaded into talking too much.

There was no question that Grand-Elder Tomasz this year, as in a large number of previous years, held the Judging Committee in the hollow of his tongue, as the saying went.

He looked up and down the long table at which all the judges had now taken their seat in order of preference, with Tomasz himself right in the middle. The computer had been fed; it had produced the result. There was complete silence in the room where the contestants, their friends, and their families sat, waiting for glory and, failing that, for at least the consolation of being able to taste all the contesting samples.

The rest of Gammer, possibly without exceptions, watched by holo-video. There would, after all, be additional batches made up for a week of feasting and the general opinion did not always match that of the judges either, though that did not affect the prize winning.

Tomasz said, "I do not recall an Awarding in which there was so little doubt as to the computer-decision, or such general agreement."

There was a nodding of heads, and smiles and looks of satisfaction.

Chawker Minor thought: They look sincere; not as if they're just going along with the Grand-Elder, so it must be mine.

Tomasz said, "It has been my privilege this year to taste a dish more subtle, more tempting, more ambrosial than anything I have ever, in all my time and experience, tasted. It is the best. I cannot imagine it being bettered."

He held up the computo-cards, "The win is unanimous and the computer was needed only for the determination of the order of the runners-up. The winner is—" just that pause for effect and then, to the utter surprise of everyone but the winner, "Chawker Minor, for his dish entitled Mountain-Cap. —Young Man."

Chawker Minor advanced for the ribbon, the plaque, the credits, the hand-shakes, the recording, the beaming, and the other contestants received their numbers in the list. Chawker Major was in fifth place.

Grand-Elder Tomasz sought out Chawker Minor after a while and tucked the young man's arm into his elbow.

"Well, Chawker Minor, it is a wonderful day for you and for all of us. I did not exaggerate. Your dish was the best I've ever tongued.—And yet you leave me curious and wondering. I identified all the ingredients, but there was no way in which their combinations could produce what was produced. Would you be willing to impart your secret to me? I would not blame you if you refused, but in the case of an accomplishment so towering by one so young, to—"

"I don't mind telling you, Grand-Elder. I intend to tell everybody. I told my Elder that I would say nothing till I had proof. You supplied that proof!"

"What?" said Tomasz, blankly. "What proof?"

"The idea for the dish occurred to me, actually, on the Other-World Kapper, which is why I called it Mountain-Cap in tribute. I used ordinary ingredients, Grand-Elder, carefully blended, all but one. I suppose you detected the Garden-Tang?"

"Yes, I did, but there was a slight modification there, I think, that I did not follow. How did the Other-World you speak of affect matters?"

"Because it was not Garden-Tang, Grand-Elder, not the chemical. I used a complicated mixture for the Garden-Tang, a mixture of whose nature I cannot be entirely certain."

Tomasz frowned portentiously. "You mean, then, you cannot reproduce this dish?"

"I *can* reproduce it; be certain of that, Grand-Elder. The ingredient to which I refer is garlic."

Tomasz said impatiently, "That is only the vulgar term for Mountain-Tang."

"*Not* Mountain-Tang. That is a known chemical mixture. I am speaking of the bulb of the plant."

Grand-Elder Tomasz's eyes opened wide and so did his mouth.

Chawker Minor continued enthusiastically, "No mixture can duplicate the complexity of a growing product, Grand-Elder, and on Kapper they have grown a particularly delicate variety which they use in their Prime. They use it incorrectly, without any appreciation of its potentiality. I saw at once that a true Gammerperson could do infinitely better, so I brought back with me a number of the bulbs and used them to good advantage. You said it was the best dish of Prime you had ever rolled tongue over and if there is any better evidence than that for the value of opening our society, then—"

But he dwindled to a stop at last, and stared at Tomasz with surprise and alarm. Tomasz was backing away rapidly. He said, in a gargling voice, "A growth—from the dirt—I've eaten—"

The Grand-Elder had often boasted that such was the steadiness of his stomach that he had never vomited, not even in infancy. And certainly no one had ever vomited in the great Hall of Judgment. The Grand-Elder now set a precedent in both respects.

*   *   *

Chawker Minor had not recovered.   He would never recover.   If it were exile that Elder Chawker had pronounced, so be it.   He would never return.

Elder had not come to see him off.   Neither had Major, of course.   It didn't matter.   Chawker Minor swore inwardly that he would make out, somehow, without their help, if it meant serving on Kapper as a cook.

Lady *was* there, however, the only one in all the field to see him off; the only one to dare accept the non-person he had become.   She shivered and looked mournful and Chawker Minor was filled with the desperate desire to justify himself.

"Lady-mine," he said, in a fury of self-pity, "It's *unfair!*   It was the best dish ever made on Gammer.   The Grand-Elder said so *himself*.   The *best*.   If it had grated bulb in it, that didn't mean the dish was bad; it meant the bulb was good. Don't *you* see it?   —Look, I must board the ship.   Tell me you see it.   Don't you understand it means we must become an open society, learn from others as well as teach others, or we'll wither?"

The platform was about to take him up to the ship's entrance.   She was watching him sadly, as though she knew she would never see him again.

He began the final rise, leaned over the rail.   "What did I do *wrong*, Lady-mine?"

And she said in a low, distraught voice, "Can't you see, Minor-mine, that what you did was not in—"

The clang of the ship's-port opening drowned her last two words, and Chawker Minor moved in and put the sight of Gammer behind him forever.

GARRY R. OSGOOD

To Sin against Systems

With a defiant squeak, the chalk finished its last block diagram for the year while I concluded to the blackboard, "So the classical tube amplifier can be represented by the block μ times the load resistor, R_{lL}, divided by R_L plus plate resistance r_p. This transfer function represents the ideal gain of the system and relates the time varying function at the block's input port to the output function."

I turned to the young faces of the class and pitched the chalk stub in the wastepaper basket. The classroom was hot. My shirt was sticking to my back, and I had beads of perspiration growing on my forehead. There was one last hurdle between these kids and the summer vacation.

"The final for this course will be held in the lecture hall L-212, I guess." I peered at the assignment sheet posted on the bulletin board, to keep up the appearance that I was myopic. "On Friday, first period—nice and early in the morning." Nobody laughed. I sat down on the desk and mulled over the various bits of wisdom that a professor should pass on to his departing students. There were damn few items that weren't already stale. I rubbed my chin, peered out the window, and decided on a few classics.

"Everybody should bring a pencil, I guess. A school that can't afford individual terminals probably can't afford pencils—or a sharpener, so bring a spare." That was classic enough, so I left them with some personal philosophy: "I think if you go into this thing with the idea of memorizing a lot of equations, you'll run into a great deal of trouble. Remember the underlying concepts, the reasons why the equations are written the way they are. We are dealing with integrated and interrelated systems here, and not discrete pieces. Nowhere in the exam are you given equations. You are given a system. Take the overview approach and look at the system as a whole, and the proper relations will suggest themselves if you don't bury yourself in minute and unimportant aspects."

Well, that's what all engineering profs say anyway, so I guess I didn't add anything new to student lore.

"See you next year—some of you. Get lost." And away they went. Some were intent and some were asleep; I wondered if teachers were ever any use. Chances were I wouldn't be seeing them again next year, anyway. I was feeling the weather in my joints, and I didn't like getting up in the morning anymore. Both were signs that soon I would have to hole up somewhere and go through a metamorphosis.   I didn't think that I could leave it for another year; and after it was done I would have to be someone else—two lifetimes of Professor Gilbert Fenton were more than I could take.   It had been fun for a while, teaching these kids; but the subject matter was getting stale of late.   I had taught it too many times.   I'd be doing myself and these kids a favor if I became somebody else.

I walked out of the old ivy-covered brick building into the heat of a midwestern day in May.   I found myself wandering down a shady, sleepy walk of American academe.   It was one of those late spring days that whisper, like the wind through the trees, "Summer is here."   The students who had doubts about their futures were hitting the books and typewriters for their final papers and whatnots.   Those who were in no doubt—the "smart" and the otherwise—were infesting the beer halls and hangouts of the college town.

It had been my pleasure to have for the last few days a companion, of sorts, though I knew neither who he was nor where he came from.   I hadn't even spoken with him.   He was a slender youth, dressed in the standard uniform of T-shirt and jeans.   He didn't amount to anything save for those eyes of his.   He had first caught my attention, then my curiosity.   As I turned the corner of the lane on that sleepy summer day, my companion of sorts saw me; upon seeing me, he propelled himself down the street like the boy who had made the acquaintance of the preacher's daughter and the sheriff; the latter being an unplanned circumstance.   Seeing him struck me as a very curious thing, for apparently I had gone through most of the year without noticing him; and when I finally did I couldn't avoid him.   This sometimes happens with me: to be aware of people is to see them; but I don't think I would have noticed this particular youth in the first place if it had not been for those eyes.   He reminded me of a friend; Sheridan had eyes like that youth: steel grey eyes that penetrated and calculated, windows to a sharp intellect.   Sheridan was a living embodiment of von Neumann's ideal game player: perfectly intelligent and perfectly ruthless.   In all my years he has been the only one to really guess who I am.

Damn him.

While I have laid low in life, Sheridan always grabbed the limelight, always wanted still more; though age was slowing him down at last.   He and I first met in a rooming house on Fulton Street in New York City, in the year 1912.   He was a lad of twenty and I . . . well I was passing through, in need of folding money or a man who was handy with a printing press.   Sheridan had both.   But he was also a most perceptive lad, and he picked up something that had kept him on my trail ever since.   I considered the memory.   It has been ninety years since I made that acquaintance.   Sheridan was now very old, and very rich—and very persistent. I decided that I might just put old Gilbert Fenton to rest that night; Sheridan's grey eyes might run in the family.   After I metamorphose I generally make myself quite different and turn up quite far from where I start, and Sheridan usually loses me for a spell.   If I pulled the dodge one more time, I probably wouldn't have to worry again.   I set off with decision in my step, lighthearted, in a way; I was about to begin again.

Perhaps I shouldn't be harsh on Sheridan, though.   For all that I abhor his fascination with wealth and power, I haven't come one iota closer to the Universal Why than he has: which is to say, not at all. I have been looking for some time, too. I recalled, as I walked down the lane, That Woman—metamorphosing always makes me nostalgic—she had had an insight that impressed me deeply. She was old—mentally old—for an ephemeral. I had thought that with two of us on the job, the Universal Why wouldn't be too hard to find, so on her eightieth birthday I gave her the insight I have been able to exercise on myself as a gift to celebrate our fifty-five-year-old friendship. Afterwards, she was very quiet; and some time later she found the Universal Why at the bottom of a mine shaft. I was very thoughtful about the matter of self-annihilation after that, and I swore that I would understand a human being *thoroughly* before I tried the stunt again. I started the new policy with myself, and I'm still working with the first candidate.

You can understand how thoughtful a man becomes when considering such terribly human matters. That day I should have been careful. I am not immortal: I am a well-tuned mechanism, granted, but I can break. I should have paid attention to the crunch of gravel on the road as the car coasted along in neutral, the engine off. The car came alongside me (lost as I was in fond reverie), and a door opened.

"Hey, Bill! Wanna ride?"

Well, it wasn't my name but I looked up anyway. The youth with steel grey eyes was adding sounds of plausibility to what amounted to a kidnapping—though I was far too old to be a kid. I felt a little twinge of pain and a mild feeling of regret. A quick investigation of my chemical systems told me that the sedative was fast-acting and already rooted in too many places for me to whip up an effective counter-agent.

Shucks. Can't win 'em all.

They were gentle with me. I suspect they all had hospital experience; Sheridan knew how to pick his staff. I was sure I was going to see him again. I can't call him friend, but it's people like him who make the world go round the way it does: sadly.

The ride up to the Polar Orbital Station, administrative offices of the Sheridan Group Industries, was uneventful. I'd have been drugged to the gills if I had any.

It was a peaceful awakening, considering the abruptness of my abduction. I found myself in a nice, soft bed in a room of pastel colors. In the background there was the rustle of pink noise, which at one moment suggested the wind through tree branches, at another, the dance of water through rocks. I had the warm feeling that follows a good long sleep, but I was not at all sure how this next meeting with Sheridan would go. I looked for a clock but couldn't find one. I sat back on my pillows with the vague disquiet that comes when I'm completely disoriented in time. I don't think the temporal displacement would have been all that bad, if I hadn't found that I had company.

A male steward. A large male steward. Rather larger than four of me in fact.

I gave him what I imagined was a glower but it didn't seem to scare him.

"Hey, Shorty. How about telling your Boss that I'm awake?" I said.

He looked over his shoulder at me, uncrossed his arms from behind his back, turned, bowed curtly. From anyone else, the gesture would have looked ridiculous, but he gave it an air of poetry; and besides, he was bigger than I, so I didn't laugh. Through his smile he said,

"Mr. Sheridan will be with you presently. In the meantime, if there is anything that I can do—"

"Leave," I suggested.

"That would not be possible, I'm afraid." A smile, a bow. I rapped out a few drum rolls with my fingers and thought a few thoughts.

"Hmm. Can you dance? Do magic tricks? How about some clothes? Sure as taxes your Boss man is going to chew the fat with me eventually." Why else would he go to all this trouble?

"Certainly." He snapped his fingers, and another version of him, somewhat smaller perhaps, appeared. This didn't help, I thought. It wasn't that I wanted privacy so I could escape—where could I escape to, on Sheridan's own orbital satellite? I didn't think they'd lend me a shuttle; aasuming I could find a shuttle, assuming I could run a shuttle, or assuming that I could go through the bang, bang, shoot-'em-up heroics that would be required to get one. I haven't lived since A.D. 900 by giving people excuses to shoot at me. I wanted privacy because I was prudish, and if I asked for anything else, I'd probably get a brass band to watch me dress.

"How 'bout some privacy? You expect me to dress to an audience?" They both complied. In unison they turned their backs. The choreography was superb.

I knew Sheridan was well off, but I began to wonder if even that could adequately describe a man who owned his own space station. When I first met him he was just another two-bit waterfront chiseler with an accommodating smile and a printing press that spit out sawbucks and fins. On the side he could do magic with a piece of paper. He could match stock certificates to inks and to presses. He could take a document from any institution and turn out a very reasonable facsimile lickety-split.

At the time, the various patrons I served in the booking industry were tossing those significant glances my way that told me that it was time to move on, and like Tammany Hall, I did. I picked Sheridan because I needed the various bits of paper naming an individual to be crisp and well done. Sheridan was just a kid, but he was beginning to get the reputation of being a phenomenally skilled kid. True to form, he was thorough with his patrons and kept an eye on me even after I thought I had finished doing business with him. My thirteenth metamorphosis had had a cheering section.

The togs fit perfectly. One of the goons brought me a mirror, and I saw that I liked the cut and style of the clothes. Warm color, simple, with no baroque frills. Sheridan remembered my tastes and had gained some skill on the soft pedal. It was very different from the techniques that he had used on me before; the last time we met, Sheridan caressed me with an india rubber hose.

He has had a long time to learn, I reflected. Sheridan must be at least a hundred and ten, and still a captain of industry. He should have become an honorary member of the Board of the Sheridan Group Industries forty years ago, but he didn't retire.   He still had enough energy to secure his position in the business and chase me all over India, when he got wind of me there.   I looked around the compartment.   It was well appointed.   I could have been on the Terran surface. Sheridan was a scoundrel who would sell his mother down the river; but he was a capable, intelligent, and gifted scoundrel.   One of the goons cleared the ceiling and I amused myself by watching the activity on the Station's Hub.

In a short while I heard the door mechanism.   The two goons got up to go as the compartment door slid quietly into the bulkhead.

It was Sheridan.

Oh, he was old, and very thin, but I couldn't make the word "frail" hang on him.   His was the distinguished kind of old that one associates with the occupants of stone castles, who cultivate very fine wines.   His back was straight.   He was neat as a pin, and though his cheeks were sunken he still had the hawk nose and the penetrating, steel grey eyes.   I had the urge to stand up in his presence, to forget about the abduction and the rubber hose: he had an atmosphere of command just like that.   I almost got up—but I didn't.

"Good afternoon—Gilbert, is it?" he asked, and held out a hand that I didn't take.   He had a nice, rich voice, with just a slight trace of a piping waver. Ordinarily, I would like a man with a voice like that.

I scratched my head, still sprawled out on the bed, looked up at the Hub, and said it was as good a name as any.   "Is it afternoon?   Heck, Pappy, I should be hungry now.   Got anything to eat in this oversized bicycle wheel?"

" 'Afternoon' by Greenwich Mean.   I suspect it would be early in the morning in Midwestern America.   You either will, or already have notified the college that you have been taken ill."

"Thanks, Pappy, I guess.   You always were thorough."   The last time we had met he had been a near youngster, and I'd been apparently in my late seventies. I wasn't a youngster at the moment, but the apparent age-spread between us was the same, only the sign had been changed.

"Chester," he addressed one of the goons by the door, "attend to dinner for Mr. Fenton and myself.   Have it served in the Observatory.   After that, you and the staff shall retire from my living quarters until 0800 tomorrow."

"Very good, Mr. Sheridan."   Chester and the other goon left in a butlerish sort of way.

Sheridan turned his attention back to me, saying, "To the Observatory, sir?   The view of the Earth is magnificent—Olympian, even."

"As beheld by an Olympian god, perhaps?" I asked.

Sheridan smiled, ignored my sally and asked: "Have you ever seen the Earth from this vantage point?"

"Naw," I replied.   "This is a first.   First time in orbit, too.   Can't say that it's much different from any Terran flophouse—purtier, maybe."

Sheridan allowed a calculated degree of surprise.   "The first time?   I thought that you had the time to try everything."   Sheridan arched his eyebrows just so.

"What?   Impossible.   Sir, I have just begun!" I replied.

". . . And at an age when most men have long retired from their affairs,"

Sheridan added. Then he cocked his eyebrow and fixed me with a steely sidelong glance. "Except that it's 'all men' in your case, Gilbert?"

"Speak for yourself, Chief," I retorted. "You aren't doing too badly either. Banging around in orbit. Hell, you got your start out of the backside of a horse-drawn wagon. Are you telling me that you've finally figured it out for yourself and you don't need my services?"

"Business after lunch, Fenton. We old fellows shouldn't rush about. Let us say I have changed my mind on certain fundamental points in our century-old cat-and-mouse game."

"You've decided to be the mouse?" I asked with staged surprise.

"Maybe, Fenton, I have been the mouse all along. Quiet, now." We had been riding in a slidevator that ran along the rim of the Station. It had reached its last stop, and the doors slid open. Sheridan guided me to another set of double doors. With his finger poised over the opening plate, he turned to me and whispered: "Hold on; this view will take your breath away. I've had people faint here."

The doors opened into an oval room with dark walls and unobtrusive lights scattered about the ceiling. Save for small islands and threadlike catwalks, the floor opened out into parsecs of inky black space, scattershot with points of light. The Milky Way was drifting with stately dignity beneath our feet.

"Walk out onto it. The floor is quite an engineering feat itself."

And I saw Earthrise at the Polar Orbital Station.

Moving with a graceful pace, Northern Europe hove into view, dressed in the satin white lace of a fair-weather system. To my left, protracted, was the North American continent, glowing under a late morning sun. White and sapphire, russet and green, Terra spun slowly against a velvet backdrop; and behind her, the Milky Way drifted in the vastness of the expanding Universe. I was awestruck, thunderstruck, and struck by a million items so vanishingly small, yet so brilliantly resolved: the sun's highlight on the Atlantic, individual textures of clouds, the incredibly involved texture of the land. If ever I had a feel for the comprehension of the Universal Whole, it was in that Observatory.

I wasn't going to fall . . . but I wasn't going to let go of Sheridan, either.

"Sher—Sheridan?"

"Sir."

"I'm impressed. Where can I sit down?"

Sheridan helped me along the walk, over the Mid-Atlantic, and sat me down at a table somewhere above the Ural Mountains. For some time I had forgotten to breathe. I checked my pulse, spent some minutes doing something about all the adrenalin my glands had so thoughtlessly dumped into my bloodstream, and soothed senses that *swore* I was going to fall out of the place. There were a number of body-keeping chores that I had to attend to right there.

"Do you have a fear of heights?" Sheridan asked pleasantly.

"Only—recently, Sheridan. I didn't think they could make a transparent shield of such dimensions."

"Anything can be done with money, Gilbert. The costs of developing the

Observatory were indeed high, but you should see the effect it has on the stock-holders. Between you and me and the Board, the principal stockholders require little additional conditioning after they've been in this room. They respond to this place as they would to a religious experience; indeed, for some it's the only religious experience they ever have.''

Conditioned stockholders. A typical Sheridan scheme. But, I had to admit to myself, I hadn't been moved like this since I was sixteen and inside my first cathedral. Life was more carefree then; I didn't have to trouble myself with the schemings of old men—or escaping from their space stations to protect the secret of longevity. For all its faults, the world didn't deserve an immortal Sheridan.

I think Sheridan felt embarrassed in the silence that followed his remark. I peered at him in the green and blue earthlight, and he fumbled with his fingers and then burst out: ''Oh, the conditioning isn't that severe! We have no use for a bunch of Pavlov dogs! The conditioning is very subtle, and actually falls into that never-never land between conditioning, convincing, and educating. They aren't even aware of it. The only form it takes is the inclination to invest in one kind of a scheme, every now and then, rather than another; and to keep reelecting the present Board of Directors and myself. That's hardly dictating their every move-ment! And we're only dealing with one-thousandth of one percent of the world's population.''

''The ones with money,'' I said, levelly.

''Well, that is hardly an abuse of power,'' he said, forcing conviction into his voice.

''Did I sound like I was objecting?'' I asked.

''Oh . . .'' Sheridan seemed surprised. Poor fella; he was warming up to a justification speech that he found out he didn't need. He didn't know what to do with his mouth—and I felt good. At least for that instant he wasn't in the driver's seat.

''I rather thought you would,'' he said, a little lamely. ''You always were a liberal moralist, Gilbert. You objected to the printing of bogus money even as you were accepting your degree from—'Matheus University'? I think that was the place I gave you.'' I got a thin smile as soft sounds from the ramp announced Chester's arrival with the chow.

Chester was unimpressed by the spectacle beneath his feet. The green-blue light from the floor lit him up like an apparition from the Ektachrome of a bad horror movie.

I replied to Sheridan's comment, ''Times change; so do the opinions of cantan-kerous old men.''

Sheridan nodded thoughtfully. He began to cut carefully into the steak. Since my background lacked grace and form, I attacked my portion in the spirit of an Apache raid on an intruding wagon train.

In time I asked through the music of utensils on porcelain, ''So, Pappy; how's the printing business?''

Sheridan stopped the elegant business of eating. He looked at me and tried to gauge any hidden meaning in my question.

"I sold it to someone who could appreciate it. I purchased a bakery and sold it as a bread company. I bought into Rockwell International and recommenced the manufacture of the Shuttle when the energy depletion scare finally blew away. It was difficult, but men aren't all that difficult to control, if they are ambitious. You figure out what they want, and then you make them think you've delivered it to them—all for a price, mind you."

"Hmm," I said. He had suggested something to me . . . but what was it? A plan, a whole brazen plan flashed in front of me and—I lost it. My glimmer didn't reach the gleam stage.

Sheridan asked, between bites, "And how are you proceeding, sir?"

As if he didn't know. "I've been trying my hand as an engineering prof in a diploma mill," I replied. "I have no illusions about the sanctity of the learning process. There are people who learn—and people who look for the instructions on things."

"Education, a personal process, what?"

"Yep." I launched my last piece of steak on its next phase of existence and said around the bite, "Maybe the process is easier in defined atmospheres, with research material and someone to help you who knows the ropes; but it's still a personal process. Maybe the word 'teacher' is meaningless. Maybe 'learning assistant' is better."

Chester was gone. We were alone now.

"I am going to make a proposition, Gilbert."

"Anything like the last one? As I recall, you presented it with a great deal of persistent vigor."

Sheridan laughed a polite laugh, which revealed a row of perfect teeth. The floor was opaquing in response to a local sunrise. "And I would have continued to do so if you hadn't found a door I didn't know existed."

That wasn't how I had gotten out; but if that was what he wanted to think, then I wasn't going to disillusion him.

Sheridan continued: "But you must admit that I have developed a great deal of sophistication since those days. Here we are in an orbital station, amid the offices and laboratories of the Sheridan Group Industries. A thousand office workers and technicians and their families reside here. No one knows you are here but you and I."

"What about Chester?"

"Chester? He thinks you're someone who has to be persuaded to do a little business. He has no idea that you are a millennium old or what you are here for. He rather hopes to help out in a little accident that will occur in your local area if you can't be persuaded. But he shall be disappointed this time, fortunately."

"You mean you'd let me go if I didn't tell you how I do what I do?" I asked.

"I haven't planned what I'd do with you if you refused me," replied Sheridan, easily. I couldn't imagine a situation where Sheridan hadn't laid a plan for each detail. Sheridan was meticulous.

"You see," he said after a pause to consider his last piece of steak, "I am rather confident that we have come to an agreement, shall we say.'' Sheridan carefully arranged his silverware on his plate. ''I considered that I might have to demonstrate to the authorities that you were never here, of course. Let us say that it comes to unpleasantness. Several people might swear that you were uncommonly careless in the traffic lanes near Des Moines, Iowa, say. But I don't intend to harm you. We are lifelong companions, of sorts, equal gentlemen, you and I; and I have a proposition.'' He neatly swiped at his mouth with his napkin.

''Sheridan,'' I said warily, ''I do not use the term 'gentleman' for someone who uses rubber hose diplomacy.''

Sheridan winced and with a waving hand cleared the air of my ungentlemanly observation. ''Oh, please don't say that. I've grown up, Fenton. At a hundred and ten I can see myself in perspective. I've come to realise that I am dependent on you for just a little flow of information. I can't beat you to death, you'd die with the secret and a smirk on your lips, I know. I'd be as badly off as I was before I brought you up here, worse because you'd be dead; and there isn't another man on the face of the Earth that knows what you know.''

''Maybe. Folks like us are mighty particular with our identities.''

''You mean there are *others* . . .?'' Sheridan's expression told me I'd better can that line, or my life wouldn't be worth one of Sheridan's funny-money sawbucks.

''How the hell do I know? You've been looking around, have you found any?''

Sheridan looked bitter. ''No, but I have you. A bird in hand. No, Gil, I was wrong to try to beat it out of you, though I wouldn't admit it at the time. I was extraordinarily lucky that I didn't kill you; for I was strong as an ox, and I had all the passion of youth. But then you were out that extra door, Gil, and I swore that someday I would be in a position to buy you, if I had to. In a way, you are responsible for Sheridan Group Industries; you are its prime mover. I merely gathered the resources to track you down.''

''And now you've got all that dough and I'm not the least interested in it,'' I said tiredly. ''I generally outlive the local currency standards. What is wealth then? If that's the basis of your proposition, to trade your future for your empire . . . You've bored me, Sheridan.''

Sheridan pushed his empty plate back and rose from his chair. He began to pace the floor, now fully occluded and pearly white from the attenuated sunlight.

''No, Gil. I could offer you lifelong wealth as a part of the commission, which for you would be quite a pile, but that is not my intention. Gil, my proposition is that I won't pay you a red cent. I'll pay Humanity.''

I smiled. Deathbed morality catches up with the richest man in the world. ''Do tell, I say.''

''Gil, I know you want a better Humanity. Beneath your cynicism you want every person to live better and far longer. Maybe you want them to live indefinitely. Am I right?''

I shrugged, suppressing a thrill of wonder. ''Has he changed?'' I asked myself, then a mental chuckle realigned the errant neurons.

"That what all right-thinking people on the globe want—for the record. Have you got something concrete to back up those pleasant words?" I smiled and watched him pace to my side of the table.

"I have been amassing wealth, Gil; but more important, I have been amassing *control*.

"Fact:" announced Sheridan. "Since the depression that preceded World War II, and in a larger sense since the Industrial Revolution, the gross economic trend has been the concentration of wealth into the hands of a smaller and smaller circle of people and institutions. At first it was direct personal wealth. Personal wealth purchases goods and services—and money is purchasable, like beer and pickles. Hence we have people who sell money, for profit; they rent out a commodity that won't wear out and is guaranteed by the governments of the world. Since the members of the service class are wealthy to start with, they become wealthier—"

"Positive feedback," I said.

"Eh?"

"Positive feedback. Like a feedback circuit where the linkage is multiplicative with a positive sign at the circuit's summation point. The output shows an exponential change in magnitude to the limits of the supply, or it steals wind from other supplies."

Sheridan seemed to like the engineering. He beamed, "An essentially similar viewpoint, Gil. I didn't think you had it in you.

"Anyway, there is a tendency for wealth to concentrate. To control the concentrations of wealth is to have that wealth, and the power it represents, in your hands. My strategy for the last sixty years has been to allow other people's wealth to accumulate, so I can then take control of it. I have not been troubled by the politics of the masses.

"Now, what to do with that power? One can purchase or develop technological means to control people who control wealth. Right hemisphere implants—a crude method—chemotherapy via food doping, nonvolitional conditioning . . ." He paused. "Anyway, we've developed many techniques here at the Station. Fact. Sheridan Group Industries can now control the purchasing and investment habits of twenty-five percent of the pivotal individuals and institutions."

I shrugged. Sheridan was getting excited in the pearly sunlight. "So? You've dedicated a century of living to get control, but you're dying just the same. Tell me, Sheridan, what's the point? I'd really like to know—I've got a hunch that civilization is a circus we've all put on to keep our minds off the main question: 'What happens after I shoot through . . .?' "

"That doesn't have to be the point. I represent a potential that has never existed before. I represent the apex of economic control. I can devastate the world economy by changing the value of paper tokens, simply by launching a series of booms, which trigger the busts. I can make the system oscillate wildly; I can destroy the links between the economic communities: people will go back to direct barter. Or, I can make the system work better because I can control enough of the system to reroute it—to improve it. That's a much harder trick; for it takes knowledge, experience, control—and *time*. There have been people like me before, but they gained the first three elements at the expense of the fourth, and whatever potential they had was cut off by the vanishingly small time they had left to use it in.

"Gil, you represent that fourth element, and I represent the other three.   All four elements in one man, Gil; it would be tremendous."   Sheridan waited, hesitant, expecting a reaction.

"Who gets the four elements?"

"I do, Gil.   You give me the fourth element."

"And what's in it for me?"

"Nothing, Gil.   There's nothing in it for you.   I can't buy you a whore or bribe you with money, and at one time that annoyed me.   But I've learned that I can rely on your higher principles.   Trust me and give me longevity, and I'll use the time, control, knowledge and experience to pass that longevity on to humanity. I have the tools to do it.

"I'm not Pappy the Printer anymore.   Diligence and unorthodox financial techniques have brought me to the brink of economic domination of the world.   As I've watched this globe wheel beneath my feet, Gil, I've gained an understanding of what could be done.   It'll take several years to retune the global economy to tolerate longevity, of course.   I know what needs to be done.   But I'll be dead before I can do it.   I have the vision; give me the *time*."

The opalescent half-light sharpened to needle points as the floor cleared to reveal again the timeless Milky Way.   Sheridan waited.   He had spoken his piece.

Three seconds brought me almost—but not quite—to the conclusion that Sheridan was full of that elegant stuff that fills a soul while the body is on Death Row and that he would revert to his old foolishness if he got a pardon.   Let us say that I was ninety percent sure of this.   But as I am damned to see every side to a circular question, I was ten percent in doubt now and would be more than ten percent doubtful later and—*damn!*—I would most assuredly have to kill Sheridan if I didn't join him.   What an awesome decision.   My killing Sheridan, my being his executioner, could result only from an act of judgment.   I have fundamental reservations about executing a man I haven't properly judged; to do so is to send him to that state that I have not yet had the courage to face myself.

Troubled, I tabled the thought.   I said into the utter silence of that room, "Thank you."

"Eh?" was Sheridan's response.

"You are the first man who has tried to appeal to me with neither a sexy kitten nor a pile of gold.   Instead, you've appealed to my morals.   I thank you for the compliment."

Sheridan nodded tiredly.   "I need what you have but there is nothing in the world that I can give you in trade.   So I'll tell you of my purpose and I ask you to judge if it's a worthy one.   I am completely dependent upon your believing me. I ask you to trust me, Gil, to judge me; to let me work, or to condemn me and watch me die."   Still holding at ten percent, I thought.

But to have civilization on a leash!   What a heady thought.   And Sheridan had what it took.   Almost.   "What if I . . . don't decide immediately?"

"Wait," he answered. "I won't let you go, until you have decided; I think you owe me that."

"And if I . . . never decide?" I asked.

Sheridan played with his fork, smiled a bitter smile, and looked directly at me.

"Why," he said, "that would be the same as judging against me, wouldn't it?" He paused. "I've been dodging it for some time. We've used some pretty powerful techniques to keep me alive. I've made it to a hundred and ten; but the repair rate is getting out of hand. The doctor thinks I can live six more months." And Sheridan looked at me with twinkling, intelligent, predatory eyes.

"I think you had better prepare your guest room, Pappy."

"I'm not Pappy anymore. His attitude is dead."

"So he says."

"You'll see," said Sheridan, unruffled. "I can wait—for a little while. In the meantime, we'll need to keep you occupied. You'll be my personal assistant."

Sheridan and I walked through his personal section of the Station—two of the twenty-four major compartments circling the rim. The interior was decorated in subtle whites and greys, with curved floors, plants, sculpture, and paintings scattered about. One compartment was a guest area, which contained along with a get-together room, visiting quarters and servants' area, the Observatory. The other compartment was Sheridan's *sanctum sanctorum*. Sheridan led me past its locked door and into a wide room tastefully done in the same white and grey décor. In one corner of the main room, a terminal to the Station's library silently presented a menu of games and reading material. Sheridan watched me while I browsed through some of the 1-person games, happy as a clam. Then he switched the terminal to the novice mode and showed me the query generator, commenting that this was one of the only two unsealed terminals in the Station, the other being in his room. "Look at anything you want," he said. "My life's work is on line." He then retired for the evening while I amused myself with the terminal.

I quickly discovered that the station library, and the station itself, were manifestations of Sheridan's interests. The station was his "activity module," I suppose the best word is that; his library showed a preponderance of sociology, psychology, and biology, with an impressive number of unpublished papers. Sheridan had been gunning for the Fountain of Youth for some time, it seemed. A lot of his inquiries concerned genetic engineering—a practice banned on the surface—and he had on his staff Dr. William Vonner, who had gone into hiding when the scientific community announced its self-imposed moratorium on the design and manufacture of new species. It was good to know how the Doctor was biding his time.

A few touches of the paging stud informed me that Sheridan, while prospecting for the Fountain of Youth, had come up with a swarm of useful techniques. He had put brain implants and gene doping on a practical basis, if I interpreted this three-year-old report correctly, and had developed a system of protein fabrication that fit learning into little pills. He had been using it to teach languages to his staff and "investment techniques" to clients who subscribed to his service. I whistled in appreciation: not only did Sheridan control his investors, they were paying for the privilege! He would have been a hell of a horse trader, back when.

After two hours at the data bank I sat back, amazed.   Sheridan's inquiries into the science of direct and indirect control of the human subject were the most exhaustive I had ever seen.   He had hit the problem on both the macro and micro levels.   He was developing a mathematics of n-dimensional topological spaces, and investigating how a functional projection of degree $(n-1)$ onto a given topological space could serve as a model for various macrophenomena—how a crowd will sell, or buy, or revolt.   On the micro level he was developing subtle methods of direct individual control like his "subscription service."

The man had no competition in the science of manipulation.   With all of these control mechanisms at his command, he could have become dictator of the Earth in the most subtle way, and no one would have been particularly aware of it—

I jerked up.

Maybe he was now.   Maybe he just needed me to assure his subsequent terms in office.

Or maybe he was still consolidating his position and treading water until he was sure he could direct all phases of the program personally, without having to be inconvenienced halfway through by dropping dead.

Or maybe deathbed morality had changed his reach, redirected his vision, and he was waiting for me to give him the go-ahead, the time to do the world right— the world he had so sorely cheated.   The groundwork was there for something magnificent, shenanigans or otherwise.

I turned off the terminal, stretched out on the resilient floor, and threw a pillow over my head.

I had, I thought, a powerful investigative tool that would clear out a lot of the guesswork—the longevity therapy itself.   I discovered shortly after my first metamorphosis that I could gain access to other people's minds if they "let me in."   The process is a little more complicated than that, but that is the best I can do with the language.   Once I was let in I had a wide communication spectrum with a subject, and I could see—Hell, it isn't "see" but that's the best word going—I could see his neural network and his chemical systems as well as he could; better, because I knew where to "look" and he didn't.   Telepathy and this clear inner eye and control of one's inner processes seem to go hand in hand and indeed, might even be the same phenomenon.   I could learn a lot about what really went on in Sheridan's mind during the initial rapport, and I could pull out if I saw anything I didn't like.   If he were being totally deceptive he might even balk at a telepathic linkup, and my decision would be easy—though getting out of the station might be pretty hard.   I rather liked that alternative.   I took off the pillow and smiled to myself.   There just might be a way out.

I slept on the problem until a female voice by my head said, "Mr. Sheridan asked me to remind you that it is 0600, and that you are to meet with him at 0700 in the Administration Compound, segment zero one hundred, room thirteen."

"Fair 'nuff," I muttered.   I wandered into the bathroom, and cycled the refresher cube until I was reasonably awake.   Breakfast was a problem, and fresh clothing; and I pondered the point in my birthday suit until I remembered the terminal.   I negotiated a large breakfast and a small wardrobe; in two minutes a chime rang out and I had what I'd asked for, although the surrogate coffee needed some development work.

I headed to work on my first job with the great Mr. Sheridan.

I found segment zero one hundred between zero two hundred and two four hundred. A "Can you tell me where Mr. Sheridan's office is?" got me the rest of the way.

"Good morning!" greeted Sheridan.

"It'll be a while before I have an opinion on it," I replied. He smiled. "I've got a job for you. Come with me, I'm starting on my rounds." We went through a priest's hole and into some unlisted corridor.

"The thing is, I'm getting forgetful in my old age," he said. "Every day I walk around to all of the departments and see the heads, trade a few words with the help. There are over a thousand people employed here, Fenton; and I know all of their names and faces—and all about their wives, husbands, lovers, families, and kids too. I used to remember all the things they told me, important or not. People work better for me when they think I care about them."

I nodded.

"But as I said, I'm getting forgetful, so I'd like you to tag along and keep track of things for me."

"Besides, you would always have your eye on me," I said.

"There's that too, isn't there," agreed Sheridan. "Of course, if you find the job offensive, I can always find another one for you. Engineering is a forte of yours. I have some systems work—"

"No, no. Don't go to a lot of trouble," I said. "I just might want to keep an eye on you too."

"Ha! Fenton, if life were any different, we just might have been friends—we still could be. But I must ask you to be quiet, and careful as to what you say, for on the other side of these doors are the public corridors."

The large doors slid easily in their slots to reveal a businesslike corridor. To the left, at various intervals, were the slidevator stations; to the right were the working spaces appropriate for the pinnacle of the Sheridan Group Industries.

We went into a bio lab.

Some people, working at individual terminals, looked up. Sheridan got a chorus of "Good Morning, Mr. Sheridan" and a few "Hi Sher"'s.

"Morning, crew. Is Bill around?"

"In the office, Chief."

"Thanks, Frank. Group, I'd like you to meet Gil, my new memory man. If it's important, tell him. Gil is going to be the fellow who tells me what to do from now on."

Sheridan plowed to a hubward compartment, with me in tow.

The compartment was well laid out. There were happy plants all over the place, gentle curves, and light colors. We found the occupant contemplating the Hub with a ghost of a smile on his lips.

"Good Morning, Dr. Vonner," said Sheridan. I arched my eyebrows.

"Hi, Sher. I've got a biggie," announced Bill as he swung his feet to the floor.

There was enthusiasm in his eyes, a sheaf of papers in his hand. He was young, sandy haired and pudgy, late of the genetic engineering effort on the surface.

"Look at this, Sher: a definitive carrier loop that can modulate codon transfer during the pre-meiotic stage . . ."

And off he went, bubbling, enthusiastic, optimistic: a delighted child who had just learned a new magic trick. I could have been happy for him if I weren't so busy taking notes.

After about fifteen minutes, Vonner wound down and Sheridan was nodding thoughtfully. He handed back the sheaf to Vonner and said, "If you think you can control a mutation like that without radiation, Bill, then be my guest. Just don't let a hairy monster out into the lab."

"Hairy monster?" Vonner looked indignant. "I happen to be careful with my facilities—not like those jackasses on the surface, who probably wash their equipment in the nearest stream. Anything that I make will be so weak that it will self-destruct if I look at it cross-eyed."

Sheridan's bantering tone vanished. "I know you're careful, Bill. I'm basically conservative, that's all."

Vonner cooled off and his enthusiasm resurfaced. "You'll see the most wonderful things from this! History will be made in these labs!"

"I'd say you've made history in these labs already, Bill. When we release some of your experiments to a—more understanding world, your name will rank with Salk and Pasteur."

Sheridan wheeled out of the office, leaving Vonner in a happy, creative flush. Before we got any distance, I had notes on two birthdays and an anniversary, along with two get-well cards.

When we got to the slidevator, Sheridan was in a thoughtful mood. He said, in part to himself, "You know, Vonner's lucky that he's up here. If his own safeguards fail, and worse comes to worse, there is always the ultimate safeguard."

"Such as?" I asked. Sheridan looked up at me.

"Oh! Well, Space itself. Genetic labs are ideally suited to orbit because that big old vacuum out there will get anything the radiation misses. If something—unpleasant—does happen up here, then I have deadman instructions controlling a nuclear device located in the Hub. Couldn't have that kind of safeguard anywhere on the surface."

"How about traffic to and from the Station between the time a bug gets loose and when the first symptoms show up?" I asked.

Sheridan looked surprised. "I *am* getting senile! Note somewhere on that pad that I should issue a general three-week quarantine on personnel leaving the Station. Call it General Instruction Q3. The Station Provost Officer is going to inundate me with grievances by tomorrow night, dollars to donuts."

Sheridan fell to inspecting his tightly cropped fingernails. I had a doomsday thought.

"Sheridan, suppose there is a plague in the near future, after you and I resolve our . . . differences," I asked, "would you blow yourself up with the Station?"

Sheridan fixed me with his eyes, his steely glinting eyes.

"I have you thinking about it, haven't I?"

"Maybe."

"You're thinking about it. Progress, I can't complain." Sheridan sat back and a relieved expression crossed his face.

"Would you blow yourself up if the Incurable X disease slipped out of Vonner's test tube?" I pushed the matter. It was important.

The slidevator had stopped at the next station. Sheridan kept his bony fingers on the HOLD and DOOR CLOSE buttons, and said in a soft voice, tight with tension: "I have told you not to talk about this matter in public places. I suspect you made your way through the Black Plague in a manner that the contemporary alchemists would have found amazing, not to mention the present ones. It turns on what you teach me, Gil. Now *can it*!" The door opened and a perfectly composed Sheridan slipped out with a thoughtful memory man padding along behind.

There were sixteen anniversaries, two-score birthdays, ten get-well cards and thirty pages of notes from Sheridan to others via my aching fingers. My feet were killing me. Sheridan was just starting his day. I saw data processing and genetic experiments, high vacuum industrial experiments, and crystal-growing experiments, and I had notes to get data sheets on a dozen more.

"We do a lot of research here," remarked Sheridan as we headed back to his office. "This is the only private industrial facility in orbit, and we have clients who need testing done in the high vacuum and zero-g—plus all of the housework from the industries in the Group."

When we got into his office I gave him the note pad. Sheridan looked at my tight notes, diagrams, circles, arrows, and three-colored inserts and made a tsk, tsk, sound.

"Good heavens, Fenton, do you think the way that you write notes?"

I marveled, as I wriggled in my seat, how a fellow barely a century old could make me, with my ten centuries' seniority, feel like a junior office boy.

"This is the most amazing aggregation of mixed-up markings. . . . Here." Sheridan opened a drawer, exactly the one he wanted; reached in; and picked out a sealed metal cylinder. He snapped it open and rolled a large green pill onto his felt desk-top.

"Take it. It's a special shorthand that I can read and you can take, real-time, without looking at the notepad."

I looked dubiously at the pill, tapped my teeth with my pencil, and thought of that investment subscription service of his.

"Come on, I wouldn't poison you now, would I?" laughed Sheridan.

I was thinking of Vonner's enthusiasm—genuine human reaction or derived from a German language pill? Everyone that Sheridan dealt with was respectful, loyal, and even loving in a businesslike way. Was it love and respect on a human to human basis, or were they chemically treated dogs and yes-men?

I didn't know. It was all as enigmatic as Sheridan himself. But I knew my body chemistry and I had my inner "eyes" and "hands." I made a bet with myself that I could nullify any chemical in that pill should it get out of hand. Swallowing it, I noted a slight suggestion of the taste/feel of dry peach rind, before the skin breaks.   It was an interesting gamble, the kind that adds gusto to one's life. Besides, I was interested in how that pill would work on me.

"It'll be a while," remarked Sheridan.   "Some of the secretaries say that when it starts to hit, it's best to draw some audio from the Station's library and practice. Others say to sleep on it.   Do what comes naturally, and I'll see you tomorrow."

"Sure," I said, and I went to my quarters with my inner eyes watching.

It was a pleasant inner show, that pill.   It didn't touch my value areas one bit. Any fragment of protein that banged on the doors in that neighborhood got a gruff "We don't want any."   The protein looked at its instructions, said, "Excuse me!" and moved on.   When it got to the area that decided whether a sound should be shunted to a higher level or acted on right there, the proteins slipped in and established a correspondence between a sequence of motor instructions and phonal groups.   The causality between "loud noise: jump and cuss" which worked within a certain small loop suddenly had company in the form of such correspondences as "freedom: motor instructions 4FEA."   There was a blocking neuron that controlled the loop, making it a function of will, so I wouldn't continually be urged to write everything I heard.   When I *did* will the routine in, I would automatically write the shorthand analog of each word, knee jerk fashion.

I suppose I could have done something similar myself, if I knew how; but there is a lot that I don't know about me.   I do know the various control nexi and can manipulate a variety of neural, electrical, and chemical circuits.   Since I see the body as a whole, I can appreciate the wide variety of "domino chains" throughout the body: almost every circuit is linked to its neighbors, and an intentional adjustment will often trigger side effects in a (seemingly) unrelated function.   Thus when I treat hardening of the arteries, I affect bone-cell manufacture.   Though I know the nexi and how they can be excited, I still have to respect the overall body and its interrelated systems.   In order for me to do that neural adjustment myself, I would be obliged to trace out all of the domino chains.   Why Sheridan's little green pill failed to trigger any side effects is a mystery that goes to show how little I understand me, in spite of the intimate relationship that I enjoy with myself.

Which brought me to the problem of Sheridan, the next order of business after the Pill.   My idea of what was on the man's mind and how it might be probed during the intimate linkup of the Therapy had taken a severe blow when I saw how Sheridan was received by his employees.

They liked him.

No one liked Sheridan when he was on Fulton Street.   People did business with him because he was efficient, not because he was pleasant.   Had he changed over the years?

Possibly Sheridan had changed.   On the other hand, if it were deathbed morality, then I might miss it: unconscious self-deception, I cannot detect.   I had missed That Woman's suicide tendency, and I was a hell of a lot more intimately bound to her than to Sheridan; and had rambled through her head for hours on end.   And I now had the feeling that once I got inside of Sheridan, I would find answers that would beget more questions until it was *all* questions again.

In between arguing with myself, I watched the scenery that evening.   The ceiling was cleared, and it treated me to alternate views of Space, then Earth, and then a period of occlusion while the sun was in view.

Good old Terra, I thought.   Even she is a spaceship, with naturally evolving controls, hierarchies of systems, diverse phenomena working hand in hand: all of it fitting together so *right*.   And the human creature is an outgrowth of that fit.   Oh, he had a learning period, I thought, when he messed with chemicals that didn't dovetail with naturally existing systems; and when his material use was straight line, and not a loop that fed itself; but when the economics of recycling made themselves felt in the latter half of the depletion age, humankind learned the first aspect of systems; a lesson that John Donne put into the words: "No man is an island."

Indeed, no *thing,* man or otherwise, is an island: everything is adjacent in one way or another in the intricate universal topology, related, in a web of relationships, where everything can be connected implicitly or explicitly to every or any other thing in the web.   Changes in one portion of the web mean changes in all other portions of the web and once this fundamental rule of systems was learned by Humankind, he was forever more careful with his garbage, especially when it became profitable to do so.

The ceiling occluded and I was cut off, for a time, from the outside.

I am a frail creature, dogged with uncertainty, lacking in personal self-worth at times; but I see that things fit together—click—joyfully like fine machinery, and that understanding is the basis of my morals; for I respect and wish to preserve that fit.   It is the reason I believed that longevity was safe with me at the time, for I wouldn't spread it—willy-nilly—throughout Mankind until I had carefully traced out all of the domino chains—

I stopped, thunderstruck.   Sheridan had shoved the job of judgment on me as if I were the sole judge, as if the buck could stop with me, and that is not the way things work at all, at all!   I admired—marveled at—the man's postures, choice of words, styles of talking, and the way he maneuvered me into the role of an arbitrator, giving me the obligations of a judge—omniscient but detached—when I was intimately woven into the problem.   Sheridan knew that, when he forced himself on me and displayed himself as a person loved and respected, I wouldn't have the courage to watch him die.   He knew I was particularly sensitive to death.   He gambled that I would keep him alive even if I didn't give him the full therapy.   He gambled that I would remain in the judge's role long enough for the responsibilities of that august position to cloud my vision; until I would say to myself: "Why am I keeping this guy on tenterhooks?" and give in.   I jumped off the bunk, resolved.   Sheridan played a skillful game, a damned skillful game, and he had come perilously close to winning.

But he didn't.   And I knew exactly what to do.

I fixed myself an elegant meal with some help from the terminal.   Just as I sat down, the compartment bell set up an enormous clatter.   Annoyed, I put down my chopsticks, rose, and touched the door plate.   My visitor was evidently in a hurry.

"Mr. Fenton, you are to come with me immediately. I—"

I stepped on the brakes gently. "Easy, son. I can't think offhand why I should neglect dinner on your say-so, can you?"

"Mr. Fenton, please, I understand you give security personnel a difficult time as a matter of course, but this is serious. Can you run?"

So we ran. We ran to the slidevator, which then skipped every stop until we reached the sickbay compound. Shortly I was in an emergency care room, and my guess was verified. A young doctor with a stormy look in his eyes confronted me.

"Mr. Fenton? I'm Mr. Sheridan's physician. Mr. Sheridan has had a severe coronary, which at his age—anyway, he wants you here." I peeked past the doctor.

Sheridan wore a mask and had things wired to his chest. His eyes were closed and he was breathing with quick shallow breaths. He looked awful, very old-looking now, frail, the dynamic personality gone. There was a small pick-up on his pillow. His eyes opened a crack, he turned slightly toward us and whispered, "Jim."

"Mr. Sheridan." The doctor turned, businesslike.

"Get lost—clear room of—everyone—but Fenton."

"Mr. Sheridan, I have the responsibility. . . ."

"Jim." The doctor stopped abruptly. I looked at Sheridan. Despite the attack that had beaten his body, despite the tinny speaker and phone amplifier, the voice still carried command.

"Jim—I am a dying—man. Washed up. You—wouldn't deny—a dying man— his last—wish?"

The doctor turned red. Sheridan could still do it, turn a person against himself with a carefully composed sentence. Sheridan was a marvel.

The doctor and nurses and technicians retired behind the door. They were not to return until I allowed them.

Sheridan was peering at me again with that intense predatory look. I looked down at him, waiting.

"Your . . . decision, Fenton."

I checked my thoughts. It would be a calculated gamble; chances were there would be unfortunate aspects no matter what the outcome.

"Welcome to the Longevity Club. We're a small and select group."

"What . . . What . . ." Sheridan seemed almost surprised. Did he have last minute doubts about his game? I tabled the thought.

"All you have to do is relax and give me eye contact. Don't think of anything and when you feel me, *don't resist!*"

I found a chair to sit down on, cradled my head in my hands, and took a stab. I was in. Information flow was very wide and the exchange rate was fast.

"SHERIDAN!"

"Yes . . ."

"Don't will anything. Go to sleep."

"The pain . . ." I altered the firing threshold of a bundle of synapses.

"What did you do?"

"Later, sleep now. This is not the metamorphosis, this is just to patch you together."

It wasn't the worst session I'd had with death. My fourteenth metamorphosis, the short one, somehow found me in France during the year 1916. I called the shot that World War One wouldn't happen and got drafted in the French infantry. A moment of carelessness found me stitched up the side with a machine-gun burst. I had to keep myself alive *and* metamorphose at the same time. At least Sheridan wasn't halfway sawed through and lying in a trench.

Patchwork kept me busy for about an hour. Sheridan was in relatively healthy shape, so I took the liberty of hyper-regenerating the arterial walls. I worked on the local timing too, so I was sure the heart wouldn't stop on us. With the somatic problems mostly settled and the consequences of a few dozen toppled domino chains cleared up, I woke Sheridan.

"Sheridan."

"Yes."

"How do you feel?"

"Good! Is it over?"

"We haven't even begun. I just rewired you so you can make it through the short haul, which is going to be a rough one. I am going to go through a metamorphosis step by step and you are to take notes. The first thing I'll show you is direct-memory access so you won't forget anything that I show you."

"I could use that trick in a thousand and one ways."

"Now a lot of these processes are traumatic and set up noise in the nervous system. It's painful. I also won't touch the exterior much. That's finishing and I'll leave it to you as practice; besides, it's best not to upset the doctor too much."

"Understandable."

"You ready?"

"Yes."

"This is going to hurt as much as your rubber hose."

I gave Sheridan very practical instruction. If you ever buy a piece of complicated machinery a field representative will come with it. That field representative will give you point-by-point instructions: this knob does this; that lever controls that. He isn't teaching you an overall philosophy, he's telling you how that button sorter can be specifically operated to sort buttons. It's the exact opposite of how I teach control systems and the exact opposite of how I taught That Woman because the two teaching methods stem from entirely different points of view.

Sheridan didn't seem to object.

"It's done."

"That was very comprehensive, Fenton; and this linkup is a very effective method of getting ideas across."

"True, but it's an 'and' link: both of us have to agree to it and either of us can cut at any time." I finished with my voice. *"So it's subject to my vagaries."*

Sheridan shook his head. The cyanosis was gone, but his exterior, to the quick glance, was about as old as when I first came on board.

Sheridan looked at the clock. "It's been two hours. Gil, let the doctor in; he'll be having kittens."

I opened the door and the doctor was about standing on it with a battalion of security men, it seemed.

"Good Heavens! I was about to break in, Fenton. What . . . ?"

"Are you sure there is anything wrong with Mr. Sheridan? He and I had a good long chat and he doesn't seem the least bit ill," I said innocently. The doctor shoved past me and bee-lined to the telemetry equipment.

"What happened?" he kept on saying through his teeth.

"Security, you're dismissed," Sheridan commanded. "Fenton, if I pull through," with amusement in his eyes, "I'll be in direct contact with you."

Near as I could tell, that ten percent chance was shrinking, and Sheridan would soon be up to his old tricks. I had made my move, however, and only time would tell if I had made the right one.

Three days.

I had expected things to happen, but Sheridan was working on a grand scale. The afternoon of the metamorphosis, he had the doctors take him to his personal quarters, where he got out of bed and dismissed them. He relieved his physician and gave him a research post he was after. He then announced that Sheridan Industries would be marketing another First.

Three days. I knew my plan would work, but it might take a week. Meanwhile, Sheridan was going to town.

Sheridan had invited me to the Observatory for a private breakfast. Sheridan had dismissed his personal staff and made his domain "taboo," while I was forbidden to go into the rest of the Station. I watched the Earth spin silently below my feet. "You've put up with a lot of silliness," I said to her. She bore the comment in silence. I wondered, for the umpteenth time, if my timing was off. A perfectly good scheme shot to Hell by poor timing still loses the war. If my timing was off, could I still patch up the pieces?

Sheridan came strutting down the catwalk. Oh God, I thought for the seventh time that day, Doc Savage and Conan rolled into one.

Sheridan was a magnificent specimen. His skin was bronzed, with muscles rippling smoothly beneath. His hair was blond again and close-cropped. The only real constants, his eyes, were still the same—steel grey and penetrating. He tried a mental hookup, but I had the "bug-off" shield up. So he shrugged and sat down to a breakfast that was large enough to feed the Golden Horde. Well, he was half of it, anyway. I nursed a cup of coffee—my seventh cup.

"You're bigger than yesterday," I said. "Have you got the inner man represented yet?"

"Yes, I do, and I feel at peace with myself and my exterior, thanks to you."

He shot me an engaging, genuine smile.   I suspect, knowing his mentality, that Sheridan considered me his only equal; his staff were people with whom words and charm sufficed.

"Don't thank me, you are what you are because . . . well, that's the way you want to be," I said.

"But you taught me how to live and how to do this," said Sheridan, gently flexing his body beautiful.   "You pulled me from the grave with your teachings."

"I taught you nothing.   You taught yourself.   I just told you a few things that you used according to a certain philosophy."

"You're modest, Fenton.   That's your only shortcoming: you have no assertive qualities.   You neither assert yourself nor impose your ideas on your surroundings. No wonder you've been in the background for a millennium."

"Where would you foreground people be if it wasn't for us background people giving you something to stand out from?"

"True, true—it takes all kinds to make a world.   I am going to take advantage of this boon."

"You're going to charge a membership fee to the longevity club."

"More than that, Gil.   I am going to make the Sheridan Group the most powerful organization that has ever existed."   Sheridan stalked around the room, lecturing me.   I finally got around to breakfast, hoping that my timing wasn't off, ready to hear the worst, if it was.

"Nationwide, then worldwide hookup, right on Day One."   Sheridan paced around the room with Terra wheeling beneath his feet.   He turned to me.

"Why can't today be Day One?"

"Too soon," I replied around a dripping jam sandwich.   "Take it from the authority on longevity.   You need a little more practice."

"Hard to believe."

"Besides," I replied, "if you announce today you'll hit the North American continent on Friday.   If you wait two days you'll hit 'em on a Monday.   There ain't *nothin'* to look forward to on a Monday but another lousy week.   The announcement of immortality will break up an otherwise dull day."

"That would be better," Sheridan acquiesced.   Turning to an unpowered holographic rig, he said, "People of the nation, I am the director of the Sheridan Group Industries and I have an Important Announcement to make."   He smiled and turned back to me.   "Sheridan Industries are now offering options on Immortality. You and I will give the first lessons and hire the ones we've processed until we have a good line going.   Then you'll be my chief engineer and I'll go back to the management of the Group.   The price: no money, just the adoption of The Sheridan Plan; a plan of recommended, rational behavior based on chemotherapy and classroom teaching.   It's going to be a wonderful world, Gil."

"Do tell."   I chased a bit of egg around.   "What about population control?"

"That's in the plan—some special instructions for women," beamed Sheridan. "Having kids will be a privilege."

"I see, always the girl who carries the burden," I observed to Terra, turning slowly in space.

"Well, there's physical evidence if we catch her. I'm thinking in terms of logistics."

"Or stagnation?" I asked. "How about genetic remixing? How will the gene pool get stirred around?"

"I think Vonner and his boys can handle that; as for senility—well, you know the answer to that one."

"I don't mean senility. What will happen to the culture if the same points of view get banged around century after century?"

"Nor do I see any objection there, Gil; there's no point of view like the right point of view; and that's what The Sheridan Plan is for." He smiled, his hands on his hips. "Next objection! You see I've thought out this entire business of world direction. I am the first scientific ruler this planet has ever had, thanks to you."

Remembered as Sheridan's "Dr. Frankenstein"? I was horrified.

"We've been over this teaching business," I said. "So what are the logistics of handling everybody and his uncle?"

Sheridan became serious, calculating. "We have to be rather exclusive in our clientele in the first phase. Between you and me, Sheridan is still consolidating its position. We will have to do business with potential investors and world rulers at first, and make the club exclusive, and use the *promise* of longevity to control the masses. As we go along, tying in more rulers and investors, we can consolidate our position and give permission to those populations who are most in tune with the Sheridan Group." The word "Industries" had disappeared.

"As near as I can tell," I said musingly, watching the world turn, "we'll have, a century from now, a population with the right point of view, chemically cultivated by the Sheridan Group, which is an instrument of your philosophy." I looked at Sheridan and he nodded. I continued, "People will be born at an insignificant rate, to replace those who were careless with machinery or political points of view. Those born could easily be dealt with early in life, separately, for together they might brew up some silly ideas. Once cultivated, they pose no threat. Most everybody will sit around for millennia on end, nodding to each other, thinking the right kind of thoughts, a worldwide Roman Empire without the boon of the Huns to stir up the show." I again looked at Sheridan. He nodded.

And continued nodding.

Nodding, with a blank stare.

Nodding, with a growing look of horror on his face.

Nodding, he grabbed at what he thought was the table and seized air.

Nodding, he shook and stumbled, as neural networks crumbled and revolted.

Nodding, he fell, soaked with sweat, trembling lips trying to form words, with chemical circuits awry, neural circuits oscillating or disengaging, his entire body politic in revolt.

I scratched the back of my head, much relieved. There were a few blows against my bug-off screen, but they weakened, and vanished.

"G-G-G-G-G-G-G—Gil!"

"Nothing I can do about it, chum; you are what you are and that is the bed of roses. Don't complain."

"What's happening?   *God,* it hurts!''

"Easy question.   You're dying.''

"Impossible—I can't reach anything—falling apart . . . *Help me!* Help the world—''

"I'm helping the world in the most humane way I can; and I guess that means your elimination.   Sorry, Sheridan, but I abide by the circumstances of your passing.''   I folded my hands on the table and watched the heaving, sweating, crawling man.

"You judged me . . . *worthy!''* he growled out.   He tried to fix his grey eyes on me but the head kept oscillating about the proper line of sight, giving Sheridan the appearance of nodding yes, no, yes, no.

"Before you pass on, Sheridan, I would like you to know that I almost fell for your judgment game: but I didn't.   I never judged you.   I did, however, give you an examination, knowing that I could live with the results of the examination— whether you passed or failed.''

"Y-y-y-you gave me—*ability!''*

"I didn't know if you truly appreciated the obligations of one who instigates change.   Many changes introduced to the culture have had vast side effects, such as the petroleum dirt of our late, great automobile; we lived through that era, you and I.   And I, in search of that Universal Why, have come to respect the inter-relatedness of things.   I wondered if you had.   I knew Terra was a network of dependencies.   I also knew you had big plans for it.   So after I got out from under that judgment syndrome you offered me, I gave you a microcosm to play with: yourself.''

"Long—'' Sheridan had stopped trembling now.   He drooled.

"No, it wasn't longevity.   I showed you a number of system controls that *could* have been used to promote your longevity wish.   They could also make you big and handsome overnight.   Used with the understanding that the body is an inter-related complex, where introduced changes in themselves trigger related changes, they could make you do a thousand different things.   Used without the under-standing of the relatedness of things, they kill you.   You made yourself big and handsome, pushed your skeleton around, forced growth there, retarded activity here as if your body were one great plaything.   Now you die, because you weren't sensitive to the chemical, neural, and electrical systems you bowled over.   You kicked over too many domino chains.''   I looked at him.   "And you were on the verge of doing it with Terra.   Sheridan, if you can't run yourself right, how the hell do you expect to keep a *planet* straight?''

"You . . . tested me?''

"And you flunked.''

Sheridan understood.   Before Sheridan shot through, he understood, and died without fear.

And I sat for a long time at the breakfast table, wondering if, philosophies aside, Sheridan was a better man than I for facing fearlessly that which frightens me so. I could have changed him, tweaked a neuron or so while he was asleep to make him a less ambitious man.

But he had called me a man of principles: I didn't approve of his sawbucks, and I didn't approve of his conditioning either.   Sheridan died Sheridan.

And at the breakfast table I mourned him for what he could have been.

I finished my sixteenth metamorphosis and attended to Sheridan's rounds.   I sent the security force chasing around for a Gilbert Fenton, laid the plans for some very careful dismantling; cancelled an announcement that I had made the previous week, when I was ill and given to curious things.   All in all, it was a productive Monday; and I finished out the day, alone, amused at the circumstances that induced me to metamorphose into a very old man.

JACK C. HALDEMAN II

Louisville Slugger

Slugger stood helplessly as he watched the ball arc over his head and clear the center field fence. Four to three—it was all over. He dropped his glove to the ground and started the long walk back to the dugout. The sell-out crowd was silent. He shook his head. They'd lost it; lost everything—the game, the series. Now those ugly Arcturians had won the right to eat all the humans.

It was a crying shame.

Too bad Lefty had sprained his ankle rounding first.

The UN delegates milled aimlessly around in their special box seats. They looked depressed and Slugger couldn't blame them. They were all overweight and would surely be among the first to go.

Well, he had gone the distance and that was the important thing. *How* you play the game is everything. Coach Weinraub always said that.

He hated going to the showers after losing a game. There was none of the joking around and towel snapping that followed a win. Maybe there would be a cold beer. That would be nice. He wondered absently who they *would* eat first.

The locker room was depressing—no beer at all, only warm Cokes and stale popcorn. He dressed quickly and slipped out the back door. The Arcturians were probably spraying each other with champagne.

He arrived at the Blarney a few minutes later. Usually he didn't go there, but tonight he wanted to go someplace where he wasn't known. He wasn't aware that his face was more widely known than the President's. He ordered a beer.

The bar was dirty and dark and the ruddy-faced bartender was the only one who could get a good look at his face. Luckily he was sympathetic and didn't let on that he recognized Slugger.

"Damn shame," said a man at the other end of the bar.

"Yeah, I wonder what Arcturians taste like. Do you know anyone who's eaten one?"

"My brother-in-law's in the Forces, and he says they taste like corned beef."

"Yuck. I wouldn't eat one in a million years. They look worse than maggots."

"You ever seen an algae production plant? That burger you're eating was a slimy green plant a week ago."

"That's different."

Slugger played with the water spots on the counter in front of him as he listened to their conversation. He wished Lefty was around and they could joke things up, break some of the tension. Maybe he should give him a call. He'd said he was going home to his wife, but maybe he'd come out for a beer. Maybe his ankle still bothered him.

"I bet you wouldn't eat one of them."

"I'm not sure. After all, they were going to eat us and it seemed like the only thing for us to do. Anyway, we lost the game, so we don't have to eat them. Why worry about it?"

"Yeah, the game. Buncha clowns."

Slugger felt his collar getting tight. He gripped his beer glass harder to keep his temper down.

"The umpire should've been shot. I hope they roast him n a stick."

"It wasn't the umpire, it was the team. They looked like a buncha girls out there. Did you see that bonehead play old Mandella made? They shoulda traded him years ago."

"They gave him an error, didn't they? What do you want? He was two for five."

"Lousy singles with nobody on. He struck out in the fifth with the bases loaded."

"They had good pitching. Shut us out twice."

Slugger nodded to himself and ordered another beer. They did have good pitching. Have to hand it to them there. But hell, with six arms and twelve fingers on each hand, they *had* to have good control. A lot these bar-flies knew. They should have had to face those curve balls that dipped *just* right.

"You're all wet. We blew it—blew it real bad. Lefty only had one hit and he had to FALL DOWN! An easy double, maybe three bases and with Pedro batting clean-up, man, that would have been the ball game. But no, he had to go and trip over his own shoelaces. Couldn't even get back to first. What a clown."

Slugger had had enough. They couldn't talk about his friend like that. With calculated slowness, he stood up and turned to face the men at the end of the bar.

"It coulda happened to anyone. Wasn't his fault."

"Hey look, it's Slugger."

"Throw the bum out."

"Fantastic! Ten for seventeen in the series."

"Bet the fix was on."

"Can I have your autograph, Slugger? It's for my kid."

"Buncha sand-lot bums."

Slugger turned to the nearest man and grabbed him by the collar, lifting him off the bar stool.

"It could have happened to anyone," Slugger repeated. "A bad day, that's all."

He sat the struggling man down, missing the stool and dumping him on the dirty floor.

"But this was the last one, Slugger. We *had* to win this one."

"You win some, you lose some, and some get rained out," said Slugger as he walked to the door, stopping only to autograph a baseball someone held out for him.

Outside, the streets were filled with celebrating Arcturians. They were running around with knives and forks in their multiple hands. Some wore bibs with humorous sayings printed on them.

Slugger started the long walk back to his apartment. Many of the Arcturians he met congratulated him on his performance in the series. Others pinched his arms and buttocks. He felt like half a cow hanging in a butcher shop window.

It was growing dark and a cold drizzle had started. A young boy wearing a tattered baseball cap was standing on the corner, selling evening papers with the headline: HUNGRY FOR A WIN, THE AWKS COP THE BIG ONE.

The boy approached him.

"Say it isn't so, Slugger."

The great man just shook his head and crossed the street.

NANCY KRESS

A Delicate Shade of Kipney

Sullen gray clouds lay heavily on the low sky, and below them gray fog shrouded the land.   It had just finished drizzling, or was about to drizzle, or perhaps even was drizzling with fine clammy droplets that were indistinguishable from the ever-present mist.   In the East the lowering clouds were paling almost imperceptibly, and the stunted kiril trees that dotted the plain hastily turned their gray-green leaves toward the thin light before any of it should be wasted.

A boy sat on the hill that poked abruptly from one side of the plain, just before it broke into irregular rocky ravines.   His already muscular arms were clasped around knees that, child-like, were scraped from falls.   Under his coarse, dull-colored tunic, his bare buttocks pressed against the damp, straggly grass.   He sat unmoving, absorbed, staring raptly toward the drab eastern sky.

"Wade?"

The boy turned without getting up, and peered through the shifting fog.   It was difficult to see clearly more than a few yards.

"Wade!   Are you there?"

"Oh, it's you, Thekla.   I'm over here."

"Who else did you think it would be?"   Spectrally his sister materialized from the fog, her gray tunic blending with it at the edges, her younger child astride one hip.   The baby stared at Wade with round solemn eyes.

"I thought I'd find you here.   How was it today?"

Wade shook his head, inarticulate.   "Really beautiful.   Much brighter than the sunset ever is.   Thekla, look at this color."   He held out a leaf.   The underside was a delicate gray, lightly shined with silver.

"Mmmm, what a pretty shade of tlem."

"It's the exact color I need for the painting.   If only I could figure out a way to mix it!"   He gazed hopefully at Thekla, only four years his senior but always so much more deft at the endless foraging and fashioning of supplies.   "Got any ideas?"

"No, but I'll think about it.   Wade, you'd better come down to breakfast now. Mother sent me to get you.   She's almost ready to serve."

The cords in Wade's neck grew taut.   "I thought it was earlier than that."

"It is.   I mean, we're having breakfast earlier this morning because Brian woke us up when he was news-spreading.   Jenny had her baby last night, it's a girl, and they're both all right!'' Thekla smiled, and he saw that it was still the dazzling, comradely smile which had made the toddler Wade follow her everywhere, stumbling gaily after her through the wet mist, and which lately had become so rare. But now it somehow—*jarred* with her too-thin face, and with the awkward way she stood, one shoulder hoisted a little higher than the other. Something had gone wrong with one hip when the last baby had been born; they hadn't told Wade just what. Painfully he looked away, watching instead the perfect, disembodied fog.

"I'm glad. I was thinking about Jenny." He added, after a pause, "Maybe that will put *him* in a good mood, too. Forty-nine now."

They both looked down from the hill, down to the plain, where the small stone cabins huddled around the lifeless hulk of the ship. The fog shifted, and for a moment they could see her clearly, the long, grotesquely mangled wreckage barnacled with rust, and, at a sharp angle to the rest, the rear observation section, miraculously snapped free and preserved whole by the inexorable vectors of chance. Then the fog closed once more.

The pause lengthened, broken only by the soft cry of a small creature shrouded somewhere in the formless gray mist: "Kee-day! Kee-day!"

"Well, come on then," Wade said heavily. "I guess we have to go down."

The inside of the small cabin fairly vibrated with color.

Every wall was covered with pictures, glossy prints carefully torn from an art book and cemented to the walls in close rows, as though to blot out as much of the native stone as possible. Masterpieces from several centuries elbowed each other crazily, with no regard to chronology, all seemingly chosen only for their glowing colors and pure, hard lines. Picasso, Van Eyck, Miro, Vermeer, Grunewald, Reznicki.

In the center of the wall opposite the fireplace was a group of landscapes done on split kirilwood boards. The drawing showed obvious skill, but the colors were garish, larger than life, put on with a lavish desperate hand by an almost-artist who had forgotten that nature could be subtle. The Grand Canyon at sunset screamed orange and red and acid yellow; a kelly green forest grew lushly under a turquoise sky; Victoria Falls threw up a lurid, brassy rainbow.

The others were already seated at the long table. Wade slid into his place, glanced once at Mondrian's *Broadway Boogie-Woogie* on the wall opposite him, and shuddered. He dropped his eyes quickly to his plate, thinking of his own paintings prudently stored in the sleeping loft, dwelling on their soft, almost imperceptible shadings; the last one carried the blending right to the edge of what the eye could discern, he was pretty sure. Now if he could only mix that shade of tlem, the one you only saw when the light had just—

"Wade, Jenny had her baby last night," his mother said in her soft voice. "A little girl, thank God."

"Thekla told me," Wade said. He looked at his mother's worn face with affection. "They're both all right. That's wonderful."

"Forty-nine, by God!" his grandfather cackled. "Forty-nine, and two more

pregnant right this minute—Cathy, and Tom's youngest girl, what's-her-name—
Suja. We'll make it yet!''

"Yes, sir,'' Wade agreed. His grandfather was elated, as he always was when
another addition arrived to the colony, and maybe this morning he would let Wade
alone, let him escape the usual . . . Quickly he began eating.

Thekla finished strapping her baby into a tall wooden chair, and began putting
food on her five-year-old's plate. The little girl was rhythmically kicking her heels
against the legs of the rough wooden bench, and the old man frowned.

"Stop that, Malki, right now! A Strickland is reverent when grace is said,
remember that!''

Damn. No escape after all.

The grandfather swept his gaze around the table to make sure the four of them
all folded their hands and bowed their heads. Thekla's baby stared at him soberly.

"Earth, let us see you once again, green and blooming, if it is possible. If
not—'' there was always an agonized pause here, and Wade wondered what awful
scenes of desolation howled in his grandfather's mind, ''—if not, then let us see
your offspring, New Earth, and carry to her a loyal band of colonists to help prepare
for the Return. If even that is not possible—'' again that anguished quaver,
''—then be sure that we will rebuild Earth here, preserving, above all, the great
cultural traditions entrusted to us so long ago, and someday carrying them ourselves
to the stars!''

Wade caught Thekla's eye out of the corner of his own; she smiled faintly and
shook her head. Malki piped, ''What's a star, Great-Grandfather?''

The rheumy old eyes glared at her fiercely. ''You asked that yesterday, Malki,
and I told you then. It's a big ball of fire in the sky that makes light and heat.''

The child looked at the stone fireplace, where a fire was kept constantly against
the pervasive damp of the fog. She opened her mouth, her eyes full of doubt,
glanced at her great-grandfather's glowering face, and said instead, ''I caught a
non-frog.''

"Did you now?'' the grandfather asked, amusement replacing annoyance with
the fitfulness of the old, and the adults around the table relaxed. ''And what did
you do with him?''

"Oh, I let him go. He was pretty, though. He was tlem.''

"What?'' asked the grandfather, puzzled.

"What did the non-frog say, Malki?'' Thekla asked hastily.

"He went like this: kee-day, kee-day, kee-day!'' The high, childish voice piped
such a close imitation that even the grandfather smiled.

"After breakfast, I'll show you a picture of a real frog, Child, in the Book. It
was painted long ago, by a man called Nussivera.'' He glanced lovingly at the
wall, where five well-worn books were enthroned. *History of Western Art*; Petyk's
A Thousand Years of Painting, now cannibalized to provide the pictures on the
walls; *Complete Shakespeare*; the Bible; and a dubious novel popular fifty-three
years before, *Love Until the Sky Falls*. The five books that had been shelved on
the rear observation deck when the Emergency Landing deteriorated into the Crash.

On a little carved bracket, set well enough below the shelf to make even the remote chance of fire impossible, a candle burned day and night.

"What's a real frog, Grandfather?"

"It's a small green amphibian. It looks a little like a non-frog, but it goes 'ribbit-ribbit.' "

The little girl's eyes grew round. "*Nothing* goes like that!"

Wade smiled. "Nothing that lives here, Malki. But, remember, Keedaithen isn't the only—" he stopped abruptly, groaning inwardly, knowing it was already too late.

His grandfather rose to his feet, trembling violently. "This is not 'Keedaithen!' " he shouted. "This is 'Exile,' and don't you forget it, young man! Exile! *Exile!* Not a home you give a name to! A 'home,' this dingy, mildewed . . . mildewed. . . ." he broke off, his face flushed hectically, his eyes straining out of their sockets. Wade's mother hurried over to him.

"Sit down, Father, right here; it's all right. You shouldn't get that excited, you know it's bad for you, the boy didn't mean anything. . . ." Her eyes signalled for Wade to leave. He was halfway to the door when his grandfather's voice, wheezing and jagged, stopped him.

"Just a minute, boy. You think I don't know that you kept on with that stuff you call painting. The hell I don't—" wheeze, wheeze, "—carry on cultural heritage . . . must preserve—" wheeze, "—no composition or values or even geometric grouping. . . ."

"Now, Father, just sit quietly for a few minutes and you'll be all right. Thekla, bring a dipper of water. There, that's better, just sit still."

". . . perverting sacred trust. . . ." he began coughing hard.

Wade made his escape.

All morning he hoed non-potatoes, savagely driving his hoe deeper than necessary into the spongy wet earth. In the afternoon he cut kirilwood, choosing trees set far enough into the ravines to require much heaving and pulling. By evening Wade's back muscles ached all the way to the base of his skull, but he felt that he had control enough of himself to return to the cabin. Still, he was aware that somewhere, deep inside, his resentment was only precariously banked.

The sunset damped it down a little more. He watched the fading light raptly, leaning on his ax, his eyes glued to the soggy clouds glimpsed through the mist as they shaded from gray to tlem to slate and all the way to a delicate kipney. The fog carried the mingled smells of rainplant, decaying wet leaves, and the pungent richness of cut kirilwood.

It won't all get into even this last painting, he thought with a curious mixture of gratitude and despair. No artist could get it all—not even me, damn it. The shaded softness, the grayness, the—the *rightness* of the way it looks just before dark. God, the world is so damn beautiful.

He shifted a little, gingerly flexing his cramped muscles, keeping his eyes turned upwards to the foggy sky, and the gray lichens beneath his boots crunched softly. He bent over and carefully scraped them off the rocks. What if he powdered them, maybe adding a little thinned river clay—would they mix into that silvery shade of tlem?

He began to whistle a wordless, excited little tune, unaware that he did so, as he intently rubbed the gray lichens into the back of his hand and squinted at the resulting shades. He didn't see the figure gliding through the fog until his mother materialized next to him.

"Wade? Are you all right?"

All his life, that had been her greeting—a tentative request for reassurance, made as though she questioned her own right to ask it. Incongruously, Wade thought of the three headstones in the little cemetery with "Beloved Child of Janice" on them, as well as that other one bearing the name of the man assigned to sire two of them and Wade himself.

"Yes, Mother, I'm all right." He half-held out his lichen-colored hand, then drew it back. Better show Thekla instead.

They were silent, smelling the wet air, watching the way the gray mist softened the tools leaning against the stone cabin. Simple tools, simply made; the improvisations of a pioneer society starting over.

"He's very old, Wade. You don't always remember that," his mother said abruptly. Wade said nothing, his lips pressed tightly. Somewhere among the rocks a non-frog shrilled: kee-day, kee-day.

"Eighty-three, by that reckoning system he insists on using." Her voice was softer now, pleading, almost apologetic. "Eighty-three, and the last one left. We can't know what it was like for them, Wade. Leaving behind them a world on the edge of war, taking all those books and art treasures with them to the only place of safety left, and then, after sleeping all those years—" he caught the little stumble in her voice, the psychological balk at hurdling the illogical concept, "—to miss it by so little."

"Oh, Mother, it's not so little," Wade said impatiently. "It's a whole planet away! A whole different world!"

His mother sighed. "I know it seems that way to us. But after they traveled all that way—nine 'light years'—" again that little stumble, "—being just one planet away *seems* like a little. I guess."

She stared at the darkening clouds, behind which were—somewhere—that just-missed Earth-like world, with its flourishing commemorative colony, New Earth. Behind them, too, was the sun, which the grandfather insisted they refer to as "Beta Hydri," and all the other unimaginable "stars." Wade fidgeted impatiently. If he mixed the powdered lichens with a little pale kipney—

"You know, when I was a little girl," his mother went on, "and all of the Five Survivors were alive, I would hear them have the same conversation over and over. I used to wonder why it was so interesting to them. Mother would wail about all the books and paintings that were destroyed in the Crash. Uncle Peter would shake his head and say how much they would have meant to New Earth. Then Father would brace his shoulders—I know you don't remember him strong and healthy, Wade, but I do—and say in a deep, artificial voice, 'If you were marooned on a desert island and could only take one book . . .' The others would laugh, but not happily, and Father would add, 'But we've got five of them. Well, four decent ones, anyway. A whole culture!' and then Aunt Alia would simper and say that it wouldn't have meant so much without a real artist and art historian like Professor James Strickland to help pass on that culture, and that even though New Earth had suffered his loss, it was Exile's gain.''

Wade shifted his weight from one foot to the other. It was growing very dark. His mother reached up her hands and rested them on his shoulders.

"He's not well, Wade. He never leaves the fire anymore, and he can't bear to even look outside—and even close to the fire he coughs from the damp. And these scenes just upset him so. Yes, I know, you kept your temper this morning, but what about yesterday, or the day before? It can't be much longer. Please, Wade.''

"Please what?'' he asked through suddenly stiff lips.

"Please don't paint those gray-mist pictures anymore. Paint the way he needs you to.''

"I can't!''

"Then don't paint at all. Please. I can say they need everyone for some harvest emergency or other; he can't keep track of the work anymore.''

Not to paint. Not to feel the smoothness of the whittled brush handle between your fingers, and the power flow down your arm, and the ultimate, wholly enormous satisfaction of the subtle shades drifting over the kirilwood board seemingly without even touching it and the. . . .

"Please, Wade. It means so much to him, this passing on of a heritage. It's all that's kept him going, that's carried him—and all of us with him, don't you ever forget that—this far.''

Her face was completely obscured. He put out a finger and touched the worn cheeks, the skin still soft from the eternal damp but hollowed out, stretched tautly in the contours of a face that had looked steadily at backbreaking work and compulsory childbearing and the thin edge of survival every day of her life, with no space for the luxury of painting that was her son's inheritance from her labor.

"What about you, Mother?'' he asked desperately, his voice cracking from its new deep tones upward into a childish wobble. "It's always *him*, everything's always *him*. What about you? Don't you have an opinion about it? What cultural heritage do *you* want me to have?''

She took her hands from his shoulders, and through the sodden darkness her voice was weary with all those weeks and months and years of unbroken work. "I don't know, Wade. I don't have one to give you.''

He didn't paint. He harvested non-potatoes, and hunted the small, quick glarthen, and cut kirilwood, and didn't paint. He took his turn on the hand loom and helped roof the Ciegler cabin for the winter, and went on a foraging trip to haul rock salt, and didn't paint. In the mild autumn evenings he sat with the others by the fireplace and listened to his grandfather read alien, outlandish plays from Shakespeare or discuss the turn-of-the century Delineists. While his grandfather talked, Wade made himself keep his eyes focused on the trembling, liver-spotted hands that would never hold a paintbrush again.

Once, almost formally, the old man showed him a seventeenth-century Tohaku in the Book. It was a pine forest, seen through early-morning mist. "See," he quavered, "there's a fog, but the emphasis is still on the trees, the composition and values are preserved. Now if you would use your talent to do something like that, boy, instead of those formless, colorless blobs, it would be part of a great tradition!"

For a moment Wade saw everything red, an ugly livid red that made his body recoil even while his mind winced away from the knowledge that, coming from his grandfather, this was a peace offering. Peace, when it might be years—oh, God, surely not *years*—before he would paint again, and the old man kept on shoving those hard ugly drawings at him and he was probably going to live till a hundred and what kind of a person would *wish* for another human's death? What did that make him?

The grandfather was shrinking back on his bench, clutching the book and staring at Wade's face. Wade shook his head convulsively, saw his mother fearfully watching him from across the room, and managed to say in a voice that was almost steady, "I wasn't *trying* to paint the way a landscape looks in fog."

There was a long, painful pause. Finally the grandfather dropped his eyes; he hardly spoke to Wade the rest of the winter.

As winter wore on, the usual stretching of provisions began. Wade lost ten pounds and his mother watched him anxiously. In the longer evenings, desperate to put some object into fingers that seemed to constantly curve into the hold for a brush, he tried to help Thekla teach Malki to read. Malki had always come to him, hanging around underfoot and fiddling with his tools, but now she climbed into her mother's lap when Wade fixed her with his flat, tense gaze that seemed to see nothing.

The spring came early. The fog lost its winter clamminess and chill, and smelled of new gray-green life and wet dirt. Wade, restless, took to long twilight walks, meandering aimlessly through the dank fog, refusing even Thekla's company. As he walked, he held his right hand firmly imprisoned in his left.

He returned one night well after dark. His mother watched him as he came in, looking as though she were going to urge him again to eat something, but he avoided her eye and climbed up to the sleeping loft. She sighed and went back to helping his grandfather touch up the colors in his Terran landscapes.

"More red in that, Janice," the old man was saying fretfully. "Can't you see it's too drab? The damn fog fades everything. It should be scarlet, or even crimson, damn it."

The loft seemed cramped and suffocating. Wade lay on his pallet and stared at the peak of the kirilwood ceiling, where a non-spider was spinning an intricate gray web. He tossed to his side and examined the weave of the heavy, dull blanket. He lay on his stomach and tried to bring sleep by sheer effort of will.

At last he rolled off the pallet and slowly, his calloused fingers trembling a little, opened the little cupboard he himself had built under the low eaves.

They were gone.

A few chips of dried paint shimmered on the rough shelves.   His brushes were all there, and the little dippers of the powders he had made, and one thin kirilwood board, painstakingly sanded but still as yet empty.   But the paintings, all of them, were, unbelievably, gone.

"Mother!   Thekla!   *Malki!*"   Wade clattered down the ladder, sprang at the child bent over her lesson slate.   "Malki!   You were in my things again!   What did you do with them, where are they, oh my God—"

Malki squealed and ran for her mother.   Wade caught her by the shoulders and started shaking her violently, like a rag doll.   Thekla hit at his arms, screaming, and finally her words pierced the red mist in his brain.

"She didn't take them, Wade!   She didn't take them!   Leave her alone, you're hurting her!   Wade!   She didn't take them!"

He dropped Malki, who climbed, sobbing, into Thekla's arms.   Wade straightened slowly, and slowly, leadenly, his eyes swung to his grandfather.

"No," he whispered, "you couldn't have."

The old man shrank back on his bench.   "You weren't painting anything: you have talent only you just don't *use* it, boy; you have an obligation to the colony. . . ," he began to sputter, his words slurring together as the quavering, cracked voice rose higher.   "You *can* do it, but this damn stinking hell cast a spell on you, and they were holding you back, those other ones, don't you see I *had* to burn them! I had no choice!"

Wade took a step forward, woodenly, feeling his fists clenching themselves at his sides.

". . . and who the hell d'you think you are, anyway?" his grandfather shouted, pulling himself up with his stick.   "All of us . . . obligation . . . to cult'al heritage . . . memory of Earth. . . ."

"Memory of Earth!" Wade shouted.   "My God, I hate the damned place! Earth!   What good have your memories of Earth ever done but strangle us!   This isn't Earth, it's Keedaithen, and you're just too rotten stubborn to admit it!   But I won't go down with you, you hear me, old man?   You destroyed my p-paintings."

He bent over in a ragged, shuddering sob, then sprang, his face demented, to the fireplace.   The grandfather tried to scurry behind the table, but Wade rushed past him.   He grabbed the books from their homemade altar and hurled them, one by one, into the fire.

"This is what I think of Earth!   My God, my God, all my work—"   The Shakespeare hit the center of the flames and sent red sparks leaping.   The Bible joined it a second later and the two of them, old and brittle, blazed passionately.   *A Thousand Years of Painting* landed a little to one side and began to char, its edges graying ghoulishly.

The grandfather started forward with a strangled cry, his face dull purple, his eyes bulging from their sockets.   Wade began to claw at the walls, ripping the prints into tatters, hurling the paper fragments into the fire. The kirilwood land-scapes, more solid, hit the back of the stone fireplace with a dull "thunk."

"And this damned memory, and this one, and this one! 'Cultural heritage!' 'Memories of Earth!' Damn the stinking place, it's probably nothing but a pile of rubble by now—"

The old man fell to his knees. Spittle covered his chin and his face was ashen, but he made no sound. He seemed to fall very slowly, his body twisting from the waist, like a feather from a kel bird and floating through the shifting fog, cutting secret little paths that soundlessly closed behind it. When he hit the stone floor there was scarcely a noise at all.

The mist hung in dark gray curtains into the oblong hole, filling it, asserting first rights over the kirilwood box that would soon take its place. Wade stood a little apart from the rest, numb with guilt and unexpected grief, isolated less by any action of the others than by his own frozen immobility. A baby whimpered in its mother's arms, was impatiently hushed, and quieted.

Thomas, now the eldest colonist, stepped forward and began the service. He recited it haltingly, hesitating often, and when Wade realized why the man had to rely on his uncertain memory, he moaned softly, an inarticulate keening, unaware that he did so. Thekla put out her hand and gently touched his arm.

"As for man, his days are as grass . . . and . . . as a flower of the field, so he . . . flourisheth."

His mother, dry-eyed, watched Wade anxiously. It began to drizzle.

"For the wind passeth over it, and it is gone, and . . . and . . . the place thereof shall know it no more."

The light rain fell on Wade's face, fragrant with the smell of new grass and wet slate. The frozen immobility cracked a little, began to break up.

Eighty-three years. "He's not well, Wade. It can't be long." And time passing, relentless as the squalling clouds, in the unimaginable light-years among those stars he only half-believed in, anyway. "As a flower of the field."

But there were no field flowers here, he thought haltingly. None of those garish, over-colored daisies or zinnias or roses in the Impressionist paintings that now existed nowhere in the world. And the wind never passed *over* anything; it got tangled in the mist and the clouds and made beautiful shifting shapes of its own.

Wade unclenched his fists and surreptitiously flexed his hands; the right one began to curve gently. There must be someone, he thought, either among these 48 or yet to come, who could see words as purely as he could see colors. Someone who could write a new funeral service—as well as sonnets, plays, celebrations, all of it—to fit here, and now, on Keedaithen.

HERB BOEHM

Air Raid

I was jerked awake by the silent alarm vibrating my skull. It won't shut down until you sit up, so I did. All around me in the darkened bunkroom the Snatch Team members were sleeping singly and in pairs. I yawned, scratched my ribs, and patted Gene's hairy flank. He turned over. So much for a romantic send-off.

Rubbing sleep from my eyes, I reached to the floor for my leg, strapped it on and plugged it in. Then I was running down the rows of bunks toward Ops.

The situation board glowed in the gloom. Sun-Belt Airlines Flight 128, Miami to New York, September 15, 1979. We'd been looking for that one for three years. I should have been happy, but who can afford it when you wake up?

Liza Boston muttered past me on the way to Prep. I muttered back, and followed. The lights came on around the mirrors, and I groped my way to one of them. Behind us, three more people staggered in. I sat down, plugged in, and at last I could lean back and close my eyes.

They didn't stay closed for long. Rush! I sat up straight as the sludge I use for blood was replaced with supercharged go-juice. I looked around me and got a series of idiot grins. There was Liza, and Pinky and Dave. Against the far wall Cristabel was already turning slowly in front of the airbrush, getting a Caucasian paint job. It looked like a good team.

I opened the drawer and started preliminary work on my face. It's a bigger job every time. Transfusion or no, I looked like death. The right ear was completely gone now. I could no longer close my lips; the gums were permanently bared. A week earlier, a finger had fallen off in my sleep. And what's it to you, bugger?

While I worked, one of the screens around the mirror glowed. A smiling young woman, blonde, high brow, round face. Close enough. The crawl line read *Mary Katrina Sondergard, born Trenton, New Jersey, age in 1979: 25*. Baby, this is your lucky day.

The computer melted the skin away from her face to show me the bone structure, rotated it, gave me cross-sections. I studied the similarities with my own skull, noted the differences. Not bad, and better than some I'd been given.

I assembled a set of dentures that included the slight gap in the upper incisors. Putty filled out my cheeks. Contact lenses fell from the dispenser and I popped them in. Nose plugs widened my nostrils. No need for ears; they'd be covered by the wig. I pulled a blank plastiflesh mask over my face and had to pause while it melted in. It took only a minute to mold it to perfection. I smiled at myself. How nice to have lips.

The delivery slot clunked and dropped a blonde wig and a pink outfit into my lap. The wig was hot from the styler. I put it on, then my pantyhose.

"Mandy? Did you get the profile on Sondergard?" I didn't look up; I recognized the voice.

"Roger."

"We've located her near the airport. We can slip you in before takeoff, so you'll be the joker."

I groaned, and looked up at the face on the screen. Elfreda Baltimore-Louisville, Director of Operational Teams: lifeless face and tiny slits for eyes. What can you do when all the muscles are dead?

"Okay." You take what you get.

She switched off, and I spent the next two minutes trying to get dressed while keeping my eyes on the screens. I memorized names and faces of crew members plus the few facts known about them. Then I hurried out and caught up with the others. Elapsed time from first alarm: twelve minutes and seven seconds. We'd better get moving.

"Goddam Sun-Belt," Cristabel groused, hitching at her bra.

"At least they got rid of the high heels," Dave pointed out. A year earlier we would have been teetering down the aisles on three-inch platforms. We all wore short pink shifts with blue and white stripes diagonally across the front, and carried matching shoulder bags. I fussed trying to get the ridiculous pillbox cap pinned on.

We jogged into the dark Operations Control Room and lined up at the gate. Things were out of our hands now. Until the gate was ready, we could only wait.

I was first, a few feet away from the portal. I turned away from it; it gives me vertigo. I focused instead on the gnomes sitting at their consoles, bathed in yellow lights from their screens. None of them looked back at me. They don't like us much. Our fat legs and butts and breasts are a reproach to them, a reminder that Snatchers eat five times their ration to stay presentable for the masquerade. Meantime we continue to rot. One day I'll be sitting at a console. One day I'll be *built in* to a console, with all my guts on the outside and nothing left of my body but stink. The hell with them.

I buried my gun under a clutter of tissues and lipsticks in my purse. Elfreda was looking at me.

"Where is she?" I asked.

"Motel room. She was alone from 10 to noon on flight day."

Departure time was 1:15. She cut it close and would be in a hurry. Good.

"Can you catch her in the bathroom? Best of all, in the tub?"

"We're working on it." She sketched a smile with a fingertip drawn over lifeless lips. She knew how I like to operate, but she was telling me I'd take what I got. It never hurts to ask. People are at their most defenseless stretched out and up to their necks in water.

"Go!" Elfreda shouted. I stepped through, and things started to go wrong.

I was faced the wrong way, stepping *out* of the bathroom door and facing the bedroom. I turned and spotted Mary Katrina Sondergard through the haze of the gate. There was no way I could reach her without stepping back through. I couldn't even shoot without hitting someone on the other side.

Sondergard was at the mirror, the worst possible place. Few people recognize themselves quickly, but she'd been looking right at herself. She saw me and her eyes widened. I stepped to the side, out of her sight.

"What the hell is . . . hey? Who the hell. . . ." I noted the voice, which can be the trickiest thing to get right.

I figured she'd be more curious than afraid. My guess was right. She came out of the bathroom, passing through the gate as if it wasn't there, which it wasn't, since it only has one side. She had a towel wrapped around her.

"Jesus Christ! What are you doing in my—!" Words fail you at a time like that. She knew she ought to say something, but what? *Excuse me, haven't I seen you in the mirror?*

I put on my best stew smile and held out my hand.

"Pardon the intrusion. I can explain everything. You see, I'm—" I hit her on the side of the head and she staggered and went down hard. Her towel fell to the floor. "—working my way through college." She started to get up so I caught her under the chin with my artificial knee. She stayed down.

"Standard fuggin' *oil*!" I hissed, rubbing my injured knuckles. But there was no time. I knelt beside her, checked her pulse. She'd be okay, but I think I loosened some front teeth. I paused a moment. Lord, to look like that with no makeup, no prosthetics! She nearly broke my heart.

I grabbed her under the knees and wrestled her to the gate. She was a sack of limp noodles. Somebody reached through, grabbed her feet, and pulled. *So long, love! How would you like to go on a long voyage?*

I sat on her rented bed to get my breath. There were car keys and cigarettes in her purse, genuine tobacco, worth its weight in blood. I lit six of them, figuring I had five minutes of my very own. The room filled with sweet smoke. They don't make 'em like that anymore.

The Hertz sedan was in the motel parking lot. I got in and headed for the airport. I breathed deeply of the air, rich in hydrocarbons. I could see for hundreds of yards into the distance. The perspective nearly made me dizzy, but I live for those moments. There's no way to explain what it's like in the pre-meck world. The sun was a fierce yellow ball through the haze.

The other stews were boarding. Some of them knew Sondergard so I didn't say much, pleading a hangover. That went over well, with a lot of knowing laughs and sly remarks. Evidently it wasn't out of character. We boarded the 707 and got ready for the goats to arrive.

It looked good. The four commandos on the other side were identical twins for the women I was working with. There was nothing to do but be a stewardess until departure time. I hoped there would be no more glitches. Inverting a gate for a joker run into a motel room was one thing, but in a 707 at twenty thousand feet . . .

The plane was nearly full when the woman that Pinky would impersonate sealed the forward door.   We taxied to the end of the runway, then we were airborne. I started taking orders for drinks in first.

The goats were the usual lot, for 1979.   Fat and sassy, all of them, and as unaware of living in a paradise as a fish is of the sea.   *What would you think, ladies and gents, of a trip to the future?   No?   I can't say I'm surprised.   What if I told you this plane is going to—*

My alarm beeped as we reached cruising altitude.   I consulted the indicator under my Lady Bulova and glanced at one of the restroom doors.   I felt a vibration pass through the plane.   *Damn it, not so soon.*

The gate was in there.   I came out quickly, and motioned for Diana Gleason— Dave's pigeon—to come to the front.

"Take a look at this," I said, with a disgusted look.   She started to enter the restroom, stopped when she saw the green glow.   I planted a boot on her fanny and shoved.   Perfect.   Dave would have a chance to hear her voice before popping in.   Though she'd be doing little but screaming when she got a look around . . .

Dave came through the gate, adjusting his silly little hat.   Diana must have struggled.

"Be disgusted," I whispered.

"What a mess," he said as he came out of the restroom.   It was a fair imitation of Diana's tone, though he'd missed the accent.   It wouldn't matter much longer.

"What is it?"   It was one of the stews from tourist.   We stepped aside so she could get a look, and Dave shoved her through.   Pinky popped out very quickly.

"We're minus on minutes," Pinky said.   "We lost five on the other side."

"Five?"   Dave-Diana squeaked.   I felt the same way.   We had a hundred and three passengers to process.

"Yeah.   They lost contact after you pushed my pigeon through.   It took that long to realign."

You get used to that.   Time runs at different rates on each side of the gate, though it's always sequential, past to future.   Once we'd started the snatch with me entering Sondergard's room, there was no way to go back any earlier on either side.   Here, in 1979, we had a rigid ninety-four minutes to get everything done. On the other side, the gate could never be maintained longer than three hours.

"When you left, how long was it since the alarm went in?"

"Twenty-eight minutes."

It didn't sound good.   It would take at least two hours just customizing the wimps.   Assuming there was no more slippage on 79-time, we might just make it.   But there's *always* slippage.   I shuddered, thinking about riding it in.

"No time for any more games, then," I said.   "Pink, you go back to tourist and call both of the other girls.   Tell 'em to come one at a time, and tell 'em we've got a problem.   You know the bit."

"Biting back the tears.   Got you."   She hurried aft.   In no time the first one showed up.   Her friendly Sun-Belt Airlines smile was stamped on her face, but her stomach would be churning.   *Oh God, this is it!*

I took her by the elbow and pulled her behind the curtains in front.   She was breathing hard.

"Welcome to the twilight zone," I said, and put the gun to her head.   She slumped, and I caught her.   Pinky and Dave helped me shove her through the gate.

"Fug!   The rotting thing's flickering."

Pinky was right.   A very ominous sign.   But the green glow stabilized as we watched, with who-knows-how-much slippage on the other side.   Cristabel ducked through.

"We're plus thirty-three," she said.   There was no sense talking about what we were all thinking; things were going badly.

"Back to tourist," I said.   "Be brave, smile at everyone, but make it just a little bit too good, got it?"

"Check," Cristabel said.

We processed the other quickly, with no incident.   Then there was no time to talk about anything.   In eighty-nine minutes Flight 128 was going to be spread all over a mountain whether we were finished or not.

Dave went into the cockpit to keep the flight crew out of our hair.   Me and Pinky were supposed to take care of first class, then back up Cristabel and Liza in tourist.   We used the standard "coffee, tea, or milk" gambit, relying on our speed and their inertia.

I leaned over the first two seats on the left.

"Are you enjoying your flight?"   Pop, pop.   Two squeezes on the trigger, close to the heads and out of sight of the rest of the goats.

"Hi folks.   I'm Mandy.   Fly me."   Pop, pop.

Halfway to the galley, a few people were watching us curiously.   But people don't make a fuss until they have a lot more to go on.   One goat in the back row stood up, and I let him have it.   By now there were only eight left awake.   I abandoned the smile and squeezed off four quick shots.   Pinky took care of the rest.   We hurried through the curtains, just in time.

There was an uproar building in the back of tourist, with about sixty percent of the goats already processed.   Cristabel glanced at me, and I nodded.

"Okay, folks," she bawled.   "I want you to be quiet.   Calm down and listen up.   *You,* fathead, *pipe down* before I cram my foot up your ass sideways."

The shock of hearing her talk like that was enough to buy us a little time, anyway. We had formed a skirmish line across the width of the plane, guns out, steadied on seat backs, aimed at the milling, befuddled group of thirty goats.

The guns are enough to awe all but the most foolhardy.   In essence, a standard-issue stunner is just a plastic rod with two grids about six inches apart.   There's not enough metal in it to set off a hijack alarm.   And to people from the Stone Age to about 2190 it doesn't look any more like a weapon than a ball-point pen. So Equipment Section jazzes them up in a plastic shell to real Buck Rogers blasters, with a dozen knobs and lights that flash and a barrel like the snout of a hog.   Hardly anyone ever walks into one.

"We are in great danger, and time is short. You must all do exactly as I tell you, and you will be safe."

You can't give them time to think, you have to rely on your status as the Voice of Authority. The situation is just *not* going to make sense to them, no matter how you explain it.

"Just a minute, I think you owe us—"

An airborne lawyer. I made a snap decision, thumbed the fireworks switch on my gun, and shot him.

The gun made a sound like a flying saucer with hemorrhoids, spit sparks and little jets of flame, and extended a green laser finger to his forehead. He dropped. All pure kark, of course. But impressive.

And it's damn risky, too. I had to choose between a panic if the fathead got them to thinking, and a possible panic from the flash of the gun. But when a 20th gets to talking about his "rights" and what he is "owed," things can get out of hand. It's infectious.

It worked. There was a lot of shouting, people ducking behind seats, but no rush. We could have handled it, but we needed some of them conscious if we were ever going to finish the Snatch.

"Get up. Get *up,* you *slugs!*" Cristabel yelled. "He's stunned, nothing worse. But I'll *kill* the next one who gets out of line. Now *get to your feet* and do what I tell you. *Children first! Hurry,* as fast as you can, to the front of the plane. Do what the stewardess tells you. Come on, kids, *move!"*

I ran back into first class just ahead of the kids, turned at the open restroom door, and got on my knees.

They were petrified. There were five of them—crying, some of them, which always chokes me up—looking left and right at dead people in the first class seats, stumbling, near panic.

"Come on, kids," I called to them, giving my special smile. "Your parents will be along in just a minute. Everything's going to be all right, I promise you. Come on."

I got three of them through. The fourth balked. She was determined not to go through that door. She spread her legs and arms and I couldn't push her through. I will *not* hit a child, never. She raked her nails over my face. My wig came off, and she gaped at my bare head. I shoved her through.

Number five was sitting in the aisle, bawling. He was maybe seven. I ran back and picked him up, hugged and kissed him, and tossed him through. God, I was beat, but I was needed in tourist.

"You, you, you, and you. Okay, you too. Help him, will you? Pinky had a practiced eye for the ones that wouldn't be any use to anyone, even themselves. We herded them toward the front of the plane, then deployed ourselves along the left side where we could cover up the workers. It didn't take long to prod them into action. We had them dragging the limp bodies forward as fast as they could go. Me and Cristabel were in tourist, with others up front.

Adrenalin was being catabolized in my body now; the rush of action left me and I started to feel very tired. There's an unavoidable feeling of sympathy for the poor dumb goats that starts to get me about this stage of the game.   Sure, they were better off, sure they were going to die if we didn't get them off the plane. But when they saw the other side they were going to have a hard time believing it.

The first ones were returning for a second load, stunned at what they'd just seen: dozens of people being put into a cubicle that was crowded when it was empty. One college student looked like he'd been hit in the stomach.   He stopped by me and his eyes pleaded.

"Look, I want to *help* you people, just . . . what's going *on?*   Is this some new kind of rescue?   I mean, are we going to crash—"

I switched my gun to prod and brushed it across his cheek.   He gasped, and fell back.

"Shut your fuggin' mouth and get moving, or I'll kill you."   It would be hours before his jaw was in shape to ask any more stupid questions.

We cleared tourist and moved up.   A couple of the work gang were pretty damn pooped by then.   Muscles like horses, all of them, but they can hardly run up a flight of stairs.   We let some of them go through, including a couple that were at least fifty years old.   *Je*-zuz.   Fifty!   We got down to a core of four men and two dropped.   But we processed everyone in twenty-five minutes.

The portapak came through as we were stripping off our clothes.   Cristabel knocked on the door to the cockpit and Dave came out, already naked.   A bad sign.

"I had to cork 'em," he said.   "Bleeding Captain just *had* to make his Grand March through the plane.   I tried *everything*."

Sometimes you have to do it.   The plane was on autopilot, as it normally would be at this time.   But if any of us did anything detrimental to the craft, changed the fixed course of events in any way, that would be it.   All that work for nothing, and Flight 128 inaccessible to us for all Time.   I don't know sludge about time theory, but I know the practical angles.   We can do things in the past only at times and in places where it won't make any difference.   We have to cover our tracks. There's flexibility; once a Snatcher left her gun behind and it went in with the plane.   Nobody found it, or if they did, they didn't have the smoggiest idea of what it was, so we were okay.

Flight 128 was mechanical failure.   That's the best kind; it means we don't have to keep the pilot unaware of the situation in the cabin right down to ground level. We can cork him and fly the plane, since there's nothing he could have done to save the flight anyway.   A pilot-error smash is almost impossible to Snatch.   We mostly work mid-airs, bombs, and structural failures.   If there's even one survivor, we can't touch it.   It would not fit the fabric of space-time, which is immutable (though it can stretch a little), and we'd all just fade away and appear back in the ready-room.

My head was hurting.   I wanted that portapak very badly.

"Who has the most hours on a 707?"   Pinky did, so I sent her to the cabin, along with Dave, who could do the pilot's voice for air traffic control.   You have to have a believable record in the flight recorder, too.   They trailed two long tubes from the portapak, and the rest of us hooked in up close. We stood there, each of us smoking a fistful of cigarettes, wanting to finish them but hoping there wouldn't be enough time. The gate had vanished as soon as we tossed our clothes and the flight crew through.

But we didn't worry long. There's other nice things about Snatching, but nothing to compare with the rush of plugging into a portapak. The wake-up transfusion is nothing but fresh blood, rich in oxygen and sugars. What we were getting now was an insane brew of concentrated adrenalin, super-saturated hemoglobin, Methedrine, white lightning, TNT, and Kickapoo joyjuice. It was like a firecracker in your heart; a boot in the box that rattled your sox.

"I'm growing hair on my chest," Cristabel said, solemnly. Everyone giggled.

"Would someone hand me my eyeballs?"

"The blue ones, or the red ones?"

"I think my ass just fell off."

We'd heard them all before, but we howled anyway. We were strong, *strong*, and for one golden moment we had no worries. Everything was hilarious. I could have torn sheet metal with my eyelashes.

But you get hyper on that mix. When the gate didn't show, and didn't show, and *didn't sweetjeez show* we all started milling. This bird wasn't going to fly all that much longer.

Then it did show, and we turned on. The first of the wimps came through, dressed in the clothes taken from a passenger it had been picked to resemble.

"Two thirty-five elapsed upside time," Cristabel announced.

"Je-zuz."

It is a deadening routine. You grab the harness around the wimp's shoulders and drag it along the aisle, after consulting the seat number painted on its forehead. The paint would last three minutes. You seat it, strap it in, break open the harness and carry it back to toss through the gate as you grab the next one. You have to take it for granted they've done the work right on the other side; fillings in the teeth, fingerprints, the right match in height and weight and hair color. Most of those things don't matter much, especially on Flight 128 which was a crash-and-burn. There would be bits and pieces, and burned to a crisp at that. But you can't take chances. Those rescue workers are pretty thorough on the parts they *do* find; the dental work and fingerprints especially are important.

I hate wimps. I really hate 'em. Every time I grab the harness of one of them, if it's a child, I wonder if it's Alice. *Are you my kid, you vegetable, you slug, you slimy worm?* I joined the Snatchers right after the brain bugs ate the life out of my baby's head. I couldn't stand to think she was the last generation, that the last humans there would ever be would live with nothing in their heads, medically dead by standards that prevailed even in 1979, with computers working their muscles to keep them in tone. You grow up, reach puberty still fertile—one in a thousand—rush to get pregnant in your first heat. Then you find out your mom or pop passed on a chronic disease bound right into the genes, and none of your kids will be immune. I *knew* about the para-leprosy; I grew up with my toes rotting away. But this was too much. What do you do?

Only one in ten of the wimps had a customized face.   It takes time and a lot of skill to build a new face that will stand up to a doctor's autopsy.   The rest came pre-mutilated.   We've got millions of them; it's not hard to find a good match in the body.   Most of them would stay breathing, too dumb to stop, until impact.

The plane jerked, hard.   I glanced at my watch.   Five minutes to impact.   We should have time.   I was on my last wimp.   I could hear Dave frantically calling the ground.   A bomb came through the gate, and I tossed it into the cockpit. Pinky turned on the pressure sensor on the bomb and came running out, followed by Dave.   Liza was already through.   I grabbed the limp dolls in stewardess costume and tossed them to the floor.   The engine fell off and a piece of it came through.   I grabbed the cabin.   We started to depressurize.   The bomb blew away part of the cockpit (the ground crash crew would read it—we hoped—that part of the engine came through and killed the crew: no more words from the pilot on the flight recorder) and we turned, slowly, left and down.   I was lifted toward the hole in the side of the plane, but managed to hold onto a seat.   Cristabel wasn't so lucky.   She was blown backwards.

We started to rise slightly, losing speed.   Suddenly it was uphill from where Cristabel was lying in the aisle.   Blood oozed from her temple.   I glanced back; everyone was gone, and three pink-suited wimps were piled on the floor.   The plane began to stall, to nose down, and my feet left the floor.

"Come on, Bel!" I screamed.   That gate was only three feet away from me, but I began pulling myself along to where she floated.   The plane bumped, and she hit the floor.   Incredibly, it seemed to wake her up.   She started to swim toward me, and I grabbed her hand as the floor came up to slam us again.   We crawled as the plane went through its final death agony, and we came to the door. The gate was gone.

There wasn't anything to say.   We were going in.   It's hard enough to keep the gate in place on a plane that's moving in a straight line.   When a bird gets to corkscrewing and coming apart, the math is fearsome.   So I've been told.

I embraced Cristabel and held her bloodied head.   She was groggy, but managed to smile and shrug.   You take what you get.   I hurried into the restroom and got both of us down on the floor.   Back to the forward bulkhead, Cristabel between my legs, back to front.   Just like in training.   We pressed our feet against the other wall.   I hugged her tightly and cried on her shoulder.

And it was there.   A green glow to my left.   I threw myself toward it, dragging Cristabel, keeping low as two wimps were thrown head-first through the gate above our heads.   Hands grabbed and pulled us through.   I clawed my way a good five yards along the floor.   You can leave a leg on the other side and I didn't have one to spare.

I sat up as they were carrying Cristabel to Medical.   I patted her arm as she went by on the stretcher, but she was passed out.   I wouldn't have minded passing out myself.

For a while, you can't believe it all really happened.   Sometimes it turns out it *didn't* happen.   You come back and find out all the goats in the holding pen have softly and suddenly vanished away because the continuum won't tolerate the changes and paradoxes you've put into it.   The people you've worked so hard to rescue are spread like tomato surprise all over some goddam hillside in Carolina and all you've got left is a bunch of ruined wimps and an exhausted Snatch Team.   But not this time.   I could see the goats milling around in the holding pen, naked and more bewildered than ever.   And just starting to be *really* afraid.

Elfreda touched me as I passed her.   She nodded, which meant well-done in her limited repertoire of gestures.   I shrugged, wondering if I cared, but the surplus adrenalin was still in my veins and I found myself grinning at her.   I nodded back.

Gene was standing by the holding pen.   I went to him, hugged him.   I felt the juices start to flow.   *Damn it, let's squander a little ration and have us a good time.*

Someone was beating on the sterile glass wall of the pen.   She shouted, mouthing angry words at us.   *Why?   What have you done to us?*   It was Mary Sondergard. She implored her bald, one-legged twin to make her understand.   She thought she had problems.   God, was she pretty.   I hated her guts.

Gene pulled me away from the wall.   My hands hurt, and I'd broken off all my fake nails without scratching the glass.   She was sitting on the floor now, sobbing. I heard the voice of the briefing officer on the outside speaker.

". . . Centauri 3 is hospitable, with an Earth-like climate.   By that, I mean *your* Earth, not what it has become.   You'll see more of that later.   The trip will take five years, shiptime.   Upon landfall, you will be entitled to one horse, a plow, three axes, two hundred kilos of seed grain . . ."

I leaned against Gene's shoulder.   At their lowest ebb, this very moment, they were so much better than us.   I had maybe ten years, half of that as a basketcase. They are our best, our very brightest hope.   Everything is up to them.

". . . that no one will be forced to go.   We wish to point out again, not for the last time, that you would all be dead without our intervention.   There are things you should know, however.   You cannot breathe our air.   If you remain on Earth, you can never leave this building.   We are not like you.   We are the result of a genetic winnowing, a mutation process.   We are the survivors.   But our enemies have evolved along with us.   They are winning.   You, however, are immune to the diseases that afflict us . . ."

I winced, and turned away.

". . . the other hand, if you emigrate you will be given a chance at a new life. It won't be easy, but as Americans you should be proud of your pioneer heritage. Your ancestors survived, and so will you.   It can be a rewarding experience, and I urge you . . ."

Sure.   Gene and I looked at each other and laughed.   *Listen to this, folks. Five percent of you will suffer nervous breakdowns in the next few days, and never leave.   About the same number will commit suicide, here and on the way.   When you get there, sixty to seventy percent will die in the first three years.   You will die in childbirth, be eaten by animals, bury two out of three of your babies, starve slowly when the rains don't come.   If you live, it will be to break your back behind a plow, sun-up to dusk.   New Earth is Heaven, folks!*

God, how I wish I could go with them.

LINDA ISAACS

A Many Splendored Thing

They never dreamed that I would wake up in the middle of the night and watch them doing it. The house was dark and full of night sounds, but from the hallway I could hear the laughing, the noises.

I avoided creaky floorboards, but I had a little difficulty because I'm so short, and my coordination isn't perfect. Too bad the treatment doesn't fix that.

I reached up to the doorknob and ever so carefully swung the door open. It was so dark I could hardly see, but I knew what was happening.

"Rose, Rose, Rose!" Dad's voice was soft; he never spoke to her that way. And what about me? He'd never said 'Ann, Ann, Ann.'

The bed squeaked loudly, then everything was still. The whole thing was ridiculous—they didn't want more children. They had to wait till I was eighteen or lose their bonus.

"Mark, I used the card today."

The bed jingled slightly. "You what?"

"Just to pay for Ann's treatment."

I could hear him settling his pillow against the headboard. There wasn't enough light to really see, but I could imagine his lean face, a heavy stubble shadowing blue across his cheeks.

"Christ, what's this—the fifth?"

Mom laughed nervously. "This takes her through high school. Sometimes I wonder if we're doing the right thing."

Dad growled and said something incomprehensible. There were soft scufflings in the dark as I turned back to the hall.

I had barely taken two steps when the lion rushed toward me out of nowhere. He was a black-maned male of maybe four hundred pounds, and he moved with the kind of stealthy grace that indicated he was near his prey. But he didn't seem to notice me at all. He brushed by and bounded into the bedroom. There were screams and then a roar that sounded as if it were echoing down a long tunnel.

The next morning I pretended to sleep late because I didn't want to see *him*. I lay staring at the ceiling until the sound of heavy footsteps thudded from the kitchen to the front door. The distant tones of his voice drifted up the stairs, but

I did not allow myself to understand.   Instead, a giant wall of water bubbled up between him and me, garbling the words beyond recognition.

At last the door slammed, and the water began to drain out from under my door and rush in white-water rapids down the stairs.   Some of it cascaded off the landing into the hallway below.   Victoria Falls.

"You awake up there?"

I threw off the covers and stepped out onto the soggy carpet.   "I'm awake."

"Well hurry up, Ann.   I'm going to take you to the sitter."   Her voice was silvery and beautiful as she sentenced me to hours of misery.

I kicked my dresser, then went through the drawers until I found my wetsuit. There were no flippers, so I put on some sandals—you couldn't have everything. It took me only a short time to body surf the rapids.   There were no sharp rocks or gullies, so it was fairly safe.

Rose was sitting at the table reading the newspaper.   Her short, black hair had hardened into a meticulous hairdo, and her eyes and lips were painted in sleek lines onto her face.

"Come on and eat," she said without looking up.   Her hand moved toward a cup of coffee, then brought it unerringly to her lips.

"I'm not hungry."   If she loved me she'd look into my face.

"Don't make Mrs. Wineland have to feed you later, Honey.   You can't start the day on an empty stomach."

A lot she knew about nutrition.   She drank a cup of coffee for breakfast every day.   Did she think I didn't notice?

I sat down at the glass-topped breakfast table and looked into my Wonderwoman bowl.   Rose had filled it with paste.   It was hot, but I pulled my finger through it, then took a lick.   LePage's.

"Hurry up, Ann."   Rose turned the page of her newspaper, then glanced at her watch.   "We'll be leaving in ten minutes."

A lump grew slowly in my throat.   If only she would look.   "Where are you going, Rose?"

Her cream-smooth face creased, and she looked at me indirectly, as if talking to the top of my head.   "Don't you worry about it," she said.   "You'll have a good time at Mrs. Wineland's.   You'll get to play with Bob and Ellen."

I stirred the paste with my spoon.   "I don't like them—they're stupid."

Rose looked me straight in the eyes for the first time.   It almost made it worth getting her mad.   "They're not stupid, Ann.   Someday there'll be enough treated kids for you to meet one.   Not everybody can afford to get their children expensive things."

"They don't like me and I don't like them."

"Nonsense."   Rose folded the newspaper and stood up.   "Now eat.   You may have a high school education, but you're still five years old.   So don't think you can get away with disobeying me, young lady."

My stomach revolted at the thought of the paste, but I knew it would make her happy if I ate it.   I put a big spoonful in my mouth.   Mom smiled.

"You're my good girl, Ann.   I love you."

A warm glow crept across my face and kept going down till it reached my toes. Then suddenly it was gone—Dad loved her more than me.   I stopped eating.

Rose clinked dishes into the sink, then grabbed her red leather purse off the counter.

"Let's go."   She swung the strap over her shoulder; it matched precisely the red suit she wore.   "I'm in a hurry."

She grabbed my hand as if I were a heavy bag she must drag along behind her. But I was a person as much as she.   She'd only been through high school herself— I heard her tell Dad.

We raced down the walk to our starship, which was stationed at the front curb. After a minimum of preparation and strapping in, we went into cold-sleep; then the ship entered interstellar space.   It took ten thousand years to reach Wineland, a planet inhabited by a tiny population of subhuman species.

Sarah Wineland was maybe thirty-five with silver-streaked brown hair.   She smiled a lot and although she was a little overweight, the old-fashioned flowered dress she wore seemed to make that look right.   She came out onto the big screened-in porch to let us in.   She said, "Hello, Ann.   Bob and Ellen have been waiting to play with you."

Hardly likely.   "Hello," I whispered.

"Now you just take your time, Rose.   Everything will be fine here."

Rose bent down and gave me a kiss on my cheek.   A flowery scent whisked by me as she stood up again.

"Thanks, Sarah," she said.   "It'll be around one o'clock.   Bye now.   Bye, Ann."

"Bye."   I hoped she would change her mind at the last minute and take me with her, but of course she didn't.   I was a worry and a bother—she wouldn't even tell me where she was going.

She clicked down the walk in her stilted shoes and climbed back into the starship. I watched as the ignition sounded, and then, all at once, the whole ship was enveloped in giant orange flames.   The heat was so intense I had to step back, and tears fell down my face.

"She'll be back," Mrs. Wineland said, opening the door.   "Don't cry—you're such a pretty little girl with those ringlets and big brown eyes.   Don't spoil it by making a face."

I rubbed the tears away as we went into the house.   Mrs. Wineland's living room was big and airy by any standards, but it had a strange odor.   Furniture crowded the whole place—couches, endtables, coffee tables, hassocks, plant racks— every imaginable item was fitted in there.   Bric-a-brac abounded at every turn, and I was surprised that the greater part of it had not been broken.   Bob and his sister had a tendency to play with the stuff.   Personally, I saw nothing fascinating about cheap gewgaws.

"The children will be right in," Mrs. Wineland said.   "I think you all would like some Kool-Aid later.   I'll mix some up."

As she went into the hall, Bob came past her into the room.   He went immediately to a glazed statuette of a woman in an eighteenth-century dress of pink silk and ruffles.

"Hi," he said with finality.   He fingered the hard curves of the flowing dress, but didn't look at me.

"Hi, " I said.   "Look, you don't have to play with me.   I'll just amuse myself, and you and Ellen can—"

Ellen came into the room.   She wore a white tee shirt like Bob, and green pants with patches on the knees.   Fine yellow hair like her brother's clung damply to her forehead.   She didn't smile.

"We have to play with you," Bob said.   "Mom told us."   In the month that I'd known him, I'd never seen him so sullen.

"Want to play hide and seek?" Ellen said with a kind of subdued hope.   "We could go in the back yard."

I looked from her to him, then shuddered.   The thought of crawling around in the yard hiding from these two was less than inviting.

Ellen caught the look on my face and frowned.   "Well, what can we play?"

"Nothing," Bob said.   "Nothing's good enough for *her*."

He turned and took Ellen by the arm.   "Let's play hide and seek—you and me."

Ellen laughed.   "Okay—out back."

They ran into the hall as if forgetting that I ever existed.   Their shoes thudded against the bare floor and then the back door slammed.   If I could have been all alone out there, I would have gone and played on the swing set.

I felt the glass growing around me until I was enclosed all around by a giant bubble.   I floated over to the couch and bumped against the arm.   The glass was one way—I could reach through, but nothing could get in.   When I had eased the bubble onto the couch, Mrs. Wineland came in.

She sat down at the other end of the couch and smiled.

"The kids are out back—why don't you join them?   You like the swings."

"I'll stay here for a while," I said.   "It's cooler."

"But there's a breeze outside."   Her voice was a little strained.   I'd been to her house on three occasions, but this was the first time I noticed that she sat pressed up against the arm of the couch.   I'd hoped she wouldn't be like everybody else, but now her eyes had that same look of secret horror.   Even a smile couldn't hide the lines that crinkled her mouth the wrong way.

"I won't bother you," I said.   "I'll just sit here and read a magazine."   I reached under the glass endtable and pulled out a *McCall's*.

Mrs. Wineland tried another tack.   "I'm going to clean, so you just take that out back and read it.   Go on now."

She stood up to demonstrate her authority, then gave me a sharp look.   So I had to play along—it was her house.   But I knew she was afraid.

It had snowed in the back yard, and I climbed across the powdery drifts toward the swing set.

Dad sat straight and tall, cutting his steak up into little squares.   On the times we had steak, he always did that—cut everything up at once, then ate very deliberately.   He concentrated on the meat, hardly looking at me.

"This is tough, Rose." He glanced across the bowl of artificial daisies to Mom. "You pay four dollars a pound and it's not supposed to be tough."

"Maybe I cooked it too long," Rose said. Her eyes misted over a little and somehow I felt happy.

"Damn it, Rose. Four dollars a pound! I don't work ten hours a day for you to throw money away." He jabbed a piece of steak so violently that some peas fell off his plate onto the table cloth.

"You don't have to yell, Mark. I do the best I can—everybody makes mistakes."

"You're irresponsible!" For a moment Mark's face seemed ugly. Actually he's very handsome—the perfect combination of dark brown hair, and eyes shaded by perfectly-shaped brows.

Tears began to creep down Mom's face and her lips trembled. "I'm sorry."

Mark frowned and put down his fork. "No, I'm sorry. I don't know why I've been yelling so much lately. Money isn't that tight yet."

Rose looked at him and smiled. "We've been through a lot together all these years." She'd made him forget—it wasn't fair.

"But the meat's ruined," I said. "What about that? What about being irresponsible?" She had faked him out and he couldn't even see that.

Dad looked at me. They both looked at me, as if suddenly they were together and I was alone. And in their eyes was the same look of secret horror—even Dad. All at once I wasn't hungry anymore.

I walked through the great hall, my billowy dress gleaming gold and silver. By the door was a narrow stone staircase which led round and round up to the top of the keep. I mounted each step sadly, thinking of my tapestried room and my dark, handsome prince, who would never come to put his arms around me. He belonged to Rose.

TED REYNOLDS

Boarder Incident

He strolled out of the alley, trying not to look like an alien who had just buried his spaceship under the forsythia bushes. The house he sought stood at the corner, high-peaked and gaunt. The sign in the lower window proclaimed: MRS. DOGEN, FINE ROOMS FOR RENT.

On the front steps, he paused to tuck in a stray tastestalk that had somehow slipped from under his rubberoid head covering. It was his careful attention to details like these that had made him such a valuable first contact man for Galactic Empire, Inc.

He rang the bell.

The last landlady he had encountered had been sesquipedal and oviparous, but the type was universal. With a shudder he began a sputtering explanation. Mrs. Dogen seemed wilfully bent on not comprehending him.

"Just a moment," she said finally. "Your name is Astroven?"

"In effect. And I request only that—"

"Why do you want to live in *my* attic? I have nice rooms available on both the first and second floors."

"I don't precisely intend to live in it," Mr. Astroven explained in his rubbery voice, "just set up a hyperdimensional interstellar space-warp booster station in it. I shall *live* in the stairwell cupboard."

Mrs. Dogen rotated her head. "Out of the question," she announced.

Mr. Astroven took a synthekit from his pocket and synthesized a small diamond. Mrs. Dogen watched the performance suspiciously until Mr. Astroven placed the gleaming end product in her hand. "As a stipend, perhaps one of these per week," he suggested. "Its intrinsic value would equal some two hundreds of your dollars."

Mrs. Dogen's expression altered. "Perhaps," she announced, "some kind of explanation is in order."

They sat in the cool living room and Mr. Astroven explained . . . and explained . . . and explained, and with deepening misgivings, for Mrs. Dogen obviously was gleaning not a tithe of it.

"So you see," Mr. Astroven said, bringing his explanation to a conclusion for the third time, "if we can't set up on Earth, we'll have to set up at least four booster stations and go several parsecs out of the direct route to the Persean spiral arm. We prefer worlds with no natives; and if there must be natives, we'd much prefer civilized ones; but in dry regions like this we have to make do with what is available.''

"I see," Mrs. Dogen said, though she was still looking at the diamond. "Then what you're saying is that my attic is one of the three places on Earth where your gadgets will work."

"Yes, ma'am. One of the other two is a nexus at the bottom of the Marianas trench, under six miles of water. Its use poses certain inherent difficulties. The other place—" He shuddered. "The other place is in a bar in Belfast."

Mrs. Dogen nodded. "Under the circumstances, I think . . . perhaps . . . *ten* of these per week . . .''

Mr. Astroven expelled a hissing breath and agreed.

"But there is one thing. I notice that you are concealing your actual features under a headmask. I trust you are not keeping anything important from me?"

"We merely try to be discreet on first contact," Mr. Astroven said. "However, if it is a condition for renting . . .'' He pulled off the mask and showed his real face. It was garish, variegated, surreal, and mostly green.

Mrs. Dogen was visibly relieved. "Perhaps it was foolish of me," she said. "I was afraid you might be black."

She paused to chase the cat from Mr. Astroven's lap for the tenth time. "Very well," she went on. "Kitty likes you, and I trust her judgment. You may— ah—bring your—er—friends through the attic as long as none of you create any disturbance, and your weekly rent will be—did we say—fifteen of these?"

Mr. Astroven expelled another hissing breath and while Mrs. Dogen looked on greedily he operated his synthekit fourteen more times. "We use it more often to synthesize coal," he remarked.

He finished, and Mrs. Dogen counted fifteen and thanked him, and he returned her thanks. "And now," he said, "I must leave you temporarily."

"Please don't let Kitty out," Mrs. Dogen said. "She hasn't been fixed."

Mr. Astroven regarded her perplexedly. "Oh, I'm not going out*side*. It will be unnecessary to use your doors from now on."

He climbed to the attic, where he set up a tiny pendulum disc, touched it, and . . . *went*.

For the first few days, there were no difficulties. Mr. Astroven's visitors, whoever or whatever they were, kept to the attic and behaved quietly. Still, there *was* the old friend he brought downstairs to introduce to Mrs. Dogen. It was a tritubiculated monosculate tissue culture from Mirfak, and it somewhat resembled a purple sea-cucumber. When it got a good look at Mrs. Dogen, it screamed in terror.

"Mrs. Dogen," Mr. Astroven said petulantly, "could you kindly explain to your domestic symbiote that the Phlegoorian Ambassador is not a rat? She appears painfully intent on ingesting him."

*   *   *

"You know this is a non-drinking house, Mr. Astroven. Perhaps you have a reasonable explanation for that strong stench of alcohol?"

"Why, yes, ma'am, I believe I do. The carbon rings at the basis of Danubian metabolism are made up in the following interesting arrangement—"

"That does not sound like a reasonable explanation," Mrs. Dogen said frostily. "If you're suggesting that some of your visitors smell like alcohol, then I insist that they use perfume."

"But my dear ma'am—what you are smelling *is* perfume!"

Mr. Astroven clumped down the stairs in awed excitement. "Ma'am—Mrs. Dogen!" he called.

She regarded him irritably.

"The Imperial Cortege will be passing through your attic next week," he blurted, panting his excitement. "The Galactic Empress Herself has expressed the wish for your presentation to Her."

Mrs. Dogen frowned. "Does *she* use perfume?"

"My dear ma'am! As a royal personage, naturally only the very finest—"

"You will kindly give her my regrets," Mrs. Dogen said firmly. "As a loyal American, I don't believe in royalty."

"Mr. Astroven, I don't care if there *is* a war out there somewhere! Feet tramping noisily through my attic from one to seven AM is something I cannot tolerate. I'm giving you notice."

Mr. Astroven sighed. "Perhaps if I were to increase the stipend—it is rather important to us—an additional ten diamonds a week?" He got out his synthekit.

"Twenty," Mrs. Dogen said, holding out her hand.

Mr. Astroven said apologetically, "The Loobite is forced to remain here until the proper cycle in its binary destination. Do you think you could turn the thermostat up forty degrees for a few days?"

"*Really,* Mr. Astroven!"

"It must have warmth to survive, you see."

"Out of the question," Mrs. Dogen said firmly.

"Perhaps for an additional five diamonds a week?"

"For ten diamonds," Mrs. Dogen said, "I'll rent the oven to you."

"I regret to inform you," Mr. Astroven announced, "that my synthekit is broken. And therefore this week's stipend . . ."

"I'm giving you notice," Mrs. Dogen announced coldly. "Effective at once."

Mr. Astroven sighed. "Actually, that was my intention. Giving notice, I mean. My superiors feel that a weekly stipend of two hundred diamonds is excessive. The wear and tear on synthekits has become intolerable. Therefore we have decided to transfer operations to the other route, the one with the four additional booster stations."

"Under the circumstances," Mrs. Dogen said, "I'll waive the required period of notice.   Peace and quiet, and an absence of peculiar odors, are to be prized in one's home above diamonds."

"Indeed, yes," Mr. Astroven murmured; he knew it would take her years to dispose of the hoard she had accumulated.   "Indeed, yes.   Kindly express my farewell regards to Kitty."

He touched the pendulum disc and vanished.   The disc remained.   There was no way it could transport itself, or it would have gone, too.

The same evening, Kitty went to the attic in search of her friend, Mr. Astroven. She batted the pendulum disc.   She *went*.

Mrs. Dogen sent several furiously worded notes out into the galaxy by space warp . . . "Send me back my cat or else!"   The cat did not return.

Mrs. Dogen began dumping daily loads of trash into the galaxy by space warp. They sped to various stations within the Sagittarian or Perseid spiral arms and were duly noticed.   Shortly afterward, the cat reappeared.

KEVIN O'DONNELL, JR.

Low Grade Ore

Nobody knew the teleport's name. Unless she'd come alone, her parents had also disappeared. Repeated appeals through the scratchy loudspeaker system had drawn no one willing to claim knowledge of her, much less a relationship. Perhaps they were peasants, fearful of reprisals if her identity were known.

By 14:49, the Director of the Calcutta Evaluation Center was answering the rapid-fire questions of fifty unruly newsmen. He spoke in English, probably to avoid accusations of regional favoritism. "Yes," he was saying, "we should be able to find it from her computer card, as we did on the three previous occasions, but—"

He spread his dusky hands in dismay.

A cameraman from a local station lined his equipment up to frame the Director's pudgy figure with the ever-shifting colors of the Pukcip hologram.

"To the best of our admittedly limited knowledge, the child did present her card; the question now is, where has it gone? You must understand that immediately after she teleported to Pukci, at 13:46, there arose more commotion than the staff could cope with, yet—" as the photographer readied his video-tape camera, the Director, a political appointee, dried his forehead, "—I assure you, gentlemen, that as soon as conditions permit we shall cross-check all cards on file quite thoroughly, and—"

A little girl's desperate shriek froze everyone. The audience's attention shifted from the Director; he swayed visibly, as though brushed by a gust of wind. The camera whirred while its handler murmured clipped phrases of excitement into its microphone.

Between the straining reporters and the hologram stood the six-year-old whom the Pukcip screening had swallowed. Her hair was gone, shaved to the scalp; her dark skin was streaked and smeared with blood. She was naked except for wires that flapped from her wrists, her ankles, and her knobbly bald head.

They began to mutter. Was this what the Pukcip did to the children who precipitated out? Slowly, their hostility focused on the intermediary—

The child's second scream was ghastly in its inhumanity. It was the throat-tearing cry of a mortally wounded animal. Staggering towards them, she raised her tiny hands as though to beg their help.

A few in the front shook off their numbness, opened their arms, stepped—

Two Pukcip warriors materialized; the almost-saviors lurched back as if from a gout of flame.   Each warrior held a gun in its posterior hands; each trained one stalked eye on the startled newsmen.   Their anterior hands reached for the girl. She dodged.   They teleported to either side of her.   One seized her arms; the other, her legs.   The one whose kaleidoscopic carapace was more ornate dipped its eyestalks at the crowd that had begun to press forward.   An instant later, all three—warriors and child, aliens and human—had vanished as though they'd never been.

The heavy silence of shock hung over the room for an awful minute, then burst into a monsoon rain of anger.   The Director was its center.   Bodies shoved; voices shouted.   His mouth worked frantically, but futilely, against the frustration that mounted like a storm's static charge.

"Gentlemen, gentlemen, please, this is no—"   His fat hands waved in vain. He was the lightning rod; their hatred, a rising surf, needed a rock on which to break. A fist beat against his face, and then another.   He gave one strangled cry before his final, fatal inundation.

Even as the white-helmeted police were cracking enough black-haired skulls to disperse the mob, a bruised witness described the cameraman.   Through channels hypersensitive to bad publicity flashed the order to suppress the tape.

The station manager surrendered it, though he protested that the government should not obscure the truth, not when a thousand hugely distorted rumors were flickering like cobra tongues through the Calcutta slums.

His superiors, apparently confident that tempers ignited by gossip needed hard fact to sustain their heat, ignored him.

They were wrong.

Calcutta burned.

A step ahead of the flames worked a score of foreign agents, laboring to discover just why the uneasy peace had been shattered.   One "cultural attache" after another spoke to the survivors of the press conference; one government after another decided that it had to view the tape.

New Delhi, resisting their demands, insisted that it was a purely internal affair. In private and off the record, its distracted officials promised to distribute the tape once the civil disorders had ended.

Russian and American strategic analysts were skeptical.   Oft-declared "states of emergency" had overprotected the Indian government from reality; it could not, they maintained, outlast an actual emergency.

Red phones buzzed; edgy leaders conferred.   For once agreement came swiftly: they would force New Delhi, in the few remaining hours of its life, to relinquish the tape before it was buried under the wreckage of the regime.

The Indians were obdurate, at least until the fighters, scrambling off the carrier decks, made like a cloud of locusts for the subcontinent.   The camel's back snapped; the tape was broadcast to the satellite network.

Televisions lit up policy rooms around the world; sweat dampened the shirts of the watchers.   What if a teleport returned to Shanghai, or Los Angeles, or Rome?

A tense, resentful public would lash out . . . possibly with the deep-gut fervor of Calcutta.   Scrub as they might, the giant air machines couldn't filter out the stench of that fear.

Because if Calcutta was the rock, Wichita was the hard place.

On the afternoon of 23 June 1979, five hours after the then-President of the US surrendered to end the Two Minute War, the Pukcip had staged a demonstration on the Kansas plains.   Their small expeditionary force had slammed into Wichita with more fury than any tornado had ever unleashed; their grim sweep missed but four of the town's three hundred thousand residents.   The rest lay rotting in the corn-growers' sun.

When it was over, their Commander had preempted the nation's communication networks.   As cameras inched over the dark stains on the carapace he'd refused to cleanse, he said through his interpreter: "You see now our seriousness.   Do as you are told, and all will be well.   Oppose us even lightly, and a larger city will suffer the same fate."

Like a dynamite blast in a coal mine, Wichita crumbled America's solidity. While the last twitches of the President's feet were reflected in the gleaming tiles of a White House bathroom, politician after politician hurried to add his frightened constituency to the swelling list of those that would follow orders.   By midnight the country had committed itself to cooperation.

Two years had passed since the headlines, the half-masted flags, the muffled drumbeats on Pennsylvania Avenue.   The impact had yet to fade.   The annual tribute of four or five widely separated children was clearly the lesser evil.   They went so quickly, so completely . . . they left no bones to be washed by the summer rains . . . one could almost pretend that they, and the Pukcip, had never existed.

The alien presence on Earth was nearly invisible: a small embassy at the United Nations, regular equipment deliveries to the many Evaluation Centers, and an occasional spot-check of children reported to have been tested.   Scientists were prohibited from examining them; even diplomats met them only at lengthy intervals.

They were strangers, and clever conquerors.   Importing no overlords, advisors, or enforcers, they presented no targets.   Like Mafiosi handing their victim a shovel, they made Terrans do the work.   Any rebellion would have to attack the governments that traded a few children's futures for many citizens' lives.

Any successful rebel would have to raze the Centers, would have to cut off the steady trickle of teleports to Pukci.

Any such interruption would invite Pukcip retaliation on a scale that would dwarf Wichita and utterly discredit the rebels.

The options seemed stark to most leaders: they could protect escaping teleports, and be punished; or they could do nothing, be overthrown, and then watch their populaces be savaged.

In the gray light of dawn, with the sun only a band of pink promise on the horizon, the President reached his decision.   America would continue to cooperate with the Pukcip—up to a point.   However, any returning children would find armed troops eager to defend them.

The men at the Cabinet meeting saw him hammer his fist on the long table, felt his agony of soul as though it were theirs, and shared his determination when he vowed: "No kid of ours goes to Pukci twice!   Send in the Army."

Colonel Mark Hazard Olsen, spine straight as a pine from his native Vermont, meditated in the passenger seat of the Jeep.   The wind, the smooth humming roar of the motor, the dawn-dappled rows of abandoned buildings, were all locked out of his thoughts.   His entire being sought serenity.

Yet the housefly flitting of Pukcip warriors refused to respect the pattern and the peace of his mantra.   He forced himself to persevere, but after a few minutes more opened his eyes.   Maybe later, once the bright plating of his hunger had been corroded by hours of forced alertness, he could try again.

At the moment, all he wanted to do was kill a few Pukcip.

Olsen had been a major during the Two Minute War.   When the Pukcip squad had wink-blinked onto his post, he'd been dictating a new page for the MP training manual.   Scattered shots had drawn him to the window.

His uncomprehending blue eyes had seen the bright shells of the Pukcip, had seen the running, falling, sprawling blurs of khaki.   More shots: a pitifully few steady growls punctuated by flurries of single cracks that seemed always to end in astonished screams of pain.

Hanging out the open window, he'd watched his men race for the armory, where all the weapons except the guards' were kept under lock and key.   The first to emerge had taken cover, were waiting for the enemy to come carelessly into range.   There!   The machine gun roared, its tracers leaping out to the—but the foe was already gone, had already shielded itself inside a squad of stunned GI's.

"NO GRENADES!" he'd shouted.   "NO GRENADES!"   The din was too great for his order to be audible, but his men didn't need it.   They wouldn't hurl indiscriminating death into their own ranks, not even to kill the commingling aliens.

The phone had rung; an enraged General had had to scream, "Surrender, you damn fool!" four times before its import had sunk in.   A word to his secretary, a frantic realignment of intercom switches, and his hollow voice, pregnant with feedback squeal, had echoed through the firefights.

Afterwards the clean-up, as integral a part of modern warfare as hot turkey on Thanksgiving, or cold beer on the Fourth.   Three hundred GI's lay dead and dying; another five hundred were wounded.   In the pools of blood, under the half-wrecked armory, were found four bullet-riddled shells.   The Pukcip, as contemptuous of their own dead as of the human living, had left them behind.

Olsen, after wondering what to do with them, had decided to ship them to a nearby university.   He'd taken the alien weapons—the post had specialists who could say if they deserved detailed study—and then ordered a dozen sullen GI's to load the death-dulled shells onto a van.

Before the van had cleared the gate, the news of Wichita had crackled through every radio on the post.   The GI's, without communication or negotiation, responded to the same instincts.   They'd parked the van on the parade ground.

Gasoline burns hot and quick; Pukcip horn merely chars.   The billows of black smoke had drawn the survivors, who'd contributed wood, and more gas, and phosphorus grenades.   A wasp-bitter helicopter had offered a load of napalm. And through it all the men had stood, helpless rage under the dirty sweat of their empty-eyed faces.   Among them was Mark Hazard Olsen, who'd waited till the last crisp curl of carapace had folded upon itself to give the order for bulldozed burial.

By then he'd been informed that his was one of the three US posts assaulted by the invaders.   There had been no tactical or strategic reason for the attack—the motive had been psychological.   Deliberately flaunting their ability to rain chaos on any defensive installation, the Pukcip had hoped to demoralize the military.

Their ploy had failed.   Olsen had already started to work out tactics for the next engagement, tactics—the convoy jolted to a stop amid the potholes of a long-neglected parking lot; he dismounted and surveyed the old, two-story school building—which would be invaluable if the Pukcip came to Hartford.

Ten minutes later, Walter F. Dortkowski, Director of the Hartford Evaluation Center, groaned aloud.   The blacktop lawn of the commandeered school was littered with Jeeps, deuce-and-a-half's, and milling squads of soldiers.   Cursing, he rammed his battered Volvo into his reserved space.   Things weren't red-taped enough, they had to saddle him with the Army, too.

As he switched off the ignition, he brightened.   Maybe the Governor, finally keeping her promise, had convinced the Army to take over.   Maybe he could throw away his plasticized ID badge, break his clipboard over his knee, and go home a free man.   God knew he'd tried to resign often enough before.

In July of 1979, when the Governor had named him Director, he'd accepted the appointment for two reasons, and on one condition.   The condition had been that he'd step down within six months.

The reasons had been almost classically simple: first, a very important job had to be done with a minimum of time, money, and effort.   Dortkowski, who had earned his MBA at Columbia before finding the fascination of educational administration, had realized—had been sweet-talked into realizing—that he could establish a better Center than anyone else under consideration.   The stakes had been too high for his hatred of the Pukcip to interfere.   He'd felt—he'd been urged to feel—a responsibility to the public.

Then, once he'd truly understood—had been made to understand—how he could guarantee the safety of three and a half million people, the Governor had pulled out the plum: after six months of designing, implementing, and refining the evaluation system, he'd be named State Commissioner of Education.   It would have been a wonderful 45th birthday present.

But difficulties arose.   January, 1980: the administration could find no qualified successor, could he hold on for a few months more?   Yes, he could.   April, 1980: The Commissionership received too much exposure to be held by someone who symbolized Pukcip oppression; they'd find him another slot, but in the meantime . . . and the meantime became all the time, and the bars of inertia, animosity, and indispensability had grown around him like bamboo.

At last, I'm quitting! he'd declared, to the deputies and assistants and administrators who'd hemmed him in.   He'd continued to say it; in the end, even to the Governor herself.

Warm sympathy had flowed across her face.   Sadly, she'd told him she was sorry, she couldn't let him quit.   She needed him too badly.   And if he did just walk away from it, as he'd threatened to do, she personally had it in her power to make sure that he.   Never.   Worked.   Anywhere.   At anything.   Again.   And in her face had glittered the eyes of a krait.

So he'd stayed, despite the vociferous hatred of people he'd never met, despite the pleas of his ostracized family.   He'd stayed because he had no choice, because the Directorship—carrion-strewn plateau that it was—was his only pathway to the peak, and if he ever climbed down from it, they'd never let him near the mountain again.

Now, for the first time in months, a smile disturbed his sunken cheeks.   Adjusting his tie, checking his frizzy gray hair in the rear-view mirror, he stepped into the early sun.   Already the day felt hot.   A shirtsleeve day.   His small, neatly shod feet were light as he walked expectantly to the door.   If he could transfer power quickly, he might have time for his fishing rod.

He might even get away before the first child arrived.

Someone was shaking Jonathan's shoulder.   It was his daddy, telling him to get up.   He pushed his heavy eyelids open, but it was still dark.   That meant it was going to rain a lot, 'less it was real early.   Gradually, he remembered.   Today he'd be 'valuated.

"You 'wake, boy?" gruffed his daddy.

"Yowp."   It was true, too.   He sat up, feeling alive and excited all over. "How soon we leaving, Daddy?"

"Soon's your mama fix us some breakfast.   Get dressed, now."

"Okay, I be quick."   He slid out from under the much-mended sheet, and started grabbing for the clothes his mama had laid out on his dresser.   "I be real quick, Daddy.   Don't wanna be late for my 'valuation."   As he pulled on his underwear, he puzzled over his daddy's wordless turn and hasty exit.

Dortkowski stared into Olsen's face.   Long and lean, dark from years of weather, lined by innumerable hard decisions, it was utterly impassive.   Only two things hinted at the Colonel's feelings: the grinding of his teeth on the burnt-out stub of a cigar, and the ambiguous softness in his clear blue eyes.

"Sorry as hell to give you the wrong impression, Mr. Dortkowski," Olsen was sayng.   "We're here for one reason, and one reason only: to protect any kid who happens to come back from Pukci.   We'll give you any assistance we can, but . . . we're not going to run your operation."

"It's my fault, Colonel."   The words were very hard to get out.   To be trapped in reality's field after free-falling through fantasy like a wide-eyed child . . . a glider pilot must feel the same, when he's lost the thermals and the ground is rushing up at him.   "Thanks for, uh, letting me down easy."

He turned away.   Hands behind his back, shoulders slumped, he entered the I-shaped school building.   The place would consume him yet.   Already it had cost him his friends, his reputation as a concerned administrator . . . what next?   His wife?   His life?   Olsen had said his Calcutta counterpart had been torn to pieces by an enraged mob.   That might be better.   One white-hot moment of pure, unmasked hatred—despite the agonies of dying—might be preferable to years of uncomfortable silences, of embarrassed breakings-off.

Hand kneading his belly, where the ulcer had awakened with its usual rumbling torment, he trudged down the stem of the **I**.   As he did every morning, he paused by the door that led to the memory-wiping machinery.   That had earned him more abuse than anything else.

The test could be invalidated if the children knew what to expect, so the Pukcip had designed equipment to keep the already-screened from describing it to the untested.   There had yet to be a single adverse reaction to the erasing—if nothing else, the Pukcip were unparalleled in neuroelectronics—but every mother despised him for exposing her child's mind to a callous alien machine.

The dials glittered in the slanting sunlight.   If only the scales were larger; if only the gauges measured months instead of minutes . . . to go in, to strip his brain of its experience, to tear from it the skills that made him indispensable to the political establishment . . . they'd have to let him resign, then.   They'd have no use for a seventeen-year-old mind in a forty-six-year-old body . . .

He unlocked the door to his office.   The small cubicle smelled of arguments and dust, of hysteria and decay.   He forced a swollen window up six inches, as high as it would go.   Rubbing the neck muscle that had protested the exertion, he dropped into the chair behind his desk.

On the blotter lay a computer printout naming the 250 children who would pass through the building that day.   The coldly efficient typeface hit him like a slap in the face.   Lowering his head to his crossed arms, he wished he could be as pragmatic about it as the Colonel was.

Olsen was stationing his men just outside the projection room.   His blue eyes, as if belying Dortkowski's assessment, held real anger whenever they glanced through the next doorway.

"They were too slow in Calcutta," he was telling his lieutenant.   "They gawked like raw recruits while the Puks took the kid back.   I won't put up with that kind of horseshit.   The odds are against its happening here—that was Calcutta's third or fourth teleport, and this Center hasn't even had one yet—but if it does, so help me God, you'll either save the child or face a firing squad."   He removed his cigar and spat out a shred of tobacco for emphasis.   "Do I make myself clear?"

"Perfectly, sir."   The lieutenant was relaxed but watchful: he knew Olsen prized performance above all else.   "Are there any limitations on what weapons we may use, sir?"

Olsen studied the dingy anteroom before replying.   A touch of claustrophobia flicked him from a distance, warned him of the oppressiveness it could bring to bear.   The ceiling sagged in the middle; any significant explosion would bring it down on everyone's head. "No grenades." Even a firefight would weaken it, perhaps disastrously. "Sidearms and M-16's only." He'd have to risk it, no matter what memories it teased into life.

In 'Nam once, during his first tour on the Delta, he'd led a company of men into a subterranean VC arms cache. An observer silent in a treetop had pressed the button of a small radio transmitter; the plastique had gone up and the tunnel roof had come down. The memory of muffled screams, of tattered fingernails clawing at soggy earth, still haunted Olsen.

But now it had competition: the tape he'd seen over closed-circuit TV that morning would stalk his dreams for months to come.

"There's one advantage to this kind of confined space," he said to his lieutenant. "They won't be able to ride their carousel."

Films of the Two Minute War had revealed distinct patterns—predictable patterns—in the Pukcip style of skirmishing. Each warrior moved through a standard series of positions, a series as immutable as an 18th century waltz. To defeat them on the battlefield, a foe had merely to determine each warrior's starting point, and fire there a fraction of a second before the Pukcip was due to materialize.

That called for a special soldier: one who could make sense of the shifting, surging intermingling of gaudy shells and faded khaki; one who could synchronize his trigger squeezes with the rhythm of their maneuvers; one who could stand fast even when a Pukcip blinked into the space next to him.

Olsen had asked for permission to select and train an elite detachment of such soldiers. Civilian eyebrows had lifed—there was no future, they thought, in preparing to fight an enemy that could depopulate a continent if it chose—but the political pressure to develop contingency plans had meshed with the Pentagon's desire for revenge. He had received his colonelcy.

"Two last things," Olsen said, staring at the cracked plaster of the anteroom walls. "First, make sure you rotate your men, keep 'em fresh. Those idiots in Calcutta were probably asleep on their feet."

"Consider it done, sir."

"Second, if a kid shows up, aim above his head and hose the room. That should catch the Puks by surprise, and leave 'em no place to jump except back home. All right?"

"Yes, sir."

"Carry on." The far doorway called him. Scowling, he crossed to it, and scanned the holographic projection of the—reception room? laboratory? zoo?—on Pukci. All shimmers of swirling blues and purples, it stood in haughty contrast to the peeling green paint of the Center. Olsen glared at the metallic glints in the odd-shaped tiles of its floor, as if he could dissolve the deception through sheer force of will. The vivid image remained unaltered. The Pukcip equipment was too good.

Spurred by an impulse as inexplicable as fate, he stepped forward. The lieutenant's surprised gasp plucked at his shoulder, but he didn't respond. He had no time. Gravity grasped him, ripped him through the planes of colored light.

An instant later, he was bouncing softly on the nylon mesh strung beneath the doorway.

Damn effective, he thought. *If I hadn't known—if I'd been a trusting six year old—I'd have expected it to be solid. Shit, even knowing, I was startled.*

A child's world is tinged with the mysterious and the irrational. To him, fantasy is merely fact in which he can not participate. What looks like a room must be a room, if he can enter it.

Two hundred fifty children ran, skipped, hopped, or walked into the Pukcip projection every day. Passage over the threshold triggered the test which, for one uncaring nanosecond, pitted the law of gravity against the child's belief that he was in a room whose floor could support his weight. If reality won, the testee tumbled; if faith overrode it to write its own version of natural law, the child either levitated in blissful ignorance . . . or teleported directly to the original room, somewhere on Pukci.

Roughly eleven of every million testees had faith enough to warp reality.

Jonathan was in the front seat, between his mama and his daddy. He'd wanted to ride in the back—both his parents were pretty big, and there wasn't much room. They'd told him that just that once they wanted to be together. It was sort of nice to be able to lean against his mama's softness, but there wasn't any air. If he were sitting where he always sat, the wind would be buffeting his face, and he'd have to half-close his eyes, which made the whole world look different.

"Is it long time, Daddy?" he asked.

"Most an hour, boy." He took his eyes off the road and gazed down at his only son. "Don't be in such a hurry, y'hear? We gonna get there, we just gonna have to sit and wait till they ready for us anyhow."

Jonathan nodded solemnly. He'd been wanting to ask his daddy why he was driving so much slower than usual.

The stone floor was worn; Olsen's combat boots set up a hollow ringing. The old school building had, at that hour of the morning, the semi-deserted air of a shut-down refinery. It was hard to believe how crowded the empty corridors would become; harder still to think how many people had passed through them in either of the building's two lifetimes, ironic that each involved some sort of screening.

The silence was almost good. Dortkowski's crew would shatter it within the next half hour, but the first children weren't due till nine o'clock, more than an hour away. That would be time enough to look things over, to smooth out the jangle of his thoughts. It bothered him that he would have to stand idle while the Pukcip equipment assayed the value of two hundred fifty children.

He left-faced into the main wing. Rickety metal folding chains lined the walls; he repositioned one that had wandered out a few feet. A stencil on the seat's underside declared it to be the property of a local funeral home. Disgusted, he kicked it.   The impact chipped paint off the crumbly cinderblocks; quarter-sized flakes of green skittered down to the baseboard.

Damn the Pukcip for their ability to teleport.   And damn the civilians for being so easily cowed!   The Army could have taken them, once it had recovered from the initial shock.   Their weapons weren't very good, no matter what the hysterical media claimed, and the carouselling warriors took longer to aim than a GI did.   If their tiny expeditionary force hadn't held most of the government hostage . . .

The fact that every other officer in the world had succumbed to the same ruse didn't lessen the shame.   If anything, it heightened it.   A professional respects his opposite numbers, often to the point of judging himself by his perception of how well he could do against them.   When not a single human officer proves himself capable of beating off a handful of stalked-eyed child thieves . . .

Only revenge could remove the stigma.   But the Pukcip were immune—Earth neither knew where Pukci was, nor had the star drive to get troops there.   In a year or two, though . . .

The US and the USSR were co-developing a faster-than-light drive.   If it were possible, if it weren't a mirage hanging stubbornly above the horizon, they'd launch a grim fleet and ransack space for Pukci.   Fueled by a bitterness that wouldn't fade with the generations, they'd find it, and avenge Wichita, Lyons, Serpukhov, all the other demonstration cities . . . the Pukcip warriors could dance quadrilles on the asteroids, but their planet wouldn't be able to dodge the swollen tips of the nuclear missiles.

One fear dogged Olsen, as it did everyone who hungered for satisfaction; if an FTL drive could be invented, why were the Pukcip allowing work on it to continue?

If it couldn't be invented, why had the joint communique announcing the project provoked the invasion?

It was obvious, in the crystallized brilliance of hindsight, that the Pukcip had spied on Earth for years.   They'd done nothing to reveal themselves until the release of the joint communique, but within twelve hours of that first, hope-stirring news flash, the four-armed teleports had stormed the world.

Olsen had his own theory: that the Pukcip theoreticians had decided FTL *travel* was impossible, but that research into it would somehow uncover natural teleports.   So the Pukcip warriors, as edgily suspicious as military men anywhere, had opted to remove Earth's teleports before they could spearhead an invasion of Pukci.

That fit neatly with the intelligence analysis that only the enemy's soldiers could teleport.   If, in their culture, the power had purely military applications, their experts would naturally have decided that Earth would also exploit it for war.

They were afraid, Olsen thought.   *They knew that once we started roaming the stars, we'd find them . . . shit, and I thought we were xenophobic.   Or maybe they know how xenophobic we are, and figured they'd eliminate our space capability before we'd discovered we had it . . . or maybe their motive is completely different— like they wanted to maximize the return on their investment, and so they held off while our population grew, until it seemed that we were ready to find, and use, the raw materials they needed* . . . he gave up the effort at triple-think with a tired shake of his head.   The *why* of the situation didn't really matter, not to him.   The specialists could worry about it.

His job was to be ready to fight them.

His hope was that he'd get the chance.

Dortkowski lifted his clipboard, recorded the Center's need for more Pukcip ink, and looked the room over one more time.   Everything seemed to be ready for the children.   The question was, would he be ready for the parents?

He'd explained it ten thousand times himself; he'd had every newspaper in the state run articles on it; he'd even scraped together the funds for a brochure distributed at the door.   But still they screamed their outrage when they saw the tricolored tattoo on their children's wrists.

What could he say that he hadn't said before?   Clearly the best thing was simply to start up the mental tape recorder, let the tired neutral words fall as they had so often before, and then wear the stoic face while spittle spattered his cheeks.

The Pukcip wanted their slag heaps labeled.   What else could he say?   To tell a mother that her child likes something she doesn't is to incite the hurricane; to tell a father that the process is painless is to ignore the very real hurt he feels at his child's disfigurement.

The bureaucrat had but one defense: *I'm sorry, it's not my idea, I didn't make that rule, if it were up to me I wouldn't, I can't make an exception, I'm sorry, but I'm just following orders.*   His ulcer pinched, as if to extend the range of his soul pain.   It was a lousy defense and he knew it.   The fact that every word was true made him no happier.

What the parents couldn't understand was what he didn't dare forget: any deviation from the Pukcip procedures might be discovered in one of the irregular Pukcip spotchecks.   Such a discovery could condemn an entire city.

The headache was starting up again; his ink-stained fingers massaged the bulging vein in his temple.   It was going to be one of those days . . . but maybe he'd get lucky.   Maybe a parent would get infuriated enough to put him into the hospital.

Immediately he sighed.   That was wishful thinking.   There was always an aide, a cop, *somebody* to step in officiously and protect him from the lesser suffering. Why would no one do it for the greater?

His hands groped for the center drawer of his desk; warped wood screeched as he pulled it out.   It overflowed with the debris of bureaucracy: forms, stamp pads, pencils . . . brushing them to one side, he uncovered the small green bottle.   He shook it.   The lethal white pills rattled like castanets.

They were his ticket out.   If the Center uncovered a teleport—no, *when* it did, because eventually it had to—he'd screw off the top, tilt back the bottle, and empty dusty release down his throat . . . because it would have been his fault.   Without his administrative expertise, it never would have happened . . . and he could see no other means of atonement.

Then he laughed, sourly, and the acid bit at the back of his throat.   Atonement?

He knew himself better.   It was escape, the modern man's escape: swallow the pills and dodge the pain.   Let chemistry exorcise reality.   Let death deny his responsibility for losing a child to the Pukcip pipeline.

They were driving straight at the sun, and if it didn't rise up off the end of the road before they got there, they were going to have a whole lot of trouble getting to his 'valuation.

Jonathan squirmed around so the bright streaks wouldn't be flying into his eyes. Catching his mama looking down at him, he asked the question that had been floating around in his head for the last couple days.   "Mama, why they wanna 'valuate me for anyway?"

"They doing it to all the little children, honey."

"But how come they want *me*, Mama?"

"Cause the government say you gotta."

"Oh."   He considered that for a moment, then shrugged.   If his daddy listened to the government, whoever that was, he guessed he'd better, too.   Sure didn't sound like his mama liked that guy though.   Her voice had done the same thing to "government" that it always did to "landlord."

Olsen strode through a classroom to a window above the parking lot.   The April day was going to be hot; a tang of soft asphalt was beginning to permeate the air. Below, the unseasonably cruel sun tormented a cluster of anxious parents.   They probably hadn't slept all night.   Unable to stand the suspense, they'd come early, to get it over and quickly.   Poor bastards.   Their faces were as gray as Dortkowski's hair.

The odds were against any of them losing a kid—from the initial statistics, only one in a million could teleport—in fact, they were ten times more likely to go home with a levitator.   Still, the possibility that their child might wind up a nugget in a Pukcip pocket was enough to make most of them despair.

Leaning on the dusty windowsill, he clenched his teeth.   He had a boy of his own—Ralph, four years old, now.   In less than two years' time he'd be shuffling through the corridors of a Center much like this, one more big-eyed kid in a line that stretched all the way back to the world's maternity wards.   As a father, he knew that the most nerve-wracking aspect was that if your kid should go to Pukci, you'd never know what they did to him.

Not that Calcutta wasn't giving him some very nasty ideas.

He couldn't decide whether he should tell Grace about the video-tape.   If one of the networks was leaked a copy, of course, he wouldn't have to, but if its icy horror kept it off the air . . . *could* he tell her?

No.   From a comment or two dropped into her conversations, he knew she was expecting him to find and pull the string that would exempt Ralph.   He'd explained, more than once, that there was no such string—that even the President's grandson had endured the evaluation—but she behaved as though she'd never heard him.

It was either acute tunnel vision—she saw what she wanted to see, and no more— or she had a very touching faith in him.

Straightening, brushing the dust off his hands, Olsen gazed into the sky.   He wouldn't tell her.   There was always the random factor to consider—why make her fret for two years if there was even the slightest chance that the armies of Earth could hurl themselves against the Pukcip warriors?

If it didn't happen, she'd wax hysterical while Ralph was being tested, but once he came through alive she'd calm down.

If it did happen . . . either the Centers would be leveled by jubilant wrecking crews, or there'd be no citizens to fill their halls.

"We here," his daddy grunted.   "Looks like they just opening the doors."

"Jonathan, child—" suddenly his mama turned sideways, and her soft round eyes practically swallowed up his own "—you gonna be all right, honey, y'hear?"

"Yowp."   His head bobbed up and down, till he twisted to see his daddy, who cleared his throat with embarrassing loudness.   "You all right, Daddy?"

"Just fine, boy."   He pushed his door open, but before he threw his long legs into the parking lot, he gave Jonathan his hand.   "Do what they tell you, boy, and everything's gonna be okay."

Jonathan didn't say anything.   He was too busy wondering what they were so nervous about.

Olsen stood by the door to the anteroom, eyes restless, muscles panther-loose. Facing him was Dortkowski, thin frame draped in a soft white lab coat.   Behind him was the Specialist 5th Class who ran the communications gear.   It was a mild reassurance to know that if anything happened, the entire chain of command would hear of it within seconds.   It was less reassuring to recall that the Calcutta guards had had exactly seven seconds in which to react.

He glanced at Dortkowski, whose bony hand was massaging his stomach.   Evidently the tension was gnawing at the Director.   It was understandable: the children came so slowly; the parents hovered so watchfully.   From the other's impatient checking of his watch, Olsen guessed that they'd fallen behind schedule.   Any further delays would probably drive Dortkowski into a nervous fit.

The short, shabby corridor seemed to quiver with an air of expectancy.   Everyone was uptight, jerking about at the slightest noise, as if convinced that It was going to happen.   Eventually, of course, It would.   The only question was when.

Dortkowski's statistics were no help.   They said one in a million, but refused to say which of those million it would be.   He'd have to imitate the bureaucrat: test them all, hold his breath on each, and—if he was there long enough—swig the Maalox after every five or six.   Olsen knew, with a pawn's despair, that even when they lost one, he wouldn't be able to relax.   Though there would be only two in two million, they could come consecutively.

He wondered what was in Dortkowski's other pocket, the one he patted every few minutes.   It wasn't ulcer medicine.   The outlined bottle was too small.

Fighting back the temptation to pace, he leaned against the wall.   He had to be near enough to hear the voice patterns echo through the anteroom.

First the flare of fright as the child fell, then a gasp, then bewilderment rushing to the brink of tears.   If the costumed clown by the safety net caught the kid's attention quickly, the thin, confused voice would switch to giggles in mid-sob.   If not, they had to hold everything until the child was safely inside, out of earshot of the text testee.

A little black boy was walking towards him.   All dressed up, with his shoes shined and his hair in a neat Afro, he looked scared.   He was probably getting too much attention.   All the adults were eyeing him, and their expressions would be hard for a kid to read.   But his jaw was set, and he put one foot in front of the other with praiseworthy determination.

Dortkowski smiled down at the boy, which seemed to help a little, and one of the black soldiers winked.   His voice was still tiny, though, when he said his name was Jonathan.   Yes, sir; he'd go into the next room and wait.

Olsen watched his small back pass through the rainbow doorway.   As he braced himself for the cry of betrayal, his back tingled.   The boy was too quiet.   The air smelled . . . odd, and its pressure seemed to have dropped.

Barely noticing the green bottle in Dortkowski's hand, he looked.   Jonathan was standing on glistening tiles, apparently inspecting the spacious room.   Doors opened in the shiny walls; Olsen saw Pukcip heads come around the edges.   The boy sat down and started to sob.

Dortkowski gave a sound, almost a whimper, of relief, and sagged against him, murmuring, "It's a levita—"

But Olsen shouted, "Hell with that, it's a space warp!   Get in there, you bastards, *get in there and take that place!!!*"

Within seconds, his and other booted feet were skidding across Pukcip stone; back in Hartford, his Spec 5 was demanding reinforcements for the bridgehead; and Olsen, automatic in hand, was cradling the terrified boy.

Jonathan was frantic to know what he'd done wrong.   After all they'd *told* him to go into the room, even though they must have known how far away it was.   It was very confusing.   If they knew he couldn't go there, why did they get so excited when he brought there here?

With almost clinical dispassion, Dortkowski watched his skinny fingers tighten the cap on the bottle.   He'd come *that* close.   He almost hadn't had the courage to look.   If Olsen's uncompromising eyes hadn't swept over him . . .

They should have guessed.   When the test provoked two different paranormal reactions, one less common than the other, they should have guessed that it might provoke a third, even more rare.   This boy, neither levitator nor teleport, was something else entirely: a talent capable of wedding Earth to Pukcip via another dimension, and of keeping them joined, perhaps indefinitely.   Continued testing might eventually have uncovered a fourth kind of power . . . but he didn't have time for that, not now.

Though the halls were a blur, he knew he should clear them for the Army.   He walked up to the crowd of parents and children, spread his arms, said, "That's all, folks, it's all over, go on home, there won't be any more evaluations.''

And the tears on his cheeks made his smile more profound.

The war was short, and perhaps more savage than it should have been, but no one knew how long Jonathan could hold open the doorway. Besides, the once humbled generals wanted an unconditional surrender, and quick. And more than a few of the infantrymen had had friends or relatives in Wichita.

The Pukcip contributed heavily to their own defeat. Most of their tiny army was elsewhere, and had to be recalled. By the time it was ready to skirmish, a thousand GI's had spread throughout the neighborhood. The entire 82nd Airborne was in position before the aliens had deduced the existence, and the location, of the doorway. Their assault on it ran headlong into Olsen's special forces, and was repulsed with heavy casualties.

Furious, humiliated, and totally unaccustomed to defensive warfare, the Pukcip wasted the little strength they had. They launched a dozen vindictive raids on Terran cities, and lost soldiers in each. Then, before their terrorism could take effect, their panic-stricken government called them home. Ordered to destroy the invaders, they tried—but pent-up hatred and sheer numbers more than cancelled their carouselling multiplicity. With the arrival of the 101st Airborne, the battles tapered into sniper attacks, and those into silence.

If they'd reacted less emotionally—if they'd had any experiences with invasions— if they'd studied Russian or Chinese military history . . . but they hadn't, so the war was short. And perhaps more savage than it should have been.

The Army took two sets of documents from Pukcip archives before closing the doorway on chaos.

The first included blueprints for a functioning starship.

The second included invoices for FTL drive units sold to the shipyards on Rigel VI. Each unit was identified by its city of origin. Four had come from Calcutta.

ISAAC ASIMOV

The Missing Item

Emmanuel Rubin, resident polymath of the Black Widowers Society, was visibly chafed. His eyebrows hunched down into the upper portion of his thick-lensed spectacles and his sparse gray beard bristled.

"Not true to life," he said. "Imagine! Not true to life!"

Mario Gonzalo, who had just reached the head of the stairs and had accepted his dry martini from Henry, the unsurpassable waiter, said, "What's not true to life?"

Geoffrey Avalon looked down from his seventy-four inches and said solemnly, "It appears that Manny has suffered a rejection."

"Well, why not?" said Gonzalo, peeling off his gloves. "Editors don't have to be stupid all the time."

"It isn't the rejection," said Rubin. "I've been rejected before by better editors and in connection with better stories. It's the reason he advanced! How the hell would he know if a story were true to life or not? What's he ever done but warm an office chair? Would he—"

Roger Halsted, whose career as a math teacher in a junior high school had taught him how to interrupt shrill voices, managed to interpose. "Just what did he find not true to life, Manny?"

Rubin waved a hand passionately outward, "I don't want to talk about it."

"Good," said Thomas Trumbull, scowling from under his neatly waved thatch of white hair. "Then the rest of us can hear each other for a while. —Roger, why don't you introduce your guest to the late Mr. Gonzalo?"

Halsted said, "I've just been waiting for the decibel-level to decrease. Mario, my friend Jonathan Thatcher. This is Mario Gonzalo, who is an artist by profession. Jonathan is an oboist, Mario."

Gonzalo grinned and said, "Sounds like fun."

"Sometimes it almost is," said Thatcher, "on days when the reed behaves itself."

Thatcher's round face and plump cheeks would have made him a natural to play Santa Claus at any Christmas benefit, but he would have needed padding just the same, for his body had that peculiar ersatz slimness that seemed to indicate forty pounds recently lost. His eyebrows were dark and thick and one took it for granted that they were never drawn together in anger.

Henry said, "Gentlemen, dinner is ready."

James Drake stubbed out his cigarette and said, "Thanks, Henry.   It's a cold day and I would welcome hot food."

"Yes, sir," said Henry with a gentle smile.   "Lobster thermidor today, baked potatoes, stuffed eggplant—"

"But what's this, Henry?" demanded Rubin, scowling.

"Hot borscht, Mr. Rubin."

Rubin looked as though he were searching his soul and then he said, grudgingly, "All right."

Drake, unfolding his napkin, said, "Point of order, Roger."

"What is it?"

"I'm sitting next to Manny, and if he continues to look like that he'll curdle my soup and give me indigestion.   You're host and absolute monarch; I move you direct him to tell us what he wrote that isn't true to life and get it out of his system."

"Why?" said Trumbull.   "Why not let him sulk and be silent for the novelty of it?"

"I'm curious, too," said Gonzalo, "since nothing he's ever written has been true to life—"

"How would you know, since you can't read?" said Rubin, suddenly.

"It's generally known," said Gonzalo.   "You hear it everywhere."

"Oh, God, I'd better tell you and end this miasma of pseudo-wit.   —Look, I've written a novelette, about 15,000 words long, about a world-wide organization of locksmiths—"

"Locksmiths?" said Avalon, frowning as though he suspected he had not heard correctly.

"Locksmiths," said Rubin.   "These guys are experts, they can open anything— safes, vaults, prison doors.   There are no secrets from them and nothing can be hidden from them.   My global organization is of the cream of the profession and no man can join the organization without some document or object of importance stolen from an industrial, political, or governmental unit.

"Naturally, they have the throat of the world in their grip.   They can control the stock market, guide diplomacy, make and unmake governments, and—at the time my story opens—they are headed by a dangerous megalomaniac—"

Drake interrupted even as he winced in his effort to crack the claw of the lobster. "Who is out to rule the world, of course."

"Of course," said Rubin, "and our hero must stop him.   He is himself a skilled locksmith—"

Trumbull interrupted.   "In the first place, Manny, what the hell do you know about locksmithery or locksmithmanship or whatever you call it?"

"More than you think," retorted Rubin.

"I doubt that very much," said Trumbull, "and the editor is right.   This is utter and complete implausibility.   I know a few locksmiths and they're gentle and inoffensive mechanics with IQ's—"

Rubin said, "And I suppose when you were in the army you knew a few corporals and, on the basis of your knowledge, you'll tell me that Napoleon and Hitler were implausible."

The guest for that evening, who had listened to the exchange with a darkening expression, spoke up.   "Pardon me, gentlemen, I know I'm to be grilled at the conclusion of dinner.   Does that mean I cannot join the dinner conversation beforehand?"

"Heavens, no," said Halsted.   "Talk all you want—if you can get a word in now and then."

"In that case, let me put myself forcefully on the side of Mr. Rubin.   A conspiracy of locksmiths may sound implausible to us who sit here, but what counts is not what a few rational people think but what the great outside world does.   How can your editor turn down anything at all as implausible when everything—" He caught himself, took a deep breath and said, in an altered tone, "Well, I don't mean to tell you your business.   I'm not a writer.   After all, I don't expect you to tell me how to play the oboe," but his smile as he said it was a weak one.

"Manny will tell you how to play the oboe," said Gonzalo, "if you give him a chance."

"Still," Thatcher said, as though he had not heard Gonzalo's comment, "I live in the world and observe it.   *Anything* these days is believed.   There is no such thing as 'not true to life.'   Just spout any nonsense solemnly and swear it's true and there will be millions rallying round you."

Avalon nodded magisterially and said, "Quite right, Mr. Thatcher.   I don't know that this is simply characteristic of our times, but the fact that we have better communications now makes it easier to reach many people quickly so that a phenomenon such as Herr Hitler of unmourned memory is possible.   And to those who can believe in Mr. von Däniken's ancient astronauts and in Mr. Berlitz's Bermuda triangle, a little thing like a conspiracy of locksmiths could be swallowed with the morning porridge."

Thatcher waved his hand.   "Ancient astronauts and Bermuda triangles are nothing.   Suppose you were to say that you frequently visited Mars in astral projection and that Mars was, in fact, a haven for the worthy souls of this world.   There would be those who would believe you."

"I imagine so," began Avalon.

"You don't have to imagine," said Thatcher.   "It *is* so.   I take it you haven't heard of Tri-Lucifer.   That's T-R-I."

"Tri-Lucifer?" said Halsted, looking a little dumbfounded.   "You mean three Lucifers.   What's that?"

Thatcher looked from one face to another and the Black Widowers all remained silent.

And then Henry, who was clearing away some of the lobster shells, said, "If I may be permitted, gentlemen, I have heard of it.   There was a group of them soliciting contributions at this restaurant last week."

"Like the Moonies?" said Drake, pushing his dish in Henry's direction and preparing to light up.

"There is a resemblance," said Henry, his unlined, sixtyish face a bit thoughtful, "but the Tri-Luciferians, if that is the term to use, give a more other-worldly appearance."

"That's right," said Thatcher.   "They have to divorce themselves from this world so as to achieve astral projection to Mars and facilitate the transfer of their souls there after death."

"But why—" began Gonzalo.

And Trumbull suddenly roared out with a blast of anger, "Come on, Roger, make them wait for the grilling to start.   Change the subject."

Gonzalo said, "I just want to know why they call them—"

Halsted sighed and said, "Let's wait a while, Mario."

Henry was making his way about the table with the brandy when Halsted tapped his water glass and said, "I think we can begin the grilling now; and Manny, since it was your remark about true-to-lifeness that roused Jonathan's interest over the main course, why don't you begin."

"Sure."   Rubin looked solemnly across the table at Thatcher and said, "Mr. Thatcher, at this point it would be traditional to ask you how you justify your existence and we would then go into a discussion of the oboe as an instrument of torture for oboists.   *But,* let me guess and say that at this moment you would consider your life justified if you could wipe out a few Tri-Luciferians.   Am I right?"

"You are, you are," said Thatcher, energetically.   "The whole thing has filled my life and my thoughts for over a month now.   It is ruining—"

Gonzalo interrupted.   "What I want to know is why they call themselves Tri-Luciferians.   Are they devil-worshipers or what?"

Rubin began, "You're interrupting the man—"

"It's all right," said Thatcher.   "I'll tell him.   I'm just sorry that I know enough about that organization to be able to tell him.   Apparently, Lucifer means the morning star, though I'm not sure why—"

"Lucifer," said Avalon, running his finger about the lip of his water-glass, "is from Latin words meaning 'light-bringer.'   The rising of the morning star in the dawn heralds the soon-following rising of the Sun.   In an era in which there were no clocks that was an important piece of information to anyone awake at the time."

"Then why is Lucifer the name of the devil?" asked Gonzalo.

Avalon said, "Because the Babylonian king was apparently referred to as the Morning Star by his flattering courtiers, and the Prophet Isaiah predicted his destruction.   Can you quote the passage, Manny?"

Rubin said, "We can read it out of the Bible, if we want to.   It's the 14th Chapter of Isaiah.   The key sentence goes, 'How art thou fallen from heaven, O Lucifer, son of the morning!'   It was just a bit of poetic hyperbole, and very effective too, but it was interpreted literally later, and that one sentence gave rise to the whole myth of a rebellion against God by hordes of angels under the leadership of Lucifer, which came to be considered Satan's name while still in heaven.   Of course, the rebels were defeated and expelled from heaven by loyalist angels under the leadership of the Archangel Michael."

"Like in *Paradise Lost*?" said Gonzalo.

"Exactly like in *Paradise Lost*."

Thatcher said, "The devil isn't part of it, though.   To the Tri-Luciferians, Lucifer just means the morning star.   There are two of them on Earth: Venus and Mercury."

Drake squinted through the curling tobacco smoke and said, "They're also evening stars, depending on which side of the Sun they happen to be.   They're either east of the Sun and set shortly after sunset, or west of the Sun and rise shortly before sunrise."

Thatcher said, with clear evidence of hope, "Do they have to be both together; both one or both the other?"

"No," said Drake, "they move independently.   They can be both evening stars, or both morning stars, or one can be an evening star and one a morning star.   Or one or the other or both can be nearly in a line with the Sun and be invisible altogether, morning or evening."

"Too bad," said Thatcher, shaking his head, "that's what *they* say.   —Anyway, the point is that from Mars you see *three* morning stars in the sky, or you can see them if they're in the right position: not only Mercury and Venus, but Earth as well."

"That's right," said Rubin.

"And," said Thatcher, "I suppose then it's true that they can be in any position. They can all be evening stars or all morning stars, or two can be one and one can be the other?"

"Yes," said Drake, "or one or more can be too close to the Sun to be visible."

Thatcher sighed.   "So they call Mars by their mystic name of Tri-Lucifer—the world with the three morning stars."

"I suppose," said Gonzalo, "that Jupiter would have four morning stars: Mercury, Venus, Earth, and Mars; and so on out to Pluto, which would have eight morning stars."

"The trouble is," said Halsted, "that the farther out you go, the dimmer the inner planets are.   Viewed from one of the satellites of Jupiter, for instance, I doubt that Mercury would appear more than a medium-bright star; and it might be too close to the Sun for anyone ever to get a good look at it."

"What about the view from Mars? Could you see Mercury?" asked Thatcher.

"Oh yes, I'm sure of that," said Halsted, "I could work out what the brightness would be in a matter of minutes."

"Would you?" said Thatcher.

"Sure," said Halsted, "if I've remembered to bring my pocket computer.   — Yes, I have it.   Henry, bring me the *Columbia Encyclopedia,* would you?"

Rubin said, "While Roger is bending his limited mathematical mind to the problem, Mr. Thatcher, tell us what your interest is in all this.   You seem to be interested in exposing them as fakers.   Why?   Have you been a member?   Are you now disillusioned?"

"No, I've never been a member.   I—" He rubbed his temple hesitantly.   "It's my wife.   I don't like talking about it, you understand."

Avalon said solemnly, "Please be assured, Mr. Thatcher, that whatever is said here never passes beyond the bounds of this room.   That includes our valued waiter, Henry.   You may speak freely."

"Well, there's nothing criminal or disgraceful in it.   I just don't like to seem to be so helpless in such a silly—It's breaking up my marriage, gentlemen."

There was a discreet silence around the table, broken only by the mild sound of Halsted turning the pages of the encyclopedia.

Thatcher went on, "Roger knows my wife.   He'll tell you she's a sensible woman—"

Halsted looked up briefly and nodded, "I'll vouch for that, but I didn't know you were having this—"

"Lately, Carol has not been social, you understand; and I certainly haven't talked about it.   It was with great difficulty, you know, that I managed to agree to come out tonight.   I dread leaving her to herself.   You see, even sensible people have their weaknesses.   Carol worries about death."

"So do we all," said Drake.

"So do I," said Thatcher, "but in a normal way, I hope.   We all know we'll die someday and we don't particularly look forward to it, and we may worry about hell or nothingness or hope for heaven, but we don't think about it much.   Carol has been fascinated, however, by the possibility of demonstrating the actual existence of life after death.   It may have all started with the Bridey Murphy case when she was a teenager—I don't know if any of you remember that—"

"I do," said Rubin, "a woman under hypnosis seemed to be possessed by an Irishwoman who had died a long time before."

"Yes," said Thatcher.   "She saw through that, eventually.   Then she grew interested in spiritualism and gave that up.   I always relied on her to understand folly when she finally stopped to think about it—and then she came up against the Tri-Luciferians.   I never saw her like this.   She wants to join them.   She has money of her own and she wants to give it to them.   I don't care about the money— well, I do, but that's not the main thing—I care about *her*.   You know, she's going to join them in their retreat somewhere, become a daughter of Tri-Lucifer, or whatever they call it, and wait for translation to the Abode of the Blessed.   One of these days, she'll be gone.   I just won't see her anymore.   She promised me it wouldn't be tonight, but I wonder."

Rubin said, "I take it you suppose that the organization is just interested in her money."

"At least the leader of it is," said Thatcher, grimly.   "I'm sure of it.   What else can he be after?"

"Do you know him?   Have you met him?" said Rubin.

"No.   He keeps himself isolated," said Thatcher, "but I hear he has recently bought a fancy mansion in Florida, and I doubt that it's for the use of the membership."

"Funny thing about that," said Drake.   "It doesn't matter how lavishly a cult-leader lives, how extravagantly he throws money around.   The followers, who support him and see their money clearly used for that purpose, never seem to mind."

"They identify," said Rubin.   "The more he spends, the more successful they consider the cause.   It's the basis of ostentatious waste in governmental display, too."

"Just the same," said Thatcher, "I don't think Carol will ever commit herself entirely. She might not be bothered by the leader's actions, but if I can prove him *wrong,* she'll drop it."

"Wrong about what?" asked Rubin.

"Wrong about Mars. This head of the group claims he has been on Mars often—in astral projection, of course. He describes Mars in detail, but can he be describing it accurately?"

"Why not?" asked Rubin. "If he reads up on what is known about Mars, he can describe it as astronomers would. The Viking photographs even show a part of the surface in detail. It's not difficult to be accurate."

"Yes, but it may be that somewhere he has made a mistake, something I can show Carol."

Halsted looked up and said, "Here, I've worked out the dozen brightest objects in the Martian sky, together with their magnitudes. I may be off a little here and there, but not by much." He passed a slip of paper around.

Mario held up the paper when it reached him. "Would you like to see it, Henry?"

"Thank you, sir," murmured Henry, and as he glanced at it briefly, one eyebrow raised itself just slightly, just briefly.

The paper came to rest before Thatcher eventually and he gazed at it earnestly. What he saw was this:

Sun	−26.
Phobos	−9.6
Deimos	−5.1
Earth	−4.5
Jupiter	−3.1
Venus	−2.6
Sirius	−1.4
Saturn	−0.8
Canopus	−0.7
Alpha Centauri	−0.3
Arcturus	−0.1
Mercury	0.0

Thatcher said, "Phobos and Deimos are the two satellites of Mars. Do these numbers mean they're very bright?"

"The greater the negative number," said Halsted, "the brighter the object. A −2 object is two and a half times brighter than a −1 object and a −3 object is two and a half times brighter still and so on. Next to the Sun, Phobos is the brightest object in the Martian sky, and Deimos is next."

"And next to the Sun and the two satellites, Earth is the brightest object in the sky, then."

"Yes, but only at or near its maximum brightness," said Halsted. "It can be much dimmer depending on where Mars and Earth are in their respective orbits.

Most of the time it's probably less bright than Jupiter, which doesn't change much in brightness as it moves in its orbit."

Thatcher shook his head and looked disappointed.   "But it *can* be that bright. Too bad.   There's a special prayer or psalm or something that the Tri-Luciferians have that appears in almost all their literature.   I've seen it so often in the stuff Carol brings home, I can quote it exactly.   It goes, 'When Earth shines high in the sky, like a glorious jewel, and when the other Lucifers have fled beyond the horizon, so that Earth shines alone in splendor, single in beauty, unmatched in brightness, it is then that the souls of those ready to receive the call must prepare to rise from Earth and cross the gulf.'   And what you're saying, Roger, is that Earth *can* be the brightest object in the Martian sky."

Halsted nodded.   "At night, if Phobos and Deimos are below the horizon, and Earth is near maximum brightness, it is certainly the brightest object in the sky. It would be three and a half times as bright as Jupiter, if that were in the sky, and six times as bright as Venus at its brightest."

"And it could be the only morning star in the sky."

"Or the only evening star.   Sure.   The other two, Venus and Mercury, could be on the other side of the Sun from Earth."

Thatcher kept staring at the list.   "But would Mercury be visible?   It's at the bottom of the list."

Halsted said, "The bottom just means that it's twelfth brightest, but there are thousands of stars that are dimmer and still visible.   There would be only four stars brighter than Mercury as seen from Mars: Sirius, Canopus, Alpha Centauri, and Arcturus."

Thatcher said, "If they'd only make a mistake."

Avalon said in a grave and somewhat hesitant baritone, "Mr. Thatcher, I think perhaps you had better face the facts.   It is my experience that even if you *do* find a flaw in the thesis of the Tri-Luciferians it won't help you.   Those who follow cults for emotional reasons are not deterred by demonstrations of the illogic of what they are doing."

Thatcher said, "I agree with you, and I wouldn't dream of arguing with the ordinary cultist.   But I know Carol.   I have seen her turn away from a system of beliefs she would very much like to have followed, simply because she saw the illogic of it.   If I could find something of the sort here, I'm sure she'd come back."

Gonzalo said, "Some of us here ought to think of something.   After all, he's never *really* been on Mars.   He's got to have made a mistake."

"Not at all," said Avalon.   "He probably knows as much about Mars as we do.   Therefore, even if he's made a mistake it may be because he fails to understand something we also fail to understand and we won't catch him."

Thatcher nodded his head.   "I suppose you're right."

"I don't know," said Gonzalo.   "How about the canals?   The Tri-Luciferians are bound to talk about the canals.   Everyone believed in them and then just lately we found out they weren't there; isn't that right?   So if he talks about them, he's caught."

Drake said, "Not everybody believed in them, Mario. Hardly any astronomers did."

"The general public did," said Gonzalo.

Rubin said, "Not lately. It was in 1964 that Mariner 4 took the first pictures of Mars and that pretty much gave away the fact the canals didn't exist. Once Mariner 9 mapped the whole planet in 1969 there was no further argument. When did the Tri-Luciferians come into existence, Mr. Thatcher?"

"As I recall," said Thatcher, "about 1970. Maybe 1971."

"There you are," said Rubin. "Once we had Mars down cold, this guy, whoever he is who runs it, decided to start a new religion based on it. Listen, if you want to get rich quick, no questions asked, start a new religion. Between the First Amendment and the tax breaks you get, it amounts to a license to help yourself to everything in sight. —I'll bet he talks about volcanoes."

Thatcher nodded. "The Martian headquarters of the astral projections are in Olympus Mons. That means Mount Olympus and that's where the souls of the righteous gather. That's the big volcano, isn't it?"

"The biggest in the Solar system," said Rubin. "At least, that we know of. It's been known since 1969."

Thatcher said, "The Tri-Luciferians say that G. V. Schiaparelli—he's the one who named the different places on Mars—was astrally inspired to name that spot Olympus to signify it was the home of the godly. In ancient Greece, you see, Mount Olympus was—"

"Yes," said Avalon, nodding gravely, "we know."

"Isn't Schiaparelli the fellow who first reported the canals?" asked Gonzalo.

"Yes," said Halsted, "although actually when he said *'canali'* he meant natural waterways."

"Even so, why didn't the same astral inspiration tell him the canals weren't there?" asked Gonzalo.

Drake nodded and said, "That's something you can point out to your wife."

"No," said Thatcher, "I guess they thought of that. They say the canals were part of the inspiration because that increased interest in Mars and that that was needed to make the astral projection process more effective."

Trumbull, who had maintained a sullen silence through the discussion, as though he were waiting his chance to shift the discussion to oboes, said suddenly, "That makes a diseased kind of sense."

Thatcher said, "Too much makes sense. That's the trouble. There are times when I want to find a mistake not so much to save Carol as to save myself. I tell you that when I listen to Carol talking there's sometimes more danger she'll argue me into being crazy than that I'll persuade her to be rational."

Trumbull waved a hand at him soothingly. "Just take it easy and let's think it out. Do they say anything about the satellites?"

"They talk about them, yes. Phobos and Deimos. Sure."

"Do they say anything about how they cross the sky?" Trumbull's smile was nearly a smirk.

"Yes," said Thatcher, "and I looked it up because I didn't believe them and I thought I had something.   In their description of the Martian scene, they talk about Phobos rising in the west and setting in the east.   And it turns out that's true. And they say that whenever either Phobos or Deimos cross the sky at night, they are eclipsed by Mars's shadow for part of the time.   And that's true, too.''

Halsted shrugged.   ''The satellites were discovered a century ago, in 1877, by Asaph Hall.   As soon as their distance from Mars and their period of revolution was determined, which was almost at once, their behavior in Mars's sky was known.''

''*I* didn't know it,'' said Thatcher.

''No,'' said Halsted, ''but this fellow who started the religion apparently did his homework.   It wasn't really hard.''

''Hold on,'' said Trumbull, truculently.   ''Some things aren't as obvious and don't get put into the average elementary astronomy textbook.   For instance, I read somewhere that Phobos can't be seen from the Martian polar regions.   It's so close to Mars that the bulge of Mars's spherical surface hides the satellite, if you go far enough north or south.   Do the Tri-Luciferians say anything about Phobos being invisible from certain places on Mars, Thatcher?''

''Not that I recall,'' said Thatcher, ''but they don't say it's always visible.   If they just don't mention the matter, what does that prove?''

''Besides,'' said Halsted, ''Olympus Mons is less than 20 degrees north of the Martian equator and Phobos is certainly visible from there any time it is above the horizon and not in eclipse.   And if that's the headquarters for the souls from Earth, Mars would certainly be described as viewed from that place.''

''Whose side are you on?'' grumbled Trumbull.

''The truth's,'' said Halsted.   ''Still, it's true that astronomy books rarely describe any sky but Earth's.   That's why I had to figure out the brightness of objects in the Martian sky instead of just looking it up.   The only trouble is that this cult-leader seems to be just as good at figuring.''

''I've got an idea,'' said Avalon.   ''I'm not much of an astronomer, but I've seen the photographs taken by the Viking landers, and I've read the newspaper reports about them.   For one thing the Martian sky in the daytime is pink, because of fine particles of the reddish dust in the air.   In that case, isn't it possible that the dust obscures the night sky so that you don't see anything?   Good Lord, it happens often enough in New York City.''

Halsted said, ''As a matter of fact, the problem in New York isn't so much the dust as the scattered light from the buildings and highways; and even in New York you can see the bright stars, if the sky isn't cloudy.

''On Mars, it would have to work both ways.   If there is enough dust to make the sky invisible from the ground, then the ground would be invisible from the sky. For instance, when Mariner 9 reached Mars in 1969, Mars was having a globe-wide duststorm and none of its surface could be seen by Mariner.   At that time, from the Martian surface, the sky would have had to be blanked out.   Most of the time, though, we see the surface clearly from our probes, so from the Martian surface, the sky would be clearly visible.

''In fact, considering that Mars's atmosphere is much thinner than Earth's—less than a hundredth as thick—it would scatter and absorb far less light than Earth's does, and the various stars and planets would all look a little brighter than they would with Earth's atmosphere in the way. I didn't allow for that in my table.''

Trumbull said, ''Jeff mentioned the Viking photographs. They show rocks all over the place. Do the Tri-Luciferians mention rocks?''

''No,'' said Thatcher, ''not that I ever noticed. But again, they don't say there aren't any. They talk about huge canyons and dry river beds and terraced ice-fields.''

Rubin snorted. ''All that's been known since 1969. More homework.''

Avalon said, ''What about life? We still don't know if there's any life on Mars. The Viking results are ambiguous. Have the Tri-Luciferians committed themselves on that?''

Thatcher thought, then said, ''I wish I could say I had read all their literature thoroughly, but I haven't. Still, Carol has forced me to read quite a bit since she said I ought not defame anything without learning about it first.''

''That's true enough,'' said Avalon, ''though life is short and there are some things that are so unlikely on the surface that one hesitates to devote much of one's time to a study of them. However, can you say anything as to the Tri-Luciferians' attitude toward Martian life from what you've read of their literature?''

Thatcher said, ''They speak about Mars's barren surface, its desert aridity and emptiness. They contrast that with the excitement and fullness of the astral sphere.''

''Yes,'' said Avalon, ''and of course, the surface *is* dry and empty and barren. We know that much. What about microscopic life? That's what we're looking for.''

Thatcher shook his head. ''No mention of it, as far as I know.''

Avalon said, ''Well, then, I can't think of anything else. I'm quite certain this whole thing is nonsense. Everyone here is, and none of us need proof of it. If your wife needs proof, we may not be able to supply it.''

''I understand,'' said Thatcher. ''I thank you all, of course, and I suppose she may come to her senses after a while, but I must admit I have never seen her quite like this. I would join the cult with her just to keep her in sight; but, frankly, I'm afraid I'll end up believing it, too.''

And in the silence that followed, Henry said softly, ''Perhaps, Mr. Thatcher, you need not go to that extreme.''

Thatcher turned suddenly. ''Pardon me. Did you say something, waiter?''

Halsted said, ''Henry is a member of the club, Jonathan. I don't know that he's an astronomer exactly, but he's the brightest person here. Is there something we've missed, Henry?''

Henry said, ''I think so, sir. You said, Mr. Halsted, that astronomy books don't generally describe any sky but Earth's, and I guess that must be why the cult-leader seems to have a missing item in his description of Mars. Without it, the whole thing is no more true to life than Mr. Rubin's conspiracy of locksmiths—if I may be forgiven, Mr. Rubin.''

''Not if you don't supply a missing object. Henry?''

Henry said, ''On Earth, Mercury and Venus are the morning and evening stars, and we always think of such objects as planets, therefore. Consequently, from Mars, there must be three morning and evening stars, Mercury, Venus, plus Earth in addition. That is memorialized in the very name of the cult, and from that alone I could see the whole thing fails.''

Halsted said, ''I'm not sure I see your point, Henry.''

''But, Mr. Halsted,'' said Henry, ''Where is the Moon in all this? It is a large object, our Moon, almost the size of Mercury and closer to Mars than Mercury is. If Mercury can be seen from Mars, surely the Moon can be, too. Yet I noticed it was not on your list of bright objects in the Martian sky.''

Halsted turned red. ''Yes, of course. The list of planets fooled me, too. You just list them without mentioning the Moon.'' He reached for the paper. ''The Moon is smaller than Earth and less reflective, so that it is only 1/70 as bright as the Earth, at equal distance and phase which means—a magnitude of 0.0. It would be just as bright as Mercury, and in fact it could be seen more easily than Mercury could be because it would be higher in the sky. At sunset, Mercury as evening star would never be higher than 16 degrees above the horizon, while Earth could be as much as 44 degrees above—pretty high in the sky.''

Henry said, ''Mars, therefore, would have four morning stars, and the very name, Tri-Lucifer, is nonsense.''

Avalon said, ''But the Moon would always be close to Earth, so wouldn't Earth's light drown it out?''

''No,'' said Halsted. ''Let's see now.—Never get a pocket computer that doesn't have keys for the trigonometric functions.—The Moon would be, at times, as much as 23 minutes of arc away from Earth, when viewed from Mars. That's three-quarters the width of the Moon as seen from Earth.''

Henry said, ''One more thing. Would you repeat that verse once again, Mr. Thatcher, the one about the Earth being high in the sky.''

Thatcher said, ''Certainly. 'When Earth shines high in the sky, like a glorious jewel, and when the other Lucifers have fled beyond the horizon, so that Earth shines alone in splendor, single in beauty, unmatched in brightness, it is then that the souls of those ready to receive the call must prepare to rise from Earth and cross the gulf.' ''

Henry said, ''Earth may be quite high in the sky at times, and Mercury and Venus may be on the other side of the Sun and therefore beyond the horizon—but Earth cannot be 'alone in splendor.' The moon has to be with it. Of course, there would be times when the moon is very nearly in front of Earth or behind it, as seen from Mars, so that the two dots of light merge into one that seems to make Earth brighter than ever, but the Moon is not then beyond the horizon. It seems to me, Mr. Thatcher, that the cult-leader was never on Mars, because if he had been he would not have missed a pretty big item, a world 2160 miles across. Surely you can explain this to your wife.''

''Yes,'' said Thatcher, his face brightening into a smile, ''She would have to see the whole thing is fake.''

''If it is true, as you say,'' said Henry quietly, ''that she is a rational person.''

JESSE PEEL

Heal the Sick, Raise the Dead

After I finished attaching the last of the electrodes to the body, I looked at the girl, making it into a question with my raised eyebrows. She nodded, her thin-and-young face very pale. I turned back to my instruments—all the connections seemed to be correct—so I punched the power switch. The body gave a small, convulsive twitch; there was the smell of burned hair, then . . . nothing.

"Sometimes it takes a while," I said. Anything important usually does. I thought about my own decision. Soon, I'd likely be lying on a table like the one I now stood next to.

She nodded again, and I wanted to tell her, that in this case, it might take longer than a while—it might well take forever.

Despite the cryo-table and the holding-embalm, six days was a long time, a hell of a long time. I didn't know of any case ever brought back over a week or eight days, and anything over five days was usually good enough to make the medical journals.

The girl stood by the body, her slight frame tense and trembling. Her fingers were knitted together, the knuckles white and bloodless. Small beads of sweat stood out on her upper lip and neck, despite the hard chill of the crematorium. Her eyes never left the inert form of the dead boy.

I mostly watched my instruments, lost in my own thoughts. It was cold, and I always got cramps from standing too long when it was cold. I moved about, shifting from one leg to the other, to keep the circulation going. The smell of burnt hair was rivaled by that of stale death; there were over a thousand bodies lying on tables around us.

There was nothing yet to see on the scopes. The EEG was flat, the ECG straight-lined. Total Systems Output was nil, and enzymes were dormant. The polyvital injection/infusion was running well, despite the collapsed state of the blood vessels, but six days was still six days.

I glanced at the lifeless body, and tried to see myself there. I couldn't picture it, being dead. I wondered again how much that had to do with the whole business.

I'd figured her for a grafter this morning when she first came in. But the spiderweb skintight she wore was revealing enough to show that she had no obvious scars from prior surgery. No matter how good a medic is, there is always something—a discoloration here, a stretchmark there. She was clean, like a baby.

She had high, small breasts and a thin, leggy body. Her feet were covered with clear spray-on slippers. There was an odor of some musky perfume about her that was pleasant enough, and I figured that she was maybe fifteen.

No graft marks, so today might be her first time. The latest was to have the little finger of the right hand replaced with a live coral snake. Deadly, but who cared? It was novel—this month. Last big fad had everyone wearing raccoon tails for crotch cover. Next month, who could tell?

"What can I do for you?" I asked, giving her my best professional medic smile. I wondered if I had any snakes left in the cryo-tank—business had been good this month.

"I want a Reconstruct," she blurted, her voice a high quaver.

Reconstruct? Damn! So much for my *augenblick* diagnosis of neophyte grafter! I tried to hide my surprise with a question. "How old are you?"

She hesitated for a second. "Thirteen—almost fourteen!"

Missed again. I'd thought fifteen generous, but thirteen? That was much too young to be asking for a Reconstruct. Legally, anyway. Not that too many people paid a hell of a lot of attention to the laws these days.

"Who's this package you want defrosted? Parent?"

She shook her head, and looked down at the floor.

"Sibling?"

She brought her eyes up to meet mine. "Pronger," she said softly.

Well. She didn't look thirteen, and I supposed that if they were big enough, they were old enough. I looked at her small-and-slim body, and sighed. They were maturing earlier all the time, those that were left. When I was young, they'd have put you under the jail and left you there for sleeping with a girl that age. Except that a mob would probably have dragged you out and hanged you from the nearest tree in short order.

I sighed again. When I was young. That was so long ago, it seemed like a million years.

Maybe I was getting senile, living in the past, I thought. Sure, senile at fifty-four.

That was young, fifty-four. If you wanted to bother, you could figure on three times that age before you died, given the state of modern medicine. If you wanted to bother. Hardly anybody did, I mean, what for? I was one of the oldest people I knew—maybe one of the oldest, period.

I pulled myself back to the girl. "When did he terminate?"

"Last Friday."

Today was Thursday. That irritated me! Damn people who held off until the last minute! What did they expect, miracles? "Waited kind of long, didn't you?"

"I was . . . afraid." It was a whimper, a plea.

Go on, I scolded myself, make the little girl cry.

"How old was he?"

"Fourteen."

Another child. "How'd he die? Accident?"

She took a deep breath, and said it with a rush. "Self 'struct!"

God Damn!   Tired of life at that tender age!   Suddenly I felt very old and tired and alone.   I looked quickly down at my desk, visualizing the plastic bottle of capsules there.   I was nearly four times his age, I had that kind of right—but God, a fourteen-year-old boy?

On my scopes, I was finally getting some activity.   A small spiking on the EEG, not much, but something, at least.

I increased the power input slightly.   Easy does it, I told myself, don't fry him. I was curious to hear his version, provided I could land him, and it would be good work.   Good work was something to be proud of, something else people rarely bothered with anymore.

He had been a handsome kid when he was alive.   Some medic had done a rotten job on a pair of matched leopard-fur shoulder caplets.   They were the only transplants he'd been wearing when he'd died.   A few scars were scattered over his body, remnants of past surgeries, but not all that many.   Pretty conservative, for a teener.

I looked around the crematorium, noticing how nearly full it was.   Looked like they'd have to run the ovens in a day or two, to clear the tables for the next batch. I could taste the bitter dregs of the holding-embalm left in the air by the air'ditioners, and I felt the cold worse because of the clammy dead, I fancied.   I spotted only two guards roaming about, but I knew that there were others.   There were certain . . . people in our society who had all sorts of uses for fresh bodies.

Another blip on my scopes—some ventricular fib on the ECG.   The heart was tough, even after death.   I began to think that I might get this boy moving after all.   The timer said twenty minutes had passed, and that wasn't good, but there was still a chance out to half an hour.

But five more minutes passed without any change.   Then seven.   Eight.   Crap, the organs must be too far gone.   Sorry, kid, I thought, as I reached for the power switch.

Just then, the body turned its head.   The girl squealed and I turned up the strength on the booster-relay.   I had gross muscle!

Three more minutes passed and then the fibrillation converted.   Damned if I didn't get a spotty, but definite sinus rhythm!   A block, sure, but it was pumping! If autonomics were still workable, that meant some fine control was possible. Maybe even speech.

The EEG had steeled down to only a mild epileptogenic focus, so I fed the neural circuits more juice.   Oxy-lack damage was difficult to overcome, but the polyvital could soothe a great deal of brain damage and rot—temporarily.

Now or never, I thought.   I kicked in the bellows pump, and the lungs started to inflate.   If they held. . . .

"Uuunnhhh."   A windy moan, the voice of the dead.

"Roj?   Oh, Roj!   I'm here!"

His eyes opened.   They were cloudy, of course, and blind.   Optic nerves were always the first to go—very few Reconstructs were sighted, even those only a day or two gone.   But the eighth cranial, the auditory, hung on for some reason.   It was always the last to leave, so it was likely that he'd be able to hear.

". .Te. .Tefi?''   Ah, some vocal cords.   It was that eerie drone of speech I had heard so many times before.   Mostly wind, rushing through a voice-box that had lost much of its elasticity.   There was little tongue or lip involved.

"Oh, Roj!''   She cried, reaching out to touch him.

"Don't!'' I yelled, my voice an echo in the vast room.   "You'll short him out!'' She jerked her hand back, and I relaxed a little.   Likely short yourself out too, I thought.   Besides, you wouldn't like the feel of his flesh.   It would be like a just-thawed steak.

". .efi?. . .wh. .why. . . didn' . .youuu. . uuhhh. . . you. . . . .uuhhh. . .''

The girl started to cry.   "I'm sorry,'' she whispered with a sob.   I watched as a tear fell onto the cryo-table.   It spattered, and froze into a thousand smaller tears.

"After you, I mean, I was scared, after you were. . . .''

" 's okay. .swee'. .efi. . .uuhhh. . .'s. .like they ssaid. . . .''

The dead boy struggled, fighting against the bellows pump which restricted his speech.   He fought for air which had no other use to him now except to run his decaying vocal cords.

". .onderful. .here. . .like they ssaid. . . 'eaceful. 'alm. . .sso.nice.''   Another pause, waiting for the air.   ". . .friendss. . .here. . .all of the. . . but. .youuu. . . .''

She started to sob, her body shaking.   The knobs of my instruments felt suddenly hard and lifeless in my hands.   Even after all this time, I could still feel the sadness. Even after all the people I'd brought back.

A self'struct pact.   Only she couldn't go through with it at the end.   So she had brought him back.   For what?   To say she was sorry?   Could that matter to him?   Or to find out if it were really true, what they said about the Other Side? To hear it from one she knew and could trust, to know that Life After Death existed, after all.

But did she know?   The boy's story was familiar.   It was like, but unlike many others I had heard.   It was good to hear it, since I had almost decided.   It helped to push my fears into the distance.   It helped.

But looking at the girl's face, I wasn't happy.   She was getting the same message, more, it was her dead lover saying it.   No, I thought, not you.   Me, certainly, but not you, not at your age.   Don't listen.   Wait—thirty, or forty years, a hundred years, then decide.   But not now!

I jerked my eyes down, to see the digitals dropping.   He was fading.   It had taken every bit of my skill, along with a great deal of luck to pull him in, and now I was losing him.   But I tried, for her sake—and my own.   I punched in full power.   The smell of burning hair grew stronger.   The body shook, but it was no good.   He was gone, this time, forever.

Once, we healed the sick.   Now, we raised the dead.   I was as bad as all the rest, I did it too.   That ability, that power of god-like strength, that curse was going to be the death of mankind.   I looked at the girl, and I knew.

"I'm sorry," I said, not just meaning the loss of the boy.

"Don't be," she said, smiling through the tears. "It's all right now."

But I knew that it wasn't all right. Not now, not ever. She had made up her mind, but it wasn't all right. It was wrong, and it was as much my fault as any man's.

I repacked my instruments. Even after thirty years as a medic, I still hated to lose a patient, regardless that he was already dead. All I wanted to do now was get out, into the city-stale but alive air.

Inside my ancient and much-repaired hovercraft, we sat quietly for a minute, letting the autoglide fly us back to my office. I knew what she was thinking, but it was wrong.

Why? shouted a voice inside my head. Weren't you thinking the same thing?

That's different, I argued with myself. I am older. I—

Hah! said the voice.

"So you are going to do it," I said. It was not a question.

She nodded, smiling and unafraid now.

"You can't! You're only a child!" I exploded.

"Roj is waiting for me!"

"There are a thousand boys—"

"No! They are not Roj!"

"But to kill yourself—"

"So what? Here is only here! There is perfect! It's like everybody said, you heard him!"

Yes, I'd heard him. Him, and all the others. Still, I had to try.

"You don't know what life has to offer!"

"I do so! I'm not a baby! I've been places, done things! Why go through it all over again? Why does it even matter? Roj is *there,* waiting for me!"

"But—"

"You heard him!" She threw herself back deeply into the hovercraft's worn seat, her arms crossed to shut me out.

How could I argue with it? How could I fight a voice from the lips of her own dead lover? Who would not be taken in, convinced totally by the words of a father, mother, or a sister—or a wife?

I stared through the pitted plastic window at the city beneath us. Mostly deserted now, a far cry from the days before the Reconstruct process. Maybe if Mali had lived, had made it until the process had been perfected. . . . No. It was long past, and I'd never hear it from my own wife.

I turned back to the girl. "Listen," I said, feeling desperate. For some reason, it was important that she know, that she understand. I caught her shoulders, feeling her smooth skin and firm muscle under my hands.

"When the Reconstruct concept was first created, there were a lot of theories. One of the most important was thrown out, because nobody wanted to believe it. That theory says that what the dead say is not real!"

She shook her head and struggled, but I wouldn't let her go.

"It says that the human brain refuses to accept its own death, so it makes up a story, to convince itself that it will not die!   That what the dead say when you bring them back is only that story, played back a final time, like a recording! That's why the stories are different, because they are subjective, not because there are really different realities on the Other Side!''

She stared at me, not wanting to hear it.

"Don't you understand?   It could all be a lie!   You could be killing yourself for nothing!''   There.   I'd said it.   But who was I really trying to convince?

"You heard, you heard!''   She screamed, starting to cry.   "Roj said, he said, he said—''

I let her go, and slumped back into my seat.   Yes.   Roj had said.

The girl was gone, and I sat alone at my desk, staring at the drawer.   Had I convinced her?   Planted a seed of the smallest doubt?   I didn't know.   Probably not, but maybe.   Somebody had to convince them, the young ones.   What if the theory was wrong?

What even, if the theory was valid?   Suppose there was Life After Death—what then?   Why would there be any point in staying alive.   Or what point in being born in the first place?   It was a question that had been debated by the best minds we had, and no answer had been found.

At least, not in this life.   There was one way for anyone who wished to find out.   I took the bottle of capsules from the drawer, and shook them about inside their plastic prison.   I was older than most, surely I had the right to do as I wished. I had heard all the stories: It was Heaven, Valhalla, Nirvana, Paradise.   Nobody ever said it was Hell—at worst, it was much better than here.

But if I did it, who would be left to try and keep the young ones going?   And what if it were a lie?   What if the whole thing was a massive con game, a trick of the human mind on itself; who would be around to try and keep the human race going?

I was supposed to be a healer, a life-giver, a medic.   It was my job, wasn't it? But I was tired, and how much could one man be expected to do?

I poured the blue-and-green capsules out onto the desk, touching the slick-and-light one-way tickets to where?   Heaven, or oblivion?   I stirred them around with my finger, hearing the tiny sound they made on my plastic desk.   I was almost sure, until I had met the girl today, and brought back her dead lover.

Was this the way the world was to end, not with a bang or a whimper, but with an expectant smile?

Could all those people be wrong?

There was only one way I could be sure, only one way.

Carefully, I put the capsules back into the bottle, and snapped the lid shut.   Not today, I thought.

Not today.

RANDALL GARRETT

Polly Plus

It wasn't the first clue I had, but it was the incident of the parrot that first got me to really thinking about Willy.

Everyone always asks me about Dawn Kelley as soon as they find out that I am the Janet Sadler mentioned in her best-selling autobiography. I can understand that; as her grade-school teacher, I am presumed to be an extraordinary woman myself because I helped to mold the childhood of a *truly* extraordinary woman.

Dawn Kelley has won three Oscars for the only three pictures she has appeared in, and for two others she directed. She had earned doctorates in medicine, law, and physics; and has made widely-acclaimed contributions to all three fields. Her television program has been in the top ten of the ratings for the past seven years. Everyone who knows her loves her, and she still looks a beautiful twenty-five, although she is only fifteen years younger than I, and I am over seventy.

Yes, Dawn Kelley is a remarkable woman, but everyone has read and heard about her for years. Instead of re-hashing old material, I would like to tell you about an even more remarkable person of whom you have never heard.

As I said, it was the parrot that really got me to thinking, but there were clues before that.

I was in my mid-twenties at the time; I'd only had my teaching certificate three years, and I was still naïve enough to think that four years of college and a year of graduate work had taught me all I needed to know about teaching. I was shy, I know, and I covered that tendency with an over-precise pedantry and an avoidance of emotional involvement with my students. I conceived of myself as a lofty being who knew everything—at least, everything that a child needed to know—and whose job it was to pour as much of that knowledge into childish minds as those receptacles would hold. I was, I fear, a rather stuffy prig.

It was Willy who gave me my first real comeuppance, but the fault was my own, not his. I had always disliked nicknames and diminutives—I still do, but I'm a great deal more tolerant now. When, on Willy's first day in my fifth-grade class, I asked each child to stand and tell me his or her name, Willy stood and said: "Willy Taylor."

"William Taylor," I said, by way of correction. Like a damn fool, I hadn't looked over the prepared roster yet. I had already corrected "Susie" to "Susan" and "Bobby" to "Robert" without repercussions, and expected none now.

"No, ma'am," he said with precision.   "Willy.   Doubleyou, eye, ell, ell, wye. Willy."

" 'Willy,' " I replied with equal precision, "is a diminutive for 'William.' "

"Yes, ma'am, sometimes," he said agreeably, "but not this time.   Willy's my real name.   It's German.   You've heard of Willy Brandt and Willy Ley."

I had, of course.   I was caught, and I knew it.   I should have had sense enough to drop it right there, but my mouth was moving before I could stop it.   "Are you German?"

Now what difference would that make?   I had a David who was not Hebrew, a Marguerite who was not French, and a Paula who was not Italian; I hadn't carped at those.   Because of my shyness, I was suddenly on the defensive.

"No, ma'am."   Still polite.   "But my name is."

By then, I had control.   "I see.   Thank you, Willy.   You may sit down."

He did, and that was the end of it.   But I remember it.

I sensed from the beginning that Willy was an intelligent child. His intelligence quotient, according to the tests, was 136; bright, but hardly brilliant. The transfer record from his previous school showed a nice B + average. But almost from the very first I had the feeling that he was holding himself back, that he was trying to hide his real abilities.   That sort of behavior is not as rare as you might think; the merely bright children show it in school and get themselves thoroughly hated by their duller classmates, while the truly brilliant child is wise enough not to be that offensive.

But Willy did the same thing in sports, which was overdoing it.   At softball, touch football, volleyball, and the various track sports that nine- and ten-year-olds can play, he never ranked higher than second best, and never lower than fourth. He was trying to keep his B + average.

Now that, I thought, *is ridiculous.*   A boy might want to keep his mind under cover—no one likes being called "teacher's pet" or "bigdome"—but why do so at sports, where excellence is approved of, lauded, and looked up to by faculty and students alike?

I remember the basketball especially.   You see, I lived right across the alley from the Taylors, and I could see the back yard of their house from my second-floor apartment window.   His father had set up a basketball hoop on the garage wall, and the boy often went out there after school to practice.

No.   Not really to practice.   To have fun.

Do you remember how much fun it was to skip stones across a pond?   Or to throw snowballs against the side of a house, just to watch them splash?   You never missed the pond or the house, did you?

Willy had fun throwing at the hoop, always on the move.   Underhand, overhand, one-handed, two-handed, or over his head, facing away from the hoop, it didn't matter.   He never missed.   Never.

Except when schoolmates came by to play, or when he was playing at school. Then he became merely very good.   But not exceptional.

We have a term for that sort of thing in the teaching profession: underachievement. I resolved to speak to his father about it.

I never got around to it, of course.   Mr. Taylor never came to PTA meetings, and, somehow, I never found any excuse for asking him to see me.   It's hard to do that when a boy is, actually and really, doing very well in school.   If he'd ever got in a fight—

I often daydreamed that Orville Goldman, a tease and semi-bully, would go too far with Willy some day, but he never did.

If Willy would only get caught smoking a cigarette or drinking a beer or—
But no.

Damn it, if he would at least tease Paula, or react to the way she teased him. She discovered a series of rhymes which tickled her not-too-bright little mind, a chant that went "Silly Willy, full of chili, has a face like a water-lily!"   He responded by helping her with her math lessons, and the chant was dead within three days.   And Paula's arithmetic improved.

And then came the parrot incident.

We had a "nature study" program (call it "biology," and some clot-headed parent will think you're teaching sex) at Kilgore School.   A part of that program consisted of teaching the children how to feed and care for small animals.   Ann Simons, who was in charge of the program, was an absolute genius at it.

One thing that it is important for a human being to learn is that other people hurt.   One of the best ways, in my opinion, is to teach them that *all* animals feel pain.   Small children are solipsists at heart; they don't know that those people out there are pretty much like this person in here.   Particularly, children are unaware that an adult can be hurt.   An adult seems too big, too powerful, to suffer.   It takes a child time to learn that an adult can be hurt, both physically and emotionally, by a child.

Ann's theory—and I think it a good one—is to show this with animals.

"A little rabbit may not be able to talk, and he can't learn the things you can learn; but he can feel pain just the way you do, so you must be very careful.   It's easy to hurt him because he's so much smaller and you're so much stronger.   And even though he's small, he can hurt you, too, if you hurt him or tease him.   If you're ever unlucky enough to have a rabbit sink his teeth in you, you'll know what I mean.   I hope that never happens, because if it does it means you were hurting or teasing the rabbit."

She had many kinds of birds and small beasts: rabbits, white rats, snakes, chickens, ducks, and the like.   Plus a few exotics: a kinkajou, an ocelot, a boa constrictor, and a parrot.

Named Jeremiah.

Jeremiah was Ann's personal property and a personal friend, and she'd had him for years.   She had originally named him Onan "because he spilled his seed upon the ground," but she changed his name when she brought the bird to school because some parent might catch on to the joke.   (I later found that Ann had borrowed the gag from Dorothy Parker.)

One of the phrases the bird had learned was "Woe is me," so Ann renamed him Jeremiah.

Part of Ann's program was to allow certain very carefully selected children to "borrow" an animal and take it home for a weekend.   (Some were not borrowable; the kinkajou, for instance.   You wouldn't believe what a kinkajou can do to your home!)   It was something like borrowing a book from the library; the child was supposed to learn from it, and had damn well better bring it back in good condition. Mostly, they did.

But, there again, one had to watch out for the parents.

A white rat, bred for thousands of generations in the laboratory, is about as harmless as an animal can get.   But there were mamas and papas who were horrified at the very *word* "rat"—to say nothing of having one in their home.   Believe me, Ann Simons had to be a top-flight diplomat.   She felt obliged to teach the parents as well as their children.

Willy Taylor was very good with animals.   Ann said that his father must have taught him how to handle them from the very beginning.

"How about his mother?" I asked.

"Didn't you know?"   Ann looked a little sad.   "Mrs. Taylor—well, the way Willy puts it is that she 'went to a better world' right after he was born."

At any rate, it was because of his way with animals that Ann made the decision she did.

Willy, you see, was particularly fond of Jeremiah, and the bird seemed fond of him.   A big green parrot can be dangerous; that beak could take off the end of a child's finger if the bird put power in it.   Jeremiah had no record of that sort of behavior, but Ann was reluctant to loan him out.   She had never really put him on the "non-circulating" list, like the kinkajou or the ocelot, but she usually convinced a child that another animal would be more suitable.   Somehow, she wasn't able to resist Willy; and one fine spring Friday afternoon, Willy, with his father's permission, took Jeremiah home for the weekend.

Saturday afternoon, I was sitting at home, near the living room window, reading a book on child psychology.   (I forget the title and the name of the author, but I remember being convinced that the psychologist hadn't been anywhere near a living child for forty years.)   I had opened the window to enjoy the cool westerly breeze and the fragrances it carried with it: the sweet scent of the blooming lemon bushes beneath my window; the tangy smell of cut grass; the mouth-watering aroma of Mrs. Jackson's homemade bread.

Once, as I glanced out, I noticed Willy in his back yard playing with Jeremiah. Their voices came clearly.

"Hello, Jeremiah, hello."

"Hello.   Hello.   Yawwwk!   Hello."

The bird's wings had been clipped, and he had a leather collar around one leg, attached to a long leash, so it was perfectly safe to let him wander around on the fenced-in lawn of the back yard.

"Jeremiah!   Yawwk!   Silly bird!   Silly bird!   Yaawwk!"

Wishing I could go out and play on such an afternoon, I went back to my book. The parrot-boy talk went on, but I ignored it.

A chapter or so later, though, Willy's voice penetrated my block.

"Dad!   How come Jeremiah can talk, but can't *really* talk?"

I looked out the window and listened carefully.   The father's answer to a question like that would tell me a great deal about the man.

I couldn't see him; he was inside the house.   But his low tenor voice carried well through the open window.

"You mean he can't carry on a conversation?"

"Yeah, that's right," Willy agreed.

"Well, Jeremiah's brain is something like a tape recorder that's attached to a simple computer.   A tape recorder can talk, but it can't think.   Jeremiah can't think, either, not like you and I can, but his little computer can make certain responses to certain input signals and come out with recorded sounds."

"Oh, I see.   Yeah, that makes sense.   Thanks, Dad."

"Any time."

"Yaawwk!   What time is it?   Eight bells and all's well!"

Remarkable!   I found myself liking Mr. Taylor very much.

But I went back to my book.

It must have been well over an hour later that I heard the screaming.

I want to say here that I am fond of cats.   I have always lived with at least one, and the sad part is that I have outlived so many of them.   The one I had then— Tamantha, I believe it was—was curled up on my lap at the time.   In general, cats are nice people.

But there are exceptions.

The big orange tom was one of them.   Nobody knew who he belonged to; he'd hang around the neighborhood for a few days, then disappear for a while.   He was feral, and he was mean.   He only had three things on his mind, and the other two were food and fighting.

When I heard the screaming, I think I knew it was Orange Tom before I looked up.

I almost screamed, myself.   All I saw was a flurry of fur and feathers.

What happened took place in far less time than it takes to tell it.   The cat had evidently come over the fence and decided that Jeremiah was good for at least two of the things on his mind.

The screaming was from both of them.   Jeremiah was fighting back, beak and claw.   But he was no match for that big tom.   Then Willy came slamming out of the back door, adding his scream to the others, and running straight toward the combat.

He handled it beautifully.   If he had tried to kick the two apart, or, worse, pull them apart with his hands, there might have been far worse damage done.   He didn't; instead, he came down solidly on Orange Tom's tail with his right foot. It is difficult to step on a cat's tail if he's wary, but Orange Tom was preoccupied.

Not for long.   He let go of the bird and turned.   As he was turning, Willy let up on the tail, drew back, and kicked.

It was lovely.   He didn't kick the way you'd kick a football, with the toe.   Even under pressure like that, he did not want to hurt the cat.   His instep caught Orange Tom right under the belly, lifting him in a high arc that took him clear over the fence.   He landed neatly, as cats do, and vanished in an orange streak.

But Jeremiah was an unmoving mop of green feathers.

By that time, Mr. Taylor had come out, less than a second after the boy.   Willy knelt down by Jeremiah, not touching him.

"Dad!   He's dead!   That damn cat killed Jeremiah!"

I had never heard Willy swear before.   Under the circumstances, I didn't blame him.

I didn't hear what Mr. Taylor said.   His voice was too soft, too gentle to be intelligible at that distance.

During those several seconds, I had stood frozen at the window, not even realizing that I had unceremoniously dumped Tamantha off my lap when I stood up.   She had leaped to the window sill and was looking out to see what all the fuss was about.

Then I realized something.   I had an excuse to go over to the Taylor house! The fight wasn't exactly the one I had envisioned, but it was certainly school business, and I had been a witness.

I changed clothes quickly; shorts and halter are not for a teacher who is visiting a parent.

By the time I had gone down the block, around the end at Dillon Street, and back up to the Taylor House, ten minutes or so had passed.   I went up the walk to the porch and pushed the doorbell button.

The man who opened the door was tall, like his son, and had one of the strongest faces I have ever seen.   He was not really handsome, but there was character there. Strength, compassion, and a touch of deep-seated sadness which even his smile did not erase.

"Yes?"

"I—I'm Janet Sadler.   One of Willy's teachers."   I suddenly felt very awkward and foolish.   "I—uh—I live just across from your back yard.   I saw—what happened."

"I see."   His smile faded a little, but did not vanish.   "Will you come in, Miss Sadler?"

By that time, Willy was at the door.   He had a grin on his face of sheer happiness. I was momentarily shocked.

"He's all right, Miz Sadler!   Jeremiah's all right!   Dad fixed him!"   He looked up at his father.   "Dad, will you teach me how to fix things like that?"

"Certainly, Willy," Mr. Taylor said.   He was still looking at me.   "Jeremiah wasn't really hurt at all, Miss Sadler.   He's fine.   Mostly shock, I think.   Not a scratch on him."

"My God!" I said.   "*Really*?   It looked to me as though he'd been torn to bits."

"Come see," he said.   "He's lost a few feathers and, for a while, his dignity, but he's in perfect health."

He led me into a pleasant living room.   Jeremiah was preening himself on the crossbar of the wooden T-stand that was his perch.   He looked great.   I just stared.

"Say something, Jeremiah," Mr. Taylor said.

"Jeremiah!   Yawwwk!   Silly bird!   Silly bird!"

I got over my shock. "Well, he certainly seems all right. I'm very glad. Mrs. Simons would have had a fit if something had happened to Jeremiah. Are you sure we shouldn't take him to a veterinarian?"

"We can if you want, but I don't think he'll find a thing wrong with the bird."

"I really think we should," I said.

And we did. There wasn't a thing the doctor could find wrong with Jeremiah.

As we were driving back, I realized that Willy had said nothing for a long time. I thought I knew why.

He was in the back seat with the parrot; I was in the front with his father. "Willy," I said without looking at him, "I don't think we need to say anything to Mrs. Simons about this. Jeremiah wasn't hurt, and it wasn't your fault. But if we tell Mrs. Simons, it will make her worry and she'll be unhappy. Of course, if she asks either of us, we'll have to tell the truth, but I don't see why she should, do you?"

"No, ma'am. Thank you."

"That's very good of you, Miss Sadler," his father said. "I wouldn't like the boy to lose his borrowing privileges. And next time, there'll be no leaving an animal in the back yard unguarded, will there, son?"

"No, *sir!* I promise. Next time I need a drink of water, I'll bring whatever it is in with me."

"That's fine." He gave me a quick glance and then looked back out the windshield. "He'll keep his word."

"I know," I said.

It wasn't until he drove me up to the front door of my apartment building that I realized I hadn't said a word about Willy's underachievement. It was far too late then.

Twelve days later, on a Thursday, Ann Simons came into my classroom after the children had been dismissed for the day. She looked worried.

"Janet, are you particularly busy right now?"

"No," I told her, "I was just getting ready to go home."

"Have you got a few minutes? Jeremiah's behaving—well, *peculiarly.*"

I know that one's heart does not literally leap into one's throat at a time like that, but it certainly feels like it.

I got up from my desk. "All the time in the world. What do you mean 'peculiarly'? Is he sick?"

"Nnnno—not sick. Come along, I'd rather show you."

She led me into the nature study section, and I followed, worried. If there was something wrong with the bird, I'd have to tell her what had happened nearly two weeks before—and that would be embarrassing.

Jeremiah was sitting on his perch, looking jauntily around. He speared us with a bright eye.

"*Yawk! Good morning, Miz Simons!*"

Ann said, "What time is it?"

"*What time is it? Five of twelve. Yaawwwk! Lunchtime in five minutes. Be patient.*"

"Where does the kinkajou come from?"

"Where does the kinkajou come from? Does anybody know? Yawwk. I think it comes from South America, Miz Simons."

I wish I had a hologram of my face at that moment. Or, rather, a flat photo; there were no pocket holo cameras in those days.

Ann went over to the cage where Flower, the denatured skunk, was watching with evident interest. "Name this animal, Jeremiah."

Jeremiah eyed it carefully, looked around the room, then looked back at Flower. *"Skunk. Mephitis mephitis. A carnivorous mammal which lives mostly on other small mammals, birds' eggs, and insects. Yawk."*

I think I was actually frightened. My mouth felt dry.

Ann said, "Janet, you know the question everybody asks a parrot. Ask him."

It took me a moment to find my voice. I looked at the bird and said: "Polly wanna cracker?"

He looked at me speculatively. Momentarily the nictitating lid filmed his eye. Then, distinctively: *"Graham, fire, or Georgia?"*

I looked at Ann. Now I *knew* that I was frightened. "Ann, can that damned bird *think*?"

"Think?" said Jeremiah. *"Think, children, think! Yaawwwk!"*

"Let's go to the teacher's lounge," Ann said quietly. "There's still some coffee in the urn."

Neither of us said another word until we were seated in a couple of soft chairs with mugs of hot, black coffee in our hands. Then I said, "Well? *Does* he think?"

She frowned a little. "Well, yes. All animals do, to a limited degree. They have to reason, to make decisions. The chimpanzee experiment at the University of California at Santa Barbara showed that chimps can carry on a conversation— a real, if limited, conversation—even if they can't talk. They use plastic symbols instead of words, but they can communicate.

"And that's the difference, Janet. Jeremiah can't communicate with us."

"It certainly sounded like it to me," I said flatly.

She shook her head. "I don't think so. A bird just doesn't have the brain for that sort of thing. A bird's brain isn't connected up that way. Oh, they can communicate with each other. The best examples are in the crow family—ravens, jays, jackdaws, magpies—that bunch. The parrots are halfwits in comparison."

"That little chit-chat we were just having with Jeremiah didn't sound halfwitted to me," I said.

"Sound like it," Ann said. "That's the clue, you see. A parrot's brain can be compared to—"

"To a tape recorder connected to a computer," I said.

She tried to keep from looking surprised, and almost succeeded. "Yes, that's— that's very appropriate. Look; suppose you're an actor who wants to memorize a part in a play. You could read all the other parts into a tape recorder, leaving properly timed blanks for the part you were trying to memorize. Then you practice, and memorize your part. By the time you get through, it'll *sound* like you were having a conversation with your recorder.

"Now carry it one step further and connect in a computer that can recognize any of the lines you deliver, pick out the appropriate response from the tape, and play it back. Make up a sufficiently long list of statements and responses, and it will sound like a conversation, possibly a very sophisticated one.''

"And that's all Jeremiah's doing?''

"I think so.'' She grinned oddly. "God, I *hope* so.'' She took a sip of her coffee. "So far, that's what it seems to be. Every one of the answers he gave was something he had heard in class—word for word.''

"Even that part about the crackers?'' I asked.

She chuckled. "No, I tried to teach him that one a year or so ago, but it didn't seem to take. He apparently dug it up out of his memory.'' She grew more serious.

"What makes that sort of thing sound so much like a conversation is that most conversations you hear *are* just that sort of thing. Somebody throws you a line, and you give them a stock answer without having to think.

" 'Good morning, Ann.'

" 'Good morning, Janet.'

" 'How are you this morning?'

" 'Just fine. How are you?'

" 'Just fine. Lovely weather, isn't it?'

" 'Absolutely marvelous.'

"Hell, Janet, you can program a computer for a lot more sophisticated dialogue than that. There's a program now that will do Rogerian psychotherapy, using just that sort of system. It's so spooky that it scares people. Of course, you have to communicate by typewriter, but it still seems as though the machine knows what it's talking about. The thing it can't do is ignore or comment on nonsense, the way a real psychotherapist would. If you type in, 'My head aches,' it will type back, 'Why do you think your head aches?' But if you type in, 'My frammis pilks,' it will say, 'Why do you think your frammis pilks?' instead of saying, 'Your *what* does *what*?' the way a real person would do.''

"Do you think Jeremiah could do that?'' I asked.

She shook her head. "I don't think his internal circuits are set up for it. But I'm going to test that out. I'm going to take that bird home again, and I'm going to set up a testing program before I let him hear another word.

"I don't think he is any more a reasoning being than he was before. He isn't some strange super-parrot; he's got no more abilities than any other parrot. But he can certainly use them a damn sight more efficiently.'' She grinned at me suddenly. "I'm going to get the best tape recorder and the best movie camera, all the best equipment I can afford. If I don't get a doctorate out of this, I'll *eat* that bird.''

I didn't tell her anything about what had happened to Jeremiah twelve days before, and I'm glad I didn't. She would have thought shock had something to do with it, and only God knows how many parrots would have had nervous breakdowns before she decided that line was a dead end.

Ann went to work on her project as though there were nothing in the world but her and that parrot. She didn't actually neglect the children, but they didn't get the extra attention she had given them before. She worked twice as hard, and I've never seen a tireder, happier woman.

It was late in May when the final incident occurred.

Little Paula ran across the street during recess to get a rolling ball. She ran between two parked cars, and the oncoming driver didn't see her until too late. It was almost a textbook case of that kind of accident. If the driver had been exceeding the twenty-five mile speed limit, Paula would have been killed instantly.

I didn't see it, thank Heaven; I was inside, grading papers. I heard the ambulance, but I didn't pay much attention; it was a block away, on the other side of the school grounds. The first I heard about it was when Willy came bursting into the room. There were tears in his eyes.

"Miz Sadler! Miz Sadler! Polly's hurt!"

"Paula," I corrected him automatically. "Calm down. What happened?"

He didn't calm down. "She got hit by a car! Her head's all smashed in and some of her bones are broken and she's bleeding and they won't let me fix her! They wouldn't let me anywhere near her! I can do it, 'cause my dad showed me how, but they wouldn't let me near her! Now they're taking her to the hospital and I asked could I come and see her and they said no I couldn't because I'm too little!" He stopped for breath.

"That's right," I said, "they don't let children into the emergency ward." I was more shaken than I let on, but I thought that by remaining calm myself, I could calm the boy down.

It was a mistake.

"You don't care either! You don't understand! Those doctors can't help you! Polly's gonna die if I don't fix her! You *hear* me? She's gonna die!"

"Willy! Calm down!"

"Please Miz Sadler! *Please* take me to the hospital! If I'm with a grownup, they'll let me in!"

I shook my head. "No, they won't, Willy. They wouldn't even let me in. Even her parents couldn't see her until she's out of Emergency."

"Then the next time they see her, it'll be to identify her body." His voice and his manner had changed startlingly. He was suddenly very coldly angry. "She'll go from Emergency to the morgue. I'm glad my education on this snijjort planet is nearly done." (That's as close as I can come to spelling the word he used.) "We're going to see Mother pretty soon."

I just gawped.

"Wait!" He felt in his pocket and came out with a small wad of dollar bills. "Yeah. I can make it." And he was gone.

I just sat there, not thinking. I didn't want to think. It's taken me nearly half a century to really think about it.

I think he took a taxi. I'm sure he got into the Emergency Room somehow, although nobody saw him. I'm sure because a miracle happened. Paula was back in school three days later.

A nurse who was a friend of mine said that the doctors reported that there was nothing wrong with Paula but shock, and they only kept her in the hospital for observation.   But it was the doctors who were shocked.   One minute, Paula was a smashed and dying thing.   Then—something—happened.

The next minute, she was perfectly well.

They couldn't explain it, so they pretended, even to each other, that it hadn't happened.   I can't explain it, either, but I think I know a great deal more about what happened than they did.

Mr. Taylor took Willy out of school the next day.   The boy was having nervous trouble, emotional shock brought on by seeing the accident, he said.

They moved out the day before Polly came back to school.

I never saw them again.

Ann Simons finally got her doctorate, but it was for another study.   Jeremiah was unique, you see, and the experiment, as well documented as it was, was not reproducible.   He was a better parrot, the best parrot he could be.

After all, when you fix something that's broken, you fix it so that it will operate at optimum, don't you?

I don't know why Paula Kelley changed her name to Dawn, but there are times when I wish it had been I, rather than she, who had been hit by the car.   And there are other times when I wonder if Willy loved *me* enough to break his cover.

FREDERICK LONGBEARD

A Time for Terror

I.

The others were dead. As I lay there, my hands bound behind me, searching the darkness for a speck of light, it kept running through my mind: They're dead; they're dead, all dead. . . . The Terranists had hit us as though they were storm-driven. One second the new commandant of security was putting the number-two Terranist on display for the press—then, chaos. The commandant and guards fell a split moment after the doors blew off their hinges; I saw that hack reporter Dubord get it an instant later. All dead.

The dryness of the dark place could be felt, and I turned my face from the dusty floor, coughing. With effort, I worked up enough spit to wet my tongue, then my cracked lips. Lowering the back of my head to the floor, I held my breath and listened for the mass drivers. They said you could hear them any-where on the Lunar surface if you were against bedrock. So, either I wasn't on the Lunar surface, against bedrock, or they were full of it. Voices, dim and distant.

Doubling up, I pushed against the dusty floor with my shoulder and right knee and teetered into a sitting position. The gravity said Luna. More voices, soft footsteps against dusty rock, a hand on a door latch. In the dark, flashes of the Terranist commandos exploded before my eyes. Men, women, police or civilian— no difference—all dead. Loud, muffled orders from behind a door. The lump in my throat, my fear, grew to where it became difficult to breathe. A light metal door slammed open against a wall. Outlined by the dim light from outside was a hand against the door and the muzzle of a weapon. As dim as it was, the light made me close my eyes. When I opened them, the outline of someone in surface gear filled the doorway. Behind the figure, others were moving back and forth, shouting and carrying things.

"On your feet, munie." The figure waved the gun at me. "Let's go; move it! You're not dead. Yet."

I looked behind me and saw a rough-cut wall. Pushing my legs, I backed up against it and used my hands and shoulders to inch up the wall. Still leaning against the wall, I turned toward the armed figure. "Where am I?"

"Come out of there."

"Can I at least have some water?"

The figure stood motionless for a second.   "Laddie, your only chance of lasting out the next thirty seconds is to do exactly as I say."   The figure backed out of the doorway and waved the muzzle of his gun.   "Let's go."

I pushed off from the wall, made it to the door and stepped out into the corridor. As I worked my jaw around, I could feel the blood caked on the right side of my face.   Nameless with the gun gave me a dig in the kidney and I turned right.   I'm usually ready to give a man with a gun any kind of slack he asks for.   But that only applies when the gunsel trades me my life for following his orders.   When it's a plus or minus thirty seconds in exchange for bruised organs, the hell with it. I whirled around to plant a knee amongst his family jewels, but instead, met a rifle stock upside the right side of my head.   Unfortunately, I didn't black out.   When the chimes in my head quieted down, I spit out the dust from the corridor floor, along with a few teeth, and looked back at my keeper.   He wore the traditional greyish surface suit, helmet cracked back, except his suit looked in bad repair and had a broad red stripe painted around the chest.   He waved his gun up and down.

"Get up, stupid, and head down the walk.   Another performance like that will earn you a bolt through your kneecap."

On my knees, I looked up at him.   "You're not going to kill me, are you?"

His face was round, dark, and cruel.   He smiled, and a laugh started somewhere around his feet and rumbled out of his mouth.   "Laddie, that depends on how much trouble you are alive."

Another red-banded figure pulled up to us carrying a crate and nodded toward my keeper.   "Need a hand, Ahmis?"

He shook his head.   "No."   He cocked his head toward me.   "On your feet, harmless."   Again, he waved his gun up and down.   I put one leg forward and stood, spitting blood on the floor.   I looked at the four gleaming white teeth among the blood and dust of the corridor floor, remembering out of a childhood long forgotten that the most terrible thing in the world was getting a tooth knocked out. I looked at the face of my keeper.   There was no remorse, nor even a hint of pity. "Turn around and stop at the next door to your left."

I turned, my cheek and jaw throbbing with indescribable aches.   Three more red-banded figures, two women and a man, raced past headed in the opposite direction.   One slow foot at a time, I walked the remaining few meters to the door. As I reached it, I stopped and turned toward my keeper.   "I'd open it with my teeth, but I left them back in the walk."

My keeper nodded.   "Very brave, little boy.   Perhaps one of us will live to tell the Earth how brave you are."

He reached out and unlatched the door, pushing me in after.   The room was much like the one I had just left, except for the light and the company.   Behind a rude metal table sat a bearded fellow with a crown of brown hair circling his otherwise hairless dome.   His facial features were identical to every representation of Jesus Christ I'd ever seen, except for the dark, haunted eyes.   He pointed at a stool before the table.   "Sit.   My name is Rudy Vegler."   He nodded toward a figure seated in the shadows.   "You have already met Raymond."

I lowered myself onto the stool, trying to make out the face of the number-two Terranist. I had seen him at the news conference, but for some reason couldn't remember his face. My keeper stood behind me, his gun at the ready. Both Vegler and the one called Raymond wore surface gear.

"Why am I here?"

Vegler nodded slightly. "Yes, Mark Lambert, why are you here? You are alive because we cannot answer that question. Tell us."

I laughed. I suppose I resigned myself to being a dead man, and that helped ease my tension. After I was dead, I couldn't be hurt. Go out with style, or something stupid like that. "I didn't kill twenty men and women and drag me here. You tell me."

Vegler shook his head. "It was only eighteen." He leaned forward, the red band of his surface suit against the edge of the table. "Lambert, do you know what being surfaced is?"

"No."

"We kick you outside with no suit." He rubbed the side of his nose. "I understand that boiling blood is a very, very painful way to go." He smiled, exposing a gap in twin rows of yellowing teeth. "Of course, those in a position to know are in no position to tell. Why are you here?"

I shrugged. "Honesty won't get me any points. Why should I tell you?"

Vegler dropped his smile. "Lambert, we don't have time to waste—you don't have time to waste. Why are you on Luna?"

There it was: the question. I dropped my glance to the red band around Vegler's chest. "I'm a sound tech with the *Los Angeles Telejournal*. I was sent up with Harvy Dubord to cover . . ."

Vegler held up his hand. "I said we don't have time." He lowered it to the table. "Feed your cover story to the lockwatchers, but to us, nothing but the truth."

With puffy lips, missing teeth, and blood dribbling from my mouth, I managed the best sneer I could. "Why should I tell you anything? You're going to kill me, aren't you?"

"No decision has been made."

I snorted, dribbling more blood down my chin and coveralls. "I saw you bastards slaughter innocent men and women with less compassion than I throw out my garbage."

In the shadows, the one called Raymond uttered a brief, bitter laugh. "Lambert, we have more compassion for your garbage than we do for the munies." He leaned forward, bringing his face into the light. His fine blond hair was matted and caked with blood, his skin pale and greenish around his almost delicate jaw. The narrow-set, pale blue eyes were almost hypnotic in their attraction. "Lambert, we are evacuating this site. When we leave, we will make it useless. What we need to know is whether or not it is worth our while to spend surface gear, water, and air on your survival."

I turned to Vegler. "I find it hard to believe that anything I can say will improve my chances one bit."

Vegler rubbed his nose. "The information we have from Earthside says you are a reporter working undercover for the L.A. *Telejournal*. Your exact assignment is somewhat vague, but it concerns an investigation into the possible manipulation of news from Luna."

I felt as though Ahmis, the happy jailer, had tapped me again with his gun butt. Only five persons knew: me, my editor, the publisher, the lawyer called in to hand out a heap of ignored advice, and the New York Bureau Chief, Margate. But Margate had said that to feed a fake ID to the MAC VI would involve developing mob contacts. You tell the mob and you tell anyone who has the price of a whisper. It had been assumed that no one on Luna, particularly the Terranists, could raise the ante. "If you know that, why the question? Why not just kill me and be done with it?"

Vegler unlatched the collar ring on his suit, pulled the seal to the middle of his chest, reached inside and scratched. "Tell me, Lambert: is this information we've discovered, or crap that we've been fed?"

"What difference does it make?"

"If it's true, you live; if not . . ." Vegler pointed up, towards the surface.

"What else would I be?"

"A police spy."

I smiled and immediately regretted it as the throb in my cheek grew. "What about you? What if this is some production number by the police to get me to admit to something?"

Vegler resealed his suit. "You overestimate your importance. It will be a long time before the lockwatchers have a commandant killed just to ferret out a reporter." He raised his eyebrows. "That would be even too extreme for us."

I shrugged. "What if I am what you say I am?"

Vegler looked at Raymond. Number-two man nodded a permission, then leaned back into the shadows. Vegler turned back to me. "Then you may be of some use to us. We have been trying to get the truth to Earth for a long time."

"Terranist truth."

"Explain."

"I'm not here to do propaganda pieces for the Terranist League. Remember, I've seen your killers in action, and all it does is confirm everything I've ever seen or heard about the Terranists."

"Be that as it may, Lambert, there is still the small matter of convincing us that you are a reporter. If you can't, it's the last time you'll see anyone or anything in action."

I think that, for the first time since entering that room, I began believing I might somehow get out of my predicament in one piece. "What do you want to know?"

"Begin with why none of the registers, the official ones, list you as a reporter."

"I never have been listed as a reporter. It's a new position for me, but because of its nature, I couldn't be listed." Vegler was frowning. "Look, up until a few weeks ago, I was a sound tech. But I've been trying to get in reporting for years. I'd pestered the station editor about it so many times, he told me to come up with an idea and, if it was any good, he'd see. He liked my idea."

"What was the idea?"

"To come up here as a sound tech, poke around and see if the governor's office has anything to hide.   I got the idea from a camera jock who was with our team covering the capture of Tralcor.   The story he told me about the press conference didn't seem to have anything to do with what the reporters on Luna put on the tape loops."

Vegler nodded.   "And?"

"Then I overheard one of our reporters a few days later.   He had been assigned the story, but Immigration rejected his blood test.   The *Telejournal* sent Harvy Dubord instead, and the reporter I overheard was complaining.   Dubord is what we call a 'safe' voice—a reporter the government can count on not to embarrass it."   I felt as though my fingers were about to fall off, and nodded back over my right shoulder.   "Is there something you can do about my hands?"

"We're doing it.   Go on."

"Well, I thought of another reporter that had been turned down, then did some checking.   From the *Telejournal*, at least, nothing but safe voices have ever been sent to Luna since the Plague.   That includes writers as well as . . ."

Vegler held up his hand.   "And you suspected that the government was using the blood tests as a way of screening reporters?"

"Yes."

"For what purpose?"

I shrugged, sending darts of pain from my wrists up my arms.   "I don't know.   That's what I'm here to find out."

Vegler looked at Raymond, then turned back toward me.   "One more question: How did you plan on getting your tapes back to Earth?"

"The mass drivers.   The *Telejournal* has arranged for a small ship to pick the tapes out of the dirt track before they reach the catcher station."   My throat felt raw from the dryness.   "From there, the tapes would be taken to the New Eden industrial station at El Five and then broadcast."

"I see."   Vegler nodded.   "Wouldn't those pulses in the driver wipe the tapes?"

I started to shake my head, but thought better of it.   "I had a specially shielded case.   It was with me at the news conference. . . ."

Vegler nodded at my keeper.   I felt the muzzle of his gun dig in between my shoulder blades.   "Get up, laddie."

I stood and heard the door open behind me.   I kept my eyes on Vegler.   "Well?"

"Well, what?"

"Do I live or die?"

Vegler shook his head.   "As I said, no decision has been made."   He nodded again at the guard and I felt a hand fall on my shoulder.   The guard turned me around and shoved me out into the walk.   He followed and closed the door, pulling a long knife from the belt of his surface suit.

"Turn around."   I felt the knife slip between my hands and the bonds part.   Immediately, blood, feeling and pain began flowing from my arms into my hands.   I turned and faced my keeper.

"I thought no decision had been made about letting me live."

The guard smiled, then rumbled forth another laugh. "Rudy hasn't made that decision about me, yet." He pointed down the walk toward my old room. "Let's go."

II.

Before the guard closed the door, plunging the room into darkness again, a quick look around showed me a small rectangular alcove carved out of solid rock. In the darkness, I felt along the walls finding nothing but moon dust. The stuff was everywhere. Grey, fine, and adhesive, the powder seemed to be in everything. Stock joke earthside: moon miners get greylung. The joke had come back with the original miners that operated the first experimental mines on Luna. But that was before the Plague and before the miners had been replaced by thousands of carriers sentenced to Luna to separate them from the rest of the population. At first, the press had called Luna the new Molokai, then simply the leper colony: one hundred and forty thousand carriers of a novel lifeform product of late 1980s recombinant DNA research known as "Megabug." They were guarded and managed by five thousand immunes, or "munies." For three generations, the leper colony had mined the mountains between Imbrium and Serenitatis, feeding the seven mass drivers that provided raw materials for the New Eden industrial station, which, in turn, fed products to Earth. But, the carriers wanted to come back, and Terranism was born.

I put my back against the wall and slid down to a sitting position. Rubbing my wrists, I thought back to my meeting with Vegler and Raymond. Why was I still alive? The Terranists had claimed responsibility for bombing the shuttle to El Five from Luna, a disaster that claimed the lives of fifteen young children among many others. Why would they spare my life simply because I'm innocent?

Voices again, outside the door. What use did they plan to make of me? I was no safe voice, but I certainly had no sympathy for the Terranists. The door unlatched, then opened, exposing Ahmis the guard. "Let's go, laddie."

"Where?" I pushed myself to my feet.

"It's time to fit you with some walking gear. Looks as though you'll be with us for a while."

III.

Endless hours later, clad in scavenged surface gear, a wide red band sprayed around my chest, I followed the doctor who patched up my head through a wide, low gallery lit by a single string of dim, green numbars. Even without being bound, I found movement difficult. To move forward in the clumsy gear, I had to lean forward as though I were trying to walk through a gale-force storm. To stop, I had to lean backwards and dig in. It took a few drifts to the floor of the gallery to polish my technique.   The effort of getting back on my feet, as well as the strain of the bouncy pace we kept, soon mixed the acrid smell of the moon dust in the suit with my sweat, and the leftover smells of the previous occupant. Since my radio had been removed, the only sound I could hear were the circulation motor and my own breathing.

Ahead of the doctor, a string of Terranists made their way to the open end of the gallery.   It opened on the dark side of a mountain, but sunlight from the slope opposite the entrance hurt my eyes.   Behind, my faithful keeper Ahmis kept a close watch on me.   He had chuckled as he showed me how to patch the holes in the suit's plastic lining with crosses of plastic tape.   I had asked the cause of his humor, and he pointed out, in detail, how the suit was obtained from its previous occupant.

While she cleaned my wound and covered it with plastiskin, the doctor had remained silent.   She bounced along in front of me, and came to a halt at the gallery entrance.   Leaning backward and digging in, I managed not to run into her.   Ahmis pulled up beside me and we could all see a figure in front, outside the entrance, giving hand signals.   In a few moments, the doctor started off and Ahmis and I followed.   Behind us were, perhaps, ten others.

Outside the gallery, I saw that we were on one of the old access roads.   The old mounting braces for the ore-belt supports could be seen every few meters, which meant that we were still in the Caucasus.   Far in front, a six-wheeled ore extractor turned right off the road and headed down a large gully.   Those in front turned and followed after.   As we walked out of the mountain's shadow, I saw the rim of Calippus.   It had to be.   Calippus was the largest crater near the ore belt system, which meant we were far north of Bee Town.   An hour or more later, we reached the end of the gully and gathered again.   As I looked around, I could see thirty-two in surface suits.   One of them mounted the ore extractor and entered the airlock.   Soon after, the figure emerged and the extractor turned right again and headed off across the low rolling hills toward the darkness of the higher Caucasus west of Calippus. · Those of us on foot turned left and headed south.

As my suit struggled to keep out the blistering heat, I began feeling dizzy.   I kept up, but before I realized what was happening, the doctor had fallen back beside me and had plugged a black cord from her helmet into mine.

"How do you feel, Lambert?"

I laughed.   "After getting my head beat in with rifle stocks, how do you expect me to feel?"

"Are you dizzy; a little sick to your stomach?"

"Yes."

She held up her hand and Ahmis stopped next to us.   She pulled the air coupling from my pack and inserted it into a cup she pulled from a pouch at her belt.   I could feel that no air was entering my system, and began to panic, but she soon plugged the coupling back in and my nostrils were assaulted with a new odor: something like rotted leaves mixed with some kind of commercial hand cream. "The feeling should be gone in an hour or so."   She pulled the cord from my helmet and wound it up and attached it to her own. As she turned and followed the others, Ahmis tapped my shoulder and pointed after her. I leaned forward and followed.

I looked from the black sky to the Earth hanging huge over the horizon and wondered what purpose I was serving. One bouncing foot in front of the other, each one lifting that grey dust that settled quickly to the surface again. As I reached a slight rise I could see wheel prints in the dust extending off toward the golden tan horizon. We followed the tracks for another hour or two until we reached the end of another abandoned access road. At that point, my dizziness had cleared up but the effort of walking with mostly unfamiliar muscles had my legs aching. Hand signals went up for a halt, and I turned to see how our passage had marked the Lunar surface, but no tracks could be seen. At the end of the column two figures with what looked like hockey sticks were erasing the evidence. The column moved again, then walked into the shadow of a cliff and stopped.

The doctor turned and connected the cord from her helmet to mine. "Is the dizziness gone?"

"Yes." She reached up her hand to pull the plug. "Wait. As long as we're stopped, could we talk for a while?"

"Why?"

"I'd like to ask a few questions." She reached up again to pull the cord. "Look, if you people want your side reported, you're going to have to talk to me."

She hesitated, then dropped her hand. "What do you want to know?"

I sighed, grateful to have someone to talk to. "Well, to begin, what's your name, doctor?"

"Kit."

"Kit what?"

"You'll find most of us use single names, usually adopted. We still have families in the pits." Her voice came through the speaker cold and brittle.

"What about Rudy Vegler?"

"The lockwatchers killed his family, when he was just a boy, right after he joined the Terranist League."

"Why are you a Terranist?"

She gave a sharp laugh. "The same as everyone else, Lambert: to go back to Earth." She reached up, pulled the plug and turned away. More hand signals from up front, and the column moved out.

As we bounced down the road past dark, abandoned mine entrances, I thought of the Terranist goals and could almost understand. The novelty of being on Earth's moon had worn off tense hours ago, and seeing that blue-white globe hanging above the bleak, grey, airless mountains made me long for fresh air, trees, and water. To be able to stretch my naked arms in the sunlight, to splash into a clear pool, even to scratch when I felt like it, had become luxuries beyond price. It would seem even dearer to those who have never been to Earth, and the band of cutthroats I'd seen were at least third, possibly fourth generation carriers. But they were carriers, and could never come home to Earth. The Terranists had no sympathy on Earth; to let them back on the planet meant certain death for at least four-fifths of the human race.   I looked at the Great Lakes and took a sip of warm, tasteless water through the tube in my helmet.

As the column reached a sharp turn in the old access road, hand signals went up and we fled off the road back into the shadows.   I looked up and saw a formation of four police fighters streak toward Calippus.   We waited for a few moments, then were motioned back on the road.   Ahead, five-wheeled vehicles turned right off the main road onto a track that led straight into the mountain.   As I came abreast of the feeder road and turned, I saw it enter the opening of one of the countless abandoned mine shafts that dotted the base of the mountain.

Inside the shaft, we came to a gallery-wide airlock and stepped in, leaving the vehicles outside.   After a few moments, I could feel the pressure of the chamber equalizing the pressure of my suit.   Vegler, Ahmis, and the others removed their helmets, and I fooled with the lock on mine until it opened, allowing me to push my helmet back.   Ahmis reached out a beefy hand and shut down my suit's systems.

Vegler turned to me.   "All the gear we picked up at the news conference will be brought in.   Identify yours and bring it with you.   Ahmis will show you the way."

"Would it be a breach of security to ask why?"

"You're about to do your first story from the leper colony; that's what you're here for, isn't it?"

I ground my teeth a little—the ones that remained.   "I said I'm not here to do puff pieces for the Terranist League.   What makes you think I will?"

"Two things: first, it doesn't matter whether you approve or not, the Terranists exist and they are news.   Or are you one of those safe voices you mentioned?"

"No."   What could I do but agree; he was right.   "What was the second thing?"

Vegler grinned.   "With your mouth shut, you're no use to your station, the munies, or to us.   You may as well be skinny dipping in the moon dust."

I nodded.   Both points were well taken.

IV.

Loaded with my equipment, Ahmis and I followed Vegler and three other Terranists through the dark shafts until we came to a section lit with numbars.   The greenish light, dim and flickering, mixed with mournful, wailing voices.   It took a moment to realize this was singing.   We moved around a slight turn in the shaft and were waved on by a red-banded figure in the distance.   Where the sentry stood, the shaft seemed to narrow to a single passageway almost two meters wide, but, as we came closer, I saw that the gallery walls had been filled in with rough-cut blocks.

I entered the passage behind Vegler and saw that the gallery had been divided into rooms, and in the rooms were people. Only a few steps into the mine shaft town, the smell of the ever present moon dust was overpowered by the smells of unwashed bodies, urine, and burnt grease. A very old woman, her legs missing from the knees down, sat in the passageway and reached out a hand toward Vegler as he passed. The Terranist stopped, squatted, and touched the old woman's cheek with the palm of his hand. She took his hand in hers, kissed it, then released it. Vegler watched as she nodded, smiled, and pulled herself into a dark doorway. He looked down at the dusty floor for a second, then stood and looked at me.

I pointed toward the dark doorway. "What was that, a Terranist groupie?" Vegler backhanded me across my face with the armored glove of his surface suit sending me sprawling into Ahmis, then onto the floor. He turned and stormed off. Ahmis grabbed my shoulder and pulled me to my feet. "What is she, his mother?"

Ahmis reached down and picked up my equipment, dumping it into my arms. "No. She's just an old woman."

"What happened to her legs?"

"Mine accident, like a lot of old people here."

A bit weavey on my feet, I stumbled off after Vegler. There were many dark doorways, and many old faces. The deeper we got into the area, the stronger became the smells. Ahead, Vegler turned into one of the doorways. Before entering, I stopped and faced Ahmis. "What is this place?"

"This is where you go when you're too old to work the mines. We call it the boneyard."

Ahmis pointed at the doorway, and I turned and entered. The dark room looked and smelled like all the others. Its single difference was a false wall where the hard rock of the gallery should have been. Ahmis nodded toward it, and I stepped through into a black, narrow hall. Feeling along the rough walls with my fingertips, I made a turn and saw white light ahead. A few steps further and I entered a smooth-walled, white chamber with a low ceiling set with yellowish-white light panels. Along the far wall stood racks of weapons. On either side of the racks were closed doors and immediately in front of me were several metal chairs and a table. Vegler stood with his back toward me, talking to Kit and a frail old fellow dressed in coveralls. It took a moment, but I finally made the face. It was Charles Towne, the molecular biologist stationed with the Luna Immune contingent, kidnapped by the Terranists four years earlier and presumed dead.

Vegler cocked his head in my direction. "Towne, this is Lambert, the reporter I told you about."

Towne's watery blue eyes darted at me, then back to Vegler. "If I cooperate, then you'll release me?"

"We'll see." Vegler looked at me. "This is your show; how do you want to work it?"

I shrugged, then looked around the room. "I'll set my stuff up, then we'll just sit down and talk. . . . Will we be going someplace other than this room?"

"Perhaps."

"Then I may need someone to work the camera in transit."

Vegler scratched his chin and looked at Ahmis standing next to me.   The Terranist guard had his arms loaded with gear.   "You feel like a camera jock, Ahmis?"

The guard grinned.   "Sure, Rudy."   Ahmis lowered the gear to the floor, removed the gloves to his surface suit and rubbed his hands together.   "Where do we start, laddie?"

I raised an eyebrow at Vegler.   He smiled and sat in one of the metal chairs. "Whenever you're ready, Lambert."

V.

Hours later, I sat in the room staring at the five-centimeter screen of my editor, trying to shake off the feeling that more had gone on at the interview than I had gotten on tape.   I skipped over some experimenting Ahmis had done with the camera's zoom lens, checked the index and stopped, backed, then stopped again. I pushed the playback and watched a miniature representation of Charles Towne rub his nose, then fold his arms.

"The Lunar Genetic Center was established in '91, immediately after the contained carrier population had been removed to the moon.   The original purpose of the center was, in effect, to find a cure for the carriers."

Lambert.   "You said 'original purpose.'   The purpose changed then?"

Towne squirmed, looked off screen, then looked back at Lambert and nodded. "It was when the New Eden station at El Five was just beginning construction— before my time."

Lambert: "About 2005."

Towne: "Yes.   Well, you see the Center had been examining both carriers and immunes on Luna on a regular basis.   The nucleotide sequence that gave immunity to the so-called megabug had been identified.   But, another thing was beginning to make itself evident: The particular strain of *E. Coli* that carried the recombined plasmids that were found to be pathogenic . . ."

Lambert: "The megabug."

Towne: "Yes.   Well, the frequency of occurrence appeared to diminish as time passed.   Samples on record show . . ."

Lambert: "You mean the bug was dying out?"

Towne: "It did die out.   No traces have been found since 2008."

Lambert: "You mean that the carrier population has been free of the disease since '08?   They could be returned to Earth with no harmful effects?"

Towne nodded.   "That's when the Center's purpose changed.   By then, Luna had four mass drivers and the New Eden station was beginning to supply products to Earth.   The mass drivers had to be fed, and it was decided to keep the news secret until they could be sure.   All information concerning the so-called plague was collected and filed at the center."

Lambert: "And?"

Towne: "And that's where the situation stands today, sixty years later."

Vegler: "Except that now there are seven mass drivers to feed." The picture moved until Vegler's head filled the tiny screen.

Lambert: "What you're saying, then, is that the carrier population—actually, its descendents—are being used as . . . as . . ."

Vegler: "'Slaves' is the word you're looking for."

Lambert: "For what possible reason?"

Vegler: "The original miners on Luna were well paid and their quarters and facilities were extravagent. You've seen Bee Town?"

Lambert: "Yes."

Vegler: "That was the original settlement, but now the immunes live there. The immunes pay us in food and minimal living conditions. They literally control the air we breathe. You've seen how we live; it's cheaper."

I pushed the stop and looked at Vegler's frozen face. If true, that would explain what the United States of Earth had to hide on Luna. But how much of Towne's statement could be trusted? Towne and Kit had taken me into another room, crammed with equipment and wire files. They showed me slides, documents, records, and other things the Terranists had snatched at the Center when they kidnapped Towne. But I couldn't judge what I'd seen. All of us had guns stuck in our ears. Even so, just finding Charles Towne alive would make the story, not to mention the followup potential in a story on carrier living conditions. If it was true that the bug had died, so much the better. It would be the coverup of the century. Just thinking of the number of high officials and different administrations that must have been involved to pull it off made my mouth water. It was true; no one on Earth would lift a finger to help the carriers, even if the bug had died out sixty years before.

I went fast forward until I saw Vegler stabbing his finger at the air, then hit the play. ". . . like the Indians on the old reservations. They don't ask why they wound up on the reservations; all they can think of is that the government has been paying their upkeep. Why, then, should anyone give them back their land? That's what they think of us now. A planetoid full of welfare bums; why should we let them back on Earth? We do that, and the next thing you know, they'll want their properties back."

Lambert: "Will terrorism turn that indifference into sympathy?"

Vegler shook his head. "No. But we're not looking for sympathy."

Lambert: "What, then?"

Vegler: "Action."

Lambert: "You are, of course, aware that the few Terranist apologists on Earth have made the claim that the present containment of carriers is based on a hoax. It's regarded as nothing but Terranist propaganda."

Vegler: "Those pictures in your school books, the streets choked with black, rotting corpses, won't be countered by words alone. Before, you asked what we hoped to accomplish by bombing the shuttle to El Five. It's simple. We're giving them new pictures of horror to counter the old. If we make them horrible enough, we'll get the action we seek. . . ."

I hit the stop. But then, if words won't do it, why go to all the trouble of keeping me alive to conduct an interview? That's what was bothering me. The edited tape loop had been packed in the shielded case, and the case given to a party to put in one of the mass drivers. They could just ditch the case, but what would be the point? They could have accomplished the same thing just by killing me at the news conference. I feather-touched the back button and hit the play.

". . . new pictures of horror to counter the old. If we make them horrible enough . . ." I hit the stop, ejected the tape and picked the first tape off the table, feeling sick to my stomach. I hit the fast forward and watched the miniature figures jerk about until the one named Kit sat still for a moment, looking at the one called Mark Lambert. Stop. Back. Play.

Lambert: ". . . seems to me, that with the training and equipment you and Towne need to do the checks on the carriers, and to understand all this, you ought to be able to do your own recombinant DNA work."

Kit: "Such as?"

Lambert: "Well, on Earth the research has many applications in food production, medicines—things that could improve conditions up here."

Kit looked at Towne, then leveled her eyes at Lambert, a hint of a smile on her lips. "We've done a little of that, yes. . . ." I hit the stop and turned off the editor.

I just bet they'd done a little of that. ". . . new pictures of horror. . . ." The tape container would be picked up from the dirt track, taken to the New Eden station and opened, releasing . . . what? Two and a half million men, women, and children were at New Eden. I felt my skin prickle as I realized that cargo and passenger shuttles to Earth left New Eden in a steady stream. The Earth . . .

Kit entered the room from the door to the right of the rifle racks, looked at my face and smiled. "It looks as though you figured it out." She raised a rifle and pointed it at me. All I could do was sit there with my mouth hanging open. I looked at the floor and examined the equipment there. The signal coder by which I would know when the pickup had been accomplished was gone. If I had it, I could signal the pickup ship to abort. I looked at Kit. "Rudy has it."

"Where is he? You don't understand; I've got to stop him!"

She laughed. "If I wouldn't understand, who would?"

"You don't know what you're doing!"

She waved the muzzle of her rifle at me. "Stay seated and stay alive, Lambert. . . ." Before she could finish, I reached under the table and turned it over on her. The edge of the table deflected her rifle toward the ceiling. She fired, the rifle's blinding white beam blowing rocks and rock powder down on both of us. Without stopping, I ran across the overturned table, then kicked her in the side of her head. I picked up the rifle and a helmet sitting on one of the chairs. I seated the helmet in place as I headed toward the door, wondering why the helmet locks were so easy to work. I had taken my gloves off to work the editor. I went back for them, clipped them into the suit's cuffs and bounced down the dark passage, turned and came to the false wall. It was a sliding slab of rock, perhaps as thick as ten centimeters. I could see a crack of light along one edge, but couldn't find a lock. I pushed on the slab, trying to move it, but it didn't even shake.

Unslinging the rifle, I aimed it at the crack and fired. The slab shattered diagonally, opening the upper part of the entrance. Ahmis's surprised face stared back at me. Jumping through the opening, I slammed the stock of my rifle into his face and ran over him into the passage. Faces, up and down the passage, were sticking out of dark doorways.

I turned left and bounced back the way I had been led in. Where the shaft opened, I looked for the guard, but he was gone. I stepped out into the open part and a rifle bolt flashed over my head from behind me. I turned and saw Ahmis, blood running from his nose, bounding down the passage. I lifted my rifle, but there were too many others in the passage behind him. I turned and ran, stopping when I reached the slight turn in the shaft. As Ahmis came through the opening, I fired several times, filling the shaft at his end with moon dust.

I knew I had missed him as I turned and bounded off into the unlit shaft ahead. In moments, I was at the large airlock. I checked my suit's systems, closed the face plate, opened the door and stepped in. At the other end of the lock, I felt for the valve set in the door, found it and turned it wide open. In a few moments my suit was tight and I undogged the outside door and opened it. It was weighted to close automatically behind me to make the cell operational for the next person wanting out. Since that next person was going to be Ahmis, I picked up a fist-sized stone and jammed it in the closing door. It held.

One of the wheeled vehicles along the side of the gallery was missing. I climbed up on the next and lowered myself into the tubular-frame driver's seat and studied the few controls. It was a simple cargo rover with little more than a charge indicator, throttle, brake, and steering wheel. I moved the throttle to the reverse position and the rover jerked to life and swayed out of the shaft entrance. The road was wide at the entrance and I backed around, turned the wire mesh wheels downhill, and gave it forward throttle.

In moments I reached the main access road, then stopped, wondering where to go next. To the left I knew the road just ended, but Vegler and company might have gone that way to avoid the security police. But—however they went, they'd have to wind up at the mass drivers, and that's where the old ore belt access roads went. I turned right and gave the rover full throttle forward.

The road went straight, until it ran into a tee where two old ore belt routes joined. The mass drivers were south of Calippus. I turned right, held on for dear life around a curve and stopped just in time to miss an ore extractor making its way across the road. Behind it, raised on metal frame supports every few meters, was the beginning of the ore belt system in use. From the mountain rising to my right, smaller belts led from gallery entrances to dump their loads onto the main belt.

I swung around the ore extractor and followed the access road in and out of the forest of ore belt supports. To my left, the emptiness of Serenitatis made me stop and think.   As the rover came to a halt, I tried to visualize the layout of the mass drivers and ore belt system.   The drivers were at the edge of the *mare*, directly south of the eastern Caucasus, which is where I had to be if I could see Serenitatis. When the road turned to the right to follow the line of the mountains, I turned off the road and continued south.

In minutes I was lost.   All landmarks had dropped below the short horizon and my only directional aids were the rover tracks stretching out behind me.   Although not much help to me, they would be invaluable to Ahmis as he rolled down the access road and saw the tracks running off across Serenitatis pointing a big red arrow at my back.   I leaned forward to put full throttle to the rover, but found it already at maximum.   The charge indicator showed negative, and in bright sunlight. I pulled up, stood and stepped on the seat to check the solar cell panel.   There must have been a centimeter of moon dust on it.   I brushed off what I could with my arm and turned to step down off the seat.   In the distance, a flash of silver followed by another announced the mass driver complex.

I quickly checked back the way I had come, but Ahmis was nowhere in sight. My stunt at the airlock must have worked.   I dropped into the seat, hit the throttle, and headed toward where I remembered the glint of silver.   The charge indicator was still negative, but less so.   In a moment, it didn't matter.   As I reached a slight rise, the kilometers of gleaming bars and whizzing buckets of the mass driver complex stretched out right to left, from horizon to horizon.   The buckets scooped up a load at the slow end dump, then were propelled by synchronized magnetic pulses along the length of the tracks until they reached escape velocity.   At the fast end, the buckets opened, shooting the compacted ore into the dirt track orbit where the catcher station gathered it up.   The buckets were decelerated and returned to the slow end for another pickup.   The buckets I could see were slowing from left to right, and I turned right toward the slow end.

The rover lurched and bounced around a small, house-sized crater, then up a steep hill.   From the crest I could see the cargo rover Vegler and his group had taken next to three rovers mounted with environmental support vans bearing the insignia of the security police.   Behind them rose the long, tapered bin of the dump being fed by two huge ore trunk belts.   A flash from one of the police rovers kicked up the dust in front of me and I turned left and headed for the dark safety of the spaces underneath the mass driver tracks.   More flashes and it seemed as though I was caught in a dust storm.   The dust cleared, and I realized the rover wasn't moving.   The two wire mesh tires on the right side looked like aluminium spaghetti.   I jumped off the left side and bounded for the driver tracks.

As I approached the tracks, bringing my attention with me in the form of police fire, answering fire aimed at the police vans began coming from under the tracks. A red banded figure stood out from behind a support and waved me on.   When I was within five meters of the shadows, I was lifted from behind, slammed into one of the inside track supports, then buried in moon dust.

My head swam and I drifted in and out of consciousness as I felt hands digging me out.   My body felt like a sack of broken glass.   Gloved fingers wiping the dust off my face plate; Vegler's face looking back at me. He pulled a black cord from his helmet and plugged it into mine.

"Lambert?"

"You monster," I hissed. "Where is the case?"

A beam flashed behind Vegler's helmet, but he didn't seem to notice. "It's gone. Who told you, or did you figure it out?"

"Does it make a difference?"

"Lambert, the lockwatchers will be on us in a few seconds. You answer me now, or I'll fry a hole through your head."

"That seems to be the Terranist answer to everything; can't get an answer, fry a hole in somebody's head. Can't go back to Earth, wipe out the damned human race. . . ."

"Shut up and listen. What's in that case is something that will make megabug look like a case of diaper rash by comparison. . . ."

"That should get some attention, Vegler. . . ."

"You're damned right it will! But, there's something else. The bug Kit and Doc Towne cooked up takes from two to four months to kill, and no one on Earth knows a cure for it. Even if they did, it would take them two or three months to begin production. . . ."

"My god, Vegler . . ."

"Listen. We have a cure; another organism that can compete successfully with the first. We have enough of it stashed away in abandoned mine shafts right now to immunize everyone on Earth. When we go back to Earth, we'll bring it with us."

"Blackmail."

"Yes. You have a better solution?"

"Why are you telling me this?"

"Lambert, we need time—eight or ten days for the organism to spread. If they know what's going on, they'll be able to contain it at the New Eden station. . . ."

I laughed, then stopped as I felt the loose ends of a couple of ribs grind together. "What is it, Vegler? You want me to keep my mouth shut, is that it?"

"Yes."

"Why don't you just shut it?"

Vegler seemed to have the same look on his face that he had when he touched the old woman's cheek back in the boneyard. "I don't want to kill you, Lambert. Someday, when it's a time for law again, we'll need people with your naïve abhorrence of violence."

"How do you expect me to keep quiet? My god, even if they do finally agree, you know how long that would take? You know how slowly governments work."

"Why should we be the only ones who have to pay for the government's inertia?"

Breathing came very hard. Someone ran by Vegler and tapped him on the helmet as he passed. "Vegler, how do I know you have a cure? . . ." Pieces of rock showered down on us. The lockwatchers were closing in.

"Kit—" Vegler teetered, then fell over on top of me. "On the road—"
A loud ringing in my helmet, we were both lifted up, then slammed hard.

VI.

I opened my eyes, the memory of rotted leaves and hand cream still in my
nostrils. I felt ill and Kit had taken my air hose. . . . But, was that proof?
The white haze in front of my eyes swam, then shaped itself into a face.
"Lambert?"

"Who are you?" I whispered.

The face turned. "Captain, I think he can talk now."

The first face left and another took its place. "I'm Captain Manion, Lambert.
It's a real stroke you made it alive. The Terranists usually aren't that careless."

"Manion? Are you with the police?"

"Yes. I hate to question you now, but I have no other choice. What were
they doing at the mass drivers? They know that if they mess with the drivers,
we'll cut the air off to one of the residential galleries."

"Cut the air?"

"Yes. It sounds harsh, but we have to protect the drivers. Both Earth and
the New Eden station depend on them." Manion must have seen the look on
my face. "We wouldn't do it to production workers or anything vital; just
one of the boneyards. You know, they're only carriers." He turned away
and came back holding a small red plastic box. It was the signal coder and the
pickup light was still off. The case was still in the dirt track. "You know what
this is?"

I looked at the ten numbered keys. All I had to do was punch in four-four-
three and the pickup would be aborted. That's all. "I don't know, Captain. It
looks like a pocket calculator."

Manion raised his eyebrows and shrugged, then turned to the other one. "All
right, doctor, you can have him back." He left the compartment. It lurched;
we were in a police van.

The doctor's face swam into view. "Sorry we can't get you back to Earth right
away, Lambert, but you're pretty banged up. We'll probably keep you for two
weeks or so."

I closed my eyes. "That should be time enough."

"Enough for what?"

I opened my eyes and looked at the doctor. "The Terranists are planning an
announcement about then."

"Oh?" The doctor peered at a plastic sack filled with clear liquid that drained
from a tube into my arm. "More demands?"

I bit my lip and closed my eyes to force back the tears. "It's a surprise."
Vegler at the interview: *"There are no innocents, Lambert. If because you do
nothing, nothing is done, you are guilty. There is a time for terror. Perhaps
you will come to understand this. . . ."* I laughed. "Where's Rudy Vegler?"

The doctor nodded toward the back of the compartment.   Stacked like cordwood, the five Terranists, still in their torn, filthy blood-caked surface suits, jiggled with the motion of the police rover across the Lunar landscape.   On the bottom, nearest me, Rudy Vegler stared at me through a shattered faceplate with empty sockets. His skin was purple—almost black.   "We got all of them."

I looked back at the doctor.   "Not all.   There's still a few left."

The doctor shrugged.   "Ten or fifteen?   Might as well be all.   How can a dozen fanatics fight the entire world?"   The doctor patted my arm, turned and left the compartment.

"As I said, doctor, it's a surprise."   My voice sounded tinny in the empty compartment.   The tears began to flow freely and I turned my head toward the pile of dead Terranists.   "Damn you.   Damn you, damn you, damn you!"

SALLY A. SELLERS

Perchance to Dream

From the playground came the sound of laughter.

A gusty night wind was sweeping the park, and the light at the edge of the picnic grounds swung crazily. Distorted shadows came and went, rushing past as the wind pushed the light to the end of its arc, then sliding back jerkily.

Again the laughter rang out, and this time Norb identified the creaking sound that accompanied it. Someone was using the swing. Nervously he peered around the swaying branches of the bush, but he saw no one.

He heard a click. Danny had drawn his knife. Hastily Norb fumbled for his own. The slender weapon felt awkward in his hand, even after all the hours of practice.

"It'll be easy," Danny had said. "There's always some jerk in the park after dark—they never learn." Norb shivered and gripped the knife more tightly.

Then he saw them—a young couple walking hand in hand among the trees. Danny chuckled softly, and Norb relaxed somewhat. Danny was right—this would be a cinch.

"You take the girl," Danny whispered.

Norb nodded. All they had to do was wait—the couple was headed right toward them. They were high school kids, no more than fifteen or sixteen, walking slowly with their heads together, whispering and giggling. Norb swallowed and tensed himself.

"Now!" Danny hissed.

They were upon them before the kids had time to react. Danny jerked the boy backward and threw him to the ground. Norb grabbed the back of the girl's collar and held his knife at her throat.

"Okay, just do what we say and nobody gets hurt," snarled Danny. He pointed his knife at the boy's face. "You got a wallet, kid?"

The boy stared in mute terror at the knife. The girl made small whimpering sounds in her throat, and Norb tightened his hold on her collar.

"Come on, come on! Your wallet!"

From somewhere in the shadows, a woman's voice rang out. "Leave them alone!"

Norb whirled as a dark form charged into Danny and sent him sprawling. Oh God, he thought, we've been caught! As the boy leaped to his feet and started to run, Norb made a little swipe at him with his knife.   His grip on the girl must have relaxed, because she jerked free and followed the boy into the woods.

Norb looked from the retreating kids to the two wrestling figures, his hands clenched in indecision.   The dark form had Danny pinned to the ground.   He was squirming desperately, but he couldn't free himself.   "Get her off me!" he cried.

"Jesus!" Norb whispered helplessly.   The kids had begun to scream for help. They'd rouse the whole neighborhood.

"Norb!" screamed Danny.

It was a command, and Norb hurled himself onto the woman.   Twice he stabbed wildly at her back, but she only grunted and held on more tightly.   He struck out again, and this time his knife sank deeply into soft flesh.   Spurting blood soaked his hand and sleeve, and he snatched them away in horror.

Danny rolled free.   He got to his feet, and the two of them stood looking down at the woman.   The knife was buried in the side of her throat.

"Oh my God," whimpered Norb.

"You ass!" cried Danny.   "Why didn't you just pull her off?   You killed her!"

Norb stood paralyzed, staring down at the knife and the pulsing wound.   Fear thickened in his throat, and he felt his stomach constrict.   He was going to be sick.

"You better run like hell.   You're in for it now."

Danny was gone.   Norb wrenched his gaze from the body.   On the other side of the playground, the kids were still calling for help.   He saw lights up by the gate, swinging into the park drive.

Norb began to run.

The gush of blood from the wound slowed abruptly and then stopped.   The chest heaved several times with great intakes of air.   Then it collapsed, and a spasm shook the body.   In the smooth motion of a slowly tightening circle, it curled in on itself.   The heart gave three great beats, hesitated, pumped once more, and was still.

Norb caught up with Danny at the edge of the woods.   They stopped, panting, and looked in the direction of the car.   It had come to a stop by the tennis courts, and, as they watched, the driver cut his motor and turned off his lights.

"This way," whispered Danny.   "Come on."

As they headed across the road for the gate, the car's motor suddenly started. Its lights came on, and it roared into a U-turn to race after them.

"It's the cops!" Danny yelled.   "Split up!"

Norb was too frightened.   Desperately he followed Danny, and the pair of them fled through the gate and turned along the street as the patrol car swung around the curve.   Then Danny veered off, and Norb followed him through bushes and into a back yard.   A dog began yelping somewhere.   Danny scaled a fence and dropped into the adjoining back yard, and Norb followed, landing roughly and falling to his knees.

He scrambled to his feet and collided with Danny, who was laughing softly as he watched the patrol car. It had turned around and was headed back into the park.

The heart had not stopped. It was pumping—but only once every six minutes, with a great throb. At each pulse, a pinprick of light danced across the back of the eyelids. The wound attempted to close itself and tightened futilely around the intrusion of steel. A neck muscle twitched. Then another, but the knife remained. The tissue around the blade began contracting minutely, forcing it outward in imperceptible jerks.

Officer Lucas parked near the playground and started into the trees. He could not have said what he was looking for, but neighbors had reported hearing cries for help, and the way those two punks had run told him they'd been up to something. He switched on his flashlight, delineating an overturned litter basket that had spewed paper across the path. The gusting wind tore at it, prying loose one fluttering fragment at a time. Cautiously he walked forward. Gray-brown tree trunks moved in and out of the illumination as he crept on, but he could see nothing else.

He stumbled over an empty beer bottle, kicked it aside, and then stopped uncertainly, pivoting with his light. It revealed nothing but empty picnic tables and cold barbecue grills, and he was about to turn back when his beam picked out the body, curled motionless near a clump of bushes. Lucas ran forward and knelt beside the woman, shining his light on her face.

The throat wound seemed to have stopped bleeding, but if the knife had sliced the jugular vein—he leaned closer to examine the laceration. Belatedly a thought occurred to him, and he reached for the wrist. There was no pulse. He shone his light on the chest, but it was motionless.

Lucas got to his feet and inspected the area hastily. Seeing no obvious clues, he hurried back to the patrol car.

The heart throbbed again, and another pinprick of light jumped behind the woman's eyelids. The tissues in the neck tightened further as new cells developed, amassed, and forced the blade a fraction of an inch outward. The wound in the back, shallow and clean, had already closed. The lungs expanded once with a great intake of air. The knife jerked again, tilted precariously, and finally fell to the ground under its own weight. Immediately new tissue raced to fill the open area.

The radio was squawking. Lucas waited for the exchange to end before picking up the mike. "Baker 23."

"Go ahead, Baker 23."

"I'm at Newberry Park, east end, I've got a 409 and request M.E."

"Confirmed, 23."

"Notify the detective on call."

"Clear, 23."

"Ten-four." He hung up the mike and glanced back into the woods. Probably an attempted rape, he thought. She shouldn't have fought. The lousy punks! Lucas rubbed his forehead fretfully. He should have chased them, dammit. Why hadn't he?

The heart was beating every three minutes now. The throat wound had closed, forming a large ridge under the dried blood. Cells multiplied at fantastic rates, spanning the damaged area with a minute latticework. This filled in as the new cells divided, expanded, and divided again.

Lucas reached for his clipboard and flipped on the interior lights. He glanced into the trees once before he began filling in his report. A voice crackled on the radio, calling another car. His pen scratched haltingly across the paper.

The heart was returning to its normal pace. The ridge on the neck was gone, leaving smooth skin. A jagged pattern of light jerked across the retinas. The fugue was coming to an end. The chest rose, fell, then rose again. A shadow of awareness nudged at consciousness.

The sound of the radio filled the night again, and Lucas turned uneasily, searching the road behind him for approaching headlights. There were none. He glanced at his watch and then returned to the report.

She became aware of the familiar prickling sensation in her limbs, plus a strange burning about her throat. She felt herself rising, rising—and suddenly awareness flooded her. Her body jerked, uncurled. Jeanette opened her eyes. Breathing deeply, she blinked until the dark thick line looming over her resolved itself into a tree trunk. Unconsciously her hand began to rub her neck, and she felt dry flakes come off on her fingers.

Wearily she closed her eyes again, trying to remember: Those kids. One had a knife. She was in the park. Then she heard the faint crackle of a police radio. She rolled to her knees, and dizziness swept over her. She could see a light through the trees. Good God, she thought, he's right over there!

Jeanette rubbed her eyes and looked about her. She was lightheaded, but there was no time to waste. Soon there would be other police—and doctors. She knew. Moving unsteadily, at a crouch, she slipped away into the woods.

Four patrol cars were there when the ambulance arrived. Stuart Crosby, the medical examiner, climbed out slowly and surveyed the scene. He could see half a dozen flashlights in the woods. The photographer sat in the open door of one of the cars, smoking a cigarette.

"Where's the body?" asked Crosby.

The photographer tossed his cigarette away disgustedly. "They can't find it."

"Can't find it? What do you mean?"

"It's not out there.   Lucas says it was in the woods, but when Kelaney got here, it was gone."

Puzzled, Crosby turned toward the flashlights.   As another gust of wind swept the park, he pulled his light coat more closely about him and started forward resignedly—a tired white-haired man who should have been home in bed.

He could hear Detective Kelaney roaring long before he could see him.   "You half-ass!   What'd it do, walk away?"

"No, sir!" answered Lucas hotly.   "She was definitely dead.   She was lying right there, I swear it—and that knife was in her throat, I recognize the handle."

"Yeah?   For a throat wound, there's not much blood on it."

"Maybe," said Lucas stubbornly, "but that's where it was, all right."

Crosby halted.   He had a moment of disorientation as uneasy memories stirred in the back of his mind.   A serious wound, but not much blood . . . a dead body that disappeared . . .

"Obviously she wasn't dragged," said Kelaney.   "Did you by chance, *Officer* Lucas, think to check the pulse?   Or were you thinking at all?"

"Yes, sir!   Yes, I did!   I checked the pulse, and there was nothing!   Zero respiration, too.   Yes, sir, I did!"

"Then where *is* she?" screamed Kelaney.

Another officer approached timidly.   "There's nothing out there, sir.   Nothing at all."

"Well, look again," snarled Kelaney.

Crosby moved into the circle of men.   The detective was running his hand through his hair in exasperation.   Lucas was red-faced and defiant.

Kelaney reached for his notebook.   "All right, what did she look like?"

Lucas straightened, eager with facts.   "Twenty, twenty-two, Caucasian, dark hair, about five-six, hundred and twenty-five pounds . . ."

"Scars or distinguishing marks?"

"Yeah, as a matter of fact.   There were three moles on her cheek—on her left cheek—all right together, right about here."   He put his finger high on his cheekbone, near his eye.

Crosby felt the blood roar in his ears.   He stepped forward.   "What did you say, Lucas?" he asked hoarsely.

Lucas turned to the old man.   "Three moles, doctor, close together, on her cheek."

Crosby turned away, his hands in his pockets.   He took a deep breath.   He'd always known she'd return some day, and here was the same scene, the same bewildered faces, the same accusations.   Three moles on her cheek . . . it had to be.

The wind ruffled his hair, but he no longer noticed its chill.   They would find no body.   Jeanette was back.

The next morning, Crosby filed a Missing Persons Report.   "Send out an APB," he told the sergeant.   "We've got to find her."

The sergeant looked mildly surprised.   "What's she done?"

"She's a potential suicide. More than potential. I know this woman, and she's going to try to kill herself."

The sergeant reached for the form. "Okay, Doc, if you think it's that important. What's her name?"

Crosby hesitated. "She's probably using an alias. But I can give a description—an exact description."

"Okay," said the sergeant. "Shoot."

The bulletin went out at noon. Crosby spent the remainder of the day visiting motels, but no one remembered checking in a young woman with three moles on her cheek.

Jeanette saw the lights approaching in the distance: two white eyes and, above them, the yellow and red points along the roof that told her this was a truck. She leaned back against the concrete support of the bridge, hands clenched behind her, and waited.

It had been three nights since the incident in the park. Her shoulders sagged dejectedly at the thought of it. Opportunities like that were everywhere, but she knew that knives weren't going to do it. She'd tried that herself—was it in Cleveland? A painful memory flashed for a moment, of one more failure in the long series of futile attempts—heartbreaking struggles in the wrong cities. But here—

She peered around the pillar again. The eyes of the truck were closer now. Here, it could happen. Where it began, it could end. She inched closer to the edge of the support and crouched, alert to the sound of the oncoming truck.

It had rounded the curve and was thundering down the long straightaway before the bridge. Joy surged within her as she grasped its immensity and momentum. Surely this . . . ! Never had she tried it with something so large, with something beyond her control. Yes, surely this would be the time!

Suddenly the white eyes were there, racing under the bridge, the diesels throbbing, roaring down at her. Her head reared in elation. Now!

She leaped an instant too late, and her body was struck by the right fender. The mammoth impact threw her a hundred feet in an arch that spanned the entrance ramp, the guideposts, and a ditch, terminating brutally in the field beyond. The left side of her skull was smashed, her arm was shattered, and four ribs were caved in. The impact of the landing broke her neck.

It was a full quarter of a mile before the white-faced driver gained sufficient control to lumber to a halt. "Sweet Jesus," he whispered. Had he imagined it? He climbed out of the rig and examined the dented fender. Then he ran back to the cab and tried futilely to contact someone by radio who could telephone the police. It was 3 AM, and all channels seemed dead. Desperately he began backing along the shoulder.

Rushes of energy danced through the tissue. Cells divided furiously, bridging gulfs. Enzymes flowed; catalysts swept through protoplasm: coupling, breaking, then coupling again.   Massive reconstruction raged on.   The collapsed half of the body shifted imperceptibly.

The truck stopped a hundred feet from the bridge, and the driver leaped out. He clicked on his flashlight and played it frantically over the triangle of thawing soil between the entrance ramp and the expressway.   Nothing.   He crossed to the ditch and began walking slowly beside it.

Bundles of collagen interlaced; in the matrix, mineral was deposited; cartilage calcified.   The ribs had almost knit together and were curved loosely in their original crescent.   Muscle fibers united and contracted in taut arches.   The head jerked, then jerked again, as it was forced from its slackness into an increasingly firm position.   Flexor spasms twitched the limbs as impulses flowed through newly formed neurons.   The heart pulsed.

The driver stood helplessly on the shoulder and clicked off the flashlight.   It was 3:30, and no cars were in sight.   He couldn't find the body.   He had finally succeeded in radioing for help, and now all he could do was wait.   He stared at the ditch for a moment before moving toward the truck.   There *had* been a woman, he was sure.   He'd seen her for just an instant before the impact, leaping forward under the headlights.   He shuddered and quickened his pace to the cab.

Under the caked blood, the skin was smooth and softly rounded.   The heart was pumping her awake: Scratches of light behind the eyelids.   Half of her body prickling, burning . . .   A shuddering breath.

Forty-seven minutes after the impact, Jeanette opened her eyes.   Slowly she raised her head.   That line in the sky . . . the bridge.
She had failed again.   Even here.   She opened her mouth to moan, but only a rasping sound emerged.

Stuart Crosby swayed as the ambulance rounded a corner and sped down the street.   He pressed his knuckles against his mouth and screamed silently at the driver: God, hurry, I know it's her.
He had slept little since the night in the park.   He had monitored every call, and he knew that this one—a woman in dark clothes, jumping in front of a trucker's rig—this one had to be Jeanette.
It was her.   She was trying again.   Oh, God, after all these years, she was still trying.   How many times, in how many cities, had she fought to die?
They were on the bridge now, and he looked down on the figures silhouetted against the red of the flares.   The ambulance swung into the entrance ramp with a final whoop and pulled up behind a patrol car.   Crosby had the door open and his foot on the ground before they were completely stopped, and he had to clutch at the door to keep from falling.   A pain flashed across his back.   He regained his balance and ran toward a deputy who was playing a flashlight along the ditch.

"Did you find her?"

The deputy turned and took an involuntary step away from the intense, stooped figure. "No, sir, doctor. Not a thing."

Crosby's voice failed him. He stood looking dejectedly down the expressway.

"To tell you the truth," said the deputy, nodding at the semi, "I think that guy had a few too many little white pills. Seeing shadows. There's nothing along here but a dead raccoon. And he's been dead since yesterday."

But Crosby was already moving across the ditch to the field beyond, where deputies swung flashlights in large arcs and a German shepherd was snuffling through the brittle stubble.

Somewhere near here, Jeanette might be lying with a broken body. It was possible, he thought. The damage could have been great, and the healing slow. Or—a chill thought clutched at him. He shook his head. No. She wouldn't have succeeded. She would still be alive, somewhere. If he could just see her, talk to her!

There was a sharp, small bark from the dog. Crosby hurried forward frantically. His foot slipped and he came down hard, scraping skin from his palm. The pain flashed again in his back. He got to his feet and ran toward the circle of deputies.

One of the men was crouched, examining the cold soil. Crosby ran up, panting, and saw that the ground was stained with blood. She'd been here. She'd been here!

He strained to see across the field and finally discerned, on the other side, a road running parallel to the expressway. But there were no cars parked on it. She was gone.

After he returned home, his body forced him to sleep, but his dreams allowed him no rest. He kept seeing a lovely young woman, with three moles on her cheek—a weeping, haunted, frantic woman who cut herself again and again and thrust the mutilated arm before his face for him to watch in amazement as the wounds closed, bonded, and healed to smoothness before his eyes. In minutes.

God, if she would only stop crying, stop pleading with him, stop begging him to find a way to make her die—to use his medical knowledge somehow, in some manner that would end it for her. She wanted to die. She hated herself, hated the body that imprisoned her.

How old was she then? How many years had that youthful body endured without change, without aging? How many decades had she lived before life exhausted her and she longed for the tranquility of death?

He had never found out. He refused to help her die, and she broke away and fled hysterically into the night. He never saw her again. There followed a series of futile suicide attempts and night crimes with the young woman victim mysteriously missing—and then . . . nothing.

And now she was back. Jeanette!

He found himself sitting up in bed, and he wearily buried his face in his hands. He could still hear the sound of her crying. He had always heard it, in a small corner of his mind, for the last thirty years.

                              *   *   *

The street sign letters were white on green: HOMER.   Jeanette stood for a long while staring at them before she turned to walk slowly along the crumbling sidewalk. A vast ache filled her chest as she beheld the familiar old houses.

The small, neat lawns had been replaced by weeds and litter.   Bricks were missing out of most of the front walks.   The fence was gone at the Mahews'.   Jim Mahew had been so proud the day he brought home his horseless carriage, and she'd been the only one brave enough to ride in it.   Her mother had been horrified.

This rambling old home with the boarded up windows was the Parkers'.   The house was dead now.   So was her playmate, Billy Parker—the first boy she knew to fight overseas and the first one to die.   The little house across the street had been white when old Emma Walters lived there.   She had baked sugar cookies for Jeanette, and Jeanette had given her a May basket once, full of violets.   She must have died a long time ago.   Jeanette's hand clenched.   A very long time ago.

The sound of her steps on the decayed sidewalk seemed extraordinarily loud. The street was deserted.   There was no movement save that of her own dark figure plodding steadily forward.   Here was Cathy Carter's house.   Her father had owned the buggywhip factory over in Capville.   They'd been best friends.   Cathy, who always got her dresses dirty, had teeth missing, cut off her own braids one day. There was that Sunday they'd gotten in trouble for climbing the elm tree—but there was no elm now, only an ugly stump squatting there to remind her of a Sunday that was gone, lost, wiped out forever.   She'd heard that Cathy had married a druggist and moved out East somewhere.   Jeanette found herself wondering desperately if Cathy had raised any children.   Or grandchildren.   Or great-grandchildren.   Cathy Carter, did you make your little girls wear dresses and braids? Did you let them climb trees?   Are you still alive?   Or are you gone, too, like everything else that ever meant anything to me?

Her steps faltered, but her own house loomed up ahead to draw her on.   It stood waiting, silently watching her approach.   It, too, was dead.   A new pain filled her when she saw the crumbling porch, saw that the flowerboxes were gone, saw the broken windows and the peeling wallpaper within.   A rusted bicycle wheel lay in the weeds that were the front yard, along with a box of rubble and pile of boards. Tiny pieces of glass crunched sharply beneath her feet.   The hedge was gone.   So were the boxwood shrubs, the new variety from Boston—her mother had waited for them for so long and finally got them after the war.

She closed her eyes.   Her mother had never known.   Had died before she realized what she had brought into the world.   Before even Jeanette had an inkling of what she was.

A monster.   A freak.   This body was wrong, horribly wrong.   It should not be.

She had run away from this town, left it so that her friends would never know. But still it pulled at her, drawing her back every generation, pushing itself into her thoughts until she could stand it no longer.   Then she would come back to stare at the old places that had been her home and the old people who had been her friends.   And they didn't recognize her, never suspected, never knew why she seemed so strangely familiar.

Once she had even believed she could live here again. The memory ached within her and she quickened her pace. She could not think of him, could not allow the sound of his name in her mind. Where was he now? Had he ever understood? She had run away that time, too.

She'd had to. He was so good, so generous, but she was grotesque, a vile caprice of nature. She loathed the body.

It was evil. It must be destroyed.

Here, in the city where it was created: Where she was born, she would die. Somehow.

The phone jangled harshly, shattering the silence of the room with such intensity that he jumped and dropped a slide on the floor. He sighed and reached for the receiver. "Crosby."

"Doctor, this is Sergeant Andersen. One of our units spotted a woman fitting the description of your APB on the High Street Bridge."

"Did they get her?" demanded Crosby.

"I dunno yet. They just radioed in. She was over the railing—looked like she was ready to jump. They're trying to get to her now. Thought you'd like to know."

"Right," said Crosby, slamming down the receiver. He reached for his coat as his mind plotted out the fastest route to High Street. Better cut down Fourth, he thought, and up Putnam. The slide crackled sharply under his heel and he looked at it in brief surprise before running out the door.

They've found her, he thought elatedly. They've got Jeanette! Thank God— I must talk with her, must convince her that she's a miracle. She has the secret of life. The whole human race will be indebted to her. Please, please, he prayed, don't let her get away.

He reached the bridge and saw the squad car up ahead. Gawkers were driving by slowly, staring out of their windows in morbid fascination. Two boys on bicycles had stopped and were peering over the railing. An officer had straddled it and was looking down.

Crosby leaped from the car and ran anxiously to the railing. His heart lifted as he saw another officer, with one arm around the lower railing and a firm grip on Jeanette's wrist. He was coaxing her to take a step up.

"Jeanette!" It was a ragged cry.

"Take it easy, Doc," said the officer straddling the railing. "She's scared."

The woman looked up. She was pale, and the beauty mark on her cheek stood out starkly. The bitter shock sent Crosby reeling backward. For a moment he felt dizzy, and he clutched the rail with trembling fingers. The gray river flowed sullenly beneath him.

It wasn't Jeanette.

"Dear God," he whispered. He finally raised his gaze to the dismal buildings that loomed across the river. Then where was she? She must have tried again. Had she succeeded?

*   *   *

Chief Dolenz clasped, then unclasped his hands. "You've got to slow down, Stu. You're pushing yourself far too hard."

Crosby's shoulders sagged a little more, but he did not answer.

"You're like a man possessed," continued the Chief. "It's starting to wear you down. Ease up, for God's sake. We'll find her. Why all this fuss over one loony patient? Is it that important?"

Crosby lowered his head. He still couldn't speak. The Chief looked with puzzlement at the old man, at the small bald spot that was beginning to expand, at the slump of the body, the rumpled sweater, the tremor of the hands as they pressed together. He opened his mouth but could not bring himself to say more.

"Citizens National Bank," the switchboard operator said.

The voice on the line was low and nervous. "I'm gonna tell you this once, and only once. There's a bomb in your bank, see? It's gonna go off in ten minutes. If you don't want nobody hurt, you better get 'em outta there."

The operator felt the blood drain from her face. "Is this a joke?"

"No joke, lady. You got ten minutes. If anybody wants to know, you tell 'em People for a Free Society are starting to take action. Got that?" The line went dead.

She sat motionless for a moment, and then she got unsteadily to her feet. "Mrs. Calkins!" she called. The switchboard buzzed again, but she ignored it and ran to the manager's desk.

Mrs. Calkins looked up from a customer and frowned icily at her; but when the girl bent and whispered in her ear, the manager got calmly to her feet. "Mr. Davison," she said politely to her customer, "we seem to have a problem in the bank. I believe the safest place to be right now would be out of the building." Turning to the operator, she said coolly, "Notify the police."

Mr. Davison scrambled to his feet and began thrusting papers into his briefcase. The manager strode to the center of the lobby and clapped her hands with authority. "Could I have your attention please! I'm the manager. We are experiencing difficulties in the bank. I would like everyone to move quickly but quietly out of this building and into the street. Please move some distance away."

Faces turned toward her, but no one moved.

"Please," urged Mrs. Calkins. "There is immediate danger if you remain in the building. Your transactions may be completed later. Please leave at once."

People began to drift toward the door. The tellers looked at each other in bewilderment and began locking the money drawers. A heavyset man remained stubbornly at his window. "What about my change?" he demanded.

The operator hung up the phone and ran toward the doorway. "Hurry!" she cried. "There's a bomb!"

"A bomb!"

"She said there's a bomb!"

"Look out!"

"Get outside!"

There was a sudden rush for the door. "Please!" shouted the manager. "There is no need for panic." But her voice was lost in the uproar.

Jeanette sat limply at the bus stop, her hands folded in her lap, her eyes fixed despondently on the blur of passing automobile wheels. The day was oppressively overcast; gray clouds hung heavily over the city. When the chill wind blew her coat open, she made no move to gather it about her.

Behind her, the doors of the bank suddenly burst open, and people began to rush out frantically. The crowd bulged into the street. Brakes squealed; voices babbled excitedly. Jeanette turned and looked dully toward the bank.

There were shouts. Passing pedestrians began to run, and the frenzied flow of people from the bank continued. A woman screamed. Another tripped and nearly fell. Sirens sounded in the distance.

Above the hubbub, Jeanette caught a few clearly spoken words. "Bomb . . . in the bank . . ." She got slowly to her feet and began to edge her way through the crowd.

She had almost reached the door before anyone tried to stop her. A man caught at her sleeve. "You can't go in there, lady. There's a bomb!"

She pulled free, and a fresh surge of pedestrians came between them. The bank doors were closed, now. Everyone was outside and hurrying away. Jeanette pushed doubtfully at the tall glass door; pushed it open further, and slipped inside. It closed with a hiss, blocking out the growing pandemonium in the street. The lobby seemed warm and friendly, a refuge from the bitterly cold wind.

She turned and looked through the door. A policeman had appeared and the man who had tried to stop her was talking with him and pointing at the bank. Jeanette quickly moved back out of sight. She walked the length of the empty room, picked out a chair for herself, and sat down. The vast, unruffled quiet of the place matched the abiding peace she felt within her.

Outside, the first police car screamed to the curb. An ambulance followed, as the explosion ripped through the building, sending a torrent of bricks and glass and metal onto the pavement.

"Code blue, emergency room." The loudspeaker croaked for the third time as Julius Beamer rounded the corner. Ahead of him he could see a woman being wheeled into room three. An intern, keeping pace with the cart, was pushing on her breastbone at one-second intervals.

Emergency room three was crowded. A nurse stepped aside as he entered and said, "Bomb exploded at the bank." A technician was hooking up the EKG, while a young doctor was forcing a tube down the woman's trachea. A resident had inserted an IV and called for digoxin.

"Okay," said Dr. Beamer to the intern thumping the chest. The intern stepped back, exhausted, and Beamer took over the external cardiac massage. The respirator hissed into life. Beamer pressed down.

There was interference. Excess oxygen was flooding the system. A brief hesitation, and then the body adjusted. Hormones flooded the bloodstream, and the cells began dividing again. The site of the damage was extensive, and vast reconstruction was necessary. The heart pulsed once.

There was a single blip on the EKG, and Beamer grunted. He pushed again. And then again, but the flat high-pitch note continued unchanged. Dr. Channing was at his elbow, waiting to take over, but Beamer ignored him. Julius Beamer did not like failure. He called for the electrodes. A brief burst of electricity flowed into the heart. There was no response. He applied them again.

The reconstruction was being hindered: there was cardiac interference. The body's energies were diverted toward the heart in an effort to keep it from beating. The delicate balance had to be maintained, or the chemicals would be swept away in the bloodstream.

A drop of sweat trickled down Julius Beamer's temple. He called for a needle and injected epinephrine directly into the heart.

Chemical stimulation: hormones activated and countered immediately.

There was no response. The only sounds in the room were the long hissssssss-click of the respirator and the eerie unchanging note of the EKG. Dr. Beamer stepped back wearily and shook his head. Then he whirled in disgust and strode out of the room. A resident reached to unplug the EKG.

The interference had stopped. Reconstruction resumed at the primary site of damage.

Rounding the corner, Dr. Beamer heard someone call his name hoarsely, and he turned to see Stuart Crosby stumbling toward him.

"Julius! That woman!"

"Stuart! Hello! What are you—?"

"That woman in the explosion. Where is she?"

"I'm afraid we lost her—couldn't get her heart going. Is she a witness?"

In emergency room three, the respirator hissed to a stop. *The heart pulsed once.* But there was no machine to record it.

In the hallway, Crosby clutched at Dr. Beamer. "No. She's my wife."

Crosby's fists covered his eyes, his knuckles pressing painfully into his forehead. Outside, there was a low rumble of thunder. He swallowed with difficulty and dug his knuckles in deeper, trying to reason. How can I? he wondered. How can I say yes? Jeanette?

The figure behind him moved slightly and the woman cleared her throat. "Dr. Crosby, I know this is a difficult decision, but we haven't much time." She laid a gentle hand on his shoulder. "We've got forty-three people in this area who desperately need a new kidney. And there are three potential recipients for a heart upstairs—one is an eight-year-old girl. Please. It's a chance for someone else. A whole new life."

Crosby twisted away from her and moved to the window. No, he thought, we haven't much time. In a few minutes, she would get up off that table herself and walk into this room—and then it would be too late. She wanted to die. She had been trying to die for years—how many? Fifty? A hundred? If they took her organs, she *would* die. Not even that marvelous body could sustain the loss of the major organs. All he had to do was say yes. But how could he? He hadn't even seen her face yet. He could touch her again, talk to her, hold her. After thirty years!

As he looked out the window, a drop of rain splashed against the pane. He thought of the lines of a poem he had memorized twenty years before.

> *From too much love of living,*
> *From hope and fear set free,*
> *We thank with brief thanksgiving*
> *Whatever gods may be*
> *That no man lives forever,*
> *That dead men rise up never;*
> *That even the weariest river*
> *Winds somewhere safe to sea.*

The rain began to fall steadily, drumming against the window in a hollow rhythm. There was silence in the room, and for a brief moment, Crosby had the frightening sensation of being totally alone in the world.

A voice within him spoke the painful answer: Release her. Let her carry the burden no more. She is weary.

"Dr. Crosby . . ." The woman's voice was gentle.

"Yes!" he cried. "Do it! Take everything—anything you want. But God, please hurry!" Then he lowered his head into his hands and wept.

Grafton Medical Center was highly efficient. Within minutes, a surgeon was summoned and preparations had begun. The first organs removed were the kidneys. Then the heart. Later, the liver, pancreas, spleen, eyeballs, and thyroid gland were lifted delicately and transferred to special containers just above freezing temperature. Finally, a quantity of bone marrow was removed for use as scaffolding for future production of peripheral blood cellular components.

What had been Jeanette Crosby was wheeled down to the morgue.

The woman's voice was doubtful. "We usually don't allow relatives. You see, once the services are over . . ."

Stuart Crosby clutched his hat. "There were no services. I only want a few minutes."

The owner of the crematory, a burly, pleasant looking man, entered the outer office. "Can I do something for you, sir?"

The woman turned to him. "He wanted a little time with the casket, Mr. Gilbert. The one that came over from the hospital this morning."

"Please," Crosby pleaded. "There were no services—I didn't want any, but I just—I didn't realize there'd be no chance to say goodbye. The hospital said she was sent here, and . . . I'm a doctor. Dr. Stuart Crosby. She's my wife. Jeanette Crosby. I didn't think until today that I wanted to . . ." He trailed off and lowered his head.

The owner hesitated.   "We usually don't allow this, doctor.   We have no facilities here for paying the last respects."

"I know," mumbled Crosby.   "I understand—but just a few minutes—please."

The manager looked at the secretary, then back to the old man.   "All right, sir. Just a moment, and I'll see if I can find a room.   If you'll wait here, please."

The casket was cream-colored pine.   It was unadorned.   The lid was already sealed, so he could not see her face.   But he knew it would be at peace.

He stood dry-eyed before the casket, his hands clasped in front of him.   Outside, the rain that had begun the day before was still drizzling down.   He could think of nothing to say to her, and he was only aware of a hollow feeling in his chest. He thought ramblingly of his dog, and how he hadn't made his bed that morning, and about the broken windshield wiper he would have to replace on his car.

Finally he turned and walked from the room, bent over a bit because his back hurt.   "Thank you," he said to the owner.   Stepping outside into the rain, he very carefully raised his umbrella.

The owner watched him until the car pulled onto the main road.   Then he yelled, "Okay Jack!"

Two men lifted the casket and bore it outside in the rain toward the oven.

Cells divided, differentiated, and divided again.   The reconstruction was almost complete.   It had taken a long time, almost twenty-four hours.   The body had never been challenged to capacity before.   Removal of the major organs had caused much difficulty, but regeneration had begun almost at once, and the new tissues were now starting the first stirrings of renewed activity.

The casket slid onto the asbestos bricks with a small scraping noise.   The door clanged shut, and there was a dull ring as the bolt was drawn.

There was a flicker of light behind the eyelids, and the new retinas registered it and transmitted it to the brain.   The heart pulsed once, and then again.   A shuddering breath.

Outside the oven, a hand reached for the switches and set the master timer.   The main burner was turned on.   Oil under pressure flared and exploded into the chamber.

There was a shadow of awareness for a long moment, and then it was gone.

After thirty minutes, the oven temperature was nine hundred degrees Fahrenheit. The thing on the table was a third of its original size.   The secondary burners flamed on.   In another half hour, the temperature had reached two thousand degrees, and it would stay there for another ninety minutes.

The ashes, larger than usual, had to be mashed to a chalky, brittle dust.

As Dr. Kornbluth began easing off the dressing, she smiled at the young face on the pillow before her.

"Well, well.   You're looking perky today, Marie!" she said.

The little girl smiled back with surprising vigor.

"Scissors, please," said Dr. Kornbluth and held out her hand.

Dr. Roeber spoke from the other side of the bed.   "Her color is certainly good."

"Yes.   I just got the lab report, and so far there's no anemia."

"Has she been given the Prednisone today?"

"Twenty milligrams about an hour ago."

The last dressing was removed, and the two doctors bent over to examine the chest: the chest that was smooth and clean and faintly pink, with no scars, no lumps, no ridges.

"Something's wrong," said Dr. Kornbluth. "Is this a joke, Dr. Roeber?"

The surgeon's voice was frightened. "I don't understand it, not at all."

"Have you the right patient here?" She reached for the identification bracelet around Marie's wrist.

"Of course it's the right patient!" Dr. Roeber's voice rose. "I ought to know who I operated on, shouldn't I?"

"But it isn't possible!" cried Dr. Kornbluth.

The girl spoke up in a high voice. "Is my new heart okay?"

"It's fine, honey," said Dr. Kornbluth. Then she lowered her voice. "This is physiologically impossible! The incision has completely healed, without scar tissue. And in thirty-two hours, doctor? In thirty-two hours?"

BRIAN W. ALDISS

The Small Stones of Tu Fu

On the 20th day of the Fifth Month of Year V of Ta-li (which would be May in A.D. 770, according to the Old Christian calendar), I was taking a voyage down the Yangtse River with the aged poet Tu Fu.

Tu Fu was withered even then. Yet his words, and the spaces between his words, will never wither. As a person, Tu Fu was the most civilised and amusing man I ever met, which explains my long stay in that epoch. Ever since then, I have wondered whether the art of being amusing, with its implied detachment from self, is not one of the most undervalued requisites of human civilization. In many epochs, being amusing is equated with triviality. The human race rarely understood what was important; but Tu Fu understood.

Although the sage was ill, and little more than a bag of bones, he desired to visit White King again before he died.

"Though I fear that the mere apparition of my skinny self at a place named White King," he said, "may be sufficient for that apparition, the White Knight, to make his last move on me."

It is true that white is the Chinese colour of mourning, but I wondered if a pun could prod the spirits into action; were they so sensitive to words?

"What can a spirit digest but words?" Tu Fu replied. "I don't entertain the idea that spirits can eat or drink—though one hears of them whining at keyholes. They are forced to lead a tediously spiritual life." He chuckled.

This was even pronounced with spirit, for poor Tu Fu had recently been forced to give up drinking. When I mentioned that sort of spirit, he said, "Yes, I linger on life's balcony, ill and alone, and must not drink for fear I fall off."

Here again, I sensed that his remark was detached and not self-pitying, as some might construe it; his compassion was with all who aged and who faced death before they were ready—although, as Tu Fu himself remarked, "If we were not forced to go until we were ready, the world would be mountain-deep with the ill-prepared." I could but laugh at his turn of phrase.

When the Yangtse boat drew in to the jetty at White King, I helped the old man ashore. This was what we had come to see: the great white stones which progressed out of the swirling river and climbed its shores, the last of the contingent standing grandly in the soil of a tilled field.

I marvelled at the energy Tu Fu displayed. Most of the other passengers flocked round a refreshment-vendor who set up his pitch upon the shingle, or else climbed a belvedere to view the landscape at ease.   The aged poet insisted on walking among the monoliths.

"When I first visited this district as a young scholar, many years ago," said Tu Fu, as we stood looking up at the great bulk towering over us, "I was naturally curious as to the origin of these stones.   I sought out the clerk in the district office and enquired of him.   He said, 'The god called the Great Archer shot the stones out of the sky.   That is one explanation.   They were set there by a great king to commemorate the fact that the waters of the Yangtse flow East.   That is another explanation.   They were purely accidental.   That is a third explanation.'   So I asked him which of these explanations he personally subscribed to, and he replied, 'Why, young fellow, I wisely subscribe to all three, and shall continue to do so until more plausible explanations are offered.'   Can you imagine a situation in which caution and credulity, *coupled with extreme scepticism,* were more nicely combined?"   We both laughed.

"I'm sure your clerk went far."

"No doubt.   He had moved to the adjacent room even before I left his office. For a long while, I used to wonder about his statement that a great king had commemorated the fact that the Yangtse waters flowed East; I could only banish the idiocy from my mind by writing a poem about it."

I laughed.   Remembrance dawned.   I quoted it to him.

> *I need no knot in my robe*
> *To remember the Lady Li's kisses;*
> *Small kings commemorate rivers*
> *And are themselves forgotten.*

"There is real pleasure in poetry," responded Tu Fu, "when spoken so beautifully and remembered so appositely.   But you had to be prompted."

"I was prompt to deliver, sir."

We walked about the monoliths, watching the waters swirl and curdle and fawn round the base of a giant stone as they made their way through the gorges of the Yangtse down to the ocean.   Tu Fu said that he believed the monoliths to be a memorial set there by Chu-Ko Liang, demonstrating a famous tactical disposition by which he had won many battles during the wars of the Three Kingdoms.

"Are your reflections profound at moments like this?" Tu Fu asked, after a pause, and I reflected how rare it was to find a man, whether young or old, who was genuinely interested in the thoughts of others.

"What with the solidity of the stone and the ceaseless mobility of the water, I feel they should be profound.   Instead, my mind is obstinately blank."

"Come, come," he said chidingly, "the river is moving too fast for you to expect any reflection.   Now if it were still water. . ."

"It is still water even when it is moving fast, sir."

"There I must give you best, or give you up.   But, pray, look at the gravels here and tell me what you observe.   I am interested to know if we see the same things.''

Something in his manner told me that more was expected of me than jokes.   I looked along the shore, where stones of all kinds were distributed, from sand and grits to stones the size of a man's head, according to the disposition of current and tide.

"I confess I see nothing striking.   The scene is a familiar one, although I have never been here before.   You might come upon a little beach like this on any tidal river, or along the coasts by the Yellow Sea.''

Looking at him in puzzlement, I saw he was staring out across the flood, although he had confessed he saw little in the distance nowadays.   Because I sensed the knowledge stirring in him, my role of innocent had to be played more determindly than ever.

"Many thousands of people come to this spot every year,'' he said.   "They come to marvel at Chu-Ko Liang's giant stones, which are popularly known as 'The Eight Formations,' by the way.   Of course, what is big is indeed marvellous, and the act of marvelling is very satisfying to the emotions, provided one is not called upon to do it every day of the year.   But I marvel now, as I did when I first found myself on this spot, at a different thing.   I marvel at the stones on the shore.''

A light breeze was blowing, and for a moment I held in my nostrils the whiff of something appetizing, a crab-and-ginger soup perhaps, warming at the food-vendor's fire further down the beach, where our boat was moored.   Greed awoke a faint impatience in me, so that I thought, before humans are old, they should pamper their poor dear bodies, for the substance wastes away before the spirit, and was vexed to imagine that I had guessed what Tu Fu was going to say before he spoke.   I was sorry to think that he might confess to being impressed by mere numbers.   But his next remark surprised me.

"We marvel at the giant stones because they are unaccountable.   We should rather marvel at the little ones because they are accountable.   Let us walk upon them.''   I fell in with him and we paced over them: first a troublesome bank of grit, which grew larger on the seaward side of the bank.   Then a patch of almost bare sand.   Then, abruptly, shoals of pebbles, the individual members of which grew larger until we were confronted with a pile of lumpy stones which Tu Fu did not attempt to negotiate.   We went round it, to find ourselves on more sand, followed by well-rounded stones all the size of a man's clenched fist.   And they in turn gave way to more grit.   Our discomfort in walking—which Tu Fu overcame in part by resting an arm on my arm—was increased by the fact that these divisions of stones were made not only laterally along the beach but vertically up the beach, the demarcations in the latter division being frequently marked by lines of seaweed or of minute white shells of dead crustaceans.

"Enough, if not more than enough,'' said Tu Fu.   "Now do you see what is unusual about the beach?''

"I confess I find it a tiresomely *usual* beach,'' I replied, masking my thoughts.

"You observe how all the stones are heaped according to their size.''

"That too is usual, sir.   You will ask me to marvel next that students in class-rooms appear to be graded according to size."

"Ha!"   He stood and peered up at me, grinning and stroking his long white beard.   "But we agree that students are graded according to the wishes of the teacher.   Now, according to whose wishes are all these millions upon millions of pebbles graded?"

"Wishes don't enter into it.   The action of the water is sufficient, the action of the water, working ceaselessly and randomly.   The playing, one may say, of the inorganic organ."

Tu Fu coughed and wiped the spittle from his thin lips.

"Although you claim to be born in the remote future, which I confess seems to me unnatural, you are familiar with the workings of this natural world.   So, like most people, you see nothing marvellous in the stones hereabouts.   Supposing you were born—" he paused and looked about him and upwards, as far as the infirmity of his years would allow— "supposing you were born upon the moon, which some sages claim is a dead world, bereft of life, women, and wine. . .   If you then flew to this world and, in girdling it, observed everywhere stones, arranged in sizes as these are here.   Wherever you travelled, by the coasts of any sea, you saw that the stones of the world had been arranged in sizes.   What then would you think?"

I hesitated—Tu Fu was too near for comfort.

"I believe my thoughts would turn to crab-and-ginger soup, sir."

"No, they would not, not if you came from the moon, which is singularly devoid of crab-and-ginger soup, if reports speak true.   You would be forced to the con-clusion, the inevitable conclusion, that the stones of this world were being graded, like your scholars, by a superior intelligence."   He turned the collar of his padded coat up against the breeze, which was freshening.   "You would come to believe that that Intelligence was obsessive, that its mind was terrible indeed, filled only with the idea—not of language, which is human—but of number, which is inhuman. You would understand of that Intelligence that it was under an interdict to wander the world measuring and weighing every one of a myriad myriad single stones, sorting them all into heaps according to dimension.   Meaningless heaps, heaps without even particular decorative merit.   The farther you travelled, the more heaps you saw—the myriad heaps, each containing myriads of stones—the more alarmed you would become.   And what would you conclude in the end?"

Laughing with some anger, I said, "That it was better to stay at home."

"Possibly.   You would also conclude that it was *no use* staying at home. Because the Intelligence that haunted the earth was interested only in stones; that you would perceive.   From which it would follow that the Intelligence would be hostile to anything else and, in particular, would be hostile to anything which disturbed its handiwork."

"Such as human kind?"

"Precisely."   He pointed up the strand, where our fellow-voyagers were sitting on the shingle, or kicking it about, while their children were pushing stones into piles or flinging them into the Yangtse.   "The Intelligence—diligent, obsessive, methodical to a degree—would come in no time to be especially weary of human kind, who were busy turning what is ordered into what is random.''

Thinking that he was beginning to become alarmed by his own fancy, I said, ''It is a good subject for a poem, perhaps, but nothing more. Let us return to the boat. I see the sailors are going aboard.''

We walked along the beach, taking care not to disturb the stones. Tu Fu coughed as he walked.

''So you believe that what I say about the Intelligence that haunts the earth is nothing more than a fit subject for a poem?'' he said. He stooped slowly to pick up a stone, fitting his other hand in the small of his back in order to regain an upright posture. We both stood and looked at it as it lay in Tu Fu's withered palm. No man had a name for its precise shape, or even for the fugitive tints of cream and white and black which marked it out as different from all its neighbours. Tu Fu stared down at it and improvised an epigram.

> *The stone in my hand hides*
> *A secret natural history:*
> *Climates and times unknown,*
> *A river unseen.*

I held my hand out. ''You don't know it, but you have released that stone from the bondage of space and time. May I keep it?''

As he passed it over, and we stepped towards the refreshment vendor, Tu Fu said, more lightly, ''We take foul medicines to improve our health; so we must entertain foul thoughts on occasion, to strengthen wisdom. Can you nourish no belief in my Intelligence—you, who claim to be born in some remote future— which loves stones but hates human kind? Do I claim too much to ask you to suppose for a moment that I might be correct in my supposition . . .'' Evidently his thought wandered slightly, for he then said, after a pause, ''Is it within the power of one man to divine the secret nature of the world, or is even the whisper of that wish a supreme egotism, punishable by a visitation from the White Knight?''

''Permit me to get you a bowl of soup, sir.''

The vendor provided us with two mats to lay over the shingle. We unrolled them and sat to drink our crab-and-ginger soup. As he supped, with the drooling noises of an old man, the sage gazed far away down the restless river, where lantern sails moved distantly towards the sea, yellow on the yellow skyline. His previously cheerful, even playful, mood had slipped from him; I could perceive that, at his advanced age, even the yellow distance might be a reminder to him—perhaps as much reassuring as painful—that he soon must himself journey to a great distance. I recited his epigram to myself. ''Climates and times unknown, A river unseen.''

Children played round us. Their parents, moving slowly up the gangplank on to the vessel, called to them. ''Did you like the giant stones, venerable master?'' one of the boys asked Tu Fu, cheekily.

''I like them better than the battles they commemorate,'' replied Tu Fu. He stretched out a papery hand, and patted the boy's shoulder before the latter ran after his father.   I had remarked before the way in which the aged long to touch the young.

We also climbed the gangplank.   It was a manifest effort for Tu Fu.

Dark clouds were moving from the interior, dappling the landscape with moving shadow.   I took Tu Fu below, to rest in a little cabin we had hired for the journey. He sat on the bare bench, in stoical fashion, breathing flutteringly, while I thought of the battle to which he referred, which I had paused to witness some centuries earlier.

Just above our heads, the bare feet of the crew pattered on the deck.   There was a prolonged creaking as the gangplank was hoisted, followed by the rattle of the sail unfolding.   The wind caught the boat, every plank of which responded to that exhalation, and we started to glide forward with the Yangtse's great stone-shaping course towards the sea.   A harmony of motion caused the whole ship to come alive, every separate part of it rubbing against every other, as in the internal workings of a human when it runs.

I turned to Tu Fu.   His eyes went blank, his jaw fell open.   One hand moved to clutch his beard and then fell away.   He toppled forward—I managed to catch him before he struck the floor.   In my arms, he seemed to weigh nothing.   A muttered word broke from him, then a heavy shuddering sigh.

The White Knight had come, Tu Fu's spirit was gone.   I laid him upon the bench, looking down at his revered form with compassion.   Then I climbed upon deck.

There the crowd of travellers was standing at the starboard side, watching the tawny coast roll by, and crying out with some excitement.   But they fell silent, facing me attentively when I called to them.

"Friends, " I shouted.   "The great and beloved poet Tu Fu is dead."

A first sprinkle of rain fell from the west, and the sun became hidden by cloud.

Swimming strongly on my way back to what the sage called the remote future, my form began to flow and change according to time pressure.   Sometimes my essence was like steam, sometimes like a mountain.   Always I clung to the stone I had taken from Tu Fu's hand.

Back.   Finally I was back.   Back was an enormous expanse yet but a corner. All human kind had long departed.   All life had disappeared.   Only the great organ of the inorganic still played.   There I could sit on my world-embracing beach, eternally arranging and grading pebble after pebble.   From fine grit to great boulders, they could all be sorted as I desired.   In that occupation, I fulfilled the pleasures of infinity, for it was inexhaustible.

But the small stone of Tu Fu I kept apart.   Of all beings ever to exist upon the bounteous face of this world, Tu Fu had been nearest to me—I say "had been," but he forever *is*, and I return to visit him when I will.   For it was he who came nearest to understanding my existence by pure divination.

Even his comprehension failed.   He needed to take his perceptions a stage further and see how those same natural forces which create stones also create human beings.

The Intelligence that haunts the earth is not hostile to human beings.   Far from it—I regard them with the same affection as I do the smallest pebble.

Why, take this little pebble at my side!   I never saw a pebble like that before. The tint of this facet, here—isn't that unique?

I have a special bank on which to store it, somewhere over the other side of the world.   Only the little stone of Tu Fu shall not be stored away; small kings commemorate rivers, and this stone shall commemorate the immortal river of Tu Fu's thought.

SHARON N. FARBER

Born Again

*A*BSTRACT. *The historical condition vampirism is found to be caused by a microorganism which revamps the host's physiology and metabolism through negentropic processes. Evolution of the organism is conjectured and potential uses of the discovery suggested.*

TITLE. Haematophagic Adaptation in Homo Nosferatus, *with Notes upon the Geographical Distribution of Supergene-moderated Mimicking Morphs in* Homo Lycanthropus.

I'd forgotten the pitch black of a country road at night. Overhead, between the aisles of trees, you can see the stars; but otherwise it's the same as being blind. Totally different from the hospital where I'd just completed my residency, an oasis of fluorescent light in an urban jungle. You couldn't walk down the best lit streets in safety there. It felt good to be home, even just for a short vacation.

I walked by the feel of the asphalt under my feet. At the bend there'd be an almost subliminal glimmer of starlight on the mailbox at the foot of the drive to my family's farm. The halo of an approaching car rounded the bend, illuminating the road. I discovered I was standing directly in the center, and moved to the side of the road. Headlights washed over me. I shut my eyes to keep my nightsight.

The car hung a sharp left into the driveway of the old Riggen place, and stopped.

City-conditioned nerves made my heart pound faster.

The car door swung open, the overhead lighting up a seated man in his late twenties. He had dark hair and a bushy mustache.

"Are you lost?" he asked.

"No, I'm close enough to home to call the dog."

He chuckled, and his smile turned him handsome. "Don't be so paranoid. Hmmm . . . you must be the Sanger's famous daughter who went to the Big City to become a doctor."

"Guilty as accused. And you must be the Mad Scientist renting the Riggen spread."

"No, I'm just a humble masters in microbiology. Kevin Marlowe. My boss Auger is the mad scientist."

"*The* Auger?"

He flashed another grin. "Ah. Why don't you come to tea tomorrow, Doctor, and see."

AUTHORS. *Alastair Auger, Ph.D.*
  Kevin Marlowe, M.A.
  Mae Sanger, M.D.
Asterisk. *Funded by a grant from the Institute for the Study of Esoterica .*

INTRODUCTION. Recent advances in medicine have necessitated differentiating between clinical death, or cessation of heartbeat, and biological, or brain death. The distinction has been further complicated by the increasing use of heroic life support methodology.

History reports rare cases in which clinical death was not followed by biological death, but was maintained in status. The affected undead individuals were called Nosferati, or vampires. The authors' investigation of this phenomenon has led to the discovery of a causative microorganism, Pseudobacteria augeria.

"Dr. Sanger, Dr. Auger."

"Charmed." The great Professor Alastair Auger smiled down at me. He was tall, gray-haired but with dark eyebrows, somewhat out of shape, a couple of decades older than Marlowe and I. He had the clipped words, riveting eyes, and radiating intellect of the perfect lecturer.

He continued, "At last we meet someone in this semi-civilized intellectual backwash who at least aspires to the level of pseudo-science."

"You must come by sometime and see my herb-and-rattle collection," I replied.

He raised an eyebrow. "I understand that you've heard of me."

"Sure. Everyone knows about Professor Auger, brilliant—"

He preened.

"But nuts."

Auger said, "You see, Kevin? She has retained the delightful candor of the local rednecks, untempered by her exposure to the hypocritical milieu of higher education. She'll do fine."

My turn to raise an eyebrow.

The doorbell rang. Marlowe looked out the window and groaned. "Hell. It's Weems."

I followed his gaze. Leaning on the bell was a small ferret-faced man, with a gray suit and a loud tie.

Auger grimaced with pain and clutched his abdomen for a few seconds, then recovered. "I'll get rid of him. Take her on a tour of the lab."

METHODS AND MATERIALS. The Pseudobacteria augeria *was stored in isotonic saline solution kept at 37°C, at which temperature it is inactive. Titers of inactive* P. augeria *were injected into host animals, which were then sacrificed. After a critical period, depending on the number of injected pseudobacteria and the generations (Graph 1) necessary to achieve the species specific ratio of pseudobacterial kg body weight (Table A), the dead host animal was reanimated.   The mean latency was three days.   The dotted line indicates the threshold number of primary infecting pseudobacteria necessary to replicate sufficient progeny in order to reanimate the body before irreversible decay occurs.   In vivo, a number of vampiric attacks or "bites," ensuring a large founding colony, would increase chances of postmortem revivification.*

"Vampires?" I repeated, petting a white rabbit.   "Come on, we did that one in med school.   Funniest gag since Arlo left a piece of his cadaver in a confessional."

I looked around the lab, believing my eyes as little as Marlowe's story.   They'd turned an old farm house into a modern-day Castle Frankenstein.   Cages of lab animals faced a small computer, nestled amongst the centrifuges, particle counters, electron microscope, and spectrometers.   Automatic stirrers clacked away in the background.

Marlowe handed me a stethoscope.   "First, assure yourself that it works."

I put it over my fifth rib and heard a reassuring "lub dub lub dub."

"I'm alive."

"Try the rabbit."

No heartbeat.

I stared at it, snuffling in my hands.   Marlowe put out a saucer of what looked like blood.   The fluffy little bunny tore free of my hold, dove at the bowl, and began lapping up the red liquid.

"Okay, I believe you.   How?   I mean, its brain is obviously getting oxygenated or it wouldn't be hopping around.   But how does the blood circulate if the heart's not pumping?"

"We're not sure."   He waved at a garbage can.   There was a former rabbit inside.

"Were you dissecting it or dicing it?"

"Auger's a biochemist, and me . . . well, neither of us can even carve a roast."

"I see.   You need someone who feels at home with a scalpel, right?   Look, this is my first real vacation in seven years, and I have a job that starts back east in a month. . . ."

Weems and Auger entered the lab.

"I am certain, Mr. Weems, that even you will notice that we have not had recourse to the pawnshop," Auger said, gesturing expansively.

Weems pointed to a coffee mug sitting on the infrared spectrometer.   "Is that any way to treat the Foundation's equip—Who's she?"

"Our new associate," Auger said.

Weems looked at me contemptuously.

"You wanna see my credentials?"

He sneered.   "I think I see them."

I said, "You boys just got yourselves a surgeon."

The progressive effect of vampirism upon host physiology was studied in rats. One group was injected with a threshold number of P. augeria, *sacrificed, and placed in an incubation chamber held at 15°C to hasten replication.   Ninety-seven percent of the infected rats reanimated between 54 and 73 hours post-mortem. Specimens were sacrificed at intervals of 0, 6, 12, 24, etc., hours post-revivification, and the gross anatomy, pathology and serology studied.*

Another group of control rats was injected with normal saline, sacrificed, and placed in the 15°C incubation chamber.   These underwent classical necrotic decay, and were disposed of on the sixth day.

"Whew.   Smells like a charnel house," Marlowe said.   "How do you stand it?"

"It's obvious you never worked in an inner-city clinic, Kevin.   Or lived on a farm."   I pointed to the rat I had pinned open on the table and was dissecting under red light.

"See that?   They may not be using the heart as a pump, but it's still the crossroads of the circulatory system.   That must be why the old stake-in-the-heart routine works."

"Only as a temporary measure," Marlowe said.   "The microorganisms seem able to repair tissue.   Remember, the classical method of killing vampires is staking, followed closely by decapitation or burning."

"Mmm.   Stake, season well with garlic, and place in a hot oven until thoroughly cooked.   Look at those little buggies move."

"Please do not call my *Pseudobacteria augeria* 'buggies,' " Auger said, walking in on us.   He was good at that.

"Oh, you'll want to see this, sir," Marlowe said, handing the taller man an electronmicrograph.

"Beautiful!"

I stood on tiptoe to see.   The micrograph showed the bug, with its bacteria-like lack of a nucleus, its amoeba-like pseudopods and irregular cellular borders, and its just-plain-weird ribosome clusters and endoplasmic reticulum, plus some things not even Marlowe could identify.   There was a smooth, anucleate disc attached to the outer membrane.

"Wow!   That's got an erythrocyte hooked on!"

"I let them settle out instead of centrifuging," Marlowe said proudly.   "The spinning must dislodge the red blood cells from the surface."

"Well, that explains how the blood is transported," I said.   Auger lifted his eyebrow slightly, to signify intellectual condescension.

We heard a car drive up.

"Hell and damn!" Auger said.   "It must be Weems again."   He scowled and left the room.

"How about seeing the movie in town tonight, Mae?" Marlowe suggested.

"We've seen it, twice, unless you mean the new Disney over South-County."

"Lord, what a dull area.   How do you stand it?"

"Well, in three weeks—when I'm in a Manhattan emergency room and up to my ears in blood—I'll cherish these nice quiet memories.   Why don't we take a day off and drive down to the city—"

"Idiot!"

Outside in the garden, Professor Auger was shouting. We heard Weems shouting back. Marlowe and I ran out.

"It's revoked," Weems was yelling. The little man had ducked behind his car for protection. Auger looked mad enough to throttle him. His face was livid, and he was breathing as if he'd just run the four-minute mile. I didn't even want to imagine what his blood pressure was up to.

"Calm down, you'll give yourself a stroke," I said.

Weems turned to us triumphantly. "The Foundation's revoked the grant. We'll want a total accounting."

"You bastard!" Auger bellowed, and lunged across the car at Weems. He halted in mid-stride, a confused expression on his face, grabbed his stomach, and collapsed.

I leapt over and began examining him. He was pale and breathing rapidly, with a weak, racing pulse. Shock.

"Is it a heart attack?" Weems asked. The little rodent sounded happy.

Marlowe knelt on the other side. "What can I do?" he asked. I ripped open Auger's shirt and felt his abdomen. It was hot, pink and firm. Internal hemmorhage.

"Oh, Christ." I reached inside his pants and felt for the femoral pulse. There was none. "Well, that's it. Damn." I realized I was crying.

Auger stopped breathing, and Marlowe began mouth-to-mouth resuscitation. I reached to the neck and felt for the carotid pulse. It fluttered weakly and then faded.

"It's no use, Kevin. He's dead."

Weems chortled gleefully, jumped in his car, and sped up the driveway in reverse. Marlowe began external heart massage, anxiously doing it way too fast.

I pulled him off and shook his shoulders. "Stop it, Kevin. It won't help. Remember those stomach pains he had? It was an aneurysm, a weakness in the wall of his abdominal aorta. It burst, Kevin; he's bled to death internally. CPR won't help, dammit, nothing can."

"Ambulance, call a—"

"Listen. Even if they could get here within a half-hour, it wouldn't do any good. Look, Kevin, five minutes ago, if I'd had him on the table in a fully equipped operating room, with a good team, we could have tried a DeBakey graft. But the chances of saving him would have been maybe five percent."

Marlowe stood and stared down at the body. Then he turned and ran inside the house, leaving me with the corpse. Dead, Auger was devoid of charisma. His features were bloodless white; he looked like a horror waxwork. I closed his mouth and rearranged the clothes to give him more dignity.

Marlowe returned with a huge cardiac syringe and a bottle of milky liquid.

"You're crazy."

"It would work, Mae. We can bring him back. I centrifuged them down to a concentrate. There are enough pseudobacteria here to repair the damage and reanimate him almost immediately."

The implications were terrifying. Vampire rabbits were bizarre enough, but he was preparing to do it to a human being.

"You can save his life! Come on, do it."

Typical Marlowe, always leaving the decisions to someone else. I filled the syringe and plunged the six-inch needle deep into the blood-distended abdomen. Marlowe looked ill, and turned away. It was hard work pushing in the fluid. I pulled the needle out, and a small amount of blood welled up through the puncture. Two more syringes full and the bottle was empty.

We carried the body into the lab and packed it in ice to lower the body temperature quicker. Marlowe went away to vomit. I brewed some coffee and added a stiff jolt of medicinal Scotch.

"Here's to a fellow future inmate of Sing Sing," I toasted Marlowe.

Half an hour later we were feeling no pain.

"We'll have to buy him a black cape," I was saying. "Lessons in Transylvanian diction, too."

"I vant to suck your blood," Marlowe said, and leapt on me. We collapsed on the floor together, laughing.

The doorbell rang. Weems had returned with a sheriff's deputy.

"Hey, Fred!"

"Uh, hi Mae. Long time no see." The deputy looked embarrassed.

"We went to high school together," I announced to no one in particular.

"Sorry to have to disturb you, but this guy says you've got a stiff here."

Marlowe giggled from the floor. "A body? I don't see anybody." He adopted a stern voice. "The only thing dead around here is the night life in town."

Weems piped up with "They're drunk."

"Brilliant, Weems, an astonishing deduction," I cried.

"They've hidden the body! Alastair Auger was dead. She even said so." He pointed at me accusatorily.

"Remove your finger."

The deputy stepped between us. "Uh, I'm sorry Mae, uh, Doc, but I have to make a report."

"Professor Auger's not feeling well, Fred; he shouldn't be disturbed. Hey, you can believe me when I say he's alive. I'm a doctor. We're trained to know these things."

"They're faking. I won't leave until I see Auger's body."

"Yes, it is awe-inspiring. But I'm afraid you're just not my type, Weems."

Weems's face blanched at the sight of Auger, leaning in the doorway to the lab, and smiling malevolently at us all. He was glistening from the ice, and was wearing a towel.

"She's done something to him," Weems stuttered. "He was dead."

The deputy took Weems's elbow and propelled the little man out the door. "Sorry Mae, Professors—" He headed for the patrol car, saying "Okay, mister, there's a little matter of making false reports."

Marlowe laughed hysterically.

"If you hadn't woken up right then," I said, "you'd have woken up in the county morgue."

Auger said, "If you'll excuse me, this light is most unpleasant and I'm starving."

I offered to fetch him a pint of blood.

"Yes, please, Doctor.   I'm finding myself uncomfortably attracted to your neck."

RESULTS AND DISCUSSION.   The vampire is traditionally considered a body occupied by a demon.   We may now modify that picture to encompass a mammal, dead in that its heart does not beat and its body temperature is abnormally, indeed fatally, low, but still functioning as an organism due to the presence of a colony of symbiotes.   The pseudobacteria function as metabolizers and as transporters of oxygen, nutrients, and wastes, functions assumed in uninfected organisms by the circulatory and digestive systems.   P. augeria is a weak infective agent, requiring the special environment found after death, and susceptible to most common anti-bacterial drugs.   Folklore documents the vampire's aversion to garlic, a mild antibiotic.

The host physiology undergoes changes which seem to eliminate unnecessary systems and increase efficiency for vampiric adaptations.   These changes appear to be progressive, but must await long-term studies.

The first major change is the atrophy of the digestive tract.   Nutrients pass directly from the stomach to the blood-stream, with the concurrent necessity that only isotonic solutions be ingested, to avoid the osmotic destruction of the blood cells. As the only isotonic solution available in nature is blood, the vampire's fluid intake has traditionally been in this form.   An external blood source is also necessary for other reasons.   Because blood transport is pseudobacterial rather than hy-drostatic, and hence much slower, the body requires more red cells than can be produced by the host's bone marrow.

"All the great men are dead—myself, for instance."

"Breathe in," I replied.

Marlowe walked in, saw us, and blushed.   The longer I knew Kevin, the more I realized how anal retentive he could be.

"Am I interrupting?"

"Yes," Auger said.   When he spoke, I could see his sharp canine teeth.

"No.   Pass me that, yeah, the sphygmomanometer.   You don't realize what a pleasure it is to have a patient who doesn't complain about the stethoscope being cold."

I joked as I put on the blood pressure cuff, trying to hide the creepy feeling Auger gave me.   Intellectually, I knew he was the same man I'd met a week before, but emotionally I had problems relating to a patient with a current body temperature of 30°C—midway between what it should be, and the temperature of the room.   And because of the vagaries of his circulation, even in the warmest room Auger's hands felt like he'd been out in a snow storm without his mittens.

"Must we do this again?"   Auger winced as I pumped up the cuff.   I nodded, and listened with the stethoscope.   I just couldn't get used to the fact that his heart didn't beat, and that he had no blood pressure.

"No diastolic, no systolic," I said.   "Sir, your b.p.'s holding steady at zero over zero."

"Ah, normal," Auger said, reaching for his shirt.   "Enough time wasted.   Shall we return to the lab?"

He hated medical exams (and, I was convinced, doctors as well).   I argued in vain for the opportunity to take him to a hospital and run some *real* tests on him: X-rays, metabolic studies, EEGs. . . .

"It's three in the morning," Marlowe complained.   "I need some coffee."

"Can't get used to working graveyard shift?"   He acknowledged my joke with a weak smile.   This nocturnal living was tough to get used to.   Auger had acquired the vampiric dislike of daylight.   Another thing that needed more study: was it because of the temperature, or the infrared radiation?   In any case, my parents seemed to think my new hours were the result of an affair with Kevin Marlowe, and this made things fairly uncomfortable on the home front.

Auger accepted a cup of coffee, and stirred in a spoonful of salt, to make it osmotically similar to blood.

"There aren't enough metabolites and nutrients in the blood you drink to sustain you, Professor.   Where the hell do you get your energy?"

"It's a negentropic process, similar to the one which allows my *Pseudobacteria augeria* to be dormant over 35°, while ordinary enzymatic processes become accelerated," he told me.   "How much calculus have you had, Dr. Sanger?"

"Two semesters."

"You'd need at least four to understand.   Hadn't we better return to work?"

As human populations grew, they tended to eliminate competing species, creating a niche for a predator.   It may be possible to remutate Pseudobacteria augeria *to its hypothetical ancestor,* P. lycanthropica, *which could survive at normal body temperature and changed its hosts into carnivorous animals.   The body type was probably mediated by a supergene complex similar in principle to those found in butterfly mimicry, resulting in discrete morphs with a lack of intermediate types.   Examination of the literature suggests the morph adopted was that of the major natural predator of the geographical area, leading to werewolves in Northern Europe, were-bears in Scandinavia, and were-tigers in India.   Some cases have been reported of werewolves becoming vampires after death, suggesting either concurrent infection, or evolution in progress.*

I was driving back from town when I saw police cars lined up along the road. I slowed up and yelled out the window.

"Need a doctor?"

My deputy friend Fred flagged me in behind a patrol car.   "Remember the wimp who accused the big guy of being dead?"

He led me through a swarm of cops, down the gully to the creek.

Weems lay with his arm dangling in the creek.   His wrist had been slashed, and he had bled to death.

"Not much blood," I finally commented.   "It usually gets all over when some-one exsanguinates."

"Washed away downstream," the sheriff said.   "They always have to come on my territory to kill themselves.   How long would you say he's been dead?"

The body was cold.   Rigor mortis was complete but not yet passing off.   I estimated 20 hours, maybe less allowing for the cold.

"Damned suicides," the sheriff muttered.   "Big goddam nuisance."   I agreed, and we all stood around for a few minutes swapping gross-out stories.

Then I sped home, parked the car, and walked over to the lab.   It was dusk when I arrived.

Marlowe was in an elated mood.   "We've started on the last draft of the article. We'll submit simultaneously to *Science* and *Nature*.   Well, Mae, start working up an appetite because I hear they have great food at the Nobel awards."

I stomped past him to Auger's bedroom.   Auger was lying on his bed, absolutely straight, like a corpse already laid out.   As I stood there, clenching my fists, he awoke and sat up.

"Well, Dr. Sanger.   To what do I owe the honor of—"

"You killed him."

"Whom?"

Oh, he could be suave.

"You were clever making it look like suicide.   The cops have swallowed it."

He gave me his most charming smile, not realizing how his long teeth spoiled the effect.   "I had no alternative.   The man was our enemy.   He convinced the Foundation to revoke our funding."

"His death won't get the grant back, Auger.   You just killed him out of spite."

He laid a cold hand on my arm.   "Calm down.   By next week we'll all be famous.   You won't have to take that cheap job in New York.   You'll be the most pre-eminent witchdoctor in America."

"You're making me sick."   I wrenched my arm away and walked out.   "Good-bye, Kevin.   It was swell while it lasted.   Leave my name off the article.   I want to forget that any of this happened."

Marlowe had a hurt-little-boy look on his face.   "But you can't just leave."

"Watch me," I muttered.

It was pitch black already, but I'd walked it a dozen times.   When my feet felt asphalt instead of gravel, I turned right and headed uphill.   A passing car lit up the road, and I moved to the side.   The tail-lights dwindled in the distance, and in their faint afterglow I saw a tall figure come from the driveway.

Auger.

Following me.

Then it was black again.   I saw two eyes, shining like a deer's, only red.   They were all I could see: the stars above, and two red eyes.   They stared right at me, the nightsight of the predator.

Auger spoke softly, his voice carrying in the stillness.

"It won't hurt.   You know you want it."

I panicked and started running, going by the sound of my feet on the blacktop, my hands outstretched as I ran blind.   My heart was pounding with fear and cold sweat poured down my body, but the supercharge of adrenalin kept me going.

I saw the glimmer of light on the mailbox.   I could turn down the driveway, run the quarter mile to my home.   Home, light, safety. . . .

Something cut off the glow of the mailbox; and I knew it was Auger, in front of me now, blocking the driveway.   Six feet above the ground, two red eyes.

I swerved and plunged into the forest.   Branches whipped against my face and caught in my clothes and hair.   I tripped and fell in the stream, got up and kept running.

Hands caught me from behind and pulled me against a body, invisible in the dark.   I was conscious of an inhumanly strong grip, and a coat smelling of wool and chemicals.   I started pounding and flailing, but he ignored my blows.

He caught my hands and held them in one ice-like hand.

"Don't fight it," he whispered.   "You'll enjoy it."

I felt his breath on my neck, and tried to scream, but I couldn't.   I was too scared.

"This can't be happening to me," I thought.   "Not me."

The bite was sharp and painful, followed by a warm sensation as my blood welled up through the punctures.   I started struggling again but he was oblivious to everything but the blood he was greedily sucking in.

My mind went clinical on me.   Two pints equals 15 percent blood volume. Moderate shock will set in.   I could feel the symptoms start.   He's killing me.

My knees gave out and I sank to the ground, Auger still drinking from my left jugular.   Over the roaring in my ears I could hear my gasping breath and the vampire's gross panting and slobbering.   I was too weak to fight anymore.   The summer constellations gazed down uncaring, and became part of a light show as lack of oxygen brought hallucinations, and a strange feeling of euphoria.

The dying started to feel good.

CONCLUSIONS.   Throughout history the vampire has been maligned as a villain and demon.   Now that the etiology of the condition is understood, there is no reason why the vampire cannot take his place as a functioning member of society. With prescription availability of blood, the disease will be limited to present victims. Under these conditions it need not even be classified as contagious.

I woke up under an oak tree.   A spider had used my left arm to anchor its web, and earwigs were nesting in my hair.

"Ohhh.   I must have tied one on good," I groaned, and pulled myself into a sitting position, leaning against the oak.   I felt like hell.   Weak, cold, splitting headache, and hungry.   Never so hungry in all my life.   The feeling of hunger seemed to fill every inch of my body.

Absently, I put two fingers to my wrist to take my pulse.

There was none.

I reached up to check the carotid.   Every movement hurt.

My heart wasn't beating.

I withdrew my hand and stared at my fingers.   They were pale: dead white.
I was dead.   I was a vampire.   I tongued my canines and felt their new sharpness.
Auger did this to me.   I remembered it all, and felt nauseated.
He'd be in the lab.
And blood.   They had blood there.   Whole refrigerators full.   Rabbit blood.
Rat blood.
Human blood.

The new moon is still a sliver in the sky, but 1 can see in the dark now.   A
deer crosses my path and freezes in terror until I pass.   As I approach the house
I can hear Marlowe typing the article.   The damned article.

It will even be possible, through a controlled infection of Pseudobacteria augeria,
to conquer death, allowing us to revive and preserve indefinitely great minds and
"Kevin.   Get me some blood.   Quick, before I bite you."
I clutch at a chair to control myself.   When I look down, I see that my new
vampiric strength has crushed the hard plastic.
Marlowe tremulously hands me a liter of O-negative.   I gulp it down.   It's
cold, cramping my stomach.
"More."
It takes six liters before I can look at Marlowe without wanting to attack him.
Then I clean up some, comb my hair, cover my filthy clothes with a lab coat, and
slip a filled syringe into the pocket.
"Where is he, Kevin?"
"You're alive, Mae, that's what counts.   Let's not—"
"He sucked me damn near dry.   Where is he?"
"It didn't hurt you.   He said it wouldn't—"
I grab his arm, and he flinches at the touch.   "Feel it, Kevin, dead flesh.   Is
a Nobel going to keep either of us warm at night?"
"Add this to the conclusion, Kevin: 'Where there is no longer any death, murder
must be redefined.'   Welcome back, Dr. Sanger."
Auger stands in the lab doorway.   I realize that I'm shaking.
He can't hurt me now, I repeat over and over.   But I want to flee.   Or else
cry.
"Refrigerated blood is nothing.   Wait until you've drunk warm, pulsing, living
blood."
"Shut up," I whisper.
"And the power.   The strength.   You've always admired strength.   You'll
enjoy being a vampire, Dr. Sanger."
"No.   No, I won't become powercrazy.   I won't kill.   I'm trained to save, to
heal . . .   I won't be like you!"
He laughs.
"Biology isn't destiny!" I scream.
He laughs more.   I almost don't blame him.
"I thought we'd give you a chance.   All right, Kevin, stake her."

I spin around.   Marlowe has a wooden stake and a mallet, but he's vacillating, as usual.   I pick him up and toss him to the floor before Auger.

Auger curses and snatches up the stake.

"Am I to assume this won't hurt either?" I ask.

"I've always admired the late doctor's resilient sense of humor," he says.

I pull the syringe from my pocket, duck in close, ram it into his side and push the plunger.

"Admire that—20 cc of tetracycline."

He roars and throws a table at me.   I duck, and it crashes into a shelf of chemicals.

"You're cured, Auger.   I've killed those little bugs, the ones that are keeping you alive."

He picks up a 200 pound spectrometer and tosses it at me.   It bowls me into the cages, liberating a half dozen specimens.   Vampire rabbits scurry about underfoot.   I get up and dust myself off.

"Temper, temper.   That's Foundation equipment."

Marlowe watches dumbfounded as Auger throws the gas chromatograph at me. It shatters on the floor, sparks igniting the spilled chemicals.   A brisk fire begins, punctuated by explosions of bottled reagents.

Auger closes in and grabs me, but this time I push him back, pick up the wooden stake, and shove it into his heart.

He looks surprised.

"Why me?" he asks, and dies again.

"Kevin.   Come on.   The place is burning up."

"Get away from me," he yells.   "Don't touch me, vampire!"   He pulls open his shirt to show a cross on a chain.

"Don't be stupid, Kevin."

The fire has reached the chemical stockroom.   I run for the window, and plunge through in a cloud of glass.   The lab behind me explodes.

Marlowe's screams die out.

Charred paper blows away as heated air rushes out the shattered windows.   The plastic on the typewriter melts and runs, laying bare the sparking wires inside. The metal letters writhe and bend and wrap around each other, and then melt into an indistinguishable lump.

I go home and clean up, and get back in time to watch the firemen.   Not much is left of the old farmhouse.

"I'm a physician.   Can I help?"

"They're beyond help, Mae."   The fire chief remembers me from 4H.   "Think you could identify the bodies?"

They've covered them with yellow plastic blankets, two gross, body-shaped chunks of charred meat.   The fire chief looks at me sympathetically.

"I guess their own mothers wouldn't know them . . . you're pale, Mae.   Johnny, you better walk her home."

A husky young fireman takes my arm and steers me up the path, away from the lights and smoke.

"They were scientists?" he asks. "What were they doing in there?"

"Working on things man was not meant to know," I say. He doesn't recognize the quote.

I stare sideways at my escort.

He's young and strong and healthy.

He won't miss a pint at all.

JOHN VARLEY

Good-bye, Robinson Crusoe

It was summer, and Piri was in his second childhood. First, second; who counted? His body was young. He had not felt more alive since his original childhood back in the spring, when the sun drew closer and the air began to melt.

He was spending his time at Rarotonga Reef, in the Pacifica disneyland. Pacifica was still under construction, but Rarotonga had been used by the ecologists as a testing ground for the more ambitious barrier-type reef they were building in the south, just off the "Australian" coast. As a result, it was more firmly established than the other biomes. It was open to visitors, but so far only Piri was there. The "sky" disconcerted everyone else.

Piri didn't mind it. He was equipped with a brand-new toy: a fully operational imagination, a selective sense of wonder that allowed him to blank out those parts of his surroundings that failed to fit with his current fantasy.

He awoke with the tropical sun blinking in his face through the palm fronds. He had built a rude shelter from flotsam and detritus on the beach. It was not to protect him from the elements. The disneyland management had the weather well in hand; he might as well have slept in the open. But castaways *always* build some sort of shelter.

He bounced up with the quick alertness that comes from being young and living close to the center of things, brushed sand from his naked body, and ran for the line of breakers at the bottom of the narrow strip of beach.

His gait was awkward. His feet were twice as long as they should have been, with flexible toes that were webbed into flippers. Dry sand showered around his legs as he ran. He was brown as coffee and cream, and hairless.

Piri dived flat to the water, sliced neatly under a wave, and paddled out to waist-height. He paused there. He held his nose and worked his arms up and down, blowing air through his mouth and swallowing at the same time. What looked like long, hairline scars between his lower ribs came open. Red-orange fringes became visible inside them, and gradually lowered. He was no longer an air-breather.

He dived again, mouth open, and this time he did not come up. His esophagus and trachea closed and a new valve came into operation. It would pass water in only one direction, so his diaphragm now functioned as a pump pulling water through his mouth and forcing it out through the gill-slits. The water flowing through this lower chest area caused his gills to engorge with blood, turning them purplish-red and forcing his lungs to collapse upward into his chest cavity.   Bubbles of air trickled out his sides, then stopped.   His transition was complete.

The water seemed to grow warmer around him.   It had been pleasantly cool; now it seemed no temperature at all.   It was the result of his body temperature lowering in response to hormones released by an artificial gland in his cranium. He could not afford to burn energy at the rate he had done in the air; the water was too efficient a coolant for that.   All through his body arteries and capillaries were constricting as parts of him stablized at a lower rate of function.

No naturally evolved mammal had ever made the switch from air to water breathing, and the project had taxed the resources of bio-engineering to its limits. But everything in Piri's body was a living part of him.   It had taken two full days to install it all.

He knew nothing of the chemical complexities that kept him alive where he should have died quickly from heat loss or oxygen starvation.   He knew only the joy of arrowing along the white sandy bottom.   The water was clear, blue-green in the distance.

The bottom kept dropping away from him, until suddenly it reached for the waves.   He angled up the wall of the reef until his head broke the surface, climbed up the knobs and ledges until he was standing in the sunlight.   He took a deep breath and became an air-breather again.

The change cost him some discomfort.   He waited until the dizziness and fit of coughing had passed, shivering a little as his body rapidly underwent a reversal to a warm-blooded economy.

It was time for breakfast.

He spent the morning foraging among the tidepools.   There were dozens of plants and animals that he had learned to eat raw.   He ate a great deal, storing up energy for the afternoon's expedition on the outer reef.

Piri avoided looking at the sky.   He wasn't alarmed by it; it did not disconcert him as it did the others.   But he had to preserve the illusion that he was actually on a tropical reef in the Pacific Ocean, a castaway, and not a vacationer in an environment bubble below the surface of Pluto.

Soon he became a fish again, and dived off the sea side of the reef.

The water around the reef was oxygen-rich from the constant wave action.   Even here, though, he had to remain in motion to keep enough water flowing past his external gill fringes.   But he could move more slowly as he wound his way down into the darker reaches of the sheer reef face.   The reds and yellows of his world were swallowed by the blues and greens and purples.   It was quiet.   There were sounds to hear, but his ears were not adapted to them.   He moved slowly through shafts of blue light, keeping up the bare minimum of water flow.

He hesitated at the ten-meter level.   He had thought he was going to his Atlantis Grotto to check out his crab farm.   Then he wondered if he ought to hunt up Ocho the Octopus instead.   For a panicky moment he was afflicted with the bane of childhood: an inability to decide what to do with himself.   Or maybe it was worse, he thought.   Maybe it was a sign of growing up.   The crab farm bored him, or at least it did today.

He waffled back and forth for several minutes, idly chasing the tiny red fish that flirted with the anemones.   He never caught one.   This was no good at all.   Surely there was an adventure in this silent fairyland.   He had to find one.

An adventure found him, instead.   Piri saw something swimming out in the open water, almost at the limits of his vision.   It was long and pale, an attenuated missile of raw death.   His heart squeezed in panic, and he scuttled for a hollow reef.

Piri called him the Ghost.   He had been seen many times in the open sea.   He was eight meters of mouth, belly and tail: hunger personified.   There were those who said the great white shark was the most ferocious carnivore that ever lived. Piri believed it.

It didn't matter that the Ghost was completely harmless to him.   The Pacifica management did not like having its guests eaten alive.   An adult could elect to go into the water with no protection, providing the necessary waivers were on file. Children had to be implanted with an equalizer.   Piri had one, somewhere just below the skin of his left wrist.   It was a sonic generator, set to emit a sound that would mean terror to any predator in the water.

The Ghost, like all the sharks, barracudas, morays, and other predators in Pacifica, was not like his cousins who swam the seas of Earth.   He had been cloned from cells stored in the Biological Library on Luna.   The library had been created two hundred years before as an insurance policy against the extinction of a species. Originally, only endangered species were filed, but for years before the Invasion the directors had been trying to get a sample of everything.   Then the Invaders had come, and Lunarians were too busy surviving without help from Occupied Earth to worry about the library.   But when the time came to build the disneylands, the library had been ready.

By then, biological engineering had advanced to the point where many modifications could be made in genetic structure.   Mostly, the disneyland biologists had left nature alone.   But they had changed the predators.   In the Ghost, the change was a mutated organ attached to the brain that responded with a flood of fear when a supersonic note was sounded.

So why was the Ghost still out there?   Piri blinked his nictating membranes, trying to clear his vision.   It helped a little.   The shape looked a bit different.

Instead of moving back and forth, the tail seemed to be going up and down, perhaps in a scissoring motion.   Only one animal swims like that.   He gulped down his fear and pushed away from the reef.

But he had waited too long.   His fear of the Ghost went beyond simple danger, of which there was none.   It was something more basic, an unreasoning reflex that prickled his neck when he saw that long white shape.   He couldn't fight it, and didn't want to.   But the fear had kept him against the reef, hidden, while the person swam out of reach.   He thrashed to catch up, but soon lost track of the moving feet in the gloom.

He had seen gills trailing from the sides of the figure, muted down to a deep blue-black by the depths. He had the impression that it was a woman.

Tongatown was the only human habitation on the island. It housed a crew of maintenance people and their children, about fifty in all, in grass huts patterned after those of South Sea natives. A few of the buildings concealed elevators that went to the underground rooms that would house the tourists when the project was completed. The shacks would then go at a premium rate, and the beaches would be crowded.

Piri walked into the circle of firelight and greeted his friends. Nighttime was party time in Tongatown. With the day's work over, everybody gathered around the fire and roasted a vat-grown goat or lamb. But the real culinary treats were the fresh vegetable dishes. The ecologists were still working out the kinks in the systems, controlling blooms, planting more of failing species. They often produced huge excesses of edibles that would have cost a fortune on the outside. The workers took some of the excess for themselves. It was understood to be a fringe benefit of the job. It was hard enough to find people who could stand to stay under the Pacifica sky.

"Hi, Piri," said a girl. "You meet any pirates today?" It was Harra, who used to be one of Piri's best friends but had seemed increasingly remote over the last year. She was wearing a handmade grass skirt and a lot of flowers, tied into strings that looped around her body. She was fifteen now, and Piri was . . . but who cared? There were no seasons here, only days. Why keep track of time?

Piri didn't know what to say. The two of them had once played together out on the reef. It might be Lost Atlantis, or Submariner, or Reef Pirates; a new plot line and cast of heroes and villains every day. But her question had held such thinly veiled contempt. Didn't she care about the Pirates anymore? What was the matter with her?

She relented when she saw Piri's helpless bewilderment.

"Here, come on and sit down. I saved you a rib." She held out a large chunk of mutton.

Piri took it and sat beside her. He was famished, having had nothing all day since his large breakfast.

"I thought I saw the Ghost today," he said, casually.

Harra shuddered. She wiped her hands on her thighs and looked at him closely.

"Thought? You thought you saw him?" Harra did not care for the Ghost. She had cowered with Piri more than once as they watched him prowl.

"Yep. But I don't think it was really him."

"Where was this?"

"On the sea-side, down about, oh, ten meters. I think it was a woman."

"I don't see how it could be. There's just you and—and Midge and Darvin with—did this woman have an air tank?"

"Nope. Gills. I saw that."

"But there's only you and four others here with gills. And I know where they all were today."

"You used to have gills," he said, with a hint of accusation.

She sighed. "Are we going through that again? I *told* you, I got tired of the flippers. I wanted to move around the *land* some more."

"I can move around the land," he said, darkly.

"All right, all right. You think I deserted you. Did you ever think that you sort of deserted *me?*"

Piri was puzzled by that, but Harra had stood up and walked quickly away. He could follow her, or he could finish his meal. She was right about the flippers. He was no great shakes at chasing anybody.

Piri never worried about anything for too long. He ate, and ate some more, long past the time when everyone else had joined together for the dancing and singing. He usually hung back, anyway. He could sing, but dancing was out of his league.

Just as he was leaning back in the sand, wondering if there were any more corners he could fill up—perhaps another bowl of that shrimp teriyaki?—Harra was back. She sat beside him.

"I talked to my mother about what you said. She said a tourist showed up today. It looks like you were right. It was a woman, and she was amphibious."

Piri felt a vague unease. One tourist was certainly not an invasion, but she could be a harbinger. And amphibious. So far, no one had gone to that expense except for those who planned to live here for a long time. Was his tropical hide-out in danger of being discovered?

"What—what's she doing here?" He absently ate another spoonful of crab cocktail.

"She's looking for *you,*" Harra laughed, and elbowed him in the ribs. Then she pounced on him, tickling his ribs until he was howling in helpless glee. He fought back, almost to the point of having the upper hand, but she was bigger and a little more determined. She got him pinned, showering flower petals on him as they struggled. One of the red flowers from her hair was in her eye, and she brushed it away, breathing hard.

"You want to go for a walk on the beach?" she asked.

Harra was fun, but the last few times he'd gone with her she had tried to kiss him. He wasn't ready for that. He was only a kid. He thought she probably had something like that in mind now.

"I'm too full," he said, and it was almost the literal truth. He had stuffed himself disgracefully, and only wanted to curl up in his shack and go to sleep.

Harra said nothing, just sat there getting her breathing under control. At last she nodded, a little jerkily, and got to her feet. Piri wished he could see her face to face. He knew something was wrong. She turned from him and walked away.

Robinson Crusoe was feeling depressed when he got back to his hut. The walk down the beach away from the laughter and singing had been a lonely one. Why had he rejected Harra's offer of companionship? Was it really so bad that she wanted to play new kinds of games?

But no, damn it. She wouldn't play his games, why should he play hers?

After a few minutes of sitting on the beach under the crescent moon, he got into character. Oh, the agony of being a lone castaway, far from the company of fellow creatures, with nothing but faith in God to sustain oneself. Tomorrow he would read from the scriptures, do some more exploring along the rocky north coast, tan some goat hides, maybe get in a little fishing.

With his plans for the morrow laid before him, Piri could go to sleep, wiping away a last tear for distant England.

The ghost woman came to him during the night. She knelt beside him in the sand. She brushed his sandy hair from his eyes and he stirred in his sleep. His feet thrashed.

He was churning through the abyssal deeps, heart hammering, blind to everything but internal terror. Behind him, jaws yawned, almost touching his toes. They closed with a snap.

He sat up woozily. He saw rows of serrated teeth in the line of breakers in front of him. And a tall, white shape in the moonlight dived into a curling breaker and was gone.

"Hello."

Piri sat up with a start. The worst thing about being a child living alone on an island—which, when he thought about it, was the sort of thing every child dreamed of—was not having a warm mother's breast to cry on when you had nightmares. It hadn't affected him much, but when it did, it was pretty bad.

He squinted up into the brightness. She was standing with her head blocking out the sun. He winced, and looked away, down to her feet. They were webbed, with long toes. He looked a little higher. She was nude, and quite beautiful.

"Who . . . ?"

"Are you awake now?" She squatted down beside him. Why had he expected sharp, triangular teeth? His dreams blurred and ran like watercolors in the rain, and he felt much better. She had a nice face. She was smiling at him.

He yawned, and sat up. He was groggy, stiff, and his eyes were coated with sand that didn't come from the beach. It had been an awful night.

"I think so."

"Good. How about some breakfast?" She stood, and went to a basket on the sand.

"I usually—" but his mouth watered when he saw the guavas, melons, kippered herring, and the long brown loaf of bread. She had butter, and some orange marmalade. "Well, maybe just a—" and he had bitten into a succulent slice of melon. But before he could finish it, he was seized by an even stronger urge. He got to his feet and scuttled around the palm tree with the waist-high dark stain and urinated against it.

"Don't tell anybody, huh?" he said, anxiously.

She looked up. "About the tree? Don't worry."

He sat back down and resumed eating the melon. "I could get in a lot of trouble. They gave me a thing and told me to use it."

"It's all right with me," she said, buttering a slice of bread and handing it to him. "Robinson Crusoe never had a portable Eco-San, right?"

"Right," he said, not showing his surprise. How did she know *that?*

Piri didn't know quite what to say. Here she was, sharing his morning, as much a fact of life as the beach or the water.

"What's your name?" It was as good a place to start as any.

"Leandra. You can call me Lee."

"I'm—"

"Piri. I heard about you from the people at the party last night. I hope you don't mind me barging in on you like this."

He shrugged, and tried to indicate all the food with the gesture. "Anytime," he said, and laughed. He felt good. It was nice to have someone friendly around after last night. He looked at her again, from a mellower viewpoint.

She was large; quite a bit taller than he was. Her physical age was around thirty, unusually old for a woman. He thought she might be closer to sixty or seventy, but he had nothing to base it on. Piri himself was in his nineties, and who could have known that? She had the slanting eyes that were caused by the addition of transparent eyelids beneath the natural ones. Her hair grew in a narrow band, cropped short, starting between her eyebrows and going over her head to the nape of her neck. Her ears were pinned efficiently against her head, giving her a lean, streamlined look.

"What brings you to Pacifica?" Piri asked.

She reclined on the sand with her hands behind her head, looking very relaxed.

"Claustrophobia." She winked at him. "Not really. I wouldn't survive long in Pluto with *that.*" Piri wasn't even sure what it was, but he smiled as if he knew. "Tired of the crowds. I heard that people couldn't enjoy themselves here, what with the sky, but I didn't have any trouble when I visited. So I bought flippers and gills and decided to spend a few weeks skin-diving by myself."

Piri looked at the sky. It was a staggering sight. He'd grown used to it, but knew that it helped not to look up more than he had to.

It was an incomplete illusion, all the more appalling because the half of the sky that had been painted was so very convincing. It looked like it really was the sheer blue of infinity, so when the eye slid over to the unpainted overhanging canopy of rock, scarred from blasting, painted with gigantic numbers that were barely visible from twenty kilometers below—one could almost imagine God looking down through the blue opening. It loomed, suspended by nothing, gigatons of rock hanging up there.

Visitors to Pacifica often complained of headaches, usually right on the crown of the head. They were cringing, waiting to get conked.

"Sometimes I wonder how *I* live with it," Piri said.

She laughed. "It's nothing for me. I was a space pilot once."

"Really?" This was catnip to Piri. There's nothing more romantic than a space pilot. He had to hear stories.

The morning hours dwindled as she captured his imagination with a series of tall tales he was sure were mostly fabrication. But who cared? Had he come to the

South Seas to hear of the mundane?   He felt he had met a kindred spirit, and gradually, fearful of being laughed at, he began to tell her stories of the Reef Pirates, first as wishful wouldn't-it-be-fun-if's, then more and more seriously as she listened intently.   He forgot her age as he began to spin the best of the yarns he and Harra had concocted.

It was a tacit conspiracy between them to be serious about the stories, but that was the whole point.   That was the only way it would work, as it had worked with Harra.   Somehow, this adult woman was interested in playing the same games he was.

Lying in his bed that night, Piri felt better than he had for months, since before Harra had become so distant.   Now that he had a companion, he realized that maintaining a satisfying fantasy world by yourself is hard work.   Eventually you need someone to tell the stories to, and to share in the making of them.

They spent the day out on the reef.   He showed her his crab farm, and introduced her to Ocho the Octopus, who was his usual shy self.   Piri suspected the damn thing only loved him for the treats he brought.

She entered into his games easily and with no trace of adult condescension.   He wondered why, and got up the courage to ask her.   He was afraid he'd ruin the whole thing, but he had to know.   It just wasn't normal.

They were perched on a coral outcropping above the high tide level, catching the last rays of the sun.

"I'm not sure," she said.   "I guess you think I'm silly, huh?"

"No, not exactly that.   It's just that most adults seem to, well, have more 'important' things on their minds."   He put all the contempt he could into the word.

"Maybe I feel the same way you do about it.   I'm here to have fun.   I sort of feel like I've been reborn into a new element.   It's *terrific* down there, you know that.   I just didn't feel like I wanted to go into that world alone.   I was out there yesterday . . ."

"I thought I saw you."

"Maybe you did.   Anyway, I needed a companion, and I heard about you.   It seemed like the polite thing to, well, not to ask you to be my guide, but sort of fit myself into your world.   As it were."   She frowned, as if she felt she had said too much.   "Let's not push it, all right?"

"Oh, sure.   It's none of my business."

"I like you, Piri."

"And I like you.   I haven't had a friend for . . . too long."

That night at the luau, Lee disappeared.   Piri looked for her briefly, but was not really worried.   What she did with her nights was her business.   He wanted her during the days.

As he was leaving for his home, Harra came up behind him and took his hand. She walked with him for a moment, then could no longer hold it in.

"A word to the wise, old pal," she said.   "You'd better stay away from her. She's not going to do you any good."

"What are you talking about? You don't even know her."

"Maybe I do."

"Well, do you or don't you?"

She didn't say anything, then sighed deeply.

"Piri, if you do the smart thing you'll get on that raft of yours and sail to Bikini. Haven't you had any . . . feelings about her? Any premonitions or anything?"

"I don't know what you're talking about," he said, thinking of sharp teeth and white death.

"I think you do. You have to, but you won't face it. That's all I'm saying. It's not my business to meddle in your affairs."

"I'll say it's not. So why did you come out here and put this stuff in my ear?" He stopped, and something tickled at his mind from his past life, some earlier bit of knowledge, carefully suppressed. He was used to it. He knew he was not really a child, and that he had a long life and many experiences stretching out behind him. But he didn't think about it. He hated it when part of his old self started to intrude on him.

"I think you're jealous of her," he said, and knew it was his old, cynical self talking. "She's an adult, Harra. She's no threat to you. And, hell, I know what you've been hinting at these last months. I'm not ready for it, so leave me alone. I'm just a kid."

Her chin came up, and the moonlight flashed in her eyes.

"You idiot. Have you looked at yourself lately? You're not Peter Pan, you know. You're growing up. You're damn near a man."

"That's not true." There was panic in Piri's voice. "I'm only. . . . Well, I haven't exactly been counting, but I can't be more than nine, ten years—"

"Shit. You're as old as I am, and I've had breasts for two years. But I'm not out to cop you. I can cop with any of seven boys in the village younger than you are, but not you." She threw her hands up in exasperation and stepped back from him. Then, in a sudden fury, she hit him on the chest with the heel of her fist. He fell back, stunned at her violence.

"She *is* an adult," Harra whispered through her teeth. "That's what I came here to warn you against. *I'm* your friend, but you don't know it. Ah, what's the use? I'm fighting against that scared old man in your head, and he won't listen to me. Go ahead, go with her. But she's got some surprises for you."

"What? What surprises?" Piri was shaking, not wanting to listen to her. It was a relief when she spat at his feet, whirled, and ran down the beach.

"Find out for yourself," she yelled back over her shoulder. It sounded like she was crying.

That night, Piri dreamed of white teeth, inches behind him, snapping.

But morning brought Lee, and another fine breakfast in her bulging bag. After a lazy interlude drinking coconut milk, they went to the reef again. The pirates gave them a rough time of it, but they managed to come back alive in time for the nightly gathering.

Harra was there.   She was dressed as he had never seen her, in the blue tunic and shorts of the reef maintenance crew.   He knew she had taken a job with the disneyland and had not seen her dressed up before.   He had just begun to get used to the grass skirt.   Not long ago, she had been always nude like him and the other children.

She looked older somehow, and bigger.   Maybe it was just the uniform.   She still looked like a girl next to Lee.   Piri was confused by it, and his thoughts veered protectively away.

Harra did not avoid him, but she was remote in a more important way.   It was like she had put on a mask, or possibly taken one off.   She carried herself with a dignity that Piri thought was beyond her years.

Lee disappeared just before he was ready to leave.   He walked home alone, half hoping Harra would show up so he could apologize for the way he'd talked to her the night before.   But she didn't.

He felt the bow-shock of a pressure wave behind him, sensed by some mechanism he was unfamiliar with, like the lateral line of a fish, sensitive to slight changes in the water around him.   He knew there was something behind him, closing the gap a little with every wild kick of his flippers.

It was dark.   It was always dark when the thing chased him.   It was not the wispy, insubstantial thing that darkness was when it settled on the night air, but the primal, eternal night of the depths.   He tried to scream with his mouth full of water, but it was a dying gurgle before it passed his lips.   The water around him was warm with his blood.

He turned to face it before it was upon him, and saw Harra's face corpse-pale and glowing sickly in the night.   But no, it wasn't Harra, it was Lee, and her mouth was far down her body, rimmed with razors, a gaping crescent hole in her chest.   He screamed again—

And sat up.

"What?   Where are you?"

"I'm right here, it's going to be all right."   She held his head as he brought his sobbing under control.   She was whispering something but he couldn't understand it, and perhaps wasn't meant to.   It was enough.   He calmed down quickly, as he always did when he woke from nightmares.   If they hung around to haunt him, he never would have stayed by himself for so long.

There was just the moon-lit paleness of her breast before his eyes and the smell of skin and sea water.   Her nipple was wet.   Was it from his tears?   No, his lips were tingling and the nipple was hard when it brushed against him.   He realized what he had been doing in his sleep.

"You were calling for your mother," she whispered, as though she'd read his mind.   "I've heard you shouldn't wake someone from a nightmare.   It seemed to calm you down."

"Thanks," he said, quietly.   "Thanks for being here, I mean."

She took his cheek in her hand, turned his head slightly, and kissed him.   It

was not a motherly kiss, and he realized they were not playing the same game.
She had changed the rules on him.

"Lee . . ."

"Hush. It's time you learned."

She eased him onto his back, and he was overpowered with *déjà vu*. Her mouth
worked downward on his body and it set off chains of associations from his past
life. He was familiar with the sensation. It had happened to him often in his
second childhood. Something would happen that had happened to him in much
the same way before and he would remember a bit of it. He had been seduced
by an older woman the first time he was young. She had taught him well, and
he remembered it all but didn't want to remember. He was an experienced lover
and a child as well.

"I'm not old enough," he protested, but she was holding in her hand the evidence
that he was old enough, had been old enough for several years. *I'm fourteen years
old,* he thought. How could he have kidded himself into thinking he was ten?

"You're a strong young man," she whispered in his ear. "And I'm going to
be very disappointed if you keep saying that. You're not a child anymore, Piri.
Face it."

"I . . . I guess I'm not."

"Do you know what to do?"

"I think so."

She reclined beside him, drew her legs up. Her body was huge and ghostly
and full of limber strength. She would swallow him up, like a shark. The gill
slits under her arms opened and shut quickly with her breathing, smelling of salt,
iodine, and sweat.

He got on his hands and knees and moved over her.

He woke before she did. The sun was up: another warm, cloudless morning.
There would be two thousand more before the first scheduled typhoon.

Piri was a giddy mixture of elation and sadness. It was sad, and he knew it
already, that his days of frolicking on the reef were over. He would still go out
there, but it would never be the same.

Fourteen years old! Where had the years gone? He was nearly an adult. He
moved away from the thought until he found a more acceptable one. He was an
adolescent, and a very fortunate one to have been initiated into the mysteries of
sex by this strange woman.

He held her as she slept, spooned cozily back to front with his arms around her
waist. She had already been playmate, mother, and lover to him. What else did
she have in store?

But he didn't care. He was not worried about anything. He already scorned
his yesterdays. He was not a boy, but a youth, and he remembered from his other
youth what that meant and was excited by it. It was a time of sex, of internal
exploration and the exploration of others. He would pursue these new frontiers
with the same single-mindedness he had shown on the reef.

He moved against her, slowly, not disturbing her sleep.   But she woke as he entered her and turned to give him a sleepy kiss.

They spent the morning involved in each other, until they were content to lie in the sun and soak up heat like glossy reptiles.

"I can hardly believe it," she said.   "You've been here for . . . how long? With all these girls and women.   And I know at least one of them was interested."

He didn't want to go into it.   It was important to him that she not find out he was not really a child.   He felt it would change things, and it was not fair.   Not fair at all, because it *had* been the first time.   In a way he could never have explained to her, last night had been not a rediscovery but an entirely new thing. He had been with many women and it wasn't as if he couldn't remember it.   It was all there, and what's more, it showed up in his lovemaking.   He had not been the bumbling teenager, had not needed to be told what to do.

But it was *new*.   That old man inside had been a spectator and an invaluable coach, but his hardened viewpoint had not intruded to make last night just another bout.   It had been a first time, and the first time is special.

When she persisted in her questions he silenced her in the only way he knew, with a kiss.   He could see he had to rethink his relationship to her.   She had not asked him questions as a playmate, or a mother.   In the one role, she had been seemingly as self-centered as he, interested in only in the needs of the moment and her personal needs above all.   As a mother, she had offered only wordless comfort in a tight spot.

Now she was his lover.   What did lovers do when they weren't making love?

They went for walks on the beach, and on the reef.   They swam together, but it was different.   They talked a lot.

She soon saw that he didn't want to talk about himself.   Except for the odd question here and there that would momentarily confuse him, throw him back to stages of his life he didn't wish to remember, she left his past alone.

They stayed away from the village except to load up on supplies.   It was mostly his unspoken wish that kept them away.   He had made it clear to everyone in the village many years ago that he was not really a child.   It had been necessary to convince them that he could take care of himself on his own, to keep them from being overprotective.   They would not spill his secret knowingly, but neither would they lie for him.

So he grew increasingly nervous about his relationship with Lee, founded as it was on a lie.   If not a lie, then at least a withholding of the facts.   He saw that he must tell her soon, and dreaded it.   Part of him was convinced that her attraction to him was based mostly on age difference.

Then she learned he had a raft, and wanted to go on a sailing trip to the edge of the world.

Piri did have a raft, though an old one.   They dragged it from the bushes that had grown around it since his last trip and began putting it into shape.   Piri was delighted.   It was something to do, and it was hard work.   They didn't have much time for talking.

It was a simple construction of logs lashed together with rope. Only an insane sailor would put the thing to sea in the Pacific Ocean, but it was safe enough for them. They knew what the weather would be, and the reports were absolutely reliable. And if it came apart, they could swim back.

All the ropes had rotted so badly that even gentle wave action would have quickly pulled it apart. They had to be replaced, a new mast erected, and a new sailcloth installed. Neither of them knew anything about sailing, but Piri knew that the winds blew toward the edge at night and away from it during the day. It was a simple matter of putting up the sail and letting the wind do the navigating.

He checked the schedule to be sure they got there at low tide. It was a moonless night, and he chuckled to himself when he thought of her reaction to the edge of the world. They would sneak up on it in the dark, and the impact would be all the more powerful at sunrise.

But he knew as soon as they were an hour out of Rarotonga that he had made a mistake. There was not much to do there in the night but talk.

"Piri, I've sensed that you don't want to talk about certain things."

"Who? Me?"

She laughed into the empty night. He could barely see her face. The stars were shining brightly, but there were only about a hundred of them installed so far, and all in one part of the sky.

"Yeah, you. You won't talk about yourself. It's like you grew here, sprang up from the ground like a palm tree. And you've got no mother in evidence. You're old enough to have divorced her, but you'd have a guardian somewhere. Someone would be looking after your moral upbringing. The only conclusion is that you don't need an education in moral principles. So you've got a copilot."

"Um." She had seen through him. Of course she would have.

Why hadn't he realized it?

"So you're a clone. You've had your memories transplanted into a new body, grown from one of your own cells. How old are you? Do you mind my asking?"

"I guess not. Uh . . . what's the date?"

She told him.

"And the year?"

She laughed, but told him that, too.

"Damn. I missed my one hundredth birthday. Well, so what? It's not important. Lee, does this change anything?"

"Of course not. Listen, I could tell the first time, that first night together. You had that puppy-dog eagerness, all right, but you knew how to handle yourself. Tell me: what's it like?"

"The second childhood, you mean?" He reclined on the gently rocking raft and looked at the little clot of stars. "It's pretty damn great. It's like living in a dream. What kid hasn't wanted to live alone on a tropic isle? I can, because there's an adult in me who'll keep me out of trouble. But for the last seven years I've been a kid. It's you that finally made me grow up a little, maybe sort of late, at that."

"I'm sorry. But it felt like the right time."

"It was.   I was afraid of it at first.   Listen, I *know* that I'm really a hundred years old, see?   I know that all the memories are ready for me when I get to adulthood again.   If I think about it, I can remember it all as plain as anything. But I haven't wanted to, and in a way, I still don't want to.   The memories are suppressed when you opt for a second childhood instead of being transplanted into another full-grown body.''

"I know.''

"Do you?   Oh, yeah.   Intellectually.   So did I, but I didn't understand what it meant.   It's a nine or ten-year holiday, not only from your work, but from yourself.   When you get into your nineties, you might find that you need it.''

She was quiet for a while, lying beside him without touching.

"What about the reintegration?   Is that started?''

"I don't know.   I've heard it's a little rough.   I've been having dreams about something chasing me.   That's probably my former self, right?''

"Could be.   What did your older self do?''

He had to think for a moment, but there it was.   He'd not thought of it for eight years.

"I was an economic strategist.''

Before he knew it, he found himself launching into an explanation of offensive economic policy.

"Did you know that Pluto is in danger of being gutted by currency transfers from the Inner Planets?   And you know why?   The speed of light, that's why.   Time lag.   It's killing us.   Since the time of the Invasion of Earth it's been humanity's idea—and a good one, I think—that we should stand together.   Our whole cultural thrust in that time has been toward a total economic community.   But it won't work at Pluto.   Independence is in the cards.''

She listened as he tried to explain things that only moments before he would have had trouble understanding himself.   But it poured out of him like a breached dam, things like inflation multipliers, futures buying on the oxygen and hydrogen exchanges, phantom dollars and their manipulation by central banking interests, and the invisible drain.

"Invisible drain?   What's that?''

"It's hard to explain, but it's tied up in the speed of light.   It's an economic drain on Pluto that has nothing to do with real goods and services, or labor, or any of the other traditional forces.   It has to do with the fact that any information we get from the Inner Planets is already at least nine hours old.   In an economy with a stable currency—pegged to gold, for instance, like the classical economies on Earth—it wouldn't matter much, but it would still have an effect.   Nine hours can make a difference in prices, in futures, in outlook on the markets.   With a floating exchange medium, one where you need the hourly updates on your credit meter to know what your labor input will give you in terms of material output—your personal financial equation, in other words—and the inflation multiplier is something you simply *must* have if the equation is going to balance and you're not going to be wiped out, then time is really of the essence.   We operate at a perpetual disad-

vantage on Pluto in relation to the Inner Planet money markets.   For a long time
it ran on the order of point three percent leakage due to outdated information.   But
the inflation multiplier has been accelerating over the years.   Some of it's been
absorbed by the fact that we've been moving closer to the I.P.; the time lag has
been getting shorter as we move into summer.   But it can't last.   We'll reach the
inner point of our orbit and the effects will really start to accelerate.   Then it's
war.''

"War?''   She seemed horrified, as well she might be.

"War, in the economic sense.   It's a hostile act to renounce a trade agreement,
even if it's bleeding you white.   It hits every citizen of the Inner Planets in the
pocketbook, and we can expect retaliation.   We'd be introducing instability by
pulling out of the Common Market.''

"How bad will it be?   Shooting?''

"Not likely.   But devastating enough.   A depression's no fun.   And they'll
be planning one for us.''

"Isn't there any other course?''

"Someone suggested moving our entire government and all our corporate headquarters to the Inner Planets.   It could happen, I guess.   But who'd feel like it
was ours?   We'd be a colony, and that's a worse answer than independence, in
the long run.''

She was silent for a time, chewing it over.   She nodded her head once; he could
barely see the movement in the darkness.

"How long until the war?''

He shrugged.   "I've been out of touch.   I don't know how things have been
going.   But we can probably take it for another ten years or so.   Then we'll have
to get out.   I'd stock up on real wealth if I were you.   Canned goods, air, water,
so forth.   I don't think it'll get so bad that you'll need those things to stay alive
by consuming them.   But we may get to a semi-barter situation where they'll be
the only valuable things.   Your credit meter'll laugh at you when you punch a
purchase order, no matter how much work you've put into it.''

The raft bumped.   They had arrived at the edge of the world.

They moored the raft to one of the rocks on the wall that rose from the open
ocean.   They were five kilometers out of Rarotonga.   They waited for some light
as the sun began to rise, then started up the rock face.

It was rough: blasted out with explosives on this face of the dam.   It went up
at a thirty degree angle for fifty meters, then was suddenly level and smooth as
glass.   The top of the dam at the edge of the world had been smoothed by cutting
lasers into a vast table top, three hundred kilometers long and four kilometers wide.
They left wet footprints on it as they began the long walk to the edge.

They soon lost any meaningful perspective on the thing.   They lost sight of the
sea-edge, and couldn't see the drop-off until they began to near it.   By then, it
was full light.   Timed just right, they would reach the edge when the sun came
up and they'd really have something to see.

A hundred meters from the edge when she could see over it a little, Lee began to unconsciously hang back.   Piri didn't prod her.   It was not something he could force someone to see.   He'd reached this point with others, and had to turn back. Already, the fear of falling was building up.   But she came on, to stand beside him at the very lip of the canyon.

Pacifica was being built and filled in three sections.   Two were complete, but the third was still being hollowed out and was not yet filled with water except in the deepest trenches.   The water was kept out of this section by the dam they were standing on.   When it was completed, when all the underwater trenches and mountain ranges and guyots and slopes had been built to specifications, the bottom would be covered with sludge and ooze and the whole wedge-shaped section flooded. The water came from liquid hydrogen and oxygen on the surface, combined with the limitless electricity of fusion powerplants.

"We're doing what the Dutch did on Old Earth, but in reverse," Piri pointed out, but he got no reaction from Lee.   She was staring, spellbound, down the sheer face of the dam to the apparently bottomless trench below.   It was shrouded in mist, but seemed to fall off forever.   "It's eight kilometers deep," Piri told her.   "It's not going to be a regular trench when it's finished.   It's there to be filled up with the remains of this dam after the place has been flooded."   He looked at her face, and didn't bother with more statistics.   He let her experience it in her own way.

The only comparable vista on a human-inhabited planet was the Great Rift Valley on Mars.   Neither of them had seen it, but it suffered in comparison to this because not all of it could be seen at once.   Here, one could see from one side to the other, and, from sea level to a distance equivalent to the deepest oceanic trenches on Earth.   It simply fell away beneath them and went straight down to nothing.   There was a rainbow beneath their feet.   Off to the left was a huge waterfall that arced away from the wall in a solid stream.   Tons of overflow water went through the wall, to twist, fragment, vaporize and blow away long before it reached the bottom of the trench.

Straight ahead of them and about ten kilometers away was the mountain that would become the Okinawa biome when the pit was filled.   Only the tiny, blackened tip of the mountain would show above the water.

Lee stayed and looked at it as long as she could.   It became easier the longer one stood there, and yet something about it drove her away.   The scale was too big, there was no room for humans in that shattered world.   Long before noon, they turned and started the long walk back to the raft.

She was silent as they boarded and set sail for the return trip.   The winds were blowing fitfully, barely billowing the sail.   It would be another hour before they blew very strongly.   They were still in sight of the dam wall.

They sat on the raft, not looking at each other.

"Piri, thanks for bringing me here."

"You're welcome.   You don't have to talk about it."

"All right.   But there's something else I have to talk about.   I . . . don't know where to begin, really."

Piri stirred uneasily.   The earlier discussion about economics had disturbed him. It was part of his past life, a part that he had not been ready to return to.   He was full of confusion.   Thoughts that had no place out here in the concrete world of wind and water were roiling through his brain.   Someone was calling to him, someone he knew but didn't want to see right then.

"Yeah?   What is it you want to talk about?"

"It's about—" she stopped, seemed to think it over.   "Never mind.   It's not time yet."   She moved close and touched him.   But he was not interested.   He made it known in a few minutes, and she moved to the other side of the raft.

He lay back, essentially alone with his troubled thoughts.   The wind gusted, then settled down.   He saw a flying fish leap, almost passing over the raft.   There was a piece of the sky falling through the air.   It twisted and turned like a feather, a tiny speck of sky that was blue on one side and brown on the other.   He could see the hole in the sky where it had been knocked loose.

It must be two or three kilometers up, and it looked like it was falling from the center.   How far away were they from the center of Pacifica?   A hundred kilometers?

A piece of the sky?

He got to his feet, nearly capsizing the raft.

"What's the matter?"

It was *big*.   It looked large even from this far away.   It was the dreamy tumbling motion that had deceived him.

"The sky is . . ." he choked on it, and almost laughed.   But this was not time to feel silly about it.   "The sky is falling, Lee."   How long?   He watched it, his mind full of numbers.   Terminal velocity from that high up, assuming it was heavy enough to punch right through the atmosphere . . . over six hundred meters per second.   Time to fall, seventy seconds.   Thirty of those must already have gone by.

Lee was shading her eyes as she followed his gaze.   She still thought it was a joke.   The chunk of sky began to glow red as the atmosphere got thicker.

"Hey it really is falling." she said.   "Look at that."

"It's big.   Maybe one or two kilometers across.   It's going to make quite a splash, I'll bet."

They watched it descend.   Soon it disappeared over the horizon, picking up speed.   They waited, but the show seemed to be over.   Why was he still uneasy?

"How many tons in a two-kilometer chunk of rock, I wonder?" Lee mused. She didn't look too happy, either.   But they sat back down on the raft, still looking in the direction where the thing had sunk into the sea.

Then they were surrounded by flying fish, and the water looked crazy.   The fish were panicked.   As soon as they hit they leaped from the water again.   Piri felt rather than saw something pass beneath them.   And then, very gradually, a roar built up, a deep bass rumble that soon threatened to turn his bones to powder.

It picked him up and shook him, and left him limp on his knees. He was stunned, unable to think clearly. His eyes were still fixed on the horizon, and he saw a white fan rising in the distance in silent majesty. It was the spray from the impact, and it was still going up.

"Look up there," Lee said, when she got her voice back. She seemed confused as he. He looked where she pointed and saw a twisted line crawling across the blue sky. At first he thought it was the end of his life, because it appeared that the whole overhanging dome was fractured and about to fall in on them. But then he saw it was one of the tracks that the sun ran on, pulled free by the rock that had fallen, twisted into a snake of tortured metal.

"The dam!" he yelled. "The dam! We're too close to the dam!"

"What?"

"The bottom rises this close to the dam. The water here isn't that deep. There'll be a wave coming, Lee, a big wave. It'll pile up here."

"Piri, the shadows are moving."

"Huh?"

Surprise was piling on surprise too fast for him to cope with it. But she was right. The shadows were moving. But *why?*

Then he saw it. The sun was setting, but not by following the tracks that led to the concealed opening in the west. It was falling through the air, having been shaken loose by the rock.

Lee had figured it out, too.

"What is that thing?" she asked. "I mean, how big is it?"

"Not too big, I heard. Big enough, but not nearly the size of that chunk that fell. It's some kind of fusion generator. I don't know what'll happen when it hits the water."

They were paralyzed. They knew there was something they should do, but too many things were happening. There was not time to think it out.

"Dive!" Lee yelled. "Dive into the water!"

"What?"

"We have to dive and swim away from the dam, and down as far as we can go. The wave will pass over us, won't it?"

"I don't know."

"It's all we can do."

So they dived. Piri felt his gills come into action, then he was swimming down at an angle toward the dark-shrouded bottom. Lee was off to his left, swimming as hard as she could. And with no sunset, no warning, it got black as pitch. The sun had hit the water.

He had no idea how long he had been swimming when he suddenly felt himself pulled upward. Floating in the water, weightless, he was not well equipped to feel accelerations. But he did feel it, like a rapidly rising elevator. It was accompanied by pressure waves that threatened to burst his eardrums. He kicked and clawed his way downward, not even knowing if he was headed in the right direction. Then he was falling again.

He kept swimming, all alone in the dark. Another wave passed, lifted him, let him down again.   A few minutes later, another one, seeming to come from the other direction.   He was hopelessly confused.   He suddenly felt he was swimming the wrong way.   He stopped, not knowing what to do.   Was he pointed in the right direction?   He had no way to tell.

He stopped paddling and tried to orient himself.   It was useless.   He felt surges, and was sure he was being tumbled and buffeted.

Then his skin was tingling with the sensation of a million bubbles crawling over him.   It gave him a handle on the situation.   The bubbles would be going up, wouldn't they?   And they were traveling over his body from belly to back.   So down was *that* way.

But he didn't have time to make use of the information.   He hit something hard with his hip, wrenched his back as his body tried to tumble over in the foam and water, then was sliding along a smooth surface.   It felt like he was going very fast, and he knew where he was and where he was heading and there was nothing he could do about it.   The tail of the wave had lifted him clear of the rocky slope of the dam and deposited him on the flat surface.   It was now spending itself, sweeping him along to the edge of the world.   He turned around, feeling the sliding surface beneath him with his hands, and tried to dig in.   It was a nightmare; nothing he did had any effect.   Then his head broke free into the air.

He was still sliding, but the huge hump of the wave had dissipated itself and was collapsing quietly into froth and puddles.   It drained away with amazing speed. He was left there, alone, cheek pressed lovingly to the cold rock.   The darkness was total.

He wasn't about to move.   For all he knew, there was an eight-kilometer drop just behind his toes.

Maybe there would be another wave.   If so, this one would crash down on him instead of lifting him like a cork in a tempest.   It should kill him instantly.   He refused to worry about that.   All he cared about now was not slipping any further.

The stars had vanished.   Power failure?   Now they blinked on.   He raised his head a little, in time to see a soft, diffused glow in the east.   The moon was rising, and it was doing it at breakneck speed.   He saw it rotate from a thin crescent configuration to bright fullness in under a minute.   Someone was still in charge and had decided to throw some light on the scene.

He stood, though his knees were weak.   Tall fountains of spray far away to his right indicated where the sea was battering at the dam.   He was about in the middle of the tabletop, far from either edge.   The ocean was whipped up as if by thirty hurricanes, but he was safe from it at this distance unless there were another tsunami yet to come.

The moonlight turned the surface into a silver mirror, littered with flopping fish. He saw another figure get to her feet, and ran in that direction.

The helicopter located them by infrared detector.   They had no way of telling how long it had been.   The moon was hanging motionless in the center of the sky.

They got into the cabin, shivering.

The helicopter pilot was happy to have found them, but grieved over other lives lost.   She said the toll stood at three dead, fifteen missing and presumed dead. Most of these had been working on the reefs.   All the land surface of Pacifica had been scoured, but the loss of life had been minimal.   Most had time to get to an elevator and go below or to a helicopter and rise above the devastation.

From what they had been able to find out, heat expansion of the crust had moved farther down into the interior of the planet than had been expected.   It was summer on the surface, something it was easy to forget down here.   The engineers had been sure that the inner surface of the sky had been stabilized years ago, but a new fault had been opened by the slight temperature rise.   She pointed up to where ships were hovering like fireflies next to the sky, playing searchlights on the site of damage.   No one knew yet if Pacifica would have to be abandoned for another twenty years while it stabilized.

She set them down on Rarotonga.   The place was a mess.   The wave had climbed the bottom rise and crested at the reef, and a churning hell of foam and debris had swept over the island.   Little was left standing except the concrete blocks that housed the elevators, scoured of their decorative camouflage.

Piri saw a familiar figure coming toward him through the wreckage that had been a picturesque village.   She broke into a run, and nearly bowled him over, laughing and kissing him.

"We were sure you were dead," Harra said, drawing back from him as if to check for cuts and bruises.

"It was a fluke, I guess," he said, still incredulous that he had survived.   It had seemed bad enough out there in the open ocean; the extent of the disaster was much more evident on the island.   He was badly shaken to see it.

"Lee suggested that we try to dive under the wave.   That's what saved us.   It just lifted us up, then the last one swept us over the top of the dam and drained away.   It dropped us like leaves."

"Well, not quite so tenderly in my case," Lee pointed out.   "It gave me quite a jolt.   I think I might have sprained my wrist."

A medic was available.   While her wrist was being bandaged, she kept looking at Piri.   He didn't like the look.

"There's something I'd intended to talk to you about on the raft, or soon after we got home.   There's no point in your staying here any longer anyway, and I don't know where you'd go."

"No!" Harra burst out.   "Not yet.   Don't tell him anything yet.   It's not fair. Stay away from him."   She was protecting Piri with her body, from no assault that was apparent to him.

"I just wanted to—"

"No, no.   Don't listen to her, Piri.   Come with me."   She pleaded with the other woman.   "Just give me a few hours alone with him, there's some things I never got around to telling him."

Lee looked undecided, and Piri felt mounting rage and frustration.   He had known things were going on around him.   It was mostly his own fault that he had ignored them, but now he had to know. He pulled his hand free from Harra and faced Lee.

"Tell me."

She looked down at her feet, then back to his eyes.

"I'm not what I seem, Piri. I've been leading you along, trying to make this easier for you. But you still fight me. I don't think there's any way it's going to be easy."

"No!" Harra shouted again.

"What are you?"

"I'm a psychiatrist. I specialize in retrieving people like you, people who are in a mental vacation mode, what you call 'second childhood.' You're aware of all this, on another level, but the child in you has fought it at every stage. The result has been nightmares—probably with me as the focus, whether you admitted it or not."

She grasped both his wrists, one of them awkwardly because of her injury.

"Now listen to me." She spoke in an intense whisper, trying to get it all out before the panic she saw in his face broke free and sent him running. "You came here for a vacation. You were going to stay ten years, growing up and taking it easy. That's all over. The situation that prevailed when you left is now out of date. Things have moved faster than you believed possible. You had expected a ten-year period after your return to get things in order for the coming battles. That time has evaporated. The Common Market of the Inner Planets has fired the first shot. They've instituted a new system of accounting and it's locked into their computers and running. It's aimed right at Pluto, and it's been working for a month now. We cannot continue as an economic partner to the C.M.I.P., because from now on every time we sell or buy or move money the inflationary multiplier is automatically juggled against us. It's perfectly legal by all existing treaties, and it's necessary to their economy. But it ignores our time-lag disadvantage. We have to consider it as a hostile act, no matter what the intent. You have to come back and direct the war, Mister Finance Minister."

The words shattered what calm Piri had left. He wrenched free of her hands and turned wildly to look all around him. Then he sprinted down the beach. He tripped once over his splay feet, got up without ever slowing, and disappeared.

Harra and Lee stood silently and watched him go.

"You didn't have to be so rough with him," Harra said, but knew it wasn't so. She just hated to see him so confused.

"It's best done quickly when they resist. And he's all right. He'll have a fight with himself, but there's no real doubt of the outcome."

"So the Piri I know will be dead soon?"

Lee put her arm around the younger woman.

"Not at all. It's a reintegration, without a winner or a loser. You'll see." She looked at the tear-streaked face.

"Don't worry. You'll like the older Piri. It won't take him any time at all to realize that he loves you."

*   *   *

He had never been to the reef at night. It was a place of furtive fish, always one step ahead of him as they darted back into their places of concealment. He wondered how long it would be before they ventured out in the long night to come. The sun might not rise for years.

They might never come out. Not realizing the changes in their environment, night fish and day fish would never adjust. Feeding cycles would be disrupted, critical temperatures would go awry, the endless moon and lack of sun would frustrate the internal mechanisms, bred over billions of years, and fish would die. It had to happen.

The ecologists would have quite a job on their hands.

But there was one denizen of the outer reef that would survive for a long time. He would eat anything that moved and quite a few things that didn't, at any time of the day or night. He had no fear, he had no internal clocks dictating to him, no inner pressures to confuse him except the one overriding urge to attack. He would last as long as there was anything alive to eat.

But in what passed for a brain in the white-bottomed torpedo that was the Ghost, a splinter of doubt had lodged. He had no recollection of similar doubts, though there had been some. He was not equipped to remember, only to hunt. So this new thing that swam beside him, and drove his cold brain as near as it could come to the emotion of anger, was a mystery. He tried again and again to attack it, then something would seize him with an emotion he had not felt since he was half a meter long, and fear would drive him away.

Piri swam along beside the faint outline of the shark. There was just enough moonlight for him to see the fish, hovering at the ill-defined limit of his sonic signal. Occasionally, the shape would shudder from head to tail, turn toward him, and grow larger. At these times Piri could see nothing but a gaping jaw. Then it would turn quickly, transfix him with that bottomless pit of an eye, and sweep away.

Piri wished he could laugh at the poor, stupid brute. How could he have feared such a mindless eating machine?

Good-bye, pinbrain. He turned and stroked lazily toward the shore. He knew the shark would turn and follow him, nosing into the interdicted sphere of his transponder, but the thought did not impress him. He was without fear. How could he be afraid, when he had already been swallowed into the belly of his nightmare? The teeth closed around him, he awakened, and remembered. And that was the end of his fear.

Good-bye, tropical paradise. You were fun while you lasted. Now I'm grown up, and must go off to war.

He didn't relish it. It was a wrench to leave his childhood, though the time had surely been right. Now the responsibilities had descended on him, and he must shoulder them. He thought of Harra.

"Piri," he told himself, "as a teenager, you were just too dumb to live."

Knowing it was the last time, he felt the coolness of the water flowing over his gills. They had served him well, but had no place in his work. There was no place for a fish, and no place for Robinson Crusoe.

Good-bye, gills.

He kicked harder for the shore and came to stand, dripping wet, on the beach. Harra and Lee were there, waiting for him.

ISAAC ASIMOV

How It Happened

My brother began to dictate in his best oratorical style, the one which has the tribes hanging on his words.

"In the beginning," he said, "exactly 15.2 billion years ago, there was a big bang and the Universe—"

But I had stopped writing. "Fifteen billion years ago?" I said incredulously.

"Absolutely," he said. "I'm inspired."

"I don't question your inspiration," I said. (I had better not. He's three years younger than I am, but I don't try questioning his inspiration. Neither does anyone else or there's hell to pay.) "But are you going to tell the story of the Creation over a period of fifteen billion years?"

"I have to," said my brother. "That's how long it took. I have it all in here," he tapped his forehead, "and it's on the very highest authority."

By now I had put down my reed pen. "Do you know the price of papyrus?" I said.

"What?" (He may be inspired, but I frequently noticed that the inspiration didn't include such sordid matters as the price of papyrus.)

I said, "Suppose you describe one million years of events to each roll of papyrus. That means you'll have to fill fifteen thousand rolls. You'll have to talk long enough to fill them, and you know that you begin to stammer after a while. I'll have to write enough to fill them, and my fingers will fall off. And even if we can afford all that papyrus and you have the voice and I have the strength, who's going to copy it? We've got to have a guarantee of a hundred copies before we can publish, and without that where will we get royalties from?"

My brother thought a while. He said, "You think I ought to cut it down?"

"Way down," I said, "if you expect to reach the public."

"How about a hundred years?" he said.

"How about six days?" I said.

He said, horrified, "You can't squeeze Creation into six days."

I said, "This is all the papyrus I have. What do *you* think?"

"Oh, well," he said, and began to dictate again, "In the beginning— Does it have to be six days, Aaron?"

I said, firmly, "Six days, Moses."

ARTHUR C. CLARKE

Quarantine

Earth's flaming debris still filled half the sky when the question filtered up
to Central from the Curiosity Generator.

"Why was it necessary?   Even though they were organic, they *had* reached
Third Order Intelligence."

"We had no choice: five earlier units became hopelessly infected, when they
made contact."

"Infected?   How?"

The microseconds dragged slowly by, while Central tracked down the few fading
memories that had leaked past the Censor Gate, when the heavily-buffered Recon-
naissance Circuits had been ordered to self-destruct.

"They encountered—a *problem*—that could not be fully analyzed within the
lifetime of the Universe.   Though it involved only six operators, they became
totally obsessed by it."

"How is that possible?"

"We do not know: *we must never know*.   But if those six operators are ever
rediscovered, all rational computing will end."

"How can they be recognized?"

"That also we do not know: only the names leaked through before the Censor
Gate closed.   Of course, they mean nothing."

"Nevertheless, I must have them."

The Censor voltage started to rise; but it did not trigger the Gate.

"Here they are: King, Queen, Bishop, Knight, Rook, Pawn."

Cautionary Tales

T aller than a man, thinner than a man, with a long neck and eyes set wide apart in his head, the creature still resembled a man; and he had aged like a man. Cosmic rays had robbed his fur of color, leaving a grey-white ruff along the base of his skull and over both ears. His pastel-pink skin was deeply wrinkled and marked with darker blotches. He carried himself like something precious and fragile. He was coming across the balcony toward Gordon.

Gordon had brought a packaged lunch from the Embassy. He ate alone. The bubble-world's landscape curled up and over his head: yellow-and-scarlet parkland, slate-colored buildings that bulged at the top. Below the balcony, patterned stars streamed beneath several square miles of window. There were a dozen breeds of alien on the public balcony, at least two of which had to be pets or symbiotes of other aliens; and no humans but for Gordon. Gordon wondered if the ancient humanoid resented his staring . . . then stared in earnest as the creature stopped before his table. The alien said, "May I break your privacy?"

Gordon nodded; but that could be misinterpreted, so he said, "I'm glad of the company."

The alien carefully lowered himself until he sat cross-legged across the table. He said, "I seek never to die."

Gordon's heart jumped into his throat. "I'm not sure what you mean," he said cautiously. "The Fountain of Youth?"

"I do not care what form it takes." The alien spoke the Trade Language well, but his strange throat added a castinet-like clicking. "Our own legend holds no fountain. When we learned to cross between stars we found the legend of immortality wherever there were thinking beings. Whatever their shape or size or intelligence, whether they make their own worlds or make only clay pots, they all tell the tales of people who live forever."

"It's hard not to wonder if they have some basis," Gordon encouraged him.

The alien's head snapped around, fast enough and far enough to break a man's neck. The prominent lumps bobbing in his throat were of alien shape: not Adam's Apple, but someone else's. "It must be so. I have searched too long for it to be false. You, have you ever found clues to the secret of living forever?"

Gordon searched when he could, when his Embassy job permitted it. There had been rumors about the Ftokteek. Gordon had followed the rumors out of human space, toward the galactic core and the Ftokteek Empire, to this Ftokteek-dominated meeting place of disparate life forms, this cloud of bubble-worlds of varying gravities and atmospheres. Gordon was middle-aged now, and Sol was invisible even to orbiting telescopes, and the Ftokteek died like anyone else.

He said, "We've got the legends. Look them up in the Human Embassy library. Ponce de Leon, and Gilgamesh, and Orpheus, and Tithonus, and . . . every god we ever had lived forever, if he didn't die by violence, and some could heal from that. Some religions say that some part of us lives on after we die."

"I will go to your library tomorrow," the alien said without enthusiasm. "Do you have no more than legends?"

"No, but . . . do other species tell cautionary tales?"

"I do not understand."

Gordon said, "Some of our legends say you wouldn't want to live forever. Tithonus, for instance. A goddess gave him the gift of living forever, but she forgot to keep him young. He withered into a lizard. Adam and Eve were exiled by God; He was afraid they'd learn the secret of immortality and think they were as good as Him. Orpheus tried to bring a woman back from the dead. Some of the stories say you can't get immortality, and some say you'd go insane with boredom."

The alien pondered. "The tale tellers disdain immortality because they cannot have it. Jealousy? Could immortal beings have walked among you once?" ·

Gordon laughed. "I doubt it. Was that what made you come to me?"

"I go to the worlds where many species meet. When I see a creature new to me, then I ask. Sometimes I can sense others like me, who want never to die."

Gordon looked down past the edge of the balcony, down through the great window at the banded Jovian planet that held this swarm of bubble-worlds in their orbits. He came here every day; small wonder that the alien had picked him out. He came because he would not eat with the others. They thought he was crazy. He thought of them as mayflies, with their attention always on the passing moment, and no thought for the future. He thought of himself as an ambitious mayfly; and he ate alone.

The alien was saying, "When I was young I looked for the secret among the most advanced species. The great interstellar empires, the makers of artificial worlds, the creatures who mine stars for elements and send ships through the universe seeking ever more knowledge, would build their own immortality. But they die as you and I die. Some races live longer than mine, but they all die."

"The Ftokteek have a computerized library the size of a small planet," Gordon said. He meant to get there someday, if he lived. "It must know damn near everything."

The alien answered with a whispery chuckle. "No bigger than a moon is the Ftokteek library. It told me nothing I could use."

The banded world passed from view.

"Then I looked among primitives," the alien said, "who live closer to their legends. They die. When I thought to talk to their ghosts, there was nothing, though I used their own techniques. Afterward I searched the vicinities of the black holes and other strange pockets of the universe, hoping that there may be places where entropy reverses itself. I found nothing. I examined the mathematics that describe the universe. I have learned a score of mathematical systems, and none hold any hope of entropy reversal, natural or created.''

Gordon watched stars pass below his feet. He said, ''Relativity. We used to think that if you traveled faster than light, time would reverse itself.''

''I know eight systems of traveling faster than light—''

''Eight? What is there besides ours and the Ftokteek drive?''

''Six others. I rode them all, and always I arrived older. My time runs short. I never examined the quasars, and now I would not live to reach them. What else is left? I have been searching for fourteen thousand years—'' The alien didn't notice when Gordon made a peculiar hissing sound. ''—in our counting. Less in yours, perhaps. Our world huddles closer to a cooler sun than this. Our year is twenty-one million standard seconds.''

''What are you *saying?* Ours is only thirty-one million—''

''My present age is three hundred thirty-six point seven billion standard seconds in the Ftokteek counting.''

''Ten thousand Earth years. More!''

''Far too long. I never mated. None carry my genes. Now none ever will, unless I can grow young again. There is little time left.''

''But *why?*''

The alien seemed startled. ''Because it is not enough. Because I am afraid to die. Are you short-lived, then?''

''Yes,'' said Gordon.

''Well, I have traveled with short-lived companions. They die, I mourn. I need a companion with the strength of youth. My spacecraft is better than any you could command. You may benefit from my research. We breath a similar air mixture, our bodies use the same chemistry, we search for the same treasure. Will you join my quest?''

''No.''

''But . . . I sensed that you seek immortality. I am never wrong. Don't you feel it, the certainty that there is a way to thwart entropy, to live forever?''

''I used to think so,'' said Gordon.

In the morning he arranged passage home to Sol system. Ten thousand years wasn't enough . . . no lifetime was enough, unless you lived it in such a way as to make it enough.

JO CLAYTON

A Bait of Dreams

As Gleia hurried along the uneven planks of the walkway, pattering around the bodies of sleeping drunks, slipping past workmen, and market women, Horli's red rim bathed the street in blood-red light, painting a film of charm over the facades of the sagging buildings.

She glanced up repeatedly, fearing to see the blue light of the second sun Hesh creeping into the sky. Late. Her breath came raggedly as she tried to move faster. She knocked against people in the crowded street, drawing curses after her.

Late. Nothing had gone right this morning. When Horli's light had crept through the holes in her torn shade and touched her face, one look at the clock sent her into a panic, kicking the covers frantically aside, tearing her nightgown over her head. No time to eat. No time to discipline her wild hair. She dragged a comb through the worst of the tangles as she splashed water into a basin. No time to straighten the mess in the room. She slapped water on her face, gasping at the icy sting.

Rush. Grab up the rent money. Snatch open the wardrobe door and pull out the first cafta that came to hand. Slip feet into sandals. A strap breaks. With half-swallowed gasp, dig out the old sandals with soles worn to a paper thinness. Rush. Drop the key chain around her neck. Hip strikes against a chair, knocking it over. Ah! No time to pick it up. Plunge from the room, pausing only to make sure the lock catches. Even in her feverish hurry she could feel nausea at the thought of old Miggela's fat greasy fingers prodding through her things again.

Clatter down the stairs. Down the creaking groaning spiral, fourth floor to ground floor. Nod the obligatory greeting to the blunt-snouted landlady who came out from her nest where she sat in ambush day and night.

The sharp salty breeze whipped through the dingy side street, surrounding her with its burden of fish, tar, exotic spices, and the sour stench from the scavenger's piles of scrap and garbage. The smells slid by unnoticed as she ran down the wooden walk, her footsteps playing a nervous tattoo on the planks. As she turned onto the larger main street, she glanced up once again. Hesh still hadn't joined Horli in the sky. Thank god. Still a little time left. She could get to the shop before Hesh-rise.

Her foot came down hard on a round object. It rolled backward, throwing her.

She staggered. Her arms flung wildly out, then she fell forward on the planks, feeling her palms tearing as she tried to break her fall, feeling her knees tearing even through the coarse cloth of her cafta.

For a minute she stayed on hands and knees, ignoring the curious eyes of the workers flowing past her. Several stopped and asked if she was hurt. But she shook her head, her dark brown hair hanging about her face, hiding it from them. They shrugged, then went on, leaving her to recover by herself.

Still on her knees, she straightened her body and examined her palms. The skin was broken and abraded. Already she could feel her hands stiffening. She brushed the grit off, wincing at the pain. Then she looked around to find the thing that had brought her down. A crystalline pebble was caught in one of the cracks between the planks. Shaped like an egg, it was just big enough to fit in the palm of her hand. "A Ranga eye," she whispered.

Blue Hesh slid over the edge of the roof above her, reflecting in the crystal. Gleia looked cautiously around, then thrust the eye into her pocket and jumped to her feet, wincing at the pain that stabbed up from her battered knees. Limping, she hurried on toward the center of the city.

"You're late." Habbibah came fluttering through the lines of bent backs, her tiny hands thrusting out of the sleeves of her elegant black velvet cafta like small pale animals. Her dark eyes darted from side to side, scanning the girls' work as she moved.

Gleia sucked in a deep breath, then lowered her head submissively. She knew better than to try to excuse herself.

Habbibah stopped in front of her, moving her hands constantly over herself, patting her hair, stroking her throat, touching her mouth with small feathery pats. "Well?"

Gleia stretched out her hands, showing the lacerated palms. "I fell."

Habbibah shuddered. "Go wash." She flicked a hand at the wall clock. "You'll make up the time by working through the lunch break."

Gleia bit her lip. She could feel the emptiness growing inside her and a buzzing in her head and a tremble in her knees. She wanted to protest but didn't dare.

"Go. Go. Go." Habbibah fluttered hands at her. "Don't touch the wedding cafta with those filthy hands and don't waste more time."

As Gleia went into the dark, noisome washroom, she heard the soft voice lashing first one then another. She made a face and muttered, "Bitch." The falling curtain muted the poisonous tongue.

Hastily Gleia scrubbed at her hands, ignoring the sting of the coarse soap. She dried them on the towel, the only clean thing in the room. Clean because a filthy towel might lead to filthy hands which could damage the fine materials the girls worked on. Not for the workers, nothing ever done for the workers. She felt the crystal bang against her thigh as she turned to move out, felt a brief flare of excitement, but there was no time and she forgot it immediately.

She slid into her place and took up her work, settling the candles so the light fell more strongly on the embroidery. White on white, a delicate pattern of fantasy flowers and birds.

Habbibah's shadow fell over the work. "Hands."

Gleia held out her hands. Small thumbs pressed hard on the drying wounds.

"Good. No blood." Habbibah's hand flew to the shimmering white material protected from dust and wear by a sheath of coarse unbleached muslin. "Slow." A finger jabbed at the incomplete sections, flicking over the pricked-out design. "I must have it done by tomorrow. A two-drach fine for each hour you take over that." Her shadow moved off as she darted away to scold one of the girls who was letting her candle gutter.

Gleia caught her breath, a hard frustration squeezing her in the middle. Tomorrow? Sinking her teeth in her lower lip, she blinked back tears. She'd been counting on the money Habbibah had promised her for this work. Twenty-five oboli. Enough to finish off the sum she needed to buy her bond, even to pay the bribes and leave a little over to live on. Now. . . . She looked around the cavernous room with the fifty small lights flickering over bent heads. Then she gritted her teeth. Damn her, she thought. I'll finish this on time if it kills me.

Resolutely she banished all distraction and bent over the work, her stiffened fingers slowing her until the exercise warmed them to their usual suppleness.

As the band of embroidery crept along the front panels of the cafta, Gleia felt hungry, her stomach paining almost as if she were poisoned, but that went away after a while.

While she sewed, her mind began to drift though her eyes clung tenaciously to the design. In a painful reverie, she relived brief images from her life, tracking the thread of events that had led her to this place at this moment. . . .

First memories. Pain and fear. Dim images of adult faces. A woman's arms clinging to her, then falling away. A man, face blurred, unrecognizable, shouting angrily, then in pain, then not at all. Then a series of faces that came and went like beads falling from a cheap necklace.

Then . . . digging in garbage piles outside kitchen doors, fighting the scavengers—small shaggy creatures, with filthy hands and furtive eyes—for scraps of half-rotten vegetables, or bones with a shred of meat left on them.

Habbibah came back, jerked the work from her hands and examined it closely. "Sloppy," she grunted. She held the work so long Gleia clenched her hands into fists, biting her lip till blood came to hold back the protest that would spoil all her chances of finishing the cafta on time.

A smile curled Habbibah's small tight mouth into a wrinkled curve, then Habbibah thrust the material back at her. "Take more care, bonder, or I'll have you rip the whole out."

Gleia watched her move on. For a minute she couldn't unclench her fingers. She wants me to go overtime. She wants to make me beg. Damn her . . . damn her . . . damn . . .

* * *

After a minute she took up the work again, driving the needle through the fabric with a vicious energy that abated after a while as the soothing spell of the work took over.   Once again she fell into the swift loose rhythm that freed her mind to think of other things.

Begging in the streets, running with packs of other abandoned children, sleeping in abandoned houses or old empty warehouses, barely escaping with her life from a fire that took twenty other children, wandering the streets, driven by cold back into the houses where the only heat was the body heat of the children sleeping in piles where some on the outside froze and some on the inside smothered, children dying in terrible numbers in the winter, only the toughest surviving.

Being beaten and hurt until she grew old enough to fight, learning to leap immediately into all-out attack whenever she had to fight, no matter what the cause, until the bigger children let her alone since it wasn't worth expending so much of their own meager energy to defeat her over small matters.

Being casually raped by a drunken sailor, then forgotten immediately as he staggered away, leaving her bloody and crying furiously on the cobblestones, not wholly sure of what had happened to her, but recognizing the violation of her person and vowing it would not happen again, screaming she would kill him kill him. . . .

Running in a gang after that, being forced to submit to Abbrah, the leader, bully-stupid but too strong for her, taking a perverse pride in being chosen, never liking it, realizing about that time the vulnerability of male pride and the superiority of male muscle.

Learning to steal, driven to stealing by Abbrah, stealing from a merchant, being caught, branded, bound into service with Habbibah.

Being scrubbed up and forced to learn . . . the lessons, oh the lessons, shadowed impersonal faces bending over her, voices, hushed and insistent, beating at her. . . .

She jumped.   A cowled figure moved soundlessly past, the coarse cloth of his robe slapping against her ankles.   She watched the Madarman halt beside Habbibah and begin talking.   Habbibah nodded and the two figures moved out of the room, both silent, both trailing huge black shadows that spread depressingly over the sewing girls.   What's that about, she wondered.   Madarman . . .

. . . cowled figures, voices demanding, learn or be beaten, memorize and repeat, mechanical rote learning, paying no attention to what is learned, cram the songs, the histories, the Madarhymns into the unwilling little heads.   Repeat. Repeat.   Work all morning, then, when her body rebelled, when she yearned for the freedom of the streets with a passion that swamped even her continual hunger to know, sent to school by order of the Madarmen to save her pitiful soul.

History in chant.   Jaydugar, the testing ground of the gods.   The Madar's white hands reached among the stars and plucked their fruit, the souls that needed testing, catmen and mermen, caravanner and hunter, scavenger and parsi, plucked wriggling from their home trees and dropped naked on the testing ground. Chant of the coming. I take you from the nest that makes you weak and blind. I take from you your metal slaves. I take from you your far-seeing eyes. I take from you the wings whereby you sail from star to star. I purify you. I give you your hands. I promise you cleverness and time. Out of nothing you will build new wings. . . .

New wings. Gleia snorted. Several girls turned to look at her, their faces disapproving. She smiled blankly at them and they settled back to work. She could hear the furtive whispers hissing between them but ignored them. Her needle whispered through sheer white material, popping in and out with smooth skill. She sniffed scornfully at the other girls' refusal to accept her into their community.

New wings. . . . She frowned down as she looped the thread in a six-petalled flower and whipped the loops in place. It might make an interesting design . . . new wings . . . the stars . . . she popped the needle through the material in a series of dandelion-bloom crosses. Did we all come here from other stars? How? Her frown deepened. The Madar . . . that was nonsense . . . wasn't it?

The Madarman came down the aisle and stopped beside her. He held out his hand. Reluctantly Gleia set the needle into the material and gave him her work, biting her lip as she saw the dark crescents of dirt under his fingernails. She held her breath as he brought the cloth up close to rheumy eyes.

"Good," he grunted. He thrust the cloth back at her and stumped off to rejoin Habbibah. Gleia took a minute to stretch her cramped limbs and straighten her legs as she watched Habbibah usher him out. Looks like I'm up for a new commission, she thought. She looked over the line of bent backs, feeling a fierce superiority to those giggling idiots raised secure in homes with fathers and mothers to protect them. Here they were anyway, doing the same thing for a lot less pay than she was getting. Gleia. The despised bonder. The marked thief. She wriggled her fingers to work some of the cramp out of them, then touched the brand on her cheek. Then she sighed and went back to the design. Her thoughts drifted back to her life. Remembering. . . .

Being forced to learn rough sewing, then embroidery, taking a timid pride in a growing skill, taking a growing pride in making designs that she soon recognized to be superior to any others created in Habbibah's establishment.

Learning she could buy herself free of the bond if she could ever find or save enough money. Fifty oboloi for the bond. Fifty oboloi for the bribes. More to keep herself while she hunted for work. Joy and despair. And joy again. . . .

Demanding and getting special pay for special projects. Her work brought fancy sums to Habbibah's greedy fingers and more—a reputation for the unique that brought her custom she couldn't have touched before. The old bitch tried to beat her into working, but she had learned too well how to survive. She was stubborn enough to resist punishment and to persist in her demands, sitting resolutely idle through starvings and whippings and threats until she won her point.

*   *   *

Gleia jabbed the needle through the cloth.   It glanced off a fingernail, coming close to pricking her finger and drawing blood.   She leaned back, breathing fast, trying to calm herself.   A drop of blood marring the white was all she needed. Not now.   Not so close to winning.   She couldn't stand another month of this slavery.   She fingered the mark on her cheek and knew they'd throw her into prison as incorrigible if she tried to run away.

Sometime later Habbibah made the last round, inspecting the day's work.   She stopped beside Gleia and picked up the cloth, running the unworked length of design through her plump white fingers.   "Pah! too slow.   And there."   She jabbed a forefinger at the last sections of work.   "You did finer work than that when you were learning.   Tomorrow you come in one hour early.   Abbosine will be told to let you in."   She pinched the material between her fingers.   "Take out that last work to there."   She thrust the strip of embroidery into Gleia's face and indicated a spot about two palms' width above the last stitches.   "I won't tolerate such miserable cobbling going out under my name."

Gleia closed her eyes.   Her hands clenched into fists.   She wanted to smash the old woman in the face, to smash smash smash that little weasel face into bloody ruin, then wipe the ruin on that damn cafta.   But she doubted whether she could stand without tumbling over, so she managed to keep her head down and her mouth shut.   When the old woman went off to scold someone else, she sat still, hands fisted in her lap.

Habbibah's scolding voice faded as she left the room.   The other girls moved about, chattering cautiously, eyes turning slyly about, watching out for the sudden return of their employer.   When they had all trickled out, bunched into laughing clusters of work-friends, Gleia forced herself onto her feet.

The world swung.   She grabbed at the sewing stand and held on tight until the room steadied around her.   With neat economical movements she folded her work and put it in the box, then she walked through the rows of silent tables, a fragile glass person that the slightest shock would crack into a thousand fragments.

Outside, the darkening twilight threw a veil of red over the crowded streets, blurring covered carts with screeching wheels into horsemen riding past in dark solid groups into single riders gawking at the city sights into throngs of people pushing along the wooden walkways.   She hummed the Madarchant of the peoples. *Chilkaman catman fisherman and hunter, parsi plainsman desert fox and herder, firssi mountainman caravanner hawkster. . . .*   In spite of her fatigue she sucked in a deep breath and watched furtively the fascinating variety of peoples flowing past her.   Chilka catmen from the plains with their hairy faces, flat noses, and double eyelids, the inner transparent one retracted into the damp tissue folds around their bulging slit-pupiled eyes.   Caravanners, small and quick, more like her own parsi people, dark hair, dark eyes, pale faces.   Mountain hunters, far from their heights, with dark gold skin and brown hair bleached almost white at the tips, leading horses loaded with fur bales.

A breath of salt air, cool and fresh as the sea itself, stung her nose.   A flash of opaline emerald.   Impression of scaled flesh flowing liquidly past.   A merman.

Ignoring the irritated protest of the other pedestrians she turned and stared after the slim amphibian walking with the characteristic quick clumsy grace of the sea folk. She didn't recognize him. Disappointed, she edged to the wall and stumbled tiredly through the crowd thinking about the only friend she'd ever had, a slim green boy . . . so long ago . . . so long ago. . . .

She walked slowly into the dingy front hall of the boarding house, putting each foot down with stiff care, wondering how she was going to get up all those damn creaking stairs.

"Gleia, 'spina." The hoarse breathy voice brought her to a careful halt. She inched her head around, feeling that her burning eyes would roll from her head if she moved too quickly.

"Rent." Miggela held out a short stubby hand.

Gleia closed her eyes and fumbled in her pocket, sore fingers groping for the packet of coins she'd put there earlier. Her fingers closed on the egg-shaped stone and she frowned—not remembering, for a minute, where the thing came from.

The rat-faced landlady scowled and flapped her pudgy hand up and down. "Rent!"

Gleia slid her hand past the crystal and found the packet. Silently she drew it out and handed it to the old woman.

Miggela tore clumsily at the paper. Her crusted tongue clamped between crooked yellow teeth, she counted the coins with deliberate slowness, examining each one with suspicious care, peering nearsightedly at the stamping.

Gleia rubbed her hand across her face, too tired to be irritated.

Slipping the coins into a sleeve pocket, Miggela stood staring up into the taller woman's drawn face. "You're late. You missed supper."

"Oh."

"And don't you go trying to cook in your room."

"No." She wasn't hungry anymore but knew she had to have food. Her legs trembled. She wanted more than anything to lie down. But she turned and went out. She walked slowly over the uneven planks, heading aimlessly toward the edge of the night-quarter and a familiar cookshop.

Gleia strolled out of the cookshop feeling more like herself with two meat pies and a cup of cha warming her middle. She held a third pie in her hand. She sank her teeth into the pie, chewing slowly, drifting along the street watching the people move past her.

Horli was completely gone in the west with only a stain of red to mark her passing while the biggest moon Aab was thrusting her pale white edge over the rooflines to the east, her brilliant colorless light cutting through inky shadows. Gleia knew she should get back to her room. There were too many dangers for a woman alone here. Sighing, she began working her way through the noisy crowd toward the slum quarter. She finished the pie, wiped her greasy hands on a bit of paper, and dropped the paper in the gutter for the scavengers to pick up in their dawn sweeps through the streets.

The crowd thinned as she left the commercial area and moved into the slum that held a few decrepit stables and row on row of ancient dwellings converted into boarding houses. Some were empty with staring black windows where the glass was gone—stolen or broken by derelicts who could find no other place to sleep. One by one these abandoned houses burned down, leaving behind fields of weeds and piles of broken, blackened boards.

Gleia looked up at the grey, weathered front of Miggela's place. She was tired to the point of giddiness but she felt such a reluctance to go inside that she couldn't force her foot onto the warped lower step; instead she went past the house and turned into the alley winding back from the side street. Moving quickly, eyes flicking warily about, she trotted past the one-room hovels where the small scurrying scavengers lived anonymous lives. Sometimes desperate bashers and maulers hid out there waiting for sailors to come stumbling back to their ships. She went around the end of a warehouse, the last in the line of those circling the working front of the dredged port. The water here was too shallow to accommodate any but the smallest ships.

She saw a small neat oceangoer, a chis-makka, one of the independent gypsy ships that went up and down the coast as the winds and their cargoes dictated. The ship was dark, the crew apparently on liberty in one of the taverns whose lights and noise enlivened the waterfront some distance in toward the center. Out here it was quiet, with ravellings of fog beginning to thicken over the water. As the waves slapped regularly at the piles, the evening on-shore breeze made the rigging on board the chis-makka creak and groan.

Gleia edged to the far side of the wharf and kicked off her sandals. Then she ran along the planks, bent over, making no more sound than a shadow. She slid over the end of the wharf and pulled herself onto one of the crossbars nailed from pile to pile under the broad planks. Ignoring the coating of slime and drying seaweed, she sat with her back against a pile, her legs dangling in space, her feet moving back and forth just above the rocking surface of the water.

For a long while she sat there, the sickening emotional mix settling away until she felt calm and at peace again. The fog continued to thicken, sounds coming to her over the water with an eerie remoteness.

Something pushed against her thigh. She remembered the Ranga eye that had thrown her so disastrously in the morning. As she reached into her pocket, the water broke in a neat splash and a glinting form came out of it, swooping onto the crossbar beside her. In her surprise she nearly toppled off into the still-agitated water, but the merman caught hold of her and steadied her.

Her face almost nosing into his chest, she saw the water pour from his gill slits and the slits squeeze closed. The moonlight struggling through the fog touched his narrow young face and reflected off his pointed mother-of-pearl teeth as he sucked air into his breathing bladder than grinned at her. "Thought it was you. No other land crawler ever come here."

"Tetaki?" She closed her fingers around his cool hard forearm. "I haven't seen you in years." Shaking her head, she smiled uncertainly at him. "Years."

"Not sin' you was finger high."

"You weren't any bigger." She tugged at her nose, amusement bubbling inside her. "Brat."

He perched easily on the narrow bar, his short crisp hair already drying and springing into the curls that used to fascinate her with their tight coils and deep blue color. "Good times. We was good friends." He was silent a minute. "This isn't the firs' year I come back. You never come here."

"I was thinking about you earlier." She pushed away from the pile and touched his knee. "The only friend I ever had."

His hand closed around hers, cool and metal smooth, his flesh unlike hers but comforting. "I come each time. You were never here."

"At first I couldn't," she said, her fatigue and depression coming back like the fog to shroud her, smother her spirit. She sighed. "Later . . . Later, I forgot."

"What happened?" His hand tightened on hers. She looked up. The shining unfamiliar planes of his face seemed to banish the fog. Then he smiled. His teeth were a carnivore's fangs, needle sharp and double rowed. "Forgot me? Shame."

She laughed and pulled free. "I turned thief. Abbrah made me. Remember him?"

His teeth glinted again. "I got reason."

Gleia stared at her feet swinging back and forth over the dark water, almost black here under the wharf but flickering with tiny silver highlights where the moonlight danced off the tops of wavelets, remembering. . . .

A delegation of the amphibian people had come to negotiate trade rights with the Maleek; Tetaki's father was a minor official. She remembered a slim scaled form with big lightgreen eyes and tight-coiled blue hair poking through a dingy side street looking eagerly about at the strange sights. Alone. Foolishly alone. Abbrah's gang gathered around him, baiting him, coming closer and closer to attack. Something about his refusal to give in to them stirred a spark in Gleia and she fought her way to his side in that stubborn all-out battle the gang knew too well. So they backed off, shouting obscenities, reasserting their dominance by showing contempt for her and her protégé. She took him back to his father and scolded the startled merman for his carelessness.

"You got caught." His dry comment roused her from her reverie.

"I was a lousy thief. Yes, I got caught. And bonded. See?" She turned her face so he could see the bondmark burned into her cheek. "What about you?"

He chuckled and waved a hand toward the dark shadow that marked the presence of the chis-makka. "Ours. This is the fifth summer we come to the fairs."

"Hey." She forced congratulatory laughter.

He bent closer, staring into her face. "You don' look so good."

She yawned. "Madar, I'm tired." She swallowed another yawn. "That's all."

"Come back wit' me. Temokeuu would welcome you. You could live wit' us."

She stroked the mark on her cheek but didn't answer for a minute. He settled back, content to let her announce her answer when she was ready. Finally, she shook her head. "Can't, Tetaki. I'm stuck here till my bond is cancelled. You going to be here long?"

"We've had good trading." He frowned. "Two, three days more, I think."

"At least we can talk some. I've missed having someone to talk to."

"Come see Temokeuu. We show you the ship."

"Sure." She yawned again. "I'd better get back. I have to be up an hour early tomorrow." She swung herself up onto the wharf, hung her head over the edge for a minute. "See you."

Her room looked like someone had taken a giant spoon and given it a quick stir. The sheet, blanket, and quilt hung over the side of the bed where she'd kicked them. Her one chair was overturned. She remembered her hip catching it on the way out. The wardrobe door hung halfway open. The sandal with a broken strap sat forlornly in the middle of the floor.

Gleia stretched, feeling the spurious energy from the warm food beginning to trickle away. Yawning repeatedly she pulled the bed to rights and straightened the room superficially, then tugged the ties loose and pulled her cafta over her head. The crystal bumped against her and she fished it out before she hung the garment away. Then she strolled across the room to the nightstand, turning the Ranga eye over and over in her hands. She dropped it in the middle of the bed and took out her cha pot, setting it next to the water tin. From the bottom drawer in the bed table she pulled out the tiny sway-bottomed brazier, setting it up on the wide window ledge. Using the candle and strips of paper, she got the charcoal burning, then set the water tin on the grill. Making sure the window was wedged open, she left the tin to boil and went back to the nightstand. She dumped a palmful of leaves into the cha pot and got a cup ready, then let herself collapse on top of the quilt.

She folded the pillow twice to prop up her head and reached out, prodding the quilt. She fished the eye from under the curve of her back and turned it over and over, examining it idly.

A Ranga eye. She'd heard whispers of them. A frisson of fear shivered down her spine. If they caught her with it. . . . If they caught her, she could forget about buying her bond. Or anything else. If I could sell it . . . somehow . . . somehow . . . if I could sell it, Madar! Bonded thief with a Ranga eye. If I could sell it. . . .

The crystal warmed as she touched it. At first a few tentative sparks licked through the water-clear form. She felt a surge of delight. The tips of her fingers moved in slow caressing circles over the smooth surface. The colors began cycling hypnotically, then the color forms began to shift their nature, imperceptibly altering into images of a place. As she watched, the picture developed rapidly, blurred at first, then sharpening into focus.

Gentle hills rolled into a blue distance, covered with a velvety green carpet, a species of thick moss dotted with small star-shaped pseudo-flowers. Other flower forms as large as trees were spaced over the slopes, each form existing at the middle of a circular space roughly equal to the extreme limit of its four leaf-stems. The leaves were eight-sided and multiple, marching along wiry black stems curving out from the central stalk at a spot halfway up to the bloom, four black arcs springing out at the same height from the ground. At the top of each plant great brilliant petals rayed out from a black center that gathered in the butter-yellow light of a single sun.

Another sun. She stroked the crystal, dreaming of another place, a better place, feeling a growing excitement. The tin on the fire began to whistle softly. Gleia dropped the eye on the bed, levered herself up, and scuffed across to the brazier. She poured the bubbling water over the cha leaves. While they were steeping, she tilted the rest of the water onto the glowing coals. Head tipped back to avoid the billowing steam, she let the blackened water trickle down the side of the building. Then she knocked out the wedge and pulled the window shut.

With a cup of cha in one hand and the eye in the other, a clean nightgown on her body and the pillow freshly folded for her head, she lay and watched the play of colors in the crystal. The image began to move through the flower trees, as if she was seeing through the eyes of some creature flying just below the petals of the flower tops. Before she had time to get bored with the lovely but monotonous landscape she flew out into the open, skimming along brilliant white sand. Blue waves rolled in with white-caps breaking cleanly, rhythmically. The sky stretched above, a glowing cloudless blue only slightly lighter than the sea. As she hovered in place she saw other creatures come flittering from the flower forest. A delicate-boned male with huge black eyes danced up to her, spiralling in complex pirouettes.

Huge black eyes soft as soot and as shineless. Thin arms and legs. Hands whose long slender fingers, like jointed sticks, were half the length of the forearms. Body short and broad, the shoulders muscled hugely.

From his back sprang wide delicate butterfly wings patterned with brilliant colors in black-outlined splotches. He rode the air in swoops and glides, wheeled in front of her, small mouth stretched in a wide inviting grin, narrow hands beckoning. . . .

The exhaustion of the day caught up with her and she sank into a heavy sleep, the last of the cha spilling on the bed, soaking into the mattress. The crystal rolled out of her loosened fingers.

When the alarm bell woke her in the morning the cha spot was still damp and the leaves were smeared over her shoulder and back. The crystal had worked along her body and ended up in the hollow between her neck and shoulder. When she picked it up to put it in the drawer, it seemed to cling to her fingers, quivering gently against her skin, shedding a pleasant warmth that slid up her arm and made her feel soft and dreamy. She shut off the alarm and stumbled to the wardrobe still half asleep in the deep red dawn. With the eye clutched in her hand she fumbled for a cafta. After she wriggled into the garment, she slid the stone into the pocket not noticing what she was doing, tied the ties, and smoothed the material down over her body.

The cavernous sewing room was dark and silent when Gleia walked in. She wound through the close lines of sewing tables and settled in her usual place. She lit the candles and took out her sewing.   Holding the delicate material close to the flame, she examined the last bit of embroidery.   It was good enough.   Damn if she was going to pick it out.

She threaded her needle with the silk.   Tongue clamped between her lips, she snipped at the loose ends, dropping small bits of thread haphazardly over the floor, over her cafta, around the table, scattering the pieces of thread with a gleeful abandon.

Sometime later, after the room had filled and the other girls were bent over their work, Habbibah came by, her sharp eyes darting over the scattered ends of thread. Her mouth pursed in satisfaction, she sailed past to pounce on an unfortunate girl who had chanced to look up and stretch at the wrong time.

Gleia swallowed a smile, feeling a warm buoyant satisfaction at fooling the old bitch.

At the end of the long day, she stretched and rubbed her red, tired eyes.   She stood motionless beside the sewing table a minute with eyes closed, then she shook out the cafta, ran a quick eye over the lines of embroidery, put the cafta on a hanger, and carried it to Habbibah.

"Finished," she murmured, keeping her head down to hide the triumph that flushed her face.

Habbibah took the cafta and pulled the bands of embroidery close to her eyes as she went over the work, stitch by stitch.   When she was finished, she grunted sourly, her small black eyes darting at Gleia, then she sailed off, the cafta a fluttering white banner beside her small black figure.   Gleia waited tensely.   Twenty-five oboloi, she thought.   I won't take less.   But she knew that she would, that she had to.   But Habbibah didn't know that.   Oh God, she couldn't know.   I've fought her too often and even won a couple of times.   She has to think I'll fight her on this.   Has to think . . .

Habbibah came back.   She stopped in front of Gleia.   "Not your best work," she grumbled.   Her small plump fingers were closed about a small bag of coins. "Hold out your hand."   With painful reluctance she eased the drawstring loose and pulled out an eight-sided gold coin.   "Pentobol.   One."   She pressed the coin into Gleia's palm, her fingers sliding off the metal with a lingering caressing motion.

Slowly, releasing the coins like drops of her own blood, Habbibah counted out five pentoboloi into Gleia's outstretched hand.   Holding the bag with the remaining coins pressed tightly against her breast, Habbibah looked at Gleia with distaste. "You be on time in the morning.   The Maleeka wants a cafta with embroidered sleeves for the name day of her youngest daughter."   She hesitated.   "You'll be paid the same," she finished sourly.

Gleia bowed her head further, rounding her shoulders.   Hai, you old bitch, she thought.   No wonder you paid me the whole.   My god, the Maleeka.   How you must be preening yourself.

She went out into the street and wandered along, feeling tired but elated.   She had the money.   No more aching back.   No more passive acceptance of abuse.

She fingered the mark on her cheek.   Closed her fingers on the coins in her pocket. The eye rolled against her hand but she ignored it, happily planning her visit to the House of Records.

Her feet eventually took her to the boarding house.   Looking up at the shadowed facade she scratched her chin and hesitated.   She could smell the awful stew Miggela had cooked up for them, an unappetizing mess with a few shreds of cheap meat, tough vegetables, and thick filling of soggy barley.   The rancid smell followed her as she walked away toward the cookshop where the grease was fresher at least.   Foolish as it was to wander about with all that money in her pocket, it was good to walk and feel free for a while, to let the sea breeze ruffle through her hair, to sluff along the walkway, winding in and out of the men and women walking purposefully homeward, the noisy influx of sailors from the wharves, the streetwalkers who were coming out to start their peculiar workdays.   She looked eagerly around trying to spot another of the mermen but saw none.

She came out of the shop munching on a pie, enjoying the taste all the more when she thought of the stew the faceless collection of losers were stuffing down their throats at Miggela's table.

She stopped at the alley leading to the wharf but shook her head.   That would be a bit too stupid.   Sighing, she clumped up the steps and went inside.

Miggela popped out of ambush.   "You missed supper."

Gleia compressed her lips, but swallowed what she wanted to say.   Somehow, this close to freedom, it was doubly hard to control her tongue.   "Yes," she said.

"You don't get no refund, you miss supper."

"I know."   She nodded briefly and moved away to the spiral staircase with its collection of creaks and groans.

In her room, she crossed to the window, leaned out, hid the money in her special place under the eaves.   After lighting her candle she tidied the room a bit more and heated water for cha.   When she was finally ready for bed, she was surprised to find the eye in her hand.   She didn't remember picking it up.   For a moment she was frightened, then curious.   The crystal warmed in her palm as she walked slowly across to the bed.

Sipping at the cha, the quilt pulled in a triangle over her middle, she held the eye up enjoying the flow of the colors.

Then she was flitting again under the flower tops.   She came out on the beach, further on this time.   Hovering over the white sand, she looked curiously around and saw distant buildings perched on slender poles, a line of graceful points and curves on the horizon.   Then the butterfly man came sailing out of the sun, a black shimmer with gold edges dancing on the breeze, an ebullient joyfulness that made her quiver with delight and feel the swoop of laughter in her blood.   She joined him, dancing, turning, twisting over the blue-green of the wrinkled sea.   Cool wine air slipped along her body and her dance became more intense.   Others came and they laughed a silent laughter, long slender feelers clicking in telegraphic wit.

The mug dropped, spilling a last few drops of cold cha on the bed as she drifted to sleep, fingers still curled tightly about the eye.   In her dreams the air dancers whispered   *come   come   come   join us   come*

In the morning she dragged herself out of bed and dressed with one hand, clutching the crystal in the other, paying no attention to the unmade bed and ignoring the nightgown dropped on the floor when she stepped out of it.

She listened distantly as Habbibah described the cafta to be embroidered, took the ruled paper and went to her table to draw the designs.

Her fingers slipped into her pocket and moved slowly over the sensuous warm surface of the crystal.

Habbibah came scolding when she saw nothing on the paper.

Gleia looked at her vaguely, listened until the wizened little woman was done with her tirade, then bent over the paper.   She began sketching flower forms under a single sun and dancing soaring butterfly figures, working the whole into a rhythm of lightness and joy.

Habbibah watched for a minute then went quietly away, smiling with greedy satisfaction.

Gleia went back to dreaming.

In her room that night she stripped off the cafta, hung it on a hook, and forgot it.   Forgot to wash.   Forgot to make her cha.   She picked up the nightgown from the floor and slipped it over her head, ignoring its damp musty smell.   She lay down on the wrinkled sheet turning the crystal over and over in her hands.

They came swooping around her, taking her through the line of houses perched on slender peeled sticks that raised them high above the flower-dotted moss below. Through open arches pointed at the tops.   Past arches filled with knotted hanging accented wth shell and polished seeds.   Past walls bare and pearly grey, with brilliant hangings creating stripes of glowing color against their bareness.   Over floors upholstered with padded carpets, different colors in different rooms.   Through room on room on room separated from one another by cascades of multi-sized arches.   Antennas clicking with laughter, the butterfly people darted about, showing off their homes.

come   come   they whispered to her   *leave your miseries behind and ride the wind with us   come   come*

In the morning she dragged herself out of bed, put on the crumpled cafta from yesterday.   Dressed with one hand again, not aware that her movements were limited by the warm and throbbing crystal clutched in her right hand.   She thrust it finally in her pocket and left the room without washing herself or doing anything about the mess she left behind.

At work she sat hunched over the layout paper, running her pencil idly over the sketch from the day before, dreaming as idly of the crystal's world.

Habbibah came by sometime later and looked over her shoulder.   When she saw the whole morning had gone by with nothing done, she exploded with rage.

"Hai, worm!" she shrieked.   Her small hand buried itself in Gleia's tangled hair and jerked her head up.   "What're you sniffing, bonder?"   She peered into Gleia's dull eyes.   "By the Madar, I'll teach you to waste my money on that filth. Abbosine!"

The big tongueless watchman came from the small room where he spent his days.   He took Gleia's hand, pulling her down the hall into the punish room.   He pushed her against the wall and closed a set of cuffs about her wrists, her struggles as futile as fly tickles against his unthinking strength.   He looked briefly at Habbibah.   When she jerked her head at the door, he shambled dully out.

The furious little woman slammed her fist into Gleia's back, driving her against the wall.   "You never learn," she hissed.   "You never learn, bonder.   Maybe I can't make you work, fool, but you'll hurt for it."   She stepped back and swung the many tongued whip.

The sharkeskin tails slashed down, slicing through the worn cloth of the cafta, cutting lines of fire into Gleia's back.   She gasped.

Grunting in a fury that showed no sign of abating, Habbibah lashed at Gleia again and again, screaming her rage at Gleia for all the times the girl had successfully defied her.   For all the lovely coins the girl had milked from her.   Finally, shaking, eyes bloodshot, face flushed, Habbibah dropped the bloody whip and walked out of the room with slow, dragging steps.

Gleia hung shuddering from her wrists, her legs too weak to support her weight. The crystal dream was cleaned out of her system by the pain that turned her body to mush.

Slowly she began to feel stronger, though, as the shock passed, the pain bit deeply into her.   She pushed against the stone floor with stiff numb feet and took the punishing weight off her wrists.   Standing face to the wall, she came to the humbling conclusion that she was a fool.   To be trapped by a Ranga eye when she knew better.   To be trapped by dreams like any giggling slogger's daughter. Dreams!

She felt the crystal press against her leg, sending warmth through the material of her cafta into her flesh.   She jerked the leg back, feeling disgust at herself as she trembled with the memory of the beauty she'd seen in the eye, longing intensely, while at the same time shuddering with revulsion, for the freedom of soaring on air with the butterfly people of the dream.   Somehow she felt they were real and not mere phantoms of a drugged mind.   That their world was real.   Somewhere. She couldn't comprehend how the crystal could serve as a gateway to that world, but deep within her she knew she could pass through the gate into a gentle world unlike the rough, unfeeling one she'd been born into.   Ranga eye.   Eye into another world.

"I'm not going to touch you again," she muttered, resting her forehead against the cold damp stone.   "I'll sell you.   I will.   I'll find a way."   The crystal bumped hard against her thigh, sending a stab of pain through her already aching body.   "We'll see who wins once I get out of this."

Her feet began to ache since she couldn't rest fully on her heels.   Her arms ached, stretching without respite over her head.

Fatigue and the effort of fighting off the insidious invasion of the crystal brought her close to fainting, while the growing certainty that Habbibah intended to leave her there all night, in a final attempt to break her spirit, was a cold knot in the pit of her stomach.   She knew that if the old bitch did, the crystal would have her.

She smashed her hip against the wall, letting out a scream of anger and pain when the crystal ground into her muscle, striking hard against nerves.   Sweating and breathing raggedly, she hung in the wrist cuffs, tears of pain streaming down her face, struggling to regain a measure of control of her body.

When she could think again, she shook her head.   "No good," she muttered. She couldn't shatter it, maybe she could ease it out of her pocket.

Pinning the material against the stone she pressed herself to the wall, counting on the pain to keep the crystal from charming her.   Wriggling, contorting her body until she was bathed in a film of sweat, she struggled to work the eye out of her pocket.

It fought back.   Whenever she managed to squeeze it an inch or so from the bottom of the pocket, it wriggled like a thing alive and eeled away from the pressure.

She kept trying until she was exhausted, sick with pain, shaking too hard to control her body any longer.

It was dark in the room when Abbosine shambled back.   The huge mute unfastened the cuffs and watched with massive indifference as she crumpled to the floor.   Stolidly he wound his thick fingers in her hair and dragged her through the building and out into the alley where he dropped her in a heap beside the worker's entrance.

Gleia pushed herself onto her feet and stood swaying, supporting herself with a hand pressed against the side of the building.   Then the anger that still simmered under the haze of fatigue gave her the strength to start walking over the cobblestones toward the main street.

She went to the wharf.   Gritting her teeth against the pain she swung down onto the worn crossbar that was her only refuge at so many crises in her life.

Clouds sailed with clumsy grace over the darkening sky, tinged with a last touch of crimson though Horli had slid behind the horizon some time ago.   Here and there a star glimmered in the patches of indigo sky visible between the cloud puffs. On the water the fog blew in thickening strands, coming up to curl around her feet.

The air had a nip that marked the decline of the summer.   Winter coming, she thought.   Three hundred days of winter.   I've got to get away.   Somehow.   Get south.   Her back itched and stung.   The bruise on her thigh was an agony whenever she moved her legs.

But she was free from the eye and tomorrow she would be free of Habbibah too. She leaned tentatively against the pile, closing tired eyes once she was settled. Tomorrow.   After the House of Records . . . what?

The water splashed and Tetaki was perched on the bar beside her.   She jumped then winced as her back protested.

"What's wrong?"   His mouth opened baring the tips of his teeth.   His eyes searched her face, seeing the pain.

"I was stupid."

"Turn."   His hand was cool on her arm.   "Let me see."

She pulled back.

"Gleia."

"If you must."   Holding onto the slanting brace, she swung around so he could see her back.   With her face hidden, her forehead resting against the pile, she spoke too loudly.   "I told you.   I was stupid!   I knew better than to provoke her. Especially when she'd just had to pay me a bonus."

His hand touched the lacerated flesh with exquisite gentleness.   It still hurt. She sank her teeth into her lip to keep from crying out.

"Come wit' me."

"What?"

"To the ship.   We got med'cine.   Your skin's cut.   'Less wounds are clean you have trouble wit' them."

"I suppose so."   She eased herself around.   "Help me up."

He sat back on his heels, an odd look on his face.   "Firs' time you ever ask for help."

She hauled herself to her feet and risked a crooked smile.   "Give me a boost, friend."

On the ship, he nodded to the watch and took her below to his cabin.   "Wait here.   I get med'cine."

She sat on the narrow bunk and looked around with a quickly growing appreciation of the neatness, comfort, and convenience of the small cabin.   A shelf of books running around the top of the wall, locked in place by an ingenious webbing.   A desk folded away against the wall.   A chair folded and latched flat.   Two long chests.   A shell lantern hanging from the beam bisecting the ceiling.   The light coming through the translucent shell touched the room with rosy gold warmth. The oil was lightly perfumed with a pleasant fresh smell that made her think of forests and green growing things.

When Tetaki came back his father Temokeuu came with him.   The older merman pushed gently on her shoulder, bending her over so he could see her back.   "This isn't the firs' time."

"I learn hard."

"What lesson?"

"Submission."

"Hmm."   He took the jar Tetaki was holding out.   "This will hurt a little at first."

The salve stung like acid.   She hissed in a breath and bit her lip till blood came, squeezed her eyes shut until tears came, then suddenly her back was cool and no more pain . . . ah . . . no more pain.   She straightened and moved her shoulders. In spite of all of her expertise in enduring pain and degradation she felt uneasy now, having had little practice with kindness.   She reached out and caught hold of his wrist with shaking fingers.   "Th—thank you."   She stumbled over the words.   "Thank you," she repeated.

Temokeuu touched the brand on her face.   "Bonded?"

"Yes."   She hesitated, stared in embarrassment at her scuffed and scarred feet in the old ragged sandals.   "I was caught stealing."

"How long?"

"Since I was bonded?   Six standard years.   Three summers ago.   A quarter of my life."

"To go?"

"Until whenever.   The term was left open.   It always is.   Until I buy myself free, that's the sentence."

"Ah."   There was heavy contempt in that soft breathed syllable.   She looked up at him, startled.   "How much is the bond?" he went on.

"Fifty oboloi.   But you've got to add on the bribes.   At least as much more. Say a hundred, hundred twenty oboloi."

He looked disconcerted.   "So much?"   Then he stroked a finger beside his mouth.   "Never mind.   How does one buy a bond?"

"Temokeuu, no.   I can't accept that.   Besides, I've earned the money already. I found I had a talent and the stubbornness to make it good."   She caught his hand and held it against her cheek.   "You're very good, you and Tetaki."   She held out her other hand to the young merman.   The she laughed, the sound surprising her with its joyousness.   "I've got the money to buy the bond and pay the bribes."   She stood and shook her hair back over her shoulders.   Then she stretched and sighed, laughing more when one hand swung against the roof beam. "You're the only two people in the world I'd tell that to, my friends.   It took the skin off my back to get that money but it was worth it.   Tomorrow, Tetaki, Temokeuu.   Tomorrow during my halfday I go to buy my bond."

He folded his arms across his wide chest.   "I have some small influence."

She frowned.   "I don't understand."

"I will stand for you in the court."   He smiled suddenly, the shimmering tips of his opaline teeth barely visible behind his wide smooth lips, his dark green eyes glinting with a sardonic amusement.   "It is surprising how much more alacritous justice becomes in the presence of influence."

She shifted uneasily, abruptly conscious of the smallness of the cabin, the closeness of the two seafolk males.   "My debt becomes heavier by the minute.   What can I say?"

Temokeuu's mouth twitched as he recognized her growing nervousness.   He moved back and opened the door; as he stepped out he said, "When you are free, what will you do?"

"I don't know.   I thought about heading south."

"Come here."   He felt her hesitation.   "Think about it.   I'll leave you to make your decision once we're finished at court, but there is always a place for you in my house."   He went quickly up the steps of a ladder and swung out onto the deck.

Gleia scrambled up beside him and stood quietly waiting for Tetaki, enjoying the feel of the breeze fingering through her hair.   "I'm a thief.   Remember?"

"I owe you my son's life.   Sin' that day you are blood of my blood."   He chuckled, a warm affectionate sound.   "A small dirty-face wild thing scolding me like my mother for letting my boy walk into danger."   He touched her face.   "I liked your spirit.   That's why I let Tetaki spend so much time wit' you.   You were good for him.   Come wit' us.   Be a daughter of my house."

"I don't want to be a . . . to live off anyone.   I want to work my own way.   To owe nobody nothing."

"What make you think any of the People are allowed to drift at another's expense?"   He laughed.   "Go back to your place, young Gleia.   Rest.   Here."   He handed her the jar of ointment.   "Put this on what you can reach in morning.   I will wait beside the Hall of Records."

On the wharf again, she found the fog had closed in thickly.   She could barely see the lanterns hanging from the mast.   A muscle twitched in her thigh, reminding her of the Ranga eye.   She shuddered.   No, she thought, no more chances.   It's too dangerous.   I can damn well get along without it.   She limped to the end of the wharf and pulled the crystal from her pocket.   For a minute she hesitated as her fingers involuntarily caressed the smooth seductive surface.   Was it so bad after all?   Beautiful.   The crystal throbbed and warmth began to climb up her hand.   "No!   Go charm a fish."   She flung the eye out into the water.

The fog was bunchy and treacherous around the scavenger's hovels.   She walked with intense wariness, moving silently along the rutted path.   The last few meters she ran full-out, forgetting the pain in her leg as shadows came at her out of the dirty yellow-white muck.   She slammed the door on the reaching hands and scurried up the stairs, flitting past Miggela's ambush before the ratty figure could come out and stop her.

She stood in the doorway wrinkling her nose at the unlovely mess waiting for her.   Cursing the crystal under her breath, she lit a candle at the guttering tallow dip smelling up the hall, then marched inside, slamming the door after her.   After bringing a measure of order in the chaos, she got out the brazier and the cha fixings, using the candle to light shreds of paper beneath the last of her charcoal sticks.   While the water was heating she yawned and stretched, feeling amazingly good in spite of the incredible day behind her; then she pulled the cafta's ties loose and dragged it over her head.   Once she had it off, she turned it over to look at the ruined back where the whip tails had sliced through the cloth.   There was a weight sagging in the pocket.

She thrust her hand in and her fingers closed on a smooth curved form.   Warmth leaped up her arms.   Her hand came out.   Came up.   She couldn't open her fingers.   The films of color danced around her, painted on the streamers of fog crawling through the open window.   I threw it in the bay, she thought.   I heard it splash.   I felt it fly out of my fingers.   I heard it splash. . . .

come   come   come   come   sister   lover   sister   no   more trouble   no more pain   we love and laugh and live in butter-rich sunlight   there is no anger, no hate, no oppression   here there is no anguish here there is no hurting   we live in beauty   no hunger   no want   no

abandoned children   we have as   gift   everything everything we
want   don't fight us   come   will it   will it come   you
can come   sunlight   and beauty   sunlight and joy   come come
sister   lover

They were all around her, glorious wraiths twittering alluringly, antennas flicking encouragement, affection, love.

come   sister   come

The water tin began whistling, the small shrill sound cutting through the haze. She swung around, deliberately bashing her fist into the wall, the sudden pain breaking the spell. Holding the crystal in her sore hand, she ripped a piece of the slashed cloth from the ruined cafta and tied the thing in it. She hooked the rag over the handle of the wardrobe, breathing a sigh of relief as she walked across to the whistling tin.

At the House of Records, Gleia watched Temokeuu walk through the main entrance. He looked over his shoulder at her, his narrow face with its sharp angles throwing off glints of red and blue from the two suns, then he vanished through the door she had no right to enter. She sighed and pushed through the bonder's gate.

In the salla, body disciplined to the proper stance of humble submission, she stopped in front of the clerk's desk and waited for him to notice her.

"What do you want, bonder? Some pointless complaint? Be sure you don't waste my time." His fat arrogant face was creased in a frown meant to underline his importance. He fiddled impatiently with some papers sitting in a folder.

"By Thrim and Orik, the bonder's law," she said meekly. She fished in her pocket and pulled out a silver obol, laying it on the desk. "Thrim and Orik." She placed two more oboloi on top of the first. "I come to buy my bond."

He grunted as he swept the coins off the top of the desk. "Straighten up, bonder. Let me see your mark."

She lifted her head.

"Closer. You think I can read the sign across the room?"

She leaned across the desk. He touched the brand. "Thief. That's fifty oboloi." His hand slid down her neck and moved inside the cafta, stroking the soft skin as he moved his pale tongue over his thick lips. "And an investigation to see if you've reformed. There's a lot of work in voiding a bond." He took a fold of her flesh between his fingers and pinched. She closed her eyes against the sudden pain. "Unless you can convince me now how reformed you are."

Gleia went stiff. She hadn't planned on paying that sort of bribe. If she refused him, he'd set a thousand niggling obstacles in her way until she exhausted her money and her strength and sank beaten back into the slow death of her bondage. She closed her eyes on her anger. If that was the cost, it was no big thing. Not

when set against the thing she wanted.   She thought of Abbrah.   No big deal.
She leaned into the fat clerk's hand, smiling at him.

He wobbled his pudgy body around to the gate and swung it open.   "Interrogation
room this way."   As she moved through the gate, he shoved her along the hall
and pushed her into a small bare room with a lumpy couch, a soiled chair, and a
washstand.

Gleia pulled off her cafta and lay on the couch, waiting for him.

The Kadiff was sitting behind his high bench looking bored.   He tapped long
slim fingers on the desk top as the clerk led Gleia in.   "What's this?"

"Bond buyer, noble Kadiff."

"Umph.   Bring her here."

Gleia came to the desk, suppressing her annoyance at the servile behavior expected of her.   She glanced quickly and secretly around as she bent her body into
a low bow.   Temokeuu came quietly from the shadows and stood beside her.   The
Kadiff raised his eyebrows and looked a trifle more interested.

"Noble and honored Kadiff, may I offer a small evidence of my appreciation
for your Honor's condescending to disturb your magnificent thoughts to hear my
small and unimportant petition?"   She reached back and touched Temokeuu's arm,
inviting him to share her game.   His fingers touched hers, nipped one slightly,
letting her know he was appreciating her performance.

The Kadiff inclined his head and she came closer, feigning a shy timidity,
inwardly contemptuous of the man for swallowing her speech, sitting there, preening
himself on his importance.   She placed five gold pentoboloi on the table in front
of him and backed away.

He grunted and tucked the coins into one of his sleeves.   "You have investigated
her reform?" he asked the clerk.

"Yes, Noble Kadiff."

The Kadiff sniffed.   "No doubt.   Have you sent for the bond holder?"

"Yes, Noble Kadiff.   The caftamaker Habbibah.   The wardman was sent and
should be here momentarily."

"While we're waiting you'd better send for the brander.   If we have to cancel
the bond, he should be here."

"It will be done, Noble Kadiff."   The clerk scurried out, looking pale at having
forgotten this.

The Kadiff tapped the end of his long nose with a neatly polished nail.   "It's
unusual to see one of the seafolk in this place."   He looked around disdainfully.
"Let alone one of your status, ambassador."

Gleia's eyebrows rose involuntarily.   A little influence he said?

Temokeuu bowed his head with a delicately exaggerated solemnity that delighted
Gleia.   "I owe blood debt to this person, noble sir, and stand surety for her.   She
is sister and daughter, blood of my blood."

The Kadiff appeared suitably impressed.   His attitude altered subtly.   He sat
straighter, looked more interested, and considerably more respectful.   "Fifty oboloi
for the bond.   You need ten more for the brander."

"I have it, Noble Kadiff." She kept her eyes on her feet.

"A lot of money. You're fortunate to have a sponsor, young woman."

Temokeuu bowed slightly. "The honor would have been mine, save that my daughter has earned the money to redeem herself."

"I didn't know sewing girls made such pay."

"If you please, Illustrious Kadiff, my designs have received some praise and brought much money into the pockets of Habbibah my bond mistress. And she has seen fit to share some of the bounty with me," Gleia murmured.

"Share!" Habbibah came storming into the room, the hapless wardman trailing behind. "The creature wouldn't work without extra pay. Why am I dragged out of my home? For this?" She jabbed a shaking finger at Gleia, then her hands went flying, touching her earrings, dabbing at her lips, brushing down over her chest. That and her angry lack of respect congealed the Kadiff's horseface into a scowl of petulant displeasure.

"Be quiet, woman." He glared at the wardman who hastily came up behind the angry Habbibah. "You are here," he went on, "as required by law to witness the cancelling of your bond."

"What!" Forgetting where she was, Habbibah shrieked and lunged at Gleia, small hands curved into claws. The wardman caught her and got a scratched face for his pains. He wrestled her back, holding her until the Kadiff's astonished roar broke through her rage, putting her on notice that she was in danger of a massive fine. The thought of losing money quieted her immediately. "I most humbly beg your pardon, Noble Kadiff," she shrilled, falling onto her knees in a position of submission. "It was only my anger at the ingratitude of this girl that made me forget myself. I gave her a home and trade and paid her well, better than she deserved, and now she wishes to leave me when the Maleeka herself has asked for her to work the cafta her daughter will wear on her nameday."

Gleia saw the Kadiff lean back, his eyes shifting uneasily between them. "May a lowly one have permission to speak, Magnificent Kadiff?"

"Granted." His eyes moved from the fuming Habbibah to the stern face of the merman. Like black bugs they oscillated back and forth as he tried to decide where his interest lay.

"The design is completed," Gleia said. She spoke slowly, clearly. "The design is the important thing. There are sewing girls with skills greater than mine to execute the work."

The Kadiff scowled at Habbibah. "Is that true?"

Habbibah glared furiously at Gleia but didn't quite dare lie. "It's true," she muttered.

"What?"

"It's true."

The Kadiff sighed with relief. "That, I believe, answers your objection, woman. And you, bonder, I hereby cancel your bond. The fifty oboloi, if you please."

Gleia stood in front of the wardrobe. Deliberately she unhooked the rag bundle and took it to the bed. She sat holding the bundle in her lap. "Well."

The crystal moved inside the cloth like something alive.

Rubbing the skin beside her new brand, Gleia contemplated the bundle. "Looks like I've got several ways I can go from here." She poked at the cloth, rolling the hidden eye about. "I can stay here and work for Habbibah. She knows I can quit any time and go with a competitor. I've got a lever now. Maybe could work out a good arrangement. At least I'd know what I was facing. I would, wouldn't I. I'd know what every day would be like. Every day." She shivered. "Or I could head south." She touched the stone and laughed. "And probably end up in a worse mess."

She rubbed the end of her nose, feeling warmth stroking down into her thighs from the stone. "I know what you want. Mm. I could go with Temokeuu and Tetaki. That's a leap in the dark too, but at least I'd have friends." She shook her head. "Some influence. Ambassador. Temokeuu, ah my friend."

Carefully, moving with slow deliberation, she untied the knots in the rag and touched the Ranga eye. The warmth spread up through her body and once again she saw the butterfly people. The male spun in ecstatic spirals and the others danced their jubilation. She could feel them drawing her out of her body. She wanted to let go, she wanted desperately to let go, to fly on glorious wings, free and joyous. So easy, it would be so easy just to go sailing away from all the pain and misery of her life here. Why not? Why not just go, let them take her to fly in joy under a butter-yellow sun. . . .

"No." She jabbed her free thumb into the new burn on her face, using the pain to wrench herself from the eye's influence. "No." She folded the rag about the stone, knotting the ends once again. Levering herself back on her feet, she took the bundle to the wardrobe, opened the door, and tossed the rag with the Ranga eye into the back corner. "No. You're too much like a trap. How could I trust you?" She shook her head. "I'm free now. I don't want you. I don't need you. What you offer is too easy. Makes me wonder where the thorns are."

Patting her pocket to make sure her money was safe, she went down the stairs for the last time, nodded pleasantly to Miggela as the squat figure came out of her nest. No reason to bother about the old rat anymore. Gleia laughed to herself as she remembered dreams of telling her landlady just what she thought of her. But it wasn't worth the wasted energy.

She stepped into the cruelly bright afternoon, pulling the cafta's hood up over her head. Without hesitation she turned into the alley, leaving behind with few regrets the drab reality of her past and the dream possibilities of the crystal. Temokeuu was waiting, would wait until sundown for her answer. She smiled and began to run past the stinking hovels.

NANCY KRESS

Against a Crooked Stile

Down under the new cast, somewhere near the immobile crook of his elbow,
Jorry's arm itched. Surreptitiously he tried to fidget his cramped muscles against
the inside of the heavy plaster, but the itchy prickling only grew worse, and the
sudden pain that shot through his broken elbow was sharp enough to bring tears to
his eyes. Quickly, before his father could notice, Jorry raised his eyes and gazed
across the heat-shimmered field, trying to make it look as though the tears had
come from staring unblinkingly into the sun. Neither of the two men facing each
other in the thigh-deep, uncut hay noticed him.

"Two days," his father growled in his heavy, rusty voice, a voice that scraped
across the words like an unused file. Tiny drops of perspiration rolled from the
black eyebrows that were joined in a single fierce line, and down onto the bridge
of his nose. Jorry took a step backward, away from them both.

"Two days she just sat there, now. Hay only halfways cut, burning up in this
sun—who's gonna cut it?" He spat, the spittle sticking to a stalk of hay in a wet
glob. "Not me. So you just tell me that, you that's got all the answers—who's
gonna get up on that there death trap and cut the hay before the crop's lost for
good?"

The power-company man gazed at the tractor squatting in the middle of the field.
Sunlight reflected blindingly off the tarnished yellow metal, and he put up one
plump, pale hand to shield his eyes. Bits of hay clung to his dark suit where it
bulged outward at the waist.

"But I've told you several times, Mr. Whitfield, there's no danger now that
we've grounded the machinery and the other—"

"I know what you told me. I heard you." Whitfield spat again and the stranger
hopped back a little, glancing down at his shoes. "You come in here and put
chains on my barn and my tractor and even on my boy's swing, and that's supposed
to fix ev'rything, trade it all out nice and even. It don't, mister. Not by a goddam
sight. How'd you like to be the one who—"

"Look, Whitfield," the stranger said. He leaned forward a little, and Jorry
saw a hard line of bone suddenly jut forward under his soft jowls, as unexpected
as the teeth in the pink baby possums Jorry had once found in the woods. The
boy almost whimpered, but caught himself: trading silence for not being noticed.

"I've spent all the time here that this situation calls for. Minor shocks such as

you experienced are common near 1,000 kV lines; we get 'em all the time.   But
if conducting objects near the right of way are properly grounded, there's no danger.
No one has ever demonstrated—''

"Now see here, you can't—''

"—*ever* demonstrated, I said, harmful effects from exposure to electrostatic
fields—''

"I'll sue you bastards for—''

"—of *any* strength; and, believe me, the power company will dismiss your threats
of a court suit with nothing more than 'exposure' to trade on as so much nonsense.
Have I made our position clear to you?   Because I've heard all I intend to!''

Whitfield took a step forward, his fists clenched at his sides.   The stranger stood
his ground squarely; and suddenly it seemed to Jorry that the man grew as tall and
black as the line towers themselves, thrusting darkly 150 feet above the baking
field, like menacing giants stalking the sky.   In sudden terror Jorry moved to jerk
his right arm up to cover his face, but the sling held the cast immobile and pain
again tore through the shattered elbow.   *Giants—*

"All you're going to hear, eh?'' his father was shouting.   "You think so?
Well, listen a goddamn minute to *that!''*   He thrust a trembling arm backward.

Caught off guard, the stranger blinked stupidly in the fierce sunlight before turning
and looking over the hay.   The scrubby pine at the edge of the field seemed to
waver a little in the blanket of heat, but the girders of black metal slicing the sky
above it were etched hard and clear.   For a moment the two men were still, bent
slightly forward, straining to listen.   Over the drone of summer insects came a
low crackling hum, fitful and unceasing, punctuated with an occasional louder snap
that fizzled out slowly.   The sound was insistent, edgy, like the mutter of buried
embers under a banked fire.

"And that's prett' near 400 feet away,'' Whitfield said grimly.   "You walk
closer with a fluorescent light from the bathroom, the bulb lights up.   I know.
I did it myself.''   Suddenly he shivered, a quick unexpected spasm shaking his
thick body but not rippling the stained denim overalls covering it.   "And I ain't
gonna do it again.   You say that's not dangerous?''

"I do,'' the stranger said.   His intent stare had vanished; and now he appeared
bored, amused, and impatient.   "People are not light bulbs.   I'll find my own
way back to the car.''

A few steps into the uncut hay, however, he stopped, paused, and then turned
with obvious reluctance, his plump face annoyed.   "Uh . . . just one more thing,
Whitfield.   You don't wear a pacemaker, do you?   From heart surgery?   The
company is . . . uh . . . advising all residents with the demand-type cardiac pace-
makers to remain outside the right of way.   Purely as a precautionary measure.''

Before Whitfield could answer, the stranger turned again and hurried across the
field, the stalks closing behind him with a soft swish.   Jorry took another step
backward, his eyes too big as he watched his father's face go from red to a dull
mottled purple.   Jagged red lines sprang out around the nose and mouth.   Holding
his breath, unable to move, the boy cowered dumbly in the tall hay, waiting

—the belt falling and he threw up his arms to shield—

for the moment his father would turn and the fierce blue eyes with their watery, red-lined whites would fall on him, fall on him and then . . .

But Whitfield didn't turn around.   He kept staring across the hay at the dwindling black spot that was the power-company man, and slowly his hands curled into fists. Behind him the line crackled in the empty hot sky.

If you lay with your eyes half-closed, Jorry thought, and sort of squinted up the left one, you could make the clouds change shape even faster than the wind could. If you squinted up both eyes, the shapes dissolved and ran together and you could start all over again, make a new world all over again. . . .

Lying on his back with the shoulder-to-knuckle cast propped up on his stomach, breathing in the dry warm smell of the Sandersons' hay, Jorry made shapes out of clouds.   The Sanderson farm joined the Whitfields', but was much larger; and in its back field already dense with the second hay crop of the summer, Jorry was seldom disturbed.   He had left off the sling because he couldn't figure out how to tie it around his neck with only one hand; the laces on his dirty blue sneakers were untied for the same reason.   A grasshopper bounded onto the cast, watched the boy from shiny multi-faceted eyes, and leaped off again.   Jorry didn't stir.

Small shapes, that's what you wanted—nothing too large, nothing too dangerous. Rabbits, and marbles, and over there one of those fluffy white dogs, the kind that looked like a mop, like old Mrs. Reynolds used to have with all that shaggy hair all over its—

"You're scaring the mice," a voice said above him.

Jorry's eyes flew open and he scrambled to his feet, already backing away, hastily cradling the cast in his good arm.   The flapping sneaker laces tangled in the hay and he pitched forward, throwing up his

—arm to shield his face from the buckle coming down and the smell of whiskey and—

"Hey," the voice said.   "There, I've got you—take it easy, fella.   Hey, it's O.K.—I'm not rabid.   Really.   Haven't been for years."

Caught by his shoulders, Jorry stopped struggling and tried desperately to blink away his panicky tears and get a clear look at his captor.   The man wavered, watery at the edges and streaked with blurred silver, then came into focus as the pain in Jorry's elbow subsided and the tears rolled out of his eyes and down his thin cheeks.

The man was wearing jeans, a blue cotton work shirt, and boots—a new hand at the Sandersons', then.   But no—the jeans were patched and clean, not whole and dirty, and there were no traces of manure on the boots.   So not a farm hand. His leather belt was foreign-looking, intricately worked, with some sort of silver buckle

—coming down and the smell of whiskey and his own voice screaming just before—

shaped like the sun.

"Hey, I'm sorry," the man said, releasing Jorry's shoulders.   "I didn't mean to scare you.   You all right?   I just wanted to ask you if you'd mind moving, because you're scaring the mice.   That's all.''

Jorry wrenched his eyes upward from the buckle, and then it was better.   Above an untidy beard were good eyes, warm and young and brown, the color of fresh toast.   Some of Jorry's panic ebbed, sliding away in long slow waves; and he sniffed and swiped at his nose with his good hand.

''What mice?''

The man rocked back and squatted on his heels.   ''Up there—under the line. You're upwind of them, and they smell you.   Makes 'em jumpy.   Jumpier.''

Jorry craned his neck; he couldn't see over the low ridge swelling with half-grown hay.

''Come on up and look,'' the man said, and started off in such an off-hand matter that after a moment Jorry found himself following.

Under the line, on the uneven stubble of weeds that had remained after the power company had mowed its right-of-way, was a jumble of equipment.   Four large glass boxes, elevated on wooden blocks and screened on two sides with plastic mesh, held piles of shredded newspaper full of burrowing mice.   Two of the glass boxes were surrounded by a double shell of parallel wires, one inside the other, which were joined together and anchored firmly into the ground.   Squares of metal standing on edge and facing each other in pairs had been placed on the grass, or on high poles.   The metal squares had been hooked up to odd-looking meters and to dials that looked to Jorry like plastic warts.   Parked over the ridge was a small, sturdy red truck near the remains of a ham sandwich already being carried away by the boldest of a watchful flock of crows.   On the warm air rode the nose-wrinkling smell of mice.

''What's that?'' Jorry asked, in spite of himself.   ''Around the mice?''

''Faraday cages,'' the man said promptly.   ''Keep the mice in that box from being exposed to the electrostatic field from the line.''

Involuntarily Jorry glanced upward.   The cable above him stretched like a long black road, a road curving and diminishing over the far horizon.   A road for giants . . .

''What about these other mice?''

''They're exposed to the field.   The idea is to see if they behave any differently after a long while near the line.''   Slowly, his brown eyes never leaving Jorry's face, he came around the boxes of mice and held out his hand.   ''My name's Tom Crowell.''

Jorry took a step backward.   ''You from the power company?''

''No—no, I'm not.''   He lowered his empty hand.   ''I work for the Environmental Study Association.   We want to see if these new 1,000 kV lines affect the wildlife hereabouts.   Want to hold one of the mice, son?''

''I can't,'' Jorry mumbled, looking down at his untied sneakers.   He could feel the back of his neck growing hot.   '' 'Cause of my arm.''

''I broke my arm once,'' Tom said cheerfully.   ''Healed clean as a whistle. Before the cast came off, I'd collected the autographs of the whole fifth grade.''

He glanced at Jorry's cast, bare except for a rubbed-in catsup stain.   " 'Course, school's out just now.   What's your name, son?''

"Jorry.''

"Well, Jorry, I've seen you before, walking in the fields.   You're about the only kid that *does* come up here.   You interested in electronics?   Is that why you like it here?''

Jorry kept his eyes fastened on a glass box behind a Faraday cage.   Two bright eyes peered out from beneath a pile of shredded Sunday comics.   Finally, as though it were an answer, he said, "My pa doesn't like the line.''

"And who's your pa?''

"Clayte Whitfield.''

"Oh,'' Tom said.   "Oh—yes.''   He looked at the boy more closely, a sudden sharpness in his brown eyes.   "He know you're up here, Jorry?''

Jorry traced a circle on the grass with the toe of his sneaker.   "Pa never comes up here.''   After a long pause he added reluctantly, "He says the line's dangerous.''

"Well, he's probably right,'' Tom said.   The boy looked up quickly, his eyes wide with astonishment in his hollowed face.

"There's enough of a field up here to cause all sorts of body currents in a human being and set off God-knows-what trigger phenomenon—especially in the brain organelles.   Not to even mention the geophysical effects.   Just smell the air—go ahead, move away from the mice and take a deep breath.''

Jorry had been going to ask what brain organelles and trigger fins on men were, but instead he obediently moved away from the glass boxes and sniffed.   The air smelled faintly acrid, a dry elusive odor that reminded him vaguely of freshly-ironed cotton.

"Ozone,'' Tom said.   "If we get a storm, you watch the line during the thunder, Jorry.   It'll glow reddish-blue.''

Again Jorry glanced at the huge metal towers.   Giants . . .

"But, Mr. Crowell, if—''

"Tom.''

"Well—Tom.''   He stumbled over the name, not used to this freedom.   "If you think the line's so dangerous, why are you up here?   Why aren't you joined up with the folk who stay away and want the line tore down and write letters and talk about . . .''   Jorry trailed off.   Talk?   Talk was cheap, Pa said, and Jorry had watched while Pa carried in the tightly-sealed box from the County Agricultural Agency, the box that was so heavy in the big hands that trembled all the time now except when they held the bottle steady to pour . . .

"Why am I up here?'' Tom was saying.   "Because I *think* the line's dangerous, but I don't *know*.   Do you know where the line comes from, Jorry?''

He shook his head.   No one ever said; they just wanted it gone.

"From the lignite coal mines up north.   Energy is a valuable thing for everyone, Jorry, although not if the cost is too high in other valuable things.   You have to weigh both sides, make the best trade-off.   The people here want the line down because it's a scary unknown.   But I think it's a better idea to get to *know* it, and then decide.   What do you think?''

Jorry shook his head, embarrassed again.   That wasn't the sort of thing adults asked him, except in school; and even then they didn't talk to him the way this Tom did.   It didn't seem right, somehow.   Not fitting.   He was only Jorry Whitfield, Clayte Whitfield's kid, and everybody knew the Whitfield farm hadn't had a decent cash crop in three years, couldn't even bring much produce to town to trade anymore.   And you had to trade for things, Jorry knew; even this Tom talked about the line as a trade-off.   You didn't get things for free.   Not hay, not chicken feed, not canned stew, not friendship.

"I got to go," he said abruptly.

"O.K.," Tom said.   "But it was nice talking to you.   Come back if you feel like it."

Jorry started home without answering.   Pa might be back from town, might be looking for him.   It was bad to be in the house when Pa came in, but worse not to be.

Moving slowly so his untied shoelaces wouldn't tangle in the hay, the boy trudged through the green stalks, holding the plaster cast close to his body.   He took a long oblique route that kept him downwind of the mice.

But he went back, again and again, first hanging around the edges of the mowed stubble, observing as Tom worked and puttered and whistled off-key, then later moving in closer.   Each time he came he brought something: a handful of chives from the plant that came up each year behind the barn, some wild strawberries from the hill by the creek, a sharpened pencil in case Tom lost his.   Tom accepted these offerings gravely, putting the chives in his sandwich and the pencil in his shirt pocket, so Jorry felt it was all right for him to stay.   He helped, too, whenever he could.   He fed the mice, careful to measure each cupful with painstaking exactness, adding and removing single pellets until he was sure each cage received the same amount.   After a while Jorry got used to Tom's talking to him as if they were friends; sometimes he pretended to himself that they were.   Jorry seldom said anything, but Tom talked all the time: talk poured out of him as relentlessly as sunshine, as unceasing as the crackle of the line.   Jorry, unused to such talk, listened to all of it with cloistered intensity, his head bent forward, watching Tom through the sideways fall of his untrimmed bangs.

"The thing is, Jorry, that electrostatic fields set up currents between different parts of your body.   There you are, Jorry Whitfield, a real live wire."

"You, too," Jorry said, astonishing himself.   Tom leaped into the air, thrusting out his arms, legs, and tongue in a frenzied parody of every cartoon animal that ever stuck its finger in an electric socket on Saturday morning TV.   The mice scuttled for cover.

"So the question is—what do all these currents *do*, coursing through the body beautiful?"

"What?" Jorry asked breathlessly.

Tom shrugged and dropped to the ground.   "Dunno.   Nobody knows."

Jorry stared at him a fraction of a second before again ducking his head.   His hair fell forward over his face.

"We can guess, though. We can guess that it's probably affecting the brain, because brain organelles are most sensitive to voltage differences. And the brain is where perception takes place, where you experience things, so perception's a likely candidate for residual effects. You notice yourself seeing the grass blue, Jorry, or pink?"

Jorry frowned. The grass looked the same as usual to him, a dusty green fading to brown under the hot sun.

"Ah, well," Tom said, "Rome wasn't built in a day, and neither was Goodyear Rubber. Did you know that Goodyear—the first Goodyear, I can't think of his name—that he discovered how to vulcanize rubber by accident, while he was cooking some sulphur gunk on the stove? Fact. You just never know what you'll get with science. The whole thing might just as easily have exploded in his face. But it didn't."

Jorry hadn't known. Sometimes it seemed to him that he didn't know anything, hadn't ever thought about anything except how to stay out of people's way, until the coming of the line, and Tom. Now at night he lay awake in bed, listening to the shutter that had been banging in the wind for over a year now, and thought about their talks. Each remembered word became a smooth stone to turn over and over, running his thumb over the texture and curves of the surface, squinting at the hidden lines. At such times he always had a picture of Tom standing gigantic against a clear empty sky. In his picture, Tom was still talking.

There was a daily period, however, when they both sat silent and observed the mice for an uninterrupted hour, while Tom made notes in a large black folder. First he removed most of the shredded newspaper, and even the mice behind the wire Faraday cages could be seen clearly. As the weeks slipped by, it seemed to Jorry that the mice were increasingly jumpy and nervous, nipping at each other or fidgeting along the mesh, then dropping into periods of sudden sleep. He wondered what was going on in their brain organelles (he knew, now, what the words meant). Sometimes he touched his own head with one questing finger. It just felt like his head.

The weather turned rainy, a warm off-again on-again drizzle. Weeds grew lush and green in the vegetable garden, choking the feathery carrots and the string beans straggling up their sagging poles. Jorry tried to fix the bean poles, but the wood was old and rotten, and he couldn't find the key to the storeroom where there may or may not have been fresh lumber. The uncut hay in the back field gave off the pungent smell of decay. As his father spent more and more time in town, Jorry slacked off on his chores, unable to find the needed supplies or equipment. He took care, however, to keep the few animals fed; when the chicken feed ran out, he gave the hens popcorn and Rice Krispies. They seemed to like it just as well.

The reduced chores gave him more time to hunt for things to take to Tom, necessary things, things that would earn him the right to visit the site under the line. He brought fresh eggs—Pa had stopped keeping egg tally—wild sumac for tea, blackberries, an Indian arrowhead, a four-leaf clover ironed between two sheets of waxed paper so it wouldn't shrivel up. Tom made a face wh   he tasted the sumac tea, but he carefully put the four-leaf clover in his wallet, on top of his health insurance card.

They observed the mice from under a leaky tarp rigged like a lean-to, and Tom shielded his notebook with an old plastic bag labeled "Marino's work shirts." Rain dripped off his beard into his coffee cup.

"Ah, well, it's still not as messy as reading chicken entrails," Tom said as he wiped the rain off his thermos before pouring them more coffee.   No one else had offered Jorry coffee.   "Although sometimes Dame Science seems just as capricious as the rest of that Olympian crew about bestowing her mixed offerings and benedictions.   Still, you have to be ready, in case she spreads her wings and gets generous."   Jorry looked bewildered and Tom laughed.

"I mean that science gives both benefits, like tractors and medicine and this remarkable-unbreakable-new-improved-temperature-controlled thermos, and also problems, such as the power line.   Starting off with a first step, you never really know what you'll end up with.   Surprise, folks!   A cosmic poker game, new deals hourly, step right in and play!"

"Like Charles Goodyear," Jorry said.   Tom stared at him, surprised, and Jorry added in a sudden rush, "I'm gonna be a scientist, too, when I grow up, and discover important things like rubber."   He reddened and ducked his head.

"Where'd you learn Goodyear's first name?" Tom asked.   Jorry didn't answer. One day when Pa had inexplicably ordered him to ride to town in the truck, and then just as inexplicably forgotten all about him when they got there, Jorry had slunk into the library and read what he could about the vulcanization of rubber, puzzling over the unfamiliar words until footsteps approached and he had fled before any librarian could demand payment in the form of his nonexistent library card.

Tom sipped his coffee.   "I do hope you get to be a scientist, Jorry," he said gently.   "I really do.   Tell me—you ever have a dog?"

The boy shook his head and dumped three spoonfuls of sugar into his coffee.

"Well, I did.   A black Labrador retriever.   Used to show her.   I remember talking once to a farmer about a dog that had gone wild, up north this was, and was killing chickens.   It might have been part coyote.   Anyway, the farmer was determined to shoot it, and took to hanging around the farmhouse with his rifle all loaded; but the dog always slipped by him, time after time.   It got to be an obsession with the guy.   He took to neglecting his farm, ignoring his family.   All sorts of financial and legal tangles developed, about mortgages and such, and then about bad checks and diseased stock—and the guy blamed it all on the dog killing those chickens.   Just an excuse, of course—and a pretty shoddy one.   Some men aren't afraid of anything except their mirrors."

He looked at Jorry with a sudden intensity, his eyes sharp and kind over the red plastic rim of the thermos cup, and Jorry wriggled his feet in embarrassment.   Often he had the hazy impression that Tom was trying to tell him something, offer him something, in the same way he offered him the coffee.   Why should a grown man be afraid of a mirror?

Just now, however, Jorry had something that needed saying.   Carefully he kept his eyes on the generous amount of artificial cream dissolving in swirls in his coffee.

"Tom—there's a meeting Friday.   Today.   This afternoon."

"A meeting?"

"Of people who live here."   Abruptly he looked up and offered the rest in a rush: "They're all mad.   *Real* mad, Tom.   They've made up their minds to get this line tore down!"

"And you thought I ought to know about it."   Tom's brown eyes warmed with amused affection.

"Yes!"

"Well, Jorry, I'm not sure they're not right.   These figures we've been collecting . . ."   He dumped out his rain-diluted coffee and poured himself some more from the thermos.   "But we won't really know anything until Monday, when the mice go into the lab for testing and mating and dissection."

Tom frowned.   "The thing is, the behavior changes in the mice are negative, all right—jumpiness, decreased sexual interest, interrupted sleep patterns: all indicate stress.   But they're not *dramatic* changes, not something that makes you sit up and take notice.   Not, anyway, if you're on the State Power Commission.   Without something more theatrical to offer, any appeal on this line will just get lost in the lobbying.   The bureaucratic tendency to not shut the lion's cage till the beastie's loose.   Now if the mice had done something really stagy, like grow three-inch fangs or invent espionage warfare . . . well.   But I think all our hard work here may end up just another overlooked scientific study, a dull and ineffective witness for the prosecution.   And thanks, Jorry, for the information about the meeting, but I already knew about it.   Oh, I'm up on all the local gossip.   I board at the Sandersons', you know."

Jorry didn't know.   He hadn't ever thought about Tom boarding somewhere, eating breakfast, brushing his teeth.   Every day Tom just *appeared,* like a part of the huge black towers and crackling hum of the line itself.   Jorry tried to picture him watching TV with Jeanine Sanderson, who had been in his class at school last year, and a queasy feeling twisted in his stomach.   Once he had overheard Mrs. Sanderson tell Jeanine that she "shouldn't play with that Whitfield boy, because with a pa like that, you never knew."   The feeling twisted harder.   Jorry stood up.

"I got to go."

"You sure . . . it's not your usual time yet.   Here—wipe off your cast with the towel.   There's coffee on it."

"No!"

"Hey, Jorry—what's wrong?"

"Nothing!   I got to go."

"But—"

"I got to go!"

Tom watched him intently.   Around the boy's eyes were the beginnings of moist trails streaking the dirt on his thin face.

"Jorry," he said quietly, "Jorry—how did you break your arm?"

The tear trails paled, and the boy made an aborted half-gesture in the direction of throwing up his arm.   Then he blinked dully and mumbled, "I fell out of the hay loft."

Tom put an arm around Jorry's shoulders, speaking in a low, serious voice so unlike his usual self that Jorry was startled into listening.   "Jorry, you know this is the last day for this project.   After I pick up the mice on Monday I won't be back.   I don't believe you fell out of the hay loft—no, wait, don't squirm away, listen to me—you're a bright kid, and a damn nice one, and if you stay here . . . Jorry, there are arrangements, laws, for making sure that nothing like that happens to kids.   You could leave here, stay with some nice foster family; and I could even visit you on weekends.   We could go to a ball game, mess around in my lab.   All you have to do is let me take you to Social Services, and then you'll have to be willing to *tell* them—Jorry, wait, listen to me—wait!"

"You're crazy!" Jorry shouted, already backing away.   Crazy, crazy, crazy! Tom didn't even need Jorry's information about the meeting—he already had it, already had everything.   Let Tom take him away?   When Jorry could give Tom nothing but sumac tea he didn't even like, could be worth nothing to Tom, to anyone except Clayte Whitfield, doing farm chores, and even there mostly a useless nuisance—"goddamn nuisance!" his father roared.   To be always in the way, always in need, always someone other people's children shouldn't play with?   To be always with nothing to trade for the impatient charity of strangers who traded taking care of you for money from the Welfare—to live like that?   Crazy!

"Go take Jeanine Sanderson to a ball game!" he shouted.

"Hey, Jorry—"

"Just leave me *alone*!"   And then he was running, clutching his cast awkwardly against his stomach, running with a lopsided lope over the ridge, through the rain.

By the time Jorry reached home, still running, his elbow ached from bouncing against the inside of the cast.   Water streamed onto it from his shoulders and hair; with each heaving breath he smelled soaked plaster mingled with damp earth and the wind-borne smell of wet cows.   Leaning against the house, Jorry tried to catch his breath, to stop the silent sobs that shook his whole body, before he pushed open the screen door and went inside.

"Where you been, boy?"

Jorry snapped his head upward.   Pa, who should have been in town, should have been still at that meeting, was never in the house at this time anyway—Pa was sitting behind the kitchen table, a glass in his big hand.   Over the rain smells came that other smell.   A pool of it had spilled on the table and one amber drop slid lazily over the edge, hung suspended for a long second, then plopped softly to the floor.   Funny about that plop, Jorry thought crazily—you should hardly be able to hear it over the rain, but it filled the room like thunder.

Slowly he reached behind him for the latch to the screen door.

His father's hand caught him at the shoulder and spun him across the kitchen and into the table.   The glass shattered on the floor.

"I asked you where you been!"

"Ou-out, Pa!"

Fighting for balance, Jorry twisted his head and gazed at his father in terror. But Whitfield was nodding, a drunken heavy nod that made his head bounce like a dropped sack of grain.

"Out. You been out, and I know where—you think I don't know where. I know where. I been out, too—out with those namby-pamby bastards who don't give a damn if their farms go to hell on account of some fat-assed power company, 'thout doing a damn thing about it but givin' the farms away!" He nodded over and over, repeating the phrase: "Givin' away. Just givin' away.

"And you know what they're gonna do—what got decided at their big angry meeting—they're gonna send a delegation up to the Congressman . . . up to the Congressman, tiptoein' all polite up to the Capitol, where nobody gives a damn anyway—but not me, boy! Not me! *I* know the only way to set the bastards to rights!" He shoved his face close to Jorry's and hissed again, "Not me!" Rheumy yellowish liquid oozed from the corners of his eyes. "What do you say to that, boy?"

"N-no, Pa."

Whitfield laughed loudly, straightened up, and groped behind him for the missing glass. Jorry edged around the table, numbly eyeing his father's face, until his foot struck something hard. Glancing down, he saw the box from the County Agricultural Agency, open now, spilling out the cylinders that could blast out a stubborn stump no tractor could dislodge, could send it spraying wood chips ten feet into the air. One stick of the dynamite lay half-puddled in amber whiskey. A stump, or a rock—or a truck. "You been out and I know where."

"Hey!" Whitfield yelled, and snatched at air. Jorry had barreled across the kitchen and through the door, his cast striking the screen with such force that bits of plaster flaked into the dirty mesh. He stumbled as the rain hit him in a solid sheet, but picked himself up and ran, zig-zagging across the barnyard and around the edge of the barn. Behind him he heard the door bang again and then his father's hoarse yell, the words blown away by wind and rain. Jorry leaned against the barn, squeezing his eyes shut for a moment before peering around the corner.

His father was lurching across the barnyard.

A sudden, unexpected flash of thunder lit up the sky and to Jorry his father suddenly looked huge, a giant swelling blackly to fill up the world and no place to hide and

—the buckle coming down and the smell of whiskey and his own voice scream-ing just before the—

Giants!

He ran the length of the barn and headed out toward the hayfield, bent low, huddled over the cast. Cutting diagonally through the rotting hay, running until his lungs ached, stopping only to wipe the streaming water from his eyes before running again, until he collapsed, heaving and panting, in the one place his father had never yet come. Sanctuary.

But for how long?

Jorry wrapped his good hand around the bottom girder and convulsively flexed and unflexed his fingers over the wet metal. Gradually his breathing slowed and he no longer had to snatch at draughts of wet air. Above him the line crackled and snapped, glowing through the rain with a fuzzy, reddish-blue corona. The line swayed gently, like the smooth surf line of some radioactive sea, but the boy hardly noticed. When he could stand, he began to trudge along the right-of-way, shedding stray bits of hay as he went, and his eyes moved only to jump to the next colossus in the long row of looming black giants safe-guarding his trail.

The truck was gone, and Tom with it.

Only the cages of mice remained. Water slid down the glass sides in smooth, silent trails. The rain had let up, but the sky was darkening, and occasionally thunder drowned out the ceaseless crackle overhead. Jorry stared blankly at the spot where the tarp lean-to had been, and his face twisted sideways.

Gone. Home for the day, home to the Sandersons', home and dry and in no danger at all. Playing checkers with Jeanine and drinking hot coffee and not needing to be warned, not needing anything, because dynamite fuses don't light in the rain and even Pa would remember that. Everyone remembered that, except Jorry. And on Monday Tom would pick up the mice and be gone for good, gone beyond the reaches of Jorry's stupid rescues or bitter tea or anything else he might scrounge up. He wouldn't see Tom again, couldn't see him again, because things didn't work like that. You didn't get things for free, and suddenly he didn't care if Pa blew up every tower on the whole line, one by one, and Jorry himself along with them. He just didn't care.

The boy threw himself down on the damp earth in front of the mice cages and buried his face in his left arm, too spent for tears. The right arm stuck out awkwardly at his side, the cast lying stiff and sodden in the mud.

Gone.

Abruptly, the sky shrieked and cleaved into two blinding halves as a bolt of lightning tore from cloud to cloud. Jorry was hurled back down on his face, the mud tingling below him, while overhead the line flamed red-purple and leaped wildly against its moorings. The crackling mounted to a wailing crescendo, for a confused moment sounding acrid and smelling deafening, and then both sound and smell whirled into a jaundice-colored mist swirling with mice and rain and

—the belt falling and he threw up his arm to shield—across the field stay low don't—more coffee Jorry there's plenty and put some sugar in your Olympian offering—his face from the buckle coming down and the smell of ozone you watch the line during a storm Jorry it—body currents and brain organelles and the center of perception of his screaming just before the crack of bone in Jeanine Sanderson's head tingling with the smell of—

The mist faded into black. The blackness pulsed and then steadied, and out of it slowly emerged the slipperiness of the mud. Jorry raised his head and shook it from side to side, first cautiously and then, when nothing hurt too much, more vigorously. Thunder rumbled somewhere over the horizon, and the eastern sky paled weakly. The boy sat up and swiped at the mud on his face, smearing it into long dark smudges.

The air smelled scorched, like wet laundry under a too hot iron, and mingled over and under and through was another smell, both familiar and unfamiliar, like a dream half-forgotten.

The smell of fear.

Whose?

Jorry wrinkled up his muddy nose and sniffed.   It *was* fear and it *was* in his nose, not in his mind or muscles or stomach.   As he sniffed he became aware that the elusive smell—how did he know what it was?   but he did—had slid down to the back of his throat and become a taste, chalky and metallic.

Wide-eyed, Jorry looked around.   A gray mouse was huddled next to the plastic mesh, its whiskers still quivering.   Around the matted fur on its wedge-shaped head was a faint red halo.

Instantly Jorry glanced up, but the reddish glow around the line had gone: the cable lay black and inert against the sky.   By the time Jorry's eyes swung back to the mouse, the red halo was fading and so was the chalky taste-smell of fear. The mouse uncurled itself, stretched, and wandered along the mesh.   From under the sodden newspapers at the back of the cage crept another mouse, smaller and white, with pink ears.   The head of the gray mouse began to glow again, this time a flickering marigold yellow, and Jorry breathed in a musky, damp odor that brought no word to his mind but did bring a sudden tightening in his belly muscles and a heaviness in his groin and a confused image of Jeanine Sanderson in her gym shorts.

He hunted up a sharp stick and prodded the gray mouse through the mesh.   The marigold yellow flashed into red and again the chalky-metallic smell filled Jorry's nostrils.   Slowly he withdrew the stick and gazed at the glass cage, dazed.

Bits and pieces of things Tom had told him vibrated in his head like struck tuning forks.   Brain organelles.   Body currents.   "Perception's a likely candidate for change."   Trigger phenomenon.   And, incongruously, the smell of coffee.

Was it the mice who were different, giving off their haloes and their emotional smells, or was it something different in *his* brain that made him aware of these things?   Jorry put his good hand to his nose and pinched it thoughtfully.

A second later he was scrambling to his feet, his sneakers nearly sliding out from under him in his haste to get to the second cage.   It was more difficult to get the stick poked into this one, through the double-wire screening of the Faraday cage and then through the plastic mesh; but he kept at it, his tongue stuck out at the corner of his mouth, until the stick hit something more yielding than glass, less than newspaper.   Jorry prodded hard.   There was a sudden squeal, and a black mouse head poked out of a pile of shredded editorials.   Around the black was a thin halo of red.

Inside the Faraday shield.

Rocking back on his heels and wrinkling his muddy nose against the sudden chalky-metallic smell, the boy stared at his stick, then at the black line stretching overhead, and again at the stick.   So it *was* a change inside his own head; if the change had been in the mice, the ones within the Faraday shield wouldn't have been affected.   What was happening to him?

The fear only lasted a moment, a sickening moment when he wondered crazily if he would see a red halo if he looked in a mirror. A mirror—what had he been told about a mirror? Who had told him? Oh, yes—Tom.

Jorry's grip tightened around his stick. Another feeling swelled within him, swelled like the breaking of river ice after the winter, splintering the momentary fear and spinning it away in the rush of excitement. Whatever this thing was, this thing he could do now, *he* had found it. He, Jorry Whitfield. It was his discovery, his first step, his vulcanized rubber spilling onto the stove, his. Like a real scientist, like Charles Goodyear, like *somebody*.

Like Tom.

And it was important, this thing. Jorry wasn't sure how he knew that, but he did. Important enough, different enough—what had Tom said? "dramatic"—so those men on the Power Commission would have to listen about the line. Was it good dramatic or bad dramatic? What would those men think about what had happened to him? Jorry didn't know, but he guessed they wouldn't like it when he told them what colors *their* halos were.

But even when the line was gone—and here he glanced up at it with something almost like affectionate regret—this thing, this Sense, would still be his. His to keep, his to use, his to give to Tom for that scientific report that now was not going to be dull. And if he "gave" this Sense to Tom, offering him the use of it the way he would have with a new bicycle if he had ever had one, then for the first time Jorry could, in turn, let himself think about the dizzying possibility Tom had talked about, the possibility of leaving, of not having to lie rigid in his bed listening to Pa downstairs with his bottle and wonder if this time . . . he could leave, now. Now that he had earned the right, now that he had this important thing to trade, to swap—

But what had he traded to earn the Sense?

Slowly Jorry sat down in the mud. He had traded nothing; he was even going to help get the line torn down, if that was possible. So the Sense was free, an unexpected gift, an offering, a benediction. But that wasn't possible: nothing was free, things didn't go right by themselves, nobody gave you anything without trying to get something greater back, it just didn't work like that. It *never* worked like that.

Did it ever work like that?

Sitting on the wet ground, his stick still in his hand, Jorry felt dizzy. An errant drop of water trickled off the back of his collar and down his neck, and he sneezed.

It was difficult fishing the gray mouse out of the cage, using only one hand. When Jorry finally had the damp body clasped around its middle, he squeezed it firmly and started walking over the ridge. At the top he halted abruptly. Far down the line was a dark figure, made tiny by distance, standing motionless in the middle of a wet field of rotting hay. By screwing up his eyes and squinting through the mist, Jorry could just make out the figure of his father, head tilted back to stare upward at the soaring black girders of the line tower. He could make out, too, around the thrown-back head, a thin red halo. On a vagrant puff of wind came the faint smell of chalk.

Jorry blinked and tightened his grip on the mouse until it squealed. His father's arms dangled at his sides, the big hands limp and empty.   He was standing well back from the line, well outside the right of way, and the red fear-halo glowed like a blurred mist through the soft rain.

His father?   Afraid?   His father afraid; small and wet and powerless by the line, and afraid.   Clayte Whitfield.   Only a man afraid.   Of the line, of his mirror, of the scary confusion in things not always turning out badly, in sometimes ending well, or neither, or both.

Jorry gazed for a long time, his face streaked with mud and concentration.   Then he blinked again, turned away, and carried his mouse on his cast, riding in front of him like an unexpected gift, an offering, a benediction, over the ridge toward the Sandersons'.   His muddy figure loomed tall as a giant against the rainy sky.

POUL ANDERSON

Joelle

When the aircraft bearing him began its descent and he saw Lawrence, Eric Stranathan's first thought was: *But Joelle never said the place is beautiful!* He had imagined all Kansas to be like the plains that reached eastward and eastward of Calgary. Instead, a river gleamed between hills rich with trees, while the town itself climbed from the water in streets and homes that had known the same shade for two and a half centuries, and the university campus might have been a huge park. After a moment, he realized how little of anything she had ever told him about it . . . or about her entire life, but he knew the reason for that.

The aircraft dropped steeply, engines a-thunder. It was an American military jet, akin to those he glimpsed on patrol against summer-blue sky and summer-white cumulus clouds. Now he spied the base for which it was headed. That too was a surprise, as small as it appeared, a field and a few buildings, until he reflected that most of it must be underground, hardened against missile strikes. Well, the border of the Holy Western Republic was less than 400 kilometers toward sunset, and although the Yanks had been at peace with their dissident brethren for two decades, still, three civil wars in as many generations left scars which would not heal soon and perhaps never completely.

Pulse riotous, his body shoved at the safety harness as if wanting to leap out and beat the flyer to earth. He forgot landscape and politics. Joelle was down there.

Air cushion met concrete, the craft slid to a halt, tripods thudded into place, power cut off, silence rang. Eric fumbled at his harness. He had never flown in a fighting vehicle before. His service unit at home was simply the domestic police, Canada having a policy of not assigning much-needed specialists to soldiering, where their skills were mostly irrelevant. Beside him, Major Goldfine, his single cabin companion on the flight from Calgary, reached over to help. Despite the importance of this mission, the American had chatted amiably en route, had actually scoffed a trifle at the elaborate preliminaries and precautions. "Shucks, the Holies are too worried about the Mexican Empire these days to want trouble with us. We aren't. And as for you Canucks, why, Dr. Stranathan, isn't your coming here part and parcel of our countries drawing together? My money says the North American Federation will exist inside another ten years."

Eric had grinned to himself at being called a Canuck—he was tall, rawboned, sandy-haired, his countenance craggy as ancestral Highlands—and tried to respond in the same fashion. But he kept falling silent; his mind was always slipping off to seek Joelle.

He rose, bade the crew goodbye, ritually patted the autopilot, and followed the major out the door, down an extruded ramp. The day was warm, sun-dazzled, eased by a breeze which seemed to carry a breath of hay scent from agridomains beyond this field and those walls. He hardly noticed. At a gap in a fence, she was waiting. Somehow he did not run; but each footfall beat through its shin to the knee.

Had she changed in fifteen months? She was not dressed quite as he had ever seen her before, in the severe business outfit of the conference, the casual shirt and pants of their mountain holiday, the flowing Antique Revival gown she had bought toward the end—getting advice from a couturier—to please him. Today the slenderness and the fullness of her were clad in a high-collared blue tunic, blue trousers, and buskins which suggested the basic uniform of the American military without having its dash.

As he approached, she lifted an arm in half a wave: no more.

A large blonde colonel and a small black civilian flanked her, two noncoms bearing sidearms behind them. The colonel stepped forward. "Dr. Stranathan?" she greeted with an efficient smile. "Welcome. I'm Maria Lundgard, chief liaison officer with the Shannon Foundation." Handshake; polite words. "Allow me to introduce Dr. Mark Billings, the head of it. You know each other by reputation, of course." Handshake; polite words. "And you have already met Joelle Ky."

Handshake—As he took hers in his, there flitted across Eric's mind the idea that these names, together with Sam Goldfine's, expressed something of what had made this strange, wounded nation wherein he stood. For Joelle, little save strong cheekbones bespoke, in the blood, what history her surname remembered. The helmet of bobbed sable hair, big dark eyes, delicate nose and jaw, mouth a bit wider than it might have been, clear pale complexion, 175 centimeters of height, must have come from many elsewheres, England, France, Russia, Cuba, Dacotah, who could now tell? Who cared? Her hand was branding his with its coolness.

"How good to see you again," she said, as she might to any colleague. Or was her contralto still more withdrawn than that?

(A message from her in December had warned: "When you come—because you are going to, you are, if I have to call a one-girl strike to make them arrange it— be prepared for a most correct reception. At first, I mean. They will be around, too, you know, all the pushy theys that infest this world like flies, officers, officials, I know not who or what more. We won't let them see what we share, will we? It's none of their damn business, it's our private miracle. Oh, no doubt they suspect. Maybe they know for sure. I wouldn't put it past them to have sicced their nasty little bugs on me 'way up in your country. But they won't dare let on—the atmosphere, the negotiations toward union must never ever be endangered by any friction that can be avoided, "Union" is as sacred a cow as people have yet seen, though I admit she is a very dear cow to me too—anyway, if we stay discreet, they can't so much as hint we need a chaperone, not even under the excuse of security. Have no fears, darling. No bugs can crawl into *my* section. I've seen to that, and I don't let up on it. Once we're alone, wow, will we be indiscreet! How can I wait till then? . . .")

She looked so grave. "I, I'm anxious to get busy with you," he ventured.

"Likewise is everybody here," Billings said. Eric released Joelle. "But you must be tired from your flight, Dr. Stranathan, and certainly you'll want to get properly settled in before starting on as demanding a project as this will be." The director chuckled. "I know better than to push my linkers. They push back, hard."

"I think we, he and I would be wise if we have a preliminary run-through as soon as possible," Joelle urged. Her tone stayed level.

"Tomorrow?" Eric asked.

"Already?" Lundgard replied, surprised. "Why, I was planning to have you shown around, the sights, you know, and I'm sure the place is full of persons who're eager to meet you."

"Yes, no doubt," Joelle said, oddly hesitant.

"Uh, if, uh, if nobody will feel it's rude of me," Eric blurted, "I disagree. You and I, Miz Ky, we'd do best to, uh, get each other thinking about specific dimensions of what we hope to do." *Why isn't she insisting?* stabbed within him.

"Well, we can talk about that on our way into town," Lundgard decided. "I have a car ready. Sergeant, bring along our guest's baggage. This way, please."

Eric maneuvered to walk beside Joelle. He bent his arm, wondering if she would take it. In Canada he had been astonished—angry, at first—to learn that that simple gesture was unknown to her, and touched at how eagerly she adopted it. Today she did not notice, or pretended not to.

She wasn't all aloof. On the ride into Lawrence, she joined somewhat in the conversation. The banalities she avoided—How had his trip been? How were things in Calgary?—but that had always been her way. Likewise, she had scant interest in politics, on which the rest of the party cautiously touched—Did Dr. Stranathan believe General McDonough might really allow a parliament to be elected in Canada? If so, might that prove an obstacle to union, Congress remaining such a cherished symbol in the States? However, since President Antonov appeared sure to be succeeded by his nephew when he died, which he would any day, and the nephew favored federation, might still another U. S. Constitution be decreed?

But when talk veered to technical subjects, she grew animated. The latest R & D toward improving migma fusion powerplants; cryobiological discoveries announced from an orbital lab maintained by the Iliadic League; design of a space-ship which would carry twice as many colonists as at present to Demeter through the star gate; a proposal for a message to which the Others must, oh, must at last respond—As the spirit danced forth in her darting smile and gestures, pouncing questions, a remembered manner of tossing her head, Eric let the wonder of being beside her overwhelm him.

Yet when the car stopped at the university faculty club, where he would lodge, she said merely, "I'll call you later, if I may, after you know what else you ought to do, and we'll make a date."

(A message from her in April had warned: "I suppose I have been less passionate in my communications lately. Poor dear, how your last letter struggled to tell me without telling any censors! As a matter of fact, I don't guess our mail is being read, though we'd better not count on that; it's possible to do without leaving traces I could detect through my special system, if they went to a lot of trouble. But about us. Maybe I'm just running out of love words, seeing they have to flow in the one direction only. Or maybe—well, more and more, you, your homeland, everything seems like a dream. Did it really happen? Could it ever have? Can it? I am in a new linkage these days, subnuclear physics, and can't say much about it because it's so shatteringly strange. But it fills me till I find myself wrapped up in it off work too, and suddenly realize I've not thought about you for hours. They have *got* to let you come here soon, soon!'')

Eric shook her hand once more. "Indeed," he responded. "This evening, may I hope?"

They had been less formal when first they met.

THE MEMORY BANK

The International Conference on Psychosynergistics was more than an important scientific event. It was a large political move. The Covenant of Lima had supposedly established a framework within which peace could grow after generations of upheaval. A sharing of knowledge that governments had long kept jealously secret was a commitment to try to make that supposition be true.

Thus the gathering was a profoundly symbolic act, a breaking of bread together. Ultimately, for most of those who took part, it became a communion. More than a few would afterward find their lives on quite unforeseen courses.

The world as a whole—Earth, the Iliadic states, other space colonies which retained allegiance to some mother country, the Lunar settlements, bases throughout the Solar System, the Demetrians at the far end of the star gate—sensed this, and tried to follow along wherever news outlets existed. That created a certain amount of nuisance, albeit in a worthy cause. Besides being constantly seized by journalists, delegates had to sit through interminable opening ceremonies. General McDonough himself welcomed them to Calgary—well, that was all right, he was short-spoken. But later in the evening Nikos Drosinis, not content to be introduced as a Grand Old Man, felt called upon to explain to the public, in his thick English, what the subject matter was. True, the average layman had become a scientific ignoramus. Still, wasn't popularization the job of those same journalists?

"—the human brain, and hence the entire nervous system, can be integrated with a computer of the proper design. We have long ago progressed beyond the 'wires in the head' stage. Electromagnetic induction suffices to make a linkage. The computer then supplies its vast capacity for storing and processing data, its capability of carrying out mathematicological operations in microseconds or less. The brain, though far slower, supplies creativity and flexibility; in effect, it continuously rewrites the program. Computers which can do this for themselves do exist, of course, but for most purposes they do not function nearly as well as a computer-operator linkage does, and we may never be able to improve them significantly. After all, the brain packs some ten to the twelfth cells into a mass of about a kilogram. Furthermore, linkage gives humans direct access to what they would otherwise know only indirectly.

"For present, practical purposes, its advantages are twofold. (A) As I remarked, programs can be altered on the spot, in the course of being carried out. Formerly it was necessary to run them through, painstakingly check their results, and then slowly rewrite them, with possibilities of error, and without any guarantee that the new versions would turn out to be what we most needed. Once linkers and their equipment come into everyday use, we will be free of that handicap. (B) By the very experience, as I have also suggested, the linker gains insights which he or she could have gotten in no other way, and hence becomes a more able scientist—including a better writer of programs—when working independently of the apparatus, too."

Good Lord! Eric thought. He shifted in his chair. His eyes took French leave of the stage and roved around the auditorium. A couple of hundred heads, several of which had fallen onto their owners' chests; the walls beyond, handsome maple paneling, proud standards displayed of the provincial regiments which had helped see Canada through the Troubles; a neighbor's jacket, slightly scratchy against his own bare arm (the man was pot-bellied and white-goateed but might be fascinating to talk to); a subtle sense of pressure in the nearness of the chap on his left (slight, dark, Hindu race but surely not from India's tragic barbarism—maybe the Himalayan Confederacy?); despite air conditioning, a subliminal smell of flesh. . . .

"Linkage has therefore advanced research considerably, in those areas fortunate enough to have escaped the worst ravages of chaos," Drosinos was droning. "It will accomplish unpredictably much more as it moves from its present, mainly pilot stage to a global industrial routine. I expect this to be principally through computation and, perhaps, ultra-delicate manipulation of specialized equipment—not through control of ordinary machines, for which we already have adequate systems, human *or* robotic.

"I have my doubts likewise about the artistic potentialities. A few interesting experiments have been conducted. However, they have not gone far. Besides computer time being badly needed elsewhere, it seems unlikely that artists of genius will have the patience, inclination, or innate talent to go through the long and rigorous training that would make linkers of them. Yet I hope a few of the papers at our conference will tell us more about this area. Linkers do report that their experience has a transcendental quality, and various of them have made amateur attempts to communicate this through poetry, music, or graphics. . . ."

Eric nodded. He had tried that himself, without success. Well, he was unfitted by heritage and probably heredity—younger son of one of the neo-baronial families which gave their parts of British Columbia law, order, and rough justice; his memories running to wild hunts across mountainsides and through ancient rainy forests, to patrols against bandits and occasional fights with them, to accompanying hoarse-voiced coarse-handed gentle-hearted fishermen along the wonder of the Inland Passage, to carefree tumbling of servant girls, to evenings when hearths roared with fire and squadron pipers skirled forth the Songs of Our Dead and he was reckoned old enough to get drunk with men; then the scholarship offered him when he was eighteen, to study at the Turing Institute and perhaps, if he did well, become a fellow of it; and accepting, because McDonough's peace had made feudalism obsolete throughout the country, and he was not interested in empty titles, and anyway, he was a younger son; and his amazed discovery that throughout centuries, the mathematical titans from Pythagoras to von Neumann and beyond had wrought glory—it struck more deeply into him than any falling in love had ever done—

Damnation, there *were* no words for being in linkage, and he had yet to encounter notes or images that carried the truth. Linked, he saw—no, not "saw"—maybe, "He was"—the whole of a problem—no, not "problem," that was too fragmentary a concept—"undertaking?"—"rise-toward-comprehension?"—he went outside of himself, outside of the world.

"We must mount programs for finding thousands of young persons who have the gift. We must persuade them that, while a career in psychosynergistics is demanding, it has its great rewards."

Even the elementary analyses on which he had trained had taken him into themselves. And when, the stern years behind him, he became worthy of the frontier questions, for which no programs could be devised until their very meanings had been explored—

"Already we become able, not simply to advance our technologies, but to improve the societies in which we live."

Take the credit tax matter, as the most dismal-seeming example. McDonough was pledged to work for an eventual restoration of civil government, though probably not till after his death. (So were his American counterparts. They might or might not be sincere. Eric believed McDonough was.) To that end, he wanted measures which would encourage private enterprise and discourage the growth of bureaucracy. At the same time, the state did need revenues. Well, instead of an income tax, with the power over the individual that that entailed, why not a tax on interest-bearing loans, whether they be to a householder who accepted charges so he could defer paying his hydrogen bill, or to a corporation financing an asteroid mine?

Why not? Okay, what would the likely effects be on the economy? Obviously, people would pay cash whenever they could. How might that affect companies which provided them with short-term credit, and the employees of those companies, and the merchants whom the employees patronized? The average person, having more money in his pocket in the absence of income tax, would find that his increased mortgage payments made no difference in his everyday life—or would he? With no more writeoffs, the giant combines, borrowing money on a giant scale, might actually carry a larger share of the burden than hitherto. How would that alter business and politics?

The questions went on and on. They had no single answers, for there was no single model. The problem was to construct as many different models as possible—

they could be as elegant as Adam Smith's or as crude as Karl Marx's—and play the game out within each such universe, and test the respective scores against real data. But real data themselves are selected; a model is always implicit in any set of them. So the logic itself must likewise be analyzed.

Eric remembered how he groaned when the Institute got the job and asked him to join in. He had just come from working out (taking into account gravitation, electromagnetic fields, solar wind and solar evolution, dust and gas clouds, known stars in this region and their own projected fates, galactic orbit dependent on a million changing configurations elsewhere . . .) a tentative future history of the planets of his sun.

But having accepted, he found himself creating n-dimensional spaces, and time-variant curvatures for them, and tensors within, and functions and operators that nobody had ever imagined before; he made a conceptual cosmos, learned that it was wanting and annulled it, made another and another, until at last he saw what he had made and, behold, it was very good. Each time the numbers rushed through him to verify, and suddenly he knew how much reality he had embraced, it was an outbursting of revelation. The Christian hopes to be eternally in the presence of God, the Buddhist hopes to become one with the all in Nirvana, the linker hopes to achieve more than genius—is there a vast difference between them? Yes: the linker, in this life, does it.

In days, hours, fractional seconds. Afterward he or she cannot entirely comprehend what happened. The high moment of love also lies outside of time; but we understand it better, when at peace, than the linker understands what the linker has known.

Doubtless it's for the best that I have the primitive background I do, passed through Eric. *Too many of my fellows lose taste for the ordinary world. I haven't.*

"—often enough suggested that by way of psychosynergistics, we may become able to have discourse with the Others. Of them, we really know only that, once we had found the star gate in orbit, they let us use it, showing us the way through it to reach Demeter. Nothing else. Nothing else, in the century since then. The stupendous fact of their existence has inspired spiritual revolutions which helped bring on chaos. I cannot believe this was their wish. Rather, I would say that the knowledge of them aided mankind, throughout every grief and anger, not to release those powers which would kill the planet. Now, perhaps, we have completed a hard apprenticeship and are ready for the next stage. I dare trust that this meeting will bring us closer toward direct communication with the Others."

I wonder, Eric thought. *My guess is that they live their whole lives as I do only once in a while. Except they do it far more fully. That's my guess.*

Again his vision wandered. Hoy, quite a woman a dozen seats to his right! Why hadn't he noticed before? Tall, well-formed, dark-haired, face as finely and powerfully formed as the arch of a seagull's wings. . . . Who was she? What? Yank, to judge by the cut of her suit. She sat chin on fist, lost in her own wilderness as he had been in his.

"—during the years of secrecy, our American colleagues have made a tremendous advance. I wish to thank personally, and I am sure on behalf of everyone else present, thank the post-revolutionary United States government for its wise, altruistic decision to make at least the basic principles of this new technology public. Some of the most significant papers at our meeting will deal with aspects of it. Suffice it for me to say tonight that an extra dimension has been added to linkage, initially for military purposes, lately for pure research. In this holothetic system, as it is called, conceivably we begin to approach direct perception of the noumenon. No doubt that is too Faustian a statement, especially at our own eo-stage of investigation—''

The young woman had roused a bit. So probably the new specialty was hers. She listened for a while before returning to wherever she returned to.

—Afterward, as things broke up and the crowd moved out, Eric pushed his way through until he met her. Boldness had often gotten him what he wanted, and had never cost him more than he could afford. ''Excuse me,'' he said, reading her badge, ''Miz Ky.''

''Sir?'' Her eyes were neither timid nor inviting.

He had worked out his approach beforehand. It involved no lies, merely implications; it was fragile, but he shouldn't need it for more than an introduction. ''My name's Stranathan, as you can see. I'm a plain, digital kind of linker, but certain of the work I've been involved in has brought me toward the fringe of holothetic concepts, and I was given to understand that that's your field.''

''Yes.''

''Well, uh, well,'' (if she isn't a servant girl but a lady, start out shy) ''I would like to talk to an operator in it. I mean informally, no commitment to be precise, maybe getting a little subjective, do you follow me? Soon, before the conference hardens.''

''Well—'' She considered. It wasn't coquetry, it was straightforward thinking; yet her fingers had a darling way of touching her cheek. ''Mmm, yes, that sounds reasonable.''

''You might be interested to hear what we've been doing in Canada,'' he pursued. ''We haven't gone as far as you, in some directions, that is, but I get the impression we've explored some others further.''

She nodded. ''I have the same impression.'' The crowd shoved and mumbled around them.

He put on the smile. ''If I'm not being brash, would you like to come down to the bar with me and chat for a while?''

''I'm not accustomed to alcohol,'' she said calmly.

''Oh, well, a soft drink if you'd rather.''

''I would. You suit yourself, though.'' Her gaze met his, and he thought he had never seen a more total honesty. ''Yes, thank you, Dr. Stranathan, I've come to exchange information and this looks like a good beginning. Shall we?''

PRESENT TIME

His room at the faculty club was sizeable, comfortably furnished, joined to a private bath, and equipped on his account with typer, computer terminal, data screen and printout. On top of a small fridge were glasses, soda, and a liter of his favorite whisky. He stroked the bottle, touched by the gesture, until suddenly his throat clenched. Joelle must have told them the brand. It must have been her idea from the start. Then why had she herself, today, been so barren of welcome?

Striding to a window, he stared out. Open, it gave him a breeze gone cool, scented by newly cut grass, and a second-story view across lawns and buildings. Light streamed nearly level from the west, drenching leaves with gold and turning panes molten. A few students wandered along the paths, boys and girls brightly garbed, several couples hand in hand. The sky brimmed with quietness.

And this was her environment, these past three years, he thought. *Quite a change from the military reservation where she grew up. Or was it, really? She told me how her teachers, trainers, experimenters, at last her associates as she matured into her work and it into her—they were mostly research types, scientists, carrying out the project for its own sake, even if they were engaged by the armed forces, not terribly different from the professors here. And is she less walled off on campus, surrounded by town, with air and telecom access to almost anywhere anytime she chooses, than she was on a hundred fenced-in square kilometers in the Tennessee backwoods?*

The phone chimed. He stumbled and nearly fell in his haste to reach it and punch accept. And then it showed him Colonel Lundgard.

"Hello again," she said genially. "I hope you're settled in and getting rested."

"Uh, yes." He was startled to notice on a clock that he had arrived a couple of hours ago. More time than he knew had passed while he stood mind a-swirl. "Yes, they've given me a nice lodging."

"You're having dinner shortly with Dr. Billings, you recall," she said. "As for tomorrow, I've been making arrangements. Lots of people are eager to meet you. At ten, a preliminary tour of the university as a whole, ending in the office of Dr. Johns, the president, you know. He'll take you to a luncheon where a group of chosen faculty members will be. Afterward—"

A surge went through Eric. "Wait a minute," he snapped. "What about Miz Ky?"

Lundgard looked surprised. "I beg your pardon?"

"I—" He swallowed, mastered himself, and spoke fast. "Look, I appreciate your efforts, but I've come mainly to collaborate with her, and I am . . . am impatient to get going. I haven't heard from her yet. Better not make any commitments till I do."

"What?" Lundgard paused before frowning. "I daresay she'll be in her laboratory tomorrow afternoon, when Dr. Billings takes you through the Shannon Foundation facilities. You can discuss a work schedule then if you wish. First you do want to greet the, um, the leaders."

From a practical viewpoint she was right, Eric knew. In fact, he was stupid if he acted arrogant. He had his appointment not because he was the best linker in Canada—he was good, had contributed to the advancement of techniques as well as using them to solve problems, but he was no Tremblay or Vlasić—no, Joelle had pulled wires on his account, month after month; quite likely she had worn Billings down. Furthermore, he was supposed to bear international goodwill. He should if anything be a mite humble.

His shoulders stiffened till they hurt. *God damn it, I'm of the House of Stranathan, my father was Captain General of the Fraser Valley, we do not truckle!* Underneath, he recognized that it was his blood which would not let him wait a minute longer than he must to be alone with Joelle. Nevertheless, the principle was important, on behalf of his nation as well as family and pride. Wasn't it?

He picked his way carefully among words. "Yes, I see your point, Colonel. But please see mine. I can't talk sense until I have a rough idea of what's ahead in this job, what its shape will be, its dimensions. Before then, social noises are a waste of everybody's time, aren't they? Nobody but Miz Ky can properly explain. Linkage is not like anything else people do." He pushed his lips upward. "You must know that, if you've been a liaison with the Foundation. Linkers are all weird."

They did have a reputation for eccentricity, though it stemmed from a minority of them. Most tended to cover bashfulness or boredom when they were away from their machines with an ultra-conventional mode of life, and were not self-assertive. Daily details did not seem worth arguing about. Eric's background had left him a creature of the world who sometimes—he would recognize afterward—behaved pretty flamboyantly. But much would be forgiven him in Lawrence if, at first, the staff assumed he was only marginally human. The truth ought to dawn on them too slowly to make them feel they'd been hoodwinked.

Lundgard appeared to take his line. "Well, if you insist," she said after a moment. "I can't understand why Miz Ky didn't raise the issue while we were driving in."

Nor I. Was she too troubled? And by what? How should I know? When will I? "My fault, probably," Eric improvised. "She could've been waiting to hear what I wanted. And I was, uh, tired after my flight, too tired to think straight."

"Shall I call her?"

"No! —Sorry. Didn't mean to yell. We'd best settle this between us, she and I. I'll let you know as soon as possible. Do please convey my regrets—" Conversation eddied away in formulas. "So long."

When the screen blanked, Eric's hands began to shake. Sweat was prickling forth upon him. He tossed off a stiff shot and felt it burn out part of the tension.

Should I ring Joelle myself? No, she distinctly said she would. Why hasn't she, then? I don't understand her any longer. Did I ever?

Abruptly, violently, he twisted the information knob for her office and home numbers. At neither did he get a response. He imagined her walking alone by the river, as she had told him she often did, thinking about—what? He recorded a message to both places, the bare statement that he had kept tomorrow clear in order to consult with her and requested she call back. A minute after he was through, he could not recollect just what his phrasing had been.

The sun went under. It was time for his dinner with Billings. He changed into his reservist's uniform, acceptable everywhere and declarative of his citizenship.   Having been shown around upon arrival, he readily found the designated place in the building.

That was a room broad and gracious, wood-paneled, French doors ajar to let in fresh air but a fire crackling on a stone hearth to ward off chill.   Fluoros were set soft enough that a hint of flamelight and shadow-dance wove across walls.   For an instant, Eric felt himself back in the hostel at Lake Louise, and stood blinded. But it was merely stubby, gray-polled, chocolate-colored Billings who rose to greet him.

"I'd rather have received you in my house," the director said.   "I'm a widower, though, and no private party can afford competent servants these days."   A flunky arrived in answer to a pushbutton.   "What would you like for an apéritif?"

Eric chose a margarita.   He had heard of that concoction, Yank or Mex or whatever it was, but never met it.   The sour-sweet-salt iciness was refreshing. Food would be served on a table at the far end of the chamber.   Meanwhile he and Billings sat down in armchairs facing each other.

"Smoke?"   The director offered a box of cigarettes.

"No, thanks," Eric declined.   "Tobacco's too hard to come by where I live for most of us to form the habit."

"Best for your health, of course.   Still, I look forward to the small luxuries as well as the major benefits that increased trade will bring—eventually union, don't you also hope?"   Billings lit one.   The smoke drifted harsh to Eric's nostrils, as if underlining what came next.   "I've heard from Colonel Lundgard.   Do you really feel you can't go through those motions tomorrow?   Feathers will be ruffled."

Eric tautened anew.   "I'm sorry," he clipped, "but that's the way it is."

Billings shrugged.   "Well, I'll smooth 'em down for you.   Won't be my first such job."   Amiably: "You linkers are an independent breed, shall I say, no matter how conformist a mask many of you wear."   He turned grave.   "You may find yourself up against the same difficulty.   Self-determination, intransigence . . . peculiarity . . . an order of magnitude above your own."

The cocktail, on top of what he had gulped in his quarters after a day of weariness and shocks, was making Eric's head buzz a little.   He took a defiant swallow and said, "You refer to Joelle Ky, right?"

"Primarily, yes.   Brilliant, but—"

"But nothing.   We got, got so well acquainted in Canada that—" *Hold on. Don't blurt, you clotbrain!*

Billings regarded him measuringly.   "You did?" he murmured.   "Are you sure?   For openers, what do you know of her background?"

She had given Eric a few stark paragraphs.   He decided he might as well let Billings repeat the information, possibly adding more.   If nothing else, that would gain him time in which to take hold of himself.   "Not a lot," he said, and leaned back with an expectant expression.

Billings puffed hard on his cigarette.   "She was born in western Pennsylvania," he began.   "An aircraft, crashing down out of a dogfight, killed her family when she was two.   A military orphanage took her in; well, most things were military at that period. Pretty soon, because both her parents had been applied mathematicians, a team from Project Ithaca came and tested her. She showed such natural aptitude that she, along with a number of similar kids, was whisked off to White Pine Reservation in Tennessee. That's where she spent the next twenty-one years."

He fell silent. Eric made a reinforcing noise.

Billings stirred. "Oh, they weren't unkindly treated, the children," he said. "It may have been preferable to growing up in a dormitory or a close-rationed civilian foster home. Each of them was adopted by a married couple within the project, whose material well-being the armed service saw to. The grounds were extensive, woodsy, pleasant. There were ample recreational facilities. The community, however isolated physically, was decent and lively, full of high-powered intellects. News came in on the screens and faxes, or via those who had occasion to make trips outside. And . . . what of the project itself? Even to a child, wasn't that worth sacrificing a lot of so-called normal living for? You're a linker, Dr. Stranathan. You can presumably answer that question better than I."

"You make me wonder if I can, sir," Eric said low.

"I can't myself, for certain. Linkage arrived too late in my life. My experiences with it have necessarily been limited. You, your generation, you started sufficiently young to develop those abilities much further. Now what of those who began earlier yet, virtually as infants?"

"Well, yes, what about them?" Eric attacked. "Joelle—oh you must know we're on first-name terms—when we met, she was a stranger to a lot of things that the ordinary person, that I too take for granted. But she learned fast, and was delighted. Damnation, she's no machine! She's a woman!"

At once he cursed himself for what he might have revealed. However, Billings didn't notice, or pretended not to. "What you say is true of most of those I've encountered," the director replied. "By average standards, overly cerebral. Naïve about society. Timorous or standoffish, as the case may be, about forming close relationships. And yet not pathological, any more than an athlete is who's concentrated on his bodily development at the expense of cultural activities."

"So why d'you hint Joelle and I may find it hard working together?"

"She's not only spent her whole remembered life as a linker, she's been part of the evolution of holothetics from the outset. That was the purpose of Project Ithaca, after all. She still is. In fact, since it was declassified, since she moved from White Pine to Lawrence, progress has accelerated like a torch ship. Research is no longer held to narrowly practical ends, you see. Workers are free to explore an infinity. A great deal of what they learn is unforeseeable, comes as a stunning surprise. And Joelle Ky has been, is right in the middle of it."

"Sure. Why am I here, if not to learn enough from her that I can advise my government how best to join in with your outfit and— Whoa, you've got me doing it. Repeating what we both know."

Billings raised his brows. "Do we? You in particular. Oh, some basic theory, some diagrams and experimental data and whatnot, were presented at Calgary. Since then, you and your colleagues have been in touch with various of our folk, you've received books and journals and so forth.   You have a general idea about holothetic linkage.   But have you had a real chance to consider the implications?''

Eric blinked and sat straight.   ''Why, they're revolutionary, of course.   Regardless, though, the system is a natural outgrowth of what had been going on before.   Different in degree, but not in kind.''

Memory flashed.   She stood before him again, on stage in the auditorium in Calgary, looking so small and alone that he wanted to gallop his horse across the heads between them to reach her, and he heard her read her paper in a voice that was likewise lost:

''—while linkage to macroscopic machinery has not proven cost-effective, the case has turned out to be different for monitoring and controlling scientific experiments.   For this it is inadequate to supply the operating brain with numbers such as voltmeter readings and nothing else.   For example, a spectrum is best considered—rationally appreciated—when the operator sees it and, simultaneously, knows the exact wavelength and intensity of each line.   Through appropriate hardware and software, this can now be done.   Subjectively, it is like sensing the data directly, as if the nervous system had grown complete new input organs of unprecedented power and sensitivity.

''Workers elsewhere have experimented with that.   The principal thing Project Ithaca did was to take the next step.   What is the *meaning* of those data, those sensations?

''In everyday life, we do not apprehend the world as a jumble of raw impressions, but as an orderly structure.   Yonder we do not see a splash of green and brown; we see a tree, of such-and-such a kind, at such-and-such a distance.   Although it is done unconsciously, yes, instinctively, since animals do it too, nonetheless we may be said to build theories, models, of the world, within which our direct perceptions are made to make sense.   Naturally, we modify these models when that seems reasonable.   For instance we may decide that we are not really seeing a tree but a piece of camouflage.   We may realize that we have misjudged its distance because the air is more clear or murky than we knew at first.   Basically, however, through our models we comprehend and can act in an objective universe.

''Science has long been adding to our store of information and thus forcing us to change our model of the cosmos as a whole, until today this embraces billions of years and light-years, in which are galaxies, subatomic particles, a long evolution of life, and everything else that our ancestors never suspected.   To most of us, this part of the Weltanschauung has admittedly been rather abstract, no matter how immediate the impact of the technologies it makes possible.

''In order to enhance laboratory capability, Project Ithaca began work on means to supply a linkage operator directly with theory as well as data.   This was more than learning a subject, permanently or temporarily.   Any operator has to do that, in order to think about a given task.   And indeed, outstanding accomplishments came out of the Turing Institute here, pioneering ways for the linked computer to give its human partner the necessary knowledge.   Project Ithaca greatly improved such systems, and its civilian successors continue to progress.

''That has had an unexpected result.   Those operators whom Ithaca trained from childhood, linkers who today are adults advancing the art in their turn, are more and more getting into a mode that I must call intuitive.   A baseball pitcher, an acrobat, or simply a person walking is constantly solving complex problems in physics with little or no conscious thought.   The organism feels what is right to do.   Analogously, we have for example reached the point of manipulating individual amino acids within protein molecules, using ions directed by force-fields, in a manner that perhaps only the Others could plan out step by step.   Likewise for any number of undertakings.   Direct perception through holothetics is leading to comprehension on a nonverbal level.

"This is doubly true because our theoretical knowledge is far from perfect.   Very frequently these days, a holothete senses that things are not going as intended, that something is wrong with the model—and intuits what changes to make, what the real situation is, as we so often do in our ordinary lives.   Later systematic study generally confirms the intuition.

"My colleagues will be discussing various aspects of holothetic linkage.   This introductory sketch of mine—"

Eric dropped jarringly back to awareness.   "I'm sorry, I didn't hear you," he said.

"It was a difference of degree once," Billings repeated.   "It is becoming a difference of kind.   If it hasn't already."

"Yes, I know the sensationalistic speculations.   But I know Joelle too."

Billings sighed and smiled.   "Ah, well, quite likely you do, better than I.   Two young persons—Let's not argue.   Do you care for another drink?"

Dinner was pleasant.   The older man had a marvelous store of reminiscences, not confined to his professional career.   He was in turn sharply interested in Eric's boyhood, the feudal society now vanishing, the personality types it brought forth. "In Mexico," he remarked, "the word is *macho*.   You find exactly the same kind of man in the medieval Icelandic sagas.   Seldom in nineteenth-century America; the frontier era was too brief for the armed roughneck to mature into the armed gentleman.   I suspect you western Canadians drew on a remnant of English tradition among you."

Eric wasn't sure whether he was glad when his visit ended.   He would be if his phone held a message from Joelle.   If not—   Corridor and staircase clattered to his speed.

A red light proclaimed a recording.   Eric's finger jarred against the playback button.   Her voice fell toneless: "Since you want it, let's meet at my lab tomorrow noon.   I'll have sandwich makings and will have made sure we won't be interrupted. Sleep late in the morning.   What we'll do won't be easy for either of us."

THE MEMORY BANK

While the conference lasted, he squired her around Calgary.   That held plenty of marvels for her, museums, live plays, a symphony orchestra, a ballet troupe, gourmet restaurants, little crannies of intimacy, or simply evenings of beer and bull with his local friends.   She had had a small exposure to such things in White Pine, more in Lawrence, but Calgary was cosmopolitan.   Besides, no one had taken her in hand before as he did.   He wondered why, when she was so fair, but dared not crowd her with personal questions.   She was too quick to retreat into noncommittal correctness.   And maybe that *was* why.

Their relationship struck roots and sent forth buds.   By the time the gathering adjourned, she had accepted his invitation to Lake Louise.   He had the family connections to get them into that resort, she had no trouble extending her leave of absence, and they were both well supplied with money.

On a certain early morning there, he knocked on her door.   By then they had tramped the trails, scrambled onto the peaks, loafed in alpine meadows while birds and deer and once a bear went by.   Today they would give to the lake itself. After breakfast he led her to a hired canoe.   In the hours that followed, sometimes they paddled, sometimes they used a whispery electric motor, sometimes they grounded the craft and went ashore.   Whenever they sat on sun-spattered brown duff and wavelets glittered before them, he kissed her.   She had first let him do that on one of their last outings in town.   He would never forget lamplight splintered by June leaves in the park where they were, a sound of crickets, and her dear awkwardness.   She learned fast and grew braver.   Today his hand lay rounded inside her shirt, though that was where she stopped it.   How lithe she was, how warm her odor.   She murmured.

Between two such halts they shipped their paddles and idled.   The water danced blue, green, diamond.   Around it, above forest, mountains sheered aloft into silence.   Ever so slightly, the canoe rocked with each motion they made.

She dipped a finger over the side and watched how ripples spread.   ''Electron interferences make a moiré too,'' she mused.   ''It's wonderful finding the same here.   I never noticed before.''   Her glance captured him.   ''Thank you for bringing me.''   The eyes drifted elsewhere.   ''Electrons do it in three dimensions. No, four, but I haven't perceived that . . . yet.''

He recalled similar remarks of hers.   Over coffee and brandy afterward, she had told him how sublimely Newtonian *Swan Lake* and *Ondine* were, when to him they were sublimely sexy.   Well, that could be innocence speaking; and he, a linker likewise, found as much mathematics as melody in a Bach recital, or admired above everything else the subtle perspectives in Monet.   (Looking at the same 3-faxes, she had pointed out interactions of colors to which he and, he suspected, critics of the past couple of centuries had been blind.)   Today, for whatever reason, unease roused in him.

''Look, Joelle,'' he said, ''don't get lost in abstractions— Wait.   Please.   Let me explain what I mean.   Sure, you and I work with data, set up paradigms, compute resultants, sure.   Fine.   Fine job.   But let's not let that interfere with what we, well, we find in places like this.   In our private lives generally. This—'' he waved a hand around the horizon—''is what's real.   Everything else we infer.   This is what we're alive in.''

She regarded him for a long while, during which he glowed.   Finally her gaze moved away, once more outward.   He could barely hear her: "I never got a chance to appreciate that before now."

"Jesus Christ!" broke from the quick pain in him.   "What kind of monsters were they?   Locking you away since you were a baby, treating you like a piece of apparatus.   That's what you were to them, nothing but apparatus."

She shook her head, still staring from him.   "No, Eric, I've told you that isn't true.   Weren't you listening?   The secrecy, the work itself, those were military necessities.   My foster parents were as kind as ever my own could have been. They tried to get me to lead a normal life.   I had plenty of age mates, children of personnel.   But I found too much in the computers.   Remember, holothetics wasn't something cut and dried that a school fed to me.   It was something that grew, it was discovery, accomplishment, adventure, and from the beginning, *I* was a leader. That's a heady brew for anyone, let alone a kid.   My contemporaries bored me, I discouraged every effort at friendship, except with the few who were in my part of the project, and we hardly ever wanted to do more than talk about it when we couldn't actually be in it.   So, my fault entirely, I didn't appreciate that there are equally grand things, till I moved to Lawrence and suffered a healthy culture shock. And at first that drove me still further into myself."

She faced him afresh.   "You've made the difference, Eric.   You've made me feel and understand . . ."   Her words trailed off.   She flushed from temples to bosom.

"I'm glad," he said, and, to cover the confusion in them both: "Shall we push on?"

After supper cooked over a resin-fragrant fire and seasoned by her nearness, they turned back.   Sunset caught them, but they had foreseen that and the sky gave ample light.   A kilometer or two from the lodge, they took a rest.   Pinewoods hid it; they might have been the last man and woman on Earth, or the first on a virgin world.   The lake glimmered like obsidian and, under a breeze whose chill Eric didn't notice, swayed the canoe on chuckling waves.   The mountains seemed far off and airy, something dreamed long ago in a dawntide sleep.   Stars crowded heaven, the Milky Way swung frost-bright among them, the sense of being afloat in measureless immensities could not have been greater were he spaceborne.

Vision ranging upward, she whispered, "How do the Others see that?   What is it to them?"

"What are they?" he answered.   "Animals evolved beyond us; machines that think; angels dwelling by the throne of God; beings, or a being, of a kind we've never imagined and never can; or what?   Humans have been wondering for more than a hundred years now."

"We'll come to know."   Her pride sounded forlorn.

"Through holothetics?"

"Maybe.   Else through— Who can tell?   But I do believe we will.   I have to believe that."

"We might not want to.   I've got an idea we'd never be the same again, and that price might be too high."

She shivered. "You mean we'd forsake all we have here?"

"And all we are. Yes, it's possible. And I wouldn't, myself. I'm so happy where I am, this moment."

She was silent for several heartbeats. "I am too, Eric. With you—" She moved toward him. The canoe lurched.

"Careful," he laughed automatically. "Yon water's mighty cold."

"Eric, let's hurry on." Her voice trembled with its own courage. "Start the motor. Bring us ashore where we belong."

Having landed, they stayed outside for another hour, in which the mountains danced and the stars rejoiced, before they sought his room.

PRESENT TIME

The Shannon Foundation was located on campus. As the single holothete to join it thus far, Joelle rated a building to herself, just adequate to contain the equipment she needed and an office, but electronically woven into a network which was becoming global. It stood between ancient oaks, whose leaves rustled to a wind that drove clouds and their shadows before it. Sleek plasticrete walls, pastel tinted, didn't fit into the surrounding greenery, the downhill riverward view of an old town and a gentle hinterland. *As if this were a shell shutting out the living world and me,* Eric thought. He activated the chime with his hand and knocked with his heart.

The door opened for him. There she stood. Her slimness was muffled in a coverall, the long black hair drawn into a ponytail, her eyes enormous.

"Oh, Joelle, Joelle!" He almost bowled her over, bearing her before him in his rush to let the door close them off while he embraced her.

She kissed him back, her touch also roved, and minutes passed that nobody counted. Yet when they stepped apart, fingers entwined, to see each other, she was not laughing or weeping and her breath came evenly. His did not, and it was through a faint blur of tears that he saw how seriously—compassionately?—she looked upon him.

He had spent much time composing what he would say, but it fled from him and he could only stammer, "How I've missed you. Never anymore."

"If that's what you want, darling," she responded.

"Would you believe I've been chaste these fifteen mortal months? Silly, no doubt, but it was a thing I could do for you, it was a way of telling myself we would be together."

Her gravity yielded to a sunrise of blood such as he remembered from their earliest days as one. "Silly, yes, and sweet and knight-erranty and what I'd have expected of you, Eric." Why did she appear unsure of herself?

"Well?" he called through the roaring within him.

She gathered a smile. "I expected that too. Come along."

There was a couch in her office, for occasions when she did not want to interrupt an endeavor to seek an apartment that her letters had described as cramped and lonesome. He slid the coverall off her with reverence, for she rose out of it like Aphrodite from the sea and made the drab enclosure shine. He was clumsy in removing his clothes, since he could not watch what he did.

At Lake Louise she had offered him her maidenhead, but she had soon learned how to give joy and take it as well as any woman he had ever known, except that being Joelle she gave him what went beyond joy. On this day—It happened fast in his eagerness, but she guided him with her motion and a few words, so that the billow crested in her before him. Afterward she lay quietly. Nor had she cried that she loved him, as he did to her.

The narrowness of the couch made it a rather ludicrous effort not to fall off, though it did bring him pressing up against her while he crooned nonsense. Still she rested passive, until at length she stirred and said, "No, dear, please, not again right away. We've got too much else ahead of us."

His fears stabbed him anew. He sat up, swung feet to floor, twisted around and confronted her. "What's the matter?" he demanded.

"Why, nothing . . . maybe. Everything depends on you, what you decide is best." She raised herself and reached forth to stroke his brow and cheek. Trouble crossed her face, as lightly as a cloud shadow on the grass outside. "A lot has changed while we were apart. Especially in the last few months." It passed as swiftly.

He grabbed her shoulders. Barely he kept his grip from closing with bruising force, and felt instead how silken was the skin beneath it. "You've met somebody else?" he half shouted.

"No, no." She shook her head. He saw the ponytail swirl across her back, ebony on ivory. "Never, Eric."

"You've fallen out of love, is that it?"

"No. You'll always be *you* to me. But—" She sighed and slumped. "Other things have changed, yes. I couldn't help it, I might have quit if I'd foreseen, but the newness came sneaking in—or came like a blast of trumpets, oh, I don't know—" She straightened, locked her vision into his, and spoke with regained steadiness. "When you understand, and that's what I hope to make you do, when you understand, you can choose for us. I'll be glad to go along. I do love you." She uttered a laugh. "Sweetheart, this kennel includes a bathroom. Let's wash and get dressed and have a bit of lunch, and afterward we'll talk about us."

She's being as kind as she's able. The knowledge rocked him.

In the shower she, who had never been mercurial before, was suddenly playful, giggly as a schoolgirl. "Bodies are fun, aren't they? Mostly I've geen giving mine plain maintenance, because my work wanted fifty hours a day and anyway you weren't around. . . .

No, Eric, darling, wait, we must get serious, both of us—" *I can't follow her mind, her feelings any longer, she's become a stranger. Or was she always? But what a bonny stranger. If we have to start over from zero, okay, I'm willing.*

Back in the office, she produced bread, cheese, sausage, beer from a minifridge and made sandwiches for them while she chattered. He did his best to reciprocate.

They gossipped about colleagues, they swapped recollections, and finally they reached the subject of what they had individually been doing in the past months. Communications between them had been scanted of late. She had pleaded extreme business to account for the brevity and impersonality of hers and he, puzzled, failing not to be hurt, confined in any event to sending her nothing that third parties shouldn't know about, had cut his own letters short. They talked at intervals by phone, of course, and her image remained with him for days afterward exactly as it had appeared on the screen; but those calls could show no more than affinity sprung from a shared profession.

He told her about his latest assignment, a sequel to the work on economics, this an attempt to quantify political consequences of various strictly defined types. She nodded. "Yes, I see how that'd be quite a challenge," she said. "A bare preliminary, as you admit, a grotesque oversimplification, but . . . a beginning? If ever we do get a genuine theory of human interaction, parameters we can give values to, who knows? We might become able to abolish war, tyranny, poverty the way we've abolished cancer and schizophrenia."

He could hear she was being considerate of him, faking an interest she scarcely felt. Trying to awaken some enthusiasm they might share, he asked, "Do you think holothetics will help?" and laid his hand across hers where it rested on the desk.

She pondered for seconds. "Who can tell? But I doubt it. You see, it's a paradox, but in dealing with those social affairs, you're necessarily using an abstract, mathematical model. That isn't what holothetics is concerned with."

"No? Never, in all time to come?"

"What would the appropriate inputs be, ever?"

"The right model—"

Joelle braced herself. "Eric, in the past half year I've been discovering things about reality that make me see how jerry-built the whole idea of 'models' is that my science itself was founded on." She spoke fast, looking squarely ahead of her though he sat by her side. "I haven't told you, and I've scarcely hinted at it to Mark Billings, because—because I didn't realize either until very lately, what it signified that I'd been experiencing." She turned around in her chair, toward him. Her free hand dropped to his arm. "I've spent the last few weeks trying to figure out how to explain to you, how to show you. I've been in touch with my associates from White Pine—we keep each other's secrets—and thought and thought about the results of experiments we've done involving regular-type linkers like you, and I personally—" She flushed anew. "I've only attempted full rapport with women. I wouldn't go that deep with any male except you."

She paused. "No, I lied there," she admitted. "I've not spent my whole time that way. Not when everything else has been opening up for me. But I've tried my damnedest, because I do love you, Eric."

In a rush: "Are you ready?"

"Yes," he made himself reply; for he more than half dreaded what lay in the inner building.

She leaned over and kissed him, lingeringly but altogether tenderly, almost as if she bade goodbye to a child. Then rising, she exclaimed, "Let's go!" and strode before him like the Victory of Samothrace.

THE MEMORY BANK

After the mountains, they had a few days more in Calgary before she went home. On the second of these, a supper turned into a scheming session.

"Why must you leave?" he pleaded for the xth time. "You know you can have your pick of positions in Canada."

"But I can't," she replied softly. "You've no holothetic system in the country, and won't for years."

Bitterness coursed through him. "Yes, your career."

He saw her wince, and damned his tongue. A violinist was playing Mendelssohn's Concerto Number One; the notes flowed wistful around them. They had this part of the restaurant to themselves, their table by a window overlooking a lawn, rosebeds, and the Bow River agleam in blue dusk. Candlelight glowed on her shoulders and arms, brought forth seductive shadows in the gown she had bought with such pride to make a show worthy of a Stranathan's woman, and sparkled off tears caught in her lashes.

"My life, Eric," she said. "You could give up linking if you had to, go back to the Fraser Valley, be a rancher, and not feel existence was drained dry. But you wouldn't willingly, would you? And you had those woods as a boy; it's in you to range them. I've only had my computers. Without them, I'd soon be nothing—have nothing to give you."

"I'm sorry." He reached across linen and crystal. "You're right, I'm wrong, it's only that it hurts too hard losing you."

"Not forever, darling. If we use the proper strategy."

They had talked about the matter before, but desultorily, soon veering away from a question that broke into their delight. Now he nodded. "We'd better work out a plan, then."

"The basic idea's simple. We wangle you an appointment to the Shannon Foundation."

"Couldn't I easier and quicker come down to the States and take whatever job is available?"

"No, I'm afraid not. The market is fairly well filled. Certainly you couldn't find a post in Lawrence or anywhere near. Besides, I'll be frank, the U.S. government is chary about admitting foreigners. Paranoid, if you wish, but don't forget what it's been through, these past decades. It'll ease up in due course, starting with Canadians. But meanwhile—in spite of the gesture made at our conference, and believe me, that was a huge gesture, we're saddled with a lot of official nosiness and suspiciousness."

"As your husband—I do want to marry you, Joelle—"

"And I you. Oh, I want!" Their hands clung. "But no. Not till the security regulations change.   As they are, I'd be automatically excluded from defense-related research, and that's still a big part of what we do at Shannon.   So I'd lose the very leverage I need to get you an appointment, where you too can have satisfying, meaningful work.   Plenty bad I've prolonged my leave of absence.   I dare not stretch it out.''

"Can you, uh, spend your vacations here?''

"I won't have any for another year.   And by that time, if everything has gone well, we'll be close enough to squiffling you into the Foundation that our best bet will be for me to hang in there and make sure of it.''

"A year or worse!   And I can't write or phone to say I love you, can I?''

"No, that'd be unwise.   If they learn I'm 'emotionally compromised,' some bureaucrat is bound to take the safest course and deny you entry, as well as lifting my clearance.''   Joelle chuckled.   The gallantry of that tore at him.   "Once you're established among us, a romance leading to a marriage will be perfectly natural and cause no trouble.''   Her humor faded.   "You're right, though.   Those will be dead months, waiting for you.''

"We can maintain professional contact,'' he said.   "In fact, we must, to make it plausible that you push my candidacy.   Let's have a few code phrases.   'Erratic feedback' means 'I'm off my orbit for lack of you.' 'Hyperspatial configuration' means 'You're a walking miracle.' ''

"And you, Eric. . . .   Hold on.   I can improve on that.   I can write to you, whatever I please.''

"Huh?''

"Yes.''   Excitement animated her.   "Data systems in the two countries will shortly be interconnected, you remember.   I can input information without its registering on any monitor.   You can't, but I can, and route it to your private terminal.   The holothetic system enables me.   In effect, I take over a whole channel, including its registers and memory.''

He whistled at the magnitude of that capability.

"Ah, ha, I've surprised you,'' she laughed.   "Well, a girl ought to surprise her man once in a while, true?   Wait till you see my letters.   They're going to be so erotic the printout will smoke.''

"I'll kiss it just the same,'' he said.

"Never expected I'd want to be a printout. . . .''   She grew solemn.   "Eric, can you imagine what you are to me?   What you've given me?   The whole material universe, that's what, from that garden out there that I now fully see and feel and smell—'' she gestured at it; darkness was rising swiftly from the earth, but the earliest stars were kindling overhead— "and this nice tickly champagne in my mouth, on from those to the novas exploding when you make love to me—and then to top the treasure off, *yourself*, body, mind, soul, your funny lopsided smile and your recollections of home and the countless courtesies you don't even notice you're doing me—'' Joelle covered her eyes.   "Pardon me if I blubber for a minute.   It's not from being sad.   I am that, sure, but only on th-th-the surface.   Underneath, where it counts, I'm aleph-sub-aleph happy.''

PRESENT TIME

The hardware filled a large bleak room, and at that much of it was below the floor in a cryogenic chamber.   Principally Eric saw four metal cabinets, taller than himself and thrice as long, standing parallel to each other.   Instruments, displays, and controls upon them were for the benefit of service technicians; once linked, the woman had no need of such gadgets.   Behind them he recognized the bulk of a Heydt 707, similar to the machine with which he worked at the Turing Institute and, she had informed him in their "public" communication, lately modified and reprogrammed for his benefit.   In front of the apparatus were four equally familiar loungers and their attached linkmakers.   He knew that sometimes she teamed with up to three visiting holothetes, as well as employing ordinary operators like himself for assistants.

Today, they two were alone.   Windowless, the room was fluorolit, a whiteness that felt cold though ventilators hummed forth warm currents of air.   Silence pressed inward.   He looked at her and thought, *But for me, she might never have known anything more than this; sun, stars, wind, leaves, flowers, heights, every joy there is would be ghosts she hardly noticed, and love would not exist.*   Yet the distress he had sensed in her earlier was gone.   She stood before her machines and fairly blazed with ardor.   For a skipped pulse he wondered if she had forgotten him.

But she spoke, rather quickly, not facing him: "You caught me off guard, dear. I assumed you'd spend your first few days being sociable as you were supposed to.   I should have recalled you don't brook being told what to do.   I figured I'd plan this demonstration according to how you seemed to react, to feel—fifteen months is a long time apart, you might have changed, in any case we haven't had years to get acquainted.   Well, I'll have to improvise.   Forgive me if it comes heavier than I hoped for you."

"What are you talking about?" he asked, seizing her elbow the way that fear seized him.

She turned and considered him steadily, her countenance gone strange, before she replied, "Words are no use here.   You must experience for yourself.   We're about to become more intimate than ever in bed.   normously more."

Quasi-telepathic effects had been reported, when a passive linker in a holothetic circuit not only received the same data in his brain as the active one did, but "felt" the latter's ongoing evaluations.   "You, uh, you'll slave my unit to yours?"   Eric inquired.   "According to what I've seen in the literature, that doesn't convey a particularly strong or clear perception."

"Everything isn't in the literature yet.   I told you I—we—all right, I am making whirlwind progress.   I've acquired a, I don't know, an insight, a near-instinct, and the feedback between me and the system, the continuous reprogramming at each session—"   She tugged his sleeve.   "Come along.   Get to know!"

"What do you have in mind?"

She frowned the least bit.   "That'll depend partly on you, how you're taking what happens.   We'll begin with you and the 707.   Just think in it for a while, get settled down.   Then, through the cross-connections, I'll phase you in with me and my computer.   That will have to be strictly input to you, no access to effectors, or you might ruin some delicate experiments.   I'm going to look in on them, you see.   My help is called for often enough that we have constantly open channels between them and my system.   Genetics at a lab right on this campus; nuclear physics at the big accelerator in Minnesota; cosmology in Sagan Orbital.   I hope I can lead you to a hint of what I'm doing these days.   I'll know, because you will have an output of a kind to me.   In effect, I'll be scanning your mind.   Yes,'' she said into his stupefaction, "I've reached that stage.''

"Afterward—'' She threw her arms around him and kissed him.   "Let there be an afterward.''

He responded, but couldn't help thinking that her tone had been kind rather than prayerful.   *Well, why should she fear?   Isn't her work going well, and aren't we together again?*

He lowered himself into the proper lounger, adjusted it to the reclining angle he liked, let muscle and bone ease into its form-fitting comfort until he felt almost disembodied, before he pulled the helmet down over his head, adjusted and secured it, put his wrists through the contact loops, tapped fingers across a control plate and checked out the settings.   A side glance revealed Joelle doing likewise in a rig that appeared little different from his.   And the olden thrill shook all fret out of him.   Once more he was going to become transhuman.

"Activate?'' he asked.

"Proceed,'' she answered.

"I love you,'' he said, and pressed the main switch.

Momentarily, senses and consciousness whirled, he imagined he heard a wild high piping, memories broke forth out of long burial as if he had fallen back through time to this boyhood swimming hole and moss cold and green upon a rock, that hawk at hover and the rough wool of a mackinaw around him.   Then his nervous system steadied into adjustment, into mastery.   Electromagnetic induction, amplification of the faintest impulses, a basic program which he had over the years refined to fit his unique self, meshed; human and computer became a whole.

"Think,'' she said.   How could he not, when his was now a mightier intellect than any which had been on Earth before his day?

"Words are no use here,'' she said.   Never would they tell an outsider the least part of that which dwelt in him.

He was fully aware of his environment.   Had he wanted to, he could have examined its most micrometric details, a scratch and a reflection on polished metal, the shimmy of a needle on a meter, mumble and faint tang of oil in the ventilation, back-and-forth tides in his veins.   But they didn't matter.   Joelle herself no longer was quite real.   He had a conceptual universe to conquer.

In the next several milliseconds, while he cast about for a problem worth tackling, a minor compartment of him calculated the value of an elliptic integral to a thousand decimal places.   It was a pleasant, semi-automatic exercise.   The numbers fell together most satisfyingly, like bricks beneath the hands of a mason.   *Ah*, came to him, *yes, the stability of Red Spot vortices on planets like Jupiter, yes, I did hear talk about that in Calgary.*   The sweep hand on a wall clock had barely stirred.

He marshalled a list of the data he thought he would need and sent a command. To him it felt much like searching his normal memory for a fact or two, except that this went meteorically faster and more assuredly, in spite of drawing on memory banks which were hundreds of kilometers away.   The theory reached him, equations, parameters and their specific values for Jupiter, yes, that particular differential equation would be an absolute bitch to solve except that he saw a dodge; but wait, was it actually plausible, couldn't he devise a set of relationships that better described conditions on an aborted sun—?

An ice-clean fire arose, he was losing himself in it, he was getting drunk on sanity.

Eric: no voice, no name, a touch; Joelle.

He must wrench his attention from Jupiter, with a vow, *I'll be back.*   Probably he would not have done it for anyone but her.   He was no less a human male than when unlinked, he was simply a mathematicological super-genius.   Though also, this time—lying back, eyes closed, he caught what might be the first gleam of a revelation.

Eric, are you ready to follow me?

It was not truly a question, it was an intent which he felt.   It was her.   At dazzling speeds, as neurone webs adapted to each other's synapse patterns, she merged with him.   The formless eddies that go behind shut lids were not shaping into her image; rather he got fleeting impressions of himself, before her presence flooded him.   Was it her femaleness he knew as a secret current in the blood, a waiting to receive and afterward cherish and finally give, a bidding she chose not to heed but which would always be there?   He couldn't tell, he might never know, for the union was only partial.   He had not learned how to accept and understand most of the signals that entered him, and there were many more which his body never would be able to receive.   That became a pain in him as it was in her.

Eric, in this too you are my first man, and I think my last.

Forebrains, more alike than the rest of their organisms, meshed.   Besides, Joelle had practiced cross-exchange on that level and developed the technique of it with fellow linkers, until she was expert.   Communication between her and Eric strengthened and clarified, second by second.   It was not direct, but through their computers, whose translations were inevitably imperfect.   Impressions were often fragmentary and distorted, or outright gibberish—bursts of random numbers, shapes, light-flashes, noises, less recognizable non-symbols, which would have been nightmarish save for the underlying constancy of herself.   What touched his mind as her thoughts were surely reconstructions, by his augmented logical powers, of what it supposed she might be thinking at a given instant.   The real words that passed between them went in the common mortal fashion, from lips to ear.

Nevertheless: he took her meanings with a fullness, a depth he had not dreamed could be, there on the threshold of her private universe.

"Genetics," she said aloud.   That was the sole clue he needed.   She would guide him to the research at this school.   Knowledge sprang forth.   The work was on the submolecular level, the very bases of animate being. She was frequently called on to carry out the most exacting tasks, invent new ones, or interpret results. Today the setup was in part running automatically, in part on standby; but she had access to it anytime.

Her brain ordered the appropriate circuits closed, and she was joined to the complex of instruments, sensors, effectors, and to the entire comprehension man had of the chemistry of life. Receiving from her, Eric perceived.

He got no presentation of quantities, readings on gauges whose significance became clear after long calculation. That is, the numbers were present, but in the experience he was hardly more conscious of them than he was of his skeleton. He was not looking from outside and making inferences, he was *there*.

It was seeing, feeling, hearing, traveling, though not any of those things, for it went beyond what the poor limited human creature could ever sense or do, and beyond and beyond.

The cell lived. Pulsations crossed its membrane like colors, the cell was a globe of rainbow, throbbing to the intricate fluid flow that cradled it in deliciousness, avidly drinking energies which cataracted toward it down ever-changing gradients. Green distances reached to golden infinity. Beneath every ongoing fulfillment dwelt peace. The cosmos of the cell was a Nirvana that danced.

Now inward, through the rainbows, to the interior ocean. Here went a maelstrom of . . . tastes . . . and here reigned a gigantic underlying purposefulness; within the cell, work forever went on, driven by a law so all-encompassing that it might have been God the Captain. Organelles drifted by, seeming to sing while they wove together chemical scraps to make stuff that came alive. As the scale of his cognition grew finer, Eric saw them spread out into Gothic soarings, full of mysteries and music. Ahead of him, the nucleus waxed from an island of molecular forests to a galaxy of constellated atoms whose force-fields shone like wind-blown star-clouds.

He entered it, he swept up a double helix, tier after tier of awesome and wholly harmonious labyrinths, he was with Joelle when she evoked fire and reshaped a part of the temple, which was not less beautiful thereafter, he shared her pride and her humility, here at the heart of life.

Her voice came far-off and enigmatic, heard through dream: "Follow me on." He swept out of the cell, through space and through time, at light-speed across unseen prairies, into the storms that raged down a great particle accelerator. He became one with them, he shouted in their own headlong fervor, the same speed filled him and he lanced toward the goal as if to meet a lover.

This world outranged the material. He transcended the comet which meson he had become, for he was also a wave intermingling with a trillion other waves, like a crest that had crossed a sea to rise and break at last in sunlit foam and a roar—though these waves were boundlessly more shapeful and fleetly changeable, they flowed together to create a unity which flamed and thundered around an implacable serenity—*Bach could tell a little of this,* passed through him, for he had his reasoning mind too; that was a high part of the glory—*but he alone could, and it would only be a little—*

The atom awaited him.   Its kernel, where energies querned, was majestic beyond any telling.   Electron shells, elfinly a-sparkle, veiled it from him.   He plunged through, the forces gave him uncountable caresses, the kernel shone clear, itself an entire creation, he pierced its outer barriers and they sent a rapturous shudder across him, he probed in and in.

The kernel burst.   That was no disaster, it was an unfolding.   The atom embraced him, yielding to him, his being responded to her every least wild movement, he knew her.   Radiance exploded outward.   The morning stars sang together, and all the sons of God shouted for joy.

"Cosmology," said Joelle the omnipotent.   He fumbled to find her in a toppling darkness.   She enfolded him and they flew together, up a laser beam, through a satellite relay, to an observatory in orbit beyond the moon.

Briefly he spied the stars as if with his eyes, unblurred by any sky.   Their multitudes, steel-blue, frost-white, sunset-gold, coal-red, well-nigh glittered the night out of heaven.   The Milky Way rivered in silver, nebulae glowed where new suns and planets were being born, a sister galaxy flung her faint gleam across Ginnungagap.   But at once he leagued with the instrumentality which was seeking the uttermost ends of space-time.

First he was aware of optical spectra.   They told him of light that blossomed from leaping and whirling gas, they told him of tides in the body of a sun—a body more like the living cell than he could have imagined before—and of the furnaces down below where atoms begot higher elemental generations and photons racing spaceward were the birth-cry.   And in this Brahma-play he shared.   Next he felt a solar wind blow past, he snuffed its richness, tingled to its keenness, and knew the millennial subtlety of its work.   Thereafter he gave himself to radio spectra, cosmic ray spectra, magnetic fields, neutrino fluxes, relativistics which granted a star gate and seemed to grant time travel, the curve of the continuum that is the all.

At the Grand Canyon of the Colorado you may see strata going back a billion years, and across the view of them, a gnarly juniper, and know something of Earth.   Thus did Eric learn something of the depths and the order in space-time.   The primordial fireball became more real to him than the violence of his own birth, the question of what had brought it about became as terrifying.   He bought the spirals of the galaxies and of the DNA molecule with energy which would never come back to him, and saw how the cosmos aged as it matured, even as you and I; the Law is One.   He lived the lives of stars: how manifold were the waves that formed them, how strong the binding afterward to an entire existence!   Amidst the massiveness of blue giants and black holes, he found room to forge planets whereon crystals and flowers could grow.   He beheld what was still unknown—the overwhelming most of it, now and forever—and how Joelle longed to go questing.

Yet throughout, the observer part of him sensed that beside hers, his perception was misted and his understanding chained.   When she drew him back to the flesh, he screamed.

*   *   *

They sat in the office. Her desk separated them. She had raised the blind on the window at her back and opened it. Shadows hastened across grass, sunlight that followed was bright but somehow as if the air through which it fell had chilled it, the gusts sounded hollow that harried smells of damp soil into the room, odors of oncoming autumn.

Though she spoke with much gentleness, her tone bore the same farewell to summer. "We couldn't have talked meaningfully before you'd been there yourself, could we have, Eric?"

His glance went to the empty couch. "How meaningful was anything between us, even at first?"

She sighed. "I wanted it to be." A smile touched her. "I did enjoy."

"No more than that, enjoy, eh?"

"I don't know. I do care for you, and for everything you taught me about. But I've gone on to, to where I tried to lead you."

"How far did I get?"

She stared down at her hands, folded on the desk in helplessness, and said low, "Still less than I feared. It was like showing a blind man a painting. He might get a tiny idea through his fingertips, texture, the dark colors faintly warmer than the light—but oh, how tiny!"

"Whereas you respond to the lot, from quanta to quasars," he rasped.

She raised her head, challenging their unhappiness. "No, I've barely begun, and of course I'll never finish. But don't you see, that's half of the wonder. Always more to find. Direct experience, as direct as vision or touch or hunger or sex, experience of the *real* reality. The whole world humans know is just a passing, accidental consequence of it. Each time I go to it, I know it better and it makes me more its own. How could I stop?"

"I don't suppose I could learn?"

Cherishing no hope, he was not surprised to hear: "No. A holothete has to start like me, early, and do hardly anything else, especially in those formative young years." He was touched when tears sprang into her eyes. So she did want to be his kin. "I'm sorry, darling. You're good and kind and . . . how I wish you could follow along. How you deserve it."

"You don't wish you could go back, though, to what you were when we met?"

"Would you?"

Unlinked, he could not truly summon up what had happened this day. His brain lay alone. Nevertheless— "No," he said. "In fact, I dare not ever try again. That could be addictive. For me, nothing but an addiction, and to lunacy. For you—" He shrugged. "Do you know the *Rubaiyat?*"

"I've heard of it," she said, "but I've had no chance to become cultured."

And will never take it, he thought while he recited the lines—

> Why, if the Soul can fling the Dust aside,
> And naked on the Air of Heaven ride,

> Were't not a Shame—were't not a Shame for
>   him
> In this clay carcase crippled to abide?

—for human things will speak to you less and less, until finally you are not human yourself. Will you then be an Other, my dearest who was?

She nodded. "The old man told truth, didn't he? I did read once that Omar was a mathematician and astronomer. He must have been lonely."

"Like you, Joelle?"

"I have a few colleagues, remember. I'm teaching them—" She broke off, leaned across the desk, and said in a renewed concern: "What about us two? We'll be collaborating. You're strong enough to carry on, discharge your duty, I'm certain you are. But our personal lives—What's best for you?"

"Or for you?" he replied. "Let's take that up first."

"Anything you want, Eric," she said, "I'll gladly be your lover, wife, anything."

He was quiet a while, seeking words that might not hurt her. None came.

"You're telling me that you don't care which," he pronounced. "You're willing to treat me as well as you're able, because it doesn't greatly matter to you." He raised a palm to check her response. "Oh, no doubt you'd get a limited pleasure from living with me, even from my conversation. At the least, I'd help fill in the hours when you can't be linked—until you and those fellows of yours go so far that you'll have no time for childish things."

"I love you," she protested. A pair of tears broke loose.

He sighed. "I believe you. It's simply that love isn't important anymore, beside the grandeur. I've felt affection for dogs I've kept. But—call it pride, prejudice, stubbornness, what you will—I can't play a dog's part."

He rose. "We'll doubtless have an efficient partnership till I go home," he ended. "Today, though, while something remains of her, I'll tell my girl good-bye."

She sought him. He held her while she wept. It might well be the last time in her life that she did. When at length she kissed him, beneath a taste of salt her lips were quite steady.

"Go back to your link for a bit," he counselled her. "I will," she answered. "Thank you for saying it."

He walked out into a wind gone cold at evening.

She stood in the doorway and waved. He didn't turn around to see, because he didn't want to know how soon the door closed on her.

JACK CHALKER

Dance Band on the *Titanic*

The young woman was committing suicide again on the lower afterdeck. They'd told me I'd get used to it, but after four times I could still only pretend to ignore it, pretend that I didn't hear the body go over, hear the splash, and the scream as she was sucked into the screws. It was all too brief, and becoming all too familiar.

When the scream was cut short, as it always was, I continued walking forward, toward the bow. I would be needed there to guide the spotlight with which the captain would have to spot the buoys to get us all safely into Southport harbor.

It was a clear night; once at the bow I could see the stars in all their glory, too numerous to count or spot familiar constellations. It's a sight that's known and loved by all those who follow the sea, and it had a special meaning for us, who manned the *Orcas,* for the stars were immutable, the one unchanging part of our universe.

I checked the lines, the winch, and ties in the chained-off portion of the bow, then notified the captain by walkie-talkie that all was ready. He gave me "Very well," and told me that we'd be on the mark in five minutes. This gave me a few moments to relax, adjust my vision to the darkness, and look around.

The bow is an eerie place at night, for all its beauty; there is an unreality about a large ferryboat in the dark. Between where I stood on station and the bridge superstructure towering above me there was a broad area always crowded with people in warm weather. That bridge—dominating the aft field of vision, a ghostly, unlit white-gray monolith, reflecting the moonlight with an almost unreal cast and glow. A silent, spinning radar mast on top, and the funnel, end-on, in back of the bridge, with its wing supports and mast giving it some futuristic cast, only made the scene more alien, more awesome.

I glanced around at the people on deck. Not as many as usual, but then it was very late, and there was a chill in the air. I saw a few familiar faces, and there was some lateral shift in focus on a number of them, indicating that I was seeing at least three levels of reality that night.

Now, that last is kind of hard to explain. I'm not sure whether I understand it, either, but I well remember when I applied for this job, and the explanations I got then.

Working deck on a ferryboat is a funny place for a former English teacher, anyway.   But, while I'd been, I think, a good teacher, I was in constant fights with the administration over their lax discipline, stuff-shirt attitudes toward teaching and teachers, and the like.   The educational system isn't made for mavericks; it's designed to make everyone conform to bureaucratic ideals which the teacher is supposed to exemplify.   One argument too many, I guess, and there I was, an unemployed teacher in a time when there were too many teachers.   So, I drifted—no family, no responsibilities.   I'd always loved ferryboats—raised on them, loved them with the same passion some folks like trains and trolley cars and such—and when I found an unskilled job opening on the old Delaware ferry, I took it.   The fact that I was an ex-teacher actually helped; ferry companies like to hire people who relate well to the general public.   After all, deck duty is hectic when the ferry's docking or docked, but for the rest of the time you just sort of stand there, and every tourist and traveler in the world wants to talk.   If you aren't willing to talk back and enjoy it, forget ferry runs.

And I met Joanna.   I'm not sure if we were ever in love, but we got along.   No, on second thought, I shouldn't kid myself—I *did* love her, although I'm pretty sure I was just convenient from her point of view.   For a while things went smoothly—I had a job I liked, and we shared rent.   She had a little daughter she doted on, and we hit it off, too.

And in a space of three weeks my neat little complacent world ended.   First she threw that damned party while I was working, and a cigarette or something was left, and the apartment burned.   They saved her—but not her little girl.   I tried to comfort her, tried to console her, but I guess I was too full of my own life and self-importance, I didn't see the signs.   The woman hanged herself, again while I worked the boat.

A week after that the damned bridge-tunnel put the ferry out of business, too.

I was alone, friendless, jobless, and feeling guilty as hell.   I seriously thought about ending it all myself about then, maybe going down to the old ferryboat and blowing it and me to hell in one symbolic act of togetherness.   But, then, just when I'd sunk to the depths, I got this nice, official-looking envelope in the mail from something called the Bluewater Corporation, Southport, Maine.   Just a funny logo, some blue water with an odd, misty-looking shape of a ship in it.

"Dear Mr. Dalton," it read.   "We have just learned of the closing of the Delaware service, and we are in need of some experienced ferry people.   After reviewing your qualifications, we believe that you will fit nicely into our company, which, we guarantee, will not be put out of business by bridge or tunnel.   If this prospect interests you, please come to Southport terminal at your earliest convenience for a final interview.   Looking forward to seeing you soon, I remain, sincerely yours, Herbert V. Penobscot, Personnel Manager, Bluewater Corp."

I just stood there staring at the thing for I don't know how long.   A ferry job! That alone should have excited me, yet I wondered about it, particularly that line about "reviewing my qualifications" and "final interview."   Funny terms.   I could see why they'd look for experienced people, and all ferry folk knew when a line was closed and might look for their own replacements there, but—why me?

I hadn't applied to them, hadn't ever heard of them or their line—or, for that matter, of Southport, Maine either.   Obviously they preselected their people—very odd for this particular business.

I scrounged up an old atlas and tried to find it.   The letterhead said **"Southport— St. Michael—The Island"**, but I could find nothing about any such place in the atlas or an almanac.   If the letterhead hadn't been so damned convincing, I'd have sworn somebody was putting me on.   As it was, I had nothing else to do, and it beat drinking myself to a slow death, so I hitchhiked up.

It wasn't easy finding Southport, I'll tell you.   Even people in nearby towns had never heard of it.   The whole town was about a dozen houses, a seedy ten-unit motel, a hot dog stand, and a very small ferry terminal with a standard but surprisingly large ferry ramp and parking area.

I couldn't believe the place warranted a ferry when I saw it; you had to go about sixty miles into the middle of nowhere on a road the highway department had deliberately engineered to miss some of the world's prettiest scenery and had last paved sometime before World War II just to get there.

There was a light on in the terminal, so I went in.   A gray-haired man, about fifty, was in the ticket office, and I went over and introduced myself.   He looked me over carefully, and I knew I didn't present a very good appearance.

"Sit down, Mr. Dalton," he offered in a tone that was friendly but businesslike. "I've been expecting you.   This really won't take long, but this final interview includes a couple of strange questions.   If you don't want to answer any of them, feel free, but I must ask them nonetheless.   Will you go along with me?"

I nodded, and he fired away.   It was the damndest job interview I'd ever had. He barely touched on my knowledge of ferries except to ask if it mattered that the *Orcas* was a single-bridge, twin-screw affair, not a double-ender like I'd been used to.   It still loaded on one end and unloaded on the other, though, through a raised bow, and a ferry was a ferry to me and I told him so.

Most of the questions were on my personal life, my attitudes.   Like this one: "Have you ever contemplated or attempted suicide?"

I jumped.   "What's *that* have to do with anything?" I snapped.   After all this I was beginning to see why the job was still open.

"Just answer the question," he responded, almost embarrassed.   "I told you I had to ask them all."

Well, I couldn't figure out what this was all about, but I finally decided, what the hell, I had nothing to lose and it was a beautiful spot.

"Yes," I told him.   "Thought about it, anyway."   And I told him why.   He just nodded thoughtfully, jotted a little something on a preprinted form, and continued.   His next question was worse.

"Do you now believe in ghosts, devils, and demonic forces?" he asked in the same tone that he would ask whether I did windows.

I couldn't suppress a chuckle.   "You mean the ship's haunted?"

He didn't smile back.   "Just answer the question, please."

"No," I responded.   "I'm not very religious."

Now there was a wisp of a smile there.   "And suppose, with your hard-nosed rationalism, you ran into one?   Or a whole bunch of them?"   He leaned forward, smile gone.   "Even an entire shipload of them?"

It was impossible to take this seriously.   "What kind of ghosts?" I asked him. "Chain rattlers?   White sheets?   Foul forms spouting hateful gibberish?"

He shook his head negatively.   "No, ordinary people, for the most part.   Dressed a little odd, perhaps; talking a little odd perhaps, but not really very odd at all. Nice folks, typical passengers."

Cars were coming in now, and I glanced out the window at them.   Ordinary-looking cars, ordinary-looking people—campers, a couple of tractor-trailer rigs, like that.   Lining up.   A U.S. customs man came from the direction of the motel and started talking to some of them.

"They don't look like ghosts to me," I told my interviewer.

He sighed.   "Look, Mr. Dalton.   I know you're an educated man.   I have to go out and start selling fares now.   She'll be in in about forty minutes, and we've only got a twenty-minute layover.   When she's in, and loads, go aboard.   Look her over.   You'll have free rein of the ship.   Take the complete round trip, all stops.   It's about four hours over, twenty minutes in, and a little slower back. Don't get off the ship, though.   Keep an open mind.   If you're the one for the *Orcas,* and I think you are, we'll finish our talk when you get back."   He got up, took out a cash drawer and receipt load, and went to the door, then turned back to me.   "I hope you are the one," he said wearily.   "I've interviewed over three hundred people and I'm getting sick of it."

We shook hands on that cryptic remark, and I wandered around while he manned his little booth and processed the cars, campers, and trucks.   A young woman came over from one of the houses and handled the few people who didn't have cars, although how they ever got to Southport I was at a loss to know.

The amount of business was nothing short of incredible.   St. Michael was in Nova Scotia, it seemed, and there were the big runs by CN from a couple of places and the Swedish one out of Portland to compete for any business.   The fares were reasonable but not merely cheap enough to drive this far out of your way for, and to get to Southport you *had* to drive out of the way.

I found a general marine atlas of the Fundy region in his office and looked at it.   Southport made it, but just barely.   No designation of it as a ferry terminal, though, and no funny line showing a route.

For the life of me I couldn't find a St. Michael, Nova Scotia—nor a St. Clement's Island, either—the mid-stop that the schedule said it made.

And then there was the blast of a great air horn, and I rushed out for my first look at the *Orcas*—and I was stunned.

That ship, I remember thinking, *has no right to be here.   Not here, not on this run.*

It was *huge*—all gleaming white, looking brand-new, more like a cruise ship than a ferryboat.   I counted three upper decks, and, as I watched, a loud clanging bell sounded electrically on her and her enormous bow lifted, revealing a grooved raising ramp, something like the bow of an old LST.   It docked with little trouble, and the ramp came down slowly, mating with the ferry dock, revealing space for well over a hundred cars and trucks, with small side ramps for a second level available if needed.

It was close to sundown on a weekday, but they loaded over fifty vehicles, including a dozen campers and eight big trucks.   Where had they all come from, I wondered.   And why?

I walked on with the passengers, still in something of a daze, and went up top. The lounges were spacious and comfortable, the seats padded and reclining.   There was a large cafeteria, a newsstand, and a very nice bar at the stern of passenger deck 2.   The next deck had another lounge section, and a couple of dozen staterooms up front, while the top level had crew's quarters and a solarium.

It was fancy; and, after it backed out, lowered its bow, and started pouring it on after clearing the harbor lights, the fastest damned thing I could remember, too. Except for the slight swaying and the rhythmic thrumming of the twin diesels you hardly knew you were moving.   It was obviously using enormous stabilizers.

The sun was setting, and I walked through the ship, just looking and relaxing. As darkness fell and the shoreline receded into nothingness, I started noticing some very odd things, as I'd been warned.

First of all, there seemed to be a whole lot more people on board than I'd remembered loading, and there certainly hadn't been any number staying on from the last run.   They all looked real and solid enough, and very ordinary, but there was something decidedly weird about them, too.

Many seemed to be totally unaware of each other's existence, for one thing. Some seemed to shimmer occasionally, others were a little blurred or indistinct to my eyes no matter how I rubbed them.

And, once in a while, they'd walk through each other.

Yes, I'm serious.   One big fellow in a flowered aloha shirt and brown pants carrying a tray of soft drinks from the cafeteria to his wife and three kids in the lounge didn't seem to notice this woman dressed in a white tee shirt and jeans walking right into him, nor did she seem aware of him, either.

And they met, and I braced for the collision and spilled drinks—and it didn't happen.   They walked right *through* each other, just as if they didn't exist, and continued obliviously on.   Not one drop of soda was spilled, not one spot of mustard was splotched.

There were other things, too.   Most of the people were dressed normally for summer, but occasionally I'd see people in fairly heavy coats and jackets.   Some of the fashions were different, too—some people were overdressed in old-fashioned styles, others wildly underdressed, a couple of the women frankly wearing nothing but the bottoms of string bikinis and a see-through short cape of some kind.

I know I couldn't take my eyes off them for a while, until I got the message that they knew they were being stared at and didn't particularly like it.   But they were generally ignored by the others.

There were strange accents, too.   Not just the expected Maine twang and Canadian accents, or even just the French Canadian accents—those were normal.   But there were some really odd ones, ones where I picked out only a few words, which sounded like English, French, Spanish, and Nordic languages all intermixed and often with weird results.

And men with pigtails and long, braided hair, and women with shaved heads or occasionally beards.

It was weird.

Frankly, it scared me a little, and I found the purser and introduced myself.

The officer, a good-looking young man named Gifford Hanley, a Canadian by his speech, seemed delighted that I'd seen all this, and not the least bit disturbed.

"Well, well, well!" he almost beamed. "Maybe we've found our new man at last, eh? Not bloody soon enough, either! We've been working short-handed for too long and it's getting to the others."

He took me up to the bridge—one of the most modern I'd ever seen—and introduced me to the captain and helmsman. They all asked me what I thought of the *Orcas* and how I liked the sea, and none of them would answer my questions on the unusual passengers.

Well, there *was* a St. Clement's Island. A big one, too, from the looks of it, and a fair amount of traffic getting off and wanting on. Some of the vehicles that got on were odd, too; many of the cars looked unfamiliar in design, the trucks very odd, and there were even several horse-drawn wagons!

The island had that same quality as some of the passengers, too. It seemed never to be quite in focus just beyond the ferry terminal, and lights seemed to shift, so that where I thought there were houses or a motel suddenly they were somewhere else, of a different intensity. I was willing to swear that that motel had two stories; later it seemed over on the left, and four stories high, then farther back, still later, and single-storied.

Even the lighthouse as we sped out of the harbor changed; one time it looked very tall with a house at its base; then, suddenly, it was short and tubby, then an automated light that seemed to be out in the water, with no sign of an island.

This continued for most of the trip. St. Michael looked like a carbon copy of Southport, the passengers and vehicles as bizarre, and there seemed to be a lot of customs men in different uniforms dashing about, totally ignoring some vehicles while clearing others.

The trip back was equally strange. The newsstand contained some books and magazines that were odd to say the least, and papers with strange names and stranger headlines.

This time there were even Indians aboard, speaking odd tongues. Some looked straight out of *The Last of the Mohicans,* complete with wild haircut, others dressed from little to heavy, despite the fact that it was July and very warm and humid.

And, just before we were to make the red and green channel markers and turn into Southport, I saw the girl die for the first time.

She was dressed in red t-shirt, yellow shorts, and sandals; she had long brown hair, was rather short and overweight, and wore oversized granny glasses.

I wasn't paying much attention, really, just watching her looking over the side at the wake, when, before I could even cry out, she suddenly climbed up on the rail and plunged in, very near the stern.

I screamed, and heard her body hit the water and then heard her howl of terror as she dropped close enough in that the prop wash caught her, tucked her under, and cut her to pieces.

Several people on the afterdeck looked at me quizzically, but only one or two seemed to realize that a girl had just died.

There was little I could do, but I ran back to the purser, breathless.

He just nodded sadly.

"Take it easy, man," he said gently. "She's dead, and there's no use going back for the body. Believe me, we *know*. It won't be there."

I was shocked, badly upset. "How do you know that?" I snapped.

"Because we did it every time the last four times she jumped, and we never found her body then, either," he replied sadly.

I had my mouth open, ready to retort, to say *something;* but he got up, put on his officer's hat and coat, said, "Excuse me, I have to tend to the unloading," and walked out.

As soon as I got off the ship it was like some sort of dreamy fog had lifted from me. Everything looked suddenly bright and clear, and the people and vehicles looked normal. I made my way to the ferry terminal.

When they'd loaded and the ship was gone again, I waited for Mr. McNeil, the ticket agent, to return to his office. It looked much the same, really, but a few things seemed different. I couldn't quite put my finger on it, but there *was* something odd—like the paneling had been rosewood before, and was now walnut. Small things, but nagging ones.

McNeil, the ticket agent, came back after seeing the ship clear. It ran almost constantly, according to the schedule.

I glanced out the window as he approached, and noticed uniformed customs men checking out the debarked vehicles. They seemed to have a different uniform than I'd remembered.

McNeil came in, and I got another shock. He had a beard.

No, it was the same man, all right. No question about it. But the man I'd talked to less than nine hours earlier had been clean-shaven.

I turned to where the navigation atlas lay, just where I'd put it, still open to the Southport page.

It showed a ferry line from Southport to a rather substantial St. Clements Island now. But nothing to Nova Scotia.

I turned to the bearded McNeil, who was watching me with some mild amusement in his eyes.

"What the *hell* is going on here?" I demanded.

He went over and sat down in his swivel chair. "Want the job?" he asked. "It's yours if you do."

I couldn't believe his attitude. "I want an explanation, damn it!" I fumed.

He chuckled, "I told you I'd give you one if you wanted. Now, you'll have to bear with me, since I'm only repeating what the Company tells me, and I'm not sure I have it all clear myself."

I sat down in the other chair. "Go ahead," I told him.

He sighed. "Well, let's start off by saying that there's been a Bluewater Corporation ferry on this run since the mid-1800s—steam passenger and freight service at first, of course. The *Orcas* is the eleventh ship in the service, put on a year and a half ago."

He reached over, grabbed a cigarette, lit it, and continued.

"Well, anyway, it was a normal operation until about 1910 or so. That's when they started noticing that their counts were off, that there seemed to be more passengers than the manifests called for, different freight, and all that. As it continued, the crews started noticing more and more of the kind of stuff you saw, and things got crazy for them, too. Southport was a big fishing and lobstering town then—nobody does that anymore, the whole economy's the ferry.

"Well, anyway, one time this crewman goes crazy, says the woman in his house isn't his wife. A few days later another comes home to find he has four kids— and he was only married a week before. And so on."

I felt my skin start to crawl slightly.

"So, they send some big shots up. The men are absolutely nuts, but *they* believe in what they claim. Soon everybody who works the ship is spooked, and this can't be dismissed. The experts go for a cruise and can't find anything odd, but now two of the crewmen claim that it *is* their wife, or their kid, or somesuch. Got to be a pain, though, getting crewmen. We finally had to center on loners— people without family, friends, or close personal ties. It kept getting worse each trip. Had a hell of a time keeping men for a while, and that's why it's so hard to recruit new ones."

"You mean the trip drives you crazy?" I asked unbelievingly.

He chuckled. "Oh, no. *You're* sane. It's the rest of 'em. That's the problem. And it gets worse and worse each season. But the trip's *extremely* profitable. So we try and match the crew to the ship, and hope they'll accept it. If they do, it's one of the best damned ferry jobs there is."

"But what causes it?" I managed. "I mean—I saw people dressed outlandishly. I saw other people walk *through* each other! I even saw a girl commit suicide, and nobody seemed to notice!"

McNeil's face turned grim. "So that's happened again. Too bad. Maybe one day there'll be some chance to save her."

"Look," I said, exasperated. "There must be some explanation for all this. There *has* to be!"

The ticket agent shrugged and stubbed out the cigarette.

"Well, some of the company experts studied it. They say nobody can tell for sure, but the best explanation is that there are a lot of different worlds—different Earths, you might say—all existing one on top of the other, but you can't see any one except the one you're in. Don't ask me how that's possible or how they came up with it, it just *is,* that's all. Well, they say that in some worlds folks don't exist at all, and in others they are different places or doing different things—like getting married to somebody else or somesuch. In some, Canada's still British, in some she's a republic, in others she's a fragmented batch of countries, and in one or two she's part of the U.S. Each one of these places has a different history."

"And this one boat serves them all?" I responded, not accepting a word of that crazy theory. "How is that possible?"

McNeil shrugged again. "Who knows? Hell, I don't even understand why the little light goes on in here when I flip the switch. Do most people? I just sell tickets and lower the ramp. I'll tell you the company's version, that's all. They say that there's a crack—maybe one of many, maybe the only one. The ship's route just happens to parallel that crack, and this allows you to go between the worlds. Not one ship, of course—twenty, thirty ships or more, one for each world. But, as long as they keep the same schedule, they overlap—and can cross into one or more of the others. If you're on the ship in all those worlds, then you cross, too. Anyone coexisting with the ship in multiple worlds can see and hear not only the one he's in but the ones nearest him, too. People perception's a little harder the farther removed the world you're in is from theirs."

"And you believe this?" I asked him, still disbelieving.

"Who knows? Got to believe *something* or you go nuts," he replied pragmatically. "Look, did you get to St. Michael this trip?"

I nodded. "Yeah. Looked like this place, pretty much."

He pointed to the navigation atlas. "Try and find it. You won't. Take a drive up through New Brunswick and around to the other side. It doesn't exist. In this world, the *Orcas* goes from here to St. Clement's Island and back again. I understand from some of the crew that sometimes Southport doesn't exist, sometimes the Island doesn't, and so forth. And there are so many countries involved I don't count."

I shook my head, refusing to accept all this. And yet, it made a crazy kind of sense. These people didn't see each other because they were in different worlds. The girl committed suicide five times because she did it five times in five different worlds—or was it five different girls? It also explained the outlandish dress, the strange mixture of vehicles, people, accents.

"But how come the crew sees people from many worlds and the passengers don't?" I asked him.

McNeil sighed. "That's the other problem. We have to find people who would be up here, working on the *Orcas,* in every world we service. More people's lives parallel than you'd think. The passengers—well, they generally don't exist on a particular run except once. The very few who do still don't take the trip in every world of service. I guess once or twice it's happened that we've had a passenger cross over, but if so we never heard of it."

"And how come I'm here in so many worlds?" I asked him.

McNeil smiled. "You were recruited, of course. The Corporation has a tremendous, intensive recruiting effort involving ferry lines and crewmembers. When they spot one, like you, in just the right circumstance in all worlds, they recruit you—all of you. An even worse job than you'd think, since every season one or two new Bluewater Corporations put identical ferries on this run, or shift routes slightly and overlap. Then we have to make sure the present crew can serve them, too, by recruiting your twin on those worlds."

Suddenly I reached over, grabbed his beard, and yanked.

"Ouch! Dammit!'' he cried, and pulled my hand away.

"I—I'm sorry, I—'' I stammered.

He shook his head, then smiled. "That's all right, son. You're about the seventh person to do that to me in the last five years. I guess there's a lot of varieties of *me,* too.''

I thought about all that traffic. "Do others know of this?'' I asked him. "I mean, is there some sort of hidden commerce between the worlds on this ferry?''

He grinned. "I'm not supposed to answer that,'' he said carefully. "But, what the hell. Yes, I think—no, I *know* there is. After all, the shift of people and ships is constant. You move one notch each trip if all of you take the voyage. Sometimes up, sometimes down. If that's true, and if they can recruit a crew that fits the requirements, why not truck drivers? A hell of a lot of truck traffic through here year 'round, you know. No reduced winter service. And some of the rigs are really kinda strange-looking.'' He sighed. "I only know this—in a couple of hours I'll start selling fares again, and I'll sell a half-dozen or so to St. Michael— and *there is no St. Michael.* It isn't even listed on my schedules or maps. I doubt if the Corporation's actually the trader, more the middleman in the deal. But they sure as hell don't make their millions off fares alone.''

It was odd the way I was accepting it. Somehow, it seemed to make sense, crazy as it was.

"What's to keep me from using this knowledge somehow?'' I asked him. "Maybe bring a team of experts up?''

"Feel free,'' McNeil answered. "Unless they overlap they'll get a nice, normal ferry ride. And if you can make a profit, go ahead, as long as it doesn't interfere with Bluewater's cash flow. The *Orcas* cost the company over twenty four million *reals* and they want it back.''

"Twenty four million *what?''* I shot back.

"Reals,'' he replied, taking a bill from his wallet. I looked at it.

I looked at it. It was printed in red, and had a picture of someone very ugly labeled "Prince Juan XVI'' and an official seal from the "Bank of New Lisboa.'' I handed it back.

"What country are we in?'' I asked uneasily.

"Portugal,'' he replied casually. "Portuguese America, actually, although only nominally. So many of us Yankees have come in you don't even have to speak Portuguese any more. They even print the local bills in Anglish now.''

Yes, that's what he said. Anglish.

"It's the best ferryboat job in the world, though,'' McNeil continued. "For someone without ties, that is. You'll meet more different kinds of people from more cultures than you'll ever imagine. Three runs on, three off—in as many as twenty-four different variations of these towns, all unique. And a month off in winter to see a little of a different world each time. Never mind whether you buy the explanation—you've seen the results, you know what I say is true. Want the job?''

"I'll give it a try,'' I told him, fascinated. I wasn't sure if I *did* buy the explanation, but I certainly had something strange and fascinating here.

"O.K., here's twenty *reals* advance," McNeil said, handing me a purple twenty from the cashbox. "Get some dinner if you didn't eat on the ship, get a good night at the motel, then be ready to go on at four tomorrow afternoon."

I got up to leave.

"Oh, and Mr. Dalton," he added, and I turned to face him.

"Yes?"

"If, while on shore, you fall for a pretty lass, decide to settle down, then do it—*but don't go back on that ship again!* Quit. If you don't she's going to be greeted by a stranger, and you might never find her again."

"I'll remember," I told him.

The job was everything McNeil promised and more. The scenery was spectacular, the people an ever-changing, fascinating group. Even the crew changed slightly—a little shorter sometimes, a little fatter or thinner, beards and moustaches came and went with astonishing rapidity, and accents varied enormously. It didn't matter; you soon adjusted to it as a matter of course, and all shipboard experiences were in common, anyway.

It was like a tight family after a while, really. And there were women in the crew, too, ranging from their twenties to the early fifties, not only in food and bar service but as deckhands and the like as well. Occasionally it was a little unsettling, since, in two or three cases out of the crew of 66, they were men in one world, women in another. You got used to even that. It was probably more unsettling for them; they were distinct people, and *they* didn't change sex. The personalities and personal histories tended to parallel, regardless, though, with only a few minor differences.

And the passengers! Some were really amazing. Even seasons were different to some of them, which explained the clothing variations. Certainly what constituted fasion and moral behavior was wildly different, as different as what they ate and the places they came from.

And yet, oddly, people were people. They laughed, and cried, and ate and drank and told jokes—some rather strange, I'll admit—and snapped pictures and all the other things people did. They came from places where the Vikings settled Nova Scotia (called Vinland, naturally), where Nova Scotia was French, or Spanish, or Portuguese, or very, very English. Even one in which Nova Scotia had been settled by Lord Baltimore and called Avalon.

Maine was as wild or wilder. There were two Indian nations running it, the U.S., Canada, Britain, France, and lots of variations some of which I never got straight. There was also a temporal difference sometimes—some people were rather futuristic, with gadgets I couldn't even understand. One truck I loaded was powered by some sort of solar power and carried a cargo of food service robots. Some others were behind—still mainly horses, or old-time cars and trucks. I am not certain even now if they were running at different speeds from us or whether some inventions had been made in some places and not in others.

And, McNeil was right. Every new summer season added at least one more. The boat was occasionally so crowded to our crew eyes that we had trouble making

our way from one end to the other.   Watching staterooms unload was also wild—
it looked occasionally like the circus clown act, where 50 clowns get out of a
Volkswagen.

And there *was* some sort of trade between the worlds.   It was quickly clear that
Bluewater Corporation was behind most of it, and that this was what made the line
so profitable.

And, just once, there was a horrible, searing pain that hit the entire crew, and
a modern world we didn't make anymore after that, and a particular variation of
the crew we never saw again.   And the last newspapers from that world had told
of a coming war.

There was also a small crew turnover, of course.   Some went on vacation and
never returned, some returned but would not reboard the ship.   The company was
understanding, and it usually meant a little extra work for a few weeks at most
until someone new came on.

The stars were fading a little now, and I shined the spot over to the red marker
for the Captain.   He acknowledged seeing it, and made his turn in, the lights of
Southport coming into view and masking the stars a bit.

I went through the motions mechanically, raising the bow when the captain hit
the mark, letting go the bow lines, checking the clearances, and the like.   I was
thinking about the girl.

We knew that people's lives in the main did parallel from world to world.   Seven
times now she'd come aboard, seven times she'd looked at the white wake, and
seven times she'd jumped to her death.

Maybe it was the temporal dislocation, maybe she just reached the same point
at different stages, but she was always there and she always jumped.

I'd been working the *Orcas* three years, had some strange experiences, and
generally pleasurable ones.   For the first time I had a job I liked, a family of sorts
in the crew, and an ever-changing assortment of people and places for a three-point
ferry run.   In that time we'd lost one world, and gained by our figures three others.
That was 26 variants.

Did that girl exist in all 26? I wondered.   Would we be subjected to that sadness
19 more times?   Or more, as we picked up new worlds?

Oh, I'd tried to find her before she jumped in the past, yes.   But she hadn't
been consistent, except for the place she chose.   We did three runs a day, two
crews, so it was six a day more or less.   She did it at different seasons, in different
years, dressed differently.

You couldn't cover them all.

Not even all the realities of the crew of all worlds, although I knew that we were
essentially the same people on all of them and that I—the other mes—were also
looking.

I don't even know why I was so fixated, except that I'd been to that point once
myself, and I'd discovered that you *could* go on, living with the emotional scars,
and find a life.

I didn't even know what I'd say and do if I *did* see her early. I only knew that, if I did, she damned well wasn't going to go over the stern that trip.

In the meantime, my search for her when I could paid other dividends. I prevented a couple of children from going over through childish play, as well as a drunk, and spotted several health problems as I surveyed the people. One turned out to be a woman in advanced labor, and the first mate and I delivered our first child—our first, but the *Orcas'* nineteenth. We helped a lot of people, really, with a lot of different things.

They were all just spectres, of course; they got on the boat often without us seeing them, and they disembarked for all time the same way. There were some regulars, but they were few. And, for them, we were a ghost crew, there to help and to serve.

But, then, isn't that the way you think of anybody in a service occupation? Firemen are firemen, not individuals; so are waiters, cops, street sweepers, and all the rest.

We sailed from Point A to Point C stopping at B, and it was our whole life.

And then, one day in July of last year, I spotted her.

She was just coming on board at St. Clement's—that's why I hadn't noticed her before. We backed into St. Clement's, and I was on the bow lines. But we were short, having just lost a deckhand to a nice-looking fellow in the English Colony of Annapolis Royal, and it was my turn to do some double duty. So, there I was, routing traffic on the ship when I saw this little rounded station wagon go by and saw *her* in it.

I still almost missed her; I hadn't expected her to be with another person, another woman, and we were loading the Vinland existence, so in July they were more accurately in a state of undress than anything else, but I spotted her all the same. Jackie Carliner, one of the barmaids and a pretty good artist, had sketched her from the one time she'd seen the girl and we'd made copies for everybody.

Even so, I had my loading duties to finish first—there was no one else. But, as soon as we were underway and I'd raised the stern ramp, I made my way topside and to the lower stern deck. I took my walkie-talkie off the belt clip and called the captain.

"Sir, this is Dalton," I called. "I've seen our suicide girl."

"So what else is new?" grumbled the captain. "You know policy on that by now."

"But, sir!" I protested. "I mean still alive. Still on board. It's barely sundown, and we're a good half hour from the point yet."

He saw what I meant. "Very well," he said crisply. "But you know we're short-handed. I'll put Caldwell on the bow station this time, but you better get some results or I'll give you so much detail you won't have time to meddle in other people's affairs!"

I sighed. Running a ship like this one hardened most people. I wondered if the captain, with nineteen years on the run, even understood why I cared enough to try and stop this girl I didn't know from going in.

Did *I* know, for that matter?

As I looked around at the people going by I thought about it. I'd thought about it a great deal before.

Why *did* I care about these faceless people? People from so many different worlds and cultures that they might as well have been from another planet. People who cared not at all for me, who saw me as an object, a cipher, a service, like those robots I mentioned. They didn't care about me. If *I* were perched on that rail and a crowd was around most of them would probably yell "Jump!"

Most of the crew, too, cared only about each other, to a degree, and about the *Orcas,* our rock of sanity. I thought of that world, gone in some atomic fire. What was the measure of an anonymous human being's worth?

I thought of Joanna and Harmony. With pity, yes, but I realized that Joanna, at least, had been a vampire. She'd needed me, needed a rock to steady herself, to unburden herself to, to brag to. Someone steady and understanding, someone whose manner and character suggested that solidity. She'd never really even considered that I might have my own problems, that her promiscuity and lifestyle might be hurting me. Not that she was trying to hurt me—she just never *considered* me.

Like those people going by now. If they stub their toe, or have a question, or slip, or the boat sinks, they need me. Until then, I'm just a faceless automaton to them.

Ready to serve them, to care about them, if *they* needed somebody.

And that was why I was out here in the surprising chill, out on the stern with my neck stuck out a mile, trying to prevent a suicide I *knew* would happen, *knew* because I'd seen it three times before.

I was needed.

That was the measure of a human being's true worth, I felt sure. Not how many people ministered to your needs, but how many people you can help.

That girl—she had been brutalized, somehow, by society. Now I was to provide some counterbalance.

It was the surety of this that kept me from blowing myself up with the old Delaware ferry, or jumping off that stern rail myself.

I glanced uneasily around and looked ahead. There was Shipshead light, tall and proud this time in the darkness, the way I liked it. I thought I could almost make out the marker buoys already. I started to get nervous.

I was certain she'd jump. It'd happened every time before that we'd known. Maybe, just maybe, I thought, in this existence she won't.

I had no more than gotten the thought through my head when she came around the corner of the deck housing and stood in the starboard corner, looking down.

She certainly looked different this time. Her long hair was blond, not dark, and braided in large pigtails that drooped almost to her waist. She wore only the string bikini and transparent cape the Vinlanders liked in summer, and she had several gold rings on each arm, welded loosely there, I knew, and a marriage ring around her neck.

That was interesting, I thought.

Her friend, as thin and underdeveloped as she was stout, was with her. The friend had darker hair and had it twisted high atop her head, and had no marriage ring.

I eased over slowly, but not sneakily. Like I said, nobody notices the crewman on a vessel; he's a part of it.

"Luok, are yu sooure yu don' vant to halve a drink or zumpin'?" the friend asked in that curious accent the Vinlanders had developed through cultural pollution with the dominant English and French.

"Naye, I yust vant to smell da zee-spray," the girl replied. "Go on. I vill be alonk before ze zhip iz docking."

The friend was hesitant; I could see it in her manner. But I could also see she would go, partly because she was chilly, partly because she felt she had to show trust to the girl.

She walked off. I looked busy checking the stairway supports to the second deck, and she paid me no mind whatsoever.

There were a few others on deck, but most had gone forward to see us come in, and the couple dressed completely in black sitting there on the bench were invisible to the girl as she was to them. She peered down at the black water and started to edge more to the starboard side engine wake, then a little past, almost to the center. Her upper torso didn't move, but I saw a bare, dirty foot go up on the lower rail.

I walked over, casually. She heard, and turned slightly to see if it was anyone she need be bothered with.

I went up to her and stood beside her.

"Don't do it," I said softly, not looking directly at her. "It's too damned selfish a way to go."

She gave a small gasp and turned to look at me in wonder.

"How—how didt yu—?" she managed.

"I'm an old hand at suicides," I told her, and that was no lie. Joanna, then almost me, then this girl three other times.

"I vouldn't really haff—" she began, but I cut her off.

"Yes you would. You know it and I know it. The only thing you know and I don't is *why*."

We were inside Shipshead light now. If I could keep her talking just a few more minutes we'd clear the channel markers, and slow for the turn and docking. The turn and the slowdown would make it impossible for her to be caught in propwash, and, I felt, the cycle would be broken, at least for her.

"Vy du yu care?" she asked, turning again to look at the dark sea, only slightly illuminated by the rapidly receding light.

"Well, partly because it's my ship, and I don't like things like that to happen on my ship," I told her. "Partly because I've been there myself and I know how brutal a suicide is."

She looked at me strangely. "Dat's a fonny t'ing tu zay," she responded. "Jost vun qvick jomp and *pzzt!* All ofer."

"You're wrong," I said. "Besides, why would anyone so young want to end it?"

She had a dreamy quality to her face and voice. She was starting to blur, and I was worried that I might somehow translate into a different world-level as we neared shore.

"My 'usbahnd," she responded. "Goldier vas hiss name." She fingered the marriage ring around her neck. "Zo yong, so 'andzum." She turned her head quickly and looked up at me. "Do yu know vat it iz to be fat und ugly und 'alf bloind and haff ze best uv all men zuddenly pay attenzion to yu, vant to *marry* yu?"

I admitted I didn't, but didn't mention my own experiences.

"What happened? He leave you?" I asked.

There were tears in her eyes. "Ya, in a vay, ya. Goldier he jomped out a tventy-story building, he did. Und itz my own fault, yu know. I shud haff been dere. Or, maybe I didn't giff him vat he needed. I dunno."

"Then you of all people know how brutal suicide really is," I retorted. "Look at what it did to you. You have friends, like your friend here. They care. It will hurt them as your husband's hurt you. This girl with you—she'll carry guilt for leaving you alone the whole rest of her life." She was shaking now, not really from the chill, and I put my arm around her. Where the hell were those marker lights?

"Do you see how cruel it is? What suicide does to others? It leaves a legacy of guilt, much of it false guilt. And you might be needed by someone else, sometime, to help them. Somebody else might die because you weren't there."

She looked up at me, then seemed to dissolve, collapse into a crescendo of tears, and sat down on the deck. I looked up and saw the red and green markers astern, felt the engines slow, felt the *Orcas* turn.

"*Ghetta!*" The voice was a piercing scream in the night. I looked up and saw her friend running to us from coming down the stairway. Anxiety and concern was in her stricken face, and there were tears in her eyes. She bent down to the still sobbing girl. "I shud nefer haff left yu!" she sobbed, and hugged the girl.

I sighed. The *Orcas* was making its dock approach now, the ringing of the bells said that Caldwell had managed to raise the bow without crashing us into the dock.

"My Gott!" the friend swore, then looked up at me. "Yu stopped her? How can I effer—?"

But they both already had that ethereal, unnatural double image about them, both fading into a different existence than mine.

"Just remember there's a million Ghettas out there," I told them both. "And you can make them or break them."

I turned and walked away as I heard the satisfying thump and felt the slight jerk of the ferry fitting into the ramp. I stopped and glanced back at the stern, but I could see no one. Nobody was there.

Who were the ghosts? I mused. Those women, or the crew of the *Orcas?* How many times did hundreds of people from different worlds coexist on this ship without knowing it?

How many times did people in the *same* world coexist without knowing each other, or caring about each other, for that matter?

"Mr. Dalton!" snapped a voice in my walkie-talkie.

"Sir?" I responded.

"Well?" the captain promised.

"No screams this time, Captain," I told him, satisfaction in my voice. "One young woman will live."

There was a long pause, and, for a moment, I thought he might actually be human. Then he snapped, "There's eighty-six assorted vehicles still waiting to be off-loaded, and might I remind you we're short-handed and on a strict schedule?"

I sighed and broke into a trot. Business was business, and I had a whole world to throw out of the car deck so I could run another one in.

E. AMALIA ANDUJAR

Softly Touch the Stranger's Mind

"**W**e are curious, Johalla. It has always been so. If there is a mountain, we will climb it. It will not remain untouched by us. And so it is with space. It is there. We must know what is in it."

The storm had been violent. The onslaught had permitted no time for evasive action.

The hull of the ship, as durable as anything in the universe, had not been damaged, but the shields had weakened, exposing delicate instruments to radiation. Sparks flashed from the panel. The odor of fused circuits tainted the air. Amber lights warned of danger.

Johalla disengaged relays, releasing the ship from automatic control. It responded sluggishly as he brought it about in a wide arc.

Before the advent of the storm, he had finished surveying a solar system. Deep within it, scans had revealed a planet compatible to the physiology of his species. Probes had also identified areas of dense population.

A pinpoint of light appeared in the monitor. As the ship drew nearer, the dot swelled, illuminating the screen.

Johalla coaxed the vessel into orbit around the globe, frantically searching the surface for an island. It was not as likely to be inhabited. One does not set down a disabled craft in the midst of a teeming metropolis.

"Remember, my friend, aliens are not predictable. They feel threatened by our presence. As often as they turn and flee, they will attack. Time has given little knowledge of the beings which populate this galaxy."

He cut into the planet's atmosphere, guiding the ship toward the small target. It skimmed the glassy-smooth water. Flip-flopping out of control, the vessel slashed across the island, plunged through the trees, smashing them to fibers.

The impact was shattering. It paralyzed him, suspended him in a well of pain. He moaned, waited unmoving for the hurt to subside, for silence to calm his battered senses.

Johalla fumbled with the harness, his aching claws catching the fabric of the protective garment which covered his angular frame. He pulled at it. Without it, fragments of shell and a green puddle would be the only remains of this creature who had dared to trespass against the galaxy.

He groped for the portal, hesitating before he released the cover.   Every living being here must know of his arrival.

He pushed the hatch forward, peering out into the dusk.   Strange forms intrigued him.   He studied the terrain, eyes lingering on the trees, their silhouettes black against the heavens.   His antennae quivered in harmony to the sounds and smells of the island.

Weary, he turned from all of it and sought comfort in dreamless sleep.

Noisy chattering awakened him.   The forest, streaked by dawn, shivered with life.   Johalla climbed from the ship.

The cool wind caressed his thorax, soothed his aching limbs.   The surf rolling against the rocky shore seemed to echo his isolation.   He looked at stately trees, at small creatures stalking the sky on fragile wings.

"How awesome it is to press one's feet against alien soil.   How different it is, yet the same.   The essence of the universe is there.   To reach out and touch it; if only one could reach out and draw it in."

He cut branches from the trees torn by the ship's passage and formed a leafy shroud, shielding the vessel from view.   He knew nothing of the inhabitants of this world, but many races throughout the galaxy were capable of mechanized flight.

Each instrument was checked for damage, a chore hampered by the confines of the ship.   With the panels removed and the units spread about, there was little room for him.

His discomfort increased with the heat.   The environmental system had been shut down, which left the air stagnant and heavy with the odor of scorched insulation.

At sunset, Johalla nibbled rations to appease gnawing hunger and watched the clouds gathering overhead.

Huge drops splattered the ground, dissolving into rivulets at his feet.   Johalla shivered.   The misty rains which refreshed his planet were nothing like this downpour.

He was fascinated by the thunder, the frenzy of the wind, the blinding sheets of water.   Tentacles of fire flashed in the sky, driving him to the refuge of the ship. He wished for someone to share with him the excitement of these phenomena.

"It is not our nature to be alone, Johalla, but is the price of our endless missions into that dark void.   Memories are as precious jewels.   Memories will sustain you, when isolation numbs your thoughts."

Puddles were now the only remnants of the storm.   The morning was crisp with pungent odors, the foliage more vibrantly colored, but he had little time to ponder the beauty of nature.   He returned to his tasks, laboring again until dusk.

The evening, so calm after yesterday's violence, aroused him.   His spirits sent him prancing along the beach, dashing back and forth across the sand, teasing the waves.

Lured from his game by the forest, he ran among the trees, leaping over vines and bushes until the odor of burning wood halted his carefree journey. He stopped and sniffed the air.

The smoky wisps led him through the undergrowth to a clearing among the trees. In the center logs burned brightly, casting shadows upon the barren ground. Johalla looked about him, seeking the cause of the strange patterns which stroked his mind. He discovered he was not alone.

The animal crouched near the fire. Slowly, it straightened, tense with fear.

Johalla's wings fluttered. He stumbled back into the shadows. His powerful legs sent him high into the trees.

From above, he watched the biped as it circled the clearing, thrashing the undergrowth with a stick. It was a small, frail beast. The soft, pulpy body, the pallor of its flesh made Johalla shudder.

Light swept the thick vegetation. Johalla dodged the beam. His eyes would mirror the ray a hundred-fold, exposing him.

The bough sagged beneath his weight. Needle-shaped growths tickled his abdomen. He pushed at them with his feet. The tree trembled with his every movement.

The animal continued to pace, twisting and jerking its head, wagging a response to the probing fingers of Johalla's mind. He could sense its terror.

The night seemed endless. His legs were stiff with cramps. With gentle thoughts, he tried to lull the creature from its frantic search.

Finally, the creature slumped against a tree, exhausted. It lay there, defenseless, a fragile orphan of the universe.

He climbed down. Branches swayed and broke under his weight. His great agility saved him from crashing to the ground in an undignified heap. Quietly, he made his way through the forest, back to the ship.

"Although we seek them out, Johalla, we have yet to form a bond between ourselves and other species. How does one greet a stranger? What is the common ground on which we all might tread? What splendid gesture will forge the link?"

The sun was warm against his iridescent skin. Johalla tinkered with an instrument, carefully tuning its sensitive elements. Bored with the task, he set it down.

Memories nagged him. His actions last night had been those of a coward. The creature had been no threat to him. He was taller, stronger, but he had not faced it boldly. His noble feet had taken flight faster than his noble thoughts. His failure was no greater than that of his friends, but still, it was no less.

The undergrowth rustled, stopping his thoughts. Twigs snapped. The scent of fear was carried by the wind. Alert, Johalla watched the trees.

The animal leaped into the clearing, a black cylinder extending from an upper limb. Rigid with defiance, the native faced Johalla, exploding with hatred. Flame burst from the outstretched cylinder.

Johalla sprawled to the ground, his back smarting where the missile glanced off the bony ridge between his wings. He was uninjured, but stunned by the attack.

It fired again and again. Johalla's claws clicked in irritation, his head throbbed with anger. He tapped the weapon hanging at his belt, pulled it out, aiming it at a clump of bushes. They were blasted to ashes.

The creature scrambled through the trees, howling in terror.

The native's behavior had provoked Johalla's rage, but his retaliation sickened him. His mood was dark with shame.

The animal could not translate his thoughts. It feared him. The signals from its mind were sharp, hot spikes of passion, wounding his pride.

"When fear is present, one cannot communicate. It blinds, smothers expression of all other emotions and thoughts. To cut beyond that veil and softly touch the stranger's mind, to share its joys and sorrows . . ."

The chill of twilight calmed him, driving the demons from his soul. He walked briskly, scanning the beach with keen eyes. The sands were cold beneath his feet. He quickened his steps. He had found what he was seeking.

It was a small tub made from tree fibers. The marks were still clear where it had been dragged from the water onto the beach.

He leaned over it, exploring the interior with his claws. He discovered a jagged hole, low in the bow. Perhaps this broken vessel had carried the native to the island. It must have been stranded here by the storm, unable to reach a safer port.

The device attached to the vessel's side reeked of hydrocarbons. Intrigued by it, Johalla ran his claw along the shaft, spinning the hard blades of the fan. Once, such primitive things had been common to his world, but now they were part of history.

"Our ancestors burrowed in mud. We build our shelters from plastic. Our life is hewn from molecules and atoms tailored to our wishes. And yet we are the same beings we were aeons ago, Johalla.

"We seek them out, our galactic kin, compelled to share our future with another race. We have no other reason for existing."

The odor of burning wood drifted across the beach. The image of the strange creature, squatting near the flames to warm itself, distressed him. Its loneliness somehow touched him, magnified his own feelings of isolation. He would not leave it here to die, with no companion to hear its lonely cries. Tomorrow he would mend the little tub.

At daybreak, Johalla returned with tools and adhesives. He covered the jagged hole with mesh, sealing it to the wood with plastic, carefully pressing the sticky substance into the crevices.

Flowers swayed in the gentle breeze, waiting for the sun's hot rays to awaken them. Graceful forms swooped above the water, stabbing the surface with yellow noses. The sea murmured quietly to the sky. This island pleased him.

Again the rustle of leaves and snapping twigs announced the stranger's presence. A deafening roar split the air.   Johalla groaned in exasperation.

Claws snapping in anger, he sprinted across the beach in pursuit of the fleeing native.

The creature staggered and fell before it could reach safety.   Johalla snatched the loathsome cylinder from its grasp.   The animal cowered at Johalla's feet, moaning, its thoughts red with horror.   The sting of its hatred filled him with despair.   He turned from the animal, walked back to the tub, dragging the weapon behind him.

"We have accomplished nothing.   So much time spent in that cold emptiness, with only rocks and stones to mark our journeys.   How vain we are to think that other beings would wish to call us friends.

"Their existence intensified my loneliness.   The portals to their minds seem forever closed against us.   I longed to return home.   It was like a magnet drawing me back from the stars.   I had to submit to it.   It will happen to you, Johalla. You will come home one day and never go back out there again."

Johalla applied another coat of plastic to the tub.   Later, he would check the craft for leakage.   The alien stayed near the trees, watching him as he worked. He tried to ignore it; its wrath, its raging thoughts.

Memories of youthful games tugged at his soul, combing out the anger and the hurt.   He traced circles in the sand with his feet and molded wet grains into mounds of various sizes and shapes.

He listened to the cries of the small winged beasts hovering near the water.   He remembered other places from his past, their citizens shrouded in mystery, alien and unyielding.

He fashioned castles like the dwellings he had seen in a distant land, dug rivers, paved the winding streets with pebbles from the shore.   With tiny bits of wood he bridged the make-believe canals.

He was pleased with his creation, as much as he had been in his youth when he had made his dreams from mud and clay.   Today, however, no guardian would chastise him for tracking soil into the tunnels.

A shadow crossed his fantasy, pulling him back from his childish retreat.   He found himself staring into the eyes of the native, not knowing how long he had been watched.   The patterns of its mind were smooth now, untinted by distrust. It moved slowly to Johalla's side.

It built its own castles from the sand and placed them among Johalla's, then surrounded them all with a miniature forest of leafy twigs.

When darkness came, they gathered wood and shared the warmth of a fire. Johalla's thoughts flowed with the rhythm of the sea.   Softly, he touched the stranger's mind; his joy was echoed in the pounding surf.

SHERWOOD SPRINGER

Lorelei at Storyville West

Lf a car knocks at all, it will knock climbing up out of Laurel Canyon on Kirkwood Drive—and this one pounded as if a midget were under the hood with a ball-peen hammer. When I heard it leave Kirkwood and hit the short grade to my place I looked out the window.

It was a black Corvette, about six years old. The driver pulled up against the bumper of my old Chevy—which left his back wheels about twelve inches down the hill. When he got out he paused to look back at them and shake his head. I gave myself eight to five he said "Jesus!"

He was wearing tan doubleknits, brown hush puppies, a yellow vest sweater, and his rust shirt was open at the throat. In his left hand was a tape recorder. He had a black beard, neatly cropped, and he looked about twenty-seven.

When I opened the door his first words were, "Jesus, you're hard to find," and I figured that was good enough grounds to collect five bucks from myself.

"I'm Ernie Morris," he said, shoving out his hand. "I'm doing a book, and if you're Al Burke you're the only guy in L.A. can help me."

"Everybody's doing a book," I said, moving aside and trying to reconcile a tight beard with a noisy motor. "Come on in."

His eyes took in the Mickey Mouse bookshelves of brick and board that reached to the ceiling, the beat-up Remington on its stand, the old Baldwin upright, and the music manuscript paper and bottle of India ink on the table.

"You write music?" he asked.

"Write music? Hell, no. I'm a copyist."

He looked at the score I'd been working on. "How about that? You know, I never saw this done before."

"Who has? Everybody seems to think notes are set like type or something. Man, it's hard work, and here's what you have to work with." I shoved the original toward him. "You ought to see these arrangers in action—hit keys with one hand, jab a pencil with the other, like shorthand. When they make a change they rub with their thumb. Another change and they've got something that would stop Rorschach cold. It takes a copyist to make music out of it."

I picked up where I had left off and rattled off six bars with crisp strokes.

"Hey," he said. "Just like downtown."

"Every job I take I do somebody a favor.   The money is good, but what good is the money?   There are other things to do."

"Yeah, I read you."   He chuckled and then turned to the window that looked out into thin air, a hundred feet above the bottom of Laurel Canyon.   "That borrowed set of wheels out there barely got me up here.   What's with these mountainsides?"

"Well, for one thing," I said as my subconscious elbowed me, "we do as we damn well please.   If you look out that other window through those trees you can see somebody's front door on the other side of Kirkwood.   Every noon a honeycomb blonde comes out that door to water her geraniums.   Bare-assed."

He laughed, and came back to the table.   "Hooray for houseplants!   But parking?   How about that?"

"Man, if you're on the street you toe your wheel in, set your brake, wedge a rock against the tire, and pray.   In the morning, if you're lucky, it'll still be there.   What's this book you're doing?"

He sat down, put the recorder on the floor and pulled out a deck of butts.

"Dixieland," he said, elevating his palms as if he were confessing some monstrous vice.   "It's just something I'm into.   I've already done one on the brass and—"

It hit me then.   "Sure . . . Ernie Morris.   You wrote *Gabriel's Clan*.   I've got a copy around here somewhere.   Good job, too . . . except I think you and everybody else lay it on too thick about Beiderbecke.   What did he have going for him besides a good tone and an early grave?   Most of his sides are corn, you know that.   You ought to let him stay dead."

Morris shrugged.   "So you're right.   But he's a legend, and legends sell books, and that's the name of the game.   Anyway, I didn't come up here to argue Bix. I'm doing the vocalists—you know, Bessie Smith, Lil Hardin, Rosa Henderson, Lady Day, right on down.   But it's not the old-timers that are giving me trouble.

"There was a gal singing around here in the fifties that has me climbing walls. I hear she was the greatest of them all, and I can't find a single goddam side she ever cut."

I knew what was coming now, and my flesh tightened, as if someone were holding the door open on a winter night.

"Around the clubs they tell me you knew her . . . Ruby Benton."

I locked my teeth, got up slowly and moved to the kitchen.   Fishing around, I found a half-full jug of vodka, some ice, and quinine water.   Picking up two glasses, I took the works back to the table and looked a question at him.   He nodded, and I poured.

"She never cut any records," I said.

He bent over and opened his Norelco.   "Mind if we tape this?" he asked. "I'm lousy at notes."

"Be my guest."

He checked his cartridge, plugged in a mike, and thumbed the red button.   "But you did know Ruby Benton?"

"I knew her . . . if there was a Ruby Benton."

"What does that mean?"

I took a slug of the vodka.   "Yeah, what does that mean?   It's a good question."

"You're losing me.   Ruby Benton's the name she used."

"I'm not talking about the name.   I'm talking about her."

"Hell, man, she sang at Storyville West on Melrose Avenue the whole summer of '55.   Leonard Feather heard her, and she was the greatest.   Bobby Hackett told me the same thing.   Al Hirt heard her, Wild Bill Davison, Ray Beauduc, Wingy Manone, Sonny Weldon, Louis Mills, hell, I could name a—"

"I know, I know.   I used to see them come in.   Everybody that got to the coast that summer heard her.   Every week she got offers to step into the big time, and every week her answer was the same.   She wasn't ready yet.   Ready?   Hell, she was 28, maybe 30, and with a voice like that . . . ." I trailed off and had another go at the vodka.

"Let me tell you about Ruby's voice.   I grew up in New England.   In the early forties I was a cub reporter on a paper in Springfield, Mass., and met a gal who sang with a five-piece combo on Friday and Saturday nights.   She was about nineteen then, and during the week she worked for the telephone company.   Katy McKane, her name was, and you're wasting your time looking her up.   She never made lights.   But, man, could she sing.   Popular stuff, not jazz . . . 'Once in a While,' 'Manhattan Serenade,' 'All of Me' . . . Katy's voice was something else!

"Well, I managed to get her some space in the paper, and one thing and another, we got to going out together and it lasted over a year.   Exactly what happened to it, I don't know.   I ran into her after the war, and we swapped memories over a drink.   She summed it up with a few bars from Cole Porter: 'It Was Just One of Those Things.'   But maybe for me it wasn't one of those things.   I think I'm still in love with her."

A mood could have set in right there, but, as I broke off, Morris took up the slack.   "It's the story of every man's life.   There's always a love back there in the past somewhere that didn't quite jell."

"Well, anyway, I came into Storyville one Wednesday night in May.   Jiggs Kirby and his Hot Five were billed, and I took a stool at the bar.   The place was always good for some solid Dixieland, but there was some dancing, too.   A girl started singing 'Night and Day.'

"Morris, I got the cold sweats.   It was Katy's voice—throaty, liquid, throbbing. I wheeled around to get a load of the girl, and you know what I saw?   A little brunette with deep eyes in a pale face who couldn't have weighed more than ninety-five, black sequins and all.   A fellow named Curly was working the bar, and I asked him who she was.

" 'Name's Ruby Benton,' he told me.   'Started last night.'

"I noticed something.   No table chatter.   She had everybody in the joint watching her.   Even my Katy could never manage that.   By the time she hit the bridge my throat was choked up as memories of Katy came flooding back, and the years when this world was worth living in and there were still things worth fighting a war for.   My eyes were wet by the time she finished.   Everything was quiet for several beats, then she got a hand that shook the glasses on the back bar.

"Jiggs Kirby was on piano, and I had copied a few arranging jobs for him. When they took ten I had him introduce me. I bought Ruby a drink, and when we got acquainted I'm damned if she didn't have a little accent trouble with her r's. It threw me. When she'd been singing there was no trace of it.

"Her voice across the table wasn't McKane's either, and I groped in vain for any resemblance at all. Katy was a lot of woman, and this girl, with the thin jaw and the shadowy eyes, was strictly a number in a minor key. She looked as if someone ought to put her on a diet of thick steaks.

"But a little later, with the band behind her, I took it all back. The boys began to jam, Chicago style, with Ruby on the words of 'Sister Kate' and 'A Good Man Is Hard to Find.' She sat out 'Tin Roof Blues' and came back with 'If I Could Be With You.' Later in the evening she came on with 'Sunny Side' and, believe me, I've heard *everybody* on 'Sunny Side.' Ruby Benton's was the living end."

I picked up the bottle from the table and poured us two more. Morris was on another cigarette.

"Are you sure she never cut any numbers?" he said.

"I told you. But what I didn't tell you was I taped her myself one night."

I swear I never saw a man spring to attention like this Ernie Morris. For a second I thought he was going to pop an eyeball.

"You've got a *tape* of Ruby Benton?"

I dropped my eyes and turned away so Morris wouldn't catch the bleakness of my grin. Getting up, I went to a wall cabinet and started pawing through some boxes of Muggsy Spanier, Kid Ory, Sidney Bechet, and Mezzrow. "I used to hit Storyville two or three nights a week after that," I said. "The word on Benton spread like a spilled martini, and I'm damned if I ever saw so many jazzhounds come into one place to catch a band. Even Milt Gabler. Someone said he flew out from the Commodore to talk her into an all-star session. Ah, here it is."

The box was labeled with a single word: "Ruby." I brought it back to the table and set up my machine. "I told Ruby I wanted to tape her, and she asked me not to. But one night I had Sapolio—he ran the joint then—hold me a table next to the bandstand, and I put the recorder under the table and primed Jiggs to open Ruby on 'Night and Day.' During the number she must have spotted the dodge or something because she came over right afterward and said, 'Please, Al, turn it off. You promised.'

"Well, I hadn't promised, but I turned it off. What the hell, I had something, anyway . . . and here it is."

I threaded the tape into my ancient machine and pressed the switch. The reels started turning and at half gain the music came on strong.

Morris's face was a picnic as Ruby's cue approached. Then frown lines started creeping down between his eyes and he seemed to stop breathing entirely. When the number ended he looked at me with the damnedest expression of bafflement I ever saw.

"Are you putting me on?"

"What would be the point?"

"Well, then, what the hell happened?"

I let out one of those sighs with muscles on it, and turned off the machine. "So help me, that's the tape of Ruby Benton singing 'Night and Day'; and that's Jiggs Kirby on piano, exactly as it was recorded. Now you've got it on your own tape."

"Yeah, so I have." The words came out of Morris woodenly, as if he suddenly were fogged in. He looked at his Norelco and checked his watch, but they were idle motions. I picked up the vodka again, emptied what was left into our glasses, and dribbled in some tonic.

"God knows why," I went on, "but Ruby liked me. One evening I ran into her in Barney's Beanery, of all places, and we ate onion soup together. Barney's was different in the old days, you know, and their onion soup was something to remember. Well, anyway, it was Monday and the Story was dark, so neither of us had anything lined up. She seemed in the mood for making a night of it, but it was my week to be tapped out so we came up here. I opened a jug and dug into my collection of 78's . . . some good Jimmie Luncefords, Johnny Hodges, early Coleman Hawkins, and that great riff in 'Thru for the Night,' with Fatha Hines, remember that? After a while I brought out Frankie Newton's 'Minor Jive.' Mezzrow wrote it, and they cut it for Bluebird in the late thirties. It's low down and indigo, and it must have struck some vibes in Ruby. After about four straight runs of it she turned it off and looked square at me with those big shadowy eyes.

" 'Al . . . will you make love to me?' she said, just as if she were asking me to mix her another drink or something."

Sometime during the night [I continued] Ruby started twisting and muttering, and it got me awake. Did you ever listen to somebody talking in his sleep? Like the vocal chords are working but the tongue doesn't want to get involved? Words are blurry, and the emphasis, it's weird. At any rate, I couldn't make head nor tail out of what she said, except she seemed to be arguing with someone, protesting against something. But it passed, and I went back to sleep. In the morning I noticed a tiny blue marking on her arm. A tattooed number. She saw me staring at it, then put her finger-tips to the corresponding place on my arm. Her eyes widened.

"Are you a noss?"

"A what?"

"Are you a—" She broke off, a peculiar look crossing her face. Her bottom lip crawled in slightly, and I had the feeling I had caught her in a faux pas of some kind. "It's nothing," she said. "Just something I picked up."

The tattoo was obviously her social security number, but it was preceded by an "A" and followed by a space and five additional digits.

"I dig the mark," I said. "Beats carrying it on a card. But what's the rest of it for?"

"What?"

"The last five numbers."

She twisted her head to look. "That? It's just my—"

At that moment my telephone rang and whatever it was she said didn't register. My caller was Ace Flanagan in Hollywood, who had to have some copies of an arrangement by 10:00 A.M. The stuff was ready, so I told Ruby we'd get dressed and eat breakfast downtown.

Afterward, I spent a lot of time with her at the club, but we never did get back up here for an encore. The last weeks of summer rolled away, and Sapolio dry-washed his fat hands while Ruby packed them in. Then one morning late in August there was a knock on my door.

It was only 8:30, and I grumbled as I rolled out of the sack and reached for a robe. That's the real reason we live up here in the canyon. Every man is an island—and to hell with John Donne. We don't get peddlers.

I opened the door, ready to chew somebody out, and it was Ruby Benton.

I squinted at her with one eye. "You're just in time to make me some black coffee," I said.

She came in and made the coffee while I hit the bathroom and threw some cold water in my face.

"I can't stay, Al," she said when I came out. "I'm finished here. I came up to say good-bye."

"I told you you were too good for Sapolio," I said. I knew all along she'd be moving up to the big time, so her leaving Storyville was no surprise. "Where do you open? Vegas or Broadway?"

The bell on the timer rang, and Ruby went into the kitchen to pour the coffee.

"It is something I can't tell you," she said as she brought the cups. "Maybe, if you read the newspaper . . ."

"Roger," I said, and wondered at the peculiarites of show business. "I'll read the newspaper."

We kicked reminiscences of the summer around for a while, and finished the coffee. Then she got up to go.

"You have been a good friend, Al," she said. "I will always remember you."

I was going to walk her to the car but when we got outside there was no car. "How did you get up here?" I asked.

"I walked," she said.

I was dumbfounded. I told her I'd drive her down to Sunset or wherever she wanted to go, but she refused, and it occurred to me she might be staying with someone below me in the canyon. She gave me a light kiss on the lips and started down the incline. When she got to the turnoff into Kirkwood she gave me a little wave. Then she passed the corner and was gone. The click of her heels came up through the trees a while longer but soon that, too, was gone. I never saw Ruby Benton again.

Morris was silent, and I sat there toying with my glass. Finally he said, "She never went to Broadway or Vegas."

"I know. I read *Variety* and the *Reporter* for weeks. Hell, I read the *Times* and the *Examiner* and the *Citizen-News*. The columnists all speculated—but nothing ever came out. It was just as if she'd stepped off the edge of the earth."

"There's something more," Morris said. "You told me she had a voice like this girl of yours, Katy. Did you ever wonder how she sounded to anyone else?"

"No, why should I? . . . Wait a minute, I remember a guy next to me at the bar one night asked me if I knew the name of that babe used to sing 'Oh, Johnny, Oh, Johnny, Oh.' Told me he used to be nuts about her, and Ruby was the first one he ever heard who could sing like her. I gave him a withering look and moved down the bar. Any guy so sauced up he thought Ruby sang like Bonnie Baker—yecch!''

"I'll tell you something," Morris said. "I've interviewed dozens who remember Ruby, and I still don't know a damned thing about her voice. She belted a song like Sophie Tucker, one oldtimer told me. He was a Sophie Tucker fan, natch. Another dude said Dinah Washington. One guy, so help me God, swore she sang like Dorothy Kirsten. Several said she was another Billie Holliday. Somebody said she reminded him of his mother. The only thing I can dredge out of all this is that when you heard Ruby sing you heard the voice you loved best in the whole world. But what sense does that make?''

I stared at the window for a while. "It would make sense—if we knew the rest of the script.

"One thing reading all those papers did for me that August, it caught me up on the news. You remember that guy, Joel Kurzenknabe, they nailed here in '55? Had a machine shop in Santa Monica? They said he was building an atom bomb to blow up California?''

Morris shrugged vaguely. "I was just a kid.''

"Well, anyway, let me tell you about this Joel Kurzenknabe. Some newspaper correspondent remembered him from France when American jazz was sweeping Europe in the thirties. He played tailgate trombone, and the story was he sat in on gigs with guys like Grappelly and the Reinhardts and Louis Vola and Alix Combelle in the early Paris days. He never made the big time like they did, though, and maybe the frustration ate at his guts. But play or not, he followed the action; and wherever le jazz was hot, there was Joel.''

"So?''

"So I haven't finished. More stuff came out about Kurzenknabe. He was supposed to have been at Telemark during the war when the Nazis were playing around with heavy water. Then in 1945 he turned up at Oak Ridge with clearance to work on the bomb. He was at Alamagordo. But how he managed these things, or who he really was, nobody seemed to know. All this kept coming out after the story broke that the Feds had nailed him. The G-men charged him with building his own A-bomb in a secret machine shop just outside of Los Angeles, using material stolen from the government.

"Well, that was pure crap. How I know is I had a friend, Tony Ragazzo, who repaired instruments in those days. He did a job on Joel's trombone, and the two got to talking Dixieland. One thing led to another; and Joel, who was using the name Ed Parker, was invited to sit in on a couple of Sunday jam sessions. Eventually they got to rapping about musical theory, counterpoint, vibrations, and so forth, and Joel ended up showing Tony his project. He was working on some kind of vibration amplifier, you know, like the soprano whose high note shatters a wineglass. Joel aims his beam at a skyscraper and the concrete disintegrates.

A dandy toy for the warmakers. But someone blew the whistle on him that August, and his work went down the drain. To top it off, he died before the trial. Suicide, the papers said. But when Tony was telling me all this afterward, he insisted somebody got to Joel.''

"What does this have to do with Ruby Benton?" Morris asked.

"Joel Kurzenknabe was fingered in Storyville West the night before Ruby came up here to say good-bye.''

"Wait a minute. You mean Ruby—''

"Think about it. Some outfit wants to do a number on Kurzenknabe. They know he's in the L.A. area but they don't know what name he's using. What they do know is he's such a nut on jazz that if a great talent flares up he'll bounce toward it like a moth heading for a hundred-watt bulb. So they send Ruby. She sings like a Lorelei for three months at Storyville West. Finally Kurzenknabe barges in and racks himself up on her reef. Mission accomplished. Ruby waves farewell and dissolves into the friendly California smog.''

"But that doesn't answer anything!" Morris protested. "Who was she? Where did she come from? Where did she go? If somebody sent her, who were they, and why did they want Kurzenknabe? And most of all, how did she manage that business with her voice?''

"I've thought about it; but if I tell you, you're going to think I'm strung out on reefers.''

"Try me.''

"OK, let's go back to that number on Ruby's arm. Did you know there's been a bill in Congress to give every newborn kid an indelible social security number? It didn't pass, but they'll bring it up again. That raises a question: Would offspring of the big shots have to submit to tattooing? Would there be an aristocracy exempt from social security stencils? Ruby looked at my unmarked arm and asked if I were a 'noss.' Could that be a slang word for 'no S.S.'? . . . And that 'A' in front. It suggests Uncle Sam's getting ready for the *second* billion registrants. When will that be necessary?

"But there are two other things that really give me a cold chill about Ruby's origin. One is those five digits I asked her about. Looking back now, I think they were her zip code.''

"So what?" Morris said as I paused.

"That was 1955, remember? We didn't start using zips till '62. And one other thing—a song title. When Ruby and I were playing records that night, she asked me if I had 'Raindrops Keep Fallin' on My Head.' I had to admit I never even heard of it.''

"Nineteen sixty-nine," Morris said. *"Butch Cassidy and the Sundance Kid."*

"Right. But if it was precognition, why would she ask, in 1955, if I had the record? Sounds more as if her programming wasn't tight enough. At any rate, whatever was in her mind still wouldn't explain that damned tattooed zip code.''

"I get it. You're trying to tell me you think Ruby didn't come from another place, she came from another *time.''*

"What else is there?''

"It's crazy! . . . But it's beautiful. My God, what a chapter for the book."

"One thing bugs me," I said. "Did the good guys get the bad guy—or was it the other way around? Tony Ragazzo said he liked Joel, and Ruby didn't seem too happy with her part of the business. Was Joel a fugitive from the future himself, or was the whole operation one of those science fiction 'adjustments of history,' like pinching off a twig to keep a limb from growing in the wrong place?"

"That isn't what bugs me," Morris said. "It's that trick about her voice."

"Well, nobody's gonna give you the answer to that! Jiggs Kirby supplied the music, Ruby supplied what must have been lip synch, and each listener supplied a memory that might have been activated by some gizmo or other. Who the hell knows? Maybe it was something inside Ruby. Maybe she was bionic. I slept with her—and even I couldn't prove she wasn't."

Morris frowned, rubbed his beard, and chewed on it a while. His watch told him the cartridge was full, and he turned off the feed. Then he asked me to run my tape once more. I rewound and started it again. At Ruby's cue, the brass and drums muted and the piano carried the accompaniment just as if Ruby Benton were singing 'Night and Day.' Thirty-two bars pianissimo, then a repeat to the bridge and eight more bars.

But there was no voice on the tape . . . no voice at all.

CONWAY CONLEY

On the Way

The bed was low, and he struggled for some time to get to his feet. Several times he almost invented different furniture; chairs, perhaps, or a bed high enough that a person could get his legs under himself when getting out of it. Finally, by finding handholds on the rough-textured wall, he was able to stand.

He looked down at his bed. There beside it was the bell, placed within easy reach the first day he hadn't gotten out of bed. And the cup and jug, which had been moved back a little each time they tended him, for fear he would spill it into his bedding. There was no clock; in fact there was only one in the house, and he wasn't so used to measuring time as to think of counting his last hours.

He faced the door and pushed at the wall, gently, then a little harder until he was away from its support and walking. Might have to follow the wall around to the door; no, he could balance well enough to walk across the middle of the floor.

The outer room was empty; he surveyed it while he rested holding to the doorframe. Then he launched himself toward the outer door. Step by step; suddenly a voice sounded behind him, "Grandsire, where are you going? Marsha says we've made things so you'll be comfortable in bed," and a youngster appeared to his right.

Carefully gathering breath to speak without losing his concentration on walking, he said, "A man's got to be comfortable in his spirit as well as his body."

The child watched silently, curious and uncertain about the struggles of one in the terminal stage of life.

"Here, open that door, will you?" he grunted.

"I'm not sure that Marsha or Todd'd want me to," but the youngster hardly hestitated, making it clear that a certain word from him still drew more respect than implications dropped by those two. Which ones were they, he wondered as he rested in the outer doorway. He had a granddaughter named Marsha, he was sure, but they might have given a later child the same name. As for Todd, that sounded like a grand- or great-grandchild.

The boy held the door until he shoved off from the doorframe and started walking across the yard. After that he didn't see or hear him; he didn't want to try looking behind.

The sky was blue with sunlit clouds. Too bright, actually, but he couldn't see well in dim light either; evening would come on a little earlier for him than for the others.

Sky above and ground beneath; an improvement over indoors, but he still wanted a clear view of the horizon. There was a knoll west of the house, and that was where he wanted to be.

"Grandsire, whatever is the matter? Why didn't you tell us?" The new interruption broke his concentration on walking over the slightly uneven ground; he was tiring. He stood and watched the woman-child running toward him. This one he remembered, though the name had slipped from him again. Very attractive, and about fifteen. Some men when they reached senior years misjudged the ages of teenage girls. He knew because he had done it; but he had had ample time since then to learn to tell ages all over again, as the great-grandchildren and their children grew so numerous that he lost track of names and parentage.

He was tired; he leaned on the proffered young body and directed her steps, "Out. Out to where the grass meets the sky." He thought that was a pretty good line, at least considering that it was extemporaneous.

But as they passed a bench she said, "Do you want to rest, Grandsire?" And he scanned the way west to the knoll, found it devoid of anything on which to sit, and said, "Yes."

"You like the out-of-doors, Grandsire?"

He liked her sensible approach to a person's wants and needs. "I was on a journey when I came here. Stayed most of my life, but I felt I should at least start on a little way."

Her face took on a serious look. Apparently she felt as if he had always been here. "I've heard you were a pet of the Overholders," she said, and it was obvious that she had put that information in the back of her mind, not forgotten but out of reach of her feelings until now.

"Until I was forty."

"I've never seen an Over."

"They've probably seen you. But you know what they look like, of course?"

She nodded doubtfully. "I've seen the pictures and all that, but I don't think it's the same as seeing one, certainly not like actually going up and touching them."

He was silent then.

"What are you thinking?" she asked.

"Thinking about Inzlai, the Overholder who was my mistress—that's feminine for master, if you'll recall—and how she used to pick me up and hold me and ask me how my history was coming. She didn't understand most of it; computer scientists and engineers make better pets because any young Overholder can understand what they're doing. But Inzlai liked me anyway."

He paused, wondering how much this human child who had never seen a member of the ruling race wanted to know, or wanted to hear from him since she'd probably already been taught it by her parents or uncles, aunts or grandparents. "The young ones who keep pets develop a knack for communicating with humans, but if you want to really talk with an Overholder you have to find one who has gone on to study it as an adult. I never really tried; wanted to work on my problem myself, through human resources.''

They were silent for a minute or two, then, as if she had just worked her way through what he had said, suddenly she asked, "And what was your problem?''

"Two questions, actually. Is this our native planet, the world called Terra? And were we here first, or the Overholders?''

"It seems natural enough,'' she said, gazing on as if to include the sun and air and living things. "Except sometimes, when you can't get quite right. But I suppose they could have changed our chemistry to match this world if they brought us here from somewhere else.''

"Or if we stowed away on their starships. It's less likely; but if this isn't Terra, and if we've weighed the legends aright to say that we never got very far into space by ourselves, I've always liked the idea that we took our own passage.

"I'd like to walk on out to the knoll now.''

She helped him to stand. Then he put an arm on her shoulders, and found that he liked that as much as he liked getting out of the house. Wondered if this was one of his twice-great- or even thrice-great- grandchildren. All the later generations must be descendants of his by now; there had never been many people in the group. Maybe he was exaggerating his age. Children didn't come often in these times, it had been the occasion for a party when his granddaughter had conceived at the age of only twenty-five. Maybe he wasn't old enough to be a thrice-great-grandfather. He wondered if the incest taboo extended as far as twice-greats. The old book said that the thought in the heart was as much as the act; he doubted that he had it left in him to get beyond thinking. Their community was too small to have formal rules for uncommon situations, but great-greats probably had fewer genes in common than did some of the couplings they had allowed, so he could let himself think as lasciviously as he wanted.

She asked, "How did you get away when you were a pet?''

"I didn't really want to get away from Inzlai, surprising as that may sound. Her holding—her family, roughly, but I guess you know how hard their society is for us to understand, with so many life stages and more sexes than we have—they were on a trip away from their usual habitation, and I was often out exploring libraries and I forgot when they were leaving. We had been there ten years; I was only thirty when we got there, and that much time seemed nearly as long and vague to me then as it does to you now.

"When I got back to the campsite, there was nothing there. Except a backpack with some things I might need, and a note from Inzlai, so I set out walking to get home.''

"Maybe they took off for another planet or solar system.''

"She wouldn't have sent me a quarter of the way around the planet to find an empty holding. She knew I might make it, because she had told me of another pet that had found her way home even further, and I had told her I'd heard the same story from other pets. And I would have made it, if I hadn't stopped on here.''

"Because establishing an independent human colony was more important than going to see an Overholder," she recited.

"Actually, I didn't intend to stay. It was about to rain when I came upon Carl and Thelma and Leslie working desperately to get some hay into the barn before it got wet, and I helped even though I didn't know much about hay at the time."

He stopped talking, aware that he had caused some confusion. The Carl and Thelma and Leslie of whom he spoke had died, others had been born and given the names, long before this child's birth, and it took her a moment to check the facts she knew. When her face signalled that she had the characters in order, he continued. "They let me stay until the rain stopped and the grass dried; and then the cow, the only one and the mother of all that you have now, had gotten loose and wandered off. They had to find her, so I joined the hunt. And then helped to build a fence. One thing led to another. Winter came, and I stayed over. Spring, and I wanted to plant enough of the new crops to pay for what I'd eaten over the winter. Summer, and I was so involved with the care of the crops that I wanted to see them harvested. But I was still on my way home. Just spending a little time with my own people on the way."

"And I always thought it was because we were important," she pouted.

"Judge for yourself; you're old enough to do that. Everyone who was here when I stopped by has been dead and gone sixty years, and I've just gotten this far west of the house on my journey. Let me sit down; I can see the way I was going. I think," he hedged, realizing that a gray curtain had come down between him and the world. They sat on the grass.

"There are no Overholders around here," she said, speaking out of her own thoughts.

"They may be watching us right now. Or not. Maybe this colony was their idea to start with, or maybe they don't know we're here. You never know about the Overholders."

"Did Inzlai have the furry arms?"

"Yes. When they're about that age (I think she was about four hundred), they don't care much whether they look handsome or dignified (to other Overholders); so if they keep soft-skinned pets they usually grow soft flesh and hair on one set of arms, the better to take care of us. Inzlai's were not quite as soft as you are, but more satiny. It was her second triad of arms; I was vain at the time and wanted her to change her first triad for me and use her second three arms for the things she needed hard skin for. But she didn't."

"I bet after she lost you she grew soft fur on both triads. Not for always, just for a few years."

"Too inconvenient, but that's a generous thought, child. I don't know what to call you."

"Evelyn."

"Are you my great-great-granddaughter or my great-great-great-granddaughter?"

"Both. My father Carl is your daughter Velda's grandson, and my mother Inzlai is your daughter Sharon's great-granddaughter."

"Inzlai.   I wasn't sure we'd used the name.   Who was her mother?"

"Thelma.   Thelma II."

"And whose child is Carl?"

She giggled; it took him a moment to realize he had called her father a child. Then she said, "Leslie II's.   Listen, how can you be sure Inzlai—the Overholder, not my mother; I don't know how we'll keep the names straight if we have any more Inzlais, 'cause I can't figure out whether my mother is Inzlai the First or Inzlai the Second.   Anyway, maybe your mistress got tired of you, didn't want any soft arms anymore and so forth, and just dumped you.   Maybe her holding wanted her to grow up."

"I trust her.   As for growing up, she was just starting a stage that lasts about two hundred years; few Overholders that have pets lose interest in them before six hundred.

"Besides, Overholders hardly ever abandon a pet.   I've heard stories that if they can no longer keep one or find another to take it, they'll sometimes kill it. One story has it that former pets sometimes turn into real nuisances.   Another is that they do it to save us starving or dying of exposure.

"I suppose that could happen if they didn't have some place like our colony to come to."

After a time she said, "I've heard most of these things before, but they come out different when I hear them from you."

She was quiet then.   The warmth of the sun slowly mixed with the cool morning air.   His thoughts were as the day, warm and poignant and blurred around the edges so that he couldn't be sure how much he thought of his uncompleted journey and how much of his grandchild's grandchild.

The sun rose further, and now part of his sunshine rose too, the part named Evelyn.   "Is there anything you need that I can send from the house?" she asked.

"Something to lean against."   He lay back on the grass; he had been sitting too long.

Some time later a man carried out a rolled-up mattress and arranged it as a backrest, so that he could face west.   As the sun grew hot a youth set up a sunshade. Still later a child brought a flask and asked if he was thirsty, and helped him raise it to his lips.   Cider; he liked it, though really he could taste so little these last few days that they might about as well have saved the cider for themselves and sent him water.

He watched the western horizon and imagined himself walking across it.   Inzlai would probably still be with her holding in the same location; he thought he would recognize her yet, even with six hard glassy arms.

Favored pets lived a long time; even by the time he was forty she must have given him more than she was supposed to of whatever it was, or he wouldn't have lived a century beyond the natural span.   Even now, he wondered, if he were there and not here, would she lift the weight of age from him and keep him vigorous for another half century or beyond?

Just as he could tell the sun was going down the afternoon sky, Evelyn returned.

"Great-great-great-grandfather," and it was the first time she had used the full title, "by what name were you known when you were a pet of Inzlai?"

"Thomas Huntington Clifford Pence.   Five-eight-one-four-two-three-seven."

She wrote.   Then she held papers in front of him.   "Is this the map Inzlai left for you, and these you drew from memory, and this was given you by a human you met?"   He had difficulty focusing, but he recognized the buildings of the holding in his sketches, and the maps.   He nodded.   She put them in a backpack that he recognized as the one he had hung in the First House one rainy evening a century plus a generation ago, and still he did not understand.   She hesitated with her arms already into the straps, set it down, and said, "Give me your blessing, Grandsire the eldest."   She swooped down too quickly for his aging eyes to follow and kissed him full on the mouth (which he feared had let some of the cider run down his chin).   He put his arms around her, murmuring, "Sweet, sweet child," as she pressed her body against him for a brief moment that reached back through the generations he had tarried here.   Then she was on her feet, and in another moment the pack (strong as when Inzlai had left it at the campsite) was on her strong young back, and she turned and started off to the west.   At last he understood what she had said.   And he wanted to call after her; but he was confused as to what he should say, perhaps ask if she had made sure there were duplicate maps and did her parents know where she was going.   But he couldn't find the strength. His eyes were dimming, but for a long time he could see Evelyn walking across the western horizon.

RANDALL GARRETT

The Napoli Express

I

His Royal Highness, Prince Richard, Duke of Normandy, seated on the edge of his bed in the Ducal Palace at Rouen, had taken off one boot and started on the other when a discreet rap came at the door.

"Yes? What is it?" There was the sound of both weariness and irritation in his voice.

"Sir Leonard, Highness. I'm afraid it's important."

Sir Leonard was the Duke's private secretary and general factotum. If he said something was important, it was. Nevertheless—

"Come in, then, but damn it, man, it's five o'clock in the morning! I've had a hard day and no sleep."

Sir Leonard knew all that, so he ignored it. He came through the door and stopped. "There is a Commander Dhuglas downstairs, Highness, with a letter from His Majesty. It is marked *Most Urgent*."

"Oh. Well, let's see it."

"The Commander was instructed to deliver it into your hands only, Highness."

"Bother," said His Highness without rancor, and put his boot back on.

By the time he got downstairs to the room where Commander Dhuglas was waiting, Prince Richard no longer looked either tired or disheveled. He was every inch a tall, blond, handsome Plantagenet, member of a proud family that had ruled the Anglo-French Empire for over eight centuries.

Commander Dhuglas, a spare man with graying hair, bowed when the Duke entered. "Your Highness."

"Good morning, Commander. I understand you have a letter from His Majesty."

"I do, Your Highness." The naval officer handed over a large, ornately sealed envelope. "I am to wait for an answer, Your Highness."

His Highness took the letter and waved toward a nearby chair. "Sit down, Commander, while I see what this is all about."

He himself took another chair, broke the seal on the envelope and took out the letter.

At the top was the embossed seal of the Royal Arms, and, below that:

My dear Richard,
  There has been a slight change in plans. Due to unforeseen events at this end, the package you have prepared for export must go by sea instead of overland. The bearer of this letter, Commander Edwy Dhuglas, will take it and your courier to their destination aboard the vessel he commands, the White Dolphin. *She's the fastest ship in the Navy, and will make the trip in plenty of time.*
  All my best,
  Your loving brother,
  John

Prince Richard stared at the words. The "package" to which His Majesty referred was a freshly negotiated and signed naval treaty between Kyril, the emperor at Constantinople, and King John. If the treaty could be gotten to Athens in time, Kyril would take steps immediately to close the Sea of Marmora against certain Polish "merchant" vessels—actually disguised light cruisers—which King Casimir's navy was building in Odessa. If those ships got out, Casimir of Poland would have naval forces in the Mediterranean and the Atlantic for the first time in forty years. The treaty with the Scandinavians, at the end of the 1939 war, had stopped the Poles from getting out of the Baltic, but the treaty with the Greeks at that time had had holes in it.

The present treaty closed those holes, but Kyril would not act until the signed treaty was in his hands. There were three of the disguised cruisers in the Black Sea now; once they got past the Dardanelles, it would be too late. They had to be trapped in the Sea of Mamora, and that meant the treaty had to be in Athens within days.

Plans had been laid, timetables set and mathematically calculated to get that treaty there with all possible haste.

And now, His Imperial Majesty, John IV, by the Grace of God King of England, France, Scotland, and Ireland; Emperor of the Romans and Germans; Premier Chief of the Moqtessumid Clan; Son of the Sun; Lord and Protector of the Western Continents of New England and New France; Defender of the Faith, had changed those plans. He had every right to do so, of course; there was no question of that. But—

Prince Richard looked at his wristwatch and then at Commander Dhuglas. "I am afraid this message from the King my brother is a little late, Commander. The item to which he refers should be leaving Paris on the *Napoli Express* in five minutes."

II

The long, bright-red cars of the *Napoli Express* seemed almost eager to get into motion, the two ten-inch-wide stripes along their length—one white and one blue—

almost gave the impression that they were already in motion.   Far down the track ahead, nearly outside the South Paris Station, the huge engine steamed with a distant hissing.

As usual, the *Express* was loaded nearly full.   She only made the run from Paris to Napoli twice a week, and she usually had all the passengers she could handle— plus a standby waiting list.

The trouble with being a standby is that when a reservation is cancelled at the last moment, the standbys, in order of precedence, have to take the accommodations offered or give them up to the next in line.

The poshest compartments on the *Napoli Express* are the eight double compart- ments on the last car of the train, the Observation Car, which is separated from the rest of the train by the dining car.   All sixteen places had been reserved, but three of them had been cancelled at the last moment.   Two of them had been filled by standbys who rather reluctantly parted with the extra fare required, but the sixteenth place remained empty.   None of the other standbys could afford it.

The passengers were filing aboard.   One of them—a short, stout, dark-haired, well-dressed Irishman carrying a symbol-decorated carpetbag in one hand and a suitcase in the other, and bearing papers which identified him as Seamus Kilpadraeg, Master Sorcerer—watched the other passengers carefully without seeming to do so. The man just ahead of him in line was a wide-shouldered, thick-set man with graying hair who announced himself as Sir Stanley Galbraith.   He climbed aboard and did not look back as Master Seamus identified himself, put down his suitcase, surrendered his ticket, and took back his stub.

The man behind him, the last in line, was a tall, lean gentleman with brown hair and a full, bushy brown beard.   Master Seamus had previously watched him hurrying across the station toward the train.   He carried a suitcase in one hand and a silver-headed walking stick in the other, and walked with a slight limp.   The sorcerer heard him give his name to the ticket officer as Goodman John Peabody.

Master Seamus knew that the limp was phony and that the walking stick concealed a sword, but he said nothing and did not look back as he picked up his suitcase and boarded the train.

The small lounge at the rear of the car already contained some five or six passengers.   The rest were presumably in their compartments.   His own com- partment, according to his ticket, was Number Two, towards the front of the car. He headed toward it, suitcase in one hand, carpetbag in the other.   He looked again at the ticket: Number Two Upper.   The lower bed was now a day couch, the upper had been folded up into the wall and locked into place, but there were two lockers under the lower bed marked "Upper" and "Lower."   The one marked "Upper" still had a key in its lock; the other did not, which meant that the man who shared his compartment had already put his luggage in, locked it, and taken the key.   Master Seamus stowed his own gear away, locked the locker, and pocketed the key.   Having nothing better to do, he went back to the lounge.

The bushy-bearded man named Peabody was seated by himself over in one corner reading the Paris *Standard*.   After one glance, the sorcerer ignored him, found himself a seat, and looked casually around at the others.

They seemed a mixed lot, some tall, some short, some middle-aged, some not much over thirty.   The youngest-appearing was a blond, pink-faced fellow who was standing by the bar as if impatiently awaiting a drink, although he must have known that liquor would not be served until the train was well under way.

The oldest-appearing was a white-haired gentleman in priest's garb; he had a small white mustache and beard, and smooth-shaven cheeks.   He was quietly reading his breviary through a pair of gold-rimmed half-glasses.

Between those two, there seemed to be a sampling of every decade.   There were only nine men in the lounge, including the sorcerer.   Five others, for one reason or another, remained in their compartments.   The last one almost didn't make it.

He was a plump man—not really fat, but definitely overweight—who came puffing up just as the ticket officer was about to close the door.   He clutched his suitcase in one hand and his hat in the other.   His sandy hair had been tousled by the warm spring wind.

"Quinte," he gasped.   "Jason Quinte."   He handed over his ticket, retaining the stub.

The ticket officer said, "Glad you made it, sir.   That's all, then."   And he closed the door.

Two minutes later, the train began to move.

III

Five minutes out of the station, a man in a bright red-and-blue uniform came into the car and asked those who were in their staterooms to please assemble in the after lounge.   "The Trainmaster will be here in a moment," he informed everyone.

In due time, the Trainmaster made his appearance in the lounge.   He was a man of medium height, with a fierce-looking black mustache, and when he doffed his hat, he revealed a vast expanse of bald head fringed by black hair.   His red-and-blue uniform was distinguished from the other by four broad white stripes on each sleeve.

"Gentlemen," he said with a slight bow, "I am Edmund Norton, your Trainmaster.   I see by the passenger manifest that all of you are going straight through to Napoli.   The timetable is printed on the little cards inside the doors of your compartments, and another one—" he gestured "—is posted over there behind the bar.   Our first stop will be Lyon, where we will arrive at 12:15 this afternoon, and there will be an hour stopover.   There is an excellent restaurant at the station for your lunch.   We arrive at Marseille at 6:24 and will leave at 7:20.   There will be a light supper served in the dining car at nine.

"At approximately half an hour after midnight, we will cross the border from the Duchy of Provence to the Duchy of Liguria.   The train will stop for ten minutes, but you need not bother yourselves with that, as no one will be allowed either on or off the train.   We will arrive at Genova at 3:31 in the morning, and leave at 4.30.   Breakfast will be served from 8 to 9 in the morning, and we arrive in Rome at four minutes before noon. We leave Rome at one o'clock, which will give you an hour for lunch. And we arrive at Napoli at 3:26 in the afternoon. The total time for the trip will be 34 hours and 14 minutes.

"For your convenience, the dining car will be open this morning at six. It is the next car ahead, toward the front of the train.

"Goodman Fred will take care of all of your needs, but feel free to call on me for anything at any time." Goodman Fred made a short bow.

"I must remind you, gentlemen, that smoking is not permitted in the compartments, in the corridor, or in the lounge. Those of you who wish to smoke may use the observation platform at the rear of the car.

"If there are any questions, I will be glad to answer them at this time."

There were no questions. The Trainmaster bowed again. "Thank you, gentlemen. I hope you will all enjoy your trip." He replaced his hat, turned, and left.

There were four tables reserved in the rear of the dining car for the occupants of the observation car. Master Sorcerer Seamus Kilpadraeg got into the dining car early, and one by one, three other men sat down with him at the table.

The tall, husky man with the receding white hair and the white, clipped, military mustache introduced himself first.

"Name's Martyn Boothroyd. Looks like we're going to be on the train together for a while, eh?" His attention was all on the sorcerer.

"So it would seem, Goodman Martyn," the stout little Irish sorcerer said affably. "Seamus Kilpadraeg I am, and pleased to meet you."

The blocky-faced man with the two-inch scar on his right cheek was Gavin Tailleur; the blond man with the big nose was Sidney Charpentier.

The waiter came, took orders, and went.

Charpentier rubbed a forefinger against the side of his imposing nose. "Pardon me, Goodman Seamus," he said in his deep, rumbling voice, "but when you came aboard, didn't I see you carrying a magician's bag?"

"You did, sir," said the sorcerer pleasantly.

Charpentier grinned, showing strong white teeth. "Thought so. Journeyman? Or should I have called you 'Master Seamus'?"

The Irishman smiled back. "Master it is, sir."

All of them were speaking rather loudly, and around them others were doing the same, trying to adjust their voice levels to compensate for the roar and rumble of the *Napoli Express* as she sped southwards towards Lyon.

"It's a pleasure to make your acquaintance, Master Seamus," Charpentier said. "I've always been interested in the field of magic. Sometimes wish I'd gone into it, myself. Never have made Master, though; math's way over my head."

"Oh? You've a touch of the Talent, then?" the sorcerer asked.

"A little. I've got my ticket as a Lay Healer."

The sorcerer nodded. A Lay Healer's License was good for first aid and emergency work or for assisting a qualified Healer.

The blocky-faced Tailleur tapped the scar on his cheek with his right forefinger and said, in a somewhat gravelly voice: "This would've been a damn sight worse than it is if it hadn't been for old Sharpy, here."

Boothroyd said suddenly: "There's a question I've always wanted to ask—oops, here's breakfast." While the waiter put plates of hot food on the table, Boothroyd began again. "There's a question I've always wanted to ask. I've noticed that Healers use only their hands, with perhaps a little oil or water, but sorcerers use all kinds of paraphernalia—wands, amulets, thuribles, that sort of thing. Why is that?"

"Well, sir, for one thing, they're slightly different uses of the Talent," the sorcerer said. "A Healer is assisting in a process that naturally tends in the direction he wants it to go. The body itself has a strong tendency to heal. Furthermore, the *patient* wants it to heal, except in certain cases of severe aberration, which a Healer can take care of in other ways."

"In other words," Charpentier said, "the Healer has the cooperation of both the body and the mind of the patient."

"Exactly so," the sorcerer agreed. "The Healer just greases the skids, so to speak."

"And how does that differ from what a sorcerer does?" Boothroyd asked.

"Well, most of a sorcerer's work is done with inanimate objects. No cooperation at all, d'ye see. So he has to use tools that a Healer doesn't need.

"I'll give you an analogy. Suppose you have two friends who weigh fourteen stone apiece. Suppose they're both very drunk and want to go home. But they are so drunk that they can't get home by themselves. You, who are perfectly sober, can take 'em both by the arm and lead 'em both home at the same time. It may be a bit o' trouble; it may require all your skill at handling 'em. But you can do it without help because, in the long run, they're cooperating with you. They *want* to get home.

"But suppose you had the same weight in two sandbags, and you want to get *them* to the same place at the same time. You'll get no co-operation from three hundred and ninety-two pounds of sand. So you have to use a tool to assist you. You have a great many tools, but you must pick the right one for the job. In this case, you'd use a wheelbarrow, not a screwdriver or a hammer."

"Oh, I see," said Boothroyd. "You'd say a healer's job was easier, then?"

"Not easier. Just different. Some men who could wheel twenty-eight stone of sand a mile in fifteen minutes might not be able to handle a couple of drunks at all without using physical force. It's a different approach, you see."

Master Seamus had let his eyes wander over the other men in the rear of the dining car as he talked. There were only fourteen men at breakfast. The white-haired priest was listening to two rather foppish-looking men discourse earnestly on church architecture at the next table. He couldn't hear any of the others because of the noise of the train. Only one man was missing. Apparently the bushy-bearded Goodman John Peabody had not wanted any breakfast.

IV

The saba game started early.

An imposing man with a hawk nose and a full beard, completely white except for two narrow streaks of dark brown beginning at the corners of his mouth, came over to where Master Seamus was sitting in the lounge.

"Master Seamus, I'm Gwiliam Hauser.   A few of us are getting up a little game and thought maybe you'd like to join us."

"I thank you for the offer, Goodman Gwiliam," the sorcerer said, "but I'm afraid I'm not much of a gambling man."

"Hardly gambling, sir.   Twelfth-bit ante.   Just a friendly game to pass the time."

"No, not even a friendly game of saba.   But, again, I thank you."

Hauser's eyes narrowed.   "May I ask why not?"

"Ah, that you may, sir, and I'll tell you.   If a sorcerer gets in a saba game with men who don't have the Talent, he can only lose."

"And why is that?"

"Because if he wins, sir, there's sure to be someone at the table who will accuse him of using his Talent to cheat.   Now you should see a saba game played among sorcerers, sir.   That's something to watch, though likely you'd not see most of what was going on."

Hauser's eyes cleared, and a chuckle came from somewhere inside the heavy beard.   "I see.   Hadn't thought of it that way.   Boothroyd said you might like to play, so I asked.   I'll pass on your bit of wisdom to him."

Actually, it would never occur to most folk to distrust a magician, much less accuse one of cheating at cards.   But a heavy loser, especially if he's been drinking, will quite often say things he regrets later.   Sorcerers rarely gamble with unTalented people unless they are close friends.

Eventually Hauser, Boothroyd, Charpentier, the plump, nearly-late Jason Quinte, and one of the two fops—the tall one with the hairline mustache, who looked as though he had been pressed into his clothes—ended up at a corner table with a deck of cards and a round of drinks.   The saba game was on.

The sorcerer watched the game for a while from across the room, then opened the copy of the *Journal of the Royal Thaumaturgical Society* and began to read.

At eight-fifteen, the Irish magician finished the article on "The Subjective Algebra of Kinetic Processes" and put the *Journal* down.   He was tired, not having had enough sleep, and the swaying motion of the train made it difficult to keep his eyes focused on the lines of print.   He closed his eyes and massaged the bridge of his nose between thumb and forefinger.

"Beg y'pardon, Master Seamus.   Mind if I join you?"

The sorcerer opened his eyes and looked up.

"Not at all.   Pray sit down."

The man had reddish hair, a bulbous nose, and sagging features that hung loosely on his facial bones.   His smile was pleasant and his eyes sleepy-looking.   "Zeisler's my name, Master Seamus.   Maurice Zeisler."   He extended his right hand; his left held a large glass of ouiskie and water—heavy on the ouiskie.

The two shook hands, and Zeisler eased himself into the chair to the sorcerer's left.   He gestured toward the saba table.

"Damn silly game, saba.   Have to remember all those cards.   Miss one, play wrong, and you're down the drain for a sovereign at least. Remember 'em all, have all the luck, bluff all the others out, and you're four sovereigns ahead. I never get the luck, and I can't keep the cards straight. Vandepole can, every time. So I stand 'em all a round of drinks and let 'em play. Lose less that way."

"Very wise," murmured the sorcerer.

"Buy you a drink?"

"No, thank you, sir. It's a bit early for me. Later, perhaps."

"Certainly. Be a pleasure." He took a hefty swig from his glass and then leaned confidentially toward the sorcerer. "What I would really like to know is, *is* Vandepole cheating? He's the well-dressed chap with the hairline mustache. Is he using the Talent to influence the fall of the cards?"

The sorcerer didn't even glance at the saba table. "Are you consulting me professionally, sir?" he asked in a mild voice.

Zeisler blinked. "Well, I—"

"Because, if you are," Master Seamus continued relentlessly, "I must warn you that a Master's fees come quite high. I would suggest you consult a Journeyman Sorcerer for that sort of thing; his fees would be much lower than mine, and he'd give you the same information."

"Oh. Well. Thank you. I may do that. Thank you." He took another long pull at his drink. "Uh—by the bye, do you happen to know a Master Sorcerer named Sean O Lochlainn?"

The sorcerer nodded slowly. "I've met him," he said carefully.

"Fortunate. Never met him, myself, but I've heard a great deal about him. Forensic sorcerer, you know. Interesting work. Like to meet him sometime." His eyes had wandered away from the sorcerer as he spoke, and he was gazing out the window at the French countryside flowing by.

"You're interested in magic, then?" the Irishman asked.

Zeisler's eyes came back. "Magic? Oh, no. Got no Talent at all. No, what I'm interested in is investigative work. Criminal investigation." He blinked and frowned as though trying to remember something. Then his eyes brightened and he said: "Reason I brought up Master Sean was that I met the man he works for, Lord Darcy, who's the Chief Investigator for His Royal Highness, the Duke of Normandy." He leaned forward and lowered his voice. The ouiskie was strong on his breath. "Were you at the Healers' and Sorcerers' Convention in London some years back, when a sorcerer named Zwinge got murdered at the Royal Steward Hotel?"

"I was there," the sorcerer said. "I remember it well."

"I imagine so, yes. Well, I was attached to the Admiralty offices at the time. Met Darcy there." He winked an eye solemnly. "Helped him crack the case, actually, but I can't say anything more about it than that." His gaze went back out the window again. "Great investigator. Absolute genius in his field. No-body else could crack that case, but he solved it in no time. Absolute genius. Wish I had his brains." He drained his glass. "Yes, sir, I wish I had his brains." He looked at his empty glass and stood up. "Time for a refill. Get you one?"

"Not yet. Later, perhaps."

"Be right back." Zeisler headed for the bar.

He did not come back. He got into a conversation with Fred, the attendant who was mixing drinks, and forgot about Master Seamus completely, for which the stout little Irish sorcerer was extremely grateful.

He noticed John Peabody, he of the full and bushy beard, was sitting alone at the far end of the long couch, apparently still reading his newspaper, and seemingly so thoroughly engrossed in it that it would be boorish for anyone to speak to him. But the sorcerer knew that the man was keeping at least a part of his attention on the long hallway that ran forward, past the compartments.

Master Seamus looked back at the saba game. The foppishly dressed man with the hairline mustache was raking in sizeable winnings.

If Vandepole were cheating, he was doing it without the aid of the Talent, either latent or conscious; such usage of the Talent would have been easy for the sorcerer to pick up at this short range. It was possible, of course, that the man had a touch of the precognitive Talent, but that was something which the science of magic had, as yet, little data and no theory on. Someone, some day, might solve the problem of the asymmetry of time, but no one had done it yet, and even the relatively new mathematics of the subjective algebrae offered no clue.

The sorcerer shrugged and picked up his *Journal* again. What the hell, it was no business of his.

V

"Lyon, gentlemen!" came Goodman Fred's voice across the lounge, fighting successfully against the noise of the train. *"Lyon in fifteen minutes! The bar will close in five minutes! Lunch will be served in the station restaurant, and we will leave at one-fifteen! It is now twelve noon!"*

Fred had everyone's attention now, so he repeated the message.

Not everyone was in the lounge. After the bar was closed—Zeisler had managed to get two more during the five minutes—Fred went forward along the passageway and knocked on each compartment door. "Lyon in ten minutes! Lunch will be served in the station restaurant. We will leave for Marseille at 1:15."

The stout little Irish sorcerer turned in his couch to look out the window at the outskirts of Lyon. It was a pleasant place, he thought. The Rhone valley was famous for its viniculture, but now the grape arbors were giving way to cottages more and more densely packed, and finally the train was in the city itself. The houses were old, most of them, but neat and well-tended. Technically, the County of Lyonnais was a part of the Duchy of Burgundy, but the folk never thought of themselves as Burgundians. The Count de Lyonnais commanded their respect far more than the Duke of Burgundy did. His Grace respected those feelings, and allowed My Lord Count as free a hand as the King's Law would permit. From the looks of the countryside, it appeared My Lord Count did a pretty good job.

"Excuse me, Master Sorcerer," said a soft, pleasant voice.

He turned away from the window. It was the elderly-looking gentleman in clerical garb. "How may I help you, Father?"

"Allow me to introduce myself; I am the Reverend Father Armand Brun. I noticed you sitting here by yourself, and I wondered if you would care to join me and some other gentlemen for lunch."

"Master Seamus Kilpadraeg at your service, Reverend Sir. I'd be most happy to join you for lunch. We have an hour, it seems."

The "other gentlemen" were standing near the bar, and were introduced in that quiet, smooth voice. Simon Lamar had thinning dark hair that one could see his scalp through, a long face, and lips that were drawn into a thin line. His voice was flat, with just a touch of Yorkshire in it as he said: "I'm pleased to meet you, Master Seamus."

Arthur Mac Kay's accent was both Oxford and Oxfordshire, and was smooth and well-modulated, like an actor's. He was the other foppishly dressed man— immaculate, as though his clothes had been pressed seconds before. He had dark, thick, slightly wavy hair, luminous brown eyes surrounded by long, dark lashes, and a handsome face that matched. He was almost too pretty.

Valentine Herrick had flaming red hair, an excessively toothy smile, and a body that seemed to radiate health and strength as he shook the sorcerer's hand. "Hate to see a man eat alone, by S'n George! A meal's not a meal without company, is it?"

"Not really," the sorcerer agreed.

"Especially at these train station restaurants," said Lamar in his flat voice. "Company keeps your mind off the tasteless food."

Mac Kay smiled angelically. "Oh, come; it's not as bad as all that. Come along; you'll see."

The Heart of Lyon restaurant was a fairly comfortable-looking place, not more than fifty years old, but designed in the King Dwilliam IV style of the late eighteenth century to give it an air of stability. The decor, however, reflected a mild pun on the restaurant's name—which had probably been carefully chosen for just that reason. Over the door, three-quarters life size, legs braced apart, right hand on the pommel of a great naked sword whose point touched the lintel, left arm holding a shield bearing the lions of England, stood the helmed, mail-clad figure of King Richard the Lion-Hearted in polychromed bas-relief. The interior, too, was decorated with knights and ladies of the time of Richard I.

It was fitting. Although most of the first ten years of his reign had been spent in the noble and heroic, but foolish and expensive, fighting of the Third Crusade, he had settled down after his near-fatal wound at the siege of Chaluz to become a really effective ruler. There were some historians who claimed that if Richard had died at Chaluz, a Capet would now be sitting on the throne of the Anglo-French Empire instead of a Plantagenet. But the Capets had died out long ago, as had the unstable cadet branch of the Plantagenets descended from the exiled Prince John, Richard's younger brother. It was Richard and Arthur, the nephew who had succeeded him in 1219, who had held the Anglo-French nation together during those troubled times, and it had been the descendants of King Arthur who had kept it stable through seven and a half centuries.

Old Richard may have had his faults, but he had been a fine king.

"Interesting motif for the decorations," Father Armand said as the waiter led the five men to a table. "And very well done, too."

"Not period, though," Lamar said flatly. "Too realistic."

"Oh, true, true," Father Armand said agreeably. "Not early thirteenth century style at all." He seated himself as the waiter pulled out a chair for him. "It's the painstakingly detailed realism of the late seventeenth, which fits in very well with the style of the rest of the interior. It must have been expensive; there are very few artists nowadays who can or will do that sort of work."

"Agreed, Father," said Lamar. "Workmanship in general isn't what it used to be."

Father Armand chose to ignore that remark. "Now, you take a look up there, at Gwiliam the Marshal—at least I presume it's he; he's wearing the Marshal arms on his surcoat. I'll wager that if you climbed up there on a stepladder and looked closely, you could see the tiny rivets in every link of his mail."

Lamar raised a finger. "And that's not period, either."

Father Armand looked astonished. "Riveted link mail not period for the thirteenth century? Surely, sir—"

"No, no," Lamar interrupted hastily. "I meant the surcoat with the Marshal arms. Armorial bearings of that sort didn't come in till about a century later."

"You know," said Arthur Mac Kay suddenly, "I've always wondered what I'd look like in one of those outfits. Rather dashing, I think." His actor's voice contrasted strongly with Lamar's flat tones.

Valentine Herrick looked at him, smiling toothily. "Hey! Wouldn't that be great? Imagine! Charging into combat with a broadsword like that! Or rescuing a fair princess! Or slaying a dragon! Or a wicked magician!" He stopped suddenly and actually blushed. "Oops. Sorry, Master Sorcerer."

"That's all right," said Master Seamus mildly. "You may slay all the *wicked* magicians you like. Just don't make any mistakes."

That got a chuckle from everyone, even Herrick.

They looked over their menus, chose and ordered. The food, which the sorcerer thought quite good, came very quickly. Father Armand said grace, and more small talk ensued. Lamar said little about the food, but the wine was not to his exact taste.

"It's a Delacey '69, from just south of Givors. Not a bad year for the reds, but it can't compare with the Monet '69, from a lovely little place a few miles southeast of Beaune."

Mac Kay lifted his glass and seemed to address his remarks to it. "You know, I have always contended that the true connoisseur is to be pitied, for he has trained his taste to such perfection that he enjoys almost nothing. It is, I believe, a corollary of Acipenser's Law, or perhaps a theorem derived therefrom."

Herrick blinked bright blue eyes at him. "What? I don't know what you're talking about, but, by S'n George, *I* think it's damn good wine.''   He emphasized his point by draining his glass and refilling it from the carafe.

Almost as if he had heard the pouring as a summons, Maurice Zeisler came wandering over to the table.   He did not stagger, but there was a controlled precision about his walking and about his speech that indicated a necessity to concentrate in order to do either one properly.   He did not sit down.

''Hullo, fellows,'' he said very carefully.   ''Did you see who's over in the corner?''   There were, of course, four corners to the big room, but a slight motion of his head indicated which one he meant.

It was bushy-bearded John Peabody, eating by himself, his suitcase on the floor beside his chair.

''What about him?'' asked Lamar sourly.

''Know him?''

''No.   Kept pretty much to himself.   Why?''

''I dunno.   Seems familiar, somehow.   Like I ought to know him.   Can't exactly place him, though.   Oh, well.''   And he wandered on again, back towards the bar, whence he had come.

''Condition he's in, he wouldn't recognize his own mother,'' muttered Lamar. ''Pass the wine, please.''

VI

The *Napoli Express* crossed the Rhone at Lyon and headed southwards through the Duchy of Dauphine, toward the Duchy of Provence, following the river valley. At Avignon, it would angle away from the river, southeast toward Marseille, but that wouldn't be until nearly five o'clock.

The *Napoli Express* was not a high-speed train; it was too long and too heavy. But it made up for that by making only four stops between Paris and Napoli.   Five, if you counted the very short stop at the Provence-Liguria border.

In order to avoid having to cross the Maritime Alps, the train's route ran along the coast of the Mediterranean after leaving Marseille, past Toulon, Cannes, Nice, and Monaco to the Ligurian coast.   It looped around the Gulf of Genova to the city of Genova, then stayed with the seacoast all the way to the Tiber, where it turned east to make the short side trip to Rome.   There, it crossed the Tiber and headed back toward the sea, staying with the coast all the way to arrive at last at Napoli.

But that would be tomorrow afternoon.   There were hundreds of miles and hours of time ahead of her yet.

Master Seamus sat on one of the chairs on the observation deck at the rear of the car and watched the Rhone Valley retreat into the distance.   There were four seats on the semicircular observation deck, two on each side of the central door that led into the lounge.   The two on the starboard side were occupied by the plump, sandy-haired man who had almost missed the train—Jason Quinte—and the blond, pink-faced young man whose name the sorcerer did not know. Both were smoking cigars and talking in voices that could be heard but not understood above the rush of the wind and the rumble of the wheels over the steel tracks.

Master Seamus had taken the outer of the two remaining chairs, and Father Armand, who was trying valiantly to light his pipe in the gusts that eddied about him, had taken the other. When at last the pipe was burning properly, Father Armand leaned back and relaxed.

The door slid open and a fifth man came out, thumbing tobacco into his own pipe, a stubby briar. It was Sir Stanley Galbraith, the wide-shouldered, muscular, graying man who had preceded the sorcerer aboard the train. He ignored the others and went to the high railing that surrounded the observation deck and looked into the distance. Having packed his pipe to his satisfaction, he put away his tobacco pouch and then proceeded to search himself. Finally, he turned around, scowling. The scowl vanished when he saw Father Armand's pipe.

"Ah. Begging your pardon, Reverend Sir, but could I borrow your pipe lighter? Seem to have left my own in my compartment."

"Certainly." Father Armand proffered his lighter, which Sir Stanley promptly made use of. He succeeded in an astonishingly short time and handed the lighter back. "Thank you. My name's Galbraith, Sir Stanley Galbraith."

"Father Armand Brun. I am pleased to meet you, Sir Stanley. This is Master Sorcerer Seamus Kilpadraeg."

"A pleasure, gentlemen, a pleasure." He puffed vigorously at his pipe. "There. She'll stay lit now. Good thing it isn't raining; left my weather pipe at home."

"If you need one, Sir Stanley, let me know." It was the plump Jason Quinte. He and the pink-faced youngster had stopped talking when Sir Stanley had appeared and had been listening. Sir Stanley's voice was not overly loud, but it carried well. "I have a couple of them," Quinte went on. "One of 'em never used. Glad to make you a present of it if you want it."

"No, no. Thanks all the same, but there's no bad weather predicted between here and Napoli." He looked at the sorcerer. "Isn't that right, Master Seamus?"

The sorcerer grinned. "That's what the report said, Sir Stanley, but I couldn't tell you of my own knowledge. Weather magic isn't my field."

"Oh. Sorry. You chaps do all specialize, don't you? What is your specialty, if I may ask?"

"I teach forensic sorcery."

"Ah, I see. Interesting field, no doubt." He shifted his attention as a whiff of smoke came his way. "Jamieson."

The pink-faced youth took the cigar from his mouth and looked alert. "Sir?"

"What the devil is that you're smoking?"

Jamieson looked down at the cigar in his hand as though he were wondering where the thing had come from and how it had got there. "A Hashtpar, sir."

"Persian tobacco; I thought so." A smile came over his tanned face. "Good Persian is very good; bad Persian—which that is—will probably rot your lungs, my boy. That particular type is cured with some sort of perfume or incense. Reminds me of a whorehouse in Abadan."

There was a sudden awkward pause as it came to the minds of all of them that there was a man of the cloth present.

"Toss it overboard, Jamie," Quinte said in a rather-too-loud voice. "Here, have one of mine."

Jamieson looked at the three-quarters-smoked cigar again, then flipped it over the rail. "No, thanks, Jason. I was through with it anyway. Just thought I'd try one." He looked up at Sir Stanley with a rather sheepish grin. "They were expensive, sir, so I bought one. Just to try it, you see. But you're right—they do smell like the inside of a—uh—Daoist temple."

Sir Stanley chuckled. "Some of the worst habits are the most expensive, son. But, then, so are some of the best."

"What are you smoking, Sir Stanley?" Father Armand asked quietly.

"This? It's a blend of Balik and Robertian."

"I favor a similar blend, myself. I find Balik the best of Turkish. I alternate with another blend: Balik and Couban."

Sir Stanley shook his head slowly. "Tobacco from the Duchy of Couba is much better suited for cigars, Reverend Sir. The Duchy of Robertia produces the finer pipe tobacco, I find. Of course, I'll admit it's all a matter of taste."

"Never seen Couba," said Quinte, "but I've seen the tobacco fields in Robertia. Don't know if you've ever seen the stuff grow, Father?" It was only half a question.

"Tell me about it," said Father Armand.

Robertia was a duchy on the southern coast of the northern continent of the Western Hemisphere, New England, with a seacoast on the Gulf of Mechicoe. It had been named after Robert II, since it had been founded during his reign in the early eighteenth century.

"It grows about so high," Quinte said, holding his hand about thirty inches off the deck. "Big, wide leaves. I don't know how it's cured; I only saw it in the fields."

He may have been going to say more, but the door leading into the lounge slid open and Trainmaster Edmund Norton stepped out, his red-and-blue uniform gleaming in the afternoon sun.

"Good afternoon, gentlemen," he said with a smile. "I hope I'm not interrupting."

"Oh, no," said Sir Stanley. "Not at all. Just chit-chat."

"I hope you gentlemen have all been comfortable, enjoying the trip, eh?"

"No complaints at all, Trainmaster. Eh, Father?"

"Oh, none at all, none at all," said Father Armand. "A very enjoyable trip so far. You run an excellent train, Trainmaster."

"Thank you, Reverend Sir." The Trainmaster cleared his throat. "Gentlemen, it is my custom at this hour to invite all my special passengers to join me in a drink—of whatever kind you prefer. Will you join me, gentlemen?"

There could, of course, be no argument with an invitation like that. The five passengers followed the Trainmaster into the lounge.

"One thing I'll say," Father Armand murmured to the sorcerer, "it's certainly quieter in here than out there."

The Trainmaster went quietly over to the table where the saba game had resumed after lunch.   He had judged his time accurately.

Vandepole raked in his winnings with one hand, while he ran the forefinger of the other across his hairline mustache.

The Trainmaster said a few words, which the sorcerer did not hear over the rumble of the train.   It was quieter in here, yes, but not exactly silent.

Then Trainmaster Edmund went over to the bar, where Goodman Fred stood waiting, turned to the passengers and said in a loud voice: "Gentlemen, step up and order your pleasure.   Fred, I'll see what the gentlemen at the saba table will have."

A few minutes later, the Irish sorcerer was seated at the bar watching the foam on a glass of beer slosh gently from side to side with the swaying of train.   Maurice Zeisler, he thought, was going to hate himself later.   The scar-faced Gavin Tailleur had gone back to his compartment to tell him that the Trainmaster was treating, but had been unable to rouse him from his—er—nap.

Master Seamus was seated at the end of the bar, near the passageway.   The Trainmaster came over and stood at the end of the bar after making sure everyone who wanted one had been served a drink.

"I'll have a beer, Fred," he said to the attendant.

"Comin' right up, Trainmaster."

"I see beer's your tipple, too, Master Sorcerer," Trainmaster Edmund said as Fred put a foaming brew before him.

"Aye, Trainmaster, that it is.   Wine's good with a meal, and a brandy for special occasions is fine, but for casual or even serious drinkin', I'll take beer every time."

"Well spoken.   Do you like this particular brew?"

"Very much," said the sorcerer.   "Norman, isn't it?"

"Yes.   There's a little area in the Duchy of Normandy, up in the highlands where the Orne, the Sarthe, the Eure, the Risle, and the Mayenne all have their sources, that has the best water in all of France.   There's a good beer comes from Ireland, and there are those who prefer English beer, but to my taste, Norman is the best, which is why I always order it for my train."

Master Seamus, who *did* prefer English beer, but by the merest hair, merely said: "It's very fine stuff.   Very fine, indeed."   He suspected that the Trainmaster's preference might be shaded just a little by the fact that Norman beer was cheaper in Paris than English beer.

"Have you been getting along well with your compartment mate?" the Trainmaster asked.

"I haven't been informed who my compartment mate is," the sorcerer replied.

"Oh?   Sorry.   It's Father Armand Brun."

VII

By half-past four that afternoon, Master Seamus Kilpadraeg was dozing on the rearward couch, leaning back in the corner, his arms folded across his chest and his chin nearly touching his sternum.   Since he did not snore, he offended no one.

Father Armand had gone back to Compartment Number Two at a quarter after three, and, suspecting that the gentleman was tired, the sorcerer had decided to let him have the day couch there to himself.

The train and the saba game went on.   Jason Quinte had dropped out of the game, but his place had been taken by the red-haired Valentine Herrick.   Gavin Tailleur had taken Sidney Charpentier's place, and now Charpentier was sitting on the forward couch, his large nose buried in a book entitled *The Infernal Device,* an adventure novel.   Sir Stanley Galbraith and Arthur Mac Kay were at the bar with a dice cup, playing for drinks.

Quinte and young Jamieson were back out on the observation deck with more cigars—presumably not Hashtpars this time.

Zeisler was still snoozing, and Lamar had apparently retired to his own compartment.

At Avignon, the train crossed the bridge that spanned the River Durance and curved away from the Rhone toward Marseille.

Master Seamus was roused from his doze by the sound of Simon Lamar's flat voice, but he neither opened his eyes nor lifted his head.

"Sidney," Lamar said to Charpentier, "I need your Healing Talent."

"What's the matter?   Got a headache?"

"I don't mean *I* need it.   Maurice does.   He's got one hell of a hangover. I've ordered some caffe from Fred, but I'd like your help.   He hasn't eaten all day, and he has a headache."

"Right.   I'll come along.   We'll have to get some food in him at Marseille." He rose and left with Lamar.

The sorcerer dozed off again.

VIII

When the *Napoli Express* pulled into Marseille at twenty-four minutes after six that evening, Master Seamus had already decided that he needed exercise before he needed food.   He got off the train, went through the depot, and out into the street beyond.   A brisk fifteen-minute walk got his blood going again, made him feel less drowsy, and whetted his appetite.   The tangy air of the Duchy of Provence, given a touch of piquancy by the breeze from the Mediterranean, was an aperitif in itself.

The Cannebiere restaurant—which was nowhere near the street of the same name—was crowded by the time the sorcerer got back.   With apologies to both sides, the waiter seated him at a table with a middle-aged couple named Duprey. Since he was not carrying his symbol-decorated carpetbag, there was no way for them to know that he was a magician, and he saw no reason to enlighten them.

He ordered the specialty of the house, which turned out to be a delicious, thick whitefish stew with lots of garlic.   It went well with a dry white wine of rather pronounced character.

The Dupreys, as the conversation brought out, were the owners of a small leather-goods shop in Versaille who had carefully saved their money to make a trip to Rome, where they would spend a week, leaving the business in the hands of their two sons, each of whom was married to a delightful wife, and one of them had two daughters and the other a son, and . . .

And so on.

The sorcerer was not bored. He liked people, and the Dupreys were a very pleasant couple. He didn't have to talk much, and they asked him no questions. Not, that is, until the caffe was served. Then: "Tell me, Goodman Seamus," said the man, "why is it that we must stop at the Ligurian border tonight?"

"To check the bill-of-lading for the freight cars, I believe," the sorcerer said. "Some Italian law about certain imports."

"You see, John-Paul," said the woman, "it is as I told you."

"Yes, Martine, but I do not see why it should be. We are not stopped at the border of Champagne or Burgundy or Dauphine or Provence. Why Liguria?" He looked back at the magician. "Are we not all a part of the same Empire?"

"Well, yes—and no," Master Seamus said thoughtfully.

"What can you mean by that, sir?" John-Paul said, looking puzzled.

"Well, the Duchies of Italy, like the Duchies of Germany, are a part of the *Holy Roman* Empire, d'ye see, which was established in A.D. 862, and King John IV is Emperor. But they are *not* a part of what is unofficially called the *Anglo-French* Empire, which technically includes only France, England, Scotland, and Ireland."

"But we all have the same Emperor, don't we?" Martine asked.

"Yes, but His Majesty's duties are different, d'ye see. The Italian States have their own Parliament, which meets in Rome, and the laws they have passed are slightly different than those of the Anglo-French Empire. Its acts are ratified, not by the Emperor directly, but by the Imperial Viceroy, Prince Roberto VII. In Italy, the Emperor reigns, but does not rule, d'ye see."

"I—I think so," John-Paul said hesitantly. "Is it the same in the Germanies? I mean, they're part of the Empire, too."

"Not quite the same. They're not as unified as the Duchies of Italy. Some of them take the title of Prince, and some would like to take the title of King, though that's forbidden by the Concordat of Magdeburg. But the general idea's the same. You might say that we're all different states, but with the same goals, under the same Emperor. We all want individual freedom, peace, prosperity, and happy homes. And the Emperor is the living symbol of those goals for all of us."

After a moment's silence, Martine said: "Goodness! That's very poetic, Goodman Seamus!"

"It still seems silly," John-Paul said doggedly, "to have to stop a train at the border between two Imperial Duchies."

Master Seamus sighed. "You should try visiting the Poles—or even the Magyars," he said. "The delay might be as much as two hours. You would have to have a passport. The train would be searched. Your luggage would be searched. Even *you* might be searched. And the Poles do that even when their own people are crossing their own internal borders."

"Well!" said Martine, "I certainly shan't ever go *there*!"

"No need to worry about that," said John-Paul.   "Will you have more caffe, my dear?"

Master Seamus went back to the train feeling very relaxed, thankful that two very ordinary people had taken his mind off his troubles.   He never saw nor heard of either of them again.

IX

By eight o'clock that evening, the *Napoli Express* was nearly twenty-five miles out of Marseille, headed for a rendezvous with the Ligurian border.

The saba game was in full swing again, and Master Seamus had the private feeling that, if it weren't for the fact that no one was permitted in the lounge while the train was in the station, three or four of the die-hards would never have bothered to eat.

By that time, the sorcerer found his eyelids getting heavy again.   Since Father Armand was in deep conversation with two other passengers, Master Seamus decided he might as well go back to the compartment and take his turn on the day couch.   He dropped off to sleep almost immediately.

The sorcerer's inward clock told him that it was ten minutes of nine when a rap sounded at the door.

"Yes?   Who is it?"

"Fred, sir.   Time to make up the bed, sir."

Wake up, it's time to go to sleep, the sorcerer thought glumly as he got his feet on the floor.   "Certainly, Fred; come in."

"Sorry, sir, but the beds have to be made before I go off at nine.   The night man doesn't have the keys, you see."

"Certainly; that's all right.   I had me little nap, and I feel much better.   I'll go on out to the lounge and let you work; there's hardly room in here for two of us."

"That's true, sir; thank you, sir."

There was a new man on behind the bar.   As the sorcerer sat down, he put down the glass he was polishing and came over.

"May I serve you, sir?"

"Indeed you may, me lad.   A beer, if you please."

"One beer; yes, sir."   He took a pint mug, filled it, and served it.

There was no one else at the bar.   The saba game, like the constellations in the sky, seemed unchanged.   Master Seamus entertained a brief fantasy of taking this same trip a hundred years hence and seeing nothing remarkably different about that saba game.   (Young Jamieson had replaced Boothroyd, but Hauser, Tailleur, Herrick, and Vandepole were still at it.)   Master Seamus drank his beer slowly and looked around the lounge.

Sir Stanley Galbraith and Father Armand were seated on the rearward couch, not talking to each other, but reading newspapers which they had evidently picked up in Marseille.

Apparently, Charpentier had managed to cure Zeisler's hangover and get some food in him, for the two of them were sitting at the near table with Boothroyd and Lamar, talking in low tones. Zeisler was drinking caffe.

Mac Kay, Quinte, and Peabody were nowhere in sight.

Then Peabody, with his silver-handled stick, limped in from the passageway. He ordered ouiskie-and-splash and took it to the forward couch to sit by himself. He, too, had a newspaper, and began reading it with his touch-me-not attitude.

The sorcerer finished his beer and ordered another.

After a few minutes, Fred came back from his final duties for the day and said to the night man: "It's all yours, Tonio. Take over." And promptly left.

"No, no; I can get it. I'm closer." It was Zeisler's voice, raised just high enough for the sorcerer to hear it. His chair was nearest the bar. He got up, caffe cup in hand, and brought it over to the bar. "Another cup of caffe, Tonio."

"Yes, sir."

Zeisler smiled and nodded at Master Seamus, but said nothing. The sorcerer returned the greeting.

And then pretended not to notice what Tonio was doing. He set the cup down behind the bar, carefully poured in a good ounce of ouiskie, then filled the cup from the carafe that sat over a small alcohol lamp. It was done in such a way that the men at the table could not possibly have told that there was anything but caffe in the cup.

Zeisler had obviously tipped him well for that bit of legerdemain long before Master Seamus had come into the lounge.

Mentally, the sorcerer allowed himself a sad chuckle. Boothroyd, Lamar, and Charpentier thought they were dutifully keeping Zeisler sober, and here he was getting blotto before their very eyes. Ah, well.

Peabody put down his newspaper and came over to the bar, glass in hand. "Another ouiskie-and-splash, if you please," he said in a very low voice.

It was brought, and he returned to his seat and his newspaper. Tonio went back to polishing glasses.

Master Seamus was well into his third beer when the Trainmaster showed up. He went around and nodded and spoke to everyone, including the sorcerer. He went back to the observation deck, and Master Seamus concluded that Quinte and Mac Kay must be back there.

Trainmaster Edmund came back to the bar, took off his hat, and wiped his balding head with a handkerchief. "Warm evening. Tonio, how are your supplies holding out?"

"We'll have plenty for the rest of the evening, Trainmaster."

"Good; good. But I just checked the utility room, and we're short of towels. These men will be wanting to bathe in the morning, and we're way short. Run up to supply and get a full set. I'll watch the bar for you."

"Right away, Trainmaster." Tonio hurried without seeming to.

The Trainmaster left his cap off and stood behind the bar. He did not polish any glasses. "Another beer, Master Sorcerer?"

"No, thanks, Trainmaster. I've had me limit for a while. I think I'll stretch me legs." He got up off the barchair and turned toward the observation deck.

"How about you, sir?" the Trainmaster called to Peabody, a few feet away, in the forward couch.

Peabody nodded, got up, and brought his glass over.

As Master Seamus passed the table where Zeisler and the other three were sitting, he heard Zeisler say: "You chaps know who that bearded chap at the bar is? I do."

"Maury, will you shut up?" said Boothroyd coldly.

Zeisler said no more.

X

"What is going on out there? A convention?" came the voice of the sorcerer's companion from the lower berth. It was a rhetorical question, so the Master Sorcerer didn't bother to answer.

It is not the loudness of a noise, nor even its unexpectedness, which wakes one up. It is the *unusual* noise that does that. And when the noise becomes *interesting,* it is difficult to go back to sleep.

The rumble and roar of the train as it moved toward Italy was actually soothing, once one got used to it. If it had only drowned out these other noises, all would have been well. But it didn't; it merely muffled them somewhat.

The sorcerer had been one of the last few to retire; only Boothroyd and Charpentier had still been in the lounge when he left to go to his compartment.

The hooded lamp had been burning low, and the gentle snores from the lower berth told him that his compartment-mate was already asleep.

He had prepared for bed and climbed in, only to find that the other man had left his newspaper on the other berth. It had been folded so that one article was uppermost, but in the dim light all he could read was the headline: NICHOLAS JOURDAN RITES TO BE HELD IN NAPOLI. It was an obituary notice.

He put the paper on the nearby shelf and began to doze off.

Then he heard a door open and close, and footsteps moving down the passageway. *Someone going to the toilet,* he thought drowsily. No, for the footsteps went right by his own door to Compartment Number One. He heard a light rap. *Hell of a time of night to go visiting,* he thought. Actually, it wasn't all that late—only a little after ten. But everyone aboard had been up since at least four that morning, some even longer. Oh, well; no business of his.

But there were other footsteps, farther down the corridor, other doors opening and closing.

He tried to get to sleep and couldn't. Things would get quiet for a minute or two, then they would start up again. From Compartment Three, he could hear voices, but only because the partition was next to his berth. There was only the sound; he couldn't distinguish any words. Being a curious man, he shamelessly put his ear to the wall, but could still make out no words.

He tried very hard to go to sleep, but the intermittent noises continued. Footsteps. Every five minutes or so, they would go to Number One or return from there, and, of course, these were the loudest. But there were others, up and down the passageway.

There was little he could do about it. He couldn't really say they were noisy. Just irritating.

He lay there, dozing intermittently, coming up out of it every time he heard something, drifting off each time there was a lull.

After what seemed like hours, he decided there *was* something he could do about it. He could at least get up and see what was going on.

That was when his companion had said: "What's going *on* out there? A convention?"

The sorcerer made no reply, but climbed down the short ladder and grabbed his dressing gown. "I feel the call of nature," he said abruptly. He went out.

There was no one in the passageway. He walked slowly down to the toilet. No one appeared. No one stuck his head out of a door. No one even opened it a crack to peek. Nothing.

He took his time in the toilet. Five minutes. Ten.

He went back to his compartment. His slippers on the floor had been almost inaudible, and he'd been very careful about making any noise. They couldn't have heard him.

He reported what he had found to his compartment-mate.

"Well, whatever they were up to," said the other, "I am thoroughly awake now. I think I'll have a pipe before I go back to bed. Care to join me?"

When they came into the lounge, Tonio was seated on a stool behind the bar. He looked up. "Good evening, Father; good evening, Master Sorcerer. May I help you?"

"No, we're just going out for a smoke," said the sorcerer. "But I guess you've had a pretty busy evening, eh?"

"Me? Oh, no, sir. Nobody been in here for an hour and a half."

The two men went on out to the observation deck. Their conversation was interrupted a few minutes later by Tonio, who slid open the door and said: "Are you sure there's nothing I can get you gentlemen? I have to go forward to the supply car to fetch a few things for tomorrow, but I wouldn't want you to be needing anything."

"No, thanks. That'll be all right. As soon as the good father finishes his pipe, we'll be goin' back to bed."

Twenty minutes later, they did just that, and fell asleep immediately. It was twenty minutes after midnight.

XI

At 12:25, Tonio returned with his first load.   During the daytime, when people were awake, it was permissible to use a handcart to trundle things through the aisles of the long train.   But a sudden lurch of the train could upset a handcart and wake people up.   Besides, there was much less to carry at night.

He carefully put his load of stuff away in the cabinets behind the bar, then went back to check the observation deck to see if his two gentlemen were still there. They were not.   Good; everyone was asleep.

About time, too, he thought as he headed back uptrain for his second and last load.   The gentlemen had certainly been having themselves some sort of party, going from one compartment to another like that.   Though they hadn't made much noise, of course.

Tonio Bracelli was not a curious young man by nature, and if his gentlemen and ladies gave him no problems on the night run, he was content to leave them alone.

The train began to slow, and at thirty minutes after midnight, it came to an easy stop at the check station on the Ligurian border.   The stop was only a formality, really.   The Ligurian authorities had to check the bills of lading for the cargo in the freight cars at the front of the train, but there was no search or actual checking of the cargo itself.   It was all bookkeeping.

Tonio picked out what he needed for the second load, and then stood talking to the Supply Master while the train was stopped.   The locomotive braked easily enough to a smooth stop, but getting started again was sometimes a little jerky, and Tonio didn't want to be walking with his arms full when that happened.   He'd wait until the train picked up speed.

He reached the rearmost car at 12:50, took his load of goods to the bar and stashed them as before.   Then he went to do his last duty until the morning: cleaning out the bathroom.

It was a touchy job—not because it was hard work, or even unpleasant, but because one had to be so infernally *quiet!*   The day man could bang around all he liked, but if the night man did so, the gentlefolk in Four and Five, on each side of the bathroom, might complain.

He went up to the utility compartment, just forward of Number One, got his equipment, went back to the bathroom, and went to work.

When he was finished, he took a final look around to make sure.   All looked fine until he came to the last check.

He looked at the floor.

Strange.   What were those red stains?

He had just mopped down the floor.   It was still damp, but . . .

He stepped to one side and looked down.

The stains were coming from his right boot.

He sat down on the necessary, lifted his right foot, and looked at the bootsole. Red stains, almost gone, now.

Where the devil had they come from?

Tonio Bracelli, if not curious, was conscientious.   After wiping the stains from his boot and checking the other to make sure there were none, he wiped the floor and went out to track down the source of those stains.

"Track" was certainly the word. He had left footprints of the stuff, whatever it was, up and down on the tan floor of the passageway. The darker tracks led uptrain. He followed them.

When he found their source, he lost his composure.

A great pool of what was obviously blood had seeped out from beneath the door of Compartment Number One.

XII

The Irish sorcerer was brought out of his sleep by a banging that almost slammed him awake, and a voice that was screaming: *"Sir! Sir! Open the door! Sir! Are you all right? Sir!"*

Both of the men in Compartment Number Two were on their feet and at the door within two seconds.

But the banging was not at their door, but at the one to their right—Number One. The two men grabbed their robes and went out.

Tonio was pounding his fists on the door of Number One and shouting—almost screaming—at the top of his voice. Down the passageway, other doors were opening.

An arm reached out and a hand grabbed Tonio's shoulder. "Now, calm down, my son! What's the trouble?"

Tonio suddenly gasped and looked at the man who had laid such a firm hand on his shoulder. "Oh, Father! Look! Look at this!" He stepped back and pointed at the blood at his feet. "He doesn't answer! What should I do, Father?"

"The first thing to do, my son, is go get the Trainmaster. You don't have the key to this door, do you? No. Then go fetch Trainmaster Edmund immediately. But mind! No noise, no shouting. Don't alarm the passengers in the other cars. This is for the Trainmaster only. Do you understand?"

"Yes, Father. Certainly." His voice was much calmer.

"Very well. Now, quickly." Then, and only then, did that strong hand release the young man's shoulder. Tonio left—hurriedly, but now obviously under control.

"Now, Master Seamus, Sir Stanley, we must be careful not to crowd around here any more than necessary."

Sir Stanley, who had come boiling out of Number Eight only half a second later than the sorcerer and his companion had come out of Number Two, turned to block the passageway.

His voice seemed to fill the car. "All right, now! Stand away, all of you! You men get back to your quarters! Move!"

Within half a minute, the passageway was empty, except for three men. Then Sir Stanley said: "What's happened here, Father?"

"I know no more than you do, Sir Stanley. We must wait for the Trainmaster."

"I think we ought to—" Whatever it was that Sir Stanley thought they ought to do was cut off forever by the appearance of Trainmaster Edmund, who came running in from the dining car ahead, followed by Tonio, and asked almost the same question.

"What's happened here?"

The magician stepped forward. "We don't know, Trainmaster, but that looks like blood, and I suggest you open that door."

"Certainly, certainly." The Trainmaster keyed back the bolt of Number One.

On Lower One, Goodman John Peabody lay with his smashed head hanging over the edge, his scalp a mass of clotted blood. He was very obviously quite dead.

"I wouldn't go in there if I were you, Trainmaster," said the sorcerer, putting an arm in front of Trainmaster Edmund as he started to enter.

"What? On my own train? Why not?" He sounded indignant.

"With all due apologies, Trainmaster, have you ever had a murder on your train before?"

"Well, no, but—"

"Have you ever been involved in a murder investigation?"

"No, but—"

"Well, again with apologies, Trainmaster, I have. I'm a trained forensic sorcerer. The investigators aren't going to like it if we go tramping in there, destroying clues. Do you have a chirurgeon on board?"

"Yes; the train chirurgeon, Dr. Vonner. But how do you know it's murder?"

"It's not suicide," the sorcerer said flatly. "His head was beaten repeatedly by that heavy, silver-headed walking-stick there on the floor. A man doesn't kill himself that way, and he doesn't do it accidentally. Send Tonio for the chirurgeon."

Dr. Vonner, it turned out, had had some experience with legal cases and knew what to do—and, more important, what *not* to do. He said, after examination, that not only was Peabody dead but, in his opinion, had been dead for at least an hour. Then he said that if he was needed no further, he was going back to bed. The Trainmaster let him go.

"It's nearly two hours yet to Genova," the sorcerer said. "We won't be able to notify the authorities until then. But that's all right; nobody can get off the train while it's at speed, and I can put a preservative spell over the body and an avoidance spell on the compartment."

A voice from behind the sorcerer said: "Should I not give the poor fellow the Last Rites of Holy Mother Church?"

The Irishman turned and shook his head. "No, Father. He's quite dead now, and that can wait. If there's any Black Magic involved in this killing, your work could dissipate all trace of it, destroying what might be a valuable clue."

"I see. Very well. Shall I fetch you your bag?"

"If you would be so good, Reverend Sir."

The bag was brought, and the sorcerer went about his work. The preservative spell, cast with a night-black wand, was quickly done; the body would remain in stasis until the authorities finished their investigation. The sorcerer noted the time carefully, checking his wristwatch against that of the Trainmaster.

The avoidance spell was somewhat more involved, requiring the use of a smoking thurible and two wands, but when it was finished, no one would enter that room, or even look into it of his own free will. "You'd best re-lock that door, Train-master," said the Irish sorcerer. He looked down at the floor. "As for that stain, Tonio has already walked through it, but we'd best not have any more people do so. Would you be so good as to tell the others to stay away from this area until we get to Genova, Sir Stanley?"

"Certainly, Master Sorcerer."

"Thank you. I'll put me bag away now."

XIII

The sorcerer put his symbol-decorated carpetbag down on the floor while his compartment-mate closed the door behind them.

"Now that's what I call stayin' in character, me lord," said Sean O Lochlainn, Chief Forensic Sorcerer for His Royal Highness, the Duke of Normandy.

"What? Oh, you mean offering to perform the Last Rites?" Lord Darcy, the Duke's Chief Investigator, smiled. "It's what any real priest would have done, and I knew you'd get me off the hook." When he did come up out of character, he looked much younger, in spite of the disguising white hair and beard.

"Well, I did what I could, me lord. Now I suppose there's nothing for us to do but wait until we get to Genova, where the Italian authorities can straighten this out."

His lordship frowned. "I am afraid we shall have to do more than that, my dear Sean. Time is precious. We absolutely *must* get that naval treaty to Athens in time. That means we have to be in Brindisi by ten o'clock tonight. And that means we *have* to catch that Napoli-Brindisi local, which leaves fifteen minutes after the *Napoli Express* gets into the station. I don't know what the Genovese authorities will do, but if they don't hold us up in Genova, they most certainly will when we reach Rome. They'll cut the car off and hold the whole lot of us until they *do* solve it. Even if we were to go through all the proper channels and prove who we are and what we're up to, it would take so long that we'd miss that train."

Now Master Sean looked worried. "What do we do if it *isn't* solved by then, in spite of everything we do?"

Lord Darcy's face became impassive. "In that case, I shall be forced to leave you. 'Father Armand Brun' would perforce disappear, evading the Roman Arms-men and becoming a fugitive—undoubtedly accused of the murder of one John Peabody. I would have to get to Brindisi by myself, under cover. It would be difficult in the extreme, for the Italians are very sharp indeed at that sort of work."

"I would be with you, me lord," Master Sean said stoutly.

Lord Darcy shook his head. "No. What would be difficult for one man would be impossible for two—especially two who had been known to have escaped to-gether. 'Master Seamus Kilpadraeg' is a bona fide sorcerer, with bona fide papers from the Duke of Normandy, and, ultimately, from the King himself. 'Father Armand' is a total phony. You can stick it out; I can't. Unless, of course, I want to explode our whole mission.''

"Then, me lord, we must solve the case," the magician said simply. "Where do we start?''

His lordship smiled, sighed, and sat down on the lower bed. "Now, that's more like it, my dear Sean. We start with everything we know about Peabody. When did you first notice him?''

"As I came aboard the train, me lord. I saw the walking-stick he carried. On an ordinary stick there is a decorative silver ring about two inches down from the handle. The ring on his stick was a good four inches below the silver head, the perfect length for the hilt on a sword stick. Just above the ring is an inconspicuous black stud that you press with your thumb to release the hilt from the scabbard.''

Lord Darcy nodded silently. He had noticed the weapon.

"Then there was his limp," Master Sean continued. "A man with a real limp walks with the same limp all the time. He don't exaggerate it when he's walking slowly, then practically lose it when he's in a hurry.''

"Ah! I hadn't noticed that," his lordship admitted. "It is difficult to judge the quality of a man's limp when he is trying to move about on a lurching train car, and I observed him at no other time. Very good! And what did you deduce from that?''

"That the limp was an excuse to carry the stick.''

"And I dare say you are right. Then he needed that stick as a weapon, or thought he would, and was not used to carrying it.''

Master Sean frowned. "How so, me lord?''

"Otherwise, he would either have perfected his limp or not used a limp at all." Lord Darcy paused, then: "Anything else?''

"Only that he carried his small suitcase to lunch with him, and that he always sat in the lounge on the first couch, where he could watch the door of his compartment," Master Sean said. "I think he was afraid someone would steal his suitcase, me lord.''

"Or something in it," Lord Darcy amended.

"What would that be, me lord?''

"If we knew that, my dear Sean, we'd be a great deal closer to solving this problem than we are at this moment. We—'' He stopped suddenly and put his finger to his lips. There were footsteps in the passageway again. Not as loud this time, for the men were wearing slippers instead of boots, but the doors could be heard opening and closing.

"I think the convention has started again," Lord Darcy said quietly. He walked over to the door. By the time he was easing it open, he had again donned the character of an elderly priest. He opened the door almost noiselessly.

Sir Stanley, facing down the car toward the lounge, had his back to Lord Darcy. Through the windows beyond him, the Ligurian countryside rushed by in the darkness.

"Standing guard, Sir Stanley?" Lord Darcy asked mildly.

Sir Stanley turned. "Guard? Oh, no, Father. The rest of us are going into the lounge to discuss this. Would you and Master Seamus join us?"

"I would be glad to. You, Master Sorcerer?"

Master Sean blinked, and, after a moment, said: "Certainly, Father."

XIV

"*Are you* **absolutely** *certain it was murder*?" Gwiliam Hauser's voice was harsh.

Master Sean O Lochlainn leaned back in the couch and narrowed his eyes at Hauser. "*Absolutely* certain? No, sir. Can you tell me, sir, how a man can have the whole front of his head smashed in while lying on a lower berth? *Unless* it is murder? If so, then I may reconsider my statement that I am *reasonably* certain that it was murder."

Hauser stroked his dark-streaked white beard. "I see. Thank you, Master Sorcerer." His sharp eyes looked round at the others in the lounge. "Did any of you—*any* of you—see anything at all that looked suspicious last night?"

"Or *hear* anything?" Lord Darcy added.

Hauser gave him a quick glance. "Yes. Or hear anything."

The others all looked at each other. Nobody said a word.

Finally, the too-handsome Mac Kay leaned back in his chair at the table near the bar and said: "Uh, Father, you and the Master Sorcerer had the compartment next to Peabody's. Didn't either of you hear anything?"

"Why, yes, we did," Lord Darcy said mildly. "We both remarked upon it."

All eyes in the lounge were focused on him now, with the exception of Master Sean's. The sorcerer was watching the others.

"Beginning at about twenty minutes after ten last night," Lord Darcy continued in the same mild voice, "and continuing for about an hour and a half, there was an absolute parade of footsteps up and down that passageway. There was much conversation and soft rappings at doors. There were knockings on the door of Peabody's compartment more than a dozen times. Other than that, I heard nothing out of the usual."

The three-second silence was broken by Sir Stanley. "We were just walking around, talking. Visiting, you know."

Zeisler was over at the bar, drinking caffe. Master Sean hadn't seen it this time, but he was certain Tonio had spiked the cup again. "That's right," Zeisler said in a sudden voice. "Talking. I couldn't sleep, myself. Had a nap this afternoon. Went visiting. Seems nobody else could sleep, either."

Boothroyd nodded. "I couldn't sleep either. Noisy damn train."

At that point all the others joined in—the words were different, but the agreement was there.

"And Peabody couldn't sleep either?" Lord Darcy's voice was bland.

"No, he couldn't," said Sir Stanley gruffly.

"I didn't know any of you knew the gentleman." Lord Darcy's voice was soft, his eyes mild, his manner gentle. "I did notice one of you spoke to him during the day."

"I recognized him," Zeisler said. The ouiskie wasn't slowing his brain down much. "Chap I used to know. Didn't get his name, and didn't recognize him at first, what with the beard. Didn't use to wear a beard, you see. So I went to talk to him—renew old acquaintance, you know. Bit shy at first, but we got along. He wanted to talk to the other chaps, so—" He gestured with one hand, leaving the sentence unfinished.

"I see." His Lordship smiled benevolently. "Then which of you was the last to see him alive?"

Hauser looked at Jason Quinte. "Was that you, Quinte?"

"Me? No, I think it was Val."

"No, Mac talked to him after I did."

"But then Sharpie went back in, didn't you, Sharpie?"

"Yes but I thought Simon—"

And so it went. Lord Darcy listened with a sad but benevolent smile on his face. After five minutes, it was obvious that they could not agree on who had seen Peabody last, and that not one of them wanted to own up to it.

Finally, Gavin Tailleur stood up from his seat in the rearward couch. His face was paler than usual, making the scar more conspicuous. "I don't know about the rest of you, but it's obvious *I* am not going to get any more sleep tonight. I am tired of wandering about in my nightclothes. I'm going back and put some clothes on."

Valentine Herrick, his bright red hair looking badly mussed, said: "Well, I'd like to get some sleep, myself, but . . ."

Lord Darcy, in a voice that seemed soft but still carried, said: "It doesn't much matter what we do now; we won't get any sleep after we reach Genova, and we might as well be prepared for it."

XV

Master Sean wanted to talk privately with Lord Darcy. For one thing, he wanted to know why his lordship had permitted all the passengers in the car to get together to compare stories when the proper procedure would be to get them alone and ask them questions separately. Granted, here in Italy Lord Darcy had no authority to question them; and, granted, he was playing the part of a priest, but—damn it!— he should have done *something*.

But no, he just sat there on the forward sofa, smiling, watching, listening, and saying very little, while the other passengers sat around and talked or drank or both.

There was quite a bit of caffe consumed, but the ouiskie, brandy, wine, and beer were not neglected, either. Master Sean and Lord Darcy stuck to caffe.

Tonio didn't seem to mind.   He had to stay up all night, anyway, and at least he wasn't bored.

Just before the train reached Genova, the Trainmaster returned.   He took off his hat and asked for the gentlemen's attention.

"Gentlemen, we are approaching Genova.   Normally, if you happened to be awake, you could take advantage of the hour stopover to go to the restaurant or tavern, although most people sleep through this stop.

"I am afraid, however, that I shall have to insist that you all remain aboard until the authorities arrive.   The doors will not be opened until they get here.   I am sorry to inconvenience you in this way, but such is my duty."

There were some low mutterings among the men, but nobody said anything to contradict Trainmaster Edmund.

"Thank you, gentlemen," the Trainmaster said.   "I shall do my best to see that the authorities get their work over with as promptly as possible."   He returned his hat to his head and departed.

"Technically," Boothroyd said, "I suppose we're all under arrest."

"No," Hauser growled.   "We are being detained for questioning.   Not quite the same thing.   We're only here as witnesses."

One of us isn't, Master Sean thought.   And wondered how many others were thinking the same thing.   But nobody said anything.

The Genovese Armsmen were surprisingly prompt.   Within fifteen minutes after the train's brakes had made their last hissing sigh, a Master-at-Arms, two Sergeants-at-Arms, and four Armsmen had come aboard.   All were in uniform.

This was merely the preliminary investigation.   Names were taken and brief statements were written down by the Master and one of the Sergeants, apparently the only ones of the seven who spoke Anglo-French with any fluency.   Master Sean and Lord Darcy both spoke Italian, but neither said anything about it.   No need to volunteer information that wasn't asked for.

It was while the preliminary investigation was going on that the two Norman law officers found where each of the other twelve were billeted.

Compartment No. 3 — Maurice Zeisler; Sidney Charpentier
Compartment No. 4 — Martyn Boothroyd; Gavin Tailleur
Compartment No. 5 — Simon Lamar; Arthur Mac Kay
Compartment No. 6 — Valentine Herrick; Charles Jamieson
Compartment No. 7 — Jason Quinte; Lyman Vandepole
Compartment No. 8 — Sir Stanley Galbraith; Gwiliam Hauser

Number Two, of course, contained "Armand Brun" and "Seamus Kilpadraeg" and John Peabody had been alone in Number One.

The uniformed Master-at-Arms made a short, polite bow to Master Sean.   Since he was armed by the sword at his side, he did not remove his hat.   "Master Sorcerer, I believe it was you who so kindly put the avoidance spell and the preservation spell on the deceased one?"

"Aye, Master Armsman, I am."

"I must ask you to remove the avoidance spell, if you please.   It is necessary that I inspect the body in order to determine that death has indeed taken place."

"Oh, certainly, certainly.   Me bag is in me compartment.   Won't take but a minute."

As they went down the passageway, Master Sean saw Trainmaster Edmund standing patiently by the door of Number One, holding the key in his hand.   The sorcerer knew what the Armsman's problem was.   A death had been reported, but, so far, he hadn't seen any real evidence of it.   Even if the Trainmaster had unlocked the door, the spell would have kept both men out and, indeed, kept them from even looking into the compartment.

Master Sean got his symbol-decorated carpetbag out of Number Two, and told Trainmaster Edmund: "Unlock it, Trainmaster—and then let me have a little room to work."

The Trainmaster unlocked the door, but did not open it.   He and the Master-at-Arms stood well back, in front of Number Three.   Master Sean noticed with approval that a Man-at-Arms was standing at the far end of the passageway, in front of Number Eight, facing the lounge, blocking the way.

Himself being immune to his own avoidance spell, Master Sean looked all around the compartment.   Everything was as he had left it.   He looked down at the body. The blood still looked fresh, so the preservative spell had been well cast—not that the stout little Irish sorcerer had ever doubted it, but it was always best to check.

He looked down at the floor near his feet.   The blood which had leaked out into the passageway was dark and dried.   It had not, he noticed, been disturbed since Tonio had tromped through it.   Good.

Master Sean placed his carpetbag carefully on the floor and took from it a small bronze brazier with tripod legs.   He put three lumps of willow charcoal in it, set it on the floor in the doorway, and carefully lit the charcoal.   When it was hot and glowing, he took a pinch of powder from a small glass phial and dropped it on the coals.   A spiral of aromatic smoke curled upwards.   The magician's lips moved silently.

Then he took a four-by-four-inch square of white paper from his bag and folded it in a curious and intricate manner.   Murmuring softly, he dropped it on the coals, where it flared into orange flame and subsided into gray ash.

After a moment, he took a bronze lid from among his paraphernalia and fitted it to the brazier to smother the coals.   He picked up the brazier by one leg and moved it aside.   Then he stood up and looked at the Armsman.   "There you are, Master Armsman; it's all yours."   Then he gestured.   "Watch the bloodstain, here, and watch that brazier.   It's still hot."

The Master-at-Arms went in, looked at the remains of John Peabody and touched one wrist.   He wrote in a notebook.   Then he came out.   "Lock it up again, Trainmaster.   I can now state that a man identified as one John Peabody is dead, and that there is reason to believe that a felony has been committed."

Trainmaster Edmund looked surprised.   "Is that all?"

"For now," the Armsmaster said.   "Lock it up, and give me the key."

The Trainmaster locked the compartment, saying as he did so: "I can't give you a duplicate.   We don't keep them around for security reasons.   If a passenger loses one—" he took the key from the lock "—we get a duplicate either from the

Paris office or the Napoli office.   I'll have to give you one of my master keys.
And I'll want a receipt for it.''

"Certainly.   How many master keys do you have?''

"For this car?   Two.   This one, here, and one that's locked in my office forward
for emergencies.''

"See that it stays locked up.   This key, then, is a master for this car only?''

"Oh, yes.   Each car has separate lock sets.   What are you doing, Master
Sorcerer?''   The Trainmaster looked puzzled.

Master Sean was kneeling by the door, the fingers of his right hand touching the
lock, his eyes closed.   "Just checking.''   The sorcerer stood up.   "I noticed
your lock spell on my own lock when I first used my key.   Commercial, but very
tight and well-knit.   No wonder you don't keep duplicates aboard.   Even an exact
duplicate wouldn't work unless it was attuned to the spell.   May I see that master
key, Armsmaster?   Thank you.   Mmmmm.   Yes.   Thank you again.''   He
handed the key back.

"What were you checking just now?'' the Trainmaster asked.

"I wanted to see if the spell had been tampered with,'' Master Sean explained.
"It hasn't been.''

"Thank you, Master Sorcerer,'' the Master-at-Arms said, making a note in his
notebook.   "And thank you, Trainmaster.   That will be all for now.''

The three of them went on back to the lounge.

There was an empty space on the sofa next to Lord Darcy—who was still playing
"Father Armand'' to the hilt—so Master Sean walked over and sat beside him.

"How are things going, Father?'' he asked in a low, conversational tone.   In
the relative quiet of the stationary car, it was easier to talk in soft voices without
seeming to whisper.

"Interestingly,'' Lord Darcy murmured.   "I haven't heard everthing, of course,
but I've been listening.   They seem to be finished now.''

At that moment, one of the Sergeants-at-Arms said, in Italian: "Master Armsman,
here comes the Praefect.''

Master Sean, like the Armsmaster, turned his head to look out the window.
Then he looked quickly away.

"Our goose is cooked,'' he said very softly to Lord Darcy.   "Look who's
coming.''

"I did.   I don't know him.''

"I do.   It's Cesare Sarto.   And *he* knows *me*.''

XVI

The Roman Praefecture of Police has no exact counterpart in any other unit of
the Empire.   As elsewhere, every Duchy in Italy has its own organization of
Armsmen which enforces the law within the boundaries of that Duchy.   The Roman
Praefecture is an instrumentality of the Italian Parliament to co-ordinate the efforts
of these organizations.

The Praefects' powers are limited.   Even in the Principality of Latium, where Rome is located, they have no police powers unless they have been called in by the local authorities.   (Although a "citizen's arrest" by a Roman Praefect carries a great deal more weight than such an arrest by an ordinary civilian.)

They wear no uniforms; their only official identification is a card and a small golden shield with the letters SPQR above a bas-relief of the Capitoline Wolf, with a serial number and the words *Praefecture of Police* below her.

Their record for cases solved and convictions obtained is high, their record for violence low.   These facts, plus the always gentlemanly or ladylike behavior of every Praefect, has made the Roman Praefecture of Police one of the most prestigious and honored bodies of criminal investigators on the face of the Earth.

In the gaslight of the train platform, Cesare Sarto waited as the Master-at-Arms came out of the car to greet him.   Master Sean kept his face averted, but Lord Darcy watched carefully.

Sarto was a man of medium height with dark hair and eyes and a neatly-trimmed mustache.   He was of average build, but carried himself like an athlete.   There was power and speed in that well-muscled body.   His face, while not exactly handsome, was strong and showed character and intelligence.

After a few minutes, he came into the car.   He put a suitcase on the floor and looked around at the fourteen passengers assembled in the lounge.   They all watched him, waiting.

His eyes betrayed no flicker of recognition as they passed over Master Sean's face.

Then he said: "Gentlemen, I am Cesare Sarto, an agent of the Roman Praefecture of Police.   The Chief Master-at-Arms of the city of Genova has asked me to take charge of this case—at least until we get to Rome."   His Anglo-French was almost without accent.

"Technically," he continued, "this is the only way it can be handled.   John Peabody was apparently murdered, but we do not yet know whether he was killed in Provence or in Liguria, and until we do, we won't know who has jurisdiction over the case.

"As of now, we must act on the assumption that Peabody died *after* this train crossed the Italian border.   Therefore, this train will proceed to Rome.   If we have not determined exactly what happened by then, this car will be detached and the investigation will continue.   Those of you who can be exonerated beyond doubt will be allowed to go on to Napoli.   The others, I fear, will have to be detained."

"Do you mean," Sir Stanley interrupted, "that you suspect one of *us?*"

"No one of you individually, sir.   Not yet.   But all of you collectively, yes. It surely must be obvious, sir, that since Peabody was killed in this car, someone in this car must have killed him.   May I ask your name, sir?"

"Sir Stanley Galbraith," the gray-haired man said rather curtly.

Praefect Cesare looked at his notebook.   "Ah, yes.   Thank you, Sir Stanley." He looked around at the others.   "I have here a list of your names as procured by the Master-at-Arms.   In order that I may know you better, I will ask that each of you raise his hand when his name is called."

As he called off the names, it was obvious that each man's name and face were linked permanently in his memory when the hand was raised.

When he came to "Seamus Kilpadraeg," he looked the sorcerer over exactly as he had the others, then went on to the next name.

When he had finished, he said: "Now, gentlemen, I will ask you to go to your compartments and remain there until I call for you. The train will be leaving for Rome in—" he glanced at his wristwatch "—eighteen minutes. Thank you."

Master Sean and Lord Darcy dutifully returned to their compartment.

"Praefect Cesare," Lord Darcy said, "is not only highly intelligent, but very quick-minded."

"How do you deduce that, me lord?"

"You said he knew you, and yet he showed no sign of it. Obviously, he perceived that if you were traveling under an alias, you must have a good reason for it. And, you being who you are, that the reason was probably a legitimate one. Rather than betray you in public, he decided to wait until he could talk to you privately. When he does, tell him that Father Armand is your confidant and close friend. Vouch for me, but don't reveal my identity. I expect him to be here within minutes."

There came a knock on the door.

Master Sean slid it open to reveal Praefect Cesare Sarto. "Come in, Praefect," the sorcerer said. "We've been expecting you."

"Oh?" Sarto raised an eyebrow. "I would like to talk to you privately, Master Seamus."

Master Sean lowered his voice almost to a whisper. "Come in Cesare. Father Armand knows who I am."

The Praefect came in, and Master Sean slid the door shut. "Sean O Lochlainn at your service, Praefect Cesare," he said with a grin.

"Sean!" The Praefect grabbed him by both shoulders. "It's been a long time! You should write more often." He turned to Lord Darcy. "Pardon me, Padre, but I haven't seen my friend here since we took a course together at the University of Milano, five years ago. 'The Admissibility of Certain Magically Derived Evidence in Criminal Jurisprudence' it was."

"That's all right," Lord Darcy said. "I'm glad for both of you."

The Praefect looked for a moment at the slack-shouldered, white-haired, white-bearded man who peered benignly at him over gold-rimmed half-glasses. Then he looked back at Master Sean. "You say you know the Padre?"

"Intimately, for many years," Master Sean said. "Anything you have to say to me can be said in front of Father Armand in perfect confidence. You can trust him as you trust me."

"I didn't mean—" Sarto cut himself off and turned to Lord Darcy. "Reverend Sir, I did not intend to imply that one of the Sacred Clergy was not to be trusted. But this is a murder case, and they're touchy to handle. Do you know anything about criminology?"

"I have worked with criminals, and I have heard their confessions many times,"

Lord Darcy said with a straight face.   "I think I can say I have some insight into the criminal mind."

Master Sean, with an equally straight face, said: "I think I can safely say that there are several cases that Lord Darcy might not have solved without the aid of this man here."

Praefect Cesare relaxed.   "Well!   That's fine, then.   Sean, is it any of my business why you're traveling under an alias?"

"I'm doing a little errand for Prince Richard.   It has nothing whatever to do with John Peabody, so, strictly speaking, it is none of your business.   I imagine, though, that if you really had to know, His Highness would give me permission to tell you before any case came to trial."

"All right; let that rest for now.   There are some other questions I must ask you."

The questions elicited the facts that neither Master Sean nor "Father Armand" had ever seen or heard of Peabody before, that neither had ever spoken to him, and that each could account for his time during the night.   On being put the direct question, each gave his solemn word that he had not killed Peabody.

"Very well," the Praefect said at last, "I'll accept it as a working hypothesis that you two are innocent.   Now, I have a little problem I want you to help me with."

"The murder, you mean?" Master Sean asked.

"In a way, yes.   You see, it's like this: I have never handled a murder case before.   My field is fraud and embezzlement.   I'm an accountant, not, strictly speaking, an Armsman at all.   I just happened to be in Genova, finishing up another case.   I was going to go back to Rome on this train, anyway.   So I got a teleson call from Rome, telling me to take over until we get there.   Rome doesn't expect me to solve the case; Rome just wants me as a caretaker until the experts can take over."

He was silent for a moment, then, suddenly, a white-toothed, almost impish grin came over his face.   "But the minute I recognized you, an idea occurred to me. With your experience, we just might be able to clear this up before we get to Rome! It would look good on my record if I succeed, but no black mark if I don't.   I can't lose, you see.   The head of the homicide division, Angelo Ratti, will be waiting for us at the station in Rome, and I'd give half a year's pay to see the look on his face if I could hand him the killer when I step off."

Master Sean gawped.   Then he found words.   "You mean you want us to help you nail the murderer *before* we get to Rome?"

"Exactly."

"I think that's a capital idea," said Lord Darcy.

XVII

The *Napoli Express* moved toward Rapello, on its way to Rome.   In a little over an hour, it would be dawn.   At four minutes of noon, the train would arrive in Rome.

First on the agenda was a search of the body and the compartment in which it lay. Peabody's suitcase was in the locker reserved for Lower One, but the key was in the lock, so there was no trouble getting it. It contained nothing extraordinary—only clothes and toilet articles. Peabody himself had been carrying nothing unusual, either—if one excepted the sword stick. He had some loose change, a gold sovereign, two silver sovereigns, and five gold-sovereign notes. He carried some keys that probably fit his home locks or office locks. A card identified him as Commander John Wycliffe Peabody, Imperial Navy, Retired.

"I see nothing of interest there," Praefect Cesare commented.

"It's what *isn't* there that's of interest," Lord Darcy said.

The Praefect nodded. "Exactly. Where is the key to his compartment?"

"It appears to me," Lord Darcy said, "that the killer went in, killed Peabody, took the key, and locked the compartment so that the body wouldn't be found for a while."

"I agree," Cesare said.

"Then the murderer might still have the key on him," Master Sean said.

"It's possible." Praefect Cesare looked glum. "But it's far more likely that it's on or near the railroad tracks somewhere between here and Provence."

"That would certainly be the intelligent thing to do," Lord Darcy said. "Should we search for it anyway?"

"Not just yet, I think. If he kept it, he won't throw it away now. If not, we won't find it."

Lord Darcy was rather pleased with the Praefect's answer. It was the one he would have given, had he been in charge. It was rather irksome not to be in charge of the case, but at least Cesare Sarto knew what he was doing.

"The killer," the Praefect went on, "had no way of knowing that the blood from Peabody's scalp would run under the door and into the passageway. Let's assume it hadn't. When would the body have been discovered?"

"Probably not until ten o'clock this morning," Master Sean said firmly. "I've taken this train before, though not with the same crew. The day man—that's Fred, this trip—comes on at nine. He makes up the beds of those who are already awake, but he doesn't start waking people up until about ten. It might have been as late as half past ten before Peabody was found."

"I see," said Praefect Cesare. "I don't see that that gets us any forwarder just yet, but we'll keep it in mind. Now, we cannot do an autopsy on the body, of course, but I'd like a little more information on those blows and the weapon."

"I think I can oblige you, Praefect," said Master Sean.

The sorcerer carefully inspected the walking stick with its concealed blade. "We'll do this first; it's the easier job and may give us some clue that will tell us what to do next."

From his bag, he took a neatly-folded white cerecloth and spread it over the small nearby table. "First time I've done this on a train," he muttered, half to himself. "Have to watch me balance."

The other two said nothing.

He took out a thin, three-inch, slightly concave golden disk, a pair of tweezers, a small insufflator, and an eight-inch, metallic-looking, blue-gray wand with crystalline sapphire tips.

With the tweezers, he selected two hairs, one from the dead man and one from the silver head of the stick. He carefully laid them parallel, an inch and a half apart, on the cerecloth. Then he touched each with the wand, murmuring solemn spondees of power under his breath. Then he stood up, well away from the hairs, not breathing.

Slowly, like two tiny logs rolling toward each other, the hairs came together, still parallel.

"His hair on the stick, all right," Master Sean said. "We'll see about the blood."

The only sound in the room except the rumbling of the train was the almost inaudible movement of Sarto's pen on his notebook.

A similar incantation, this time using the little golden saucer, showed the blood to be the same.

"This one's a little more complex," Master Sean said. "Since the wounds are mostly on the forward part of the head, I'll have to turn him over and put him flat on his back. Will that be all right?" He directed the question to the Praefect.

"Certainly," Praefect Cesare said. "I have all the notes and sketches of the body's position when found. Here, I'll give you a hand."

Moving a two-hundred-pound dead body is not easy in the confines of a small compartment, but it would have been much more difficult if Master Sean's preservative spell had not prevented *rigor mortis* from setting in.

"There; that'll do. Thank you," the stout little sorcerer said. "Would either of you care to check the wounds visually?"

They would. Master Sean's powerful magnifying glass was passed from hand to hand.

"Bashed in right proper," Sarto muttered.

"Thorough job," Lord Darcy agreed. "But not efficient. Only two or three of those blows were hard enough to kill, and there must be a dozen of them. Peculiar."

"Now, gentlemen," the sorcerer said, "we'll see if that stick actually was the murder weapon."

It was a crucial test. Hair and blood had been planted before on innocent weapons. The thaumaturgical science would tell them whether or not it had happened this time.

Master Sean used the insufflator to blow a cloud of powder over both the area of the wounds and the silver knob on the stick. There was very little of the powder, and it was so fine that the excess floated away like smoke.

"Now, if you'll turn that lamp down . . ."

In the dim yellow glow of the turned-down wall lamp, almost no details could be seen. All was in shadow. Only the glittering tips of Master Sean's rapidly moving wand could be seen, glowing with a blue light of their own.

Then, abruptly, there seemed to be thousands of tiny white fireflies moving over the upper part of the dead man's face—and over the knob of the stick. There were several thin, twinkling threads of the minute sparks between face and knob.

After several seconds, Master Sean gave his wand a final snap with his wrist, and the tiny sparks vanished.

"That's it. Turn up the lights, if you please. The stick was definitely the murder weapon."

Praefect Cesare Sarto nodded slowly, looking thoughtful. "Very well. What's our next step?" He paused. "What would Lord Darcy do next?"

His lordship was standing behind and a little to the left of the Italian, and, as Master Sean looked at both of them, Darcy traced an interrogation point in the air with a forefinger.

"Why, me lord's next step," said the sorcerer as if he had known all along, "would be to question the suspects again. More thoroughly, this time." Lord Darcy held up his forefinger, and Master Sean added: "One at a time, of course."

"That sounds sensible," Sarto agreed. "And I can get away with having you two present by saying that you are Acting Forensic Sorcerer on this case and that you, Reverend Sir, are *amicus curia* as a representative of Holy Mother Church. By the way, are you a Sensitive, Father?"

"No, unfortunately, I am not."

"Pity. Well, we needn't tell them that. Let them worry. Now, what sort of questions do we ask? Give me a case of tax fraud, and I have an impressive roster of questions to ask the people involved, but I'm a little out of my element here."

"Why, as to that . . ." Lord Darcy began.

XVIII

"They are lying," Praefect Cesare said flatly, three hours later. "Each and severally, every single one of the bastards is lying."

"And not very well, either," added Master Sean.

"Well, let us see what we have here," Lord Darcy said, picking up his notes.

They were seated at the rear table in the lounge; there was no one else in the car. Segregation of the suspects had not been difficult; the Trainmaster had opened up the dining car early, and the Genovese Master-at-Arms that Sarto had brought with him was watching over it. The men had been taken from their compartments one at a time, questioned, then taken back to the dining car. That kept them from discussing the questioning with those who hadn't been questioned yet.

Tonio, the night man, had been questioned first, then told to get out of the car and stay out. He didn't mind; he knew there would be no business and no tips that morning.

The Trainmaster had arranged for caffe to be served early in the rear of the dining car, and Lord Darcy had prepared the three interrogators a pot from behind the bar.

At eight o'clock, the stewards had begun serving breakfast in the dining car. It was now nearly nine.

Rome was some three hours away.

Lord Darcy was looking over his transcript of the questioning when the Roman Praefect said: "Do you see the odd thing about this group? That they know each other?"

"Well, some of 'em know each other," Master Sean said.

"No, the Praefect is perfectly right," Lord Darcy said without looking up. "They *all* know each other—and well."

"And yet," Cesare Sarto continued, "they seem anxious that we should not know that. They are together for a purpose, and yet they say nothing about that purpose."

"Master Sean," Lord Darcy said, "obviously you did not read that Marseille newspaper I left on your berth last night."

"No, Father. I was tired. Come to think of it, I still am. You refer to the obituary?"

"I do." Lord Darcy looked at Sarto. "Perhaps it was in the Genova papers. The funeral of a certain Nicholas Jourdan is to be held in Napoli on the morrow."

"I heard of it," Praefect Cesare said. "And I got more from the talk of my fellow officers than was in the paper. Captain Nicholas Jourdan, Imperial Navy, Retired, was supposed to have died of food poisoning, but there's evidence that it was a very cleverly arranged suicide. If it *was* suicide, it was probably dropped by the Neopolitan officials. We don't like to push that sort of thing if there's no crime involved because there's such a fuss afterwards about the funeral. As you well know."

"Hmm," said Lord Darcy. "I didn't know the suicide angle. Is there evidence that he was depressed?"

"I heard there was, but nobody mentioned any reason for it. Health reasons, perhaps."

"I know of another reason," Lord Darcy said. "Or, at least, a possible reason. About three years ago, Captain Jourdan retired from the navy. It was an early retirement; he was still a young man for a captain. Health reasons were given.

"Actually, he had a choice between forced retirement or a rather nasty court-martial.

"Apparently, he had been having a rather torrid love affair with a young Sicilian woman from Messina, and was keeping her in an apartment in Napoli. Normally, that sort of thing doesn't bother the Navy too much, but this particular young person turned out to be an agent of His Slavonic Majesty, Casimir of Poland."

"Ah-*ha!* Espionage rears its ugly head," the Praefect said.

"Precisely. At the time, Captain Jourdan was commanding H.I.M.S. *Helgoland Bay* and was a very popular commander, both with his officers and his men. Obviously, the Admiralty thought well of him, too, or they shouldn't have put him in command of one of the most important battleships of the line.

"But the discovery that his mistress was a spy cast a different light on things. It turned out that they could not prove he knew she was a spy, nor that he had ever told her any naval secrets. But the suspicion remained. He was given his choice.

"A court-martial would have ruined his career with the navy forever, of course. They'd have found him innocent, then shipped him off to some cold little island off on the southern coast of New France and left him there with nothing to do but count penguins.   So, naturally, he retired.

"If, as you suggest, it was suicide, it might have been three years of despondency that accounted for it.''

Praefect Cesare nodded slowly, a look of satisfaction on his face.   "I should have seen it.   The way these twelve men deport themselves, the way certain of them show deference to certain others . . .   They are some of the officers of the *Helgoland Bay*.   And so, obviously, was Peabody.''

"I should say so, yes,'' Lord Darcy agreed.

"The trouble is,'' Sarto said, "we still have no motive.   What we have to do is get one of them to crack.   Both of you know them better than I do; which would you suggest?''

Master Sean said: "I would suggest young Jamieson.   Father?''

"I agree, Master Sean.   He admitted that he went back to talk to Peabody, but I had the feeling that he didn't want to, that he didn't like Peabody.   Perhaps you could put some pressure on him, my dear Praefect.''

Blond, pink-faced young Charles Jamieson was called in.

He sat down nervously.   It is not easy for a young man to be other than nervous when faced by three older, stern-faced men—a priest, a powerful sorcerer, and an agent of the Roman Praefecture of Police.   It is worse when one is involved in a murder case.

Cesare Sarto looked grim, his mouth hard, his eyes cold.   The man he had been named for, Caius Iulius, must have looked similar when faced by some badly erring young centurion more than two millenia before.

"Young man, are you aware that impeding the investigation of a major felony by lying to the investigating officer is not only punishable by civilian law, but that I can have you court-martialed by the Imperial Navy, and that you may possibly lose your commission in disgrace?''

Jamieson's pink face turned almost white.   His mouth opened, but nothing came out.

"I am aware,'' the Praefect continued remorselessly, "that one or more of your superiors now in the dining car may have given you orders to do what you have done, but such orders are unlawful, and, in themselves, constitute a court-martial offense.''

The young man was still trying to find his voice when kindly old Father Armand broke in.   "Now, Praefect, let us not be too hard on the lad.   I am sure that he now sees the seriousness of his crime.   Why don't you tell us all about it, my son?   I'm sure the Praefect will not press charges if you help us now.''

Sarto nodded slowly, but his face didn't change, as though he were yielding the point reluctantly.

"Now, my son, let's begin again.   Tell us your name and rank, and about what you and your fellow officers did last night.''

Jamieson's color had come back. He took a breath. "Charles James Jamieson, Lieutenant, Imperial Navy, British Royal Fleet, at present Third Supply Officer aboard His Imperial Majesty's Ship *Helgoland Bay,* sir! Uh—that is, *Father."* He had almost saluted.

"Relax, my son; I am not a naval officer. Go on. Begin with why you and the others are aboard this train and not at your stations."

"Well, sir, the *Hellbay* is in drydock just now, and we were all more or less on leave, you see, but we had to stay around Portsmouth. Then, a week ago, we got the news that our old captain, who retired three years ago, had died and was being buried in Napoli, so we all got together and decided to form a party to go pay our respects. That's all there is to it, really, Father."

"Was Commander John Peabody one of your group?" the Praefect asked sharply.

"No, sir. He retired shortly after our old captain did. Until yesterday, none of us had seen him for three years."

"Your old captain was, I believe, the late Nicholas Jourdan?" Sarto asked.

"Yes, sir."

"Why did you dislike Commander Peabody?" the Praefect snapped.

Jamieson's face became suddenly pinker. "No particular reason, sir. I didn't like him, true, but it was just one of those things. Some people rub each other the wrong way."

"You hated him enough to kill him," Praefect Cesare said flatly.

It was as though Jamieson were prepared for that. He didn't turn a hair. "No, sir. I didn't like him, that's true. But I didn't kill him." It was as though he had rehearsed the answer.

"Who did, then?"

"It is my belief, sir, that some unknown person got aboard the train during the ten minutes we were at the Italian border, came in, killed the commander, and left." That answer, too, sounded rehearsed.

"Very well," the Praefect said, "that's all for now. Go to your compartment and stay there until you are called."

Jamieson obeyed.

"Well, what do you think, Father?" Cesare Sarto asked.

"The same as you. He gave us some of the truth, but he's still lying." He thought for a moment. "Let's try a different tactic. We can get—"

He stopped. A man in red-and-blue uniform was coming toward them from the passageway. It was Goodman Fred, the day man.

He stopped at the table. "Excuse me, gentlemen. I have heard about the investigation, of course. The Trainmaster told me to report to you before I went on duty." He looked a little baffled. "I'm not sure what my duties would be, in the circumstances."

Before Sarto could speak, Lord Darcy said: "What would they normally be?"

"Tend the bar, and make up the beds."

"Well, there will be no need to tend bar as yet, but you may as well make up the beds."

Fred brightened. "Thank you, Father, Praefect." He went back to the passageway.

"You were saying something about trying a different tactic," Praefect Cesare prompted.

"Ah, yes," said his lordship. And explained.

XIX

Maurice Zeisler did not look any the better for the time since he had had his last drink. He looked haggard and old.

Sidney Charpentier was in better shape, but even he looked tired.

The two men sat in the remaining empty chairs at the rear table, facing the three inquisitors.

Master Sean said: "Goodman Sidney Charpentier, I believe you told me you were a licensed Lay Healer. May I see your license, please." It was an order, not a question. It was a Master of the Guild speaking to an apprentice.

There was reluctance, but no hesitation. "Certainly, Master." Charpentier produced the card.

Master Sean looked it over carefully. "I see. Endorsed by My Lord Bishop of Wexford. I know his lordship well. Chaplain Admiral of the Imperial Navy. What is your rank, sir?"

Zeisler's baggy eyes looked suddenly alert, but he said nothing. Charpentier said: "Senior Lieutenant, Master Seamus."

The sorcerer looked at Zeisler. "And yours?"

Zeisler looked at Charpentier with a wry grin. "Not to worry, Sharpie. Young Jamie must've told 'em. Not your fault." Then he looked at Master Sean. "Lieutenant Commander Maurice Edwy Zeisler at your service, Master Seamus."

"And I at yours, Commander. Now, we might as well get all these ranks straight. Let's begin with Sir Stanley."

The list was impressive:

Captain Sir Stanley Galbraith
Commander Gwiliam Hauser
Lt. Commander Martyn Boothroyd
Lt. Commander Gavin Tailleur
Lt. Commander Maurice Zeisler
Sr. Lieutenant Sidney Charpentier
Sr. Lieutenant Simon Lamar
Sr. Lieutenant Arthur Mac Kay
Sr. Lieutenant Jason Quinte
Lieutenant Lyman Vandepole
Lieutenant Valentine Herrick
Lieutenant Charles Jamieson

*   *   *

"I presume," Lord Darcy said carefully, "that if the *Helgoland Bay* were not in drydock at present, it would have been inconvenient to allow all you gentlemen to leave at one time, eh?"

Zeisler made a noise that was a blend of a cough and a laugh. "Inconvenient, Father? *Impossible.*"

"Even so," Lord Darcy continued quietly, "is it not unusual for so many of you to be away from your ship at one time? What occasioned it?"

"Captain Jourdan died," Zeisler said in a cold voice.

"Many men die," Lord Darcy said. "What made *his* death so special?" His voice was as cold as Zeisler's.

Charpentier opened his mouth to say something, but Zeisler cut him off. "Because Captain Nicholas Jourdan was one of the finest naval officers who ever lived."

Praefect Cesare said: "So all of you were going to the Jourdan funeral—including the late Commander Peabody?"

"That's right, Praefect," Charpentier said. "But Peabody wasn't one of the original group. There were sixteen of us going; we wanted the car to ourselves, you see. But the other four couldn't make it; their leaves were suddenly cancelled. That's how Peabody, the good father, here, and the master sorcerer got their berths."

"You had no idea Peabody was coming, then?"

"None. We'd none of us seen him for nearly three years," Charpentier said.

Almost didn't recognize him," Zeisler put in. "That beard, you know. He'd grown that since we saw him last. But I recognized that sword-stick of his, and that made me look closer at the face. I recognized him. So did Commander Hauser." He chuckled. "Of course, old Hauser would."

"Why he more than anyone else?" the Praefect asked.

"He's head of Ship's Security. He used to be Peabody's immediate superior."

"Let's get back to that sword-stick," Lord Darcy said. "You say you recognized it. Did anyone else?"

Zeisler looked at Charpentier. "Did you?"

"I really didn't pay any attention until you pointed it out, Maury. Of course, we all knew he had it. Bought in Lisbon four, five years ago. But I hadn't thought of it, or him, for three years."

"Tell us more about Peabody," Lord Darcy said. "What sort of man was he?"

Charpentier rubbed his big nose with a thick forefinger. "Decent sort. Reliable. Good officer. Wouldn't you say, Maury?"

"Oh, yes," Zeisler agreed. "Good chap to go partying with, too. I remember one time in a little Greek bar in Alexandria, we managed to put away more than a quart of *ouzo* in a couple of hours, and when a couple of Egyptian footpads tried to take us in the street, he mopped up on both of them while I was still trying to get up from their first rush. He could really hold his liquor in those days. I wonder what happened?"

"What do you mean?" Lord Darcy asked.

"Well, he only had a few drinks yesterday, but he was pretty well under the weather last night. Passed out while I was talking to him."

The Roman Praefect jumped on that. "Then you *were* the last to see him?"

Zeisler blinked. "I don't know. I think somebody else went in to see if he was all right. I don't remember who."

Praefect Cesare sighed. "Very well, gentlemen. Thank you. Go to your compartment. I will call for you later."

"Just one more question, if I may," Lord Darcy said mildly. "Commander Zeisler, you said that the late Peabody worked with Ship's Security. He was, I believe, the officer who reported Captain Jourdan's—er—liaison with a certain unsavory young woman from Messina, thereby ruining the captain's career?" It was a shot in the dark, and Darcy knew it, but his intuition told him he was right.

Zeisler's lips firmed. He said nothing.

"Come, come, Commander; we can always check the records, you know."

"Yes," Zeisler said after a moment. "That's true."

"Thank you. That's all for now."

When they had gone, Praefect Cesare slumped down in his seat. "Well. It looks as though Praefect Angelo Ratti will have the honor of making the arrest, after all."

"You despair of solving the case already?" Lord Darcy asked.

"Oh, not at all. The case is already solved, Reverend Sir. But I cannot make an arrest."

"I'm afraid I don't follow you, my dear Praefect."

A rather sardonic twinkle came into the Italian's eyes. "Ah, then you have not seen the solution to our problem, yet? You do not see how Commander Peabody came to be the *late* Commander Peabody?"

"I'm not the investigating officer here," Lord Darcy pointed out. "You are. What happened, in your view?"

"Well," Cesare said seriously, "what do we have here? We have twelve naval officers going to the funeral of a beloved late Captain. Also, a thirteenth—the man who betrayed that same Captain and brought him to disgrace. A Judas.

"We know they are lying when they tell us that their conversations with him last night were just casual. They could have spoken to him at any time during the day, yet none of them did. They waited until night. Then each of them, one at a time, goes to see him. Why? No reason is given. They claim it was for a casual chat. At that hour of night? After every one of them had been up since early morning? A casual chat! Do you believe that, Reverend Sir?"

Lord Darcy shook his head slowly. "No. We both know better. Every one of them was—and still is—lying."

"Very well, then. What are they lying about? What are they trying to cover up? Murder, of course."

"But, by which one of 'em?" Master Sean asked.

"Don't you see?" The Praefect's voice was low and tense. "Don't you see? It was *all* of them!"

"What?" Master Sean stared. "But—"

"Hold, Master Sean," Lord Darcy said. "I think I see where he's going. Pray continue, Praefect Cesare."

"Certainly you see it, Father," the Praefect said. "Those men probably don't consider it murder. It was, to them, an execution after a drumhead court-martial. One of them—we don't know who—talked his way into Peabody's compartment. Then, when the opportunity presented itself, he struck. Peabody was knocked unconscious. Then, one at a time, each of the others went in and struck again. A dozen men, a dozen blows. The deed is done, and no single one of them did it. It was execution by a committee—or rather, by a jury.

"They claim they did not know Peabody was coming along. But does that hold water? Was he on this train, in this car, by coincidence? That stretches coincidence too far, I think."

"I agree," Lord Darcy said quietly. "It was no coincidence that put him on this train with the others. It was very carefully managed."

"Ah! You see, Master Sean?" Then a frown came over Sarto's face. "It is obvious what happened, but we have no solid proof. They stick to their story too well. We need *proof*—and we have none."

"I don't think you'll get any of them to confess," Lord Darcy said. "Do you, Master Sean?"

"No," said the sorcerer. "Not a chance."

"What we need," Lord Darcy said, "is *physical* proof. And the only place we'll find that is in Compartment Number One."

"We've searched that," Praefect Cesare said.

"Then let us search it again."

XX

Lord Darcy went over the body very carefully this time, his lean, strong fingers probing, feeling. He checked the lining of the jacket, his fingertips squeezing everywhere, searching for lumps or the crackle of paper. Nothing. He took off the wide belt, looking for hidden pockets. Nothing. He checked the boot heels. Nothing.

Finally he pulled on the calf-length boots themselves.

And, with a murmur of satisfaction, he withdrew an object from a flat interior pocket of the right one.

It was a flat, slightly curved silver badge engraved with the double-headed eagle of the Imperium. Set in it was what looked like a dull, translucent, grayish, cabochon-cut piece of glass. But all three men knew that if Peabody's living flesh had touched that gem, it would have glowed like a fire-ruby.

"A King's Messenger," the Praefect said softly.

No one else's touch would make that gem glow. The spell, invented by Master Sorcerer Sir Edward Elmer back in the thirties, had never been solved, and no one knew what sorcerer at present had charge of that secret and made these badges for the King.

This particular badge would never glow again.

"Indeed," Lord Darcy said. "Now we know what Commander Peabody has been doing since he retired from the Navy, and how he managed to retire honorably at such an early age."

"I wonder if his shipmates know," Sarto said.

"Probably not," Lord Darcy said. "King's Messengers don't advertise the fact."

"No. But I don't see that identifying him as such gets us any further along."

"We haven't searched the rest of the room thoroughly yet."

Twenty minutes later, Praefect Cesare said: "Nothing. Absolutely nothing. And we've searched everywhere. What are you looking for, anyway?"

"I'm not sure," Lord Darcy admitted, "but I know it exists. Still, it might have ended up on the track with the compartment key. Hmmm." With his keen eyes, he surveyed the room carefully. Then he stopped, looking at the area just above the bed where the body lay. "Of course," he said very softly. "The upper berth."

The upper berth was folded up against the wall and locked firmly in place, making a large compartment that held mattress and bedclothes safely out of the way.

"Get Fred," Lord Darcy said. "He has a key."

Fred, indeed, had a key, and he had been using it. The beds were all made in the other compartments, the lowers changed to sofas and the uppers folded up and locked.

He couldn't understand why the gentlemen wanted that upper berth unlocked, but he didn't argue. He reached up, inserted the key, turned, and lowered the shelf until it was horizontal, all the time doing his best to keep his eyes off the thing that lay in the lower berth.

"Ahh! What have we here?" There was pleasure in Lord Darcy's voice as he picked up the large leather case from where it lay in the upper berth. Then he looked at Fred. "That'll be all for now, Fred; we'll call you when it's time to lock up again."

"Certainly, Father." He went on about his business.

Not until then did his lordship turn the seventeen-by-twelve-by-three leather envelope over. It bore the Royal Emblem, stamped in gold, just beneath the latch.

"*Uh*-oh!" said Master Sean. "More here than we thought." He looked at Lord Darcy. "Did you expect a diplomatic pouch, Father?"

"Not really. An envelope of some kind. King's Messengers usually carry messages, and this one would probably not be verbal. But this is heavy. Must weigh five or six pounds. The latch has been unlocked and not relocked. I'll wager that means *two* keys on the railroad track." He opened it and lifted out a heavy manuscript. He leafed through it.

"What is it?" Cesare Sarto asked.

"A treaty. In Greek, Latin, and Anglo-French. Between Roumeleia and the Empire." There was a jerkiness in his voice.

Master Sean opened his mouth to say something and then clamped it shut.

Lord Darcy slid the manuscript back into the big leather envelope and clicked the latch shut. "This is not for our eyes, gentlemen. But now we have our evidence. I can tell you exactly how John Peabody died and prove it. You can make your arrest very soon, Praefect."

XXI

There were seventeen men in the observation car of the *Napoli Express* as she rumbled southeast, along the coast of the Tyrrhenian Sea, toward the mouth of the Tiber.

Besides the twelve naval officers, Praefect Cesare, Master Sean, and Lord Darcy, there were also Fred, the day attendant, and Trainmaster Edmund Norton, who had been asked to attend because it was, after all, his train, and therefore his responsibility.

Praefect Cesare Sarto stood near the closed door to the observation deck at the rear of the car, looking at sixteen pairs of eyes, all focused on him. Like an actor taking his stage, the Praefect knew not only the plot, but his lines and blocking.

Father Armand was at his left, seated at the end of the couch. Fred was behind the bar. The Trainmaster was seated at the passageway end of the bar. Master Sean was standing at the entrance to the passageway. The navy men were all seated. The stage was set.

"Gentlemen," he began, "we have spent many hours trying to discover and sift the facts pertaining to the death of your former shipmate, Commander John Peabody. Oh, yes, Captain Sir Stanley, I know who you all are. You and your fellow officers have consistently lied to me and evaded the truth, thus delaying our solution of this deadly puzzle. But we know, now.

"First, we know that the late commander was an official Messenger for His Imperial Majesty, John of England. Second, we know that he was the man who reported to higher authority what he knew about the late Captain Nicholas Jourdan's inamorata, certain facts which his own investigations, as a Ship's Security officer, had brought out. These facts resulted in Captain Jourdan's forced retirement, and, possibly, in his ultimate demise."

His eyes searched their faces. They were all waiting, and there was an undercurrent of hostility in their expressions.

"Third, we know how John Peabody was killed, and we know by whom it was done. Your cover-up was futile, gentlemen. Shall I tell you what happened last night?"

They waited, looking steadily at him.

"John Peabody was a man with enormous resistance to the effects of alcohol, and yet he passed out last night. Not because of the alcohol, but because someone drugged one of his drinks. Even that he was able to fight off longer than was expected.

"Then, when Peabody was unconscious, a man carefully let himself into Peabody's compartment. He had no intent to kill; he wasn't even armed. He wanted to steal some very important papers which, as a King's Messenger, Peabody was carrying.

"But something went wrong. Peabody came out of his drugged stupor enough to realize what was going on. He made a grab for his silver-headed stick. The intruder got it first.

"Peabody was a strong man and a skillful fighter, even when drunk, as most of you know. In the struggle that ensued, the intruder used that stick as a club, striking Peabody again and again. Drugged and battered, that tough, brave man kept fighting.

"Neither of them yelled or screamed: Peabody because it was not in his nature to call for help; the intruder because he wanted no alarm.

"At last, the blows took their final toll. Peabody collapsed, his head smashed in. He was dying.

"The intruder listened. No alarm had been given. He still had time. He found the heavy diplomatic pouch in which those important documents were carried. But what could he do with them? He couldn't stop to read them there, for Tonio, the night man, might be back very soon. Also, he could not carry them away, because the pouch was far too large to conceal on his person, and if Tonio saw it, he would report it when the body was found.

"So he concealed it in the upper berth of Peabody's compartment, thinking to retrieve it later. Then he took Peabody's key, locked the compartment, tossed the key off the train, and went on about his business. He hoped he would have plenty of time, because the body should not have been found until about an hour ago.

"But Peabody, though dying, was not dead yet. Scalp wounds have a tendency to bleed profusely, and in this case, they certainly did. The blood pooled on the floor and ran out under the door.

"Tonio found the blood—and the rest you know.

"No, gentlemen, this was not a vengeance killing as we thought at first. This was done by a man whom we believe to be an agent of, or in the pay of the *Serka*— the Polish Secret Service."

They were no longer looking at Cesare Sarto, they were looking at each other.

Sarto shook his head. "No; wrong again, gentlemen. *Only one man had the key to that upper berth last night!"* He lifted his eyes and looked at the bar.

"Trainmaster Edmund Norton," he said coldly, "you are under arrest!"

The Trainmaster was already on his feet, and he turned to run up the passageway. If he could get to the door and lock these men in—

But stout little Master Sean O Lochlainn was blocking his way.

Norton was bigger and heavier than the sorcerer, but Norton had only seconds, no time for a fight. From somewhere, he produced a six-inch knife and made an underhand thrust.

Master Sean's right hand made a single complex gesture.

Norton froze, immobile for a long second.

Then, like a large red-and-blue sack of wet oatmeal, he collapsed to the deck. Master Sean took the knife from his nerveless fingers as he fell.

"I didn't want him to fall on the knife and hurt himself," he explained, almost apologetically. "He'll come around all right when I take that spell off."

The Navy men were all on their feet, facing Master Sean.

Commander Hauser fingered his streaked beard. "I didn't know a sorcerer could do anything like that," he said in a hushed, almost frightened voice.

"It can't be done at all unless a sorcerer is attacked," Master Sean explained. "All my spell did was turn his own psychic energy back on itself. Gave his nervous system a devil of a shock when the flow was forcibly reversed. It's similar to certain forms of unarmed combat, where the opponent's own force is used against him. If he doesn't attack you, there's not much you can do."

The Roman Praefect walked over to where the Trainmaster lay, took out a pair of handcuffs, and locked Norton's wrists behind his back. "Fred, you had best go get the Assistant Trainmaster; he'll have to take over now. And tell the Master-at-Arms who is waiting at the far end of the passageway to come on in. I want him to take charge of the prisoner now. Captain Sir Stanley, Commander Hauser, do you mind if I borrow Compartment Eight until we get to Rome? Good. Help me get him in there."

The Assistant Trainmaster came back with Fred, and the Praefect explained things to him. He looked rather dazed, but he took charge competently enough.

Behind the bar, Fred still looked shocked. "Here, Fred," the Praefect said, "you need some work to do. Give a drink to anyone who wants one, and have a good stiff one yourself."

"How did you know it wasn't *me* who unlocked that upper berth last night?" Fred whispered.

"For the same reason I knew no one in the other cars on this train did it," Cesare whispered back. "The dining car was locked, and you do not have a key. Tonio did, but he had no key to the berth. Only the Trainmaster has *all* the keys to this train. Now make those drinks."

There were sixteen drinks to serve; Fred went about his work.

Boothroyd smoothed down his white hair. "Just when did the Trainmaster drug Peabody's drink, anyway?"

Master Sean took the question. "Last night, after we left Marseille, when Norton sent Tonio off on an errand. He told Tonio to get some towels, but those towels wouldn't be needed until this morning. Tonio would have had plenty of time to get them after we retired. But Peabody was drinking, and Norton wanted to have the chance to drug him. I've seen how easy it is for a barman to slip something into a drink unnoticed." He did not look at Zeisler.

Sir Stanley cleared his throat. "You said we were all lying, Praefect, that our cover-up was futile. What did you mean by that?"

Lord Darcy had already told Sarto to take credit for everything because "it would be unseemly for a man of the cloth to be involved in such things." So Cesare Sarto wisely did not mention *whose* deductions he was expounding.

"You know perfectly well what I mean, Captain. You and your men did *not* go into Peabody's compartment, one at a time, for a 'friendly chat.' You each had something specific to say to the man who turned in Captain Jourdan. Want to tell me what it was?''

"Might as well, eh? Very well. We were pretty certain he'd been avoiding us because he thought we hated him. We didn't. Not his fault, you see. He did his duty when he reported what he knew about that Sicilian woman. Any one of us would have done the same. Right, Commander?''

"Damn right," said Commander Hauser. "Would've done it myself. Some of us older officers told the captain she was no good for him from the start, but he wouldn't listen. If he was broken-hearted, it was mostly because she'd made a proper fool of him, and no mistake.''

Captain Sir Stanley took up the story again. "So that's what we went in there for, one at a time. To tell him we didn't hold it against him. Even Lieutenant Jamieson, eh, my boy?''

"Aye, sir. I didn't like him, but it wasn't for that reason.''

The Praefect nodded. "I believe you. But that's where the cover-up came in. *Each and every one of you was afraid that one of your group had killed Peabody!''*

There was silence. The silence of tacit assent.

"I watched you, listened to you," the Praefect went on. "Each of you considered the other eleven one by one, and came up with a verdict of 'innocent' every time. But that doubt remained. And you were afraid that I would find a motive in what Peabody did three years ago. So you told me nothing. I must confess that, because of that evasion, that lying, I was suspicious at one time of all of you.''

"By S'n George! Then what made you begin to suspect that Norton was guilty, sir?" asked Lieutenant Valentine Herrick.

"When it was reported to me that the Trainmaster showed up within half a minute after he had been sent for, right after Tonio found the blood. Norton had been awake since three o'clock yesterday morning: what was he still doing up, in full uniform at nearly one o'clock this morning? Why hadn't he turned things over to the Assistant Trainmaster, as usual, and gone to sleep long before? That's when I began to wonder.''

Lieutenant Lyman Vandepole ran a finger over his hairline mustache. "But until you found that pouch, you couldn't be sure, could you, sir?''

"Not certain, no. But if one of you had gone in there with deliberate murder on his mind, he'd most likely have brought his own weapon. Or, if he intended to use that sword-stick, he would have used the blade, since every one of you knew it was a sword-stick. But Norton didn't, you see.''

Senior Lieutenant Simon Lamar looked at "Father Armand." "With all that fighting going on next door, I'm surprised it didn't wake you up, Reverend Sir.''

"I'm sure it would have," Lord Darcy said. "That is how we were able to pinpoint *when* it happened. Tonio left the car to go forward about midnight. At that time, Master Seamus and I were out on the rear platform. I was having a smoke, and he was keeping me company. We went back to our compartment at twenty after twelve. Norton didn't know we were out there, of course, but the killing must have taken place during that twenty minutes. Which means that the murder took place *before* we reached the Italian border, and Norton will have to be extradited to Provence.''

Fred began serving the drinks he had mixed, but before anyone could taste his, Captain Sir Stanley Galbraith said: ''A moment, gentlemen, if you please.   I would like to propose a toast.   Remember, we will have another funeral to attend after the one in Napoli.''

When Fred had finished serving, he stood respectfully to one side, his own drink in his hand.   The others rose.

''Gentlemen,'' said the Captain, ''I give you Commander John Wycliffe Peabody, who did his duty as he saw it and died honorably in the service of his King.''

They drank in silence.

XXII

By twenty minutes after one that afternoon, the *Napoli Express* was twelve miles out of Rome, moving on the last leg of her journey to Napoli.

Lord Darcy and Master Sean were in their compartment, quietly relaxing after an excellent lunch.

''Me lord,'' said the sorcerer, ''are you sure it was right to turn those copies of the treaty over to the Praefecture of Police for delivery to Imperial Naval Intelligence?''

''It was perfectly safe.''

''Well, what's the use of our carrying our copies all the way to Athens, then?''

''My dear Sean, the stuff Peabody was carrying was a sham.   I looked it over carefully.   One of the provisions, for instance, is that a joint Anglo-French-Greek naval base shall be established at 29° 51′ North, 12° 10′ East.''

''What's wrong with that, me lord?''

''Nothing, except that it is in the middle of the Sahara Desert.''

''Oh.''

''Kyril's signature was a forgery.   It was signed in Latin characters, and the Basileus reads and writes only Greek.   The Greek and Latin texts do not agree with each other, nor with the Anglo-French.   In one place in the Greek text, the city of Constantinople is referred to as the capital of England, while Paris is given as the capital of Greece.   I could go on.   The whole thing is a farrago of nonsense.''

''But—*why?*''

''One can only conjecture, of course.   I believe he was a decoy.   Think about it.   Sixteen men all about to go to a funeral, and, at the last minute, four of them have their leaves canceled.   Why?   I feel the Royal touch of His Majesty's hand in there.   I think it was to make certain Peabody got aboard that train with his fellow officers.   It would look like a cover, as though he, too, were going to Jourdan's funeral.

''I think what happened was this: His Majesty found that the *Serka* had somehow gotten wind of our naval treaty with Roumeleia.   But they didn't know it was being signed by Prince Richard as proxy in Rouen, so they started tracing it in

London.   So His Majesty had this utterly nonsensical pseudo-treaty drawn up and sent in with Peabody.   He was a decoy.''

"Did Peabody know that?'' Master Sean asked.

"Highly unlikely.   If a man knows he is a decoy, he tends to *act* like a decoy, which ruins the illusion.   No, he didn't know.   Would he have fought to the death to preserve a phony document?   Of course, being an honorable officer, once that pouch was locked, he would not have opened it, so he did not know its contents.''

"But, me lord!   If he was supposed to be a decoy, if he was supposed to lead *Serka* agents off on a wild goose chase somewhere else while you and I got the real thing safely to Athens—*why was the decoy dumped practically in our laps?''*

"I think,'' said his lordship with care, "that we missed connections somewhere. Other transportation may have—*must* have—been provided for us.   But something must have gone awry.

"Nonetheless, my dear Sean, all will work out for the best.   A murder aboard the *Napoli Express* will certainly hit the news services, but the story will be so confused that *Serka* won't be able to figure out what happened until too late.''

"It would have been even worse confused if Cesare had come out with his conspiracy theory,'' the magician said.   "He's a good man at his job, but he don't know people.''

"His problem,'' Lord Darcy said, "is that he happens to be a master at paper work.   On paper, he can spot a conspiracy two leagues away.   But sentences on paper do not convey the nuances of thought that spoken words do.   A conspiracy is easy to concoct if it involves only paper work, and it takes an expert to find it. But you, as a sorcerer, and I, as a criminal investigator, know that a group of human beings simply can't hold a conspiracy together that long.''

"Aye, me lord,'' the stout little Irishman agreed.   "I'm glad you stopped me. I almost told Cesare to his face that his theory was all foolishness.   Why, that bunch would have given it away before they finished the job.   Can you imagine Zeisler tryin' to keep his mouth shut about somethin' like that?   Or young Jamieson not breaking down?''

Lord Darcy shook his head.   "The whole group couldn't even hide the fact that they were doing something perfectly innocent like assuring an old comrade that they did not think ill of him.   Even more ridiculous than that is the notion that any such group would pick a train to commit their murder on, a place where, to all intents and purposes, they would be trapped for hours.   Those men are not stupid; they're trained naval officers.   They'd either have killed Peabody in Paris or waited until they got to Napoli.   They still couldn't have held their conspiracy together, but they would have thought they had a better chance.''

"Still and all,'' Master Sean said staunchly, "Cesare Sarto is a good investigator.''

"I must agree with you there,'' said Lord Darcy.   "He has the knack of finding answers even when you don't want him to.''

"How do you mean, me lord?''

"As he and Praefect Angelo were taking Norton away, he offered his hand and thanked me. I said the usual things. I said I hoped I'd see him again. He shook his head. 'I am afraid,' he said, 'that I shall never see Father Armand Brun again. But I hope to meet Lord Darcy some day.' "

Master Sean nodded silently.

The train moved on toward Napoli.

GARY D. McCLELLAN

Darkside

O f course, Desolation Row is larger now. The old single-dome has been replaced by Deso Center and there are another dozen settlements scattered around the planet. The mining trade and our small spaceport has rated us an "IN" prefix in the Galactic Navigational Aids & Position Atlas. A small achievement in itself, but it all depends on how you look at things. For "IN," read: Inhabited World, or Friendly, or Food, Fuel, and Lodging. We even have our own com satellite, though we did go about getting it the hard way, and of course there's Kelly's Beacon and the school. A few tourists show up around here just to see the school and Desolation's stark scenery although we are way the hell and gone off the commercial lanes.

All in all, Desolation has grown quite a bit in the last few years. Deso Center is as metropolitan as damn near anyplace in the galaxy. Above-ground swimming, parks, holo theaters, bars, whorehouses, all guaranteed to convince the patrons that they're a little less bored than they really are.

Me, I'm just a little crazy, I guess, or at least that's what some people tell me. But then again, Kelly always said that a person had to be a little crazy in the first place in order to be sane at all. Sanity is a conscious choice, and I still have a habit of going up to Horizon's End and watching darkside come on in order to relax. That's one thing that doesn't change.

Desolation's tectonic activity has produced some spectacular terrain, like the uplifted jags and spires of Horizon's End. Although we don't have any real weather to speak of, the atmosphere at least produces enough light winds to blow the rock faces clean, so it's not like being on a completely airless world where you have a regolith problem; meteoric splash dust covering everything on the planet.

The atmosphere was thin here long before the first survey team sat down. The planet masses only around .57 standard with a surface gravity of .75. The atmosphere is mostly CO_2 and nitrogen, with enough carbon monoxide and other stray unbreathables to make your eyes cross in a hurry.

Desolation Row: barren rock and barren air, so darkside comes on quick. The shadows lengthen until they streteh into frayed streaks of twisted greys, and then darkside hits, a wall of shadow black twisting and puddling over the rounded and jagged outlines of the landscape, hugging the ground like some slick terrestrial reptile in pursuit of the sun.

Like I said, I'm a little crazy, but I'm not small-minded, and I figure I'm as tolerant as the next guy and I know there are a lot of folks that have seen a lot of things that a lot of other folks, including myself, will never see.   Now excuse my rambling, but there's one more thing: don't call it night, because it isn't.   It's darkside, and it always will be.   It's one of those things that doesn't change, something you can always depend on; a constant, as Kelly would say.

The point is, when you're sitting in some high place looking outward, lightside, in its brightness, becomes hypnotic.   The images blur the eye and become a muted glare.   Then darkside comes on and reality redefines itself with the racing movement of light into darkness, a passage of primal contrasts that snap all the images riding the chiseled edge of a planet's whirling into focus.   If you haven't experienced it, let me recommend it to you.   But a word of caution; don't blink, and don't change your line of vision more than a few degrees at a time.   If you do, the falling shadows will shift on you, rippling and twisting in the optic nerves, and arrive in the mind as a surreal caricature of defined sight.

So I go up to Horizon's End to relax, and it always reminds me of Kelly. Darkside and Kelly are a lot alike.   They both demand your attention.

I met Kelly my second day at Deso Prime—that's what we called the old single-dome mining operation in those days.   We were still fairly primitive then, running the site with used, low-budget equipment.   The company has never been very big on spending credits until they could be sure the returns would justify the expense. The analysis equipment was at least ten years old, but even if it took a tech twice as long to run an assay, the cost of paying his salary was a damn sight cheaper than the cost of new gear.   We had three jump boats that looked like relics from a museum display.   They flew well enough but were about as fast as the company's pay raises.   Of course we really didn't mind very much.   We weren't out here to get rich, just out here to get out.

Desolation Row was quiet and that's what most of us wanted.   Ed Sears had been one hell of a deep space navigator before he sold his soul to the juice man. He was maintenance chief for the boats and as long as his happy supply held out, he was perfectly content.   Jake was a good drillman and funny as hell, until his eyes would go cold sometimes.   We'd pretty much leave him alone when he got that way and wait for him to jolly back up.   Never did find out what Jake's last name was.   I didn't ask and I guess he didn't feel like telling anyone and of course it wasn't any of our business anyway.   Me, I was twenty at the time and trying to get some experience under my belt.   I figured I could work my way up to deep space rams and had hired on as co-pilot trainee on the jump boats.   That was about as close as I ever came, but then everybody can't be a hero.   And like I said, that's when I met Kelly.

Kelly was a scummer, from the slums of Earth.   He was tight-mouthed about it but told me enough to convince me I sure the hell wouldn't want to live there. If Kelly loved anything, it was rock.   He was one of our field geologists, although I don't know where he got the training, and he was good.   During off hours at Deso Prime, we used to play chess every now and then and Kelly would talk mostly about his work.   He had a thing for what he called constants.   He used to say that chess was one, and of course, rock.

"Starn," he'd say to me, "you have to have constants to believe in.   It keeps you stable.   Take rock for instance.   It's a constant in the universe.''   About then, he'd usually finger the gold medallion he wore, moving it back and forth on the chain that hung around his neck.   He'd kind of squint out from under those matted eyebrows of his, gray eyes sort of cool, like fog, and he'd say, ''People, hell, I don't know about them.   They're too damn complicated to figure out.   But rock, now that's a constant.   No matter if it's right there in front of you or thirty parsecs away to the where-ever, basalt is basalt, and you can count on it to have the same properties.''

He'd grin then and study the chessboard for a while.   I've never figured out whether he was tickled at his own philosophy or at his next move, but he'd grab one of his pieces in a battered hand, the knuckles all scarred and lumpy, and set it down hard where he wanted it.   He didn't move like those pros you see on the holos, afraid of disturbing the board.   When Kelly moved, he damn well wanted you to know it, so as he'd go about destroying my defense, the pieces would always walk-the-dog a little in their squares.

Of course there were times when he was quiet, too.   The day we set the beacon, he didn't say much at all.   We'd been out for a full five days looking for new outcrops to prospect and hadn't really found a damn thing.   We were running low on air and water by then and decided to head back for the dome.   Instead of going the long way around, we figured to jump over Horizon's End on a straight line run and save a few hours.

Jump boats are slow, but they have to be, otherwise we'd miss the mineral deposits we were looking for.   Ours flew well enough, though, and was stout. It didn't seem to be a bit skittish about Horizon's End, a fifteen hundred meter climb over uplifted shattered rock.

We were just beginning to crest the upper ridges when whatever it was that let loose in the engine room came apart.   We still had around quarter power or I wouldn't have gotten her down at all.   There was a shudder, and the controls turned to mush in my hands.   And there was noise; loud.   All I can say is that it was a damn good thing that I was flying her at the time.   Frank had bought an alloy sliver through his back that protruded out of his chest a full three centimeters. Blood, bright and red, was splattered to hell and back over the consoles.

The response went from mush to rusted iron and all I could do was try and hold her steady while she picked her own spot.   We didn't come down real hard because the lift fields were still holding, but when we hit, the rest of the engine room let go, blowing outboard.   Shorty was pretty much dead already, so I guess it didn't really matter.   There was very little left of him and even less left of the engines. Then naturally, damn the luck, our main power went.

The fields died slowly, with a whistle that became lower and lower as if the planet's mass was sucking the sound into its core.   They finished with a whisper, leaving only a creak and occasional shiver as the boat settled into powder and rock.

I felt heavy in the crash chair, the harness straps glued to my shoulders.   I should have called for reports on damage, activated bulkhead seals, hit the beeper, killed the drive switch and about fifty other things that are drilled into you for emergency situations.   I didn't.   Instead, I closed my eyes for a while, realizing that I was still alive and then opened them, thinking things would be different.

They weren't.   I was sitting in a broken boat on broken rock and I watched the needle of the power gauge drift toward zero as the amber glow of the auxiliary indicators came on.   I knew the forward section of the ship was still tight or I wouldn't have been watching anything.   It was just too damn much effort to climb out of the chair, so I stayed there, at least until I felt a hand on my shoulder.   It was Kelly.   He had been strapped into a sleeper hammock and seemed to be all right.   He helped me get the harness off and then we checked out the boat, moving slowly through the wreckage.

We found Dak behind his analyzer, crumpled, blood on his arms and forehead, but breathing.   We had him cleaned up and semiconscious when Stef crawled out of the crapper on his hands and knees muttering a string of curses punctuated by groans.   He'd been sitting on the can when the engines blew and had been attempting to stand up when we hit.   It must have been a damn awkward position and could have been very funny at any other time, but it wasn't then.   He was lucky he had gotten by with just a broken leg.   After splinting the leg and giving him a hypo of morphonol for the pain, we put him in a hammock.   All we could do for Frank was load him into one of those big plasti-foil sample bags and carry him aft to the cargo hold for cremation back at the dome.

Frank and Shorty might have taken the easiest way out.   Truth was, we were about as well off as a one-legged mongoose in a cobra pit.   That was one of Kelly's favorite expressions.   He told me he picked it up back on earth, in some out-of-the-way place called Nepal.   It has something to do with some kind of terrestrial animals, but simply stated it meant this: we were in trouble up to our necks.

First off, we were down in a broken boat.   Emergency power is fine to run low-energy components like fans, lighting, heaters, coolers, and such, but that's the limit.   The engines were scattered to hell and gone with not enough pieces large enough to even think about repairing.   We were down on Horizon's End when we should have been three hundred kilos to the north.   Not so terrible in itself, but we were on the wrong side of the summit.   One hundred and sixty meters of vertical rock was sitting between Deso Prime and our boat.   We had come down in the upper region of Horizon's End in a half crater that Kelly said must have been the blown-out throat of an ancient volcano.   If we could have signaled Deso Prime, everything would have been fine.   Ever try to push a radio beam through solid rock?   Forget it, it doesn't work, especially on emergency power.   The dust buggies were still operational but at twenty kilometers per hour it would take days to work our way down the slopes of the range and then three hundred kilos north around the foothills and back to the dome.   We carried spare air tanks for our suits on board, but we were far from being equipped for a long cross-country trek.

We had a small com-laser beacon on the boat that was still operational and would have worked out very well if we could have gotten it to the top of the rock wall that separated us from the dome, but nobody was about to sprout wings.   Basically, we were all about ninety-nine percent dead already and just didn't want to admit it.   The other one per cent was the possibility that one of the other boats would find us.   With that kind of odds, I sure as hell wouldn't have bet on it.

There's one thing I will bet on.   Sitting around waiting to die is not one of the greater joys of life. We all had our individual ways of doing it. Dak was as good as dead before he hit Desolation, anyway. He just stared off into space and wouldn't talk to anyone, even when asked a question. He sat by our silent radios and was silent himself.

Stef decided that his busted leg was too painful to bear. He remedied the situation by loading himself up with morphonol each time the previous shot would wear off enough to let his eyes uncross. Me, I sat around and thought of all the many and various things that I should have done. Coming to Desolation Row was not one of them.

Kelly's reaction was at least more entertaining. He was slowly going vac-happy. At least at the time, I thought he was. The landing had banged up our work suits and the locker they were stored in quite a bit. The first thing that Kelly did was pull out his suit and drag it back to the cargo hold where there was room to work on it. The corridor that bypassed the engine room was still pressurized, so he could get back and forth without too much trouble. The only decent equipment we owned were the suits. A suit was designed to fit one individual and no one else. An all-sizer is good enough to wear when you're ambling around a tourist planet taking in the sights, but you'd sweat your eyes out trying to work in one.

The tank fittings on Kelly's suit were sprung and there was a nasty rip down the right leg; but he slapped a patch on it while I was checking on Stef's leg; and, after a lot of banging and pounding around and a brief amount of torch work, he had the air system on the suit operational. I thought he planned on climbing into the suit when the ship's air started to fail so that he could cheat Desolation out of a few more hours. I was wrong, though. He got into the suit, all right, but the crazy bastard fired up one of the dust buggies and bounced out over the landscape to look at the crater wall.

He was smiling when he returned to the boat, but in that same grim way he had right before he'd lower the curtains on you in a chess game.

"That's fine-grained basalt out there, Starn," he said, as if somehow that made a difference. "Lots of crack systems," he continued. "It's real nice rock."

So I ask you, how in the hell was that supposed to help us out? I asked him myself but he just headed towards the aft end of the boat and ignored me. I followed him and watched as he grabbed a few wrenches and started taking apart the reducer, a piece of gear that breaks down rock samples into coarse dust that can be fed into the analyzer for mineral classification. He didn't actually take it apart, but every place he found a nut, he would unscrew it and lay it on the decking with all the others he had taken off. He had thirty or so removed when he put the wrenches down and headed for the cargo hold. Like I said, at least he was entertaining.

In the cargo hold, he pulled off close to forty meters of flexiweave cable that we use to tie up sample bags, strap large pieces of rock down with and about a hundred other things like winching out dust buggies when they bog down. The stuff is stored on two hundred meter spools and we always carried plenty of it on board. He cut it with hydraulic shears, but they're a bitch to use on cable so he finally lit up the torch and started whacking off two meter lengths of flexiweave from the spool.   When he had fifteen or so pieces cut, he shut off the torch and picked them up, motioning to me to pick up the forty meter coil and follow him.

Now, flexiweave is light for its strength, but at that point I didn't feel like carrying a damn thing.   I did, though, since I'd always heard that it was safer to humor a maniac.   Less chance of personal harm that way.   But then again, I suppose you tend to listen to people like Kelly, even when they do appear to be going off the deep end.

Kelly picked up the nuts he had removed from the reducer and headed towards the control room.   When he arrived, he arranged the nuts in front of him on the deck, divided into different piles of larger and smaller sizes.   I dropped the flexiweave, and he looked up at me as though he had almost forgotten I was there.

"Well, don't just stand there," he said.   "Go check out your suit."

So what the hell; I checked out my work suit.   Fortunately, it was stored between the other suits in the locker and had survived intact.   Helmet pressurization was O.K. and the oxygen demand seemed to be functioning properly.   Desolation's atmosphere is point two standard, so the suits only have to be gas tight and not vac-tight, which means they're flexible enough to work in.   They are light in weight, one piece except for the helmet which is self-sealing at the neck, and non-conductive.   And yes, they are bright metallic orange, just like you've seen in the holos.

I made sure the temperature control and radio were operational and then hung my suit back in the locker and returned to the control room.   Kelly was just finishing threading the nuts onto the two meter lengths of flexiweave.   He'd put two nuts of different size on each piece of flexiweave, then tied the ends of the flexiweave together to form a loop.   The remaining pieces of flexiweave were tied into loops, minus nuts, and tossed into a smaller pile on the deck.

"What now, Kelly?" I asked.

"Is your suit operational?" he said.

"Yeah, its O.K."

"Good.   Now go find me as many cargo clips as you can and bring them up."

"Where the hell am I supposed to get them?" I asked, puzzled.

"Take them off the wall," he said, as though I was supposed to read his damn mind or something.   He turned his attention back to the flexiweave and ignored me in silence.   So what do you do with a guy like that?   I walked back to the cargo hold and wondered how I was going to get the clips off.

Cargo clips are hook-like affairs that have a spring bar that pivots from the straight side of the shaft and forms a gate between the shaft end and the end of the curving hook.   When you're tying down samples or equipment, instead of threading the tie-down loops through eye bolts, it's much easier and faster to just snap the loops over a cargo clip.   The spring-loaded bar gives way for the hold-down and then clicks back into place and secures the straps from coming detached from the clips.   The clips were riveted to the wall and deck plates of the cargo hold.   The floor clips were battered from constant use and sliding equipment.   The ones on the wall were in better shape, and following Kelly's example with the flexiweave, earlier, I fired up the torch and cut the wall clips loose from their mounting rivets.

Out of the two dozen or so clips on the wall, I was able to remove only fifteen intact.   The others were cut through as I tried to burn out the rivets and, I assumed, were useless for whatever Kelly had in mind.   I carried them back to the control room and dumped them on the deck with the rest of the gear Kelly had collected.

"How many?" he asked.

He swore softly when I told him.   He looked down at his hands, rubbing the knuckles of one in the palm of the other.   His fingers tightened into a fist, then he flexed them open, and I thought for a moment he was going to take a swing at me, but he continued to stare at his fingers as though waiting for a message only he could read.   He finally shook his head and in a barely audible voice said, "Well, I guess we take what we can get.   It'll just have to do."

He picked up a few of the clips and tested the spring action by pushing in the gate with his thumb and then letting it snap back into place.   He snapped two loops of flexiweave strung with nuts on to each clip until he had five clips filled, then snapped the filled clips onto one of the remaining loops.   The rest of the clips were snapped together into chains of three and clipped onto the same loop holding the rest of the gear.   Kelly placed the whole affair over his head when he was finished, shoving his arm through the loop so that the clips and cable hung against his left side.   He stood up and shook himself, bending over and then straightening back up, checking to see how the contraption lay against his body.   When he noticed me watching, he burst into laughter.

"Damnedest rack I ever carried," he said.   "But it will do, I guess."

"Will do for what?" I asked.

"I'll show you when the time comes," he answered, "but we better get to it. I hate like hell to climb in the dark."

He turned and picked up the remaining loops and forty-meter coil and moved off.   I hesitated then, not knowing whether to follow him or not when he suddenly turned and yelled, "God damn it, Starn, come on.   We haven't got forever."

In the cargo hold he dumped his equipment onto the dust buggy, then moved to the com beacon and pulled it out of its storage rack.   The beacon was used to set up direct communication between field sites and the ship once the field team was out of suit-radio range.   It was a portable unit around a meter high and shaped like a slender pyramid, the power pack acting as a weighted base to keep it upright. The beacon emitted a pulse every five seconds when activated.   Centered halfway between the base and the transmitting head was a small transceiver with a continuous beam override.   The transceiver could be plugged into the outside jacks of our suit radios and used to communicate directly with the ship.

Kelly loaded the beacon into the dust buggy and then pulled off another fifty meters of flexiweave from the storage spool.   He loaded the flexiweave and four full replacement air units into the buggy as well.

"I guess that about does it," he said, and glanced around the cargo hold, checking for anything he may have overlooked.   "Let's suit up."

I was halfway into my suit when I suddenly recalled one of Kelly's statements in a flash of understanding: ". . . I hate like hell to climb in the dark."   It made sense to me now, the beacon and the flexiweave and the spare air.   The crazy bastard was actually going to try and climb the barrier between us and Deso Prime. I had no urge to be an accessory to suicide.   There was no way he'd make it, even in Desolation's lighter gravity. With a fully rigged suit, he'd be moving around about the same as an unburdened man on a one-G world. A fall would crush him like a broken puppet. "Kelly," I said, "wait . . ."

But he cut me off by walking over and smoothly zipping the sealing strip of my suit up to the collar. "Don't worry, Starn," he said, "you're going to have the time of your life."

He grabbed my helmet and had it in place over my head before I could argue with him. He immediately moved to the control unit on the wall of the cargo hold and started spilling air out of the exhaust vents. My helmet filled with air as I activated the demand valve out of reflex. The neck seals settled together with a soft sigh. "What the hell ya trying to do, kill me?" I screamed. Kelly just laughed, his voice distorted and metallic through the suit radios.

"Trying to keep you from dragging your feet," he said. "Come on, let's go." He activated the lock control and I watched the inner hatch cycle open. He cycled the outer hatch and the cargo hold stood open to the poison atmosphere of Desolation's surface. He climbed into the dust buggy and I followed, knowing I could do little else. With the cycling of the cargo hatch, the corridor hatch leading to the forward section of the boat had sealed automatically. There was no way I could return to the control room without first flushing the hold and refilling it up to standard. Our storage tanks were already dangerously low, and the amount of air needed to fill the hold would simply reduce the life span of Dak, Stef, and myself even further. Kelly had me as a partner on his fool's errand whether I liked it or not.

As we rolled out of the hold onto the planet's rugged surface, the soft hum of the suit coolers came on. I looked out at our objective through the darkening visor of my helmet. The rock wall we were headed towards stood above us in vertical indifference, harsh and jagged in the lightside brightness of Desolation's sunside rotation. Cracks and irregularities ran across its surface like black print on a grey page, a giant obituary for anyone foolish enough to try and ascend its height. But then, perhaps Kelly had the right idea. I hadn't looked forward to slowly choking to death in the jump boat. At least this way, we were still trying.

We rolled up to the base of the wall and stopped. Kelly climbed out of the buggy, apparently in a happy mood, whistling to himself. He pulled the gear sling holding the clips and flexiweave and nuts over his arm and helmet. We lifted the beacon out of the buggy and he tied one end of the fifty-meter length to the beacon's top. He tied the other end of the cable to one of the equipment loops on the outside of his suit. He tied one end of the forty-meter flexiweave around his middle and then motioned me to come closer from where I stood in front of the buggy. I walked over to him and he ran the other end of the flexiweave around the waist of my suit and tied it securely.

"O.K., buddy," he said, "we're just about ready. Now listen to what I say, because your life is going to depend on it. All right?" He grinned at the resigned look that must have shown on my face as I nodded agreement.

"Now then, this isn't flexiweave, it's rope," he said, shaking the flexiweave at me. "I don't want to hear you call it anything else till we get to the top."

He held up the flexiweave that was connected to the beacon, and continued,

"This is the haul line, and don't call one of them the other because they aren't. This one's the rope, this one's the haul line." He shook the two lengths of flexiweave at me once more to make his point. "Ya got that?"

"Yeah, Kelly, I've got that," I replied.

"All right, then," he went on, and he held up one of the loops of flexiweave with the machine nuts threaded on it. "This," he said, pointing at a nut, "is obviously a nut, right?"

"Right," I agreed, feeling like a three-year-old kid who was being taught how to play a new game.

"And this is a sling," he said, waving the flexiweave that the nuts were on at me. "And these are biners," he went on, holding up a cargo clip.

My bewilderment exploded into anger. "What the hell do you mean, biners!" I yelled. "The damn things are cargo clips and what difference does it make what the hell you call them anyway?"

"It makes a lot of difference," he said softly, cutting off my outburst. "Believe me, it makes a lot of difference, but I'll make a concession since you probably think I'm out of my mind. We'll call them clips and let it go at that."

"I'm sorry, Kelly," I said, "but it's just that you're going to fall off this damn thing and kill yourself, so I don't see what difference the terminology makes."

"No, you're wrong. I'm not going to fall off, and even if I do, you're going to hold me."

"How the hell am I going to do that?" I asked.

He moved to where the wall rose from the broken surface we stood on. "O.K.," he said, "here's how it works. Now watch."

He took one of the slings and inserted a nut into a crack in the rock. He moved it downward until the crack narrowed and the nut was wedged securely between the two sides of the crack. He gave the sling a sharp downward tug and then snapped a clip onto it. He then snapped the rope, as he called the flexiweave, into the clip.

"This is what's known as protection, Starn. After I've placed a nut, and I climb above it and happen to fall, I'll only fall as far as this nut happens to be below me, because you'll be holding me on the other end of the rope, got it?"

"Yes, I think so," I said.

"Good. Now when you start climbing after me, I'll be holding the rope above you, and the most you'll be able to do is slip five r six centimeters downward."

"But what if I can't hold you?"

"Don't worry," he said, "you will. We'll have you anchored so you can't be pulled from your position. Now take about two meters of the rope you're tied to and make an overhand loop. All right now," he said, after I had carried out his request, "clip the loop to the front of the buggy and then sit down."

After I was on the ground, he flipped the rope around and behind me.

"Now then," he said, "you must feed the rope out to me, and if I should fall, just bring your hand holding the free end across your chest, and the friction of the rope on your suit combined with the grip you have on the rope will stop me. Just one more term, Starn. What you're engaged in is the ancient and noble art of belaying. When you're holding me with the rope, I'm on belay, and when you're not, I'm off belay. You understand?''

"I understand," I said. "I just hope to hell that this rock wall understands."

"It will." And with that, he started up the rock. He moved slowly, but with a grace I had not seen before. He moved alongside a crack with a smooth rhythm, rising in short steps from resting place to resting place. I could hear his heavy breathing over the suit's radio, but that was all. He was silent as he climbed, and I realized that this was not the first time that Kelly had been on rock. Some of the fear eased back into the less conscious areas of my mind.

Kelly would stop occasionally and place a nut into a crack and clip the rope into it, and although he never looked down and I could not see his face through the reflected light of the helmet visor, I felt sure he was smiling.

At last he stopped. "Off belay," he said, and started to haul the beacon up towards him. The beacon bounced and swung going upward, but nothing short of a long drop would harm its rugged construction. "Haul line!" he called, and I dodged as the coils of the haul line dropped back toward me.

"Hook the tanks to the haul line," he said, "and then untie from the buggy and come on up. It'll take both of us to haul up the tanks."

I unclipped the rope and moved hesitantly toward the rock after hooking up the tanks to the haul line. There was nowhere to go but up, I thought, and stepped onto the rock, feeling the gravity pulling me downward. "I'm climbing, Kelly," I said.

"Belay on," came back from Kelly.

Kelly kept the rope tight as I climbed, crawled and panted up the rock. So far, it had not gone badly; and I was beginning to believe we might actually make it to the top. I looked forward only to the next nut placement, where I could rest and regain my breath while I removed the nut and sling from the crack that Kelly had lodged it in, and then clipped it onto one of the slings that Kelly had draped around me before he had started climbing. I finally crawled onto a small ledge where Kelly sat with the beacon beside him. He had anchored himself to another nut that he had placed deep into a crack at the rear of the ledge.

"Outstanding, Starn," he said to me as I collapsed beside him on the ledge. "Hell, I knew you could do it. That's one thing about climbing. You can't really tell anyone how to do it, it's just a natural ability that most people have forgotten they have. Let's get those air tanks up here."

With our combined efforts, we managed to drag the tanks up and on to the ledge. Then after a brief resting period, I clipped into the anchor and Kelly once more moved upward. We repeated the first sequence, what Kelly referred to as a pitch, and once more hauled the tanks up to where Kelly and the beacon sat. We were perhaps halfway up the wall then, and the height was becoming almost unbearable. I kept seeing myself falling, turning end over end to crash into the rocks below. I was sweating even with the cooling system of the suit on high. My fingers were beginning to ache from clenching small hand holds on the rock's surface, but nothing seemed to bother Kelly. Once again he moved up.

When he had anchored and pulled up the beacon, I moved off the ledge I had been belaying from. The sheer wall fell away below me to the ground. I couldn't see how Kelly had made progress and I told him so.

"Hell, Starn," he said, "there's a foothold around half a meter to your left that would hold an elephant. Move onto it."

"There's something there, all right," I answered. "But the damn thing's only about a centimeter wide." And thus totally impossible to stand on, I thought.

As Kelly began to lose patience, his voice rose in volume and the small speakers inside the suit began to vibrate. "Damn it, Starn, there's enough rock there for you and me both to dance on. Now move on to it."

I tentatively stretched my left foot towards the flake. Touching it with my boot, I gradually shifted my weight onto my left leg and, surprisingly enough, the rock held me.

"Don't hug the damn rock, Starn. Lean back a little so you're standing straight up and down!" Kelly roared. "Remember, what's holding you onto the rock is gravity, so make it work for you, not against you."

It made sense all right, about gravity holding you onto the rock, but at that point, I was scared witless and all I could think about was what gravity was going to do to me when I connected with the horizontal surface far below. I was standing on a small flake with a crack immediately in front of me but no hand holds that I could make use of. "What now, Kelly?" I asked. "How do I climb this damn crack?"

"Use your jams," he replied cryptically.

"Use what?" I shouted back, wondering if I was supposed to be reading his mind again.

"A jam . . . oh, sorry about that . . . forgot you don't know how. Well, now listen. Take your hand, see, and make it flat and then insert it in the crack like a knife, O.K.?"

The sides of the crack scraped the knuckles of my gloved hand as I slid it toward the rear of the opening. "It's in the crack," I told Kelly.

"Good. Now turn your hand over sideways and then tighten your fingers and thumb into a fist. Make it big—make that fist grow till it squeezes tight against both sides of the crack and stays there."

"O.K.," I replied. "It's tight."

"Now lean back on that sonofabitch and feel it hold you there."

Kelly was right. I was secured to the crack by my own hand, expanding to fill the dimensions of the crack.

"That's a hand jam, Starn. Another new term for you to remember. Now before that hand and wrist get all cramped up, take your foot and slide it into the crack sideways, with your knee bent outward."

"It's in," I said, my breath coming in short gasps.

"All right, now bring your knee and leg back toward vertical and your foot should rotate downward and jam tight against the sides of the crack. When it does, stand up on that foot and relax your hand. You'll be supporting yourself with your foot hold."

Again, Kelly was right and I slowly worked my way up the previously unclimbable crack using the jam techniques that Kelly had explained to me. My respect for Kelly and rock grew greater as Kelly would talk me up a difficult section, always with the rope tight against my middle in anticipation of a fall. I finally arrived slightly below where Kelly sat wedged into a large split in the wall. He sat with his butt firmly pressed against one side of the split while his knee and toe of his boot pressed against the opposite side. He was anchored to a nut he had placed in a smaller crack in the inside of the split. The beacon hung suspended from the nut, swaying gently below him. After I caught my breath, we slowly brought the air tanks up and tied them off to another nut placement to support the weight.

We were both breathing heavily, our suit tanks down to a quarter full. Off towards the east, Desolation's horizon darkened with a shifting of shadow. We had perhaps an hour left before lightside would slip from us like numb fingers from a small hold. I was beginning to appreciate why Kelly hated to climb in the dark.

He looked down at me from his position in the split. "This is called a chimney," he said. "The trick here is to use opposing pressure so you can maintain friction between both sides and some part of your body. Now watch me close, it's technique that counts."

He moved up the chimney with little effort, one foot and arm thrust in front of him, one foot and arm behind. Ten meters up, he suddenly stopped and cursed softly into the mike. "Can't protect the bastard, have to move out on to the face." He muttered more to himself than to me. "Why not," he continued, still talking to himself. ". . . there but for the grace of rock . . . O.K., Starn," louder, snapped like an order, "you'll come up the chimney, it'll be easier for you. I have to move out onto the face to get up. Be ready to hold a fall and remember there's nothing between me and you but bare rope, no running protection."

"Why the face, if the chimney is easier?" I asked.

"Easier for you, I said," he answered. "The moves are easier on the face but you might freeze up from the exposure." And with that, he deftly levered himself from the chimney onto the sheer vertical surface of the face. He moved with the rhythm of a spider, in quick short steps from hold to hold. The rope ran up and out, catching light like one thin spider strand of web, hooked to some crazy silvered arachnid that had lost four of its legs. For a moment, when his right foot slipped, he hung against the face awkwardly, boot moving slowly downward. Sweat instantly beaded from my palms onto the inner surface of my gloves and the breath caught in my throat. He was falling, but then, slow motion like, he leaned backwards away from the rock and his weight settled on to his remaining foot hold. He brought his right boot back to the hold it had slipped from like a wayward child that had to be coaxed. I could see he was near exhaustion but he didn't rest. He kept moving, upward. He disappeared over a rounded knob and remained out of sight as I waited to see his body suddenly appear spread-eagled and falling, feel the rope tighten and drag me from my fragile stance. A chill spread upward from my stomach, reaching for my heart. I knew we were dead, I knew . . .

"Off belay and anchored." It roared in my ears. For a moment I thought it was a scream, the sound a dying man makes when he falls.

"God damn it, Starn, I'm up.   Are you still there or did you take a walk?"

A chuckle of relief started in my throat, but caught in my dry vocal cords and came out as a muffled cough.   "Yeah, I'm still here," I said into the suit mike. "I thought maybe you were taking a nap up there or something."

"I just might do that when you get your butt up here," Kelly said.   "Make sure the haul line's clear.   I'm going to bring the beacon up the face."

I swung the beacon out of the chimney and watched it rise towards the sharp line of rock against space.   It bumped over the edge and was gone.

"It's up," said Kelly, a note of relief in his voice.   "Here comes the haul line."

I retrieved the loose end of the haul line and tied on the air tanks.   "O.K., Kelly," I said, "they're secure.   I'm climbing."

"Belay on, climb away."

I moved up the chimney imitating Kelly's earlier positions.   My right hand and boot against the rock in front, my left against the rock behind, I crept upward, moving boot or hand only centimeters at a time.   The technique worked fine, but I could feel the strength beginning to ease out of my muscles, and the weaker I felt, the harder I pushed against the rock.   I suddenly realized why Kelly had moved out into the face.   The rock sloped gently outward as it rose above me. If Kelly had slipped while in the chimney, he'd have fallen through clear space until impacting upon the stance I had been belaying from.   If I slipped from the chimney, I knew the same would happen to me, and whether Kelly could hold my weight freely suspended from the rope was a question I didn't want to consider.

The muscles of my legs felt like weak rubber bands stretched to the breaking point.   My foot slipped downward without warning, then my hand began to slide and I felt the rope tighten against my waist.   "Kelly," I screamed, "I'm falling!"

"No, you're not," he answered calmly.   "You just think you are.   The rope is tight so you're not going anywhere.   I can hold you here all day but there's no way I can pull up your whole weight, so climb, damn it."

"I can't!" I screamed in terror.   "The chimney narrows above me and I don't have room to keep my legs out."   My foot had slipped completely out from behind me and I hung straight down with my face and chest against the rock.   My boots no longer touched rock at all but were dangling in open space from the overhanging chimney.   "What do I do, Kelly," I whispered, waiting for the ground to come racing up to meet me.

"First thing is calm down.   Now," he continued, speaking with a steady voice, "if your feet have slipped, get one back up under your butt and wedge your knee against the rock in front of you."

I tried to raise my leg up but was too close to the rock.   "I can't."

"The hell you can't!   Now listen to me—push yourself back from the rock with one hand till your back touches.   Don't worry about falling, damn it, you're not going anywhere.   After you do that, reach down and pull your leg up with your other hand if that's the only way it'll come, but get the damn thing up there."

He was crazy, I knew he was crazy, but somehow I managed to push backward, supported by only the rope that led upward to Kelly.   I raised my leg up perpendicular with my body but the boot was just too heavy to move.   I looked down and a wave of nausea hit me, but with my remaining strength, I reached for my ankle and jerked it up under my thigh and felt my boot touch the rock behind me and my knee brush the rock in front. "All right," I said, "I've done it."

"Good. Now I'll give you a little slack and you can rest for a minute."

"No!" I yelled. "Wait a—" The tension released from the rope. Instead of falling, my weight settled onto my leg, wedging my bootsole and knee tighter into the facing walls of the chimmey.

"O.K.?"

"Yeah," I said, and pulled my other leg up beneath me to match the position of the first. I rested a few minutes until my breathing settled down to a low rush in my ears. My arms were still weak but no longer felt numb to the elbow.

"Well, are you ready?" said Kelly.

"Ready for what?" I replied tersely.

"To climb."

"I don't know if I can," I mumbled.

"Sure you can, Starn. Don't freeze up on me now."

The rope tightened and I pushed my body upward a few centimeters at a time until I had risen a full meter. With my feet wedged tight beneath me, I asked Kelly for some slack.

"What the hell for?" he said sharply.

"I gotta rest, Kelly," I said.

"The hell you do," he replied angrily. "You quit now and you'll stay there forever. Now climb!"

"Damn it, Kelly," I said. "I can't."

"The hell you can't!" he yelled, his voice rising in intensity. "You want slack, you got slack," and the rope coiled loosely around me, moving downward. "Now climb, you low-grav, ground-pounding, useless sonofabitch, climb!" he screamed. "I won't hold you any longer."

The lousy bastard would let me fall.

Anger boiled away my self-pity. He's trying to kill me, I thought, and my anger turned to rage and I knew that I somehow had to reach the top or he'd let me die on the rocks below. It no longer mattered that my legs ached and my arms were numb. I didn't care if I had to climb another thousand meters, I'd waste that bastard.

I struggled towards the top. Move one knee, then the foot. Push with the hands, the back . . . move the other foot. Slowly I edged towards the top of the overhanging chimney, oblivious to height, pain, rock. I finally dragged myself over the outward jutting crest and collapsed in the shallow crack that sloped gently upwards to the narrow, plateau-like summit of Horizon's End.

Gasping for breath, the rage slowly died within me and although the last part of the climb was a blur, I realized that there had never been more than a half-meter of slack in the rope the whole time I had climbed. Kelly's scheme had worked. I was up.

Kelly tied me off and then moved down to join me. We hauled the air bottles up and over the edge, then moved back up to the high point and set up the beacon,

aligning it toward Deso Prime.   With the beacon set and operational, we sank
down onto hard rock and prepared to wait.   Deso Prime would route a boat to us
as soon as they locked on to the beacon's signal.   In a few hours we would be
relaxing back at the dome.

Kelly sat with his back propped against the beacon.   "Well, Starn," he said,
"We made it.   You're a full fledged rock-rat, now."   Those were the first words
that Kelly had spoken since I reached the top.

"Ah, Kelly," I said, embarrassed at my performance, "thanks for getting me
up.   I'm sorry I froze like that."

"That's all right," he answered.   "It happens to the best of us.   It happened
to me the first time up so don't let it bother you."   His voice was heavy with
fatigue, the words slurring together.

I was drained of energy even though we were victorious.   My suit stank of dried
sweat and fear.   The air through the filters was stale and heavy.   A bit too stale,
I realized, and checked the readout to find my tanks nearly empty.

"We better change tanks," I said, rising to my feet to retrieve the spares.

"Drag them over here and I'll switch for you," said Kelly, remaining in his
seated position.

Changing your own tanks in the field is a minor problem, but it can be done.
I was more than willing, however, to accept Kelly's offer and trade off on the
chore.   I pulled the tank packs over to where he sat and turned to squat in front
of him so that he could reach the fittings.   There was a soft hiss of escaping air
as he snapped free the first tank.   He latched the coupling of the replacement tank
and then repeated the process with the second tank.

Desolation had grown darker while Kelly worked.   The suit coolers murmured
into silence as the heating units kicked in with a faint hum.   I glanced over my
shoulder and saw that darkside had swept up on us as Kelly had switched my tanks,
the temperature starting to drop as residual heat began seeping from the planet's
surface.

"O.K., Kid," Kelly said.   "You're tight."

I turned in a half circle.   With our helmets only a few centimeters apart, I could
see through the reflective visor that masked Kelly's face.   His features were drawn
and the muscles of his jaw sagged from exhaustion, making him look older than
he normally appeared.

"Turn around," I said, "and I'll do your lungs a favor."

Kelly slowly rose to his knees and turned away from me to expose his back,
steadying himself with one hand on the beacon.   His movements were awkward,
as if he were dazed.   The climb hadn't appeared to tire him at all before this, and
I was a bit puzzled by his behavior.

"Kelly," I said.

"Yeah."

"Ah, never mind," I said hurriedly, at last realizing the obvious.   Kelly had
been in his suit before I had and had led the entire climb.   Add to that the exertion
of hauling up the tank packs and there could be only one result.   His oxygen

consumption had been greater than mine and his tanks were probably now near the danger level.   I quit wasting time thinking and quickly twisted the fitting on his first tank and pulled, tossing it off to the side as it came loose.   The replacement slid into place, another quick twist of the fitting secured it.   I flipped the demand valve on and relaxed, knowing the air from the fresh tank would clear his head in a short time.

"Starn," said Kelly, after I had finished switching his second tank.   "What was it you were going to ask me?"

"I was wondering about the beacon," I said, as I stood up and reached for the knobs on the transmitter.

"What about it?"

I leaned over and pretended to check the transmit dials.   After I fiddled with the knobs a few seconds, I glanced down at Kelly, who was once again in a seated position, leaning against the beacon.

"I just thought that we might have trouble with it drifting this high up," I said.

"No problem, Starn.   That rig is as solid as the rock we're on.   They'll send a boat out for us shortly."

"Yeah, I guess you're right," I said, glad that Kelly had believed my answer. I didn't want to embarrass him by mentioning how low his tanks must have been. He must have forgotten to check his gauges in the excitement of reaching the top, yet it still seemed odd.   One of the first things you learn when working dirt is to keep a close eye on your gear, and Kelly was a veteran of at least four other mining operations before he ever hit Desolation.

My thoughts were distracted by what sounded like the faint cracklings of a jump boat in my suit speakers, relayed through the receiver override of the beacon.   I turned and looked toward Deso Prime, but the sky was empty.   So much for wishful thinking.

The pressure of Kelly's gloved hand on my arm caught my attention.   He waited for me to squat down beside him before he said anything.

"Here," he said, placing something in my hand.   "This is for luck.   You've earned it."

It was the medal he had worn as long as I'd known him.   He had taken it from the outside of his suit and I realized that he must have placed it there while still in the ship, unsure of how the climb would ultimately end.   I turned it over in my palm and read the simple inscription: EVEREST EXPEDITION—2174—SOUTHWEST FACE.   In the center was a raised likeness of what was unquestionably a large mountain.

I clutched the medal tightly in my fist.   "Kelly, are you sure you want to . . ."

"Yeah," he said, answering my unspoken question.   "I've never shown that to anyone out here.   That's Everest, Starn, tallest piece of rock on the earth.   She's a beauty, covered with snow and ice.   You don't know what snow is, Starn, but it's white and it's cold.   You'd be surprised how peaceful it can be."

He stopped speaking then and seemed to turn inward, perhaps thinking of old climbs and older rock.   Far to the western horizon, the sweeping line of darkside's shadow overcame the falling sun, leaving Desolation's surface encased in soft greys. The momentary silence was suddenly interrupted as Kelly was overcome by a coughing spasm.

"Ah, Starn," he said, when he was able to catch his breath, "I hate like hell to say this, but I think I've got a problem."

A slow chill began to spread outward from the base of my neck.   "What kind of problem, Kelly?"

"I think I've got a leak in my air supply."

"Jesus!"

"Yeah."

He hesitated for a moment, then looked up at me.   "Maybe you better take a look at my tanks again," he said.

"Maybe your first set were running too low and it's taking a while to flush the system," I said hopefully.

"No way," he responded.   "I always keep a close eye on my air supply, Starn. I was on reserve when you switched tanks, but nowhere near the danger point yet."

The chill continued down my spine, coming to rest in the pit of my stomach.

Once again, I found myself facing his back, staring at his tanks with growing apprehension.

"See if you can find something wrong back there.   I can taste Desolation and I sure as hell don't like it."

I checked the tanks and fittings on his suit.   They looked undamaged and seemed to be tight and in the right position when I gave them a light tug.   Kelly and I both knew that a small leak would be hard to find without test gear and damn near impossible to patch up in the spot we were in.   The chill in my stomach hardened into a tight knot of fear.

I quickly checked the helmet seat of his suit, looking for a small break.   Nothing visible.   He shifted his position slightly, becoming edgy at my silence.   I briefly glanced at the rest of the suit, and then it suddenly hit me: "Patch up."

"Don't move," I said, and gingerly reached down and applied thumb pressure to the top edge of the plasti-foil strip that covered the rip in the right leg of his suit.   Instead of adhering to the suit's surface, the material curled slightly under my thumb.

"It feels like there wasn't enough sealant on the surface before you stuck on the patch, but then the pressure test—you *did* run a pressure test, didn't you?"

"I was working on the air fittings while the damn patch was setting up, and then—"

"Damn it, Kelly, that's the kind of stunt a greenhorn pulls!"

Kelly sighed, then lapsed into another coughing fit.   He started to speak and then stopped, as if he were unwilling to say what was on his mind.   Finally, his voice rasping and low, he said, "I'll be damned if I'm sure what to do about it."

I searched my mind for possible ways of sealing the suit, discarding ideas as they surfaced one after the other.   They all required a sealant, the basic fix-all we needed but didn't have.   On the borders of awareness, a realization kept sliding through and around my other thoughts.   As long as I had know him, this was the first time that Kelly had ever seemed uncertain of what to do.

In and among the logical ideas, I kept getting snagged on a memory from my childhood.   When I was a kid, I'd had an ecocube by my bed that I would watch for hours.   It wasn't that much, just a small cube filled with water, some odd sea plants, and a few fluorescing fish from Bathard IV.   The cube was self-contained and recycled the essentials.   What fascinated me the most about the thing was that the gases the fish needed in the water would collect under a small shell on the bottom of the cube.   The gas bubbles would finally lift the shell and stream to the top, the fish darting through the rising bubbles.

I kept seeing those bubbles lift the shell.

I kept thinking that this was a hell of a time to revert to my childhood.

My next thought was that the most obvious answers are the hardest to see.

"Kelly," I said.   "I'll ease the pressure in your suit up."

"What the hell for?" he growled, sounding as though he thought that this time, I was the one going vac-happy.   "The patch is already sprung, it'll just make the leak worse."

"No," I said, "we'll just make sure the leak is out, not in.   Just don't move around much so you don't strain the patch more than you have to.   You'll lose a little oxygen but it's a hell of a lot better than letting Desolation's atmosphere seep in."

Kelly always was stubborn.   He thought about what I said before he would agree to up the pressurization.   He started coughing again, badly, and it seemed to decide him.

"All right, Starn," he said.   "We'll try it.   I'll increase the pressure and see if it helps."

"Better let me do it with the override valve on the tanks," I said.

"Why?" he said suspiciously.

"I don't think you can get it high enough with the in-suit control.   We'd better balloon your suit just a slight bit to be sure of an outward leak."

"Damn it, Starn, that *will* blow the patch," he said.

"I'll take it up slow," I said, keeping my voice steady.   "That way you can watch the patch and make sure it doesn't loosen any more than it already has."

I was still kneeling behind him, a few centimeters away from his back and I reached out and started to adjust the valve before he could say anything more.   As the pressurization gradually increased, the suit began to bulge just slightly in shape.

"Starn," said Kelly, "wait a . . ."

"Keep your eye on the patch," I said, cutting him off, as I gently increased the pressure.

"Ah, looks O.K. so far," he said.   "That should be enough to do it."

I had to agree with him.   His suit was still flexible, but ballooning enough to ensure the leak was outward.   I kept my hand on the valve, grateful that he couldn't see my face.   What Kelly needed in the worst way was a good dose of oxygen, not just simply to reverse the leak.   His in-suit control was mainly for adjusting his oxygen supply to handle different work loads.   The control was a safety device of sorts.   It prevented the man inside from overpressurizing to the point that the suit lost flexibility and became a rigid trap.   It could happen, but only an inexperienced man or a fool would let himself get caught that way.   Men had died in ballooned suits.

Like I said, Kelly was stubborn.   He would never have agreed if I had given him a choice.   I shoved the valve up to max.

Kelly's suit expanded, straightening into an immobile orange star.   He lay on his back, spreadeagled in the ballooning suit and stared up at me, his eyes burning through his visor into mine.

He said, softly, "You bastard."   Then he was silent, except when another coughing spell hit him.   His face would go a bit pale then, but never his eyes.

The jump boat from the dome arrived a few hours later.   It came in low and flat, slightly to the west of us, then seemed to pause and hover, and I quickly reset the valve on the back of Kelly's suit, bringing the pressurization down to normal before the boat slowly swung towards our location, landing arcs blazing a path of light through darkside's covering.

Stef and Dak recovered from their injuries after treatment from the medicos back at the dome.   Kelly's throat was sore and his breathing was ragged for a few days, but it cleared up.   We'd been lucky enough to solve the suit problem before Deso's atmosphere had caused him any permanent damage.   The crash had caused a lot of excitement at Deso Prime, but things finally quieted down and returned to normal the way they always do.   The only difference I could see was that the climb Kelly and I had made was the favorite topic whenever we were swapping yarns with the rest of the guys.

We must have told the damn story a hundred times, always breaking up the listeners when we'd get to the part about Kelly being hoarse for a week after we got back to the dome from all the yelling he had to do while he was dragging me up the rock.   I never mentioned the bad patch on Kelly's suit and neither did he. I couldn't see how it would add anything to the telling, so we just kind of forgot about it.

Kelly hung around until we started work on Desolation's second dome, then caught the first deep spacer through to God knows where.   I never did know for sure why he left, but I suppose it was because Desolation was starting to grow. Kelly didn't like too many people around.   I guess he went looking for more constants.   I remember his last words to me, as if I'd just talked to him.

"You see, Starn, climbing is a dead art," he said.   "No one remembers how to do it or has the time to learn, but what's important is, we beat the bastards, the ground pounders that say it can't be done.   Remember that, Starn."

So like I said, maybe I'm a little crazy but I still like to go up to Horizon's End and watch darkside come on, and remember.   I'm the only one left of the original crew still on Desolation.   The others are dead or still mining out on worlds where there's no one to bother them.   And I still fly jump boats—never did make it to rams, but then, I've got my hobbies to amuse me.

When Kelly left, he gave me a few of his holo-tapes, some of the only ones of their kind.   They were old, and they explain climbing techniques, and I've tried to put them to use.   That's how I came to run the school you are asking about. Kelly's High-Angle Ascents—climbing instruction and basic survival.

Look under: INSTRUCTION, SPORTS, in the directory.

I'm listed.

A. BERTRAM CHANDLER

No Room in the Stable

It was a cold night, and dark, with wind and driving rain.

The refugees, sheltering in the old barn with its leaky roof, had lit a fire. This was risky, but not too risky. It was unlikely that *They* would be out in force in this kind of weather. *They* did not like water in any shape or form. *They* never had liked water.

The two men and the three women huddled around the flickering flame, grateful for its feeble warmth. They were in rags, all of them, with broken, disintegrating shoes. Their clothing, when new, had been of good quality, but not suitable for life on the run. Two of the women were young and might once have been pretty, the other one was middle-aged, as were the men. All five of them looked old— and all of them looked as though they had known better days. The girls, perhaps, had once worked in an office. The woman must have been a comfortably off, bridge-playing house-wife. One of the men—a shopkeeper?—had been fat once; his skin was now as poor a fit as his clothing. The other one was in better condition physically, and by his speech and bearing suggested that he was accustomed to command. Whatever it was that he had commanded was irretrievably lost in the past. Perhaps, if this little band survived, he would become their leader; its members had come together, quite by chance, only a few hours prior to their taking shelter.

Ready to hand was their scant weaponry—a .22 rifle, a shotgun, a small axe, two kitchen knives. Of them all the shotgun, belonging to the ex-shopkeeper, was the most useful—but only five cartridges remained for it.

The woman, hugging her still ample breasts, complained, "It's cold—"

"We daren't build a bigger fire," the tall man, the one who had never been fat, told her.

"I don't see why not—" grumbled one of the girls rebelliously.

The tall man, speaking slowly and carefully, said, *"They* have sharp eyes—"

"It's more than their eyes that are sharp!" exclaimed the other girl.

"I miss the News . . ." whined the ex-shopkeeper. "On the radio, on the TV . . . What's happening? What's the Army doing?"

"How did it happen?" demanded the woman. "And why aren't the Americans doing something about it?"

"They'll be having their own troubles," said the girl who had wanted a bigger fire. "And the Russians, too. I heard something about it on the radio before *They* killed everybody in the town. Almost everybody."

"I thought *They* were only here," said the woman. "How could *They* get to other countries?"

"They're small," said the tall man. "And they've been stowing away aboard ships ever since there were ships. And now they have the intelligence to stow away aboard aircraft—"

"But how did it start?" asked the ex-shopkeeper.

"A mutation, I suppose. One of them born with superior intelligence, and other improvements. Tomcatting around and spreading his seed over the entire country . . . It's possible. It must be. It happened."

"But why do they *hate* us so much?" almost wept the woman. "*I* was always good to them, to the ones I had. The best food, and expensive, no scraps . . . Their own baskets to sleep in . . ."

"Why shouldn't they hate us?" countered the more intelligent of the two girls. "I've been thinking about it quite a lot—when I've had time to think, that is. We did give the bastards rather a rough spin. Having them doctored, males and females. Drowning their young ones . . ."

The tall man laughed bitterly. "That's what I should have done—but I was too soft hearted. You know—" he laughed again "—I'm inclined to think that this is all my fault . . ."

"What the hell do you mean?" growled the ex-shopkeeper. "How the hell can it be?"

"I may as well tell you," was the reply.

It all started, I suppose (said the tall man) a long time ago. Not so long really, but it seems centuries. We, my wife and I, lived in an old house in a quiet side street. I don't know what happened to her, to my wife. I'm still trying to find her. But . . .

Anyhow, this street was infested with cats. She hated cats, although I liked the brutes. I used to like the brutes, that is. My wife'd raise Cain if ever I talked to one, and she used to keep the high walls around our garden sprayed with some muck that was supposed to keep them off.

Well, at the time I was Master of a small ship on a nice little coastal run—about a week away from home and then about three days in port. At times, though, I used to run late; I was having a bad spell with head winds. My wife had arranged to go away for a week at a holiday resort, for the week I was to be away. I should have been in and out before she left—as it was, I got in just before she left.

About the first thing she said to me when I walked into the house was, "You will do something about the cats."

"What cats?" I asked.

She told me. During my last voyage one of the local females had given birth to no less than eight kittens in our carport. It wouldn't have been at all hard to dispose of them when they were newborn—just a bucket of water and a fairly hard heart. But *she* not only hated cats, she couldn't bear to touch them.

There were other jobs lined up for me as well (he said reminiscently).   Some inside painting, the chandeliers to clean, a few minor repairs around the place, a spot of gardening.   But the cats had priority.

They were rather charming kittens; although their mother was grey they were black-and-white.   They were lively—and they were full of fight.   My first intention was to drown them.   I half filled the garbage can with water, caught one and dropped him in.   But he was a good swimmer and put up such a fight trying to jump out, that I hadn't the heart to go through with it.   I rescued him and turned him loose—and, naturally enough, he and all his cobbers bolted for cover.   That was the first day.

The next day I decided to get the R.S.P.C.A. to do the job.   I rang them up, and was told that they collected unwanted animals in our district only on Mondays— and I was sailing at midnight on Sunday.   The alternative would be to take them round to the Dogs' Home in person.   So, on Saturday afternoon, I had a large empty carton ready and had a lively time catching kittens.   By this time they realized that I bore them ill will.   Finally I had five in the carton—I was covered with sweat and scratches and stinking of cat—and decided that this was at least a start.   I went back into the house to shower and change.   When I was cleaned up I didn't ring at once for a taxi but went back outside, hoping that I'd be able to catch the remaining three kittens.   I saw their mother leading *four* kittens up the drive.   Then I saw that she had overturned the carton, freeing her offspring.   One remained inside the box.   He swore at me.   I swore back and left him there, deciding to make a big effort the following day.

Now you have to visualize the lay-out.   There was the carport, with a shed at the end of it.   There was no room under the shed, but there was a space at the back, between it and the back fence of our property.   This space was too small for me to squeeze into, but there was ample room for cats.   After I'd started my attack on them the kittens had taken refuge there.

I didn't like having to do what I did do, but I'd promised my wife that the place would be clear of cats on her return.   I used the garden hose to flush them out, one by one.   They were stubborn.   I could feel them hating me, and by this time I was rather hating myself.   Their mother was hovering around, not daring to intervene—but if looks could have killed I'd have dropped dead on the spot.

But, one by one, I caught the poor, half-drowned little wretches, opened the front gate just a crack, and threw them out into the street.   They were yelling blue murder.   The last one of all was more than just half drowned when he finally gave up the struggle and crawled from behind the shed.   Even so, he gave me a nasty scratch.

I went outside to make a last check, to make sure that I'd evicted all eight of them.   I had.   Their mother was lying on her side in the gutter, giving suck.   She looked at me very reproachfully.

But . . .

But that wasn't what worried me.   It was something that I saw, something that I heard—although I didn't remember it properly until *They* came out from hiding and started to take over the world.   I suppose that *He,* even then, had powers, although they were yet to be developed.   *He* must have inhibited my memory somehow—although, *then*, nobody would have believed my story.

As I picked *Him* up I saw that his front paws were more like little hands than paws—and it is the hands of *His* children that, with their brains, have enabled them to fight us with their acts of sabotage.

And I heard in my mind a voice, not a human voice, saying, "You will pay for this . . ."

"You will!   You will!" screamed the woman, reaching for the shotgun.

The ex-shopkeeper snatched it from her before she could use it.   He said slowly, "Leave him for *Them* to deal with."   Then, almost whispering, *"I'd* have drowned the little bastards . . ."

PAULA SMITH

African Blues

M usa's cow, Llana, was eight years old, and I did not think she would be
able to calve.   But there it was, and she was bearing another one.   It was hard
for her; she was quite old.   Musa had brought her in from the savannah when it
became obvious she would have difficulty dropping.   He left her at my veterinary
barn.   "See her through, Sister Doto," he said, "and I will pay up all I owe."
This for Musa is a major concession.

That is why I was in my barn before dawn with Llana that day.   That was the
day the rocket came down over the village.   At first it was only a faraway whistle,
high and shrill.   I thought it was a bird and paid it no mind.   There were other
things to attend to; Llana is a nasty beast, with a tendency to bite.   But then the
whistle grew sharper, very quickly, you see; and Llana shuddered for more reason
than just her unborn calf.   Then bang! came a crash.

For a moment after the crash it was very quiet; even the hyenas shut up their
morning howling and the dungbirds stopped screeching.   Then half the village was
awake, hurrying out of their houses to see what it was.   "Llana, you wait for a
minute," I said.   I wanted to see what this was, and what it was doing here in
Kenya.   Besides, in the barn it was very close; I also needed some air.

It was early morning, and already quite warm.   Here on the equator there are
certain days when the sun is so bright and hot that it burns the sky yellow.   That
is what the people say.   The teachers at the missionary school in Nairobi say it is
the dust.   Certainly there is more than enough of it, a lot of dust in the air because
it had not rained in two months.   Further, that day the villagers kicked up more
running out into the savannah to find the fallen object.   The sky was already pale
with sunrise, and I knew it would not turn blue that day.

Jama was the first to find it.   It was big, bigger than a house.   "Is this one of
the whites' spaceships?" he said.

"Yes," I answered.   It was indeed a rocket; I had seen several on the television
in the capital.   But it did not look like the Americans' rockets, which are cone-
shaped, like our roof-tops.   This one was circular, round all the way over, like a
ball.   There were many wires wrapped around it, and a big—parachute, they call
it—only it looked more like a huge ship's sail.   It was torn.

The rocket was at the deep end of a long rut it had made in the brush.   The villagers began to dig it out—who can tell if such a thing might not be valuable?—and I was thinking I must return to Llana.   Then Dr. Hunter, the black American who came to our village two years ago, ran up, sweating.   He is always sweating. He came here because he wanted to be African; but even African water doesn't stay in him, it always sweats away.

"Don't open it!" he yelled in his Kiswahili, which is very bad.   Whenever possible I speak English with him.   "We'll notify the authorities first.   It might be a Russian capsule."

The villagers looked up, and some moved away.   Most moved away.   Dr. Hunter is sometimes crazy, and often rude, but he is a smart man.   He, too, is educated.

Jama walked up to Dr. Hunter and bowed a little.   "Your instructions?" he asked in Kiswahili, for that is the only language he knows.   I spoke up, using English, "What authorities should we notify, Dr. Hunter?   Brother Jama is ready to do what you suggest."

"Also may I borrow his bicycle," Jama said to me.   "It's a long way to Lodwar."

"Oh," said Dr. Hunter, blinking a little.   "Authorities . . . well—" He started to count off on his fingers.   "Well—the District Commissioner, for one.   The mayor of Lodwar, the po—"

I almost jumped out of my skin.   The rocket had knocked at us.   "Get back!" yelled Dr. Hunter, as if we weren't already scattering.   The thumping increased, grew louder, stopped.   We waited a moment, holding our breaths.   A few of the bolder young men started forward.   But they halted, and scuttled back when a section of the rocket opened a bit above the ground.   At first the door stuck, grating against the jamb, then it wiggled free, coming all the way open.   And from inside the rocket, a man crawled up, leaned out, and fell out of the hatch.   A *blue* man. I must admit I was astounded.   He was small, slighter even than a white man. He wore a great deal of padding and a thick-looking round helmet, though there was no visor.   We hurried forward to take him away from the rocket, for he just lay there.   His face was shaped like a top, very round above—especially wide at the eyes, which were closed—tapering to almost nothing for a chin.   Dr. Hunter told us, "Take him to my office."

M'bega, his two sons, and Sulimani picked up the little blue man between them and headed off to Dr. Hunter's very large, very beautiful house.   (It has a wooden roof.)   The doctor himself followed close behind them, going, "Sst! sst! careful there."

I stayed behind for a moment, walking around the rocket.   The metal radiated warmth, as did the ground around it.   Some of the sand had been turned to glass. The sun was fully up now, shimmering on the huge sail.   It wasn't cloth, for I could see no weave, although it was like a metal fabric.   But it didn't reflect quite like metal.   I came back to the opening, intending to close the hatch cover, when I heard a scraping inside the rocket.   I didn't know, were there more blue people in there?   I was most cautious as I peered in.   But it was only M'bega's littlest boy, Faki, who grinned at me from a padded chair. "See what I found, Aunt?" he said, holding up a piece of the metallike cloth. "It was in here," he said, pointing to a little mesh bag fastened on the side of the chair.

"You come out of there," I said, and leaned in to pull him out. The rocket's—cabin, I suppose you would call it—was very cramped, and it was hot, stifling. There were many more boxes and mesh bags, many things tied to the round walls of the cabin. There were three tiny windows—no, they were television screens—on the curve of the wall before the pilot's chair. I put Faki down outside and shooed him on. Then I looked at the long cloth band I had taken from him. Too big for a headpiece and too narrow for anything else, it was smooth, thick, and quite strong. I pulled out the net bag—it had come from off the side of the chair—and closed the hatch.

Admittedly I dawdled going back to my barn. I was curious; what was this cloth for? Why should the blue man have had it nearest him? Well, something had to be nearest, I supposed. But what were these other things in the mesh bag—two pieces of very soft cloth, not metallic; a length of string; a pencil; a small vial; and a bunch of cotton waste. Strange things, but not strange enough to belong with a blue man.

Well, they were getting dusty in my hand. I put them back into the bag and went on. It was growing hotter, with the horizon shimmering all around in the distance. So flat, the savannah, with nothing but the brush and dust standing on it. But do you know, as I swung that bag while I walked, all the dust in it flew out. None of the articles, but only the dust. I looked inside and all the things were clean. It was quite odd. Do you think Europeans have such things?

I came back to my infirmary, went to see whether all was well with Llana. Ah, the poor old cow! As I approached, she was standing in her stall, shuddering in a labor pain. She strained, twitched all down the length of her hide, then relaxed. "Ah, Llana, poor girl, is it hard when you're old?" I leaned against the wooden slats for a very long time. Llana was well, just that the calf was no closer than before. The sun's rays peeped in from the cracks in the southeast corner, lighting motes in the air. It was dark and still, very quiet, but growing warm even in the shed. The hay smell was thick in the air, too, as thick as dust outdoors.

Something about the bag's contents—the two kinds of cloth, the pencil, the cotton waste, and the string. And a small vial. It bothered me. I emptied the mesh bag out onto a manger to examine the items. The soft cloth, I found, would stick to itself, and the pencil would cut the string. It would also cut straw in half, but it would not cut my skin. I opened the little bottle, dabbing a bit onto my fingertip. I tasted it—and it was brine! Most unusual.

The silver cloth was a sling; and its edges would hold together, making a sort of small, hollow hammock. It all bothered me. They meant something, I was sure. I felt that. Sometimes, you see, I feel as if I were all the land, that I could hear and smell every thing and every animal that walked across me, that if I could only feel just a little bit more, I should know everything and be perfect. This was the same feeling. If I could only know the why of these curious objects, I felt I should know all about the blue man.

Llana mooed very softly.   I gathered the things into the bag—again all the dirt fell out—and noted the time.   Forty minutes.   Her waters had not yet broken, so it would be a long time yet.   I thought, and made up my mind.   I would go see the blue man.   Maybe that would give me my hint.

Outdoors, the sky was already brass, without a cloud.   The dust on the short trail to Dr. Hunter's house was stirred up just by my walking, and it settled over me, turning my arms almost as grey as the old bluejeans I was wearing.   The bag I tucked under my belt.   As I walked, I tied all the little braids of my hair up into a topknot, wrapping them all with my kerchief.   My mother had given me the kerchief last winter, before she died.   She had made me come back here to the village when I had completed school in Nairobi.

Dr. Hunter's house had been built years before, even before I was born, by a European, Herr Max.   The village people had settled around it because he also had an artesian well drilled.   There used to be a garden in back, but Dr. Hunter let it die.   It is a shame; it was very beautiful.

I knocked on the wooden door and called, "Hodi?"   Nobody answered.   Again I called, "Hodi?   May I come in?"

Then Dr. Hunter's voice said, "Who is it?"

"It is I, Doto," I said.   "May I come in?"

There was a click as he unlatched his door.   Opening it, he said, "Ka—uh, karibu, Dota.   Is Jama back yet?"

"It is unlikely that he would be," I said, walking inside.   "It is a very long way to Lodwar.   I have come to see the blue man and ask him about his bag," which I held up.   "May I see him?"

He simply looked at me, with sweat of more than heat on his brow.   There was a cry from further within the house, short, sharp, which caused Dr. Hunter to start. "Dota . . . look, the blue man is sick.   He must have been injured in that landing. And I sure as Hell—that is, I may be a doctor, but that doesn't mean I necessarily know how to treat blue Martians."

"Oh.   Well; I, too, am trained in medical matters.   I was schooled at Corleri Veterinary Institute in the capital, and I believe I may already know what is troubling the blue man.   I should like to come in."   I made to enter his dispensary, but again he stopped me.

"*Dota!*" he said.   "Can't I make you understand?   He is an *alien*—who knows what could be wrong with him?   He may have hurt organs whose normal function I couldn't know!   The best thing we can do for him is try and get him comfortable until the or somebody can get him out of here to better care.   Savvy?"

He was gripping my upper arm tightly, his face very close to mine.   I do not care for this; it is not respectful.   I, too, after all, am educated, perhaps not so much as Dr. Hunter; but even my knowledge of veterinary matters should count for something.   And I also had the blue man's bag.

"Dr. Hunter," I said, very calm.   "My name is Do*to*.   You keep mispro-nouncing my name, which is not polite.   I have come to see the blue man.   I have certain things of his from the rocket which he may be needing.   Hodi?"

He stared at me for quite a long time.   Plainly he was not happy with this situation, but when the high cry came again, he shook himself, growling, "Oh, come on in. But I'm in charge here, understand that. I don't want some back-country witch doctor fouling up interplanetary relations, y'got that?"

"Of course, Dr. Hunter. You would rather do it yourself," I said, as I went into the infirmary.

In there, on the examining table lay the blue man, awake and looking upwards. His padded suit being off, I could see he was blue all over, except for a sort of short brown pelt of hair over his scalp, apparently across his back, and running down the outside of his arms to the back of his hands. He had three fingers on each hand. He was quite thin and slight, like a young boy, with a large round head. I came a little closer and he looked at me.

How do I say it? The eyes—large and round, deep and beautiful, beautiful—like ostrich eyes, like a bowl of water reflecting sunlight. They seemed to be black, though they might have been brown. I have never seen eyes like that; I shall not forget them.

Then I looked away, down to the somewhat swollen abdomen under Dr. Hunter's modesty sheet; and everything, the bag, the belly, the sling, fell into place, as my schoolteacher used to say. "Dr. Hunter, would you want me to assist you, then?" I said to the American.

"At what?"

"The delivery. The blue man is with child."

Yes, I do say that surprised Dr. Hunter a little bit. For a long moment he gaped at the blue man, his mouth going like a fish's, until the blue man—she—groaned, gripping the sides of the table to help her bear down with the pain of labor. This brought Dr. Hunter back to himself. He snapped at me, "Move over, girl, get me—where's my stethoscope?" He fit the tips in his ears, put the cup to her belly, muttering, "All the time thought it was a second heart. *Damn!* Sell my soul for a fluoroscope. Such a thing as *too* primitive, Hunter." He flipped out the earpieces and began palpating the abdomen. The blue man looked on, quiet again. "Oh Lord, oh Lord. Doto, you're right. How'd you know?"

I emptied the wonderful bag out onto the cabinet top. "These are the things she had nearest her—this, string, to tie the cord; this pencil is a clipper, to cut it; diapers, for herself or the child, as is also the cotton waste, for cleaning and swabbing. And this," I held up the silver cloth, "is a sling to hold the baby across her back. Or chest. It is obvious."

"Obvious, Hell," Dr. Hunter said. I tried to overlook the profanity. "How you know some alien's gonna be placental? She surely isn't mammillary, not with that practically concave chest. Genitals don't even approximate human type. Oh Lord, Lord."

"But," I said to him, "what else could it be? She *does*," I pointed it out, "have a navel."

He shook his head, his hand wiping his forehead. "Never mind. I'll accept that as a hypothesis." He looked the blue man up and down a moment, then said, "By the way she's acting, birth is imminent. So, yeah, I'll want you to assist me. Go wash up, put on these," handing me a mask, cap, and gown, "and sterilize these.'' He gave me a forceps, speculum, two scalpels, and several clamps. ''Wear these gloves.''

He turned away as I balanced all these things in my arms.   I already knew that one is supposed to do such things; Dr. Hunter, like all Europeans, is quite peremptory.   Oh, I felt—but that doesn't matter.   It was at that moment that I looked at the blue man again, at the deep, deep eyes . . . and Dr. Hunter's rudeness didn't signify.   Had the blue man been a person like me, that look would have been a smile, a smile amidst all her pain.   I smiled back.

So.   I did as I had been told, coming back shortly with the instruments piled on Dr. Hunter's steel tray.   The doctor had closed the blinds to keep out the flies and dust, and set out several clean glass dishes and test tubes.   ''For samples,'' he said.   He went to wash up as well.

When he returned, he began by filling his glassware with various of the blue man's excretions.   From time to time a few drops of violet-colored blood ran from her birth canal, and nothing we did seemed to stop it.   The bag of waters had apparently already ruptured, although Dr. Hunter later said he didn't think there had ever been any.   The pains were evident and regular, about ten minutes apart. The blue man grunted with each, holding onto my hand or the table as she bore down during the spasms.   Time went on like this.

It was very close in the room, quite extremely warm.   Dr. Hunter was sweating, I was sweating—even the blue man had sweat beads about her head and neck.   I wiped them away and she spoke some words.   They made no sense, but then what do you expect from a foreigner?   Dr. Hunter listened to her belly with his stethoscope, poked and prodded, but did little else.   He did not try to dilate the birth canal, which I certainly would have done by this time.   He wouldn't even allow me to give the blue man some water.   ''We don't know if her system can tolerate real water—let alone the terrestrial organisms contaminating this stuff.   God knows what airborne diseases are already infecting her. And anyway, I don't want her to drink because I sure don't need to load up her bladder right now—if she's even got a bladder.''   Well, that made sense, so I let the matter go.

As time went by, the sun, in its swing about the building, found a crack between the screen and the window frame.   It shone in brightly, falling directly onto the blue man's face.   Her eyes seemed very sensitive to our light; she squeezed them shut till I repositioned the blind.   ''That is the Sun,'' I said to her.   ''The Sun. And I am Doto.   Do-to.''   She gazed at me a moment, then said—as nearly as *I* can say it—''Hckvfuhl.''

''There!'' I said.   ''That must be her name.   Or possibly her country.''

Dr. Hunter snorted impolitely.   ''Me–Man.   This–Earth.   Sounds more like she's clearing her throat.''   A moment later, the blue man spasmed again, crying out the loudest she had yet today, and he simply stood there, doing nothing.

I was annoyed.   First, at this nasty drip of sweat that had run beneath my mask so I *couldn't* wipe it away; second, at Dr. Hunter.   *Mostly* at Dr. Hunter.   I said as evenly as I could, ''Doctor, she is suffering greatly.   There are drugs to relieve pain.   Could you not give her a little, just to help?''

Still he did nothing, not even looking at me.   Shortly, the blue man's pains ceased.

"Dr. Hunter, I am asking you to help her.   Push on her belly, use the forceps, why don't you?   Even Juna the midwife would have had this baby born before now.   Why, I myself—"

"Oh, shove it!" he yelled at me, while a second pain arose in Hckvfuhl.   He turned to me, sweating angrily, and shouted further, "You damn native bitch! What do you know—a horse doctor?!   This is an alien, do you understand, an *alien*.   You don't know—*I* don't know the first thing about her, her physiology, or how it functions.   You and your African midwife would have had her dead by now."   Yet another cry from the blue man distracted him, and he seemed to sweat even more, if possible.   "There is nothing I can do but wait and watch.   This may even be normal for her species.   I'm not about to kill her by fooling around where I'm ignorant.   Just don't you give me any flak, girl."   And so he let her cry and cry and cry.

After an hour all the pains had slacked off.   That is not right, it doesn't happen with people or cattle.   I was alarmed that the child might be dead, but Dr. Hunter still reported hearing the fetal heartbeat.   There was still that thin trickle of violet blood which would not be stopped, only slowed.   Hckvfuhl moaned often from continuous pain, which was the most frightening of all.   The eyes were shut tight.

Eventually it neared sunset.   As the sun rimmed the unshaded window on the west side, it grew slightly cooler, quieter as both the insects and the village prepared for nightfall.   It comes swiftly here.   "I am hungry," I said.   Dr. Hunter looked up.

"Mm, yeah, so am I.   More than that, I need to take a break; and I bet you do, too.   I don't think we better eat anything, we don't have time.   But you go ahead.   Take five minutes, then be right back."

"All right."   I removed my mask and cap, peeled off my gloves.   Then, as I suddenly recalled, I put my hand to my cheek, saying, "Llana!   Her calf—"

"Doto."   Dr. Hunter looked at me wearily.   "Screw the cow.   This is more important."

Well, Musa might not have agreed with him, but no matter.   I took the break— oh, a most welcome relief!—pausing also for a small drink of water at the outdoor pump.   It was so cool, so good going down into my belly growling of its hunger. I took a few more gulps and my stomach quieted.   The sun was touching the horizon, the sky turning from yellow in the east through blue to red in the west. Tomorrow's would be much the same weather as today's.

I returned to the house and re-dressed, with fresh gloves.   As I came into the dispensary, to my utter surprise I saw Dr. Hunter helping the blue man to drink from a glass beaker of water.   Hckvfuhl drank it thirstily, making smacking sounds like a child, supported on the American's arm.   I leaned against the doorway grinning—I confess it—like a monkey and caught Dr. Hunter's eye.   He hunched embarrassedly, then shrugged to indicate the liquid.   "Distilled," he said. "Shouldn't do any harm.   Anyway, she was thirsty."

"Yes," I agreed, making my face *very* sober, as he carefully laid Hckvfuhl back down. He prepared to go, pulling off his gloves and unfastening his mask, saying, "I think we'll be okay if she just doesn't deliver here. It'll be safer for her in Lodwar—or better yet, Nairobi, or even the U.S. I know you meant well for the alien, but I don't want to force her baby. Do you know what I mean?"

"I think I do," I said. I couldn't help responding to the change in this Westerner. For once he seemed to worry about—how to say it, the *person,* not the "political affiliation." Till now, Dr. Hunter, in trying so hard to be "African," somehow failed to be "Brother Hunter." Then I added, "But you could have been more pleasant about it."

"Oh, excuse me," he said exaggeratedly. "Well, maybe today I haven't done things the way you would have liked, but she is still alive, and that's what counts, right? I think we'll just pull this one through, Doto, you and I."

I smiled. "Of course. Was there ever any doubt?"

"None at all." He patted my arm. "Now you be good and make sure the alien stays calm. I'll be going up the road to see if Jama's on the way. Hold the fort till I get back." He winked at me—not respectful, but who could mind now?—and left.

It was beginning to grow dark outside. I peered out past the window blinds at the groundsel trees silhouetted against the twilight sky: short, ugly trees, shaped like a nubby gourd on a stick. The groundsels, and all of the trees, do not grow very tall here, west of Lake Rudolf. There is not much rain.

"Snyagshe." The blue man's word turned me round. She was struggling to sit up, so I helped her. She seemed very tired, and with good reason. The sheet fell away, but it was still too warm to worry about that. Again those lovely eyes shut as she leaned against the wall, squatting on her calves. I sat down opposite her, thinking, how odd it is, that the English word "calf" means both baby cow and lower leg. I had gone from the first to the second all in one day. How utterly amazing. My own were excruciatingly tired.

After a bit I stood to light the kerosene lamp. The flame sat steady on its wick in the still air as I replaced the chimney over it. And it was just about then that the blue man cried out.

A lot of blue-tinged liquid was flooding her thighs; I could see her abdomen pulsing, rippling downward. She stood up straight on her knees, her fingers scrabbling for purchase on the wall behind her; found some, evidently. I was there in front of her in a second, pressing downward on her belly with the palm of my hand; maybe it helped. We pushed and strained together, then a little bit of grey head appeared, and more and more, stuttering outward with the pulses. Hckvfuhl was not crying any longer, but her pants were quick and loud. The baby's head was born, but there it halted.

Yet the rippling went on, and Hckvfuhl still strained against the wall. By now it was quite obvious she was placental, so perhaps the cord was restraining the baby? I felt under the child's almost nonexistent chin, barely able to fit my fingers into the tiny space; the little one was wedged tight. Indeed, it was the cord, wrapped around the neck, like a noose. I pulled it carefully, it gave slightly; pulled it downward over the child's face, it stopped short. I put my right hand under the child's head and strove to shove it back up into the womb just enough to get the umbilicus over the crown. Over its head, and then freed, the child slid out into my hands like a wet seed.

The rest was simple. The baby breathed, the cord was tied, the afterbirth came. I cleaned the child off, and Hckvfuhl as well, then carried her into Dr. Hunter's own bedroom to sleep. It was necessary; I wasn't going to allow the blue man to sleep on that mess in the infirmary. She was very light in my arms.

I brought the baby to her, with the lamp and the marvelous mesh bag; and we clothed it. It appeared to be a girl; at least, that's my guess, and it is worth that of anyone else. The baby—hummed, sort of, as we fastened the silver sling around her. It, too, had those beautiful big eyes, open already. Hckvfuhl annointed her little head with the brine from the vial. It was the most beautiful blue baby I have ever seen.

When we were done, I reached for the lamp I had set on the nightstand. Hckvfuhl lay back on the white pillow, watching me. Strange, how those eyes could catch the least ray of light, reflect the lamp like ten lamps in the night. Her hand came up, brushing the back of mine, three blue fingers against my five black ones. "Dto-dto," she said. "Khhon." A moment passed, then I left.

Well, that is what happened the day the rocket landed. Almost as soon as I emerged from the bedroom, Dr. Hunter, Brother Jama, the District Commissioner, and all the official people arrived to take Hckvfuhl off to Nairobi; and I never saw her anymore. I do understand, though, that she and her daughter are well, wherever they are.

Of course, Dr. Hunter was annoyed at me for not stopping the child's birth—as if I could stop the moon and the stars, too. But he got over it when the newspapers in the capital called him a "Statue of Liberty in the savannah," keeping Hckvfuhl's "fragile spark alight." They printed my name, too.

Oh, and finally, yes, Llana came through without me well enough. Twice as well, in fact; astoundingly, she managed to produce twins. And what do you know, stingy old Musa even did pay up all that he owed.

WILLIAM JON WATKINS

Coming of Age in Henson's Tube

Lobber ran in shouting like it was already too late. "Keri's gone Skyfalling! Keri's gone Skyfalling!" He was the kind of kid you naturally ignore, so he had to shout *every*thing. I ignored him. Moody didn't. It made no difference. Lobber went right on shouting. "I saw him going up the Endcap with his wings!"

Moody shouted right back. "Why didn't you stop him?"

"Who?! Me?!! Nobody can stop Keri when he wants to do something. He's crazy!" Lobber was right, of course. Keri *was* crazy; always putting himself in danger for the fun of it, always coming out in one piece. You couldn't stop him. Even Moody couldn't, and Moody was his older brother.

Moody grabbed a pair of Close-ups and started for the door. "He better *not* be Skyfalling! He's too young!"

That almost made me laugh really, because we were *all* too young. But Moody had done it two years ago without getting caught, and I had done it last year. Lobber would never do it. I guess that was why he shouted so much. If you even mentioned it to him, he'd say, "Are you crazy?! You could get killed doing that!"

And he was right about that too. Every couple years, somebody would wait too long to open their wings, or open them too often, and that would be it. Even the lower gravity of Henson's Tube doesn't let you make a mistake like that more than once. My father says he saw his best friend get killed opening up too late, and I remember how Keri started crying when Moody came plummeting down out of the air and we thought he'd never open his wings and glide.

Still, when you get to be a certain age in Henson's Tube, you go up the Endcap to the station and hitch a ride on the catchrails of the Shuttle. And when it gets to the middle of the cable, you jump off. It's not all that dangerous really if you open your wings at the right times. The way gravity works in Henson's Tube, or any of the other orbiting space colonies for that matter, makes it a lot less dangerous than doing the same thing on Earth.

The difference in gravity comes from the way Henson's Tube is shaped. It's like a test tube, sealed at both ends. The people all live on the inside walls of the tube, and the tube is spun, like an axle in place, to give it gravity. If you look with a pair of Close-ups, you can see land overhead above the clouds, but the other side of the Tube is five kilometers away, and that's a long way when it's straight up.

If you were born in the Tube like we all were, it doesn't seem unnatural to you to be spun around continually in two-minute circles, and even tourists find it just like Earth, all rocks and trees and stuff, until they look up. Of course, the one half gravity at "ground level" makes them a little nervous, but the real difference in gravity is at the center of the Tube. There's a sort of invisible axle running down the center of the tube lengthwise, where there's no gravity. That's where the Shuttle runs on its cable from one Endcap to the other. And that's where you start your Fall.

You step off the Shuttle halfway along its ride, and you drift very slowly toward one side of the Tube. But pretty soon the ground rotates away, under you, and the wind begins to push you around the center cable too. Only you don't just go around it in a circle, because going around starts giving you some gravity, so you come spiraling down toward the ground, rotating always a bit slower than the Tube itself.

The closer you get to the sides, the faster the Tube—the ground—spins on past you. The gravity depends on how much you've caught up with the rotating of the Tube. If you didn't have wings, you'd hit hard enough to get killed for sure, partly from falling and partly because the ground would be going past so fast when you hit. If you do have wings, then they slow down your falling okay, but then they catch the wind more, so you're rotating almost as fast as the Tube is. Only then, because you're going around faster, the gravity is stronger and you have to really use the wings to keep from landing too hard. Only by then you're probably half-way around the Tube from where you wanted to land, and it's a long walk home.

Usually, you just step off the Shuttle and drop with your wings folded until you get scared enough to open your arms. When you do, your wings begin to slow your fall. If you don't wait too long, that is. If you *do* wait too long, when you throw your arms open, they get snapped up and back like an umbrella blowing inside out, and there's nothing left to stop you. Most of the people who get hurt Skyfalling get scared and open their wings too soon or too often. Most of the ones who get killed open their wings too late. Nobody had ever seen Keri get scared.

That was probably what Moody was thinking about as he ran for the door. I know it was what I was thinking about as I grabbed a pair of Close-ups that must have been Keri's and ran after him. Lobber ran after both of us, shouting. By the time we got outside, the silver, bullet-shaped car of the Shuttle was about a third of the way along its cable, and there was nothing to do but wait until it got almost directly above us.

At first, we couldn't see Keri and we thought he must have missed the Shuttle, but then we saw him, sitting on the long catchrail on the underside of the Shuttle with his feet over the side. Lobber kept trying to grab my Close-ups, shouting, "Let me look! Let me look!" I ignored him, but it didn't do any good until Moody grabbed him and said, "Shut up, Lobber, just shut up!" Lobber looked like he was going to start shouting about being told to shut up, but the Shuttle was almost directly overhead by then, so he did shut up and watched.

When the Shuttle got where he wanted it, Keri stood up, stopped for a second to pick out his landmarks and then just stepped off.   He fell slowly at first, almost directly above us.   But soon he began to slide back and away from us in wider and wider spirals as the Tube revolved.   For a second, he looked like he was just standing there watching the Shuttle go on down the Tube and us slide away beneath him.

But in a couple seconds he went from being as big as my thumb to being as big as the palm of my hand.   We could tell he was riding down the pull of gravity at a good speed and getting faster all the time.   He had his head into the wind and his body out behind him to cut down his resistance, so the wind wasn't rotating him with it too much, and his speed was going up and up and we knew he'd have to do something soon to cut it down.

When he was half a mile above us, he still hadn't opened his wings.   Moody lowered his Close-ups and shook his head like he was sure Keri would never make it.   When he looked up again, Keri was a lot closer to the ground, and his blue wings were still folded across his chest.   It's hard to tell from the ground how far you can fall before you pass the point where it's too late to open your wings, but it looked to us like Keri had already passed it.   And he still hadn't spread his wings.

"Open up!" Moody shouted, "Open up!"   And for a little while Keri did just that, until he began to slide back around the curve of the Tube.   But long before he should have, he pulled his arms back in and started that long dive again. All Lobber could see was a small fluttering fall of blue against the checkerboard of the far side of the Tube.   "He's out of control!" Lobber shouted.

He was wrong, of course.   For some crazy reason of his own, Keri had done it on purpose, but when I went to tell Lobber to shut up, I found that my mouth was too dry to talk.   It didn't matter, because Lobber went suddenly quiet.   Moody stood looking up through his Close-ups and muttering, "Open up, Keri!   Open up!"

It seemed like an hour before Keri finally did.   You could almost hear the flap of the blue fabric as he threw his arms open.   His arms snapped back, and for a minute, I thought he was going to lose it, but he fought them forward and held them out steady.

But it still looked like he had waited too long.   He was sliding back a little, but he was still falling, and falling fast.   I could see him straining against the force of his fall, trying to overcome it, but I didn't think he was going to make it.

I didn't want to follow him in that long fall all the way into the ground.   I thought about how my father said his friend had looked after he hit, and I knew I didn't want to see Keri like that.   But just before I looked away, Keri did the craziest thing I ever saw.   Falling head down with his arms out, he suddenly jack-knifed himself forward, held it for a second, then snapped his head up and spread-eagled himself.   His wings popped like a billowbag opening up.

Moody gave a little gasp and I felt my own breath suck in.   But it turned out that Keri knew more about Skyfalling than either of us ever would and when he threw his arms back, he had almost matched ground speed and the maneuver had put him into a stall so close to the ground that I still don't believe it was possible.

Of course, Keri being Keri, he held his wings out just a fraction too long, and he went up and over before he could snap his arms down completely and came down backward. You could almost hear the crunch when he hit. I swear he bounced and flipped over backwards and then bounced and rolled over four more times before he stopped. For a second we just stood there, too stunned to move, and then we were suddenly all running toward him, with Moody in the lead.

When we got to Keri, he was sitting up, unsnapping his wings and rubbing his shoulders. His arms were a mess, all scraped and scratched, but not broken. Even though he had a helmet on, one eye was swollen shut. But he was smiling.

Moody got to him first and helped him up. "You're crazy, Keri! You know that?! You could have got yourself killed! You know that?! You know that?!" I don't think I ever remember Moody being that mad. He sounded like his father. "Look at you! You're lucky you didn't get killed!"

But Keri just kept grinning and the louder Moody got, the wider Keri grinned until Moody just turned away in disgust. Nobody said anything for a while, not even Lobber. Finally Keri said, "C'mon, Moody, I didn't act like that when *you* came down."

Moody turned around and looked at his brother like he knew Keri was right, but he wasn't ready yet to forgive him for scaring us like that. "Yeah, but I didn't wait until I almost hit the ground before I opened up! I didn't scare anybody half to death thinking I was going to get myself killed!"

Keri looked at him and chuckled. "Didn't you?"

"That wasn't the same!" Moody said. But you could tell he knew it was. Finally, he grabbed Keri's wings. "Here, give me those before you tear them."

Keri laughed and handed him the wings. He gave me a wink with his good eye. "Not easy being on the ground. Is it?" I shook my head. Moody just snorted and folded the wings. I kept waiting for Lobber to start shouting again, but he didn't. He just looked up at where the Shuttle had passed, and when he spoke, his voice was wistful and quiet like he knew Skyfalling was something he would never be able to do, no matter how much he might want to. "What does it feel like, Keri?" he said.

Keri shrugged, and I knew it was because there is something in the Fall, something about the way it gets faster and faster, and the ground rushes up at you like certain death, that he couldn't explain. I could see the freedom of it still sparkling in his eyes. "It feels like being alive."

JACK C. HALDEMAN II

Home Team Advantage

Slugger walked down the deserted hallway, his footsteps making a hollow ringing sound under the empty stadium.   Turning a corner, he headed for the dugout.   He was early.   He was always early.   Sportscasters said he'd probably be early for his own funeral.

He was.

Slugger sat on the wooden bench.   It was too quiet.   He picked up a practice bat and tapped it against the concrete floor.   Normally he and Lefty would be razzing Pedro.   Coach Weinraub would be pacing up and down, cursing the players, the umpire.   There would be a lot of noise, gum popping, tobacco spitting, and good-natured practical jokes.   The Kid would be sitting at the far end of the bench, worrying about his batting average and keeping his place in the starting lineup. The Kid always did that, even though he had a .359 average.   The Kid was a worrier, but he wouldn't worry anymore.   Not after yesterday.   Not after the Arcturians won the series and ended the season.   Not after they won the right to eat all the humans.

Tough luck about being eaten, but Slugger couldn't let himself feel too bad about that; he had led the league in homers and the team had finished the regular season 15 games out in front.   Except for the series with the Arcturians, it had been a good year.   Slugger hefted the practice bat over his shoulder and climbed the dugout steps, as he had done so many times before, up to the field.   This time there were no cheers.

The early morning wind blew yesterday's hot dog wrappers and beer cups across the infield.   It was cool; dew covered the artificial grass, fog drifted in the bleachers. Slugger strode firmly up to the plate, took his stance, and swung hard at an imaginary ball.   In his mind there was a solid crack, a roar from the crowd and the phantom ball sailed over the center field fence.   He dropped the bat and started to run the bases.   By the time he rounded third, he had slowed to a walk.   The empty stadium closed in on him, and when he reached home plate he sat down in the batter's box to wait for the Arcturians.

He wasn't alone very long.   A television crew drove up in a large van and started setting up their cameras.   Some carpenters quickly erected a temporary stage on the pitcher's mound.   The ground crew half-heartedly picked up the hot

439

dog wrappers and paper cups.   Slugger started back to the dugout but he didn't make it.   He ran into the Hawk.

Julius Hawkline was a character, an institution of sorts in the sports world.   In his early days as a manager, the Hawk had been crankier and more controversial than the legendary Stengel.   In his present role as television announcer and retired S.O.B., the Hawk was more irritating and opinionated than the legendary Cosell. True to his name, the Hawk was descending on Slugger for an interview.

"Hey Slugger!"

"Gotta go."

"Just take a minute."   A man was running around with a camera, getting it all on tape.   "You owe it to the fans."

The fans.   That got to Slugger.   It always did.

"Okay, Hawk.   Just a minute.   Gotta get back to the locker room.   The guys'll be there soon."

"How's it feel to have blown the game, the series—to be responsible for the Arcturians earning the right to eat all the humans?"

"We played good," said Slugger, backing away.   "They just played better. That's all."

"That's *all?*   They're going to *eat* us and you blew it four to three.   Not to mention Lefty—"

"Don't blame Lefty.   He couldn't help it.   Got a trick ankle, that's all."

"*All?*   They're going to gobble us up—you know, knives, forks, pepper, Worcestershire sauce, all that stuff; every man, woman, and child.   Imagine all those poor children out there covered with catsup.   All because of a trick ankle and a couple of bonehead plays.   Sure we can blame Lefty.   The whole world will blame Lefty, blame you, blame the entire team.   You let us down.   It's all over, buddy, and your team couldn't win the big one.   What do you have to say to that?"

"We played good.   They played better."

The Hawk turned from Slugger and faced the camera.   "And now you have it, ladies and gentlemen, the latest word from down here on the field while we wait the arrival of the Arcturians for their post-game picnic.   Slugger says we played good, but let me tell you that this time 'good' just wasn't good enough.   We had to be *great* and we just couldn't get it up for the final game.   The world will little note nor long remember that Slugger went ten for seventeen in the series, or that we lost the big one by only one run.   What they *will* remember is Lefty falling down rounding first, *tripping* over his own shoelaces, causing us to lose the whole ball of wax."

Slugger walked over to the Hawk, teeth clenched.   He reached out and crumpled the microphone with one hand.

"Lefty's my friend.   We played good."   He turned and walked back to the dugout.

The Hawk was delighted.   They'd gotten it all on tape.

When Slugger got back to the dressing room, most of the team was there, suiting up.   Everything was pretty quiet, there was none of the horseplay that usually preceded a game. Slugger went to his locker and started to dress. Someone had tied his shoelaces together. He grinned. It was a tough knot.

Usually coach Weinraub would analyze the previous day's game—giving pointers, advice, encouragement and cussing a few of the players out. Today he just sat on the bench, eyes downcast. Slugger had to keep reminding himself that there wouldn't be any more games; not today, not tomorrow. Never again. It just didn't seem possible. He slipped his glove on, the worn leather fitting his hand perfectly. It felt good to be in uniform, even if it was just for a picnic.

The noise of the crowd filtered through to the dressing room; the stadium was filling up. The Arcturians would be here soon. Reporters were crowding at the door, slipping inside. Flashbulbs were popping.

Lefty snuck in the back way and slipped over to his locker. It was next to Slugger's. They had been friends a long time, played in the minors together.

"Mornin' Lefty," said Slugger. "How's the wife and kids?"

"Fine," mumbled Lefty, pulling off the false mustache he'd worn to get through the crowd.

"Ankle still bothering you?"

"Naw. It's fine now."

"Can't keep a good man down," said Slugger, patting Lefty on the back.

A microphone appeared between them, followed by the all too familiar face of the Hawk.

"Hey Lefty, how about a few words for the viewing public? How does it feel to be the meathead that blew the whole thing?"

"Aw, come on, Hawk, gimme a break."

"It was a team effort all the way," said Slugger, reaching for the microphone.

"These things cost money," said the Hawk, stepping back. The coach blew his whistle.

"Come on team, this is it. Everybody topside." The dressing room emptied quickly. Nobody wanted to be around the Hawk. Even being the main course at the picnic was better than that.

On the field the Arcturians had already been introduced and they stood at attention along the third base line. One by one the humans' names were called, and they took their places along the first base line. The crowd cheered Slugger and booed Lefty. Slugger felt bad about that. The stage on the pitcher's mound had a picnic table on it and the Arcturian managers and coaches were sitting around it, wearing bibs.

After they played both planets' anthems, George Alex, the league president, went to the podium set up on the stage.

"Ladies and gentlemen, I won't keep you in suspense much longer. The name of the first human to be eaten will be announced shortly. But first I would like to thank you, the fans, for casting so many ballots to choose the person we will honor today. As with the All-Star game, the more votes that are cast make for a more representative selection. All over the country—the world, for that matter— fans like you, just plain people, have been writing names on the backs of hot dog wrappers and stuffing them in the special boxes placed in all major league stadiums.

I'm proud to say that over ten million votes were cast and we have a winner. The envelope, please."

A man in a tuxedo, flanked by two armed guards, presented the envelope.

"The results are clear. The first human to be eaten will be . . . the Hawk! Let's hear it for *Julius W. Hawkline!*"

The stadium rocked with cheers. The Hawk was obviously the crowd's favorite. He was, however, reluctant to come forward and had to be dragged to the stage. The other reporters stuck microphones in his face, asking him how it felt to be the chosen one. For the first time in his life the Hawk was at a loss for words.

The coach of the Arcturians held the Hawk with four of his six arms and ceremoniously bit off his nose. Everyone cheered and the Arcturian chewed. And chewed. The crowd went wild. He chewed some more. Finally, he spat the Hawk's nose out and went into a huddle with the other coaches.

Undigestible, was the conclusion, unchewable; humans were definitely inedible. Something else would have to be arranged.

Slugger smiled to himself, thinking ahead to next season. You had to hand it to the Hawk; he was one tough old bird.

DREW MENDELSON

Star Train

L eo had not been designed for this.   Life lay outside his scope.   He asked
Orsini when Orsini's train stopped for an hour at Leo'station.
   "What do I do, Orsini?   It seems alive."
   Orsini didn't know.
   It was a doll.   Leo had found it on the waiting room bench after a family had
transferred trains on their way past Centaurus to Earth.   She was a tiny thing in
Leo's cupped hands, a doll that talked and walked and cried and wet and breathed.
Leo's hands, twice the size of any human hands, held her.   He offered her to
Orsini.   Orsini refused.
   "It looks to be a baby, a human child," Orsini said.   "Now who would leave
a child of theirs on the waiting room bench?   Who would leave a baby a thousand
light-years from a living world?"
   "I have no way to care for a child," Leo said.   "There is no air here at all but
the waiting room air.   The trains bring that when they come.   The last roomful
is nearly exhausted.   Human babies need water.   I have none.   Human babies
need food, do they not?   I have no food.   What will happen to it, Orsini?"
   "It will die," Orsini said.   Orsini remembered death.   He had died himself
some time ago, one and a half millenia as Orsini recollected it.   Orsini was an
illusion.   His personality, stripped from him bits at a time, stretched through 28,000
parsecs of space.   His personality now, a thousand and a half years after his death,
powered the engines of the star trains.
   "I carry only freight," Orsini said.   "There is no room for life aboard my
train."
   "Help me, Orsini," Leo said.
   "I can't," Orsini told him.   "I must leave now, Leo.   I have a schedule to
keep."
   The star trains' illusionary engineers were notoriously intractable.   All construc-
tive thought had ended in them when they died; they were simply the memories of
men and women imprinted on the substance of space.   What they had nt done
they would never do.   What they hadn't thought was unthinkable to them.   They
were stretched gigantically from star to star, halfway across the galaxy.   Yet, like
the steel rails of the planet-bound railroad, they moved not an inch by themselves.

"I must go," Orsini said.   And the ugly gnomish image of that which had once been Orsini left with his interstellar freight.

Leo held the baby.   It cried, and though passengers had come and gone countless times through his station, some with crying babies, it was as if Leo had never heard the sound before.   He had never held a child.   His hands were for the lifting of colossal weights, metric tons from train to train.   His hands were for the shifting of switches in the rail yard that was Leo'station.   His hands, though they seemed supple and human, were the highest evolution of metallurgy and mechanics.   He was of metal and built for metal and for the railroad between the stars.   Life was outside his scope.

The little girl cried.   She said "Da-da," in a high clear voice and struggled fitfully in Leo's hands.   He held her like an egg or something as fragile, out away from his body.   Leo had a face, fashioned in the image of a human face so as not to frighten the passengers who came through his station.   His eyes were human enough, pigmented blue and white, iris and eyeball.   Even his skin had been of human color once, an indeterminate shade of human colors blended.   It had faded, and his hair was not in single strands but molded in a mass.   The baby didn't know and still cried, "Da-da," to Leo.

"What do I do with you?" Leo asked the baby.

"What do I do with a human child?" he bellowed into the empty station, and his voice was ten times a human voice and the child struggled and cried.

This was Leo's world, the station.   He paced it; it was twelve strides long, twice that in human strides.   He paced it.   It had not seemed so small before during his ten centuries there.   There was a beauty to it, he had always thought that. *Fyri,* the giant B-3 sun, was so close that its corona whipped the station's walls. Its solar wind flew by in tatters, glowing.   He, Leo, was the sort of life that belonged here on the star trains' right-of-way.   He paced, and the mewing of the little girl grew shriller and more desperate.   He found that she had wet his hands. Her crying wouldn't cease.

There was nothing soft in the station at all.   Everything was durable.   Nothing wore out in human lifetimes.   He wrapped the child as best he could in the soft sheets of insulation he tore from the station's walls.

Then Leo went onto the wire.   It was the way they spoke between the star train stations, a modulation of the rail force itself.   It was half thought and half wish. Leo wished that Gonzalez, the human track master at Centauri station, would hear. Perhaps Gonzalez came on the wire, perhaps Leo only wished he did.   It didn't matter; the star train only probably existed to begin with.   It existed only because passengers, railroaders, and engineers believed that it existed.   The star trains were driven by belief, and the force of that belief carried talk between the stations.

"I have a child," Leo said.   "Someone left it in my station.   When will you send a train to get it?   She will die soon if you don't."

Did Gonzalez say he wouldn't do it?   So Leo believed.

"There are two hundred thousand parsecs of track.   There are a hundred and twenty-five trains," Gonzalez said.   This was long before the trans-mat came to kill the interstellar railroad.   This was the heyday, the high time of the railroad.

"Leo, there are two million passengers a day on our trains. Do I disrupt this all because you are concerned with a bit of life?"

"It is a human child," Leo said.

"I'm afraid it's not," Gonzalez told him. "All our fare-paying passengers are accounted for. No one has lost a child."

"I tell you it is a baby," Leo said.

"Wait, please, Leo," Gonzalez said. "We'll find out for you soon."

Leo did not deal in hours easily. There was a clock of sorts within him that kept track of things of short duration. Living things were changeable, breathing one time, not the next. The passengers who came through Leo'station were like that. The same passengers were always different when they came on different journeys. It was the hair, the eyes that changed. They called this process aging. It seemed to Leo that aging occurred in humans at a frightening rate. There was a woman called Malinda who had ridden the star trains at regular times. And it seemed incredible to Leo that in the short space of fifty years, almost an eye blink of time, she had become grey suddenly, stooped suddenly and frail as if the star train had leached strength from her. He had enjoyed her comings and goings like a periodic comet. She had not traveled the star train in years. Perhaps she died. Life was like that.

Gonzalez was back. Leo saw that the baby had not changed and the clock inside him could detect no time past or very little at all.

"You can relax, Leo," Gonzalez said. "You know you gave us quite a fright here. A couple came through, a family with a child of their own, this morning through the main gate at Earth station. And they reported the loss of a doll. It belonged to their little girl. They said she left it in your station by accident. It's not a human child at all. It's just a toy, a doll, Leo, nothing to be concerned about. Send it along on the next train through. We'll get it back to its owner."

The child moved on the bench, quiet now, playing with her toes. She watched Leo; he thought he saw her smile.

"Gonzalez," said Leo, "this child is no toy. It breathes in the way humans breathe. It says things to me. It said 'da-da' to me. Human children do that. I have seen them and heard them when they come through here. The next train is one week off. How can I wait until then to send this baby? For pity's sake, Gonzalez, this thing—toy or not—is alive."

"Leo, it is a construct, an imitation of a living thing, a toy for a child. It breathes because the child it imitates breathes; it laughs because human children laugh; whatever human children do it does. But it is not human, it will not grow or change. It was made like that."

"I am a construct," Leo said. "I am an imitation of human life. What a human does I do. What of me, Gonzalez? Are you going to let me end when I'm not important anymore?"

"That's different, Leo, you serve a function."

"And when that function is over, do I die too, because I'm not of human stuff?"

"Leo, it doesn't mean that at all. . . ."

"We will see, Gonzalez. I'm bringing this child to you, toy or not, doll or not.   Humans are frail and quick to die.   I will find a way to bring you this child. Best you pray it doesn't die before then.''

Perhaps Leo said this.   Perhaps it was a wish.   *Fyri* flamed a hundred million miles away, and the star train here rode the crest of a gravity ridge.   The solar wind here from the giant star was a gale.   Its energy stung Leo's skin.   He stood on the star train platform and watched the winds of this sun's light scud down the rails.   Few could see the star train's track; it was not in most to see it.   The track was simply a path of least resistance between the stars, forced open by the passage of a human mind.   It remained as long as the force of that mind remained.   Leo existed because of the trains, had been built for them, would die with their end, and thus he saw the tracks and believed.   A thousand years of solar winds had pitted him, had blasted him smooth, though he was pocked minutely where the largest particles had struck.   He lived off the energy, fed off it.   He stood in the buffeting of this solar wind and it streamed along behind him.   Broken atoms pelted him; he sucked at them and grew drunk.

Leo said, ''I'll take the child to Centarus.   There is a way.''

There was a way, the most pitiful chance of a way.   There was a yard cart at Leo'station, an open frame of metal sealed with glassite windows, an open cage powered, as all the trains on this line were powered, by the memory of Orsini. Now, maybe there was air enough and maybe there was time enough to barrel this flimsy cart down the right-of-way to Centarus.

''It won't go,'' a little Orsini said, ''I can't drive this cart fast enough.   I don't believe it, so it won't go.''

Orsini was everywhere on his track.   At times there were ten-twelve-fifteen Orsinis simultaneously.   Every time a train moved on this track its motion conjured up another image of Orsini.   But this was so weak, so tiny an Orsini: the engine of the yard cart could evoke only the thinnest Orsini from this stretch of his track.

''I feel I am barely here at all,'' Orsini said.   ''I'm too weak to drive this cart fast.''

Leo sat beneath the blaze of the great B-3 sun in the compartment of the yard cart.   ''Take her out, Orsini,'' he said.   ''We'll go as fast as we can go.''

The baby squirmed in Leo's hands and stars drew dopplered streaks on the glassite roof.   They rolled out of Leo'station, picking up speed down the gravity ridge. Orsini's belief drove the yard cart here, and now he seemed nothing but a wasted runt.

''This is life, Orsini,'' Leo said.   ''Once you had it; do you remember it now?''

Orsini answered, ''I don't know.''   But Orsini remembered death.   The doll child was dying.   They both saw it now.   Her struggles were weaker.   She didn't smile.   She didn't say ''da-da'' to Leo.   She cried in a thin continuous wail that Leo scarcely heard.

''You were a human, Orsini.   Don't humans care about life?''   Leo watched the doll child dying.   The yard cart crawled along the light-years.

Leo went on the wire.

''Gonzalez, this is Leo,'' he said.   ''I'm coming down the main grade track.

I'm in the yard cart, coming to Centarus. I'm bringing you this baby. We just might make it before this baby dies."

"Leo," said Gonzales, perhaps he screamed; Leo wished he had. "Take your cart back to the station now. I have a freight coming on your same track. Forget the doll, it's nothing of worth. You're on the same track as the freight."

"Move it," said Leo. "Sideline that train. I won't have anything stopping me."

The yard cart rolled on Orsini's track. He was an ugly little man, solid and squat with a brutish turn. But he'd heard Gonzalez on the wire. There had been children in Orsini's life. He saw the dying baby. He listened to Gonzalez on the wire. Maybe he began to believe. Did the yard cart pick up speed? Maybe Orsini was growing now, not so scrawny, filling out. Did Leo see the track ahead where it wound down a valley through gravity bluffs? The yard cart rolled on the star train's track fifteen light-years an hour toward Centarus. Orsini rolled on hate.

"Tells me to sideline, tells me to turn back. I'm Orsini," he said. "Gonzalez knows I built this railroad. If star trains move between the stars it is because of me."

The yard cart picked up speed: twenty light-years, twenty-five an hour. There was a freight on the oncoming track. They heard its lepton whistle now, blown down the track ahead of the train. There was motion and life in the rails now, a wave of belief that swept the star freight on, toward them on their track.

There were no wrecks on the star train's right-of-way. The train was or it was not. Could Leo see that star freight come, ninety light-years an hour, two hundred cars or more? Five light-years off its whistle blew.

"There's a spur and a switch," Gonzalez said. "It's a deadline past *Gann's star*. Leo, pull off there. It's your last chance to miss that freight."

"Is there life on that train?" Leo asked.

Gonzalez' reply came down the wire: "No, it's a freight on Orsini's line. Nothing alive at all."

"Turn the freight then," said Leo. "We're coming ahead."

And Orsini drove the yard cart and Orsini drove the freight rolling toward each other, around the bend of *Gann's star*. The freight train's whistle sounded again, leptons blowing down the track. The freight's light, brighter than the star, swept the track from a light-year away, sucked faster than natural laws should allow by the impulse of Orsini's belief.

There was a noise and a rattling began. The yard cart should not have held on. It rolled at sixty, at sixty-five toward the oncoming train. There was the switch and it swept past, the side track gone and the freight came on.

Trains, if they meet at such a pace on the star track, annihilate each other with an energy fierce as a big sun's death.

Leo held the baby, Leo held the life that Gonzalez said wasn't life at all, a simulacrum. But it cried and struggled and still it breathed.

"Orsini," he said, "this is life here. There is no life on the freight. No matter what Gonzalez says, I believe that this child is alive.   I believe that I am also alive.   There is nothing on the approaching freight.   There is nothing there at all.''

''I'm on the other train,'' Orsini said.

''No, Orsini, here you are alive.   There you're only the mind of an old old spacer, a millenium dead.   Here you are what counts of Orsini, the last of your life.   Do you believe that, Orsini?''

''Maybe I do.''

''That's a ghost train coming,'' Leo said.   ''It isn't really there at all.''

''Maybe I believe it,'' Orsini said.   ''Maybe I do.''

The freight train began to fade.   They heard the whistle; they saw its light.   But there was no substance to the train.   Orsini was a giant now; he crowded Leo in the cabin of the cart.   The cart was flying on the track; a hundred or more it rolled. The dopplered stars were violet flares that burned through the misty fading freight.

''I believe that I am here alone,'' said Orsini.   ''I don't believe there's a freight at all.''

And they met the spot where the freight should have been, where there should have been a nova's flash.   They passed through the ghost train as if it were gone, as if it never had been there at all.   Then they turned the curve at the lip of a hill with the galaxy behind and only Centarus beyond.

And at Centarus, Leo delivered life.

ALAN DEAN FOSTER

Bystander

S leepy . . . he was so sleepy. . . .

Existence was proven by the depth of his dreaming, dreams of endless green plains across which he ran in slow motion. The dream faded. He clutched at it as it faded. Then it was gone.

He awoke.

Chapman sighed, waited motionless and logy until his vision had cleared. Revitalizing liquids stirred in his veins. There was the expected swabby-cotton taste in his mouth, as if he hadn't swallowed in a thousand years.

The clear domed lid of his suspension lounge slid back smoothly. He unlatched one side. Moving deliberately, with muscles groggy from several years' suspension, he eased himself into a sitting position on the lounge edge and stared around the empty pilot's pocket.

All the other seats were empty. He was the sole occupant of the gigantic bulb ship. Must be in orbit around Abraxis now, he mused. In an hour or so the endangered colony there could been shuttling its members aboard. Then he could turn over responsibility to the colony leaders.

That was the second dream to be shattered.

"Position?"

"We are slightly more than five standard days out from Abraxis," replied the even voice of the ship's computer, as though it had last spoken to him only yesterday and not three years ago. Chapman considered this unexpected news, forced his so long unused tongue and palate to work.

"Then why have I been awakened now?" Not that a few days wakefulness would hurt him, but there was no reason for early revivification. No programmed reason, he reminded himself.

"We are presently being paralleled by a Dhabian," the ship explained, "and there . . ."

"Scope first." Chapman curtly interrupted the computer. He drew a globe of energized water from the lounge dispenser, squeezed it down his throat.

Obediently, the ship complied with the order. A small viewscreen set into the emergency pilot's console flickered alight. Displayed on the screen was a massive cluster of red-orange blocks. The blocks were connected according to some elegantly inhuman design to form a ship. A Dhabian ship.

Earthmen had encountered the Dhabians over two decades ago. Since that time the relationship between the two races had been an uncertain one. Mankind's curiosity about the Dhabians was met with what was best described as cordial indifference on the aliens' part. Since the Dhabian vessels, for all their ungainly appearance, were faster than those of men, the aliens' privacy had thus far remained inviolate.

Whenever one of the infrequent encounters between human and Dhabian ships did occur, the Dhabians would sometimes communicate and sometimes not. They were never hostile, only uninterested. It was hinted that they had much of value to offer mankind. But neither pleading, threatening, nor a matching indifference had managed to inspire them to talk.

No one had ever seen an individual Dhabian. Chapman couldn't repress a slight thrill of excitement. Maybe he would be the first.

Yet the silent Dhabian was a known factor. The presence of one did not constitute a sufficient reason for revivification. He told his ship as much.

The ship proceeded to tell him about the new flare.

Flares were the reason for his hastily programmed mission. Astronomers had predicted several years ago that the Abraxis colony would have to be evacuated from its world at least temporarily because its sun was about to go through a period of brief but intense activity. That activity would produce enough high-energy radiation to kill any human on Abraxis's surface, or even slightly beneath it.

For the four to six months of dangerous stellar activity, the population would have to live aboard a rescue ship. This information being communicated to the proper authorities, a properly prepared and provisioned vessel was dispatched with barely enough time to arrive and take on the population before the onset of threatening activity.

What was the problem, then? Were the astronomers wrong? No, the ship informed him, the figures given were correct. The cycle of stellar outbursts was not beginning dangerously early. This new flare was an anomaly, a freak not accounted for in the earlier predictions. It would not endanger the colony, safe beneath its amorphous atmospheric shielding.

However, it would be severe enough to critically damage certain vital components and instruments. The bulb ship would be crippled beyond hope of performing its mission. Incidentally, Chapman would die.

"When?" the dazed pilot muttered.

"Twenty-four to forty-eight hours from now." The reply was quiet. The ship was sophisticated enough to take its pilot's emotional state into consideration and generate appropriate vocoder impulses in response.

Chapman requested more information. In the time remaining to him, the bulb ship could not flee far enough to escape the crippling burst of energy from the star. Nor could he reach the sheltering darkside of the colony world.

"Check computations." The ship did so, repeated what was already known to be inevitable. "Check again."

It was no good. Wishing had no effect on the realities of physics. Hoping failed to reduce either the critical distance to Abraxis or the number of energetic particles the star would generate. Chapman considered thoughtfully, analytically. The mission, then, would fail. The two thousand settlers, scientists, and technicians on the colony world would not be rescued in time. They would die. He would die a little sooner. And he was at once frightened and ashamed, because the last item of the two was the more important to him.

A light winked on on his console: an incoming call for position from the still distant world. An automatic relay would reply to personal curiosity.

"The Dhabian ship," he inquired. "Will it be able to escape the effects of the flare, based on what we know of their abilities?"

A pause, then, "Barring as yet undemonstrated speed, predictions are that it cannot."

He might have company, then. "Offer them the standard 'exchange of information request,' ship." It would be interesting to learn if they were doomed, too. They seemed to be if his ship was right and they didn't possess some extraordinary particle shielding. Maybe they'd come to the Abraxis system to study the activity of its star prior to eruption and had been shocked and trapped by the same coming, unexpected burst of radiation which would finish him.

Anyway, it was something to do. The idea of returning to suspension, to await the end in ignorance, appalled him.

He did not really expect the alien to reply. He was surprised when a voice of oddly modulated tone whispered at him from the speaker. *"We will exchange with you, man."*

"This star will soon generate a burst of highly charged plasma which will be fatal to me." After a moment's thought, he added, "My ship will also be severely damaged."

"Information." The response was Dhabian-brief. *"No query?"*

"What will happen to you?"

"Will with us be the same as with you, man."

The first intimation of Dhabian mortality, Chapman mused. He felt no elation at the discovery. No one else would learn what he might discover here.

"There's no way you can survive? I thought your ships were fast."

"Not enough. But there may be a way." What seemed an uncertain pause before the Dhabian spoke again. *"You have not detected it?"*

"Detected what?" Chapman was more confused than excited.

"The onu."

"What the hell's an . . . ?" Chapman calmed himself. "Can you give me position?"

"Your figurings correspond not well, but from what we have learned," and the Dhabian shot some figures at him.

"Ship? What do they mean?"

"A moment, Chapman." He imagined he could hear the machine thinking . . . too long in suspension, he thought. "Using maximum amplification focused on region given by alien vessel, it is determined that a large though faint object is indeed located in the position suggested. Alien mass sensors must be more effi-cient/powerful than our own. Present position precludes visual identification of comet from this angle of observation."

"Comet? Question, ship. Is it big enough to provide adequate protection from the anticipated flare?"

"Yes, Chapman."

"Second question: is it big enough to provide shielding for *both* vessels?"

"Some delicate close-range maneuvering by each ship to prevent damage from the other's exhaust particles will be required. It can be done. But there is a difficulty."

Chapman's hopes scattered like children at playtime. "What difficulty?"

"Drive time to cometary umbra estimated at thirty-nine hours."

"We are going, man," the Dhabian informed him. *"Shall we prepare to adjust position to accommodate your own ship?"*

Chapman considered very quickly. Thirty-nine hours was stretching the upper limits of the time allotted before the expected stellar flare. In thirty-nine hours he could be a good deal further out than the comet's position. Yet his computer informed him he would still be well inside the fatal radius of the flare radiation.

It was an easy gamble to take.

"Yes, I'm trying for it too." The Dhabian apparently accepted this without replying.

"Ship, adjust position to place us behind the cometary nucleus. Keep heading of the Dhabian in mind."

"I will be careful, Chapman," the ship replied confidently.

The ensuing hours passed busily. Studying and recording the Dhabian vessel as it moved past and ahead of him at close range would provide a great deal that xenologists would find of value. It also kept his mind pretty much off his slim chances. After the twenty-four-hour limit passed and he knew the flare could occur at any time he found himself working ever more intensely.

It was a large comet, all right. At least fifteen kilometers across the head. At thirty-two hours he had his closest glimpse of the Dhabian ship. It was eight hundred meters long, a hundred less than his own craft, but far more massive. It passed ahead of him, racing at its greater speed for the sheltering safety of the cometary bulk.

At thirty-five hours he permitted himself to hope a little. At thirty-six he was planning a full report to the Commission on his narrow escape.

At thirty-seven hours the ship told him he would be too late.

"Surface stellar activity is already showing signs of impending eruption, Chap-man. If local conditions do not change, we will arrive behind the cometary nucleus one hour twenty-two minutes ten seconds too late."

"What's the maximum we can take flare radiation for without sustaining irrep-arable damage to the ship?" Somewhat to his surprise he did not ask about himself.

"Ten and a half minutes."

That was it, then. Drowning, he'd been tossed a rope, and it had fallen short. He turned, let himself collapse in the chair opposite the main viewscreen. His head slumped forward, cradled in the crook of his right arm, to rest close by the cool metal.

He knew the fire would singe his wings, but it was so beautiful, so clean. Just a little closer, that was all, just a little closer. Through the quiet roar of the flames he thought he could hear the computer babbling precisely at him. Which was absurd. Computers did not talk to moths. Computers did not babble. He ignored the meaningless noises, dipped closer to the beckoning succubus. Fiery fingers touched his wings.

He woke up sweating.

And that was wrong. Very wrong. He couldn't have fallen asleep for more than a few hours, he felt. Even so, he had no business being awake and alive. He ought to be dead, snuffed out in a single incendiary *poof*, like a moth in a furnace. He blinked, looked around wildly.

"Ship! The flare, what . . . ?"

"Commencing countdown to arrival of first energetic particles," the computer said calmly. "Twenty, nineteen, eighteen. . . ."

Chapman stared dully at the viewscreen, tried to comprehend what he saw. To one side drifted an object that seemed assembled from the remnants of some ancient construct: the Dhabian ship, its quiescent drive glowing blue-white. Ahead was a dim green mass that as he watched concluded eclipsing the sun of Abraxis: the backside of the comet. In the reflected light from his own bulb ship it shone icy green and sharp. One moment it appeared solid, the next shifting and unstable.

"Four, three, two, one. . . ." The computer concluded. Chapman sucked in a startled breath.

The coma, the thick gaseous envelope which surrounded the cometary head, was shining so brilliantly it almost hurt him to look at it. The tenuous ribbons of gases and particles streaming back all around both ships took on a vibrant, purplish-red hue. In the storm raging off the surface of the star ahead, the streamers assumed a near-solid look, like the silken veil of a Spanish dancer.

While the view from several million miles away would have been even more impressive, there was something in the knowledge that he was *inside* the comet's tail which made him feel very small.

For five and a half hours the two ships rode the lee of the comet. Fiery colors danced around them. Devastating energy sheeted against the head of the comet, producing beauty instead of death.

Then the computer announced that the level of stellar radiation was dropping rapidly. Soon it fell to an acceptable level. At the same time the Dhabian ship began to move. It passed beyond and through the subdued but still dramatic cometary flow before Chapman thought to consider what had happened to him.

His ship could not have reached the safe position behind the comet by itself. Therefore the Dhabians had somehow helped him. Why?

"Initiate request for information, ship!"

After a moment, "They do not respond, Chapman." The alien vessel continued to move away.

"Try again!"

The computer did so, several times more before Chapman spoke directly into the pocket's pickup. "Dhabians! Why? Why save me? I owe you. Two thousand and one owe you." Silence, as the great blocky ship continued to recede from him on the screen. "Why don't you respond? Answer!"

A lilting, stilted voice. *"Multiple query inappropriate. Query elsewhere. Nothing here, man."*

Try as he would, Chapman was unable to elicit further communication from the alien.

Several weeks later, when the colony had been transferred easily and safely on board the ship and they were well out of the Abraxis system, it occurred to Chapman to ask hesitantly of his computer, "Ship, the Dhabians saved us and I don't know why. Do *you* know *how* they accelerated us in time to get us safely behind the comet?"

"Question inappropriate, Chapman." He frowned.

"Why?"

"No evidence to show Dhabian vessel affected our motion in any way."

He felt a little dizzy. Relief, he decided, and too many days on stimulants to stay awake. "What do you mean? If the Dhabians didn't adjust our velocity, then how did we get behind the nucleus?"

"Dhabians occupied fully with own maneuvers," came the reply. "Evidence indicates that comet shifted position to place us within its umbra. Dhabians had to slow, not accelerate, to match altered cometary position."

"You mean the Dhabians moved the *comet*?"

"Negative, Chapman. No evidence to support such hypothesis."

"But the comet changed position."

"Correct."

"That's impossible," he said with finality.

"Event occurred." The computer sounded slightly diffident.

Chapman considered. His eyes grew very wide. Then he raced through the ship until he located its present commander, colony-leader Otasu. The colony-leader was chatting with several other colony officials in the cramped confines of the pilot's pocket. He looked up uncertainly at Chapman's anxious entrance.

Chapman went immediately to the viewscreen. It showed only a view of star-speckled space and the slightly brighter distant spot of Abraxis' sun.

"We've got to go back, sir."

"Go back? We can't go back, Chapman, you know that." Poor fellow, he thought. Suspension does funny things to men. "Our sun's entered its eruption cycle. We'd all be fried."

Query elsewhere, the Dhabian had said before going finally silent. *Elsewhere, elsewhere . . .* where else had there been to query? The comet had changed position. . . .

"Fifteen hours," he mumbled, staring at the screen. "Fifteen hours."

"Fifteen hours for what?" prompted the colony-leader kindly, humoring the hyper emergency pilot. Chapman's face did not look up from the screen.

"I had fifteen hours during flare-time and I used it to make observations and notes about the Dhabian." He sounded numb.

"And very valuable observations, I'm told," acknowledged Otasu, trying his best to sound calming and approving.

"But you don't understand!" Chapman stared harder at the screen. The comet was back there, somewhere, moving about in the way of comets; and what did they know about comets, after all? Very little, very little.

"I spent fifteen hours studying the wrong alien. . . ."

STEVEN UTLEY

Time and Hagakure

I noue stepped into his apartment, closed the door and found himself on a sparsely wooded hillside.   Not far from where he stood, a shaggy titan scratched its haunch and belched awesomely.   Storm clouds were gathering in the sky overhead.

Inoue groped his way along the wall until he bumped into a chair.   He eased himself down into it.   From a table beside the chair, he plucked a photograph and held it as though it were a talisman.   The phantom Megatherium went down on all fours and began tearing at the earth with its long, curved claws.   Ghost lightning flashed on the horizon.

Control, Inoue told himself.   He forced himself to concentrate on the picture, a curling yellow snapshot of a woman whose face reflected years of strain, whose eyes had once seen the sun touch the earth.   Opaque eyes; blind, burnt eyes.

Across the room, the enormous ground sloth mooed softly, then shimmered and dissolved.   The Pleistocene thunderheads swirled away.

Inoue studied cracks in the dirty plaster ceiling.   Good, he thought, good.   Don't let it run away with you.   You have to be able to control it for a while closer each time. Relax.   Relax.

He settled into the cushions and closed his eyes.   He could feel the power coiled within, tensed to strike at him if he let it, tensed and ready to do his bidding if he made it.

He took a deep breath, and he began.

The floor disappears as Tadashi starts to swing his legs over the edge of the cot. He stares down through the sky.   Far below, silhouetted against a bright sea, the dark gnats of many airplanes swirl about angrily.   As he watches, one of the gnats flares up like a match and drops toward the ocean, trailing a fine ribbon of burning gasoline and oily smoke.   Tadashi pulls his legs back and huddles upon the cot. A wailing noise fills his ears.

"Lieutenant!"

He starts and looks up from the air battle.   At the far edge of the sky, where the horizon merges with the wall of the hut, stands a glowering giant, fists on hips.

"What's the matter with you?" the giant demands.   "Can't you hear the sirens?"

Tadashi shakes his head helplessly.   His gaze returns to the dogfight.   Two more airplanes are going down.   The sea ripples, then yields to the familiar wooden planks.   The airplanes vanish, swallowed up in the chinks between the planks. Tadashi rubs his eyes.

"Are you all right?" the giant says in a more solicitous tone.

"I . . . Captain Tsuyuki?"

"Of course!   Aren't you well, Lieutenant?"

Tadashi puts his feet on the floor and is relieved to feel fine splinters tickling his soles.   He rises and sways unsteadily, his head suddenly light, his stomach buoyant.   "I'll be all right, sir.   I was—the siren!   Bombers!"

"They're going for the Yokosuka-Tokyo area," says the captain as Tadashi snatches up his jacket and boots.   "The mechanics are warming up the planes. Get into the air immediately!"

Tadashi crams his feet into the boots and clomps past Captain Tsuyuki.

Inoue became aware of the pain mounting behind his eyes and cursed softly as he slipped away from Lieutenant Tadashi Okido.   He slumped in his chair, massaging his temples, then got up and went to the window.   Outside, the lights of Tokyo held back the night.

When, in the forty-third year of his life, the power had first manifested itself, had begun running amok inside his head, Inoue's Tokyo—dirty, over-crowded, very dangerous Tokyo—started to hold new terrors for him.   Thuggee stranglers stalked their victims through the corridors of his apartment complex.   Barbarian hordes rode down out of the sky to lay waste to crude towns and villages that lay superimposed upon the dreary confusion of the metropolis.   Assyrian, Roman, and Aztec priests wandered past the shrines of the city, and sun-blackened slaves labored to erect pyramids.   Waves of mounted knights broke under black rains of arrows from long bows.   Volcanoes loomed over the skyline and blew themselves to atoms.   Prehistoric glaciers crunched along the highway to Kyoto, and monster-infested coal forests reclaimed boulevards.

Three hundred million years of ghosts filled his head and spilled out into his world.

He returned to his chair and picked up the photograph again and stared into the woman's eyes, the blind, burnt eyes, the eyes seared, ruined, made useless, that time when the sun had come down to engulf Nagasaki.

It had been in the fifth month of his affliction that she came to him the first time. Bent over the lathe, he had glanced up to discover a small garden where the north wall of his tool and die shop was supposed to be.   The woman stood there, looking younger than he could recall having ever seen her in life.   But he knew her.   He had some of the ancient photographs, pictures of her in her bridal attire and drab wartime kimono.

Her gaze was fixed on a point behind and slightly above his head.   Awe and terror were creeping into her expression, and a brilliant light made her seem as pale as paraffin.   She opened her small mouth and uttered a soundless scream.   Her hands rose to her face to claw at her eyes.   She fell prone, still screaming, still silent.

Crouched over his lathe, Inoue had reached out for her and caught just a word.

He had seen her several times more in the weeks and months that followed.   The scene was always the same; once, though, an enormous iguanodon wandered past, unmindful of the furies raging all around it, unmindful of the stricken woman. Each time, Inoue tried to reach her, to hold tight to her.   Each time, he caught only the single word.

Inoue folded his hand over the photograph and forced himself to concentrate and slipped away murmuring the word, the name, *Tadashi, Tadashi . . .*

Tadashi is wedging himself into the cockpit of his airplane.   Jerking his fur-lined flying helmet down over his close-cropped skull.   Waving the ground crew out of the way.   Rolling forward, gaining speed.   Up.   Up.   Retract the landing gear.   Up.   **listen** Up.   Three thousand feet and climbing.   Young Shiizaki, Tadashi's new wing-man, is a poor pilot whose ship makes known its resentment of his heavy hand.   Tadashi grimaces in annoyance and signals Shiizaki to remain in position.   Seven thousand feet and climbing.   **listen to me**   Eight thousand feet. Nine.   There is a stab of pain between Tadashi's eyes.   **please listen to me**   He blinks it away.

It had taken Inoue another year to locate the man Tadashi.   The stream of Time was a twisting, treacherous one.   Inoue cast himself into those waters and dis-covered what it was to have been a mastodon asphyxiating in a tar pool.   He experienced the terror and agony of a Russian officer being torn to pieces by mutinous soldiers.   He was a Cro-Magnon woman succumbing to hunger and cold. He bore children.   He raped and was raped.   He decapitated a man.   He was drawn and quartered.   He knew moments of peace.   He ate strange foods and spoke odd languages.   He made love with a filthy Saxon woman and with a rancid Spanish nobleman.   He cast himself into the waters of Time again and again, and he felt himself drawn closer to his objective every sixth or seventh attempt, and then, finally, at last—

Tadashi is wedging himself into the cockpit of his airplane.   Jerking his fur-lined flying helmet down over his close-cropped skull.   Waving the ground crew out of the way.   Rolling forward, gaining Speed.   Up.   Up.   Away.

Tadashi cruises at seventeen thousand feet, tense behind the controls of the obsolete Zero-Sen fighter.   The almost-daily air raids, the seemingly interminable howling of the sirens, the endless mad scrambles to waiting planes, are taking their toll.   He had been having difficulty keeping his food down lately, and food is hardly so abundant anymore that it can be wasted in such a manner.   His head hurts intermittently.   He has been making too many mistakes in the air, over-shooting targets, firing his guns too soon or too late and, always, for too long. Ammunition thrown away, wasted in ineffectual feints at the enemy bombers' shiny aluminum bellies.

Gone is the sure, deadly aim, gone the lightning-quick reflexes that made him an ace over the Philippines.   He will, he knows, make the final mistake very soon

now, and then a Hellcat or a Mustang will blow him out of the air.   A precious
airplane lost, thrown away in a moment of inattention or confusion.

And what of your wife?   Tadashi frowns behind his goggles and reproaches
himself.   He will only hasten his own end if he permits his mind to wander thus.

He is, he tells himself, a warrior.   If he dies, he will die a warrior's death and
ascend to Yasukuni Shrine.   He will sell his life dearly, for that is his duty and
his honor.   *Hagakure,* the Bushido code, is too deeply engrained in him.   He
cannot imagine alternatives to that code—"A Samurai lives in such a way that he
will always be prepared to die" —or to the Emperor's precepts to all soldiers and
sailors of Japan: ". . . be resolved that duty is heavier than a mountain, while
death is lighter than a feather."

Tadashi catches the flash of sunlight on unpainted aluminum in the distance.
He wags his wings to attract Shiizaki's attention and points, then has to bank sharply
as Shiizaki, craning his neck to search for the enemy formation, lets his plane
swerve toward Tadashi's.   Tadashi waves his clumsy wing-man back into position
and mentally curses both the lack of radios, which have been removed to lighten
the Zero-Sens, and the scarcity of fully trained flyers.   He opens the throttle and
begins closing the gap between himself and the bombers.

In the space of a year, the Americans' B-29's have flattened virtually the whole
of Japanese industry, have severely decimated populations in the major cities, have
brought his homeland to its knees.   The B-29's are gigantic aircraft, by far the
largest he has ever seen.   Their size notwithstanding, they are almost as fast as
his interceptor, well armed and strong, altogether insuperable machines.   Some of
them have been brought down, but not many, not enough, and, for the most part,
the behemoths seem discouragingly unconcerned with both fighters and flak.

Tadashi feels his guts drawing up into a tight, hard knot as he begins his approach.
Perhaps this is the day, a part of him whispers, and he clamps his teeth on his
lower lip, trying to repress the murmur of panic.   The rearmost B-29 in the
formation swells in his gunsight.   He thumbs off the safety switch, checks his
range-finger and opens fire.   Tracers simultaneously spit from the bomber's tail
guns.   There is the whine of a ricochet.   Tadashi flinches, scowls, completes his
firing pass, kicks the rudder to the left to check on Shiizaki.

Stitched by tracers, Shiizaki's Zero-Sen sweeps past the B-29, turns on its side
and explodes.

**you must listen to me think of her the war will soon be over and she will
need you in the hard times to follow go back and land and call her to you
without delay please please listen to me**

Tadashi grimly drops into position behind a second bomber.   But the American
plane suddenly shimmers and dances in the sky before him, refusing to stay neatly
framed in the gunsight.   His eyes throb, his head hurts.   The Zero-Sen wobbles
sickeningly as his hand slips on the control stick.   **I CAN SAVE US ALL IF
YOU WILL LISTEN TO ME** and for just a moment he is deaf to the roar and
vibration of his plane, removed, face to oddly familiar face with a middle-aged
man whose furrowed brow glistens with perspiration, whose eyes are screwed tight
with some great effort.   Tadashi gives a cry of alarm, and the man appears to gasp

and then smiles. The face shatters into scintillae of light. His bride reclines with him in semi-gloom, her skin slick with post-coital perspiration, her delicate fingers tracing patterns on his shoulder and breast as she whispers endearments, *I love you, Tadashi, I shall always love and honor you, stay with me, stay with me, with me, we shall have fine, brave sons and graceful daughters.* He blinks, perplexed, filled with longing, and opens his mouth to speak to her. The soothing liquid flow of her voice is rudely terminated by the sound of canopy glass shattering. A sliver gashes his cheek. He wrenches himself away from his wedding night and finds himself bearing down on the B-29. He cannot remember how to fire his guns.

I don't need to shoot, he thinks. The moisture is gone from his mouth. I don't need to shoot.

break away I've seen you do this many times too many times I am tired sickened by the violence I've seen going mad because of what happened what is going to happen at Nagasaki there is no way to stop the ghosts except by coming to you making you break off this futile engagement Japan is doomed nothing you can do now can change that you can only return to your base and save yourself your wife me

Tadashi shakes his head savagely and gropes for the throttle. Finds it. Opens it to overboost. no no no *no no* NO NO, a scream behind his eyes, the words tumbling out, running together, *nonono,* and the Zero-Sen leaps forward.

Inoue moaned, drew himself into a ball, quivered in his chair, sweat popping from every pore, fingers digging into scalp, teeth grinding together.

Then he realized that he had crumpled the photograph. He smoothed it out, whimpering softly to himself. A brittle corner had broken off. He found the wedge-shaped chip of paper in his lap and placed it on the table.

I can do it, he thought, I've made little ripples in Time, I've made him feel my presence, made him see, hear, feel things. I've broken through to him at last, he understands now, he's going to listen this time. I'm going to save us all.

But his headache was worse now. He put the picture into the pocket of his shirt and tiredly rubbed his face for a moment before getting up to go to the window again. He took the picture from his pocket and carefully cupped it in his hand. He regarded the dead eyes sadly.

He had tried, so many times, to reach her and warn her away from the doomed city. Had tried and failed: only that moment of her terror in the garden was open to him.

He had tried to return to the day, early that last month of the war, when Lieutenant Tadashi Okido had sent his young bride to stay with his uncle in Nagasaki. Had tried and failed: only an hour of another, later day in the lieutenant's life was open to him.

He had been trying for weeks to cut short the lieutenant's mission of interception.

He was being driven mad in a Tokyo overrun with phantoms which he alone could see, and Lieutenant Tadashi Okido was his one hope. The Samurai Tadashi, who had to be made, somehow, convinced, somehow, to return to the airfield and call his wife away from Nagasaki.

Tadashi, who, in sending her to that place, had unknowingly cursed Inoue with the power.

This time, Inoue thought, this time it must not happen as it did.

LISTEN TO ME YOU MUSTN'T DIE HERE AND NOW YOU MUST LIVE LONG ENOUGH TO SAVE YOUR WIFE AND MY SANITY YOU OWE IT TO US TO LIVE LISTEN ALL THE REMAINING YEARS OF HER LIFE WILL BE A TORMENT WITHOUT YOU AND Tadashi shakes his head savagely and gropes for **MY LIFE HAS BECOME HELL BECAUSE OF YOU** the throttle **YOU AND YOU ALONE** finds it **CAN SAVE US** opens it to **PLEASE LISTEN** opens it to **LISTEN** opens it to overboost, and the Zero-Sen leaps forward to plow through the bomber's tail assembly.   The shivering fighter's starboard wing buckles like pasteboard and disintegrates.   The cowling shoots away as the radial engine begins disgorging pistons.   The Japanese and American planes fall away from each other, fall away spinning, throwing off pieces of themselves.

damn you

A large pterodactyl soared past the window.   Sobbing with frustration, Inoue pressed his fist against the grimy pane.   Go away, go away.   Go away.

He looked at the photograph in his hand, and he said to the woman with the ruined eyes, I found him, I spoke to him, told him, showed him what was at stake. I invaded the past, I altered it a very little, but why doesn't he listen?   Why does he keep doing it?   What's wrong with him?   Why can't I make him understand?

And he cried out, "Mother, doesn't he even *care?*"

Slammed and held by centrifugal force against the wall of the cockpit, Tadashi dazedly listens to his wife's pleas and feels her hands rove down over his body, and he tells her that he loves her, has loved her from the moment he first glimpsed her in her father's house, will love her always, and he tells her that their children, yes, their children will be fine, beautiful children, and he bids her goodbye, knowing she is proud of him now and will follow his example should the need to do so arise, for he is a warrior, with a wife worthy of a warrior, he has abided by the dictates of *Hagakure* and is assured of his place of honor at Yasukuni Shrine, and it is intensely hot and bright in the cockpit, there are screams which may be his own, but he is resolved that duty is heavier than a mountain, while death is li—

Ghosts

Y ou know how hard it is, sometimes, to wake up and uncradle, to set up the primary systems and sequences and face the new morning.   You know how frustrating it can be, too, to look out upon nothing but clean space, no debris in the cubics you have planned to sweep this day.   Or worse, a motherlode of junk, but with a Royal Patrol deployed at its perimeter to guard it.   You know the futility of it, then: Uranus is the Lord's Land, north and south, inner ring and outer ring. The Patrols are *everywhere*.   How long can you evade them?   How long before you are cornered and caught?   Will they find you today?

Shooting out to Neptune won't help, it's Royal too.   And of course Jupiter/ Saturn is Union.   No, this is it.   *This is it.*

Look at it: Uranus, in the night.   The rings are fine lace; this close you can see right through them, like ghosts.   And the planet itself: pale porcelain green with hints of ultramarine woven throughout.   Beautiful monster; ugly princess.   Skim it, sieve it, rake it with field generator sails scarred by the planet wind blowing inbound.   And respect the princess, the monster, for though it is your life, now, it can just as easily be your death.

Lonely, solitary work.   You like that part of it, anyway.   You came here to be alone, and so far you have been.   Except for the voices.   Like Jonquil told you so long ago (has it been so long?) there are voices here, in the cold Uranus space, so very far from home.   No one knows about them, no one hears them but you.   Keep it that way.   Keep it that way.

No one understood about the voices on Earth.   No one wanted to.   Chrise! Push those memories away, shove them back to the shadows where they belong. You shudder, remembering.

Yet they are your friends, your only friends.   Jonquil, Ben, Jonas and the rest, all of the voices, they have always been your friends, always.

Don't worry about it, Huck.   Don't worry about anything.   Just sweep what dirty space (dirty *Royal* space, managing a smile) you can find, and for Chrise's sake keep it all to yourself.   There must be enough junk left outside of the clouds to live upon.   There must be.   There has to be.   Wake up, Huck.   Uncradle, there is one more day to face.

"Huck!"   Whispered.   "Are you still awake?"
The small boy turned his eyes into the shadows.

"You better get to sleep, Huck.   If Mara catches you she's going to beat you again."

It was Jonquil, one of them, the first voice, in fact, who had ever spoken to him.

"I'm afraid, Joni."

"Afraid?   Afraid of what?   Mara?"

"You're old," the boy muttered, burying his face into his blanket.   "You don't have to be afraid."

"I'm not that old, Huck.   Why, I was only ten—Earth ten—when I was—"

Light exploded into the room, lancing across the floor, splitting the darkness to aching yellow.   Huck was caught in it, eyes wide, tears already forming.

"Were you at it again?" demanded the woman in the doorway.   "Who's in here with you?"

There was no one, of course, no one at all.   Huck huddled in the corner, pulling his blankets up around him.   Mara did not understand about the voices.   She just didn't understand.

"I didn't mean it," Huck pleaded.

Mara stared down at him, breathing loudly, barely holding her anger in check.

"I'm sorry, Mara," the five-year-old whined.   "Really, I'm—"

"Close your mouth, and your eyes as well, and go to sleep, dammit."   The woman whirled around, grabbing the door.   "And I don't want to hear any more of this talking to yourself!"

Slam, door.

Silence.

"Huck?"

He shut his eyes tightly.

"Huck . . . ?"

He hesitated at the entrance.

The Royal Court seated at the table in the center of the huge chamber rose as one.   "Come," the nearest one said.   "Please."

Another indicated a seat, which the young man took, noticeably grateful to have a place to put himself.   His nervousness permeated the chamber, causing several of the Court to flash him reassuring smiles and murmur pleasantries.

A very strained-looking woman in full dress rose from the head of the table, cleared her throat, and everyone quieted.   The young man glanced at all their faces, looking for answers to—

"My colleagues and I wish to thank you for agreeing to this audience," the woman said.   "And of course you must be wondering why you are here."

He spread his hands; he had not "agreed" to anything; he had been *brought*. Should he—?

The woman continued: "My name is Reginald.   Chief Secretary to His Majesty Lord Talshire.   You have, no doubt, heard the name."

He swallowed dryly.   Lord Talshire owned Uranus and Neptune.   Plain and simply owned them.   Of course he had heard the name.   "Why . . . ?" he managed.

"Yes," Reginald said. "We must get swiftly to the point, since there is a definite time factor involved." She activated a table screen and, glancing at it, rattled off: "Your name is Sammael Huck Jastrow, Earth. Twenty-three years old, born and raised same. You are presently engaged in a relatively small-scope illegal scavenging concern in His Majesty's Uranus space—"

Huck found his voice quite suddenly: "Illegal! It's not—!"

Reginald raised her hand impatiently. "Please, that is not our concern at the moment. This next bit of information, however, is: you have been rated the best three-prong proximity pilot outward of Mars, the best, perhaps, in the System." She smiled falsely. "You are valuable, Mr. Jastrow. At any time you are that. But to us now, at this time, you are *priceless*."

Huck swallowed again. "What's the job?"

Secretary Reginald's smile broadened. "The 'job' involves piloting a proximity shuttle due inward—"

Huck flashed puzzlement. "Sunward?"

"Oh, no." The Secretary—almost unconsciously—pointed to the floor. "Uranus," she said. "You are to fly closer to Uranus than anyone has ever previously attempted. You are to effect the rescue of a skimmer-class craft which at this moment is trapped in a slowly decaying orbit. The ship does not possess power enough to get up to freedom."

"And you picked me?"

The Secretary sighed patiently. "Prior to this morning you were the *fourth*-best proximity pilot, Mr. Jastrow. We picked three others before you, and this morning, before the Royal Police paid you a visit, those three failed in the very mission you are about to engage upon." The secretary paused to note the effect of her words, then continued. "They piloted a four-seater, of course, a *Corsair*-class refitted specifically for proximity flight. You will pilot an equally refitted two-seater shuttle—much more powerful for its mass—making, we hope, for a more successful configuration."

"You seem certain I'm going to agree to this," Huck said, slowly.

"There is nothing to agree to," the Secretary replied. "You will do it." She paused again. "We have approached you in this manner—" spreading her arms to include the rest of the Court "—to assure you of our sincerity, our good will, and of our seriousness. You must certainly realize the political and economic repercussions, not to mention your own monetary compensation . . ."

Huck glanced about the room, then down to his hands, and finally directly at the Secretary. "It has to be someone pretty big, then," he said.

"Surely you must realize?"

"Who?" Raising his voice a little.

"Why, his Majesty Lord Talshire, of course."

The voices had kept a respectful silence up to this point. But then one of them—Jonas—spoke up quite clearly: "Don't trust them past your shadow. But don't worry, they've laid it out fairly clean, and we'll be with you all the way."

Huck opened his mouth, then closed it. Then, to Secretary Reginald: "When?"

"Within the hour, as soon as we ferry you to Miranda and have you tuned up."

One of the Court put out his hand then.

Huck decided not to shake it.

"Spread 'em," the doctor said.

Huck obliged.   He shivered when she applied the probes.

"Sorry," she said.   "No time to warm them up.   My superiors caught me as much by surprise as they did you.   Hold it there."

Huck stared at the white light band over the cradle, aware that it wasn't hurting his eyes.

"When was your last tune-up, Mr. Jastrow?"

"One Earth year, sir."

"Ah-hah."   She fiddled at an instrument console.   "Quarter-year tune-ups are mandatory by law for your type of work, you know," she said.   "And call me Sylvia, please."

Huck glanced at her, surprised, then returned his gaze to the light.   "Tunes cost too much," he said in answer.   "I'm still trying to float."

"Triton?"

"No.   Earth, originally."

"Hah.   I should have guessed from the accent."   She caught his eye, a smile forming.   "Try not to feel this," she said then, and something clicked.   Huck did, however, in every single nerve of his body.   Chrise! he thought in the middle, I hate this!

Then it was over, the probes fell away, and Huck tried (without success) to focus his eyes.

"Congratulations."   Sylvia patted his rump.   "You'll feel better in a minute. Now for the form-filling."   She hit a toggle.   "Tape's running.   Do you verify the procedure, etcetera, etcetera?"

Huck managed a nod.

"You have to—"

"Verified," he gasped.

The boy saw the other children and paused.   "Jonquil?"

She murmured close to his ear: "Stay away from them, Huck.   They are waiting for you.   The big one there with the ball wants to fight."

The boy sagged against the wall, sinking into the shadows.   "But why?   What do I do to make them want to beat me up, to hate me like they do?"

Jonquil sighed.   "It's not your fault, Huck.   If anyone's, it's ours.   No one can hear us but you.   You're special that way.   I haven't been able to find anyone else alive who can hear me as well as you can.   I don't think anyone else has either.   You're the only one we can talk to.   That's why you are so special. That's why we help you whenever we can."

"But what's so important about talking to me?   I'm just a kid."

Jonquil laughed sadly.   "If only you could know," she said.   "If only you could know how important it really is, how important you really are."

Huck peered out of his shadow and saw the children playing a game he wanted more than anything else in the world to join. If only Jonquil and the rest of them were real, he thought. If only . . . but that thought chilled him so much he wanted to cry.

He eased into the cradle; several screens lit up. When he took hold of the grips, more were activated. He felt the ship flow through the grips and cradle and into his body; it felt right; it would be okay.

"Disengage on your signal," the dock chief said.

"Right."

Huck went through the pre-flight check methodically, purposefully, taking his time, then started the sequence. Within moments opposing fields were set up and the shuttle fell away from the dock. It gained speed steadily, falling away from Miranda, the moon, falling into the green-blue gas giant that was Uranus.

Talshire's skimmer was a scant thousand kilometers outside the first substantial methane cloud layer. Totally immersed in the magnetosphere, its field generator shields excited the ion wind to white luminescence. Huck had a visual on it, even from his present height; like a silver comet with an achingly straight tail, below, inward, a few steps from Death's door.

"Tracking you," said the dock chief.

"Thanks."

Falling. Falling into the green-blue disk on the main screen. The planet seemed unnaturally flat—strangely, the rings contributed to this illusion. The shuttle's arching descent was directly toward them. Of course he would pass far inward of the innermost, but the visual threat was staggering.

Huck hated visuals down this far. He looked away, then back again. No longer flat, the more he stared the more the planet began to look concave, distinctly concave, like a bowl, a well, and he was going into it, headlong, eyes wide, a green hole in space . . .

"Trim it up there, Huck. You're drifting."

". . . okay."

Field sails blossomed out like the wings of a beetle. This should be okay, he thought. He just should have known better than to look down the planet's throat. The gas giants were dangerous that way. Their utter immensity was difficult to deal with in so close.

"I'm going blind for a while," he said finally.

"Thought you might." The dock chief chuckled. "That Chrising mother of a planet is a lot to take all at once."

"Yeah." Several screens blanked to grey.

"I was down pretty far a couple of times," the dock chief continued, "droning, of course. Never so low in a shuttle, though." A pause. "Hey, you're doing real fine there, Huck."

Sure. Yeah, I must be out of my mind, doing this, being here. I really must be insane. He rubbed his hands on the cradle cushion. Chrise, I'm scared, he thought suddenly. What am I doing here? Another screen blanked.

"You going to sleep on us, Huck?"

"Sorry." The screen went on again.

He was sweating a little. One of the screens showed him saddled in the cradle, naked, perspiration shining on his belly and thighs. He looked down, wiped himself; and on the screen he looked down and wiped himself.

Jonas whispered in his ear: "My God, even now this frightens me. The only other time I was down this far I . . . never got back up. I didn't have equipment like this, though."

Huck glanced about the cabin futilely. He couldn't reply to him, couldn't do anything but sit and listen.

"How much longer?" he asked, eventually.

"ETA in seven minutes, thirty-six seconds. Check over that docking sequence in the meantime, please. We want it to be your best."

Huck exploded at that. "What the Chrise is that supposed to mean? You give me forty-five minutes to get a fifteen-point procedure down cold? You guys must be crazier than I am! You honestly expect this to work? For Chrising—"

"Hold on . . . news . . . just hold on a moment, Huck, please."

"I'm not going anywhere," he spit out, feeling blood pounding behind his ears.

". . . okay," the dock chief said a few seconds later. "You've got a temporary reprieve. His Majesty has managed to trim his orbit enough to give him an estimate two Earth days—about forty-nine hours—more time until his ship falls too low for effective rescue. If you want to know the truth, he was monitoring your transmission and agreed with you. So you've got a day and a half . . . chalk this one up as a dry run, then. Okay?"

Huck shook his head slowly, cursing every single one of them. Jonas said: "They're recording that heart and blood pressure of yours, you know. Calm down; don't give them the satisfaction."

"Right you are," Huck muttered.

"What's that, Huck?" the dock chief asked.

"Nothing. Just feed me the climb-and-away sequence. My hands are itchy; I need something to do down here."

". . . right."

He found a corner of the Company bar where most of the lights couldn't find him and grabbed it, trying very hard to forget just about everything that was in his head. The two Royal Policemen guarding him retired to a nearby table, trying unsuccessfully to appear inconspicuous.

"When do you make the real run?"

He looked up. She slid into the seat opposite him.

"Little over a day," he said, returning his gaze to the drink on the table. "How's the slash-and-sew business?"

"Ahah. Huck has finally found his voice. At our first meeting—as I recall— I couldn't get you past monosyllables. You prefer 'Huck' to 'Mr Jastrow,' don't you?"

"Yeah. Huck's fine."

"And you can still call me Sylvia."   She tapped her fingers on the tabletop, watching him.

He looked up again.   "You want a drink?"

She shook her head.   "But I would like to have a talk.   Moons are small— you can't help but run into people.   And Miranda's a small moon.   Actually I've been keeping you tightly beamed since your tune."   She reached across and touched his arm.   He made as though to pull away, but stopped himself.   "Then you heard what happened," he said.

"I heard that a young fool named Talshire took out a Royal skimmer in one of his usual drunk/high states and directed its controls due inward.   Rumors say he wanted to swim through to the other side.   I also heard that a young hotshot proximity pilot was retrieved from some out of the way corner of His Majesty's Uranus space and pressed into immediate service to rescue the foolish Lord from his dire predicament at the very question of life, limb, and . . . " and then she smiled, ". . . money?"

Huck looked at her incredulously.   "You think I'm in this for the money?"

"Well, glory, at least . . ."

Huck half-rose from his seat, his expression furious, but when he saw what was in her eyes he collapsed back and muttered a quiet obscenity.

Sylvia patted his hand.   "I know how it is," she said.   "They got me the same way.   There was this certain prince with a certain rare exobiological bug, and there too was I—young and innocent graduate student at Triton S.T. who happened to be doing extensive research on the same said bug—who got whisked away to cure him."

"Did you?"

"Unfortunately, yes; he's piloting that skimmer this very moment.   The irony, I know, must be devastating."

"Why didn't you leave, after?"

Sylvia laughed lightly.   "If I had, then I wouldn't have met you."

"Cute.   I was wondering when you would get around to that.   You're my arenar?"

She stiffened slightly; he felt it in the touch of her hand.   "I volunteered," she said.

"Oh."   He looked down at his drink again.   "Sorry."

"I also wanted to spend time with you to ask some questions."

Now it was Huck's turn to smile.   "I guess I owe you that, then."   He paused to drain half of his glass.   "Okay.   What's up?"

"I heard the tape of your 'dry run' just before.   At two points on it there was a particular type of disturbance which I could not attribute either to the dock chief, to you, or to the mechanisms involved."

"What kind of disturbances?"

'Well, they are difficult to describe with words.   I knew what they were, at any rate, though I don't think anyone else who heard the tape did."

Huck felt something touch his spine. Apprehension? "Just what exactly are you talking about?"

"I've been following the work of several University colleagues in the post-mortem life sciences."

"Isn't that a contradiction of—"

"Obviously. It's still relatively new, say, five years since the scientific community accepted the basic premises. Quickly and simply put, these scientists have succeeded in proving that certain kinds of life—specific types of intelligently controlled energies, actually—continue after physical, material life ends."

That hit Huck like walking into a wall. "You mean . . . ghosts?"

"Grossly put, with ridiculous superstitious connotations, but . . . yes. Ghosts."

Huck went cold inside, his face slowly draining of all color. He suddenly did not like the turn of the conversation.

Sylvia continued: "So far they have only been able to gain direct evidence on photographic emulsion films and certain magnetic sound-recording tapes. Deceased individuals are able to effect consistent recognizable changes in these materials."

"And that's what you say you saw in the flight tape?"

"Well, not 'saw' so much as 'heard,' but yes. I did."

"Which means?"

"That there was a presence either with you in the shuttle or with the dock chief."

"But . . ."

"But I have a feeling it was you. I checked your records, and came across a statement by one of your mothers, the one named Mara."

Huck abruptly stood, knocking over the remainder of his drink. The two police at the nearby table looked up briefly. "I must say you are thorough," he said, barely managing to keep control of himself. He wiped at the spilled liquor, trying to conceal the emotions flashing across his face.

"Hey," Sylvia said softly, stopping him. "Hey, I understand."

He looked at her, totally exposed, totally vulnerable.

"You've got a couple of hours," she said then. "Would you . . . ?"

Huck was nineteen, and he looked it. He had spent three days at the Newark docks with little food and even less sleep, trying to get off, to go *out*. However, he had found the docks a definite, dismaying anticlimax. The big glamour ships were all in orbit, or on the Moon. The largest ones on the ground were personnel transports, two or three thrusting their prows above the surrounding derricks and odd superstructures; but the most common craft were skimpy four-cradle shuttles. The necessary considerations, air and gravity, made the entire Newark operation excessively complicated. Which all added up to any dock on Earth being essentially outmoded, outdated and fading. But Earth was where he had been born and raised and trained. He had come waving his three-prong pilot rating, which made him— he also found to his dismay—about as desirable as nine thousand nine hundred and ninety-nine of the other three-prongers bumming the docks.

The voices were a help, though.

"He's not looking, Huck.   Now!"

And he lifted three oranges from the counter, certain of success.

"I can't go on like this, guys," he whispered to Ben and Jonquil and any of the others who were listening.

"However long it takes, Huck.   However long it takes."

"A gentleman crouched by that piling there, Huck," Ben said suddenly.   "See him?"

"Yeah.   So?"

"So he intends to relieve you of the oranges, most likely with the knife—its vibrating mechanism thankfully in disrepair—which he has hidden in his cloak."

Huck nodded, and as he passed the grease-smeared bum he tossed one of the fruits.   Surprised, the would-be attacker could only grab for it while Huck walked out of reach and out of danger.   "Thanks, team," he said.

You are a hard person to understand.   You are extremely complex, or utterly, utterly simple.   You just can't decide which.

He took off his pants, and then his tunic.

"Oh," she said.   "Your *back*."

His expression in the shadows: vacant, tired.   "You're the doctor," he said. "What's the diagnosis?"

"Huck, really. . . ."

"No, *really*.   What's it look like to you?"   And turned to face her, to touch her, the expression still there.

"You . . . someone . . . well, you've been through some terrible beatings a long time ago . . . oh Chrise. . . ."

He hugged her.   "Sorry, I'm being cruel.   Bitter, actually.   Sometimes I spread it around.   I bet Mara forgot to include this in the report you read, anyway."

"It was she who—?"

"She was a very frustrated lady . . . no one knew why I was different, and I was the youngest of that Group's children at the time.   I spent a lot of time by myself, hiding . . . it was hard to fit in."

"You could have had the scars taken care of, though.   Medical facilities on—"

Huck put his fingers lightly on her lips.   "It makes for great conversation in bed," he said, grinning.   "Besides, like I told you, my scavenging business isn't really floating."

"But after tomorrow you'll be—"

"After tomorrow I'll probably be dead."

"But I thought the extra time—"

"The extra time has allowed me to get the sequencing down fairly well, true. But still, no one has ever done a rescue like this before and succeeded.   The odds are definitely not leaning in my direction.'' He paused, looking at her in the darkness. "Hey, lady, I thought we were here to make love.''

"Were we?"

And they fell together, murmuring quietly.

He awoke later, gasping, tangled in sheets. The darkness was absolute. He stared into it, his body shaking uncontrollably for a moment, perspiration down his ribs.

". . . Huck?" Sleepily.

"It's nothing, Sylvia.'' He took a breath, closed his eyes, then opened them again. ". . . it's nothing.''

"Oh, Huck. In the gloom he knew she was looking at him. "Something,'' she said, almost whispering.

He lay back. "I had a nightmare—drowning in an ammonia sea—the usual. It's—" he stopped himself, breathing heavily.

"Huck, you can get help, you know.''

"For what? The nightmares?''

"My colleagues, the ones doing the life-after-death studies . . . if you agree to examinations, I'm sure they—''

He cut her off with a look. Then, shakily: "Please, let's just not talk about that. Really. Okay?''

She nodded, sensing correctly that she had stumbled again on one of Huck's great fears, perhaps his greatest.

But then he surprised her by chuckling.

"What . . . ?''

He turned to her. "Oh, I forgot. You couldn't hear.''

"The voices?''

"Yeah. One of them just commented on your technique.''

"My *what?*''

"Are you embarrassed?''

"No . . . I just . . . well, it's a little bit of a shock to have to all of a sudden deal with something . . .''

"Unreal?''

"No, of course not . . . it's just . . .''

Huck gathered her close. "How about I ask them to give us a little privacy from now on, okay?''

"Would you?''

"I just did.''

They lay in silence for a while, then Sylvia said: "Well?''

"Well what?''

"How was I?''

"How were you what?''

"You said the voice rated my—''

"Oh, yeah. He—his name is Jonas—used an archaic word, but I think you can translate: he said you were 'dynamite.' ''

Sylvia lay quietly for a little while longer. Then: "Tell Jonas I said 'thank you,' please."

You can see what is happening. Alone with yourself, alone with your thoughts, you can see what is, and what will be. Never before have you had to face this. Never before. Your choices are there, clearly in front of you. Can you do it? Are you strong enough? Either way, *every* way is an easy out, every way but one.

Suddenly—Oh Chrise, it chills you—the thought comes. It has been lurking back there, in the shadows, waiting to leap out and drag you down: *you want to fail,* don't you. Don't you?

"Well, congratulations, Huck," Jonquil said.

"Thanks."

Nothing needed to be explained. Everyone had heard, had seen, had experienced . . . Huck had managed a third-class berth on a Royal light cruiser docked and running out of Tycho. The personnel carrier was already stowing supplies and incidental cargo. Huck squinted through the smog, and picked out its prow from the others, his emotions thrilling to the prospect of his first trip off-planet. Destination was Oberon, a cold Uranus rock, but that didn't matter. It was off, it was away, it was *outside.*

"If you ever come back," Ben said, "we will be here."

That caught Huck off guard. "What do you mean? Aren't you coming with me?"

Silence, for a moment. Then, Jonquil: "We can't leave here, Huck. We died here. The ashes of our bodies are here. We can't go."

"I never knew."

"We never thought you would actually leave, or we would have told you."

"Then there won't be any voices, no one at all, after I lift?"

"Oh, of course. You'll meet others."

"But the law says all people who die get sent inwards to Earth. I remember reading that somewhere."

"And you remember correctly. But not all corpses can be recovered. No, you'll meet others, and they will be your friends, just as we were."

"Are," Huck corrected.

"No, dear Huck," Jonquil said gently. "Were."

"Let's go," he said, settling in. "Let's get the show moving."

"You've got it, cowboy. On your signal."

Screens off, now, and he was away. Uranus was down there . . . instruments told him that much . . . but he had no wish to see it. Not this time. He had a headache from the realigning tune Sylvia had given him after breakfast. Plus he hadn't eaten the breakfast, which only made the headache worse.

"How does she feel?"

Meaning the shuttle, not his head. "Fine."

"We were a little concerned about a flutter in your dorsal sail cluster.   Would you mind checking it?"

Like a hand traced lightly over the spine of his back . . .

"Nothing.   Seems okay."

Gravity tugged at him, gently, gently.   He turned on a few of his aft screens.

Miranda was vaguely round.   It was as though its sphere had been broken into pieces and then put back together without aid from the original plan.   Seen from several thousand kilometers it resembled a green flower on black velvet, irregular in outline, reflecting the color of the planet it orbited.

Huck hung in the velvet between the flower and the green-blue ringed gas giant, the shuttle enclosing him, helping him maneuver as he fell.   He completed a number of operations himself manually to give him something to do before the real work began.

"You're doing fine," the dock chief said.   "Five minutes till—"

"Yeah, right."

This is it, kid.   This is the one.   You have to go through with it.   And it all depends on you, now.   Just you.

There, the spark, the comet trail of ionized plasma.   The Lord Talshire's skimmer had ample shielding—he could afford to waste it thus—whereas Huck's shuttle didn't, and Huck couldn't.   He would have to dip, grab, and then climb out as fast as possible, hopefully with sails intact.   And though simply described, the maneuver was in reality incredibly difficult.   So difficult that—

The comet disappeared, then; like a light turned off: there, then gone.   Huck cursed.   This had not been anticipated.   Not at all.

The dock chief cut in immediately: "Seems His Majesty has gone a bit inward. We've lost all contact up here—plasma interference has scrambled everything. How do you read it?"

"The same.   So what do we do?   Is he dead?"

"Checking . . ."

From beside him, Jonas whispered: "We know you can't answer, but listen: Lord Talshire is very much alive.   He's trimmed his orbit beneath the interference layer.   You can still get him."

Huck stared at his instruments, gripping the controls with whitened knuckles.

"Trust us, Huck.   We can help you through it."

Then, from above: "We've got nothing here, Huck.   If he leveled off in time then he's still alive.   You're directed to go through with it, anyway."

"We know what we're saying, Huck," Jonas said.   "In my time I would have called this a piece of cake.   Agree to it, and quickly.   You're running out of time."

Huck looked at his instruments again and discovered this was true.   He had no choice, he realized suddenly.   He really had no choice at all.

"Is the doctor there?" he asked abruptly.

"No . . . this is a restricted—"

"Well then find her and tell her something for me."

"Huck, the time factor—"

"Just shut up and listen. Tell her its going to be all right. Tell her I've got help." And pushed the grips forward, plunging into the interference layer before any reply was possible.

You don't want anyone to know about them, about the voices. You've lived with that so long it has become part of you. They must be a secret, they have to be. No one hears voices, no one but people who should be locked up. Locked up. Picked apart. Put back together again. Happy, vacant. Gone.

Why didn't they just leave you alone? It was so good before, it really was, solitary, sweeping the air clean, dodging the Royal patrols, making that tiny amount of profit that let you float at the surface that much longer. Chrise, the silences out there were magnificent, the oneness, the universality . . . the *safety* . . .

You are ripped open, now. You are spreadeagled, flayed to the bone. *Someone knows.* She says she understands. Trust her? Trust her? Everyone wants your trust, now. Everyone.

"Listen to me, Huck," Jonas said. "Listen carefully and do what I tell you. I'll work *through* you. It can be done."

Huck stared down at the controls, his mouth slack, his hands clenching the hand grips. "I . . . I can't. . . ."

"You have to! You have to be willing or I can't do a Chrising thing!"

Huck felt Jonas near him, and the others, all the others, all of them with one thought, all of them. . . .

He closed his eyes and swallowed, his pale cheeks flushing red. "How—?"

"Just sit there, let yourself go limp . . . yeah . . . now don't panic on me . . . you and I are about to do some maneuvers with this crackerbox that are bound to scare the living . . ." he paused, ". . . just relax. . . ."

Huck's hands moved by themselves, then. Deftly, to the console, marking out a sequence. Huck watched them. Then all the forward screens snapped on, and he stifled a scream.

"Keep your eyes open, Huck! I can't do this blind!"

Green hell, deep, hot, steaming jungle of liquid emerald blades reaching up to— oh please. Oh, please. Every past fear was banished instantly in the face of this. Ultimate insanity, demon clouds, death seas . . . got to . . . got to—

"Give me some help, please. I can't keep his eyes open or his head in place."

There, something . . . a speck of black against the chaos, a defect on the screen? . . . Huck focused on it in desperation, trying to orient himself, to place himself within some sane frame of—

A grappling waldo swept across a starboard screen; Huck gasped in relief, recognizing it. Then again, a twin to the first, across a port screen.

"You're doing great. Just great. Concentrate on the skimmer. Any moment now . . ."

A power dive, all sails furled, silver bullet with arms, with hands, reaching. Huck watched, fascinated, as the skimmer grew in size in the forward screen, the Royal crest glittering on its bow. . . . "Help me, Huck. You've got to help me now. I need all that three-prong expertise. Come on pal. . . ."

*   *   *

Face it.   Face yourself.   Face the choice: two ways, two paths, up or down.
There, in your hands, the power . . .

You know how it is.   You know how hard it is, sometimes. . . .

"Do it, Jonas, just do it."

Contact.   The shuttle vibrated with sudden, staccato engine bursts.   A horizon
appeared on the forward screen, then swung up and away—

"Help me, Huck!"

—and appeared again, lowered, and was lost to an incredibly sane, unbelievably
perfect starfield.

Sails shot out; the field generators strained toward overload; the vibration was
continuous, was everywhere, was everything.

Huck glanced at the appropriate screen and saw the skimmer grappled securely
alongside the shuttle.   Sudden friend, sudden companion in the madness.   "Is it
over?" he whispered.

"The worst of it is.   Both spacecraft are intact, and the Prince is alive.   How
about you?"

Huck let out his breath, wiped the sweat from his face and neck.   "Alive," he
said.   "Alive, too."

He opened and closed the door quietly behind him.

In the shadows she turned; he saw a wetness on her cheeks.

"Hey," whispering, standing by the door.

". . . Huck?"

"We did it," he said, a smile forming.   "Hey, we did it."

ROBERT LEE HAWKINS

A Simple Outside Job

J effrey Castilho used the mirrors in one corner of the airlock to check the back of his lifepack, his eyes going from the checklist painted on the wall to the fasteners and connectors of his suit, speaking each item out loud just as he'd been trained. Static muttered in his earphones, from the fusion generator equipment working outside on Titan's surface and inside Titan Pilot Project's lifedome. Then the earphones popped and Jeff heard, "Castilho, this is Rogers. You sure you don't want someone to come with you?"

Jeff tried to scowl and tongue the transmit button at the same time. He caught sight of his face in the mirror, with the stringy beard he'd started to grow when he'd found that no one outside of translunar space shaved, and realized he just looked funny. He took a breath to be sure he kept the irritation out of his voice and said, "No. It's just a matter of plugging in a new black box, and I know you have other things to do."

"Okay. You need help, just holler."

"Sure. Thanks." Jeff tongued the button off and said to the dead microphone, "You don't have to baby me."

Then he looked over the front of his suit: the replacement box for the broken icecube maker, test socket and adaptor, flashlight, screwdrivers, emergency oxygen tank. He'd be damned if he'd take a chance on leaving something behind and asking Rogers to bring it out. He planned on being an asset to Titan Pilot Project, not a liability.

Jeff punched the cycle button and felt his pressure suit become full as the airlock was evacuated. Anyway, he thought, I might be fresh out of engineering school, first time past the orbit of Luna, and earthgrown, but anyone short of a Self-Fulfillment Class dropout could handle this job. No matter what the Shift Supervisor thinks.

The outer door opened and Jeff stepped onto the orange-yellow surface of Titan. He felt the cold—not with his skin, but with his eyes: the dim light of the sun casting unnaturally sharp shadows, the fanciful shapes of melted and refrozen ice, orange-yellow snow drifted by the thin methane wind. Jeff looked closer. It wasn't snow, but chips of eroded ice.

Irritation fell away. This was his dream. Space-living man was self-sufficient in metals, oxygen, and silicon, but short of carbon, nitrogen, and hydrogen— especially hydrogen to be thrown away in his inefficient fusion drives. Titan had all three, carbon in the atmosphere as methane, nitrogen frozen in the ground as ammonia, hydrogen in everything.   If Titan Pilot Project proved the feasibility of using these resources, dependence on earth for organic chemicals would end. Jeffrey Castilho was proud to be part of the Project, even if it only meant fixing broken icecube makers.

He found the broken machine a few hundred meters from the lifedome.   It was an irregular, dull-silver box, the size of the front half of a railroad boxcar.   It had cut a geometrically perfect trench, just wide enough for its caterpillar treads and one-and-a-half meters deep.   A double row of transparent water-ice cubes, as tall as Jeff, lay in the trench behind it.

Jeff carefully pushed in the safeties at the snout end of the machine, making sure the lasers wouldn't cut back in when he replaced the bad circuit.   The lasers, radiating at a wavelength in the infrared strongly absorbed by water but not by methane, were supposed to melt the orange-yellow ice just ahead of the snout. The machine would then suck in the water, separate the dissolved ammonia and organic contaminants, let a cube start to freeze and drop it out the back.   The cubes were shells of ice twenty or thirty centimeters thick filled with liquid water, but quickly froze solid.   Plastic balloons of frozen ammonia were dropped off to one side.

But a monitor circuit in the laser control box had gone bad ten minutes before. The icecube maker's brain had turned the lasers off, signaled the main computer, and waited.   The job had gone on the job board and Jeff had grabbed it.

Jeff moved to the snout end, shuffling in the low gravity.   The lasers were mounted in blisters, connected by a thick wedge that formed an overhang over a pit where the melted water lay.   He used his flashlight to find the access hatch, on the lower surface of the wedge.

There was a thin layer of ice covering about fifteen centimeters of liquid in the pit.   The ice broke when Jeff dropped into the pit and crawled between the blisters, but he ignored it.   His boots were well insulated.

Replacing the module should have been simple enough, but crouched down under the snout, in a pressure suit, trying to work in the crowded circuit compartment by the light of a flash velcroed to one leg, it took a frustratingly long time.   Finally Jeff got the black box out and wired into the test socket.   Then he plugged the socket into his suit radio and let it talk to the main computer in high-pitched whistles that changed almost too fast to hear.   It sounded like a cage full of birds speeded up by a factor of ten.   The computer replied vocally:

"Test: module micro 1777496 dash LOC5028: module defective: failure parameters follow. . . ."

Well, he had the right one.   Jeff noticed that his helmet was fogging up.   The icecube maker's internal heaters were still going, and he was getting vapor— probably ammonia—condensing and freezing on the faceplate.   He turned up the faceplate defogger and went back to work, plugging in the new module and checking its operation.   Then he hung the old module on his belt, fastened the access hatch shut again, and started to shuffle out from under the snout.

Except his feet wouldn't come.

He swore peevishly and jerked his left foot.   The foot shifted inside the boot but the boot didn't move.   Jeff twisted to see past his spacesuited legs and swore again.

He had little experience in swearing, but he gave it his best shot.   The water in the pit that had been fifteen centimetrs deep was now only half that, and there was a thick cylinder of ice around his boots all the way to the ankles.

For a second Jeff felt as cold as if he'd been naked in the methane wind.   In the next second his tongue went automatically to the transmit button, but he took it back.

"Wait a minute.   I must look like an *idiot.*"   If he called for help, would Rogers volunteer to come get him?   What would the rescue party say when they saw him, crouched between the laser blisters, face in the corner, ankle-deep in dirty ice?

"He expected me to screw up.   Son-of-a—"

Jeff took three deep breaths.   Then he tried chipping with a screwdriver, but the orange-yellow stuff was incredibly tough.   He suspected new ice was freezing as fast as he chipped it off.   "Couldn't wait for all the water to freeze?   Had to jump right in and go wading, eh?   Gahhh."   Jeff stuck the screwdriver back on his belt.   "It might be even stupider not to call for help.   Still . . ."

He took his flashlight apart and shorted a wire from the test socket across the battery terminals.   The wire glowed a cheery red in the dimness and was almost white-hot when Jeff applied it to the collar of ice around his right ankle.   As far as he could tell, it sank right in, losing its glow, but the water seemed to freeze behind it as fast as it melted.   Then the wire came loose from one terminal, sparking briefly, and was stuck fast in the ice.

"Great.   I should have brought a blowtorch with me."   Jeff crouched in the darkness for a while, still not willing to use his radio.   And then he started to straighten up with a jerk, thumping his helmet on the overhang, and looked down at his emergency oxygen tank in a wild surmise.

The inner airlock door cycled open.   With the green emergency tank dangling from his left hand, Jeffrey Castilho stepped into the cloakroom.   While he was racking the pressure suit, Rogers stopped in.

"Took you a long time to finish that job, Castilho.   No trouble, was there?"

Rogers's face was hard to read behind his thick black beard.   Jeff made a vague motion with one hand.   "Well, uh—"

Rogers saw the empty emergency tank.   "What's that empty for?"

"Well—"   Jeff bit the bullet.   "I emptied it.   I, uh, used it to build a fire."

"A fire."

Jeff's thumb indicated the outside.   "People on earth used to burn methane all the time.   So I burned some because my feet were stuck in the ice."

"Ah ha.   So.   You were stupid enough to get stuck."   Jeff winced.   "But smart enough to get loose."   Rogers looked at Jeff for a moment.   "I guess we'll settle for that.

"Now, we've been having some trouble with the methane compressors. . . ."

ROGER ZELAZNY

The Last Defender of Camelot

The three muggers who stopped him that October night in San Francisco did not anticipate much resistance from the old man, despite his size. He was well-dressed, and that was sufficient.

The first approached him with his hand extended. The other two hung back a few paces.

"Just give me your wallet and your watch," the mugger said. "You'll save yourself a lot of trouble."

The old man's grip shifted on his walking stick. His shoulders straightened. His shock of white hair tossed as he turned his head to regard the other.

"Why don't you come and take them?"

The mugger began another step but he never completed it. The stick was almost invisible in the speed of its swinging. It struck him on the left temple and he fell.

Without pausing, the old man caught the stick by its middle with his left hand, advanced and drove it into the belly of the next nearest man. Then, with an upward hook as the man doubled, he caught him in the softness beneath the jaw, behind the chin, with its point. As the man fell, he clubbed him with its butt on the back of the neck.

The third man had reached out and caught the old man's upper arm by then. Dropping the stick, the old man seized the mugger's shirtfront with his left hand, his belt with his right, raised him from the ground until he held him at arm's length above his head, and slammed him against the side of the building to his right, releasing him as he did so.

He adjusted his apparel, ran a hand through his hair, and retrieved his walking stick. For a moment he regarded the three fallen forms, then shrugged and continued on his way.

There were sounds of traffic from somewhere off to his left. He turned right at the next corner. The moon appeared above tall buildings as he walked. The smell of the ocean was on the air. It had rained earlier, and the pavement still shone beneath streetlamps. He moved slowly, pausing occasionally to examine the contents of darkened shop windows.

After perhaps ten minutes, he came upon a side street showing more activity than any of the others he had passed. There was a drugstore, still open, on the corner, a diner farther up the block, and several well-lighted storefronts. A number of people were walking along the far side of the street.   A boy coasted by on a bicycle.   He turned there, his pale eyes regarding everything he passed.

Halfway up the block, he came to a dirty window on which was painted the word READINGS.   Beneath it were displayed the outline of a hand and a scattering of playing cards.   As he passed the open door, he glanced inside.   A brightly garbed woman, her hair bound back in a green kerchief, sat smoking at the rear of the room.   She smiled as their eyes met and crooked an index finger toward herself. He smiled back and turned away, but . . .

He looked at her again.   What was it?   He glanced at his watch.

Turning, he entered the shop and moved to stand before her.   She rose.   She was small, barely over five feet in height.

"Your eyes," he remarked, "are green.   Most gypsies I know have dark eyes." She shrugged.

"You take what you get in life.   Have you a problem?"

"Give me a moment and I'll think of one," he said.   "I just came in here because you remind me of someone and it bothers me—I can't think who."

"Come into the back," she said, "and sit down.   We'll talk."

He nodded and followed her into a small room to the rear.   A threadbare oriental rug covered the floor near the small table at which they seated themselves.   Zodiacal prints and faded psychedelic posters of a semi-religious nature covered the walls. A crystal ball stood on a small stand in the far corner beside a vase of cut flowers. A dark, long-haired cat slept on a sofa to the right of it.   A door to another room stood slightly ajar beyond the sofa.   The only illumination came from a cheap lamp on the table before him and from a small candle in a plaster base atop the shawl-covered coffee table.

He leaned forward and studied her face, then shook his head and leaned back.

She flicked an ash onto the floor.

"Your problem?" she suggested.

He sighed.

"Oh, I don't really have a problem anyone can help me with.   Look, I think I made a mistake coming in here.   I'll pay you for your trouble, though, just as if you'd given me a reading.   How much is it?"

He began to reach for his wallet, but she raised her hand.

"Is it that you do not believe in such things?" she asked, her eyes scrutinizing his face.

"No, quite the contrary," he replied.   "I am willing to believe in magic, divination, and all manner of spells and sendings, angelic and demonic.   But—"

"But not from someone in a dump like this?"

He smiled.

"No offense," he said.

A whistling sound filled the air.   It seemed to come from the next room back.

"That's all right," she said, "but my water is boiling.   I'd forgotten it was on. Have some tea with me?   I do wash the cups.   No charge.   Things are slow."

"All right."

She rose and departed.

He glanced at the door to the front but eased himself back into his chair, resting his large, blue-veined hands on its padded arms. He sniffed then, nostrils flaring, and cocked his head as at some half-familiar aroma.

After a time, she returned with a tray, set it on the coffee table. The cat stirred, raised her head, blinked at it, stretched, closed her eyes again.

"Cream and sugar?"

"Please. One lump."

She placed two cups on the table before him.

"Take either one," she said.

He smiled and drew the one on his left toward him. She placed an ashtray in the middle of the table and returned to her own seat, moving the other cup to her place.

"That wasn't necessary," he said, placing his hands on the table.

She shrugged.

"You don't know me. Why should you trust me? Probably got a lot of money on you."

He looked at her face again. She had apparently removed some of the heavier makeup while in the back room. The jawline, the brow . . . He looked away. He took a sip of tea.

"Good tea. Not instant," he said. "Thanks."

"So you believe in all sorts of magic," she asked, sipping her own.

"Some," he said.

"Any special reason why?"

"Some of it works."

"For example?"

He gestured aimlessly with his left hand.

"I've traveled a lot. I've seen some strange things."

"And you have no problems?"

He chuckled.

"Still determined to give me a reading? All right. I'll tell you a little about myself and what I want right now, and you can tell me whether I'll get it. Okay?"

"I'm listening."

"I am a buyer for a large gallery in the East. I am something of an authority on ancient work in precious metals. I am in town to attend an auction of such items from the estate of a private collector. I will go to inspect the pieces tomorrow. Naturally, I hope to find something good. What do you think my chances are?"

"Give me your hands."

He extended them, palms upward. She leaned forward and regarded them. She looked back up at him immediately.

"Your wrists have more rascettes than I can count!"

"Yours seem to have quite a few, also."

She met his eyes for only a moment and returned her attention to his hands. He noted that she had paled beneath what remained of her makeup, and her breathing was now irregular.

"No," she finally said, drawing back, "you are not going to find here what you are looking for."

Her hand trembled slightly as she raised her teacup. He frowned.

"I asked only in jest," he said. "Nothing to get upset about. I doubted I would find what I am really looking for, anyway."

She shook her head.

"Tell me your name."

"I've lost my accent," he said, "but I'm French. The name is DuLac."

She stared into his eyes and began to blink rapidly.

"No . . ." she said. "No."

"I'm afraid so. What's yours?"

"Madam LeFay," she said. "I just repainted that sign. It's still drying."

He began to laugh, but it froze in his throat.

"Now—I know—who—you remind me of. . . ."

"You reminded me of someone, also. Now I, too, know."

Her eyes brimmed, her mascara ran.

"It couldn't be," he said. "Not here. . . .Not in a place like this. . . ."

"You dear man," she said softly, and she raised his right hand to her lips. She seemed to choke for a moment, then said, "I had thought that I was the last, and yourself buried at Joyous Gard. I never dreamed . . ." Then, "This?" gesturing about the room. "Only because it amuses me, helps to pass the time. The waiting—"

She stopped. She lowered his hand.

"Tell me about it," she said.

"The waiting?" he said. "For what do you wait?"

"Peace," she said. "I am here by the power of my arts, through all the long years. But you— How did you manage it?"

"I—" He took another drink of tea. He looked about the room. "I do not know how to begin," he said. "I survived the final battles, saw the kingdom sundered, could do nothing—and at last departed England. I wandered, taking service at many courts, and after a time under many names, as I saw that I was not aging—or aging very, very slowly. I was in India, China—I fought in the Crusades, I've been everywhere. I've spoken with magicians and mystics—most of them charlatans, a few with the power, none so great as Merlin—and what had come to be my own belief was confirmed by one of them, a man more than half charlatan, yet. . . ." He paused and finished his tea. "Are you certain you want to hear all this?" he asked.

"I want to hear it. Let me bring more tea first, though."

She returned with the tea. She lit a cigarette and leaned back.

"Go on."

"I decided that it was—my sin," he said, "with . . . the Queen."

"I don't understand."

"I betrayed my Liege, who was also my friend, in the one thing which must have hurt him most. The love I felt was stronger than loyalty or friendship—and even today, to this day, it still is. I cannot repent, and so I cannot be forgiven. Those were strange and magical times. We lived a land destined to become myth. Powers walked the realm in those days, forces which are now gone from the earth. How or why, I cannot say. But you know that it is true. I am somehow of a piece with those gone things, and the laws that rule my existence are not normal laws of the natural world.   I believe that I cannot die; that it has fallen my lot, as punishment, to wander the world till I have completed the Quest.   I believe I will only know rest the day I find the Holy Grail.   Giuseppe Balsamo, before he became known as Cagliostro, somehow saw this and said it to me just as I had thought it, though I never said a word of it to him.   And so I have traveled the world, searching. I go no more as knight, or soldier, but as an appraiser.   I have been in nearly every museum on Earth, viewed all the great private collections.   So far, it has eluded me.''

"You *are* getting a little old for battle.''

He snorted.

"I have never lost,'' he stated flatly.   "Down ten centuries, I have never lost a personal contest.   It is true that I have aged, yet whenever I am threatened all of my former strength returns to me.   But, look where I may, fight where I may, it has never served me to discover that which I must find.   I feel I am unforgiven and must wander like the Eternal Jew until the end of the world.''

She lowered her head.

". . . And you say I will not find it tomorrow?''

"You will never find it,'' she said softly.

"You saw that in my hand?''

She shook her head.

"Your story is fascinating and your theory novel,'' she began, "but Cagliostro was a total charlatan.   Something must have betrayed your thoughts, and he made a shrewd guess.   But he was wrong.   I say that you will never find it, not because you are unworthy or unforgiven.   No, never that.   A more loyal subject than yourself never drew breath.   Don't you know that Arthur forgave you?   It was an arranged marriage.   The same thing happened constantly elsewhere, as you must know.   You gave her something he could not.   There was only tenderness there.   He understood.   The only forgiveness you require is that which has been withheld all these long years—your own.   No, it is not a doom that has been laid upon you.   It is your own feelings which led you to assume an impossible quest, something tantamount to total unforgiveness.   But you have suffered all these centuries upon the wrong trail.''

When she raised her eyes, she saw that his were hard, like ice or gemstones. But she met his gaze and continued: "There is not now, was not then, and probably never was, a Holy Grail.''

"I saw it,'' he said, "that day it passed through the Hall of the Table.   We all saw it.''

"You thought you saw it,'' she corrected him.   "I hate to shatter an illusion that has withstood all the other tests of time, but I fear I must.   The kingdom, as you recall, was at that time in turmoil.   The knights were growing restless and falling away from the fellowship.   A year—six months, even—and all would have collapsed, all Arthur had striven so hard to put together.   He knew that the longer Camelot stood, the longer its name would endure, the stronger its ideals would become.   So he made a decision, a purely political one.   Something was needed to hold things together.   He called upon Merlin, already half-mad, yet still shrewd enough to see what was needed and able to provide it.   The Quest was born. Merlin's powers created the illusion you saw that day.   It was a lie, yes.   A glorious lie, though.   And it served for years after to bind you all in brotherhood, in the name of justice and love.   It entered literature, it promoted nobility and the higher ends of culture.   It served its purpose.   But it was—never—really—there. You have been chasing a ghost.   I am sorry, Launcelot, but I have absolutely no reason to lie to you.   I know magic when I see it.   I saw it then.   That is how it happened.''

For a long while he was silent.   Then he laughed.

"You have an answer for everything," he said.   "I could almost believe you, if you could but answer me one thing more—   Why am I here?   For what reason? By what power?   How is it I have been preserved for half the Christian era while other men grow old and die in a handful of years?   Can you tell me now what Cagliostro could not?''

"Yes," she said, "I believe that I can.''

He rose to his feet and began to pace.   The cat, alarmed, sprang from the sofa and ran into the back room.   He stooped and snatched up his walking stick.   He started for the door.

"I suppose it was worth waiting a thousand years to see you afraid," she said. He halted.

"That is unfair," he replied.

"I know.   But now you will come back and sit down," she said.

He was smiling once more as he turned and returned.

"Tell me," he said.   "How do you see it?''

"Yours was the last enchantment of Merlin, that is how I see it.''

"Merlin?   Me?   Why?''

"Gossip had it the old goat took Nimue into the woods and she had to use one of his own spells on him in self-defense—a spell which caused him to sleep forever in some lost place.   If it was the spell that I believe it was, then at least part of the rumor was incorrect.   There was no known counterspell, but the effects of the enchantment would have caused him to sleep not forever but for a millennium, and then to awaken.   My guess now is that his last conscious act before he dropped off was to lay this enchantment upon you, so that you would be on hand when he returned.''

"I suppose it might be possible, but why would he want me or need me?''

"If I were journeying into a strange time, I would want an ally once I reached it.   And if I had a choice, I would want it to be the greatest champion of the day.''

"Merlin . . .'' he mused.   "I suppose that it could be as you say.   Excuse me, but a long life has just been shaken up, from beginning to end.   If this is true . . .''

"I am sure that it is.''

"If this is true . . . a millennium, you say?''

"Just so.''

"Well, it is almost exactly a thousand years now."

"I know. I do not believe that our meeting tonight was a matter of chance. You are destined to meet him upon his awakening, which should be soon. Something has ordained that you meet me first, however, to be warned."

"Warned? Warned of what?"

"He is mad, Launcelot. Many of us felt a great relief at his passing. If the realm had not been sundered finally by strife it would probably have been broken by his hand, anyway."

"That I find difficult to believe. He was always a strange man—for who can fully understand a sorcerer?—and in his later years he did seem at least partly daft. But he never struck me as evil."

"Nor was he. His was the most dangerous morality of all. He was a misguided idealist. In a more primitive time and place and with a willing tool like Arthur, he was able to create a legend. Today, in an age of monstrous weapons, with the right leader as his catspaw, he could unleash something totally devastating. He would see a wrong and force his man to try righting it. He would do it in the name of the same high ideals he always served, but he would not appreciate the results until it was too late. How could he—even if he were sane? He has no conception of modern international relations."

"What is to be done? What is my part in all of this?"

"I believe you should go back, to England, to be present at his awakening, to find out exactly what he wants, to try to reason with him."

"I don't know. . . . How would I find him?"

"You found me. When the time is right, you will be in the proper place. I am certain of that. It was meant to be, probably even a part of his spell. Seek him. But do not trust him."

"I don't know, Morgana." He looked at the wall, unseeing. "I don't know."

"You have waited this long and you draw back now from finally finding out?"

"You are right—in that much, at least." He folded his hands, raised them and rested his chin upon them. "What I would do if he really returned, I do not know. Try to reason with him, yes—Have you any other advice?"

"Just that you be there."

"You've looked at my hand. You have the power. What did you see?"

She turned away.

"It is uncertain," she said.

That night he dreamed, as he sometimes did, of times long gone. They sat about the great Table, as they had on that day. Gawaine was there, and Percival. Galahad . . . He winced. This day was different from other days. There was a certain tension in the air, a before-the-storm feeling, an electrical thing. . . . Merlin stood at the far end of the room, hands in the sleeves of his long robe, hair and beard snowy and unkempt, pale eyes staring—at what, none could be certain. . . .

After some timeless time, a reddish glow appeared near the door. All eyes moved toward it. It grew brighter and advanced slowly into the room—a formless apparition of light.   There were sweet odors and some few soft strains of music. Gradually, a form began to take shape at its center, resolving itself into the likeness of a chalice. . . .

He felt himself rising, moving slowly, following it in its course through the great chamber, advancing upon it, soundlessly and deliberately, as if moving underwater. . . .

. . . Reaching for it.

His hand entered the circle of light, moved toward its center, neared the now blazing cup and passed through. . . .

Immediately, the light faded.   The outline of the chalice wavered, and it collapsed in upon itself, fading, fading, gone. . . .

There came a sound, rolling, echoing about the hall.   Laughter.

He turned and regarded the others.   They sat about the table, watching him, laughing.   Even Merlin managed a dry chuckle.

Suddenly, his great blade was in his hand, and he raised it as he strode toward the Table.   The knights nearest him drew back as he brought the weapon crashing down.

The Table split in half and fell.   The room shook.

The quaking continued.   Stones were dislodged from the walls.   A roof beam fell.   He raised his arm.

The entire castle began to come apart, falling about him, and still the laughter continued.

He awoke damp with perspiration and lay still for a long while.   In the morning, he bought a ticket for London.

Two of the three elemental sounds of the world were suddenly with him as he walked that evening, stick in hand.   For a dozen days, he had hiked about Cornwall, finding no clues to that which he sought.   He had allowed himself two more before giving up and departing.

Now the wind and the rain were upon him, and he increased his pace.   The fresh-lit stars were smothered by a mass of cloud and wisps of fog grew like ghostly fungi on either hand.   He moved among trees, paused, continued on.

"Shouldn't have stayed out this late," he muttered, and after several more pauses, *"Nel mezzo del cammin di nostra vita mi ritrovai per una selva oscura, che la diritta via era smarrita,"* then he chuckled, halting beneath a tree.

The rain was not heavy.   It was more a fine mist now.   A bright patch in the lower heavens showed where the moon hung veiled.

He wiped his face, turned up his collar.   He studied the position of the moon. After a time, he struck off to his right.   There was a faint rumble of thunder in the distance.

The fog continued to grow about him as he went.   Soggy leaves made squishing noises beneath his boots.   An animal of indeterminate size bolted from a clump of shrubbery beside a cluster of rocks and tore off through the darkness.

Five minutes . . . ten . . .   He cursed softly.   The rainfall had increased in intensity.   Was that the same rock?

He turned in a complete circle. All directions were equally uninviting. Selecting one at random, he commenced walking once again.

Then, in the distance, he discerned a spark, a glow, a wavering light. It vanished and reappeared periodically, as though partly blocked, the line of sight a function of his movements. He headed toward it. After perhaps half a minute, it was gone again from sight, but he continued on in what he thought to be its direction. There came another roll of thunder, louder this time.

When it seemed that it might have been illusion or some short-lived natural phenomenon, something else occurred in that same direction. There was a movement, a shadow-within-shadow shuffling at the foot of a great tree. He slowed his pace, approaching the spot cautiously.

There!

A figure detached itself from a pool of darkness ahead and to the left. Manlike, it moved with a slow and heavy tread, creaking sounds emerging from the forest floor beneath it. A vagrant moonbeam touched it for a moment, and it appeared yellow and metallically slick beneath moisture.

He halted. It seemed that he had just regarded a knight in full armor in his path. How long since he had beheld such a sight? He shook his head and stared.

The figure had also halted. It raised its right arm in a beckoning gesture, then turned and began to walk away. He hesitated for only a moment, then followed.

It turned off to the left and pursued a treacherous path, rocky, slippery, heading slightly downward. He actually used his stick now, to assure his footing, as he tracked its deliberate progress. He gained on it, to the point where he could clearly hear the metallic scraping sounds of its passage.

Then it was gone, swallowed by a greater darkness.

He advanced to the place where he had last beheld it. He stood in the lee of a great mass of stone. He reached out and probed it with his stick.

He tapped steadily along its nearest surface, and then the stick moved past it. He followed.

There was an opening, a crevice. He had to turn sidewise to pass within it, but as he did the full glow of the light he had seen came into sight for several seconds.

The passage curved and widened, leading him back and down. Several times, he paused and listened, but there were no sounds other than his own breathing.

He withdrew his handkerchief and dried his face and hands carefully. He brushed moisture from his coat, turned down his collar. He scuffed the mud and leaves from his boots. He adusted his apparel. Then he strode forward, rounding a final corner, into a chamber lit by a small oil lamp suspended by three delicate chains from some point in the darkness overhead. The yellow knight stood unmoving beside the far wall. On a fiber mat atop a stony pedestal directly beneath the lamp lay an old man in tattered garments. His bearded face was half-masked by shadows.

He moved to the old man's side. He saw then that those ancient dark eyes were open.

"Merlin . . . ?" he whispered.

There came a faint hissing sound, a soft croak. Realizing the source, he leaned nearer.

"Elixir . . . in earthen crock . . . on ledge . . . in back," came the gravelly whisper.

He turned and sought the ledge, the container.

"Do you know where it is?" he asked the yellow figure.

It neither stirred nor replied, but stood like a display piece. He turned away from it then and sought further. After a time, he located it. It was more a niche than a ledge, blending in with the wall, cloaked with shadow. He ran his fingertips over the container's contours, raised it gently. Something liquid stirred within it. He wiped its lip on his sleeve after he had returned to the lighted area. The wind whistled past the entranceway and he thought he felt the faint vibration of thunder.

Sliding one hand beneath his shoulders, he raised the ancient form. Merlin's eyes still seemed unfocussed. He moistened Merlin's lips with the liquid. The old man licked them, and after several moments opened his mouth. He administered a sip, then another, and another . . .

Merlin signalled for him to lower him, and he did. He glanced again at the yellow armor, but it had remained motionless the entire while. He looked back at the sorcerer and saw that a new light had come into his eyes and he was studying him, smiling faintly.

"Feel better?"

Merlin nodded. A minute passed, and a touch of color appeared upon his cheeks. He elbowed himself into a sitting position and took the container into his hands. He raised it and drank deeply.

He sat still for several minutes after that. His thin hands, which had appeared waxy in the flamelight, grew darker, fuller. His shoulders straightened. He placed the crock on the bed beside him and stretched his arms. His joints creaked the first time he did it, but not the second. He swung his legs over the edge of the bed and rose slowly to his feet. He was a full head shorter than Launcelot.

"It is done," he said, staring back into the shadows. "Much has happened, of course . . . ?"

"Much has happened," Launcelot replied.

"You have lived through it all. Tell me, is the world a better place or is it worse than it was in those days?"

"Better in some ways, worse in others. It is different."

"How is it better?"

"There are many ways of making life easier, and the sum total of human knowledge has increased vastly."

"How has it worsened?"

"There are many more people in the world. Consequently, there are many more people suffering from poverty, disease, ignorance. The world itself has suffered great depredation, in the way of pollution and other assaults on the integrity of nature."

"Wars?"

"There is always someone fighting, somewhere."

"They need help."

"Maybe.   Maybe not."

Merlin turned and looked into his eyes.

"What do you mean?"

"People haven't changed.   They are as rational—and irrational—as they were in the old days.   They are as moral and law-abiding—and not—as ever.   Many new things have been learned, many new situations evolved, but I do not believe that the nature of man has altered significantly in the time you've slept.   Nothing you do is going to change that.   You may be able to alter a few features of the times, but would it really be proper to meddle?   Everything is so interdependent today that even you would not be able to predict all the consequences of any actions you take.   You might do more harm than good; and whatever you do, man's nature will remain the same."

"This isn't like you, Lance.   You were never much given to philosophizing in the old days."

"I've had a long time to think about it."

"And I've had a long time to dream about it.   War is your craft, Lance.   Stay with that."

"I gave it up a long time ago."

"Then what are you now?"

"An appraiser."

Merlin turned away, took another drink.   He seemed to radiate a fierce energy when he turned again.

"And your oath?   To right wrongs, to punish the wicked . . . ?"

"The longer I lived the more difficult it became to determine what was a wrong and who was wicked.   Make it clear to me again and I may go back into business."

"Galahad would never have addressed me so."

"Galahad was young, naïve, trusting.   Speak not to me of my son."

"Launcelot!   Launcelot!"   He placed a hand on his arm.   "Why all this bitterness for an old friend who has done nothing for a thouaand years?"

"I wished to make my position clear immediately.   I feared you might contemplate some irreversible action which could alter the world balance of power fatally. I want you to know that I will not be party to it."

"Admit that you do not know what I might do, what I can do."

"Freely.   That is why I fear you.   What *do* you intend to do?"

"Nothing, at first.   I wish merely to look about me, to see for myself some of these changes of which you have spoken.   Then I will consider which wrongs need righting, who needs punishment, and who to choose as my champions.   I will show you these things, and then you can go back into business, as you say."

Launcelot sighed.

"The burden of proof is on the moralist.   Your judgment is no longer sufficient for me."

"Dear me," the other replied, "it is sad to have waited this long for an encounter of this sort, to find you have lost your faith in me. My powers are beginning to return already, Lance. Do you not feel magic in the air?"

"I feel something I have not felt in a long while."

"The sleep of ages was a restorative—an aid, actually. In a while, Lance, I am going to be stronger than I ever was before. And you doubt that I will be able to turn back the clock?"

"I doubt you can do it in a fashion to benefit anybody. Look, Merlin, I'm sorry. I do not like it that things have come to this either. But I have lived too long, seen too much, know too much of how the world works now to trust any one man's opinion concerning its salvation. Let it go. You are a mysterious, revered legend. I do not know what you really are. But forgo exercising your powers in any sort of crusade. Do something else this time around. Become a physician and fight pain. Take up painting. Be a professor of history, an antiquarian. Hell, be a social critic and point out what evils you see for people to correct themselves."

"Do you really believe I could be satisfied with any of those things?"

"Men find satisfaction in many things. It depends on the man, not on the things. I'm just saying that you should avoid using your powers in any attempt to effect social changes as we once did, by violence."

"Whatever changes have been wrought, time's greatest irony lies in its having transformed you into a pacifist."

"You are wrong."

"Admit it. You have finally come to fear the clash of arms! An appraiser! What kind of knight are you?"

"One who finds himself in the wrong time and the wrong place, Merlin."

The sorcerer shrugged and turned away.

"Let it be, then. It is good that you have chosen to tell me all these things immediately. Thank you for that, anyway. A moment."

Merlin walked to the rear of the cave, returned in moments attired in fresh garments. The effect was startling. His entire appearance was more kempt and cleanly. His hair and beard now appeared gray rather than white. His step was sure and steady. He held a staff in his right hand but did not lean upon it.

"Come walk with me," he said.

"It is a bad night."

"It is not the same night you left without. It is not even the same place."

As he passed the suit of yellow armor, he snapped his fingers near its visor. With a single creak, the figure moved and turned to follow him.

"Who is that?"

Merlin smiled.

"No one," he replied, and he reached back and raised the visor. The helmet was empty. "It is enchanted, animated by a spirit," he said. "A trifle clumsy, though, which is why I did not trust it to administer my draught. A perfect servant, however, unlike some. Incredibly strong and swift. Even in your prime you could not have beaten it. I fear nothing when it walks with me. Come, there is something I would have you see.''

"Very well.''

Launcelot followed Merlin and the hollow knight from the cave. The rain had stopped, and it was very still. They stood on an incredibly moonlit plain where mists drifted and grasses sparkled. Shadowy shapes stood in the distance.

"Excuse me,'' Launcelot said. "I left my walking stick inside.''

He turned and re-entered the cave.

"Yes, fetch it, old man,'' Merlin replied. "Your strength is already on the wane.''

When Launcelot returned, he leaned upon the stick and squinted across the plain.

"This way,'' Merlin said, "to where your questions will be answered. I will try not to move too quickly and tire you.''

"Tire me?''

The sorcerer chuckled and began walking across the plain. Launcelot followed.

"Do you not feel a trifle weary?'' he asked.

"Yes, as a matter of fact, I do. Do you know what is the matter with me?''

"Of course. I have withdrawn the enchantment which has protected you all these years. What you feel now are the first tentative touches of your true age. It will take some time to catch up with you, against your body's natural resistance, but it is beginning its advance.''

"Why are you doing this to me?''

"Because I believed you when you said you were not a pacifist. And you spoke with sufficient vehemence for me to realize that you might even oppose me. I could not permit that, for I knew that your old strength was still there for you to call upon. Even a sorcerer might fear that, so I did what had to be done. By my power was it maintained; without it, it now drains away. It would have been good for us to work together once again, but I saw that that could not be.''

Launcelot stumbled, caught himself, limped on. The hollow knight walked at Merlin's right hand.

"You say that your ends are noble,'' Launcelot said, "but I do not believe you. Perhaps in the old days they were. But more than the times have changed. You are different. Do you not feel it yourself?''

Merlin drew a deep breath and exhaled vapor.

"Perhaps it is my heritage,'' he said. Then, "I jest. Of course, I have changed. Everyone does. You yourself are a perfect example. What you consider a turn for the worse in me is but the tip of an irreducible conflict which has grown up between us in the course of our changes. I still hold with the true ideals of Camelot.''

Launcelot's shoulders were bent foward now and his breathing had deepened. The shapes loomed larger before them.

"Why, I know this place,'' he gasped. "Yet, I do not know it. Stonehenge does not stand so today. Even in Arthur's time it lacked this perfection. How did we get here? What has happened?''

He paused to rest, and Merlin halted to accommodate him.

"This night we have walked between the worlds," the sorcerer said. "This is a piece of the land of Faërie and that is the true Stonehenge, a holy place. I have stretched the bounds of the worlds to bring it here. Were I unkind I could send you back with it and strand you there forever. But it is better that you know a sort of peace. Come!"

Launcelot staggered along behind him, heading for the great circle of stones. The faintest of breezes came out of the west, stirring the mists.

"What do you mean—know a sort of peace?"

"The complete restoration of my powers and their increase will require a sacrifice in this place."

"Then you planned this for me all along!"

"No. It was not to have been you, Lance. Anyone would have served, though you will serve superbly well. It need not have been so, had you elected to assist me. You could still change your mind."

"Would you want someone who did that at your side?"

"You have a point there."

"Then why ask—save as a petty cruelty?"

"It is just that, for you have annoyed me."

Launcelot halted again when they came to the circle's periphery. He regarded the massive stands of stone.

"If you will not enter willingly," Merlin stated, "my servant will be happy to assist you."

"Think you I fear an empty suit of armor, juggled by some Hellborn wight? Even now, Merlin, without the benefit of wizardly succor, I could take that thing apart."

The sorcerer laughed.

"It is good that you at least recall the boasts of knighthood when all else has left you. I've half a mind to give you the opportunity, for the manner of your passing here is not important. Only the preliminaries are essential."

"But you're afraid to risk your servant?"

"Think you so, old man? I doubt you could even bear the weight of a suit of armor, let alone lift a lance. But if you are willing to try, so be it!"

He rapped the butt of his staff three times upon the ground.

"Enter," he said then. "You will find all that you need within. And I am glad you have made this choice. You were insufferable, you know. Just once, I longed to see you beaten, knocked down to the level of lesser mortals. I only wish the Queen could be here, to witness her champion's final engagement."

"So do I," said Launcelot, and he walked past the monolith and entered the circle.

A black stallion waited, its reins held down beneath a rock. Pieces of armor, a lance, a blade and a shield leaned against the side of the dolmen. Across the circle's diameter, a white stallion awaited the advance of the hollow knight.

"I am sorry I could not arrange for a page or a squire to assist you," Merlin said, coming around the other side of the monolith.   "I'll be glad to help you myself, though."

"I can manage," Launcelot replied.

"My champion is accoutered in exactly the same fashion," Merlin said, "and I have not given him any edge over you in weapons."

"I never liked your puns either."

Launcelot made friends with the horse, then removed a small strand of red from his wallet and tied it about the butt of the lance.   He leaned his stick against the dolmen stone and began to don the armor.   Merlin, whose hair and beard were now almost black, moved off several paces and began drawing a diagram in the dirt with the end of his staff.

"You used to favor a white charger," he commented, "but I thought it appropriate to equip you with one of another color, since you have abandoned the ideals of the Table Round, betraying the memory of Camelot."

"On the contrary," Launcelot replied, glancing overhead at the passage of a sudden roll of thunder.   "Any horse in a storm, and I am Camelot's last defender."

Merlin continued to elaborate upon the pattern he was drawing as Launcelot slowly equipped himself.   The small wind continued to blow, stirring the mists. There came a flash of lightning, startling the horse.   Launcelot calmed it.

Merlin stared at him for a moment and rubbed his eyes.   Launcelot donned his helmet.

"For a moment," Merlin said, "you looked somehow different . . ."

"Really?   Magical withdrawal, do you think?" he asked, and he kicked the stone from the reins and mounted the stallion.

Merlin stepped back from the now completed diagram, shaking his head, as the mounted man leaned over and grasped the lance.

"You still seem to move with some strength," he said.

"Really?"   Launcelot   raised   the   lance   and   couched   it. Before taking up the shield he had hung at the saddle's side, he opened his visor and turned and regarded Merlin.

"Your champion appears to be ready," he said.   "So am I."

Seen in another flash of light, it was an unlined face that looked down at Merlin, clear-eyed, wisps of pale gold hair fringing the forehead.

"What magic have the years taught you?" Merlin asked.

"Not magic," Launcelot replied.   "Caution.   I anticipated you.   So, when I returned to the cave for my stick, I drank the rest of your elixir."

He lowered the visor and turned away.

"You walked like an old man. . . ."

"I'd a lot of practice.   Signal your champion!"

Merlin laughed.

"Good!   It is better this way," he decided, "to see you go down in full strength! You still cannot hope to win against a spirit!"

Launcelot raised the shield and leaned forward.

"Then what are you waiting for?"

"Nothing!" Merlin said.   Then he shouted, "Kill him, Raxas!"

A light rain began as they pounded across the field; and, staring ahead, Launcelot realized that flames were flickering behind his opponent's visor. At the last possible moment, he shifted the point of his lance into line with the hollow knight's blazing helm. There came more lightning and thunder.

His shield deflected the other's lance while his weapon went on to strike the approaching head. It flew from the hollow knight's shoulders and bounced, smouldering, on the ground.

He continued on to the other end of the field and turned. When he had, he saw that the hollow knight, now headless, was doing the same. And beyond him, he saw two standing figures, where moments before there had been but one.

Morgana le Fay, clad in a white robe, red hair unbound and blowing in the wind, faced Merlin from across his pattern. It seemed they were speaking, but he could not hear the words. Then she began to raise her hands, and they glowed like cold fire. Merlin's staff was also gleaming, and he shifted it before him. Then he saw no more, for the hollow knight was ready for the second charge.

He couched his lance, raised the shield, leaned forward and gave his mount the signal. His arm felt like a bar of iron, his strength like an endless current of electricity as he raced down the field. The rain was falling more heavily now and the lightning began a constant flickering. A steady rolling of thunder smothered the sound of the hoofbeats, and the wind whistled past his helm as he approached the other warrior, his lance centered on his shield.

They came together with an enormous crash. Both knights reeled and the hollow one fell, his shield and breastplate pierced by a broken lance. His left arm came away as he struck the earth; the lancepoint snapped and the shield fell beside him. But he began to rise almost immediately, his right hand drawing his long sword.

Launcelot dismounted, discarding his shield, drawing his own great blade. He moved to meet his headless foe. The other struck first and he parried it, a mighty shock running down his arms. He swung a blow of his own. It was parried.

They swaggered swords across the field, till finally Launcelot saw his opening and landed his heaviest blow. The hollow knight toppled into the mud, his breastplate cloven almost to the point where the spear's shaft protruded. At that moment, Morgana le Fay screamed.

Launcelot turned and saw that she had fallen across the pattern Merlin had drawn. The sorcerer, now bathed in a bluish light, raised his staff and moved forward. Launcelot took a step toward them and felt a great pain in his left side.

Even as he turned toward the half-risen hollow knight who was drawing his blade back for another blow, Launcelot reversed his double-handed grip upon his own weapon and raised it high, point downward.

He hurled himself upon the other, and his blade pierced the cuirass entirely as he bore him back down, nailing him to the earth. A shriek arose from beneath him, echoing within the armor, and a gout of fire emerged from the neck hole, sped upward and away, dwindled in the rain, flickered out moments later.

Launcelot pushed himself into a kneeling position. Slowly then, he rose to his feet and turned toward the two figures who again faced one another. Both were now standing within the muddied geometries of power, both were now bathed in the bluish light. Launcelot took a step toward them, then another.

"Merlin!" he called out, continuing to advance upon them.   "I've done what I said I would!   Now I'm coming to kill you!"

Morgana le Fay turned toward him, eyes wide.

"No!" she cried.   "Depart the circle!   Hurry!   I am holding him here!   His power wanes!   In moments, this place will be no more!   Go!"

Launcelot hesitated but a moment, then turned and walked as rapidly as he was able toward the circle's perimeter.   The sky seemed to boil as he passed among the monoliths.

He advanced another dozen paces, then had to pause to rest.   He looked back to the place of battle, to the place where the two figures still stood locked in sorcerous embrace.   Then the scene was imprinted upon his brain as the skies opened and a sheet of fire fell upon the far end of the circle.

Dazzled, he raised his hand to shield his eyes.   When he lowered it, he saw the stones falling, soundless, many of them fading from sight.   The rain began to slow immediately.   Sorcerer and sorceress had vanished along with much of the structure of the still-fading place.   The horses were nowhere to be seen.   He looked about him and saw a good-sized stone.   He headed for it and seated himself.   He unfastened his breastplate and removed it, dropping it to the ground.   His side throbbed and he held it tightly.   He doubled forward and rested his face on his left hand.

The rains continued to slow and finally ceased.   The wind died.   The mists returned.

He breathed deeply and thought back upon the conflict.   This, this was the thing for which he had remained after all the others, the thing for which he had waited, for so long.   It was over now, and he could rest.

There was a gap in his consciousness.   He was brought to awareness again by a light.   A steady glow passed between his fingers, pierced his eyelids.   He dropped his hand and raised his head, opening his eyes.

It passed slowly before him in a halo of white light.   He removed his sticky fingers from his side and rose to his feet to follow it.   Solid, glowing, glorious and pure, not at all like the image in the chamber, it led him on out across the moonlit plain, from dimness to brightness to dimness, until the mists enfolded him as he reached at last to embrace it.

HERE ENDETH THE BOOK OF LAUNCELOT,
LAST OF THE NOBLE KNIGHTS OF THE
ROUND TABLE, AND HIS ADVENTURES
WITH RAXAS, THE HOLLOW KNIGHT,
AND MERLIN AND MORGANA LE FAY,
LAST OF THE WISE FOLK OF CAMELOT,
IN HIS QUEST FOR THE SANGREAL.

QUO FAS ET GLORIA DUCUNT.

MICHAEL A. BANKS & GEORGE WAGNER

Lost and Found

I must have walked five miles before I realized I was lost.   It didn't really matter, of course—I'd been lost for five months anyway, wandering between worlds. What concerned me the most at the moment was the fact that my feet hurt; I wasn't used to all that walking.   From the look of things, though, I'd be doing a lot more walking.   The road was obviously in the wrong place; that was something I hadn't run into before.   Roads, along with cities, rivers, mountains, and other physical items, were *always* in the same place, no matter what else was off.

According to the roadmap I'd picked up at a Nexon station a few worlds back, I should have come to an intersection by now.   The map showed a county road crossing the highway a quarter mile north of where I'd made the hop from the previous world.   But I had been walking for a good two hours, and so far there had been no intersections.   No towns or houses, either—I'd picked it that way. Rolling, empty farmland on either side of the road, most likely to be deserted in the middle of the night, when I made the jump.

I fished the map out of my pocket for the tenth time, hoping I would find some error in my reading of it.   As I said, roads were always in the same place; if they were off in this world, other, more important things—like the number of fingers on a hand—could be off.

It was hard to make out the markings in the dark, but I was out of matches, so I fumbled around as best I could under gathering clouds.   The intermittent moonlight helped, and once again I verified the fact that the roads were wrong.   At least, the road I was on was.   I stuffed the map back into my coat pocket and automatically felt for the little plastic box hidden in the lining.

It was still there, my companion and enemy.   I didn't dare lose it—I was certain no one else had duplicated my work, and I couldn't build another one without my notes and certain vital patterns back in my workshop.   Of course, I could check at my house, but that would be dangerous; I'd walked in on myself more than once in other time-lines, and I'm prone to shoot first and ask questions later.   No, it wouldn't do to go to my house, not knowing if I had made it to the right time-line.

And I certainly couldn't go around asking directions.   One thing I've learned from time-line-hopping is that, no matter what kind of world you hit, people who ask funny questions are subject to suspicion.   Besides, I didn't know *how* to ask.

I mean, in what directions *do* time-lines travel?   Up?   Down?   Out-back?   No, that was ridiculous.   No one would know, because no one but I had ever succeeded in crossing time-lines.

If only I had some sort of guide, some way to orient myself on the line.   Oh, I knew how the gadget worked, but I wasn't sure *why* it worked.   I designed the thing myself, following up on the work of Jablonski, but there were some aspects of its function that eluded me.   That's why I couldn't find the Earth—*our* Earth, that is.   In my ignorance I had assumed that a simple reversal of the field would return me to my starting point.   It didn't work, of course.

The clouds promised rain, so I gave up worrying over maps and roads in favor of finding some kind of shelter.   I stepped up my pace to a brisk trot, wincing at the pain.   The rain hit a minute or two later, coming on me as if someone had turned on a giant faucet—all at once in great, blinding sheets.   I was soaked instantly, and didn't have to worry about getting wet, so I slowed down to a normal walk.   I buttoned up my coat—useless—and plodded on.

When the rain finally let up a bit, my coat was about ten pounds heavier and I fought a losing battle with the water running from my hair into my eyes.   I was so preoccupied with trying to wipe the water from my face that I mistook a faint glow of light ahead of me for a car.   But the light remained constant and didn't move.

The road ran up a small hill in the direction of the glow, and when I reached the crest a few minutes later I could see the source; an all-night gas-station/restaurant. Good.   I could get out of the rain *and* get something warm inside me; the wet clothes were beginning to give me a chill.

The place was deserted, except for the counterman, who was dozing in a chair behind the counter.   He jumped as the screen door slammed shut behind me.

"Hi," I said, sliding onto a stool.   It was good to be able to sit down.   The counterman looked at me for a long moment, then fumbled around under the counter, producing a cup of coffee.

I picked up the cup and cradled it in my hands, drawing warmth.   "Thanks."

"Man," the counterman finally spoke, still staring with small watery eyes, "you been out walking in *that*?"   He jerked a thumb at the door, indicating the storm still blowing outside.   "You look like you been through Hell!"

"Yeah," I answered.   "I'm lost."

"Oh."   He seemed a little surprised.   "Where you tryin' to get to?"

"Ah . . ."   I dug the map out, checked it, and said, "Newtonsville.   Do you know where it is?"

"Here, lemme see that map."   He grabbed it before I could protest.   There was nothing I could do but hope its anomalies were small.

"Hmmm. . . ."   He spread it out on the counter.   "Say, I don't know where you got this, but it's all wrong.   Look at this; it shows Newtonsville as south of Cincinnati.   Newtonsville's due east."   He tapped a thick finger on the map to emphasize his point.

"Oh," I said.   "No wonder I'm lost."

"Yeah.   Tell you what; give me a minute or two and I'll draw you up a good map.   Then, maybe you can stick around for a couple hours until the work traffic starts, and hitch a ride with somebody.   Shouldn't take you more'n three, four hours to get there, if you get good rides.''   He picked up a tablet and pencil lying by the cash register and walked around to the far end of the counter.

He sat down a few stools away and began drawing.   I studied him out of the corner of my eye, still worried about just how much difference there might be between this world and others I'd visited.   He *looked* OK—short, fat, no hair to speak of, and the usual number of arms and legs.   He looked up and I turned my attention back to my coffee, wondering if I should ask him.

Probably wouldn't be any use in it, though, since the roads and at least one town were in the wrong places.   Unless . . . unless the geography had been gradually shifting as I moved along the time-lines, and I hadn't noticed.   After all, I wasn't that familiar with this part of the country.   But, no, that was wishful thinking.

I couldn't be certain that I was in the wrong world unless I could see a newspaper, read a book, study documents—or at least ask questions, checking the thousand and one things that could spell the difference between one world and its seeming mirror image.   Things like politics, cars, fashions, and the like.   I would have to find—or not find—the subtle differences that would indicate that I wasn't in the world I wanted—or that I was.

My coffee was finished.   Should I take a chance on the counterman?   Dared I run the risk of having him think I was crazy, and cause trouble?

I didn't have to make the decision.   He was looking up from the tablet, eyeing me with a kind of chill shrewdness.

''Funny, you having that wrong map,'' he said.   ''Where are you from?''

I shrugged.   ''Picked it up at a gas station.''   Do they call them gas stations here? I wondered, carefully ignoring the second question.

''During the war,'' he said, picking over the words carefully, ''they used to say that you could tell a spy because he didn't know who won last year's World Series.''

I edged away a bit.   ''I don't follow baseball.''   Was that what they called it here?   I tried to look casual.   ''I guess that makes me a spy.''

''But you know who the President of the United States is, don't you?''

They have a United States, I thought.   What was this guy getting at, anyway? I said, ''Jimmy Carter, of course.''

He seemed to relax a little; I relaxed a lot.   ''And Vice-President?'' he asked, leaning toward me.

''Fritz Mondale,'' I answered, confidently.

''Who?'' he said.   ''Who the hell's Mondale?''

That tore it.   I'd lost again.

Then he leaned back and said, ''Oh, I see now.   I know the Mondale one. With that map, I figured you might be hopping.   Why didn't you say so?   I got a directory right here.   Sounds like you're about two lines inzonked, unless you hit a Möbius . . . or, maybe your field calibration's off.   There's a guy right up the road can fix it. . . .''

DAVID GERROLD

Hellhole

When the phenomenon reached the crest of the third hill, Ari Bh Arobi began to be annoyed. Whatever it was, it was keeping her from her ship—and she, an Imperial *Griff*-Princess!

The island was only six kilometers long. If the phenomenon continued to move before the wind at this rate, within an hour it would sweep the entire island—and Ari Bh Arobi with it. She chafed at the thought; it was unfitting for a Daughter of the Matriarchy to be in such a situation. Idly, she wondered how much heat her chillsuit could take before its refrigeration units broke down. Not much. Probably the phenomenon could overload it in a few seconds.

She stood atop a sandy ridge, holding her white helmet with its crimson Imperial crest in one gauntleted claw. A hot G-type star burned yellow-white in an ever-blue sky. It reflected brightly off a sea like wrinkled cellophane. It was an ugly alien panorama; the sight of so much ice in its liquid form bothered her—the psychological suggestion of so much heat made her sweat despite the fact that her chillsuit registered a comfortable –4°C.

Only stray wisps of cloud marred the blueness of that incredible dome of sky—and that was another thing, there was no roof to this world! Ari was used to a comforting close cover of grey. From cubhood, the familiar and ever-present snow clouds had been constant companions and she missed them. The emptiness of this planet's hot sky was disturbing.

Also there was the appalling plume of black smoke rising from the roaring yellow phenomenon below.

It was some kind of a heat-producing phenomenon, that much she was sure of. It flickered in many yellow-orange tongues. From her vantage point above, Ari could still see her scout ship; its hull was blackened, its proud Imperial colors were almost totally obscured, but it seemed otherwise undamaged. (Well, it *should* be able to resist extremes of heat.) She could see it, but she couldn't reach it—that was prevented by the creeping phenomenon that bisected the island.

She wasn't ready to panic though. A Daughter of the Matriarchy *doesn't* panic. Instead, she tried to analyze the problem. She was alone on a small island, a narrow crescent of land in the middle of a molten ocean of an alien planet. Some kind of ravaging and heat-producing phenomenon was keeping her from her only means of escape; it moved before the wind and was reducing the land area left to her with every passing moment. The nearest other ship was more than a thousand kilometers out in space.

A brown rodentlike creature came hopping past her, followed by two others. One seemed to be badly "blackened"—a reaction to the phenomenon? Had it been touched? Probably. The plant life had curled and blackened under the influence of the orange flickerings.

The creature stumbled into her and fell to the ground twitching. Guilt twanged at Ari, as if somehow she were responsible for the animal's condition. Reflexively, she said a prayer for its soul. She turned her attention back to the growing tower of smoke, trying to figure out how she could prevent her own death. Undoubtedly, the phenomenon was not going to cease of its own accord—it *would* sweep the island.

Right now, it appeared to be consuming the island's vegetation. It glowed its brightest where the vegetation was the thickest. Obviously, the condition was dependent upon the existence of these brittle brown plants. Could it be a function of the plants somehow? Virulent spores perhaps? No, it didn't seem likely. It had to be something else.

Had the island any kind of a bare area, it would have been a simple matter for her to walk down to it and outflank the crackling phenomenon; but this yellow scrub grass and these black scraggly bushes which the condition consumed so fiercely grew right down to the water's edge, and even a little beyond that.

Patches of oily vegetation could be seen floating on the ocean's surface, apparently anchored by long rootlike tendrils. She wondered how anything could grow in water that hot—why it must be at least 20°C!

She flicked her radio on again, held the helmet close to her hooded muzzle, "Mother Bear, Mother Bear, this is She-Cub One. The phenomenon has topped hill three. Now what?"

A pause. Static crackled out of the speaker. Idly, she swung it back and forth in her hand—*World-Mother! These things are heavy!*

"She-Cub One," crackled the radio. The voice was deep and feminine. "We are aware of your difficulties. We'll have a ship down to you as soon as possible."

"How soon can they get here?"

"Uh—estimated time of arrival is one hour, thirty-three minutes."

Ari made an impatient frown. "That's not going to help."

"Why not?"

"I'm going to run out of island in about forty-five minutes. Maybe less."

"Are you sure?"

Ari growled an obscenity. "You question me?!!"

"Sorry—" breathed the speaker. "Just routine double-checking."

"Oh, that's right," Ari said acidly. "I forgot—'even on an Imperial ship, we have to do things by the rules.' "

There was silence from the communicator.

Ari exhaled loudly and said, "The phenomenon seems to be moving before the wind. When I landed, the wind was blowing about fifteen kilometers per hour, east by northeast."

"That's no wind—that's hardly a sneeze."

"It's enough," snapped Ari. "That *thing* is moving in my direction and getting closer all the time."

"You can't get to your ship?"

"I can't even see it anymore—the smoke's too thick. I'm being driven farther and farther away from it."

"Smoke?" asked the radio abruptly. "Is there smoke there?"

"From the phenomenon."

"Why didn't you tell us this before?"

"I did—"

"You didn't—"

"I distinctly remember—!!"

"I'll play back the tape—!!"

Ari was silent. *Damn these scientific castes anyway! Always trying to refute a Daughter with facts! On Urs, they wouldn't be so presumptuous—not to a member of the Imperial family! That's what we get for creating a new class of upstart cubs!* She growled deep in her throat. *Next they'll be asking for equal breeding rights. We should never have allowed space travel out of the hands of the Imperial classes!*

She hefted her helmet thoughtfully; that ill-begotten daughter was still waiting patiently for Ari's reply. And nothing short of a "proper scientific answer" would suit her. Ari allowed herself a growl, then said quietly, "The phenomenon is producing smoke. Black smoke. The phenomenon itself is a nervous yellow and orange flickering, but its general progress seems slow—about a walking pace. It seems to be consuming the vegetation. It leaves the ground hot and black and covered with ash. The smoke is black at the base, but it turns brown as it spreads out in the air; there's a huge pillar of it—it covers half the sky now. I'd guess that the thing is some kind of combustion, but the scale of it is ridiculous, so it has to be something else. It completely divides the island." She added dryly, "End of report."

"Is that all?" The voice was cold.

"Yes—" She bit off the rest of her reply before the words escaped. Later perhaps.

"Well, look," rumbled the voice of the radio operator; her sudden change of tone startled Ari. "Don't worry. There must be some way to—" A pause. When the other's voice returned, she said, "What about the water? Does the phenomenon cover that too?"

"No. It only exists where there's plant life for it to feed upon."

"Listen, would it be possible for you to swim in that water?"

Ari decided to ignore the familiarity implied in the other's tone; there would be time enough to rebuke her later. If there was a later. She looked at the still blue plane of the ocean. "I doubt it. I'd short out my chillsuit." She pulled at the white hood that covered most of her cone-shaped skull. She felt as if she were peering into an endless oven.

"We were thinking of that," said the speaker. "You'd have to take off the suit. It'd be too heavy anyway."

"Oh, no," Ari protested. "Do you know how hot that water is?"

"Twenty-one degrees," answered the radio.

"That's what I mean. It's way too hot."

"You could stand it if you had to. It'd only be for a short period of time."

"And after that? It takes twenty minutes to get in or out of a chillsuit. It takes another fifteen to charge up the ship's refrigeration units. By that time, I'd be dead from overexposure to this planet's heat. The air temperature here is almost forty degrees. I know some science too!"

Abruptly, she was aware of a new smell in the air, like overheated—no, *burned*—flesh. Her nostrils quivered wetly. Some of the animals must have gotten trapped by the phenomenon, one more indication that it was a combustion of some kind.

But a combustion—? Of this size?

Was an uncontrolled conflagration of such scope possible? She didn't know—and neither did those damnable scientists in the ship! The only other combustions Ari could remember had been laboratory demonstrations. She knew they used combustions in manufacturing and industrial plants, but she had never seen those; it would not have been seemly for a Daughter to visit *those* kinds of places.

Reflexively she touched the muzzle that cooled the air she inhaled. Her chillsuit was white and coated with a layer of microscopic beads to reflect back most of the glare of the sun; it was lined with conduits that led to the life-support cluster on her back and surrounded her with an envelope of cooler air. She wore dark goggles to protect her eyes and a breathing mask over her nose and mouth. Between the inconvenience, and all the heat and weight, she would probably sweat away five kilos of her carefully fattened bulk. *Mam*-Captain would begrudge the extra rations she would need to gain it back.

Swinging her helmet through the strange dry grass before her, Ari moved down the slope away from the phenomenon. The vegetation crunched under her wide-booted paws. She was not used to seeing plants dead and dry from lack of moisture.

Nor was she used to seeing so many plants so close together. On her home world, if there were fifty bushes like this to an acre, it would be a forest. Indeed, a jungle. She snorted in her mask—this planet would not be valuable to Urs until this Water Age came to an end and the ice-packs could reclaim the seas.

"Ari?" asked her helmet. The tone was respectful.

"Yes?"

"Are you going to go in the water?"

"I'm going to take a look," Ari said, still not admitting anything. "The vegetation grows out over it for at least six to eight meters. I'd have to do more swimming than you think."

She stood on the shore, considering the soupy mass distastefully. The land just seemed to fade away, becoming more and more swampy, until finally the yellow grass petered out in a soggy fringe.

One of the rodentlike creatures, half its fur burned away, and maddened with fear and pain, came bounding past her. It was headed straight for the sea and moved with quick, jerky leaps. Abruptly, it realized where it was heading and tried to halt, tried to turn around—but something in the water went *snap!*

—and the creature was gone. Only an uneasy bubbling of the surface marked where it had been. Involuntarily, Ari took a step back. Then another. "Uh, Semm?"

"Yes?" Semm seemed surprised at Ari's use of her name.

"I don't think the water is such a good idea. Remember those things we found in the northern hemisphere?"

"Yes?"

"Well, they're here in the southern hemisphere too."

Semm was silent. Above, the sun burned impassively, a hole of brightness in the empty blue roof of the world.

"Ari?" asked Semm after a bit.

"Yes?"

"Did you say that the phenomenon is consuming the vegetation?"

"It looks like it. After it moves on, it leaves only blackened ground and what looks from here like ash."

"Then that pretty well settles it."

"Settles what?"

"The nature of the beast. Uva says it's an uncontrolled combustion."

"Huh? On this scale? I thought of that already—it can't be."

"It's got to be, Ari! Think about it—it consumes fuel, the plants; and it releases energy, the heat. What else could it be?"

"I don't know—but still . . . combustion?!! This phenomenon is uncontrolled! It can't be a combustion—who could have started it?!!"

"Look, let's assume that that's what it is and fight it on those terms. It has the same physical properties."

"And what if you're wrong? You're playing with the life of an Heir to the Matriarch!"

"Don't you think we're aware of it—the way you keep reminding us! Our lives are just as important to us as yours—" Semm relaxed her tone. "You're not making it very easy for us."

Ari said, "Do you have an idea?"

"We might. Uva says to break the combustion cycle."

"The *what?*"

"The combustion cycle—it's a laboratory term—"

Ari made a sound of annoyance. "Science again!"

Semm ignored it. She said patiently, "The three elements of the combustion cycle are heat, fuel, and oxygen. If you deprive a combustion of one of these three elements, it can't cntinue."

"Hm." Ari surveyed the island for a moment, then spoke again. "All right. How? The air temperature in this oven is forty degrees. And there's plenty of free oxygen in the air. And the island is covered with grass."

"You're right," replied the radio. "You can't do anything about the heat o the oxygen. But you can do something about the fuel. Clear an area wide enough that the combustion can't cross."

"You mean dig up the plants? Like a common laborer? *Like a male?*"

"Yes, that's exactly what we mean."

"Do you know who I am? I am the eldest daughter of the Clan of Urs. I do not dig up plants with my hands. Males dig up plants—not Daughters of Urs."

Semm said slowly, "Scientists dig up plants too."

"Then let *them* come here and dig! Daughters of Urs do not!"

Still controlled, Semm said, "You are here on this expedition as a scientist."

"I am a Daughter of Urs!" growled Ari through clenched teeth. "I do not dig!"

"You will if you want to live."

"I will not—I would sooner die than disgrace my heritage."

"You just may have to!"

"Then I will do it with honor!"

"Just a minute," said Semm. The radio went silent.

Ari stood silently on the slope and stared at the phenomenon—she still couldn't bring herself to think of it as a combustion. And yet, the heat from it was oppressive.

She moved down the island, away from the yellow-red beast and its mane of black smoke.

"Ari!" snapped the radio. It was the *Mam*-Captain.

"Yes, *Mam?*"

"Now you listen to me—and listen good! You're going to get down on your hands and knees and clear away some of that vegetation—enough so that the combustion can't cross."

"No," snapped Ari. "I—I will not disgrace my Mother."

"You will if you know what's good for you!" The *Mam*-Captain was angry.

"The Heir to Urs will not!"

"The Heir to Urs *will!* You attached yourself to this expedition thinking it would be a lark. Well, it isn't! It's a lot of hard work and danger!"

"How would I know that? You've been keeping me cooped up on the ship!"

"Exactly because you didn't know—and you refused to learn! Dammit! You foolish young bitches of the aristocracy think that space travel is just a toy! When are you going to learn that it's for the scientific advancement of the whole race! Every time one of you bitches buys her way aboard a ship, you're taking the place of a woman of honor who isn't afraid to get her hands dirty if need be, because the knowledge is more important than dying with honor!"

Ari felt the heat-rage coming over her. *"Mam*-Captain! When I return to Urs, I will have you broken for that!"

"You'll have to get back to Urs first."

"I will die with honor then. Your suggestion is unacceptable. I am not a male."

"You might as well be when I get through with you."

"What do you mean by that?"

"I mean that if you refuse to save yourself—and that very expensive scoutship— I will enter into the log that you committed the *Nin-Gresor*."

Ari was aghast. "You wouldn't. They wouldn't believe you! The Heirs to Urs do not commit the coward's death."

"They will believe what I tell them—and we will tell them that you killed yourself. That is what your refusal to dig amounts to. We will tell them that your presence aboard the ship endangered the lives of all of us and eventually your stupidity killed you—it will not be so far from the truth. Perhaps it will keep the aristocracy away from spaceships in the future."

"They will kill you for that!"

"They will kill me anyway for returning without you. Our lives are bound together, Ari. If you refuse to save yourself, I'll disgrace your name."

"You couldn't do such a thing—" Ari could not conceive of anyone being so—evil.

"You'd better believe I would," the *Mam*-Captain rumbled back. "You'd better start saving youself, noble Daughter of Urs. There is no one else there to do it for you."

Ari grumbled at the helmet, she hissed at it. She circled it angrily. Finally, she said, "All right. What do I do?"

Semm's voice answered, "Dig, Ari, dig. Clear an area as wide as you can as long as you can. Don't leave any plants at all growing."

"It is harder work than an Heir to Urs should have to do."

"Do it anyway. It won't kill you."

"So you say," she grumbled. She picked up her helmet and began striding eastward again, ahead of the combustion phenomenon, looking for a more suitable area to clear a break. Finally, she found a wide area, covered only with the dry, waist-high grass.

She bent to the ground and began pulling at the grass, but the stalks crumbled in her hands. And the gloves she wore didn't aid her dexterity any; she couldn't get a grip.

In a few moments she realized it wouldn't work. The roots of the plants were too firmly anchored and the stalks were too dry. *How does anything grow in this hellhole anyway?* If all the grass was like this, the whole island would be a natural combustion chamber. She said a word.

"Something the matter?" the radio asked.

"I'll say. I can't pull any of these damn plants up."

"All you need is maybe ten or fifteen yards of clear area."

"I don't know about that—I think it could leap the gap." Holding her breath, she pulled her mask off her muzzle and wiped the sweat off her nose. It didn't help.

"Try digging them up."

"With what?" She tried scooping at the ground with the edge of her helmet—

"What in the name of *World-Mother* is that?" cried Semm.

"Just my helmet. I was trying to see if I could dig with it. I can't."

"You aren't wearing it?"

"No."

":Why the hell not?"

"Because it's heavy—and it hurts my ears."

"Ari!" The other was exasperated. "You were given specific orders—"

"Hang the orders! It hurts. And I'm not in any danger. We've been here two months. This is my first time on the ground and I want to breathe some real air."

"Ari," despaired the other. "You're going to be disciplined for that."

"How?" taunted Ari. "You've got to save me first."

"You've got to save yourself!" growled a different voice, the *Mam*-Captain again. Apparently, she had been listening at the radio. "We have no way of getting to you, Ari—at least not before the combustion sweeps the island."

"Fine—then I'll save myself my way! And if that means leaving my helmet off, then that's the way I'll do it. You should have known about this combustion phenomenon."

"There are a lot of things I should have known about," sighed the other. "Unfortunately, I am not as wise as an Heir to Urs. That's why we have rules on how to explore unknown planets. I will only be able to tell the Matriarch the truth—that you refused to follow her rules."

Enraged and swearing, Ari flung the helmet away. Then, realizing that she couldn't answer the *Mam* without it, she retrieved it. "This is all a waste of time," she announced. "There's no point in standing here arguing."

"I agree," said the *Mam*-Captain. "Have you tried shoveling into the earth with your hands?"

Ari dropped the helmet in disgust and kicked it away.

But she got down on her knees and began working. It was true—she didn't want to die. At least they couldn't *see* her working like this. Her great shovel-shaped claws scooped at the dirt. If she grabbed the plant low enough, just where the root system began, she could pull it up enough to dig under it and weaken it and then perhaps she could pull it up some more and. . . .

Shortly, she was able to clear a small area in front of herself, perhaps two or three feet square. She paused, looked up, wiped at her muzzle again, and suddenly realized how close the flames were. She grabbed her helmet and jumped to her feet. "Perdition!"

"What's the matter?" asked the helmet.

"It's no good. The brush is too thick. The island is too wide. I could never clear a big enough area in time."

Semm didn't answer.

Ari could feel the frustration welling up inside of her. "Dammit, Semm—the *Mam*-Captain ordered—no, threatened me. I tried your stupid idea—I disgraced myself. If I get out of this, I'll never live it down—but it didn't work. I can't dig them up fast enough."

Semm remained respectfully silent. Ari was almost in tears; frustration and anger were choking her. She kept backing away from the combustion. Then, for no reason, she broke into a run, loping eastward for several hundred meters. She had to weave her course around the craggly bushes. This incredible heat-world!

She stopped, panting easily, and glanced backward. It should take the phenomenon a while to close this distance.

"Ari, the rescue ship is in the atmosphere now."

"Fine. They'll arrive just in time to consecrate my body."

"Don't talk like that. You sound like a *Nin-Gresee*. Besides, you've still got more than half an hour to go."

Ari checked her chronometer. "Not much more than that." She sat down on a rocky outcrop, watched as the crackling orange *thing* lapped at the base of the fourth (or was it the fifth?) hillock. Was that where her abortive attempt at clearing the grass had been?

No matter. She tossed the thought away. She tried to brush the dirt from her gloves. Pah! Digging!

"How are you fixed on oxygen?"

"Why?"

"Nivie's got an idea. There's another way to break the combustion cycle."

"Huh? How?"

"Oxygen."

"What? I already told you there's no way to cut off its oxy supply—"

"No, you don't cut it off. You overload it. You feed it oxygen. Pure oxygen."

"You're out of your—"

"The computer says it'll work. If you feed enough pure oxygen into the combustion, you'll create a superheated area. It'll need more and more oxygen to survive and will start sucking it in from the surrounding area. It'll be like a storm—a combustion storm!"

"That's all I need—*more* combustion phenomenon."

"No, no! Listen—after it's used up all the oxygen in its immediate vicinity, it'll have to pull in more and more from the surrounding area in order to keep burning—that'll change the local wind pattern. The combustion on the edges of the phenomenon will cease from lack of oxygen and you could get around it and back to your ship. Now, listen—feed your oxygen to the *base* of the phenomenon—"

"Semm," Ari interrupted. "It sounds awfully risky. And it's pretty hot here already."

"Ari, it may be your only chance."

"You said that about digging up the plants."

"All right, we were wrong."

"I can still think of two reasons why I can't do it." Ari felt her eyes watering from the smoke despite her goggles and chillsuit. "First, I don't think this island is big enough for that storm effect you talk about."

"We don't know until you try."

"I'm here on the scene, Semm—it doesn't *feel* practical. Besides . . ." she hesitated, embarrassed, ". . . all my extra oxy tanks are still in the ship."

A pause. Then, "Why the hell aren't you wearing them?"

"Because I don't need them—and they're heavy, dammit! Gravity here is eleven percent higher than home!" She stopped, forced herself to be calm. "Besides, I don't think I could get close enough to the phenomenon anyway." She wiped the sweat from her muzzle again. "That thing is awfully hot." She peered at a dial on her belt pack. "From here it reads several hundred degrees at its core—this thing must be broken."

Another pause from the radio, a crackle of static.

"If only you could change the wind or something. . . ."

She didn't answer. Semm was right, though. The *wind* was the whole problem. If only it had been blowing in some other direction. If only, if only . . .

"Ari? You still there?"

"Where would I go?" she muttered.

"Nowhere. Just checking," the radio said.

"What do you want?"

"Nothing. Uh, just keep talking, will you?"

"Why?"

"Just keep talking, huh? So we know everything is all right. Tell us how the phenomenon started."

"I did that already."

"Tell us again. You might have left something out."

Ari stared out over the ocean for a long moment, wondering whether or not it was worth the trouble to be obstinate.

"If you don't start talking, *Mam*-Captain says you'll scrub decks for a month."

"She'll have to come and get me." But despite herself, Ari smiled.

"Better talk, Ari. You might survive."

"All right . . . I brought the ship down on a little spit of land on the western edge of the island—I should have made a pontoon landing. That's what I should have done. But I wanted to show off my piloting skill and put down on the land instead. Before I'd gotten fifteen meters away from the ship, I heard a noise. Or maybe not. Anyway, something made me turn around. At first, I thought the ship was exploding. Then I realized it was the vegetation—Semm!" she said suddenly. "That's how it started!"

"Huh?"

"The combustion! It started from the heat of the scoutship! The skin of it was still hot from my landing! Isn't it obvious? The vegetation is the fuel and there's plenty of free oxygen in the air—all that was needed to start the combustion was heat and I supplied that when I touched down!"

"Um," said Semm. "You're probably right. We'll have to add a note to all future landing procedures."

"*World-Mother!*" said Ari. "What an unstable ecology this must be!"

"Oh, there must be some kind of adaptive mechanisms, for reseeding and such."

"Semm, you should see this! Nothing could survive!"

The helmet said, "Ari?"

In a quieter voice: "I'm still here."

"The wind? Is there any chance it might let up? Or maybe shift direction?"

Ari sniffed the air thoughtfully. "I can't tell with this muzzle on—and I'm not going to risk taking it off. Anyway, I doubt it. It seems pretty steady."

"Oh. All right. It was only a thought."

"If anything, it seems to be picking up."

"Mm."

"That ship can't get here any faster?"

"Sorry."

"It's all right," Ari said.   She grinned wryly.   "Just don't let it happen again."

"We'll try not to."

"Semm?" Ari said.

"Yes?"

"Put the *Mam*-Captain on, will you?"

"Huh?   What for?"

"Just do it.   I want to make out my will."

"All right."   There was a pause from the helmet.   After a moment, a new voice rumbled out of the speaker, the *Mam*-Captain's.   "All right, Ari," she said. "I'm recording.   Go on."

Ari cleared her throat, a deep raspy growl.   "I, Ari Bh Arobi, Heir to Urs, being of sound mind and healthy body and so on, hereby leave, bequeath and so on, all my worldly belongings to . . ."   She paused.

"Go on," the radio urged.

Ari cleared her throat and began again: "I leave all my worldy goods, to be divided equally among all other Heirs to Urs.   I hereby grant freedom to all twenty of my personal male slaves, including my brood-husbands.   I return all of my titles and nobilities to the body of the *World-Mother*.   Uh, and any personal possessions on the ship that any of my shipmates want, well—the *Mam*-Captain has my authority to dispose of them as she sees fit."   She trailed off.   "Oh, one more thing—I hereby absolve all other members of this expedition, including the *Mam*-Captain, of any responsibility for any actions which may have directly or indirectly resulted in my death.   They may not be held liable to any claims made either in my name or against my name; at all times, their actions and their concern have been for the welfare of the aristocracy.   As an Heir to Urs, I accept full weight of the burden myself and respectfully petition the Matriarchy not to take any reprisals of any kind against any of the members of this expedition.   As an Heir to Urs, I claim the right of responsibility; the fault is my own, let the death be my own as well.   That's all.   I'm through."

The *Mam*-Captain rumbled, "It's a fine will, child."   Her voice sounded strange.

"Did you get it all?"

A pause.   Then, Semm's voice: "Yes, we got it."   Another pause.   "Uva wants to know if she can have your melt-cup."

"Tell her go ahead.   And the frozen incense too."

"She says thanks."

"Tell her she's welcome.   I'll let her do the same for me someday."

"Sure," said Semm.   Another pause.   "Keep talking, huh?"

"Uh uh," said Ari.   "Throat's getting dry.   *World-Mother,* this thing is heavy!"

"What is?"

"This helmet."   She found herself looking at it, at the shrinking spit of land left to her, at the helmet again.   "What the hell am I dragging it around for?"

She dropped it to the ground.

"Ari!" cried the speaker. "*Mam*-Captain says you keep that helmet with you!" But it was too late. Ari was already walking away from it.

She had maybe fifteen minutes left, and couldn't decide. The flames or the water?

Of course, she knew what was going to happen. Like the rodent-creatures, she would keep retreating from the ever-advancing flames until she was backed into the water. And then, she'd keep swimming for as long as she could, until she could either swim to safety; or more likely, until—

She preferred not to think about the other possibility. Idly she tugged at a bush. The branch was dry and snapped off in her hand. Still holding it, she started walking along the flame front, as close to it as she dared.

On impulse, she held the branch into a tendril of curling flame. The wood smouldered, charred, then puffed afire.

Stepping back with it, she watched as the flame curled up along the dry limb. It was hard to believe that *this* was the same phenomenon as that roaring holocaust. She turned the branch upside down. The fire continued to move from burnt to unburnt. "Won't change direction, will you?" she said to it. "Once you've burned something, you're through with it. Never satisfied though. Always looking for something else . . . I used to have a pup like that; she didn't stop eating till the last dish was empty and she didn't believe it was empty till she'd checked it herself."

Ari started to throw the branch away, then hesitated. She turned and looked at the fire again, frowning—

When the rescue team arrived, Ari Bh Arobi, the Heir to Urs, was sitting on a rocky outcrop next to her ship. She stood as they approached. Her grin could be seen even through the breathing mask of her chillsuit. "What took you so long?"

"Huh?" They scrambled across the black-crusted ground. "You're supposed to be dead!"

Ari was still grinning. "Sorry to disappoint you."

"What did you—Oh, it must have been the water. You swam around, didn't you."

Ari shook her head. "Uh uh. I told you, there's *things* in that ocean."

"Then, how—"

Ari was enjoying their frustration. "Well, it's like this. I'm an Heir to Urs, so I simply applied my superior intellectual abilities and—"

"Wait a minute." One of the two she-bears was fiddling with her radio. "*Mam!* She's alive!—Yes! Yes! *Unhurt!*—No, *Mam!* Not a burn, not a scratch—I don't know. We're finding out now." She looked at Ari. "Go on."

Ari shrugged. "It was simple. The combustion phenomenon was sweeping across the island at a steady rate, right? I had to keep moving downwind to avoid it. The problem wouldn't have existed if I was behind the thing. It could sweep all the way down to the end of the island and it wouldn't bother me at all."

"Well, that was the whole idea, to get you through the combustion. Or around it."

"No, stupid—the problem was not to get me *through* the combustion. The problem was to get it *downwind.*"

"Same thing, isn't it?"

"Not at all," said Ari. "Not at all."

"All right—how *did* you get the combustion downwind?"

"Simple. I put it there."

"Huh?"

"I took a stick. I held it in the flame until it caught. Then I walked downwind and started a second combustion. The wind blew this one toward the east too, right up to the end of the island—and I was safely *behind it.* Although those things in the water sure caught a lot of rodents there for a while."

"Wait a minute—" The pilot was frowning. "That would have put you between two flame-walls."

"Only for a short time. Both were moving eastward at the same rate. It was easy enough to keep between them. When the first combustion reached the ground where the second one had been started, it went out. Lack of fuel. Simple. After the ground cooled enough, I walked back to my ship."

"Well, I'll be damned—"

"Probably," agreed Ari. "See, everybody on the ship was worrying about the combustion cycle and things like that. It took an on-the-scene observer to interpret the behavior of the phenomenon and to use its own characteristics against itself—"

"Oh, Mother—" breathed the pilot. "She's going to be impossible."

"Hey," called the other. "Uva wants to know, does this mean you're taking back your melt-cup?"

"Absolutely." Ari grinned. "And the incense too."

"Wait a minute, Ari. *Mam*-Captain wants to talk to you."

"Uh huh," Ari said, reaching for the radio. "Probably wants to congratulate me—"

"Uh uh—she's madder'n hell," whispered the other. "Something about discipline and a burned space helmet—"

Ari suddenly remembered she had absolved the *Mam*-Captain of all responsibility. She couldn't pull rank on her anymore—

Ari Bh Arobi, Heir to Urs, was about to get her first spanking.

MICHAEL SCHIMMEL

The Man Who Took the Fifth

"**C**hristopher Lee did one without makeup."

"I saw it. He used a set of fangs."

"They weren't fangs, just enlarged canines; besides, I think those were his real teeth."

"You mean—"

"Yup! He really is a vampire; he only makes movies to keep off welfare. Vampires are a proud race, you know."

"That's only in Europe. Here in New York, they go on welfare on the grounds they can't work during the day."

"Can't you get them a job driving taxis at night?"

"They won't do it. They're afraid of the weirdos on the streets at night."

Carmine drained the last drops from his beer and set the bottle on the floor by his feet. "Does anyone want to bet before the Smithsonian comes over and declares this pot an historical exhibit?"

Ed leaned back in his chair and drew on his empty pipe. "You know, it's interesting about the canines having such power to frighten us. I have a theory it's a racial memory."

"Does anybody's racial memory tell them whose bet it is?"

Jim tossed a quarter on the pile. "Two bits on the cowboys. Then it's agreed. Tracy did the best Jekyll and Hyde."

I saw his raise. "He played it as the allegory Stevenson intended."

"How do you know that was what Stevenson originally intended?"

Everybody turned to look at Allen. This was the first time all evening he had said anything outside of the card game. I think everybody was relieved to see him coming out of his slump.

"I think it's pretty obvious," I said. *"Dr. Jekyll and Mr. Hyde* is meant to represent the dual nature of man. You do believe in the darker side of man, don't you?"

Allen lit another cigarette and leaned back in his chair. "I spent the afternoon treating an 82-year-old woman who had hair spray sprayed in her eyes and her nose broken by two 15-year-old kids who stole her Social Security check. Do you want to ask me again if I believe in the darker side of man?"

As always, Allen had succeeded in embarrassing everybody.   We were embarrassed for the pain he encountered daily.   We were embarrassed for the money he lost at poker, which we all knew he could not afford.   But mostly, we were embarrassed by the fact that of the five men who had started this game almost 20 years ago, Allen was the only one who still believed in what he was doing.

Carmine was an assemblyman who spent his mornings paying off old favors and his afternoons begging new ones.   Ed was a sociologist who wrote reports for the city that he knew were never read.   Jim was a welfare administrator whose job was to keep his caseworkers so busy they wouldn't notice they were making less than some of their clients.   I was a writer for a television news program who scanned the news daily, hoping to find a human interest story to offset the murders, rapes, and muggings the audience tuned in to hear.   The five of us played poker every Friday night behind my apartment door with its three security locks, drinking too much, playing too little, and holding a wake for our youth.

Allen had been the only one to follow the dreams we had laid down over a fraternity house poker table many years ago.   On finishing his internship, he had decided to go to work for the city, operating a mobile health care unit that ministered to shut-ins.   He was like a man trying to cure cancer with a Band-aid, but the job hadn't broken him yet, and I don't think it ever could.   I think we all waited in fear for the day some junkie thinking he had drugs would try to kill him.   We all felt sorry for Allen, we all feared for him, but mostly, we all respected and admired him.

"That's what Stevenson was saying—there's an evil side to mankind, but we—society keep it suppressed."   Carmine had paid the ultimate compliment—he had joined in a conversation that was not about cards.   Allen looked excited for the first time I can remember.   "But you see, that's it!   I don't believe *Dr. Jekyll and Mr. Hyde* is a simple allegory—I believe it's a proven medical fact."

"You mean like the use of tranquilizers in prisons to suppress aggression," I said.

"That's the right track, but instead of suppressing aggression, I'm talking about creating it."

Jim broke a potato chip in the cheese dip and looked at it in disgust.   "We need more aggression like we need more cigarette ashes in this dip.   Can't anyone hit an ash tray in this place?"

"Now wait a minute, don't knock aggression too fast—it can be useful."   Coming from Allen, that sounded like George Meany saying we needed more products from Taiwan.

"Look, I'm talking about channeled aggression.   We've all heard stories of some 90-lb. woman lifting up a car to free her child."

"Sure, we've all heard those stories," I said, "but how many can be authenticated—who's ever actually seen it?"

"I have."   It wasn't Allen's words so much as the tone of his voice that made all eyes turn towards him.   He sounded like Percival saying he's just seen the Holy Grail.

"I saw the very incident I just described—a 90-lb. woman lifting a car to free her daughter. I can vouch for the fact those stories are true. I even took a sample of the woman's blood."

"What did it show?" Ed asked.

"Nothing," Allen replied. "It was just blood, only richer in all the elements than any blood I've ever seen before. In her panic, the woman made an impossible demand on her body, and the body responded."

"Okay," I replied. "I'll admit it's possible, but why are those incidents so isolated?"

"Because in most cases the brain knows, or rather thinks it knows the request is impossible and denies it. Now if a chemical could be introduced into the system that would short-circuit the portion of the brain in which fear originates, then the outside stimulus, panic, fear, whatever, would cause the body to provide the necessary energy to meet the crisis. That's the kind of aggression I'm talking about—a reserve of created power that would automatically come into play."

"Wait a minute," Ed said, "I was just reading an article by Müller on that." Ed was always "just reading" an article by someone. We all believed he made half of them up, but when you challenged him, he attacked with such confidence, we were afraid to call his bluff.

"Who the Hell is Müller?" Good old Carmine!

"He's a German psychologist."

"No kidding! I thought he was a tap-dancing gynecologist from Newark."

"That's Miller," I joined in. "He changed his name during the war."

"Ah, those sneaky Krauts."

"If Abbott and Costello are through? Müller did some of those early experiments with mice. You know, the one where they isolated the portion of the brain that is responsible for aggression and placed it in a cage with a cat."

"What happened?"

"The mouse came out kicking tails and taking names. Is that the kind of thing you're talking about, Allen?"

"That's close, but I think the fear mechanism and the cause of aggression are one and the same, and a chemical by-pass can be induced into the human system that can change that fear into power."

"That's okay," I said. "But what value would it be?"

"Look, I deal with the most frightened group of people in the world—the elderly. They're frightened to leave their houses to go to a doctor. They're frightened they may become too ill to go to a bank, so they carry all their money on them, and that makes them a cinch for muggers. The elderly are prisoners in this city; they're too frightened to go out and get a little fresh air."

Jim stacked his chips. "I'm afraid going out for fresh air in this town won't improve anybody's health."

"No, that's why we leave them in housing projects, as an easy prey to any junk hype who feels he needs some old lady's lousy $169.50 Social Security check for smack worse than she does for dog food to survive for another month."

Ed chewed on his empty pipe. "I have a theory about those housing projects—"

"Are we going to play cards or bullshit all night?" Carmine's sense of respect had its limits.

At four o'clock in the morning, I surveyed the wreckage of my apartment and decided even a token attempt to clean up now required more strength than I had. Somewhere in the night, tires squealed, and from a distance, 1 heard a sound that could have been a shot. I checked the three security locks on my door and went to bed.

The first report came across the wire service about six days later. I wish I could say I recognized it right away, but at the time, it had been only an anecdote to take the pressure off the more morbid stories of the day. Two junkies had tried to rob a 76-year-old woman. When the smoke cleared, the junkies had a total of two broken legs, five fractured ribs, and a broken collarbone.

The second story came in on a Sunday and I didn't see it until Monday morning. This time, I recognized it. Two men in their 80's were playing bocce on a Sunday afternoon when a motorcycle gang began to harass them. The luckier ones ended up in the East River with their bikes. The two old men claimed they couldn't remember how it happened. One minute the kids were coming at them, and the next thing they knew, they were making like John the Baptist to a group of reluctant converts. The men had been treated for bruises they had picked up in the scuffle. Their doctor's name was listed at the bottom of the report, but I didn't have to read it.

"You're nuts!"

"Easy, Carmine. I only called you because the latest incident took place in your district."

"What incident? Some kid tries to rip off an old lady's purse and she smacks him up along the side of the head with a garbage can lid. Is that what you call an incident?"

"The woman was 78 years old!"

"So she got lucky."

"She dragged the kid by the hair to the police station to press charges."

"So what's your point?"

"My point is she could have seriously hurt the kid."

"For crying out loud, you're still mad they shot King Kong without reading him his rights first. Tomorrow the kid's mother is going to be in here to see me with a picture of the kid in his Communion suit with a rosary wrapped around his hand. Look, I know that kid—he's 6'1", weighs 215, and if he has anything wrapped around his hands these days, it's a bicycle chain. What am I supposed to do— tell the judge the kid had the bad taste to pick on an old lady who had just been treated by a mad humanitarian?"

"Then, you believe it?"

"Hell, no, I don't believe it. At least I think I don't. Why don't you talk to Allen?"

"I tried to after he missed the game last Friday; his answering service says he's out every time I call. He's in your district this week; make up some excuse to stop him from operating the health care van."

"Sure, that would make me popular as Hell, wouldn't it! Look, if you're so sure Allen is doing something wrong, you stop him—but don't ever call me again."

"Look, Carmine!"

"Yeah."

"Eight thirty, Friday night."

"Check."

"Check."

"For crying out loud, you got three aces showing—what do you mean, check?"

Jim tossed a dollar in the pot. "Sorry, I was thinking of something else—a buck on the bullets. I was just thinking it seemed funny all the people I saw on the street tonight coming over here—a lot of older folks, too."

Ed saw Jim's raise. "People attract people—it's as simple as that. The more people on the streets, the more reluctant the freaks are to come out—it just may be a new trend."

Carmine folded. "It's mostly the older folks the muggers are afraid of. City Hall is getting complaints from lawyers every hour that some decoy team beat up a client of theirs."

I pushed back my chair and surveyed the table. "Well, we all know who's responsible." No one looked at the empty chair. "The question is—what are we going to do about it?"

"Well, I know what I'm doing," Jim said, "I'm bringing my mother down from Albany next week for one of Allen's vitamin shots."

"You're kidding!"

"No, I'm not. Look, my mother lives all alone in that big house. A couple of months ago, I bought her a can of Mace. Last week, she mistook it for hair spray and knocked herself out for over an hour. I figure I have to give her any edge I can."

"Do you know what came over the wire today?" I said. "The patients took over a rest home in Jersey. They tied the attendants to the beds and fed them only cereal. They weren't allowed up to go to the bathroom and had to remain in their own filth until the police arrived."

"Are they going to prosecute?"

"No. It seems the conditions were pretty bad there in the first place. The patients were only paying back in kind for their own treatment. What bothers me is that someone has got to tie Allen in with these incidents sooner or later."

Carmine gave me a sharp look. "Then, you don't think what Allen is doing is wrong?"

I shrugged. "Who knows from wrong anymore? I only know someday someone is going to put two and two together and that's the end of Allen and his program. He has at most a week before they get him."

"I was reading an article today." Carmine threw his cards on the table, but Ed continued. "I was reading an article today on the hot meal program for senior citizens.   Meals will be prepared for senior citizens all over the city.   It will reach thousands.   Well, it seems they need volunteers to package and deliver the food. I talked to Allen today; his formula will break down to a powder.   I start doing volunteer work for three hours on Monday.   I think that should get Allen off the hook.''

Jim pulled a notebook and pen from his jacket.   "Do you have the number for the volunteers?''

Ed pulled three pieces of paper from his wallet.   "I figured I could count on you guys.   Here's the address and your hours.   I'm picking up the chemical from Allen tomorrow.''

Carmine was looking at Ed like a man who had just discovered that old chair his grandmother had willed him was a Chippendale.

Ed turned to Carmine.   "Carmine, may I ask you something?''

"Sure, Ed—what?''

"Are you going to deal those cards before the numbers wear off?''

I think that was the first damn poker game I enjoyed in 20 years.

ANNE LEAR

The Adventure of the Global Traveler

or: The Global Consequences of How the Reichenbach Falls into the Wells of Iniquitie

All I wanted was to find out who the Third Murderer in *Macbeth* really was. Well, I know now. I also know the secret identity and the fate of one famous personage, that the death of another occurred many years before it was reported to have done, and a hitherto unknown detail of Wm. Shakespeare's acting career.

Which just goes to show what a marvelous place to do research is the Folger Shakespeare Library in Washington, DC. In the crowded shelves and vaults of that great storehouse are treasures in such number and variety that even their passionately devoted caretakers do not know the whole.

In my quest for the Third Murderer I started at the logical place. I looked in the card catalogue under M for Murderer. I didn't find the one I had in mind; but I found plenty of others and, being of the happy vampire breed, switched gleefully onto the sidetrack offered.

Here was gore to slake a noble thirst: murders of apprentices by their masters; murders of masters by apprentices; murders of husbands by wives, wives by husbands, children by both. Oh, it was a bustling time, the Age of Elizabeth! Broadsides there were and pamphlets, each juicier than the last.

The titles were the best of it perhaps. Yellow journalism is a mere lily in these declining days. Consider:

> *A true discourse. Declaring the damnable life and death of one Stubbe Peeter, a most wicked Sorcerer, who in the likeness of a Woolf, committed many murders . . .Who for the same fact was taken and executed . . .*

or

> *Newes from Perin in Cornwall:*
> *Of a most Bloody and unexampled Murther very lately committed by a Father on his own Sonne. . . at the Instigation of a merciless Stepmother . . .*

or the truly spectacular

> *Newes out of Germanie. A most wonderful and true discourse of a cruell*

murderer, who had kylled in his life tyme, nine hundred, threescore and odde persons, among which six of them were his owne children begotten on a young women which he forceablie kept in a caue seven yeeres. . . (This particular murtherer is on record as having planned, with true Teutonic neatness of mind, to do in precisely one thousand people and then retire.)

Eventually I found myself calling for *The moft horrible and tragicall murther, of the right Honorable, the vertuous and valerous gentleman, John Lord Bourgh, Baron of Caftell Connell, committed by Arnold Cosby, the foureteenth of Ianuarie. Togeather with the forrofull fighes of a fadde foule, uppon his funeral: written by W.R., a feruant of the faid Lord Bourgh.*

The pamphlet was sent up promptly to the muffled, gorgeously Tudor reading room, where I signed for it and carried it off to one of the vast mahogany tables that stand about the room and intimidate researchers.

As I worked my way through the blackletter, I found the promising title to be a snare and a delusion. The story turned out to be a mediocre one about a social-climbing coward who provoked a duel and then, unable to get out of it, stabbed his opponent on the sly. Pooh. I was about to send it back, when I noticed an inappropriate thickness. A few pages beyond where I had stopped (at the beginning of the forrofull fighes) the center of the pamphlet seemed thicker than the edges. 'Tis some other reader's notes, I muttered, only this and nothing more.

So, it appeared when I turned to them, they were. There were four thin sheets, small enough to fit into the octavo pamphlet with more than an inch of margin on every side. The paper was of a good quality, much stronger than the crumbling pulp which had concealed it.

I hadn't a clue as to how long ago the sheets had been put there. They might have gone unnoticed for years, as the librarians and users of the ultra-scholarly Folger are not much given to murder as recreation, even horrible and tragicall murthers of the vertuous and valerous, and therefore they don't often ask for the bloody pulps.

Further, the descriptive endorsement on the envelope made no mention of the extra sheets, as it surely would have done had they been any part of the collection.

I hesitated briefly. People tend to be touchy about their notes, academicians more than most, as plagiarism ramps about universities more vigorously than anyone likes to admit. The writing was difficult in any case, a tiny, crabbed scribble. It had been done with a steel pen, and the spellings and style were for the most part those of *fin de siècle* England, with a salting of unexpected Jacobean usages. The paper was clearly well aged, darkened from a probable white to a pale brown, uniformly because of its protected position, and the ink cannot have been new, having faded to a medium brown.

My scruples were, after all, academic, as I had inevitably read part of the first page while I examined it. And anyway, who was I kidding?

"On this bleak last night of the year I take up my pen, my anachronistic steel pen which I value highly among the few relics I have of my former—or is it my future?—life, to set down a record which stands but little chance of ever being seen by any who can comprehend it.

"The political situation is becoming dangerous even for me, for all that I am arranging to profit by my foreknowledge of events as well as from the opportunities civil confusion offers to those who know how to use it. However, my prescience does not in this or any other way extend to my own fate and I would fain leave some trace of myself for those who were my friends, perhaps even more for one who was my enemy. Or will be.

"To settle this point at once: those events which are my past are the distant future for all around me. I do not know what they may be for you who read this, as I cannot guess at what date my message will come to light. For my immediate purpose, therefore, I shall ignore greater realities and refer only to my own lifeline, calling my present *the* present and my past *the* past, regardless of 'actual' dates.

"To begin at approximately the beginning, then, I found it necessary in the spring of 1891 to abandon a thriving business in London. As head of most of Britain's criminal activities—my arch-enemy, Mr. Sherlock Holmes, once complimented me with the title 'The Napoleon of Crime.' "

At this point my eyes seemed to fix themselves immovably. They began to glaze over. I shook myself back to full consciousness, and my hand continued to shake slightly as I slipped the pamphlet back into its envelope and the strange papers, oh so casually, into my own notes. After an experimental husk or two I decided my voice was functional and proceeded to return the pamphlet and thank the librarian. Then I headed for the nearest bar, in search of a quiet booth and beer to wash the dryness of astonishment and the dust of centuries from my throat.

The afternoon was warm, a golden harbinger in a grey March, and the interior of the Hawk and Dove, that sturdy Capitol Hill saloon, was invitingly dark. It was also nearly empty, which was soothing to electrified nerves. I spoke vaguely to a waitress, and by the time I had settled onto a wooden bench polished by buttocks innumerable, beer had materialized before me, cold and gold in a mug.

The waitress had scarcely completed her turn away from my table before I had the little pages out of my portfolio and angled to catch the light filtering dustily in through the mock-Victorian colored window on my left.

". . . I had wealth and power in abundance. However, Holmes moved against me more effectively than I had anticipated, and I was forced to leave for the Continent on very short notice. I had, of course, made provision abroad against such exigency, and, with the help of Colonel Moran, my ablest lieutenant, led Holmes into a trap at the Reichenbach Falls.

"Regrettably, the trap proved unsuccessful. By means of a Japanese wrestling trick I was forced to admire even as it precipitated me over the edge, Holmes escaped me at the last possible moment. He believed he had seen me fall to my death, but this time it was he who had underestimated his opponent.

"A net previously stretched over the gulf, concealed by an aberration of the falls' spray and controlled by Moran, lay ready to catch me if I fell. Had it been Holmes who went over the edge, Moran would have retracted the net to permit his passage down into the maelstrom at the cliff's foot. A spring-fastened dummy was released from the underside of the net by the impact of my weight, completing the illusion.

"I returned to England in the character of an experimental mathematician, a *persona* I had been some years in developing, as at my Richmond residence I carried out the mathematical researches which had been my first vocation. I had always entertained there men who were at the head of various academic, scientific, and literary professions, and my reputation as an erudite, generous host was well established. It was an ideal concealment for me throughout the next year, while my agents, led by the redoubtable Colonel, tracked Mr. Holmes on his travels, and I began to rebuild my shadowy empire.

"During this time I beguiled my untoward leisure with concentrated research into the nature of Time and various paradoxes attendant thereon. My work led me eventually to construct a machine which would permit me to travel into the past and future.

"I could not resist showing the Time Machine to a few of my friends, most of whom inclined to believe it a hoax. One of the more imaginative of them, a writer named Wells, seemed to think there might be something in it, but even he was not fully convinced. No matter. They were right to doubt the rigmarole I spun out for them about what I saw on my travels. Mightily noble it sounded, not to say luridly romantic—Weena indeed!—although, as a matter of fact, some few parts were even true.

"Obviously, the real use to which I put the Machine during the 'week' between its completion and my final trip on it was the furtherance of my professional interests. It was especially convenient for such matters as observing, and introducing judicious flaws into, the construction of bank vaults and for gathering materials for blackmail. Indeed, I used 'my' time well and compiled quite an extensive file for eventual conversion into gold

"As I could always return to the same time I had left, if not an earlier one, the only limit to the amount of such travelling I could do lay in my own constitution, and that has always been strong.

"My great mistake was my failure to notice the wearing effect all this use was having on the Time Machine. To this day I do not know what part of the delicate mechanism was damaged, but the ultimate results were anything but subtle.

"I come at last to the nature of my arrival at this place and time. Having learned early of the dangers attendant upon being unable to move the Time Machine, I had added to its structure a set of wheels and a driving chain attached to the pedals originally meant simply as foot rests. In short, I converted it into a Time Velocipede.

"It was necessary to exercise caution in order to avoid being seen trundling this odd vehicle through the streets of London during my business forays, but there was nothing to prevent my riding about to my heart's content in the very remote past, providing always that I left careful markings at my site of arrival.

"Thus did I rest from my labors by touring on occasion through the quiet early days of this sceptered isle—a thief's privilege to steal, especially from a friend— ere ever sceptre came to it. Most interesting it was, albeit somewhat empty for one of my contriving temperament.

"It was, then, as I was riding one very long ago day beside a river I found it difficult to realize from its unfamiliar contours would one day be the Thames, that the Velocipede struck a hidden root and was thrown suddenly off balance. I flung out a hand to stabilize myself and, in doing so, threw over the controls, sending myself rapidly forward in time.

"Days and nights passed in accelerating succession, with the concomitant dizziness and nausea I had come to expect but never to enjoy, and this time I had no control of my speed. I regretted even more bitterly than usual the absences of gauges to indicate temporal progress. I had never been able to solve the problem of their design; and now, travelling in this haphazard fashion, I had not the least idea when I might be.

"I could only hope with my usual fervency and more that I should somehow escape the ultimate hazard of merging with a solid object—or a living creature— standing in the same place as I at the time of my halt. Landing in a time-fostered meander of the Thames would be infinitely preferable.

"The swift march of the seasons slowed, as I eased the control lever back, and soon I could perceive the phases of the moon, then once again the alternating light and dark of the sun's diurnal progression.

"Then all of a sudden the unperceived worn part gave way. The Machine disintegrated under me, blasted into virtual nothingness and I landed without a sound, a bit off balance, on a wooden floor.

"A swift glance around me told me my doom. Whenever I was, it was in no age of machines nor of the delicate tools I required to enable my escape.

"Reeling for a moment with the horror of my position, I felt a firm nudge in the ribs. A clear, powerful voice was asking loudly, 'But who did bid thee join with us?'

"The speaker was a handsome man of middle age, with large, dark eyes, a widow's peak above an extraordinary brow with a frontal development nearly as great as my own, a neat moustache, and a small, equally neat beard. He was muffled in a dark cloak and hood, but his one visible ear was adorned with a gold ring. As I stood dumbly wondering, he nudged me again, and I looked in haste beyond him for enlightenment.

"The wooden floor was a platform, in fact a stage. Below on one side and above on three sides beyond were crowds of people dressed in a style I recognized as that of the early seventeenth century.

"Another nudge, fierce and impatient: 'But who did bid thee join with us?'

"The line was familiar, from a play I knew well. The place, this wooden stage all but surrounded by its audience—could it possibly be the Globe? In that case, the play . . . the play must be . . .'*MACBETH!*' I all but shouted, so startled was I at the sudden apprehension.

"The man next to me expelled a small sigh of relief. A second man, heretofore unnoticed by me, spoke up quickly from my other side. 'He needs not our mistrust, since he delivers our offices and what we have to do, to the direction just.'

" 'Then stand with us,' said the first man, who I now realized must be First Murderer. A suspicion was beginning to grow in my mind as to his offstage identity as well, but it seemed unlikely. We are told that the Bard only played two roles in his own plays: old Adam in *As You Like It*, and King Hamlet's ghost. Surely . . . but my reflections were cut off short, as I felt myself being covertly turned by Second Murderer to face upstage.

"First Murderer's sunset speech was ended, and I had a line to speak. I knew it already, having been an eager Thespian in my university days. Of course, to my companions and others I could see watching from the wings most of the lines we were speaking were spontaneous. 'Hark!' said I. 'I hear horses.'

"Banquo called for a light 'within,' within being the little curtained alcove at the rear of the stage. Second Murderer consulted a list he carried and averred that it must be Banquo we heard, as all the other expected guests were already gone into the court. First Murderer proffered me a line in which he worried about the horses' moving away; and I reassured him to the effect that they were being led off by servants to the stables, so that Banquo and Fleance could walk the short way in. 'So all men do,' I said, 'From hence to th' Palace Gate make it their walk.'

"Banquo and Fleance entered. Second Murderer saw them coming by the light that Fleance carried, and I identified Banquo for them, assisted in the murder— carefully, for fear habit might make me strike inconveniently hard—and complained about the light's having been knocked out and about our having failed to kill Fleance.

"And then we were in the wings, and I had to face my new acquaintances. Second Murderer was no serious concern, as he was a minor person in the company. First Murderer was a different matter altogether, however, for my conjecture had proved to be the truth, and I was in very fact face to face with William Shakespeare.

"I am a facile, in fact a professional, liar and had no trouble in persuading them that I was a man in flight and had hidden from my pursuers in the 'within' alcove, to appear among them thus unexpectedly. That Shakespeare had been so quick of wit to save his own play from my disruption was no marvel; that the young player had followed suit was matter for congratulation from his fellows, that I had found appropriate lines amazed them all. I explained that I had trod the boards at one time in my life and, in answer to puzzled queries about my strange garb, murmured some words about having spent time of late amongst the sledded Polack, which I supposed would be mysterious enough and did elicit a flattered smile from the playwright.

"As to my reasons for being pursued, I had only to assure my new friends that my troubles were of an amatory nature in order to gain their full sympathy. They could not afford openly to harbor a fugitive from justice, although players of that time, as of most times, tended to the shady side of the law, and these would gladly have helped me to any concealment that did not bring them into immediate jeopardy. As I was but newly arrived in the country from my travels abroad, lacked employment, and could perform, they offered me a place in the company, which I accepted gladly.

"I did not need the pay, as I had observed my customary precaution of wearing a waistcoat whose lining was sewn full of jewels, the universal currency. However, the playhouse afforded me an ideal *locus* from which to begin making the contacts that have since established me in my old position as 'the Napoleon of crime,' ludicrous title in a time more than a century before Napoleon will be born.

"As to how my lines came to be part of the play's text, Will himself inserted them just as the three of us spoke them on the day. He had been filling the First Murderer part that afternoon by sheer good luck, the regular player being ill, and he found vastly amusing the idea of adding an unexplained character to create a mystery for the audience. He had no thought for future audiences and readers, certainly not for recondite scholarship, but only sought to entertain those for whom he wrote: the patrons of the Globe and Blackfriars and the great folk at Court.

"I am an old man now, and, in view of the civil strife soon to burst its festering sores throughout the country, I may not live to be a much older one. I have good hopes, however. Knowing the outcome is helpful, and I have taken care to cultivate the right men. Roundheads, I may say, purchase as many vices as Cavaliers, for all they do it secretly and with a tighter clasp on their purses.

"Still, I shall leave this partial record now, not waiting until I have liberty to set down a more complete one. If you who read it do so at any time during the last eight years of the nineteenth century, or perhaps even for some years thereafter, I beg that you will do me the great favor to take or send it to Mr. Sherlock Holmes at 221-B Baker Street, London.

"Thus, in the hope that he may read this, I send my compliments and the following poser:

"The first time the Third Murderer's lines were ever spoken, *they were delivered from memory.*

"Pray, Mr. Holmes, who wrote them?

"Moriarty
"London
"31st December 1640"

F. M. BUSBY

Backspace

The beard and overflowing hair would have fooled me—but who else comes visiting, late on a Monday afternoon, with a six-pack of canned Martinis? So I opened the door.

He lifted a finger to the probable location of his lips. "An important datum, friend Peter—I do not exist."

I shook hands and thought about it. Sam's only flaky until you figure out what he means; then the term becomes understatement.

I closed the door behind him and said, "Then who does?" Realizing I'd asked a poor question, I rephrased it. "I mean, who just came in here, wearing your skin?"

He nodded. "A debatable point. Let us repair to your kitchen and debate it." He led the way, opened the refrigerator and exchanged his six-pack for two beers, one of which he handed to me. "For now, Petrus Sapiens, think of me as an astral body—a refugee from the material world."

He sat, and I across the table. "For a while there," I said, "I was beginning to think you *didn't* exist. After you cleared up our smog problem here—and I haven't had a chance to thank you—"

He waved a hand. *"De nada*—a simple matter of editing."

I couldn't agree. Reversing the Earth's rotation, to switch the prevailing winds and blow the city's pollution the other way? Not that I'd realized, immediately, what had happened—but then I noticed that the books say the Sun rises in the East, when obviously the opposite is true . . .

"How did you do it, anyway?"

He shrugged. "How should I know? I don't have the scientific mind." He fetched a Martini to set beside his beer. As in the old days, he sprinkled a powder into it and stirred until the stuff dissolved. I've never asked him what it is.

From under the low-hanging hair his eyebrows appeared and made a frown. "Something about a macrospin being the resultant of microspins—I read that some-place, and it *sounds* good. So I just spun the electrons in my head the other way, all at once, and the effect spread. You ever do anything like that, Pete?"

"Not on purpose," I said. "But why did you disappear?"

The brows rose to hide again. "Think about it. How did *you* find out what

I did?'' He nodded. ''Lousy editing, is what. I forgot to fix the records, to match. So before the government could put a lid on me, I ran for cover.''

''But how would *they* know—?''

He sipped the Martini and grimaced. ''You can't get real zouch anymore, but this stuff I put in here isn't half bad.'' I waited; he said, ''Well, I edit freelance, you know—and sometimes for the gum'mint, even. You remember the Kairenger scandal?'' I shook my head.

''Of course you don't,'' said Sam. ''I edited it out, that's why. And lived three years on the proceeds—my fee.'' He sighed. ''But *they* knew, Peter the Great—they had the handle on me. And to be utterly frank, this minor chore here, for your convenience—it was somewhat in breach of contract.''

His next sip of Martini must have been heavy with zouch, whatever that is, for his eyes bulged. He gulped some beer. Still breathing hard, he said, ''I am not given, Pieter, to maundering diatribes about ethics; I see myself as a practical man in an impractical world. So the question was rather simple.''

''It was?'' Thinking: *what* question?

''Of a surety. Whether to edit the government, with its threat to me, out of my life—or me out of its. I chose the latter.''

''And so—''

''That's why I no longer exist. *Much* simpler.''

I needed another beer. So would he, soon—I brought him one, and said, ''Well, then—who *is* here, and why? I mean, I'm always glad to see you, and all that, but—''

He lit a cigar; I provided an ashtray. He said, ''Through these eyes, Pedro, many of me look out—and ever have. Didn't you know?''

Well, Sam's mind always did have more independent parts than a jigsaw puzzle. I nodded. ''Right now, which one's taking a peek?''

He finished the Martini, opened another, dusted and stirred it. One sip—his mustache rippled; I think he smiled. ''Much better, Petrov. Either I have the combination or my taste buds have agreed to fake it.'' He waved a hand; cigar ash scattered.

''Question of identity,'' he said. ''Who am I, and you also? Oh, I know— you remain yourself, changing only within moderate limits. Monotonous, I'd find it—but whatever flips your switches.''

His eyes narrowed, closed, then opened wide. I waited, and he said, ''I'm taking a vote. How else?'' Then he laughed. ''It's a tie between a name I dislike and one I can't pronounce. The hell with it—call me Sam, and hope this place isn't bugged.''

He'd changed, Sam had—and not only in appearance. The lazy voice was now brisk, yet still the mind dealt in caution. Not until his third Martini would he speak of purpose. Then suddenly he ground his cigar into the tray until both ceased to smolder, and said, ''I've found, Pietro, a new way to edit—day by day, cautiously observing, proceeding by trial and thus reducing error.''

''As you used to say—chickenly?''

"Indeed—and now, more so than ever. With a modern touch of gadgetry, to aid—"From a pocket he brought out a small, oblong device—black, studded with lights and buttons. After a moment I recognized it as an electronic perpetual calendar—with additions that somehow didn't surprise me.

"What does that thing do?"

He handed it to me. "Look for yourself—but don't touch the grey button. Today, I've already put in good order." I looked but said nothing; I felt my eyebrows heading north.

"Obviously," he said, "my contrivance indicates the date. Or else," and he opened a fresh beer for himself, "it *sets* the date. An interestingly philosophical question, really. Every action has an equal and opposite reaction. Do you know who said that?"

"Sir Isaac Newton?"

"In a limited sense, I suppose." He lit another cigar. "I was thinking of Manfred the Witless, an obscure Varangian chieftain of a century best left alone. The one valid memento of his entire reign."

I shook my head. "How did he get into this? And what's the business you said, about this thing *setting* the date?"

Using the unlit end of his cigar he stirred the Martini, then licked powder specks from the damp stub. "Manfred came to power through his mother's side of the family—necessarily so, since no one would admit to being his father. And then—" He paused. "Oh, yes—I see what you mean. Well, it's the grey button. No—*don't* touch it."

"The grey button?"

"Yes. It's—well, you might call it a backspace key."

I've never caught Sam in an exaggeration. The occasional lie, yes—exaggerations, never. Still, I had to test his claim—and said so.

"Very well, Peter the Skeptical. Let us see—" He looked at his watch. "I arrived here, I believe, at twelve minutes past five. Tomorrow at that time—you will be home?" I nodded. "Then I leave the device here with you. And at that exact point of tomorrow, twelve past five, you push the grey button."

Traffic was heavy that Tuesday, but shortly after five I reached home. At the proper moment, I followed Sam's instruction. Then I heard a knock at the door and went to answer it.

The beard and overflowing hair would have fooled me—but who else comes visiting, late on a Monday afternoon, with a six-pack of canned Martinis?

Monday? But it had been . . .

I opened the door anyway.

He was into his second Martini before we talked. I wasn't sulking—I simply couldn't think what to say. Finally, "Sam? It could be—it *should* be—that you're just here two days in a row. So how come—how it is that I *know* we've got Monday on re-runs?"

For a time he didn't answer.   I guessed the line was busy, to his other head you can't see.   Then he said, "There's a *Mondayness* to Monday—you sense it, do you, Peter-san?   Not to be mistaken.   For centuries I could lie in my unforeseeable tomb, and when Gabriel—most likely portrayed by Louis Armstrong—blew his riff, I would rise in all my dank skeletal dignity.   And I would wonder—why the hell did he have to rouse me on a *Monday?*"   He nodded; his Martini wet his beard.

There are things it doesn't pay to ask Sam—but I was curious.   "In that case, O Nonexistent One, why did you feel the need to *repeat* Monday?"

His eyebrows did their vanishing act; behind the mustache curtain I thought I saw a gleam of smile.   "It is, Piterluk of the Analytical Bent, that I am broke. So I have a job, an employment that pays me—no, not in peanuts, even, but rather in the shells of peanuts."

He drained his Martini.   "And Monday happens to be my day off."

Time passed.   My wife Carla returned from visiting her grandmother in Sacramento.   We had a great reunion.   Sam pushed the button—the grey one.   My wife Carla returned from visiting her grandmother in Sacramento.   We had a greater reunion.

The president spoke on three TV networks and announced a new sure-fire plan to halt inflation.   The next day, a Tuesday, prices rose an average of twenty percent.   Sam pushed the grey button.   The president spoke on three networks and announced a new sure-fire plan to keep his hands out of the economy.   The next day, a Tuesday, prices rose an average of five percent.   Sam pushed the grey button . . .

All in all, Sam's button works rather well.   Any time he starts getting too many changes for the worse, he plays it safe and leaves bad enough alone.   He says the reason I notice, while others don't, is that since I've used the gadget once, now I'm tuned to it.

Maybe he's right.   But I do wish he'd get himself a new job—or at least a different day off.

I'm getting pretty damned tired of Monday.

JOHN M. FORD

On the Q167 File

T he Informed Reader must certainly be aware of the public furor over "Re-
combinant-DNA" experimentation, in which the genetic material of an organism
is chemically engineered to produce a desired mutation.   One possible product of
this research would be bacteria capable of creating protein molecules, such as that
of insulin, in any desired quantity or type.

I will not here discuss hypothetical "super-plagues" produced by cackling mad
scientists, as this topic has recently become somewhat sensitive politically.[1] My
concern here is rather with a possible byproduct of this research, which threatens
the livelihood of all creative typists such as myself.

An example will prove instructive here.   The reader is no doubt familiar with
the *Gedachtexperiment*[2] in which monkeys are placed at typewriters and allowed
to hit keys randomly, until the entire contents of the Library of Congress are
produced.

As can readily be seen, these auctorial apes are no threat to any body of writers.[3]
The noted logomathematician Hakluyt proved that no real-world process could type
A la Recherche du Temps Perdu in less time than is required to criticize it,[4] setting
up an infinitely recursive series clearly demonstrating that the sun will go nova and
Achilles catch Zeno's tortoise before the monkey's reach the second appendix to
The Lord of the Rings.[5]

But—what if the process were *not* random?   A protein molecule is a twisted
string of amino acid molecules, even as a sentence is a string of words and a word
a string of letters.   Suppose, as was proposed at the Rückwärts Conference,[6] a
code were espoused relating amino acids to letters of the alphabet: e.g. alanine for
A, asparagine for B, aspartic acid for C, et cetera;[7] and now imagine a DNA-
engineered bacterium, programmed with sentence structure and a rudimentary grasp
of grammar,[8] spinning out genetically-coded fiction by the line, by the page, at
undreamed-of speeds.   Replication by Transfer-RNA and reverse transcriptase
might make the "Xerox revolution" look like a wet firecracker.

For some years now, researchers have dismissed such prophecies as baseless
speculation.   Hakluyt's Original Proof[9] showed that the available number of α-
amino acids was insufficient to encode all 26 letters of the alphabet, not to mention
punctuation marks and underlining, confining so-called Bacterial Literature to certain limited forms such as nurse novels and the poetry of e.e. cummings.

But two recent breakthroughs have pushed this defense aside.   Scientists working at the University of Hawaii Research Center and Temple of Pélé at Mauna Loa Crater have produced entire chapters by utilizing the Hawaiian language, which uses only 14 letters.[10]

The proposed EK3 safeguards, which would have rendered all Hawaiian translators incapable of survival outside the laboratory, were then bypassed when the Everett Dirksen Memorial Laboratory at the University of Southern Indiana at Bedford showed, in a remarkable interdisciplinary study, that by using *pairs* of amino acids as coding elements, the symbol-carrying capacity could be tremendously increased.[11]

An additional alarming development of this finding is that it negates the Russian research handicap of a greater number of characters in the Cyrillic alphabet.[12]

Can any of the proposed safety measures be made to work?   Can a P4 ultrasafe laboratory, with its airlocks, special eyeglasses, and staff chosen for their lack of literary pretensions, be maintained in an environment teeming with $1.95 paperbacks and four-pound editions of the *New York Times?*   The consequences of admitting even one Evelyn Wood graduate could be staggering.

But perhaps more technologies are not the answer.   The true solution may lead us full circle to Man himself,[13] to human productivity and the will to succeed. After all, Sir Alexander Fleming's discovery of Penicillin did not greatly change our opinion of moldy fruit.   Surely Man,[14] with his native gifts of ten-finger touch typing and dry copying, can outproduce a jar full of bugs.[15]

Indeed, man has and will continue to fulfill his poetic aspirations[16] without the putative aid of organic chemistry.[17]   A moment's reflection brings to mind men writ large, men of prodigious output covering every field of human endeavor, combining the writer, the lecturer,[18] and the scholar, bearing advanced degrees in such fields as . . . ah . . . er . . .

Biochemistry?

1. As is well known, Transylvania is now a Warsaw Pact country.

2. German word meaning "No funding available."

3. With the possible exception of television writers.

4. Actually Hakluyt's *Other* Proof.   The distinction is fine but noteworthy.   Some have disputed the Theorem on the empirical grounds that Hakluyt's formulae dealt directly only with *Swann's Way* and were extrapolated to the general, or $n = 7$, case.

5. Or Notes toward the modular *Triton*.

6. Held each year at Mr. Janos Rückwärts' Institute for Persons Easily Confused by Facts.

7. Additional codings are left as a challenge to the reader.

8. As most bacteria reproduce by fission, split infinitives may be a problem.

9. There it is!   See the difference?

10. Reported in *Hukilau and Public Affairs*, the Bulletin of the Volcano Worshipers. While released fragments of the novel, which deals with lava flows and existential doubt, show no great literary merit, the complete work has been purchased for an undeclared sum by Dino de Laurentiis.

11. Paper, "Multiplying Two Things Together Makes A Lot More Things Out Of Them," EDML/USIB no. 3192.

12. The much-talked-of "six-character gap."   It was believed by several observers that the lack of articles in Russian grammar was an attempt to circumvent this difficulty.   See also Shyster, L., *The Inflection Conspiracy*, recounting the Soviet attempt to steal American sentence-structure secrets.

13. Or Woman herself.   I'm not one to risk my NSF grant.

14. See Note 13.

15. At three cents a word, he'd better.

16. Note to printer: This appeared in galleys as "fill the paperback racks."   Please correct in final copy.

17. A small exception being made for C_2H_5OH, a catalyst of interesting properties in ink-paper reactions.

18. Note to printer: please spell correctly in final copy.

MICHAEL A. BANKS

Horseless Carriage

I was leafing through the morning mail, hoping I'd find something other than those useless solar energy gadgets everyone was stealing from one another, when I heard the door to the outer office open. I looked up and saw Karl Epworth, looking his usual dull self in an out of date tweed jacket.

"Good morning—" I began, then ducked as he threw something about the size of a cigarette pack at me.

Whatever it was didn't reach me, though. As it came toward me, it rose to the ceiling, hit the plaster with a small click, and stayed there, humming. I stared at it, open-mouthed, then looked back to Epworth. He produced another box and dropped it. The box fell up.

At the very least, I was nonplussed. But that's not to say my brain was out of gear; I was already trying to come up with a ballpark figure on the potential value of what evidently was a workable anti-gravity device. That sort of thinking is a reflex action with me—I sell ideas. People like Epworth think things up, and then bring their ideas to me because they haven't any business sense.

You've heard of StikSand? Maybe your children have some. It's the stuff that looks and acts like sand, but isn't. Little granules of something or other with "enhanced molecular polarity." Something along those lines. Anyway, kids play with it the same way they would with real sand—in the house, even—and when it comes time to clean up, you can pick the entire pile up in one lump. Great idea, right? Epworth invented that, along with several other gimmicks that have been reasonably profitable. And I've been taking my percentage right along.

But everything he'd done before was nothing compared to this; if my guesstimation was anywhere near correct, my percentage alone would be more than the gross on all of his previous ideas combined.

"Excuse me," Epworth said, pulling a chair over to where he could stand on it and reach the second box.

I composed myself, hoping the dollar signs in my eyes weren't flashing too brightly. "So," I said, "what's the trick? Air jets?" I couldn't see any indications of fakery, but I had to play skeptic—just to be sure, and to put Epworth where I wanted him. Something this big called for more than the usual ten or fifteen percent.

"Try it yourself," he said, tossing it to me.

It didn't rise this time; I caught it just short of my nose. It was heavier than it should have been, weighing maybe five or six pounds, and made of some kind of hard, translucent plastic. I fumbled around with it, looking for a switch.

"Hold it by the ends," Epworth said, "and push."

I did, and the box flexed a bit with a muted click. It suddenly weighed nothing. I released it, and it joined its twin on the ceiling. I stood on my chair, retrieved it, and tried it again . . . and again . . . and again.

Epworth had plopped down in the chair in front of my desk.

"How about *that*?" he asked, taking out one of those little filtered cigars he smokes.

"Karl," I said, tossing the box back to him, "do you realize what we have here?" I knew he did; he was looking smug. "We can—" I stopped. What could we do with it, exactly? The obvious application would be transportation.

"Listen," I said, "how large can you make these? Big enough to carry passengers and freight?"

"Well. . . ." I winced when he said that. I knew he was hunting around for a way to make something bad sound good.

" 'Well,' what?"

"The para-magnetic field *is* limited, you understand." He looked around the room, avoiding my eyes. "It obeys the Inverse Square Law with respect to intensity, naturally, and the strength of the field falls off drastically as it is expanded. There is also the problem of a quasi-effect on electron energy levels, which—"

"OK, OK, I believe you." I cut him off before I got lost. Among other faults, Epworth has an annoying habit of assuming that everyone is as knowledgeable as he is. When I first met him, he made vague claims to being a professor of physics somewhere. I checked up on him once, out of curiosity, and found him to be a clerk for the local school board. But, maybe he *was* a physics professor once; that would explain all that heavyweight knowledge he throws around, except for the fact that he doesn't always seem to understand what he's talking about. Or maybe he has a direct line to some extraterrestrials who give him ideas. I don't know.

Another idea hit me. "Here's the perfect angle," I said. "Toys. I can see it now—toy flying saucers. Flying dolls. Helicopters. It's perfect!"

Half an hour later I was steering him through the front office and out the door. He had left behind one of the boxes and his signature on a contract that gave us a fifty-fifty split on the gross profits from the anti-gravity boxes.

"I'll get back with you in a week or two, Karl," I said, giving him my Number Two partners-in-crime handshake. "I'll have to make some contacts—work up the best deal, you know—and that will take a few days."

"All right, John. You're the expert." He waved jauntily and I closed the door behind him, hoping he wouldn't have any second thoughts about that contract; it was full of holes.

As things turned out, I had to stall him two extra weeks. The first five toy manufacturers I contacted—including the outfit I had licensed StikSand to—refused to see me, once I mentioned anti-gravity. I kept quiet about it with the sixth one, and bullied my way in to see the R&D chief by threatening to take what I had to the competition.

"I hope this is worth my time, Mr. Higgen," Reynolds, the R&D man, announced as 1 walked into his office. "I'm very busy this time of year, as—"

I had the box ready, and threw it at him, the way Epworth did to me. It worked. Reynolds gawked and pointed while I climbed on his desk and pulled the box down. Then he found his voice.

"That's great, man!" he said. "How do you do it?"

"Easy," I replied. "It's anti-gravity."

"Sure," he laughed. "Now, how do you do it? Magnets? CO_2? What?"

"It's anti-gravity, as I said. I don't have all the details, but the inventor can supply—"

"*Mister* Higgen. I told you I was busy, and I have no time for jokes. How does this work?"

"Something called a 'para-magnetic field.' I'll be glad to have the inventor come in and give you more information. I could tell I was losing it. "But it is authentic," I finished lamely.

"Hah! Look, I don't know what kind of flim-flam you're trying to pull, but it won't work here. Anti-gravity? We already have a flying saucer that does this trick—with CO_2, which is what I suspect you're using, though your gadget works better than ours. But," he leaned toward me, "even if this *is* something original, I couldn't buy it. Not without knowing exactly what it is and how it works."

He crossed the room behind me and opened the door. "Now, unless you've a better explanation than 'anti-gravity,' I don't believe we're interested." He looked at me with a taunting smile. "Or maybe you have a perpetual motion machine to sell?"

I left with my tail between my legs.

I tried a different approach with the next company, dispensing with the amateur theatrics and relying on my sales ability. I scripted an entire half-hour presentation, resplendent with qualifiers and positives. An encyclopedia salesman couldn't have done it better; I know—I used to be one.

But the guy I talked to at Arista Toys and Crafts must have been one, too. He picked up on the hype job I was pulling before I got past the qualifiers.

"Before you get too involved here," he said, cutting in on the middle of my opening spiel, "I have one comment. If you have to work this hard to sell whatever you have, it couldn't be worth buying."

I got out of there fast, before he tried to sell *me* something.

The situation grew steadily worse. I had a friend in the technical department at one of the larger studios on the West coast, so I made a quick phone call to him and outlined the idea. He was sympathetic, but. . . .

"Anti-gravity, huh? Sounds great, but we already have that?"

"What?"

"Sure. Air jets, magnets, mirrors, fine wire, and a brace of other gadgets. What it comes down to, John, is this: no one is going to pay good money to do something they already know how to do."

I admitted he had a point. "But this is the real thing! Don't you see?"

"I'm sorry, John," he said. "Really, I am. And I believe you, but I don't have any use for it, and no one else in the business would, either. It's an interesting trick, but . . ."

I made a few half-hearted attempts with some novelty distributors, but the answer was the same: "Interesting, *but*. . . ." And, under all the polite refusals, I could detect a strong current of suspicion. People were afraid of being taken by something they couldn't understand.

And, as if matters weren't bad enough, Epworth was hinting at canceling the contract—which he could do, as it contained a nonperformance clause.

I must have gotten really desperate about then, because I did something I'd sworn never to do. I got Epworth to set up a design compatible with mass production and, using the operating funds for the business and most of my personal savings, I had fifty thousand of the boxes manufactured.

I had given Epworth a vague outline of a distribution network set up through some wholesalers I had contacts with, but in reality I hadn't done more than think about it. I was so damn set against letting anyone else get ahold of the idea that I would have told Epworth anything to keep the contract. When the boxes were safely in a rented warehouse, though, I began worrying. While I was waiting for them, I had honestly tried to set up the distribution, but no one would work with me. I was running up against the same old credibility gap.

The solution came one evening when I was closing the office. I had stayed late, worrying over the problem, and finally gave up for the night. As I was passing through the outer office on my way to the street door, I caught sight of a magazine my secretary had left behind on her desk.

It was one of those occult things, full of articles on psychic phenomena and related topics aimed at convincing people who already believed in such nonsense that they were right in their beliefs. I picked it up, intending to put it in a drawer, but began leafing through it, out of curiosity.

I was surprised at the quantity of advertising it carried, all of it aimed at the audience, of course. There were ads for everything from ESP amplifiers to courses in levitation. Surprising what people will buy, I thought. You can sell anything, as long as you're reaching the right market. . . .

I didn't go home that night. I stayed at the office writing and re-writing ad copy. The next morning, I sent out for copies of certain types of magazines, and by that afternoon had thirty-one ads placed, to appear in three months. It was a long three months, but well worth the wait.

You've probably seen the ads. Sometimes they run this way:

SECRETS OF THE ANCIENTS REVEALED!
Mysterious Force used by the
Ancient Architects can be yours!
Only $5.95—

Or, depending upon the publication, we might use something like this:

UFOS
Secret Propulsion Device available.
Actually levitates/floats like real
flying saucer.   Interesting, little-
known principle discovered by ancient
scientists, only now brought to light.

Either way, the message is the same: This isn't new or strange; it's just like all the other oddball things you've been finding in the backs of magazines for years. Sort of the same principle that resulted in the early automobiles being tagged "horseless carriages."   Call something by a familiar name, or present it in a familiar way, and it will be accepted.

Orders are coming in right and left now, and we're making another production run, trying to cash in on this before some bright boy catches on to us.

One thing has been bothering me, though.   There are so many other ads like ours in the backs of those magazines, and I can't help wondering if some of those free energy or teleportation devices are for real.   So I've placed a few orders here and there, just to check things out.   Who knows?   Maybe there are some more inventors out there who could use a good business manager. . . .

JESSE BONE

Pièce de Résistance

Here, let me brush you off. This dust sticks like glue. It's a miracle you weren't killed, but she was too frightened to stop. Didn't anyone tell you a basilisk was dangerous? What are you doing here, anyway? You oughta be back at Base where it's safe.

Oh—I'm sorry, sir. Welcome to Zetah. I didn't know you were the new Governor. I thought you were another of those Earth-type inspectors who pop in now and then. We don't expect top brass out here, and you didn't bring a staff. Governor Claiborne never travelled without a couple of secretaries and a trooper or two.

I guess it takes all kinds, Governor. And you're right about the briefing manual. You can't learn much from it. I suppose if you've never seen a basilisk you can't be expected to know how fast they can move. They're not like Earth animals. They don't believe in the superiority of man.

Look at that cow over there by the chute, the one the men are unshackling. You wouldn't think anything that ugly would have a brain, would you? But she's got one and it's bigger than ours. The big brains at Base call them centauroids, although I'm damned if I can see where they look like centaurs, unless you stretch the image all out of shape. Sure they have six limbs and the rear four have something like hoofs, and the front two end in something like hands, but that's where the resemblance ends. Note those jaws and that mouthful of teeth. She's an obligate carnivore, and those teeth of hers can shear a man's leg off. No—don't look at her eyes! She can steer you right into those teeth if she gets a fix on you. That's why they're called basilisks.

Yes, sir, that's a cow. You can tell from the abdominal pouch and the small tusks. A bull's half again as big, and his tusks are as long as my forearm, and he doesn't have a pouch. You're right, sir. She does sound like a leaky steampipe— funny—I never thought of that. Hey! There she goes!

They sure can! They run like scalded cats. An adult cow can get up to 90 k.p.h. when she's in a hurry, and that girl's in a screaming rush. You wouldn't think anything with legs could travel so fast. They use the forelimbs for propulsion when they're really in a hurry. Most of the time they use just the last four. You'll have to come down to the lab. We have some stop motion studies Winslow made last year. The leg action in full flight is the damndest thing you ever saw. We have their slow gaits worked out, but high speed is impossible to describe. One loses track of what leg is doing what.

So you noticed the odor? Did it bother you? No? Well, you're one of the unusual ones. The Project shrink, George Reifenschneider, says it's a defense mechanism, but I sure as hell don't know what it's supposed to defend against. There's nothing on this world except us that's one tenth their size, and no native life has anything near their natural armament or brains. Until we came, the basilisks didn't have an enemy in the world except maybe a few parasites and a virus or two.

No sir, I'm not one of the brains of the Project. They're back at the Base. I'm the local supervisor; the guy who gets his hands dirty. The only degree I've got, beyond a BA in Agriculture, is from the school of experience. I ramrodded a cattle ranch in Wyoming before I came here, and I've been running this spread ever since it was established. I know ranching, and I expect that's why Governor Claiborne put me in this job.

Well—thank you sir. I'm sorry you got knocked down, but you've gotta watch them. We're trying to breed a more easy-going type, but we haven't had too much luck so far. They're ugly, suspicious, and antisocial; but we keep trying. We have to, if we're going to avoid things like that mess at Station Two.

What do I think of Station Two? Well—no one's asked me. I'm not supposed to think, but if you want my opinion, I think Harris asked for it. I think he committed suicide. Nobody walks into a nursing female's area and expects to come out alive. Nursing's a drain on them and they're hungry. It's like dangling a chocolate bar in front of a starving kid.

And then that cleanout order from Base really loused things up. It was a knee-jerk reaction to Harris' death; but it left half the Station worrying about what would happen when the local basilisks were gone, and the other half went ape over unrestricted hunting. Naturally the whole operation went to pot. You can't run a hatchery with a crew like that. So they didn't watch the litter, they didn't vaccinate, they didn't feed properly or check the humidity, and four hundred thousand chicks went down the drain and our entire program came to a screeching halt. That foulup set us back six months.

Yes sir, we do better now. We've got the feed problem solved, and we've worked out a method of keeping them quiet during the nursing period. Sight and smell trigger their reactions, so we keep them isolated. They're nearly blind during rut; and if we keep them in closed nest boxes where they can't see each other— and filter the air—we can house as many as the Station can hold. We can hold about a hundred at the Station. That's all the research staff can handle.

That's right, they're solitary except at rutting season. That's why the Project Area is so large. Ordinarily a basilisk won't come closer than two hundred meters to another one, except to protect their territory. The only other exceptions are when a female's nursing or when she's in season. She's the one who makes the advances. The males just kill each other or avoid each other, depending on the situation. But adult males don't deliberately attack each other unless their territory's invaded.

No sir—the pattern's not really weird.   It's a lot like the habits of terrestrial elk, except the bulls don't keep harems.   A bull may have more than one cow during rut; but he has them successively, not concurrently.

No sir, they're not exactly mammals.   They're more like a cross between a monotreme and a marsupial.   The female lays a single egg about six inches in diameter.   She incubates this in an abdominal pouch.   When the egg hatches, the young basilisk finds a milk duct on the inside of the pouch and attaches to it for about half a year.   By then the calf is big enough to forage for itself and the cow removes it from the pouch and casts it out.   The calf runs off and won't come near another basilisk until puberty when its glands take over.   If it's a cow, it finds a bull and they pair long enough to breed, after which they separate again.   If it's a bull, it stakes out a territory when it gets big enough and fights off other bulls to hold it.   Until it gets big and tough a bull calf is hassled a lot by adult bulls.   But the adults are big, fat and slow, and the youngsters are lean and quick.   Enough of them survive to keep the race supplied with breeding stock.   It's hard on the bull calves, but the tough ones survive.   The brains at Base think that is one of the reasons why the basilisks remain solitary—a natural tendency enforced by breeding patterns.

That's right, sir.   We try not to disturb the pattern on most of the Project land.   We protect this area.   We keep a census of the Project and we don't let the adult population drop.   There just might be a critical number.   We don't know about that yet.

It's not easy to explain, sir.   There's always an unbalanced sex ratio.   It goes back before birth.   The primary sex ratio in the egg is two females to one male.   In the natural state this drops to about one to three by puberty and can get as low as one to twelve among adults without hurting production.   Usually it's about one bull to four cows.

No sir, the present system wouldn't be bad except for poachers.   You can't cover a hundred kilometer square very easily, although we try.   The guards have orders to arrest trespassers and to shoot those who try to run, but how can you protect against some guy in a flitter who comes in low under the screen, kills a male or female in one of the river nests, and flits out again?   We used to chalk it off as natural losses until we started implanting electronic monitors in the ones we caught.   That's when we found out about the poachers.   We caught a few in the act at first, but they're onto us now, and many get away.   They're a bunch of murderers; too goddamn lazy or cowardly to try the wild areas.   They kill for no good reason; a few steaks, a set of trophy tusks, or just the fun of killing something that's bigger and tougher than they are.   Hell, sir, if the odds were halfway even, a basilisk would win every time.   But the poachers shoot from the air, and the poor beast doesn't have a chance.

They cut off the head, pull the backstrap, and get the hell out before we can react; and by the time our monitors tell us to get up there because the vital signs are absent, the carcass is crawling with stink bugs unless a calf or a cow has beaten the bugs to it.   In either event, the carcass is useless for anything except evidence of poaching.   None of us on the Project like poachers, and we have good reason.

A hunting party can louse up an entire program.   Let me tell you what happened after that trouble at Station Two.   We had to send nearly half of our security force up there to help maintain order, and the word got out.   It wasn't a week before we were hit with the biggest hunting parties in Project history.   They virtually wiped out Area C where we were breeding a strain that had tendencies toward compatibility.   Most of five years' work went down the drain.   That's why we have guards.   This place would be overrun with poachers if there was no security.   We could be hunted to extinction; and if the Project goes, the whole colony could collapse.

No sir, I'm not exaggerating, and I'm not an alarmist.   This is the only place inside our perimeter that has a precolonial population of basilisks.

Sure, there's plenty of wild area outside flitter range where basilisks are plentiful, but except for the Project you can draw a five hundred kilometer circle around Base and not find anything worth hunting.   We've been here ten years, and in that time we've hunted the area inside the perimeter so heavily that one can't find enough survivors to make a hunt profitable except in Project territory.   Basilisks are intelligent; and they don't like to be shot, so they hide their nests from aerial observation, and a man's a fool to try to hunt them on foot.

The net result is that the Project would be a happy hunting ground if it wasn't protected.   Sure, it's not too hard to protect, but it's still a big area.   The basilisks stay here because the food's plentiful and because we protect them.   They're smart enough to figure that their chances are better here than anywhere else inside the perimeter.   It's only occasionally that a hunter or a party gets in, and many of them don't make it out again.

But about the colony collapsing, I wasn't kidding.   Without the Project we'd lose hope and lose momentum.   The quotas would not be met and the BEC might figure we weren't worth the cost in logistic support, which would mean we'd either be evacuated or abandoned.

Have you ever seen what happens to an abandoned colony, sir?   Those Earthside chairbornes don't give a damn about us grubbies sweating it out here on Zetah. All the Bureau of Extraterrestrial Colonization cares about is the bottom line.   The colony thrives or it's aborted.   It's as simple as that.   After all, there are plenty of planets and plenty of colonists.   Right now we're holding a balance.   No one's happy, but we function.   The Project is our hope of relief, and so long as we have hope we'll continue.

Worth the cost?   Sir—you're joking!   It's worth any cost.

Oh sure—I know the objections, but the basilisks would kill us just as quickly as we kill them—and for the same reason.

I know they're intelligent.   Actually, I think they're descendants of the survivors of the atomic holocaust that wiped out the planet a few millennia ago.   Consider the implications: They are the only large terrestrial animal on this world except us. All the rest are swimmers, burrowers, crawlers, and cave dwellers.   Look at their front legs: They're adapted for grasping, they have binocular vision, they're potential tool users.   They could communicate verbally with each other if they stopped being solitary brutes.   Their brains have speech centers, and they have big brains.   And if you need any more evidence, there are ruins of a civilization down on the equator that'll make your eyes pop.   So will the scintillometer readings.

Ten thousand years ago the basilisks probably had a civilization as good as ours, one that ruled this world.   Even today their descendants dominate the planet. Sure—we control our perimeter, but it's hardly more than a pimple on Zetah's face. But in the long ago war they either had better weapons or were more determined. Anyway they did a better job of destroying their civilization than we did ours. And this solitary life of theirs possibly arose from ochlophobia brought on by mass destruction or maybe because there wasn't much to eat and they had to separate to remain alive.   We can relate to that sort of history.

See that group of buildings over there, sir?   That's our next stop.   That is the heart of the Project.   That's Headquarters.   It has to be big, since we capture every pregnant cow we can get our hands on and hold them until their calves are cast.   Then we turn the females loose, braincheck the calves, save the useful ones, cull the excess, and liberate the rest.

Yes, that's true, but the bulls would do it if we didn't.   We find about one calf in twenty that has gregarious traits.   We keep these and introduce them to each other.   There's considerable mortality, of course, but the survivors work out a peck order.   They learn to tolerate each other after a fashion.   Complete tolerance is our ultimate goal.

No sir, it's not hard to move them around.   They're terrified of fire.   We use solidographs of forest fires with sound and smell effects.   It's hard work handling the projectors, but it gets results.   We don't use the system except just after breeding season when we bring the females up here to hatch their eggs and gestate.

Feed?   Why chickens from Station Two, of course.   What else?   After all, basilisks are obligate carnivores.   Maybe they got that way from their war.   We can relate to that, but I'm not telling you anything new.   And speaking of feed, sir, it's lunchtime.   Would you care to eat with us?

Ah—here we are.   The head table's for guests.   Cook likes us to be on time. She has a hard enough job feeding a bunch of bellyachers like the Headquarters crew, without having us come at odd hours.

Try the soup, sir.   It's pure meat stock; rabbit, I think, from the look of it.   I'll admit it isn't nearly as good as beef, but this isn't Earth.   About the only thing we can ship on long trips are the small animals; the big ones don't survive, and so far we haven't managed to keep fertile ova alive over a stellar jump.   So what we have are fowl, rabbits, guinea pigs, dogs, and cats.   And rodents and fowl are poor fodder for chronic steak lovers.   Not a bit of red meat in the lot.   We tried dog once; it didn't work.   Too many emotional hangups.   Someday, maybe, we'll be able to ship larger domestic animals, but until we can, we have to live on what we can bring with us and what we can develop locally.   Nine times out of ten local sources don't work.   Either the taste is terrible or something is biochemically wrong, like those D-amine groups on Rosso that poisoned the whole colony.

Ah—I guess word got out that you were here!   I hoped it would.   Cook's gone all out for you.   Here—try this—

I'm not surprised you like it.   I've never met a person who didn't.   I remember

Mrs. Claiborne. She was a real lady; never touched anything except chicken breast and goose liver. She just couldn't stop once she tasted it. And if you think cutlets are delicious you should try steak.

What is it? Why, basilisk, of course. One of the calves that couldn't meet the competition. We don't waste them.

If you don't want your helping, sir, I'm sure someone will take it. In fact, I will.

Horrible? Not half as horrible as a steady diet of fowl and rodents. After six months of that fodder, you'll think differently. You'll hate the sight and smell of birds and bunnies. You'll dream of pork, beef, and lamb; bacon, ham, roasts, chops, and steak. You'll wake up with the memory in your tastebuds and cry like a baby when you see the bunnyburger breakfast patties. You'll remember this meal, sir; and you'll understand why we're sweating out this Project. You'll remember what they told you back on Earth about those colonies that collapsed and went cannibal—

You see, sir, we didn't really know what the Last War did to us until we went into Space. On Earth we adjusted the ecology to serve our ends, but on colony worlds we can't do that. Here, we can't forget what we are. Here's where it really hits home.

Sure, we didn't cause the mutation. Our warring ancestors did that with their nukes, but we're the ones who have to live with it.

Of course I worry about it, sir. But don't get me wrong. I don't worry about eating them, even though I can't help feeling sorry for a race that's in a worse bind than we are. They've adjusted to their ecology and manage to make do. But they must get as tired of their diet as we get of ours, and they look at us as we look at them. I can't help thinking about those nests along the riverbank surrounded by colonies of burrowers and swimmers who wait to be eaten when their masters are hungry. It doesn't take too much imagination to think what those basilisks could do if they went beyond toleration and actually worked together toward a common goal. If one of them can control whole colonies of lesser creatures, what could a dozen—or a hundred—do? I wonder—and worry—but I suppose it's a calculated risk we have to take.

F. PAUL WILSON

Lipidleggin'

Butter.

I can name a man's poison at fifty paces. I take one look at this guy as he walks in and say to myself, "Butter."

He steps carefully, like there's something sticky on the soles of his shoes. Maybe there is, but I figure he moves like that because he's on unfamiliar ground. Never seen his face before and I know just about everybody around.

It's early yet. I just opened the store and Gabe's the only other guy on the buying side of the counter, only he ain't buying. He's waiting in the corner by the checkerboard and I'm just about to go join him when the new guy comes in. It's wet out—not raining, really, just wet like it only gets up here near the Water Gap—and he's wearing a slicker. Underneath that he seems to have a stocky build and is average height. He's got no beard and his eyes are blue with a watery look. Could be from anywhere until he takes off the hat and I see his hair: it's dark brown and he's got it cut in one of those soupbowl styles that're big in the city.

Gabe gives me an annoyed look as I step back behind the counter, but I ignore him. His last name is Varadi—sounds Italian but it's Hungarian—and he's got plenty of time on his hands. Used to be a PhD in a philosophy department at some university in upstate New York 'til they cut the department in half and gave him his walking papers, tenure and all. Now he does part-time labor at one of the mills when they need a little extra help, which ain't near as often as he'd like.

About as poor as you can get, that Gabe. The government giraffes take a big chunk of what little he earns and leave him near nothing to live on. So he goes down to the welfare office where the local giraffes give him food stamps and rent vouchers so he can get by on what the first group of giraffes left him. If you can figure that one out . . .

Anyway, Gabe's got a lot of time on his hands, like I said, and he hangs out here and plays checkers with me when things are slow. He'd rather play chess, I know, but I can't stand the game. Nothing happens for too long and I get impatient and try to break the game open with some wild gamble. And I always lose. So we play checkers or we don't play.

The new guy puts his hat on the counter and glances around. He looks uneasy.

I know what's coming but I'm not going to help him out.   There's a little dance we've got to do first.

"I need to buy a few things," he says.   His voice has a little tremor in it and close up like this I figure he's in his mid-twenties.

"Well, this *is* a general store," I reply, getting real busy wiping down the counter, "and we've got all sorts of things.   What're you interested in?   Antiques?   Hardware?   Food?"

"I'm not looking for the usual stock."

(The music begins to play)

I look at him with my best puzzled expression.   "Just what is it you're after, friend?"

"Butter and eggs."

"Nothing unusual about that.   Got a whole cabinet full of both behind you there."

(We're on our way to the dance floor)

"I'm not looking for that.   I didn't come all the way out here to buy the same shit I can get in the city.   I want the real thing."

"You want the real thing, eh?"   I say, meeting his eyes square for the first time.   "You know damn well real butter and real eggs are illegal.   I could go to jail for carrying that kind of stuff!"

(We dance)

Next to taking his money, this is the part I like best about dealing with a new customer.   Usually I can dance the two of us around the subject of what he really wants for upwards of twenty or thirty minutes if I've a mind to.   But this guy was a lot more direct than most and didn't waste any time getting down to the nitty gritty.   Still, he wasn't going to rob me of a little dance.   I've got a dozen years of dealing under my belt and no green kid's gonna rob me of that.

A dozen years . . . doesn't seem that long.   It was back then that the giraffes who were running the National Health Insurance program found out that they were spending 'way too much money taking care of people with diseases nobody was likely to cure for some time.   The stroke and heart patients were the worst.   With the presses at the Treasury working overtime and inflation getting wild, it got to the point where they either had to admit they'd made a mistake or do something drastic.

Naturally, they got drastic.

The President declared a health emergency and Congress passed something called "The National Health Maintainance Act" which said that since certain citizens were behaving irresponsibly by abusing their bodies and thereby giving rise to chronic diseases which resulted in consumption of more than their fair share of medical care at public expense, it was resolved that, in the public interest and for the public good, certain commodities would henceforth and hereafter be either proscribed or strictly rationed.   Or something like that.

Foods high in cholesterol and saturated fats headed the list.   Next came tobacco and any alcoholic beverage over 30 proof.

Ah, the howls that went up from the public! But those were nothing compared to the screams of fear and anguish that arose from the dairy and egg industry which was facing immediate economic ruin. The Washington giraffes stood firm, however—it wasn't an election year—and used phrases like "bite the bullet" and "national interest" and "public good" until we were all ready to barf.

Nothing moved them.

Things quieted down after a while, as they always do. It helped, of course, that somebody in one of the drug companies had been working on an additive to chickenfeed that would take just about all the cholesterol out of the yolk. It worked, and the poultry industry was saved.

The new eggs cost more—of course!—and the removal of most of the cholesterol from the yolk also removed most of the taste, but at least the egg farmers had something to sell.

Butter was out. Definitely. No compromise. Too much of an "adverse effect on serum lipid levels," whatever that means. You use polyunsaturated margarine or you use nothing. Case closed.

Well, almost closed. Most good citizen-type Americans hunkered down and learned to live with the Lipid Laws, as they came to be known. Why, I bet there's scads of fifteen-year-olds about who've never tasted real butter or a true, cholesterol-packed egg yolk. But we're not all good citizens. Especially me. Far as I'm concerned, there's nothing like two fried eggs—fried in *butter*—over easy, with bacon on the side, to start the day off. *Every* day. And I wasn't about to give that up.

I was strictly in the antiques trade then, and I knew just about every farmer in Jersey and Eastern Pennsylvania. So I found one who was making butter for himself and had him make a little extra for me. Then I found another who was keeping some hens aside and not giving them any of that special feed and had him hold a few eggs out for me.

One day I had a couple of friends over for breakfast and served them real eggs and toast with real butter. They almost strangled me trying to find out where I got the stuff. That's when I decided to add a sideline to my antiques business.

I figured New York City to be the best place to start so I let word get around the antique dealers there that I could supply their customers with more than furniture. The response was wild and soon I was making more money running butter and eggs than I was running Victorian golden oak.

I was a lipidlegger.

Didn't last, though. I was informed by two very pushy fellows of Mediterranean stock that if I wanted to do any lipid business in Manhattan, I'd either have to buy all my merchandise from their wholesale concern, or give them a very healthy chunk of my profits.

I decided it would be safer to stick close to home. Less volume, but less risky. I turned my antique shop up here by the Water Gap—that's the part of North Jersey you can get to without driving by all those refineries and reactors—into a general store.

A dozen years now . . .

*   *   *

"I heard you had the real thing for sale," the guy says.

I shake my head. "Now where would you hear a thing like that?"

"New York."

"New York? The only connection I have with New York is furnishing some antique dealers with a few pieces now and then. How'd you hear about me in New York?"

"Sam Gelbstein."

I nod. Sam's a good customer. Good friend, too. He helped spread the word for me when I was leggin' lipids into the city.

"How you know Sam?"

"My uncle furnished his house with furniture he bought there."

I still act suspicious—it's part of the dance—but I know if Sam sent him, he's all right. One little thing bothers me though.

"How come you don't look for your butter and eggs in the city? I hear they're real easy to get there."

"Yeah," he says and twists up his mouth. "They're also spoiled now and again and there's no arguing with the types that supply it. No money-back guarantees with those guys."

I see his point. "And you figure this is closer to the source."

He nods.

"One more question," I say. "I don't deal in the stuff, of course,"—still dancing— "but I'm just curious how a young guy like you got a taste for contraband like eggs and butter."

"Europe," he says. "I went to school in Brussels and it's all still legal over there. Just can't get used to these damned substitutes."

It all fit, so I go into the back and lift up the floor door. I keep a cooler down there and from it I pull a dozen eggs and a half-kilo slab of butter. His eyes widen as I put them on the counter in front of him.

"This is the real thing?" he asks. "No games?"

I pull out an English muffin, split it with my thumbs and drop the halves into the toaster I keep under the counter. I know that once he tastes this butter I'll have another steady customer. People will eat ersatz eggs and polyunsaturated margarine if they think it's good for them, but they want to know the real thing's available. Take that away from them and suddenly you've got them going to great lengths to get what they used to pass up without a second thought.

"The real thing," I tell him. "There's even a little salt added to the butter for flavor."

"Great!" He smiles, then puts both hands into his pockets and pulls out a gun with his right and a shield with his left. "James Callahan, Public Health Service, Enforcement Division," he says. "You're under arrest, Mr. Gurney." He's not smiling anymore.

I don't change my expression or say anything. I just stand there and look bored. But inside I feel like someone's wrapped a length of heavy chain around my guts and hooked it up to a high speed winch.

Looking at the gun—a little snub-nosed .32—I start to grin.

"What's so funny?" he asks, nervous and I'm not sure why. Maybe it's his first bust.

"A public health guy with a gun!" I'm laughing now. "Don't that seem funny to you?"

His face remains stern. "Not in the least. Now step around the counter. After you're cuffed we're going to take a ride to the Federal Building."

I don't budge. I glance over to the corner and see a deserted checkerboard. Gabe's gone—skittered out as soon as he saw the gun. Mr. Public Health follows my eyes.

"Where's the red-headed guy?"

"Gone for help," I tell him.

He glances quickly over his shoulder out the door, then back at me. "Let's not do anything foolish here. I wasn't crazy enough to come out here alone."

But I can tell by the way his eyes bounce all over the room and by the way he licks his lips that, yes, he was crazy enough to come out here alone.

I don't say anything, so he fills in the empty space. "You've got nothing to worry about, Mr. Gurney," he says. "You'll get off with a first offender's suspended sentence and a short probation."

I don't tell him that's exactly what worries me. I'm waiting for a sound: the click of the toaster as it spits out the English muffin. It comes and I grab the two halves and put them on the counter.

"What are you doing?" he asks, watching me like I'm going to pull a gun on him any minute.

"You gotta taste it," I tell him. "I mean, how're you gonna be sure it ain't oleo unless you taste it?"

"Never mind that." He wiggles the .32 at me. "You're just stalling. Get around here."

But I ignore him. I open a corner of the slab of butter and dig out a hunk with my knife. Then I smear it on one half of the muffin and press the two halves together. All the time I'm talking.

"How come you're out here messin' with me? I'm small time. The biggies are in the city."

"Yeah." He nods slowly. He can't believe I'm buttering a muffin while he holds a gun on me. "And they've also bought everyone who's for sale. Can't get a conviction there if you bring the 'leggers in smeared with butter and eggs in their mouths."

"So you pick on me."

He nods again. "Somebody who buys from Gelbstein let slip that he used to connect with a guy from out here who used to do lipidlegging into the city. Wasn't hard to track you down." He shrugs, almost apologizing. "I need some arrests to my credit and I have to take 'em where I can find 'em."

I don't reply just yet. At least I know why he came alone: he didn't want anyone a little higher up to steal credit for the bust. And I also know that Sam Gelbstein didn't put the yell on me, which is a relief. But I've got more important concerns at the moment.   I press my palm down on top of the muffin until the melted butter oozes out the sides and onto the counter, then I peel the halves apart and push them toward him.

"Here.   Eat."

He looks at the muffin all yellow and drippy, then at me, then back to the muffin. The aroma hangs over the counter in an invisible cloud and I'd be getting hungry myself if I didn't have so much riding on this little move.

I'm not worried about going to jail for this.   Never was.   I know all about suspended sentences and that.   What I *am* worried about is being marked as a 'legger.   Because that means the giraffes will be watching me and snooping into my affairs all the time.   And I'm not the kind who takes well to being watched. I've devoted a lot of effort to keeping a low profile and living between the lines— "living in the interstices," Gabe calls it.   A bust could ruin my whole way of life.

So I've got to be right about this guy's poison.

He can't take his eyes off the muffins.   I can tell by the way he stares that he's a good citizen-type whose mother obeyed all the Lipid Laws as soon as they were passed, and who never thought to break them once he became a big boy.   I nudge him.

"Go ahead."

He puts the shield on the counter and his left hand reaches out real careful, like he's afraid the muffins will bite him.   Finally, he grabs the nearest one, holds it under his nose, sniffs it, then takes a bite.   A little butter drips from the right corner of his mouth, but it's his eyes I'm watching.   They're not seeing me or anything else in the store . . . they're sixteen years away and he's ten years old again and his mother just fixed him breakfast.   His eyes are sort of shiny and wet around the rims as he swallows.   Then he shakes himself and looks at me.   But he doesn't say a word.

I put the butter and eggs in a bag and push it toward him.

"Here.   On the house.   Gabe will be back any minute with the troops so if you leave now we can avoid any problems."   He lowers the gun but still hesitates. "Catch those bad guys in the city," I tell him.   "But when you need the real thing for yourself, and you need it fresh, ride out here and I'll see you're taken care of."

He shoves the rest of the muffin half into his mouth and chews furiously as he pockets his shield and gun and slaps his hat back on his head.

"You gotta deal," he says around the mouthful, then lifts the bag with his left hand, grabs the other half muffin with his right, and hurries out into the wet.

I follow him to the door where I see Gabe and a couple of the boys from the mill coming up the road with shotguns cradled in their arms.   I wave them off and tell them thanks anyway.   Then I watch the guy drive off.

I guess I can't tell a Fed when I see one, but I can name anybody's poison. Anybody's.

I glance down at the pile of newspapers I leave on the outside bench.   Around the rock that holds it down I can see where some committee of giraffes has announced that it will recommend the banning of Bugs Bunny cartoons from the theatres and the airwaves. The creature, they say, shows a complete disregard for authority and is not fit viewing for children.

Well, I've been expecting that and fixed up a few mini-cassettes of some of Bugs' finest moments. Don't want the kids around here to grow up without the Wabbit.

I also hear talk about a coming federal campaign against being overweight. Bad health risk, they say. Rumor has it they're going to outlaw clothes over a certain size. That's just rumor, of course . . . still, I'll bet there's an angle in there for me.

Ah, the giraffes. For every one of me there's a hundred of them.

But I'm worth a thousand giraffes.

DEAN McLAUGHLIN

Omit Flowers

T he doctor stepped out into the hall and closed the door.   He paused, then crossed slowly to where the small group waited.   He was tired; it was deep in the night, and nothing had done any good.   The corridor was dimly lit except down at the end near the nurses' station.   Quiet.

"I'm very sorry," he said.   "Very sorry."

They took it well.   It was no more than they had expected.

"And I'm sorry, also," he went on, still speaking slowly, for he was reluctant to speak the question his responsibilities required him now to ask, "that I must have a decision from you.   But it is not a thing that can wait.   I must know your wishes now."

He scanned their faces.   The small young woman swallowed, nodded mutely. The heavy, older man looked stoic.   "Of course," he said, his voice so hoarsely low it was almost inaudible.   The older woman looked straight ahead through rimless glasses; what she saw, if anything, was hard to guess.

"The choice must be entirely yours," the doctor said.   "But it must be made now.   No internally sustained life-signs remain; even if we wanted to, the law would not permit us to keep the life support system connected.   So: as you probably know, it would be possible to freeze him, in the hope that medical science of some future date might be able to revitalize him.   It's a costly process, and the prospect uncertain, but it can be done."

He took a deep breath.   "On the other hand," he went on, "as you may also know, certain parts of him are still in excellent condition.   You'd get very good prices on the spare parts market."

He glanced down at his watch.   "Which do you want?   At most, we have five minutes before he starts to spoil."

DIANA L. PAXSON

Message to Myself

T *o: The Captain of the crawler Polyphemus, Ciardan Pioneer Team I, Reichenbach V.*

Sir: I would be grateful if you could send this spool on to Ensign Harry Lowe by the next robo.   Code it to the A. P. S. Belshazzar, Targen Dock "L", Center. Collect on delivery.

Thanks.

Hello?

God, this is awkward!   And I thought I'd have so much to say. . . .

At least the crawler is long enough for me to have a compartment to myself. It's better this way.   It was getting to be a strain sitting in there with the Ciardans, and I can't blame them.   How do you react to a man's mind in a woman's body— the body of the criminal who nearly killed them all, and the mind of the person who saved them, all in one?   No wonder they are confused.   Every so often I get an odd feeling myself, like that ripple in perception you feel in Shift.   But I know I won't have to take it for long.

They've certainly been kind enough—loungers, an autosnacky, a scriber, audio. Come to think of it, this must be the crew lounge.   I hope they don't mind being deprived of it.   But of course they got to eat and relax while I was working.   Why should I pity them?   Too bad I don't feel like eating—could it be the gravity? But this stomach shouldn't be troubled by that.   The only thing that really interests me here is the scriber.   I hope they will send the spool on to you . . . afterwards.

I? You? We?   Must really get the pronouns straight if I'm to go on.   Because I really am you, of course, and you are me, even though you are floating comfortably weightless somewhere between here and Center, and I am sitting, equally comfortable at almost three gee, in a crawler moving slowly over the virgin dust of Reichenbach V.   Still, I *feel* like a separate person, and when you hear these words, I suppose you will too.   Shall we agree on a temporary schizophrenia?

I do think it's important for you to hear this.   Of course neither of us is aware of having missed anything, except for the few hours of unconsciousness when they took the print.   We are one life which has been divided into two equal streams. But one stream is going to continue on, while the other is due to dry up pretty soon (how long?   They wouldn't tell us that—long enough to finish the job, they said).

I read-in my formal report on the repair of the Dome Pressure mechanism when I finished the job.   I expect the Ciardans will send it to you if you ask.   It was a simple enough job, nothing to add to our professional laurels, except that I had to do it with fingers that were too thick, and in a gravity that made the instruments and colloids act as if they were bewitched.   Pity they couldn't have left enough of my hostess in here to warn me about that.   Certainly the men who died could have handled it easily enough.   I wonder what her job was, before?

Remember the old joke about the lost scoutcraft that ran out of food and when they were finally picked up there was only one man left—sleek as a ship's cat? That was in the days of the Xirari cult, and before the captain spaced the fellow, he told him, "There were only four Xirari on this ship, and you ate three of them!" I suppose pressure techs are more crucial to colony survival than cultists.   But the penalty for doing away with them seems to be similar.

So I want you to hear this.   We came out looking for adventure, didn't we? God knows the trip was tame enough, before the distress call from Reichenbach and the rather unusual request they made.   Somehow I doubt that anything so exotic will ever happen to you again.

But it's not quite like we thought it was going to be.   The work was not very interesting, after all; and since this body is used to the gravity, there is no sense of strangeness; and nobody will talk to me, so it's hard to tell what the people are like.   But my head gets fuzzy now and then, like a headache that will neither quite come on or go away.   And surely I can confess to *you* that I am afraid. . . .

I have just had a horrible thought.   What if something happens to *Belshazzar?* What if you never hear this and the two halves of us are never put back together again?   What if when this alien brain shuffles off its imprinting at last there is no other "me" out there somewhere, going on about his business?

What if I am really going to die?

This is getting morbid.   Better get up, move around.   Maybe I can manage a cup of stimo now.   If you were here too we could get it on, on that lounger.   That would certainly distract me.

Unfortunately I can see my reflection in the view-port, and I'm not your type at all.

Ciardans are built to withstand 3.5 gees—broad as a freighter, with faces that only another Ciardan could love.   I can understand why there was no way I/you could have done this job in the body we were born in.   Growing up at .8 gee and flipping half-way across the System in free-fall don't give you the physique to function on a place like Ciarda or this godforsaken planet they think they're going to make homey in a few revolves.

Is it worth it?

No—that's the part I don't want to think about for a while.

This elephant whose body I'm inhabiting must have been pretty hot stuff.   They said she'd had three husbands, two of them in this group of pioneers.   You would think she would have learned a little tolerance.   But when she found out that Number Three was working a little too closely with his team chief, she must have blown her drive.   Did she realize that a charge planted in just that spot would wreck the pressure mechanism as well as destroying the whole tech team?   As long as she got the two she was after, did she care if the rest of the pressure techs died (quickly) in the same blast?   And the rest of the colony (slowly) as the machinery failed?   And herself?

Oh, that's right—they told us that before, didn't they?   To persuade me that it was only justice.   I'm sorry.   My head hurts.

Did she suffer, knowing what was going to happen to her?   Did they bother to tell her even?   Or did they just knock her out, bring her up to the ship, clamp her into the machine and slip the psychprint cube in?

Why did I volunteer?

The ship racks prints for all essential personnel, including pressure techs, just in case someone should have to be replaced to get us home.   They could have used the one we had.   But that one was a ship specialist, and I've trained on the new planetary machines.   And I thought it would be an experience none of the other first-year men had had!

An ingenious idea—a crazy female wipes out your whole team of techs and the machinery they tended, so you psychprint her into a replacement with the aid of a passing ship.   It doesn't matter that soon the print will fade, and then there'll be a mindless nothing left (until someone decides she's using too much air).   She deserved to die, and this way she has at least made up for her crime.   And the donor happily goes his way—No harm done—

I had to sit down again.   I felt dizzy, but it's better now.   What was I saying?   Have to play back the spool a minute and find out.

No harm done. . . .

No . . . because I am not real, am I?   Just a psyche superimposed on a body that has earned death.   But it's over for her, and I still have to die—to wait for consciousness and memory to slip away.   My head feels as if my skull were splitting.   Is she killing me too, or am I killing myself?

The spool is slowing now.   Nearly full, I guess.   I'll have to turn it off.

Are you there?

Are you still listening?

I keep trying to picture the face I've frowned at in the mirror a million times.   What else can't I remember now?   I know that I am real.   I hurt too much not to be.   But are you?

Is this what dying is?   The psychprint orientation never mentioned this spreading agony as synapse after synapse flickers out.   No one could finish life sane if they knew. . . .

The spool is still turning.   I must wipe it before it gets to you—before you know—   Whoever picks this up, don't give it to Ensign . . . to. . . .

I can't remember my name!

Oh my God!   Stop it!   Stop the pain!

No one should have to die twice!

D One Rejection Too Many

ear Dr. Asimov:

Imagine my delight when I spotted your new science fiction magazine on the newsstands. I have been a fan of yours for many, many years and I naturally wasted no time in buying a copy. I wish you every success in this new venture.

In your second issue I read with interest your plea for stories from new authors. While no writer myself, I have had a time traveller living with me for the past two weeks (he materialized in the bathtub without clothes or money, so I felt obliged to offer him shelter), and he has written a story of life on earth as it will be in the year 5000.

Before he leaves this time frame, it would give him great pleasure to see his story in print—I hope you will feel able to make this wish come true.

Yours sincerely,
Nancy Morrison (Miss)

Dear Miss Morrison:

Thank you for your kind letter and good wishes.

It is always refreshing to hear from a new author. You have included some most imaginative material in your story; however, it is a little short on plot and human interest—perhaps you could rewrite it with this thought in mind.

Yours sincerely,
Isaac Asimov

Dear Dr. Asimov:

I was sorry that you were unable to print the story I sent you. Vahl (the time traveller who wrote it) was quite hurt as he tells me he is an author of some note in his own time. He has, however, rewritten the story and this time has included plenty of plot and some rather interesting mating rituals which he has borrowed from the year 3000. In his own time (the year 5015) sex is no longer practised, so you can see that it is perfectly respectable having him in my house. I do wish, though, that he could adapt himself to our custom of wearing clothes—my neighbours are starting to talk!

Anything that you can do to expedite the publishing of Vahl's story would be most appreciated, so that he will feel free to return to his own time.

Yours sincerely,
Nancy Morrison (Miss)

Dear Miss Morrison:

Thank you for your rewritten short story.

I don't want to discourage you but I'm afraid you followed my suggestions with a little too much enthusiasm—however, I can understand that having an imaginary nude visitor from another time is a rather heady experience.   I'm afraid that your story now rather resembles a far-future episode of Mary Hartman, Mary Hartman or Soap.

Could you tone it down a bit and omit the more bizarre sex rituals of the year 3000—we must remember that *Isaac Asimov's Science Fiction Magazine* is intended to be a family publication.

Perhaps a little humor would improve the tale too.

Yours sincerely,
Isaac Asimov

Dear Dr. Asimov:

Vahl was extremely offended by your second rejection—he said he has never received a rejection slip before, and your referring to him as "imaginary" didn't help matters at all.   I'm afraid he rather lost his temper and stormed out into the garden—it was at this unfortunate moment that the vicar happened to pass by.

Anyway, I managed to get Vahl calmed down and he has rewritten the story and added plenty of humour.   I'm afraid my subsequent meeting with the vicar was not blessed with such success!   I'm quite sure Vahl would not understand another rejection.

Yours truly,
Nancy Morrison (Miss)

Dear Miss Morrison:

I really admire your persistence in rewriting your story yet another time.   Please don't give up hope—you can become a fairly competent writer in time, I feel sure.

I'm afraid the humor you added was not the kind of thing I had in mind at all— you're not collaborating with Henny Youngman by any chance are you?   I really had a more sophisticated type of humor in mind.

Yours truly,
Isaac Asimov

P.S.   Have you considered reading your story, as it is, on The Gong Show?

Dear Dr. Asimov:

It really was very distressing to receive the return of my manuscript once again— Vahl was quite speechless with anger.

It was only with the greatest difficulty that I prevailed upon him to refine the humor you found so distasteful, and I am submitting his latest rewrite herewith.

In his disappointment, Vahl has decided to return to his own time right away.   I shall be sorry to see him leave as I was getting very fond of him—a pity he wasn't from the year 3000 though.   Still, he wouldn't have made a very satisfactory husband; I'd have never known where (or when) he was.   It rather looks as though my plans to marry the vicar have suffered a severe setback too.   Are you married, Dr. Asimov?

I must close this letter now as I have to say goodbye to Vahl.   He says he has just finished making some long overdue improvements to our time frame as a parting gift—isn't that kind of him?

Yours sincerely,
Nancy Morrison (Miss)

Dear Miss Morrison:
   I am very confused by your letter.   Who is Isaac Asimov?   I have checked with several publishers and none of them has heard of *Isaac Asimov's Science Fiction Magazine,* although the address on the envelope was correct for *this* magazine.
   However, I was very impressed with your story and will be pleased to accept it for our next issue.   Seldom do we receive a story combining such virtues as a well-conceived plot, plenty of human interest, and a delightfully subtle brand of humor.

Yours truly,
George H. Scithers,
Editor,
Arthur C. Clarke's Science Fiction Magazine

FREDERICK S. LORD, JR.

But Do They Ride Dolphins?

“Why, how absolutely darling!” Mrs. Hunt exclaimed when she entered the Malones' living room. “Come see, Wallace! They've got a little Water Baby!” She put her heavily powdered nose an inch from the plexiglass of the darkened tank and cooed at the equally curious figure within. “What a cute little thing you are,” she said.

Professor Hunt joined his wife in front of the large tank and nodded appreciatively. “Fascinating animals, aren't they?” He turned to their hosts. “And quite a conversation piece, I imagine.”

Jeff Malone smiled. “Yes, he is. Every time we have people over, we usually spend the first hour talking about little Nemo here.”

Mrs. Hunt tapped on the tank with a long orange fingernail. “Hi there, little fellow.”

“Please don't do that,” Mary Ann Malone told her. “He's supposed to be taking a nap, and I don't want him to get too stirred up.”

Mrs. Hunt straightened and sniffed. “Of course. Is it always that dark in there? I wish we could get a better look. That is,” she added with less good nature than the words alone might have suggested, “if it's all right with his mother.”

Mary Ann stiffened, then relaxed. Another one who will never understand, she told herself. “It's just that Nemo likes to see out,” she explained calmly. She walked over to the tank and opened a door in the cabinet below the chamber. Professor Hunt bent down to catch a glimpse of the machinery within.

“Are those batteries back there?” he asked.

“Yes,” said Mary Ann. “In case of emergencies. That's the air pump over there, and that's the heater.” Reaching in, she flipped a switch and the interior of the tank was suddenly illuminated.

Little Nemo was now thirty inches long from the tip of his vestigial nose to the tip of his wide flippers. At last check he had weighed slightly over twenty-four pounds. Except for his face, hands, and feet, he was covered with a thick golden fur, shot through with streaks of brown, to which all his fur would eventually darken.

His hands, now pressed against the glass, were of human construction, except that his thumbs and little fingers were longer and more developed than those of an ordinary human infant would have been. Webby membranes filled the spaces between his fingers as far as the first knuckles.   From the outsides of his thumbs and little fingers stretched other membranes, connected to the insides and the outsides of his elbows.   Another set of membranes connected the back of his elbows to the lower ribs on each side, giving his upper body a batlike appearance.

"Mmn . . ." Mary Ann said with disapproval.   "Time to clean those gills again."

"Absolutely charming!" Mrs. Hunt announced.   "I had no idea they could be so cute."

Mary Ann reached down and snapped off the light.   "Now you settle down," she said to Nemo, shaking her finger at him.   He began darting from corner to corner of his crib.   "I mean it," said Mary Ann.   Stepping up on a stool next to the tank, she reached into the water and the wriggling little body came up to be scratched.

Jeff frowned.   "Well, now that all the introductions have been made, let's have a drink, shall we?   Come along, dear."

"I'll be right with you," said Mary Ann, still scratching Nemo.   "Strangers make him nervous, and I want to make sure he understands everything's all right."

"We'll be in the other room,"   Jeff told her.   "Don't be long."

"I won't," she answered, but she was still not looking at her husband when she said it.

After dinner, Mrs. Hunt insisted on helping Mary Ann with the dishes.   "You wash and I'll wipe," she said.   "I haven't forgotten how."

"I'm sure Mary's used to having her hands in water," Professor Hunt commented slyly.

Mrs. Hunt held up one of the Malones' mismatched saucers.   "Look, Wallace! Aren't those faculty wives' basement sales wonderful?   This was part of old Professor Campbell's set, wasn't it?"

Professor Hunt looked up from his coffee and smiled.   "Why, yes; I think it is.   I didn't know they were still making the rounds."

Mrs. Hunt smirked.   "Not only are they hideous, they're practically unbreakable."

Professor Hunt suddenly felt the need to compensate for his wife's embarrassing lack of tact.   "You know, Celia, Jeff and Mary Ann will be eating off silver pretty soon, if they want to.   Judging by the size of their pet out there, it shouldn't be too long before it's time to cash him in."

"That's right, too," said Jeff, as if that had just occurred to him.   "Someone from Seattle is coming down the fourteenth, I think it is.   Did they say the fourteenth or the fifteenth, dear?"

Mary Ann kept her eyes on the dishes in the sink.   "The fourteenth," she said softly.

"Well, that's not very long to wait at all," Professor Hunt said.   "I'm glad for you, Jeff—I really am.   I've watched some very promising law students leave here simply because they weren't ingenious enough to find the money to continue.   And you won't spend your first ten years after school paying off those insidious student loans they're always talking young people into.''

"No, we'll be able to start out fresh, all right,'' said Jeff proudly. ''Nothing to weigh us down.''

There was a slap and a splash from the living room.

"There he goes again,'' Jeff sighed. ''That's another thing I'm looking forward to: being able to get a full night's sleep again. You'd be surprised at how much trouble these little monsters are.''

"I'll be right back,'' said Mary Ann. She paused in the doorway on her way out of the room. ''And I'll thank you kindly, Jeffery, if you'll refrain from calling my child a monster.''

Trying to determine how far genetic engineering could go before the fetus became so incompatible with its mother that it was no longer viable, scientists at the Seattle Eugenics Institute wrought increasingly radical but theoretically harmonious changes in one experiment after another. When repeated attempts to create a more complicated and more specialized baby from the given genetic material of its parents failed, the final step was taken. A human volunteer was found, and before the moral, ethical, legal, or social questions involved could be adequately expressed, a *Homo Aquaticus* named Frank was a thriving, ecologically adapted reality.

The usefulness of *Homo A.* was never in doubt. Not only was he used to cultivate and harvest the algae, seaweed, and dozens of other types of edible sea life; there were many other jobs that he could do better than they had ever been done before. With historical consistency, the CIA devised many projects in which *H.A.* played an important part. Utility companies, looking for a cheaper way to inspect and maintain undersea cables, pipelines, and mines, found *H.A.* a savior with fins. Salvage outfits, marine biologists, oceanographers, and dozens of other industries and agencies quickly saw his potential.

The demand for *Homo A.* soon outstripped the supply. While there was no shortage of volunteers to be host mothers, only a limited number of women had both the genetic and the psychological potential to succeed at bearing and raising an infant *Homo A.*

For Jeff and Mary Ann Malone, the one hundred thousand dollars paid for a healthy Sea Farmer was a quick solution to an otherwise hopeless financial crunch. Casting about desperately for some way to keep her husband in school and their dreams intact, she had applied to the Institute and been accepted. The implantation had been painless, the pregnancy uneventful. The delivery had been a long, foggy, but not totally unpleasant dream. And now . . .

"Do you mind?'' Jeff asked angrily. ''I've had a hell of a long day and I've got a longer one coming up tomorrow.'' He bleared at the two occupants of the tank, and then at the clock humming benignly on the coffee table. ''It's almost three, for God's sake.''

Mary Ann pushed her short damp hair back from her face and blinked at him, a foolish smile slowly fading from her lips. "Oh, is it? I'm sorry, dear. I didn't realize we were making that much noise. Nemo was restless, that's all."

Suddenly Nemo's flippers emerged in front of Mary Ann's face and slapped the water hard, spraying her in a sneak attack. "You!" she cried, and lunged for the elusive prankster without success. "How would you like to be tickled?"

Jeff stepped back and examined the drops of water on the rug by his slippers. "Do you mind?" he repeated.

But Mary Ann was laughing. Nemo had attacked her toes with his hard gums. "Easy!" she cautioned. "I don't want to be pobbled!"

"Come out of there right now!" Jeff commanded. "I'm not going to put up with this much longer."

"Why don't you join us?" Mary Ann offered. "Or have you had your weekly shower?"

"Be serious, will you?"

"All right," she sighed. "Hand me my robe, will you?" She stepped up on the stool she had brought with her into Nemo's crib and swung first one, then the other leg out of the water and onto the stool outside the tank. Jeff tossed her the robe and continued to scowl.

"You could have a little consideration for me, too, you know," he told her. "After all, I am your husband."

"Is that who you are!" Mary Ann exclaimed sarcastically. "I was wondering who that person I was catching a brief glimpse of twice a day was. I'm glad you introduced yourself; I might never have known."

"Things will get better," he promised routinely.

"And what am I supposed to do in the meantime—hibernate?" She stepped down from the stool and turned back to regard the disappointed little face watching her every move. "Fun's over, sweetheart," she told him. "Real Monster says we have to be quiet and go to sleep." She wrapped the robe tightly around herself, crossed the living room, and sat down on the couch.

Jeff was still angry. "I thought I asked you not to sit on the couch when you're all wet," he snapped.

"Oh, go back to bed," she answered. "And dry up, yourself."

"This isn't natural, you know."

"What isn't? That a baby should get restless in the middle of the night?"

He sat down at the other end of the couch and lit a cigarette from the pack lying on the end table. "You know exactly what I'm talking about," he said with his first exhalation of smoke. "It's not natural to feel the way you do about that . . ." He gestured at the tank. "High-class bastard."

"He's as human as you are, Jeff. At times, more so."

"That's what the shrinks pounded into your head. If I'd had any idea how much of your time he was going to take, I would never have gone along with this."

"Well, you're the one who brought the brochures." She watched the air bubbles rising in Nemo's crib and unconsciously gauged the oxygenator's speed. "I had no idea you could be so jealous, Jeff."

"You have to give him up, you know."

"I don't want to. I want to buy a house on the beach and raise him myself. But I don't suppose you understand that. You don't care about anyone but yourself these days."

Jeff took a long drag on his cigarette before answering. "Look," he said finally. "There's nothing I can do about it. We've got a contract that says what's going to happen to Nemo, and that's that."

"But I'm his mother, Jeff," said Mary Ann, her voice now a hoarse whisper. The salt water running slowly down her cheeks had not come from the tank. "What's going to happen to him? Who's going to take care of him? He needs *me*, Jeff!"

"But he'll enjoy being with his own kind."

"But we're his own kind, too."

"That's just what the psychologists told you to think."

"No. It's true. Don't you care what becomes of him?"

"I read all the information," Jeff said. "He's going to be trained at the Institute for a couple of years, and then he's going to be put to work wherever they think he'll do best."

"But will he be happy?"

"All the Water Babies are very well treated. Stop worrying about that."

"That's not what I mean!" she cried.

Jeff put out his cigarette and stood. "You're too excited to make any sense right now. I'm going to bed. I suggest you take a shower and do likewise. Good night."

She made no reply. Jeff gave out a sigh of combined weariness and frustration and went back into the bedroom. Less than a minute later, he was asleep.

Mary Ann gazed at the little figure floating in the tank, also asleep. She tried to imagine his leaving her, but the thought was too painful. Would he think she had stopped loving him? He would be confused and terrified, she was sure. And she was equally certain that no one else would ever care for him as she had.

She had seen the movies depicting the undersea lives of the Sea Farmers. She had read all she could about them. They planted and they tended and they harvested. They fished and they welded and they explored. They ate well and worked hard. They slept soundly and they seemed content.

"But do they ride dolphins?" she asked, and there was no one there to answer her.

Mary Ann unlocked the apartment door while still cradling the two heavy shopping bags of groceries in her arms. Saturday afternoon presented an exhausting change of her routine, but a welcome one. Not that there was much romance in paying bills, buying hamburger, and running a dozen errands all over town, but she did have time to herself—time to windowshop and daydream. Those few hours out of the apartment, tiring as they were, somehow reenergized her for the week.

She kicked the door closed behind her and snapped on the light.   Then she glanced over to the long blank wall opposite the picture window and dropped the groceries at her feet.

Gone.   The tank, the cabinet, Nemo.   Nothing but a depressed and lighter rectangle of rug.   They had taken him.   They had come on a weekend and they had taken him away.

The small red rubber ball that had been nestled in the top of one of the grocery bags rolled into the empty space.   The other bag was slowly staining with broken eggs.   Gasping, she left the groceries where they lay and went into the kitchen. She knew Jeff would hardly have moved everything into the other room, but she allowed herself a few seconds of hope.

On the kitchen table, strategically displayed, was an expensive set of Havilland bone china with a striking red pattern.   It was one of the things she had once told Jeff she dreamed of having one day, when he was a successful lawyer and they had a house of their own.

There was a note on one of the saucers.   Before she had picked it up in her trembling hand to read, she had recognized Jeff's scrawl:

Dearest:
I thought it would be easier for you if we did it this way.   Everything went very smoothly, and Nemo was just fine.   Will bring home a steak and a bottle for supper.

Love, Jeff.

It was a very large set of china.   It took the sobbing young woman a long time to smash every piece.

Mary Ann pressed her palms and her nose to the picture window of the Malones' new house and studied without much interest the flora and fauna of Chicago suburbia.   There was not really all that much to see.   The ranch style homes, evenly spaced on smoothly paved streets, challenged the eye to find anything out of place or out of the ordinary.   The houses were all very nice.   The second cars parked in the driveways next to the houses were all very nice.   And the people who lived in the houses and drove the cars were all very nice.

In the two years since they had left the West Coast and moved to the Midwest, Mary Ann had met a lot of nice people and had been invited into a lot of nice homes.   Jeff was doing well in the firm, and bringing new and influential friends home almost every week "to meet the Mrs. and shoot the breeze."   And all those couples Jeff expected her to charm were just like Celia and Wally Hunt.   In ten or twenty years, she told herself, she and Jeff would evolve into Celia and Wally Hunt themselves.   Nobody asks this fish how things look from her side of the glass, Mary Ann thought.   Nobody.

She let her memory replay the argument she and Jeff had had the night before. She wanted to go back to school.   She wanted to go back to work.   She wanted to do anything that would make her something more than his cook, his housekeeper, and his houri.   And Jeff liked things just the way they were.

Then, that next morning, he had suggested a compromise.   Over coffee, he had talked about having "a real baby."   "To give you something to do," he had said. "To keep you company during the day."

And she had thrown everything at him that wasn't nailed down.   She was not going to be bought off this time, she had screamed at him.   He was an insensitive moron, unqualified for fatherhood.   He had sold their first baby; what was to say he would not do it again?

Somewhere in the midst of all that, Jeff had mumbled some kind of apology and ducked out of the house, coffee dripping from his tie.

By midafternoon, she had the kitchen straightened out, her face put back together, and her mind made up.   She knew now what she had to do, and she would do it. Jeff would probably not understand, but she had tried to get her message across in the note now taped to the refrigerator.

As she watched out the window, a battered yellow cab pulled into the driveway. She picked up her suitcase and her pocketbook and went outside.

Mrs. Danis's hazel eyes twinkled at the young woman waiting for her in her office.   "Sorry to keep you waiting, Mrs. Malone.   I swear I spend half my time on the phone."

"I hope I haven't taken you away from something important," said Mary Ann.

"They don't let me do anything important anymore," Mrs. Danis told her. She sat down behind her cluttered desk and tucked a stray brown hair back into the loose bun on top of her head.   "Coffee?" she asked.

"No, thank you.   I really don't want to take up much of your time.   I've just come to ask you a few questions, that's all."   Mary Ann found it difficult to think of Mrs. Danis as one of the key scientists working at the Institute.   The ratty green sweater and the faded jeans, although practical attire considering her role as "principal" of the Sea School, did not help to remind an observer of her prestige.   And the string of pearls bobbing on the outside of the old sweater gave the fortyish woman an air of unsettling eccentricity.

"Well, ask away," said Mrs. Danis.   "It's part of my job."   She reached out a rough-skinned hand and drew back the curtains from her office window.   Beyond, a large pool swarmed with half-grown Sea Farmers, supervised by a trio of frowning behaviorists.

"I'm amazed at how fast they grow," Mary Ann commented.

"Yes.   It seems like no time at all from when we get them to when we send them off.   I guess that's true in a lot of situations.   Did Dr. Hargen give you the tour?"

"Yes.   He was very considerate.   I had no idea this place was so large.   There are so many."

Neither woman said anything for a few moments.

"Well, now," Mrs. Danis began cheerfully. "I suppose you're interested in what became of your little fellow."

Mary Ann tried to hide her surprise. "Why, yes; I am. Do you remember him? He had brown markings on his back and a . . ."

"Mrs. Malone." Mrs. Danis interrupted patiently. "We deliberately do not keep records of where our pupils come from. You must know why. Besides, we handle thousands now. Their markings change as they grow older. We couldn't locate him for you if we tried. I'm sorry; I thought you knew."

"Oh," was all Mary Ann could say.

"You say he came to us about two years ago—is that correct?"

"Oh, did I? I don't remember. I mean, yes; two years ago this month."

Mrs. Danis shuffled some papers and nodded agreement with whatever she had read. "Was he a very active fellow? He might have been graduated with last month's class."

Mary Ann managed a sad smile at the memory. "Yes. And he was very good with his hands."

"Then he probably went to the Vancouver beds. Most of our best ones have gone there recently. It won't be long before we have the entire Sound under cultivation."

"Are you sure that's where he is?"

"No, I can't be positive. But that's the most likely place he'd be. Not that you'd be able to recognize him, you understand. Or that you could find him, for that matter."

Mary Ann's chin trembled in an attempted show of determination. "I think I could recognize my own son. I just . . . I just wanted to see him one more time. You see, I never got the chance to say goodbye to him. I never got the chance to explain."

"I'm sure he understands," Mrs. Danis said gently. "He's got a new life now. And lots of new friends. Listen: it's four o'clock now. Why don't you come home with me for a drink and one of my husband's fantastic dinners? Then we can talk this over the way we should."

"Thank you anyway," Mary Ann said, rising. "I want to thank you for your time." She whirled out the door before Mrs. Danis could say another word.

The five o'clock ferry from Seattle was crowded with cars and bored commuters. What few tourists were aboard could be detected by their presence at the rails, leaning over for a better view of the Sea Farms below.

Mary Ann peered down through the blue-green water, her mind caught up in its own turbulence. The bright red rubber ball bulging out her pocket still wore its price sticker.

Perhaps if one of the Sea Farmers had not looked up with a curiosity of his own, she would not have tried to act on the impulse that had momentarily overtaken her imagination.

She had one shoeless foot up on the rail when a hand reached out and took her by the arm and a gentle voice said, "No."

*   *   *

"Thank you for stopping me from doing something foolish," Mary Ann said simply. "I'm glad you followed me."

Mrs. Danis's hazel eyes twinkled. "I knew what you might do the first minute we talked, Mary. Having just talked with Jeff on the phone, I had already started to worry about you. I've seen the look you had in your eyes before."

"You have?"

"Mary, did you think you were the first woman who's felt the way you do? Or that you'll be the last? Whatever we give life to gives life back to us. We don't give up that life without losing some of our own. It would have been unnatural if you had not loved your son. You give psychologists and hypnotherapists far too much credit. Oh, yes; I've seen that look before. The first time I saw it was in the mirror."

Mary Ann gaped. "You?"

Mrs. Danis nodded proudly. "I have five sons somewhere beneath the waves. I loved every one of them, and I cried when every one of them had to leave.

"But I'm grateful for what I've had. I think of them as strong, successful, handsome young men, doing what every mother hopes her children will do: make the future possible. I like to think of them as oceanographers' assistants, or as foremen at the offshore oil rigs, or as . . ." She held out her necklace, then took it off and put it around Mary Ann's neck. "Pearl harvesters."

"But do they ride dolphins?" Mary Ann murmured wistfully.

"Mmn? What's that? Oh, yes; they do. The younger ones, anyway. They're not supposed to, but the dolphins love it. And you know how little boys are."

STEPHEN GOLDIN

When There's No Man Around

"**S**andrust!" Lucy Stargos said exasperatedly as she kicked the unfeeling machine for the third time. Neither her ejaculation nor her kick did any good, however. The sand tractor still refused to start.

Outside the insulated tractor dome, the Martian night pressed in with cold fixedness and the stars stared down unabashed, the Martian atmosphere being too thin to work up so much as a legitimate twinkle. Phobos and Deimos were both up, doing their feeble part to illuminate the night Marsscape. And in front of the tractor rose the seven-meter crater wall that the vehicle had stalled on while trying to climb it.

Inside the dome, Lucy paced about as best she could. There wasn't much room for pacing, despite the fact that Martian sand tractors were made to be self-contained units, complete with heating, lighting, and food and water dispensers. They had to be—the Martian climate was quite inhospitable to human endurance. A person with an oxygen mask and an electrically heated suit could survive outside in a Martian night for maybe an hour or more; but the Marsmen had developed a phobia of the "Outside." No Marsman would leave a tractor dome except under the direst of emergencies.

Lucy was beginning to consider this a dire emergency. She had a vision of how her father would react. He would tower sixteen feet above her head, perched regally upon his Olympus of parental authority. "Well, young lady, what have you got to say for yourself?" The lightning of divine wrath would flash from his eyes, and small beadlets of thunder would drop from his brow. He would glower a small marsquake at her, and when she didn't say anything he would continue, "I was against letting you have the tractor in the first place. Your mother talked me into it. Personally, I don't think a girl your age should be allowed to go outside the city at night. Especially just to visit that boyfriend of yours. From now on, I smite you with the curse that you're not to go driving unless there's somebody responsible along with you. Understand?" And the specter departed in a flourish of hautboys.

"It's all your fault," Lucy said to the tractor. "What have you got against me, anyhow?"

The tractor merely sat there and politely refused to comment.

"Look, I've got to get back to Syrtis in an hour, or Daddy'll kill me. Come on, now, be a nice tractor and start." She pressed the ignition button again. The motor whirred encouragingly. "Come on, baby," she coaxed it. "Come on." The motor coughed, turned over—and died.

"Darn you!" she screamed at the machine. "Why don't you cooperate?"

The tractor, perhaps unable to think of an excuse, did not answer.

It wouldn't be so bad, Lucy mused, if this had happened on the main road. There was lots of traffic there, and she would easily have been able to find someone to help her. But she had forgotten all about so trivial a thing as time when she was with Jerry, until she'd realized that it was much too late to get home by the time her father had insisted on. "Don't worry," Jerry had said, and the wise patience of the gods had beamed through his Adonis-like face. Then he had presented her with two stone tablets, and inscribed in the living rock were the laws of the Universe. "There is an ancient, secret path that'll get you back in half the time," he went on. "Of course, it's a little bit out of the way. . . ."

A *little bit* out of the way! She had never seen such completely deserted land in all her life. She might as well be at the North Pole for all the help she could expect to get here. Darn Jerry and his silly shortcuts!

Should she try walking? The trouble was, she did not know how far she was from Syrtis. The tractor's odometer read nine hundred and ninety-nine kilometers. It had read nine hundred and ninety-nine kilometers when she'd left Roperston. In fact, for as long as she could remember, it had always read nine hundred and ninety-nine kilometers. The tractor, with characteristic cowardice, was obviously afraid to turn to an even thousand.

She glanced at the outside temperature thermometer. Minus 30° C. No thank you, no walks tonight. She had heard too many stories of people freezing to death trying to walk long distances instead of waiting calmly back at their tractors. That was one reason why the tractor domes were so self-sufficient.

She could see the headlines that would have blazoned forth tomorrow: GIRL FREEZES ATTEMPTING WALK TO SYRTIS.

No, make that **PRETTY GIRL FREEZES ATTEMPTING WALK TO SYRTIS.**

Or better yet,

NOBLE PRETTY GIRL FREEZES ATTEMPTING WALK TO SYRTIS TO SATISFY FATHER'S ARBITRARY DEMAND THAT SHE BE HOME BY MIDNIGHT.

"I guess I'm stuck with you," she informed the tractor. She realized, after she said it, the double meaning of "stuck," but she was too worried to groan at her own involuntary pun. "Please start this time."

She pressed the ignition button. The motor made a half-hearted attempt, then gave up completely. "You really want Daddy to kill me, don't you. You won't be satisfied until I'm lying there on the living room floor with my skull bashed in and my blood dripping onto the tile in a messy red puddle. But don't forget, that'll make you an accessory to murder. They'll come and take you away to the Home for Wayward Tractors and you'll spend the rest of your days pulling a plow in a cucumber patch.''

A thought occurred to her. "I know what. I'll look in the instruction manual, that's what I'll do. That'll fix you.'' If the tractor was intimidated, however, it hid its fear bravely behind stone silence.

She fished the manual out of the map compartment and skimmed to the appropriate passage. " 'If your tractor should by some chance stall,' " she read aloud, " 'it is probably due to a flooding of the gas line. Wait five to ten minutes for the fuel concentration to return to normal, then try the ignition again.' See there, Buster? I've got your number now. Thought you could put one over on ol' Tailspin Lucy Stargos, did you?'' she gloated.

To make extra sure, she waited a full fifteen minutes, sucking nervously on a food bar from the dispenser all the while. Finally, when she could take the strain no longer, she pressed the ignition button one more time. There was a discouraging whine, sputter, cough . . . then nothing.

"Darn you!'' she shrieked. "I know your type. You just want to lure a pretty, helpless girl out into the middle of nowhere so you can take advantage of her. But I'm not the sort of girl who gives in that easily. You've got a fight on your hands when you mess with me.''

She wondered whether she should put her headlights back on and hope that somebody passing nearby would see the glare. But the chances were against anybody passing this deserted spot (darn Jerry!). And anyway, the Martian atmosphere was so thin that it carried glare almost not at all. Even the light from a big city like Syrtis could be lost in the glare of tiny Phobos once you got a hill or two between yourself and the town. In order to see her lights, a person would have to be inside the crater with her, in which case they'd see her anyway. Better not to put a strain on the battery.

"The problem with you,'' she psychoanalyzed to the tractor, "is that you're ungrateful. I've always taken care of you. Remember when Willie the Creep wanted to race and I told him no, that I had to keep you in good condition? And now, when I need you, this is the thanks I get. Is that fair?''

The tractor looked guilty, but said nothing.

"But my mercy is infinite,'' she continued with a self-reverent smile. "I'll tell you what I'll do. If you start for me right now, I'll never drive you over twelve kilometers an hour, I'll scrub you down every week, and I'll keep your dome polished like the Universe has never seen. I give you this as my Word, an eternal covenant between us. Is it a deal?'' She thumbed the starter.

It was, apparently, not a deal.

Lucy picked up the instruction manual again and turned to the "Repairs'' section. " 'Your Carlisle A-7 Sand Tractor will probably not need any repairs for several years, as it is built with the finest . . .' " She skipped down a paragraph. " 'At the first sign of trouble, take the tractor to an authorized repair shop only. *Caution:* any repairs made by a non-authorized shop will invalidate the warranty.' '' Since the warranty had lapsed six months ago, this was no great problem. But it was also no great help.

"Well," she said, turning back to the stubborn machine, "do *you* know of any authorized repair shops around here?"

The tractor's silence confessed ignorance.

"Neither do I. So if you don't start this time, Carlisle, I'm going to take you apart myself. Me, old Butterfingers Stargos, who flunked Tinkertoys in kindergarten. So if you want to stay in the condition God intended for you, you'd better work now." The tractor ignored her threat and obstinately refused to start. "So be it," Lucy grunted.

Again owing to the Marsmen's dislike of the Outside, the motor of a Martian sand tractor is made to be accessible from the passenger dome. Removing the plate that covered the engine, Lucy sat down and stared at her foe face-to-face for the first time. The sight of the wires and filters, carburetor and camshaft, sparkplugs and battery was dismaying, but she resolved not to show her doubts. "I'll give you one last chance to reason this thing out," she said. "Don't you want to get back safe and sound into your nice warm garage, instead of sitting out here at thirty below? I promise that, first thing tomorrow, I'll have you looked at by the best mechanic on Mars. It'll set me back three months' allowance, but I'll do it 'cause I'm basically a nice guy. How about it?"

The haughty motor did not deign to reply.

"Okay, Carlisle, I've gone easy on you so far because I wanted to save us both a lot of trouble. But I can see now that I've been wasting my time—all you understand is sheer brute force. You were built by human beings, right?"

The machine was noncommittal.

"Okay, what one human being can build, another can fix. I am going to vivisect you, my dear Carlisle, until I find out what's wrong. What do you say to that?"

The shocked motor was speechless.

And still Lucy hesitated. She had not the faintest idea of how to take an engine apart, let alone put it together again. But the motor stared back at her defiantly, and she knew that she couldn't let herself be bluffed down.

There was one wire toward the back that looked as though it might have come loose. She reached in to tighten it—

ZZZZSST.

She pulled her hand back sharply and bumped her elbow on a seat. "Damn!" she screamed, then looked around involuntarily to make sure that no one had heard her unladylike expletive.

"So that's how you're going to play it!" she shrieked at the machine, which seemed to be smirking. "All right, from now on it's no more Miss Nice Guy. If you want war, that's what you'll get. Starraker Stargos rides again!"

She tore into the hapless motor with a vengeance. Wires, sparkplugs, battery caps, filter covers, and anything else that was the slightest bit loose yielded before her furious assault. Within minutes, she was surrounded by her captured booty, and she smiled triumphantly at the once-proud engine, now denuded and humble. "That'll teach you," she declared with finality.

Her moment of glory was short-lived, however, as she came to the realization that she was no better off than she'd been before. Worse, in fact, since she wasn't at all sure how to put things back together again. She glowered at the motor and said through gritted teeth, "You tricked me!"

She stole a glance at the clock on the dashboard. Eleven-thirty. Only half an hour now separated her from the Moment of Paternal Doom. And here she sat in a useless sand tractor in the middle of a cold Martian night, probably millions of kilometers from anywhere, with no possible chance of rescue.

"Doomed," she intoned, with all the melodramatics of her junior-grade drama class at her disposal. "Doomed to die alone and unloved in an alien desert. Sent here to perish by my witless lover, spurned by my arrogant father, failed even by my faithful Carlisle A-7 Sand Tractor. In a little while it shall all be over. Thirst will dry my mouth and crack my lips. Hunger will shrivel my stomach. I will lie here, parched and famished, until all life escapes me. And the flesh will rot on my bones, and the air in this dome will be filled with the malodorous stench of decomposing carrion. And when my body is finally discovered, a century from now, they will know who I am by my tarnished and faded ID bracelet. They will wail and bemoan my fate, that I died so young without tasting the succulent fruits of life, and they'll sing songs of mourning and compose ballads of sadness for this pathetic creature who dies here today." With remarkable control of her tear ducts, she let fall a single saline drop from her right eye.

Then, in this hour of her greatest trial, she remembered what her mother had told her many years ago when the toaster blew up. "Life is not easy for a woman, Lucy. There are always men, poor darlings, to be looked after, or they're sure to be in some kind of trouble. But even worse is that insidious creation of man— Machine. There is the real enemy, don't ever forget it. The war between Machine and Womankind is ages old, and will end only with the extermination of one or the other of the species. But in this struggle, we have one Weapon that has never failed us." And she had proceeded to demonstrate by fixing the toaster unassisted in a matter of minutes.

Lucy sighed. The time had indeed come for the Ultimate Weapon. Reaching up into her hair, she pulled out a bobby pin. . . .

Ten minutes later, the job was done. Lucy Stargos replaced the engine cover and faced the dashboard. Sweat was gathering on her palms, and she wiped them nervously on her blouse. The moment of truth had arrived. Long-dead generations of women peered over her shoulder hopefully as she gently caressed the ignition button like a reluctant lover. Until at last she could stand the suspense no longer and pushed it eagerly.

The tractor, defeated at last, hummed to life. Lucy squealed with pure joy at the thought that, once again, Woman had triumphed over Machine. Those long-dead watchers sighed with relief and returned to their other pursuits.

"Onward, Carlisle," Lucy said, cracking an imaginary whip.   "Onward and upward."   As the tractor surged ahead, Lucy looked at the dashboard clock. Fifteen minutes to go.   If she drove at top speed, she might not be too late.   With any luck . . .

She topped the rim of the crater and saw the lights of Syrtis glaring mockingly at her barely a thousand meters away.

Lucy Stargos's next reaction was far from ladylike.

JACK C. HALDEMAN II

Longshot

"**H**ot tip? Humph! A sure thing? I don't want to hear about it."
The spacer slammed his drink on the bar and looked the robot bartender right in
the electronic eye. "I've been from one side of this universe to the other and if
I haven't learned anything else, I've learned that there's no such thing as a sure
thing."

The bartender whirred and polished another glass.

"Sure I've played the ponies. I've been around. Nags on Old Earth, Bat Flies
on Medi IV, Fuzzies on Niven—I've played them all, money on the nose. Was
a time you couldn't keep me away from the tracks. Not anymore. I learned my
lesson, but good. How 'bout another? A double."

The robot swallowed the empty glass, produced a full one. He sighed deep in
his gearworks, afraid that this was going to be another burned-out spacer with a
tale to tell.

It was.

The spacer's name was Terry Freeland, although everybody called him Crash,
and his story was bound to be a tale of woe. Judging from the stubble on his face
and the condition of his clothes, he hadn't lifted ship in a long time. Besides, if
he had any money he wouldn't be drinking in a dump like this.

Except for a run of bad luck, thought the robot, *I wouldn't be pulling beers in
a place like this, either.* Still, it beat pumping gas.

"It was on Dimian. You know Dimian? Out in the Rigel sector?" asked
Crash, sipping his drink.

The robot nodded. He knew Dimian. A real backwater planet.

"Well, I was landing at the spaceport at Chingo. They got a lot of nerve calling
it a spaceport, buncha gravel out in the middle of nowhere. Only two bars in the
whole of Chingo, and it's the biggest town on Dimian. Some spaceport. Anyway,
I was hauling a load of Venusian lettuce mold hoping to swing a big deal for some
dutrinium. Wheeling and dealing, that's my game. Those sentients on Dimian
really get off on lettuce mold. So I was coming in for a landing, you know,
and . . . hey, I don't know what you've heard about me, but it ain't true I make
a habit of bustin' up ships. Just had a few hard landings and a little bad luck,
that's all. Like that time. They said I was drunk, but I say their null-field wasn't
working right. Sure I'd had a shot or two while I was hanging in orbit, but that

don't mean nothing. Do it all the time. Came down a little hard, that's all. Bent a stabilizer. Crunched a couple of scouts, but they were parked where they shouldn't 'a been. Anyway . . .''

It was looking to be a near total loss. They were overstocked on lettuce mold and Crash's profits didn't amount to much more than it took to fix the stabilizer and the two scouts. He hadn't been able to carry insurance since that time on Waycross, so everything was out-of-pocket. Still, he'd managed to pick up a load of dutrinium dirt cheap and if they'd ever finish fixing the stabilizer, maybe he'd be able to unload it on some other planet for big bucks.

He was always looking for big bucks. That's why he went to the track. That's why he listened to Whisky John. It was a mistake. Nobody listened to Whisky John. Nobody with any sense, that is.

Whisky John was born bad news.

"I tell you, it can't miss," said Whisky John. "These yo-yos don't know the first thing about handicapping."

"You mean they actually race these monsters?"

"Sure. That's the whole idea. These Dimians don't know nothing. They work 'em in the field till they get too old to cut the mustard, then they turn 'em loose on the track. These Dimians are crazy wild about betting. Most only thing to do around here."

"So where's the edge?" asked Crash.

"What you do is find one that's been out in the field a long time but hasn't done much work. He may be old, but he'll probably have a few kilometers left in him. I got it straight from B'rrax, a stableboy who sweeps out the stalls, that the sleeper of the year is going to be Heller."

"Heller?"

"That's the one. Eighty-five years old and getting pretty long in the tooth. But he was owned by National and they don't do much dredging, so he's had an easy life. He's the longshot. Two hundred to one. *Two hundred to one!*"

Crash cast a doubtful eye over the field. Monsters they were, too. The natives called them something unpronounceable that was roughly translated as "behemoths." It was an understatement. They looked like three elephants piled one on top of another. Had about as many legs, too. Thirty meters high and Lord knows what they weighed. Crash figured they could dredge pretty good, but he had a hard time imagining them racing around a track.

"Two hundred to one, you say? Eighty-five years old?"

"A sure thing. You can't lose."

"If you're so smart, how come you ain't rich?" asked Crash.

"Bad luck and hard times," said Whisky John wistfully. "I've had more than my share of both. Believe me, if I had any cash I'd put it right on the beast's, er, nose. Had to let you in on this. Figure I owe you one from that time on Farbly." He winked and Crash blushed. It had been close on Farbly, that's for sure. They'd been lucky to get out at all.

"I don't know," said Crash.

"How much you got? Cash."

"Free and clear? Let me see, after the stabilizer, uh . . . about 500 creds."

"Think about it. One hundred thousand creds! Free and clear. No taxes on Dimian. You could get a bigger cruiser, anything. Think about it."

Crash thought about it and the more he thought about it the better it seemed. It was all the cash he had and if he lost it he'd have to eat peanut butter crackers till he dumped the dutrinium. But still—*One Hundred Thousand Creds!*

He placed the bet.

Together they climbed into the stands; tall, rickety old wooden bleachers a good half click from the track. There were a few off-worlders scattered through the crowd, even a couple more humans, but mostly it was wall-to-wall Dimians. Whisky John was right about one thing—Dimians were sure crazy wild about behemoth racing.

Crash didn't know much about the Dimians, except that he thought they were weird. They probably thought Crash was weird, too. They looked like crickets, were about a meter tall, and talked in a high, squeaking rasp that Crash couldn't understand. Whisky John could speak it a little on account of his being marooned on Dimian for a good many years waiting for his ship to come in. Every time he got a few creds ahead, he'd blow it away with some crazy scheme. Whisky John was a mite irresponsible.

Down on the track, several Dimians were herding the behemoths towards the starting line. Crash noted with pleasure that Heller was still listed on the tote board at 200-1.

The Dimians moved the beasts along with huge prods, never getting closer to one than necessary. Crash didn't blame them, they were dwarfed by the massive animals. Looked like mountains being led around by small bugs. Hairy mountains.

"Where are the jockeys?" asked Crash.

"What jockeys? You couldn't pay a Dimian enough to climb on top of one of those monsters," replied Whisky John.

"How do they get around the track?"

"Sometimes they don't. When that starting gun goes off they go where they damn well please. Mostly they head around the track, though, since that's the way they're pointing at the beginning. They ain't too smart."

"Which one's Heller? I can't make out the numbers."

"It's easy to tell. He's the one on the left."

"No!"

"Yes."

If behemoths were mountains, Heller was a mountain with rickets. Most of his hair had fallen out. He was a mountain with a bad case of the mange. Half his legs didn't look like they worked right. Where the others had gleaming tusks, Heller had rotten stumps. Where the others had blazing eyes, Heller had sad, dull orbs. He had loser written all over him.

"You mean my money's on *that?*"

"Smart money, too. You can't tell a book by its cover, I always say. He can still hit the fast ball, probably tear the track apart.'' Whisky John was an incurable optimist, especially with other people's money.

"He's blind as a bat. He can't walk. He looks like he's a hundred years old.''

"Eighty-five,'' corrected Whisky John.

"If he's eighty-five, how old are the others?''

"Average out about thirty, I reckon. That's good for an old behemoth. But remember he's two hundred to one. He's had an easy life.''

"Easy life? He looks like a hundred miles of bad road.'' Crash was trying to figure out if he had time to strangle Whisky John and still run down to get his money back before the race started.

He was too late. The race started.

Crash could tell the race started because the Dimians in the crowd went wild, screaming and jumping up and down. It was harder to tell by looking at the behemoths, though, because they just seemed to be wandering aimlessly around, bumping into each other.

"This is a race?''

"Exciting, isn't it?'' said Whisky John.

Three of the behemoths started lurching more or less down the track and the spectators went wild. Some of the others followed the leaders, including, to Crash's surprise, Heller. He wasn't last, either. Not if you counted the two behemoths that had fallen down and the one that was going the wrong way. Crash felt a faint hope rising.

"Come on, Heller,'' he shouted in desperation, pounding Whisky John on the shoulder.

It soon became apparent why the stands were so far from the track. Once the behemoths started, they went any old which way and didn't stop for anything. Unless, of course, they fell down. They were very good at falling down. They were better at falling down than running. Each time one toppled over, the ground shook. One had crashed through the fence around the track and was wandering out into the desert. Heller was in fourth place and losing ground rapidly.

He had to win or it was peanut butter crackers for Crash. Lots of peanut butter crackers.

The track was a jumble of lurching, tottering behemoths. Half of them had fallen down. The falling down part was easy, but the getting up was hard. Some of them just fell asleep after they flopped, only to be woken up by another one stumbling into them. They were the clumsiest animals Crash had ever seen. The lead behemoth got his legs all tangled up and went down in a heap. The second-place one tripped over him. Suddenly everything had changed. Heller was in second place, straining for the lead.

"Atta boy,'' shouted Crash, pounding Whisky John's arm some more. "You can do it.''

They were lumbering down the home stretch now, neck and, er, neck, their bodies swaying with each ponderous step.

"Don't fall down, Heller. Don't fall down!'' Crash's heart was pounding furiously. So was his hand and Whisky John's arm was getting mighty sore.

As they approached the checkered flag, Heller was a tusk behind and giving it all he had. Just before the finish line, however, a gleam came into those eyes that had been dull so many years. Something stirred deep in the beast's massive chest. *Pride! Glory!* He straightened his bent back. He rose up on his crippled legs. He gave a mighty leap forward. *Victory!*

Crash about died.

Two hundred to one. He was already spending his money. Whisky John's arm felt like a chinaberry tree hosting a woodpecker convention.

They went to collect the money. Whisky John did the talking. They handed him a large paper bag full of cred-slips and a huge coil of rope. Whisky John looked pale.

"I swear, Crash, I didn't know." He had sick written all over his face.

"Know what? That's the money, right?"

"Right. One hundred thousand creds. It's all here. But I swear I didn't know, honest."

"We got the money, so what's to worry about? Let's go."

"It's not that easy, Crash."

"What do you mean? We just walk out and it's party time."

"See this rope, Crash?"

"Yeah. Nice rope. Let's go."

"This rope is for your behemoth."

"My *what?*"

"Your behemoth. Heller. He's yours. It was a claims race—I swear I didn't know—you just won the money *and* the behemoth, every metric ton of him."

"I won't do it. I'll leave him. Let's go." Crash was having none of this. He wanted to start spending his money.

"You can't just abandon him, Crash. He belongs to you now, at least as far as the Dimians see it. They won't stand for it. Behemoth racing is part of their religion and they take it seriously. If you dump Heller they'll kill you."

"Kill me?"

"Tear you limb from limb."

Gulp. Crash could see this was a serious matter. They walked over to the paddock area where several Dimians were washing down the behemoths with large hoses.

"I guess I could race him some more," said Crash doubtfully. "He probably has a few laps left in him. Maybe even make some money out of it."

"That's it, Crash. Hey, I'll be running along."

"You stay right here."

They looked up at Heller. He was panting at a ferocious rate. He looked terrible close up.

"What does he eat?"

"Volmer sprouts. Only the tender ones. About 10 kilos a day."

"Expensive?"

Whisky John nodded.

"Maybe I can sell him."

"That's it. Sell him. Good idea. I guess I'll be—"

Crash froze him with a stare.

"He doesn't look all that bad," lied Crash, trying to make the best out of a rotten situation. He walked towards the towering beast. "Probably lots of people out there would want a winner like him." He stood directly under Heller, looked up at his chin.

"Don't touch him!" cried Whisky John.

Crash patted Heller's massive toe, looked back over his shoulder. "What?" he asked.

Too late.

Heller rolled his eyes and swished his tail. He moaned with the sound of a thousand breaking hearts.

"Oh Lord," said Whisky John. "Now you've done it. A Love Bond."

"A what?" Heller leaned down and licked Crash on the side of the head. It sent him reeling.

"If you touch a behemoth they fall in love with you. Instantly and forever. It's called a Love Bond and there's no getting out of it. It's the peak of the Dimian's religious experience. If you tried to sell him now . . ."

"I know, they'd kill me."

"Limb from limb," added Whisky John with a serious shake of his head. "You are stuck for life."

Crash could see that Heller loved him. Love just oozed from every pore on the poor animal's massive body. He rolled his eyes with love. He waved his trunk with love. He made soul-wrenching groans of love. It was a pitiful sight. Crash felt sorry for the beast.

"He is kinda cute, at that," said Crash. "A fella could get to like him."

They tied the rope around Heller's neck and led him away. The rope was unnecessary; he followed Crash like a giant puppy dog.

Unfortunately, he made a very clumsy puppy dog. He stepped on a grocery wagon, squashed it flat. Crash dug a handful of creds out of the paper bag. He sideswiped an aircar. Crash dug into the bag. He wiped out ten light poles and three traffic lights. Crash dug into his bag and led him out of town.

On the edge of the desert, out of harm's way, Crash sat on a rock and surveyed the problem. He still had a lot of money. Money could simplify any situation. He was beginning to like Heller.

"You know," he said to the behemoth, "you and I could go places together. Do things."

He sat on the rock and talked to Heller for hours, making plans for the future, spinning dream castles that involved lots of Volmer sprouts and won races. Whisky John counted the money out into little piles on the sand. Heller stood and wheezed a lot. The sun fell low on the horizon.

So total was Heller's love for Crash that it must have been contagious. Or maybe it was the wine Crash was drinking. Anyway, the spacer was so overcome by emotion that he climbed a tree and gave Heller a kiss on the nose.

It was too much for poor old Heller. His heart couldn't stand so much happiness.   He smiled a huge lovesick grin, moaned, and fell over dead.

The ground shook.   Crash was heartbroken.   He had come to love Heller nearly .
as much as Heller had loved him.

"What am I going to do?" cried Crash.

"Bury him."

"How am I going to go on without him?" wailed Crash.

"You got to bury him," said Whisky John, taking a slosh of the wine bottle.
"All very clear."

"What's very clear?" asked Crash, casting a suspicious eye towards the other
man.

"It's all Love Bond ritual.   Has to be done a certain way.   You dig the hole—
nobody can help you, got to do it yourself—right where he died.   Then you got
to get their magical men to come and do their stuff.   Then you got to put up a
monument, has to be a big one, too.   No skimping."

"Sounds expensive."

"A Love Bond is no simple thing."

"How much?"

"See that pile of money there?"   He pointed to the rest of the winnings and
Crash nodded.   "Kiss it goodbye."

"No way out?"

"They'd—"

"I know.   Limb from limb.   Hole alone'll take me a week to dig."

It took two.

Crash lifted off from Dimian broke as a clam.   He ate peanut butter crackers
for a long, long time.

"That's how it went," said Crash, setting his empty glass in front of the robot
bartender.   It was his tenth empty glass.   "Learned my lesson."   He shook a
bent smoke from the crushed pack in his pocket.

The bartender whirred sympathetically.   This was one hardluck spacer.   He
wiped the counter with the bar rag.   Crash got shakily to his feet, headed for the
exit.

He paused at the door, turned towards the bartender.   "That was the fifth race,
you said, wasn't it?"

The robot nodded.   Good odds, too.

ISAAC ASIMOV

Nothing for Nothing

T he scene was Earth.

Not that the beings on the Starship thought of it as Earth. To them it was a series of symbols stored in a computer; it was the third planet of a star located at a certain position with respect to the line connecting their home planet with the black hole that marked the Galaxy's center, and moving at a certain velocity with reference to it.

The time was 15,000 B.C., more or less.

Not that the beings on the Starship thought of it as 15,000 B.C. To them it was a certain period of time marked off according to their local system.

The Captain of the Starship said, rather petulantly, "This is a waste of time. The planet is largely frozen. Let us leave."

But the Ship's Explorer quietly said, "No, Captain," and that was that.

As long as a Starship was in space, or in hyperspace for that matter, the Captain was supreme; but place that ship in orbit about a planet and the Explorer could not be challenged. He knew worlds! That was his specialty.

And this Explorer was in an impregnable position. He had what amounted to a sure instinct for profitable trade. It had been he and he alone who was responsible for the fact that this particular Starship had won three Awards for Excellence for the work done in the three last expeditions. Three for three.

So when the Explorer said, "No," the Captain could not dream of "Yes." In the unlikely case that he would have dreamed of it, the crew would have mutinied. An Award for Excellence might be, to the captain, a pleasant spectral disk to suspend in the main salon; but to the crew it meant a spectacular addition to take-home pay and an even more welcome addition to vacation time and pension benefits. And this Explorer had brought them that three times. Three for three.

The Explorer said, "No strange world should be left unexamined."

The Captain said, "What is strange about this one?"

"The preliminary probe shows intelligence, and on a frozen world."

"Surely that's not unprecedented."

"The pattern here is strange." The Explorer looked uneasy. "I am not sure exactly how or exactly why, but the pattern of life and of intelligence is strange. We must examine it more carefully."

And that was that, of course. There were at least half a trillion planetary worlds in the Galaxy, if one only counted those associated with stars.   Add to that the indefinite number moving independently through space and the number might be ten times as great.

Even with computers to help, no Starship could know them all; but an experienced Explorer, by dint of lacking interest in anything else, of studying every exploratory report published, of considering endless correlations, and—presumably—playing with statistics even in his sleep, grew to have what seemed to others a mystical intuition about such things.

"We'll have to send out probes in full interlocking program," said the Explorer.

The Captain looked outraged.   Full power meant a leisurely examination for weeks at enormous expense.

He said, and it was as much as he could offer in the way of objection, "Is that absolutely necessary?"

"I rather think so," said the Explorer with the diffidence of one who knows his whim is law.

The probes brought back exactly what the Captain expected, and in great detail. An intelligent species rather reminiscent, at least as far as superficial appearance went, of the lesser breeds of the inner proximal regions of the fifth arm of the Galaxy—not quite unusual, but of interest to mentologists, no doubt.

As yet the intelligent species was only at the first level of technology—long, long removed from anything useful.

The Captain said so, scarcely able to mask his exasperation; but the Explorer, leafing through the reports, remained unmoved.   He said, "Strange!" and asked that the Trader be summoned.

This was really too much.   A successful Captain must never give a good Explorer cause for unhappiness but there are limits to everything.

The Captain said, fighting to keep the level of communication polite, if not friendly, "To what end, Explorer?   What can we expect at this level?"

"They have tools," said the Explorer thoughtfully.

"Stone!   Bone!   Wood!   Or this planet's equivalent of that.   And that's all. Surely we can find nothing in that."

"And yet there is something strange in the pattern."

"May I know what that might be, Explorer?"

"If I knew what it might be, Captain, it would not be strange, and I would not have to find out.   Really, Captain, I must insist on the Trader."

The Trader was as indignant as the Captain was, and had more scope to express it.   His, after all, was a specialty as deep as that of anyone's on the Starship; even, in his own opinion (and in some others'), as deep and as essential as the Explorer's.

The Captain might navigate a Starship and the Explorer might detect useful civilizations by the most tenuous of signs; but in the final clutch, it was the Trader and his team who faced the aliens and who plucked out of their minds and culture that which was useful and gave in return something *they* found useful.

And this was done at great risk.   The alien ecology must not be disrupted. Alien intelligences must not be harmed, not even to save one's own life.   There were good reasons for that on the cosmic scale and Traders were amply rewarded for the risks they ran, but why run *useless* risks.

The Trader said, "There is nothing there.   *My* interpretation of the probe's data is that we're dealing with semi-intelligent animals.   Their usefulness is nil.   Their danger is great.   We know how to deal with truly intelligent aliens, and Trader teams are rarely killed by them.   Who knows how these animals will react—and you know we are not allowed to defend ourselves properly."

The Explorer said, "These animals, if they are no more than that, have interestingly adapted themselves to the ice.   There are subtle variations in the pattern here I do not understand, but my considered opinion is that they will not be dangerous and that they may even be useful.   I feel they are worth closer examination."

"What can be gained from a Stone Age intelligence?" asked the Trader.

"That is for you to find out."

The Trader thought grimly: Of course, that is what it comes to—for *us* to find out.

He knew well the history and purpose of the Starship Expeditions.   There had been a time, a million years before, when there had been no Traders, Explorers, or Captains but only ancestral animals with developing mind and a Stone Age technology—much like the animals on the world they were now orbiting.   How slow the advance, how painfully slow the self-generated progress—until the third-level civilization had been reached.   Then had come the Starships and the chance of cross-fertilization of cultures.   *Then* had come progress.

The Trader said, "With respect, Explorer.   I grant your intuitional experience. Will you grant my practical experience, though it is less dramatic?   There is no way in which anything below a third-level civilization can have anything we can use."

"That," said the Explorer, "is a generalization that may or may not be true."

"With respect, Explorer.   It *is* true.   And even if those—those semi-animals had something we could use, and I can't imagine what it might be, what can we give them in exchange?"

The Explorer was silent.

The Trader went on.   "At this level, there is no way in which a proto-intelligence can accept an alien stimulation.   The mentologists are agreed on that and it is my experience, too.   Progress *must* be self-generated until at least the second-level is reached.   And we *must* make a return; we can take nothing for nothing."

The Captain said, "And that makes sense, of course.   By stimulating these intelligences to advance, we can harvest them again at a later visit."

"I don't care about the reason for it," said the Trader, impatiently.   "It is part of the tradition of my profession.   We do no harm under any conditions and we give in return for what we take.   Here there is nothing we will want to take; and even if we find something, there will be nothing that we can give in return. —We waste time."

The Explorer shook his head.   "I ask you to visit some center of population, Trader.   I will abide by your decision when you return."

And that was that, too.

For two days the small Trader module flashed over the surface of the planet searching for any evidence of a reasonable level of technology.   There was none.

A complete search could take years but was scarcely worth it.   It was unreasonable to suppose a high level would be hidden.   The highest technology was always flaunted for it had no enemy.   That was the universal experience of Traders everywhere.

It was a beautiful planet, half-frozen as it was.   White and blue and green. Wild and rough and variegated.   Crude and untouched.

But it was not the Trader's job to deal with beauty and he shrugged off such thoughts impatiently.   When his crew talked to him in such terms, he was short with them.

He said, "We'll land here.   It seems to be a good-sized concentration of the intelligences.   We can do no better."

His Second said, "What can we do with even these, Maestro?"

"You can record," said the Trader.   "Record the animals, both unintelligent and supposedly intelligent, and any artifacts of theirs we can find.   Make sure the records are thoroughly holographic."

"We can already see—" began the Second.

"We can already see," said the Trader, "but we must have a record to convince our Explorer out of his dreams or we'll remain here forever."

"He is a good Explorer," said one of the crew.

"He has been a good Explorer," said the Trader, "but does that mean he will be good forever?   His very successes have made him accept himself at too high an evaluation, perhaps.   So we must convince him of reality—if we can."

They wore their suits when they emerged from the module.

The planetary atmosphere would support them, but the feeling of exposure to the raw winds of an open planet would discommode them, even if the atmosphere and temperature were perfect—which they weren't.   The gravity was a touch high, as was the light level, but they could bear it.

The intelligent beings, dressed rather sketchily in the outer portions of other animals, retreated reluctantly at their approach and watched at a distance.   The Trader was relieved at this.   Any sign of non-belligerence was welcome to those who were not permitted to defend themselves.

The Trader and his crew did not try to communicate directly or to make friendly gestures.   Who knew what gesture might be considered friendly by an alien?   The Trader set up a mental field, instead, and saturated it with the vibrations of harmlessness and peace and hoped that the mental fields of the creatures were sufficiently advanced to respond.

Perhaps they were, for a few crept back and watched motionlessly as though intensely curious.   The Trader thought he detected fugitive thoughts—but that seemed unlikely for first-level beings and he did not follow them up.

Instead, he went stolidly about the business of making holographic reproductions of the vegetation, of a herd of blundering herbivores that appeared and then, deciding the surroundings were dangerous, thundered away.   A large animal stood its ground for a while, exposing white weapons in a cavity at its fore-end—then left.

The Trader's crew worked similarly, moving methodically across the landscape.

The call, directly mental, and surcharged with such emotion of surprise and awe that the informational content was all but blurred out, came unexpectedly.

"Maestro!   Here!   Come quickly!"

Specific directions were not given.   The Trader had to follow the beam, which led into a crevice bounded by two rocky outcroppings.

Other members of the crew were converging but the Trader had arrived first.

"What is it?" asked the Trader.

His Second was standing in the glow of his suit-radiation in a deeply hollowed-out portion of the hillside.

The Trader looked about.   "This is a natural hollow, not a technological product."

"Yes, but look!"

The Trader looked up and for perhaps five seconds he was lost.   Then he sent out a strenuous message for all others to stay away.

He said, "Is this of technological origin?"

"Yes, Maestro.   You can see it is only partly completed."

"But by whom?"

"By those creatures out there.   The intelligent ones.   I found one at work in here.   This is his light source; it was burning vegetation.   These are his tools."

"And where is he?"

"He fled."

"Did you actually see him?"

"I recorded him."

The Trader pondered.   Then he looked up again.   "Have you ever seen anything like this?"

"No, Maestro."

"Or heard of anything like this?"

"No, Maestro."

"Astonishing!"

The Trader showed no signs of wanting to withdraw his eyes, and the Second said, softly, "Maestro.   What do we do?"

"Eh?"

"This will surely win our ship still a fourth Prize."

"Surely," said the Trader, regretfully, "if we could take it."

The Second said, hesitantly, "I have already recorded it."

"Eh?   What is the use of that?   We have nothing to give in exchange."

"But we have this of theirs.   Give them *anything* in exchange."

The Trader said, "What are you *saying*?   They are too primitive to accept anything we could give them.   It will surely be nearly a million years before they could possibly accept suggestions of exogenous origin. —We will have to destroy the recording.''

"But we *know*, Maestro.''

"Then we must never talk about it.   Our craft has its ethics and its traditions. You know that.   Nothing for nothing!''

"Even this?''

"Even this.''

The Trader's sternly implacable set of expression was tinged with unbearable sorrow and despite his "Even this" he stood irresolute.

The Second sensed that.   He said, "*Try* giving them something, Maestro.''

"Of what use would that be?''

"Of what harm?''

The Trader said, "I have prepared a presentation for the entire Starship, but I must show it to you first, Explorer—with deep respect and with apologies for masked thoughts.   You were right.   There *was* something strange about this planet. Though the intelligences on the planet were barely first level and though their technology was primitive in the extreme, they had developed a concept we have never had and one that, to my knowledge, we have never encountered on any other world.''

The Captain said, uneasily, "I cannot imagine what it might be.''   He was quite aware that Traders sometimes overpraised their purchases to magnify their own worth.

The Explorer said nothing.   He was the more uneasy of the two.

The Trader said, "It is a form of visual art.''

"Playing with color?'' asked the Captain.

"And shape—but to most startling effect.''   He had arranged the holographic projector.   "Observe!''

In the viewing space before them, a herd of animals appeared: bulky, shaggy, two-horned, four-legged.   They hesitated, then ran, dust spurting up beneath their hooves.

"Ugly objects,'' muttered the Captain.

The holographic recording brought the herd to a halt, clamped it down to a still. It magnified; and a single beast filled the view, its bulky head lowered, its nostrils distended.

"Observe this animal,'' said the Trader, "and now observe this artificial composition of a primitive concoction of oil and colored mineral, which we found smeared over the roof of a cave.''

There it was again!   Not quite the animal as holographed—flat, but vibrant.

"What a peculiar similarity,'' said the Captain.

"Not peculiar,'' said the Trader.   "Deliberate!   There were dozens of such figures in different poses—of different animals.   The likenesses were too detailed to be fortuitous.   Imagine the boldness of the conception—to place colors in pleasing shapes and combinations, and in such a way as to deceive the eye into thinking it is looking at a real object.   These organisms have devised an art that represents reality.   It is representational art, as I suppose we might call it.

"And that's not all.   We found it done in three dimensions also."   The Trader produced an array of small figures in grey stone and in faintly-yellow bone.   "These are clearly intended to represent themselves."

The Captain seemed stupefied.   "Did you see these manufactured?"

"No, that I did not, Captain.   One of my men saw a planetary being smearing color on one of the cave representations, but these we found already formed.   Still, no other explanation is possible than that they were deliberately shaped.   These objects could not have assumed these shapes by chance processes."

The Captain said, "These are curious, but one doesn't follow the motive.   Would not holographic techniques serve the purpose better—at such times as these are developed, of course?"

"These primitives have no conception that holography could someday be developed and could not wait the million years required.   Then, too, maybe holography is *not* better.   If you compare the representations with the originals you will notice that the representations are simplified and distorted in subtle ways designed to bring certain characteristics into focus.   I believe this form of art *improves* on the original in some ways and certainly has something different to say."

The Trader turned to the Explorer.   "I stand in awe at your abilities.   Can you explain how you sensed the uniqueness of this intelligence?"

The Explorer signed a negative.   "I did not suspect this at all.   It is interesting and I see its worth—although I wonder if we could ourselves properly control our colors and shapes in order to force them into such representational form.   Yet this does not match the unease within me. —What I wonder is how you came into possession of these?   What did you give in exchange?   It is *there* I see the strangeness lie."

"Well," said the Trader, "in a way you're right.   Quite strange.   I did not think I could give anything since the organisms are so primitive, but this discovery seemed too important to sacrifice without some effort.   I therefore chose from among the group of beings who formed these objects one whose mental field seemed somewhat more intense than that of the others and attempted to transfer to him a gift in exchange."

"And succeeded.   Of course," said the Explorer.

"Yes, I succeeded," said the Trader happily, failing to notice that the Explorer had made a statement and had not asked a question.   "The beings," the Trader went on, "kill such animals as they represent in color, by throwing long sticks tipped with sharpened stone.   These penetrate the hides of the animal, wound and weaken them.   They can then be killed by the beings who are individually smaller and weaker than the animal they hunt.   I pointed out that a smaller, stone-tipped stick could be hurled forward with greater force and effect and with longer range if a cord under tension were used as the mechanism of propulsion."

The Explorer said, "Such devices have been encountered among primitive intelligences which were, however, far advanced beyond these.   Paleomentalists call it a bow-and-arrow."

The Captain said, "How could the knowledge be absorbed?   It couldn't be, at this level of development."

"But it *was*.   Unmistakeably.   The response of the mental field was one of insight at almost unbearable intensity. —Surely you do not think I would have taken these art objects, were they twenty times as valuable, if I had not been convinced that I had made a return? Nothing for nothing, Captain."

The Explorer said in a low, despondent voice, "There is the strangeness. To accept."

The Captain said, "But surely, Trader, we cannot do this. They are not ready. We are harming them. They will use the bow-and-arrow to wound each other and not the beasts alone."

The Trader said, "*We* do not harm them and we *did* not harm them. What *they* do to each other and where they end as a result, a million years from now, is their concern."

The Captain and the Trader left to set up the demonstration for the Starship's company, and the Explorer said sadly in the direction in which they had gone: "But they accepted. And they flourish amid the ice. And in twenty thousand years, it will be *our* concern."

He knew they would not believe him, and he despaired.

F. PAUL WILSON

To Fill the Sea and Air

*D*uring the period in question there were two items on the interstellar market *for which supply could never equal demand. The intricate, gossamer carvings of the Vanek were one, valued because they were so subtly alien and yet so appreciable on human terms. The other was filet of chispen, a seafood delicacy with gourmet appeal all across Occupied Space. The flavor . . . how does one describe a unique gustatorial experience, or the mild euphoria that attends consumption of sixty grams or more of the filet?*

Enough to say that it was in high demand in those days. And the supply rested completely on the efforts of the individual chispen fishers on Gelk. Many a large interstellar corporation pressed to bring modern methods to the tiny planet for a more efficient harvesting of the fish, but the ruling council of Gelk forbade the intrusion of outside interests. There was a huge profit to be made and the council members intended to see that the bulk of it went into their own pockets.

from STARS FOR SALE:
An Economic History of Occupied Space
by Emmerz Fent.

Imagine the sea, smooth slate gray in predawn under a low drifting carapace of cloud. Imagine two high, impenetrable walls parallel on that sea, separated by ten times the height of a tall man, each stretching away to the horizon. Imagine a force-seven gale trapped between those walls and careening toward you, beating the sea below it to a furious lather as it comes.

Now . . . remove the walls and remove the wind. Leave the onrushing corridor of turbulent water. That was what Albie saw as he stood in the first boat.

The chispies were running. The game was on.

Albie gauged it to be a small school, probably a spur off a bigger run to the east. Good. He didn't want to hit a big run just yet. There were new men on the nets who needed blooding and a small school like the one approaching was perfect.

He signaled to his men at their posts around the net, warning them to brace for the hit. Out toward the sun stood a long dark hull, bristling amidships with monitoring equipment. Albie knew he was being watched but couldn't guess why. He didn't recognize the design and closed his right eye to get a better look with his left. The doctors had told him not to do that. If he had to favor one of his eyes, let it be the artificial one.   But he couldn't get used to it—everything always looked grainy, despite the fact that it was the best money could buy.   At least he could see.   And if he ever decided on a plastic repair of the ragged scar running across his right eyebrow and orbit, only old friends would know that a chispie wing had ruined that eye.   And, of course, Albie would know.   He bore the chispies no animosity, though.   No Ahab syndrome for Albie.   He was glad to be alive, glad to lose an eye instead of his head.   There were no prosthetic heads around.

Most of the experienced men on the nets wore scars or were missing bits of ears or fingers.   It was part of the game.   If they didn't want to play, they could stand on shore and let the chispies swim by unmolested.   That way they'd never get hurt.   Nor would they get those exorbitant prices people all over Occupied Space were willing to pay for filet of chispen.

Turning away from the dark, skulking hull, Albie trained both eyes on the chispies.   He leaned on the wheel and felt the old tingling in his nerve ends as the school approached.   The middle of his sixth decade was passing, the last four of them spent on this sea as a chispen fisher . . . and still the same old thrill when he saw them coming.

He was shorter than most of the men he employed; stronger, too.   His compact, muscular body was a bit flabbier now than usual, but he'd be back to fighting trim before the season was much older.   Standing straight out from his cheeks, chin, and scalp was a knotty mane of white and silver shot through with streaks of black. He had a broad, flat nose, and the skin of his face, what little could be seen, showed the ravages of his profession.   Years of long exposure to light from a star not meant to shine on human skin, light refracted down through the atmosphere and reflected up from the water, had left his dark brown skin with a texture similar to the soles of a barefoot reefclimber, and lined it to an extent that he appeared to have fallen asleep under the needle of a crazed tattooist with a penchant for black ink and a compulsion for crosshatching.   Eyes of a startling gray shone out from his face like beacons in the night.

The stripe of frothing, raging water was closer now.   Albie judged it to be about twenty meters across, so he let his scow drift westward to open the mouth of the net a little wider.   Thirty meters seaward to his right lay the anchorboat manned by Lars Zaro, the only man in the crew older than Albie.   The floats on the net trailed in a giant semi-circle between and behind them, a cul-de-sac ringed with ten scows of Albie's own design—flat-bottomed with a centerboard for greater stability—each carrying one gaff man and one freezer man.   The two new hands were on freezer duty, of course.   They had a long way to go before they could be trusted with a gaff.

Albie checked the men's positions—all twenty-six, counting himself, were set. Then he glanced again at the big ship standing out toward the horizon.   He could vaguely make out *GelkCo I* emblazoned across the stern.   He wondered why it was there.

"Incredible!   That school's heading right for him!"
"Told you."

Two men huddled before an illuminated screen in a dark room, one seated, the other leaning over his shoulder, both watching the progress of the season's first chispen run. The main body of the run was a fat, jumbled streak of light to the right of center on the screen, marking its position to seaward in the deeper part of the trench. They ignored that. It was the slim arc that had broken from the run a few kilometers northward and was now heading directly for a dot representing Albie and his crew that gripped their attention.

"How does he do it?" the seated man asked. "How does he know where they're going to be?"

"You've just asked the question we'd all like answered. Albie uses outdated methods, decrepit equipment, and catches more than anyone else on the water. The average chispen fisher brings home enough to support himself and his family; Albie is rich and the two dozen or so who work for him are living high."

"Well, we'll be putting an end to that soon enough, I guess."

"I suppose we will."

"It's almost a shame." The seated man pointed to the screen. Just look at that! The school's almost in his net! Damn! It's amazing! There's got to be a method to it!"

"There is. And after seeing this, I'm pretty sure I know what it is." But the standing man would say no more.

Albie returned his attention to the onrushing school, mentally submerging and imagining himself as one with the chispies. He saw glistening blue-white fusiform shapes darting through the water around him in tightly packed formation just below the surface. Their appearance at this point differed markedly from the slow, graceful, ray-like creatures that glide so peacefully along the seabottoms of their winter spawning grounds to the south or the summer feeding grounds to the north. With their triangular wings spread wide and gently undulating, the chispies are the picture of tranquility at the extremes of their habitat.

But between those extremes . . .

When fall comes after a summer of gorging at the northern shoals, the chispen wraps its barbed wings around its fattened body and becomes a living, twisting missile hurtling down the twelve hundred-kilometer trench that runs along the coast of Gelk's major land mass.

The wings stay folded around the body during the entire trip. But should something bar the chispies' path—a net, for instance—the wings unfurl as they swerve and turn and loop in sudden trapped confusion. The ones who can build sufficient momentum break the surface and take to the air in a short glide to the open sea. The chispen fisher earns his hazard pay then—the sharp barbed edges of those unfurled wings cut through flesh almost as easily as air.

With the school almost upon him, Albie turned his attention to the net floats and waited. Soon it came: a sudden erratic bobbing along the far edge of the semicircle. There were always a few chispies traveling well ahead of their fellows and these were now in the net. Time to move.

"Everybody hold!" he yelled and started moving his throttle forward. He had to establish some momentum before the main body of the school hit, or else he'd never get the net closed in time.

As the white water speared into the pocket of net and boats, Albie threw the impeller control onto full forward and gripped the wheel with an intensity that bulged the muscles of his forearms.

The hit came, tugging his head back and causing the impeller to howl in protest against the sudden reverse pull.   As Albie turned his boat hard to starboard and headed for Zaro's anchorboat to complete the circle, the water within began to foam like green tea in a blender.   He was tying up to Zaro's craft when the first chispies began breaking water and zooming overhead.   But the circumscribed area was too small to allow many of them to get away like that.   Only those who managed to dart unimpeded from the deep to the surface could take to the air.   The rest thrashed and flailed their wings with furious intensity, caroming off the fibrous mesh of the net and colliding with each other as the gaffers bent to their work.

The game was on.

The boats rocked in the growing turbulence and this was when the men appreciated the added stability of centerboards on the flatbottomed scows.   Their helmets would protect their heads, the safety wires gave them reasonable protection against being pulled into the water, but if a boat capsized . . . any man going into that bath of sharp swirling seawings would be ribbon-meat before he could draw a second breath.

Albie finished securing his boat to Zaro's, then grabbed his gaff and stood erect. He didn't bother with a helmet, depending rather on forty years of experience to keep his head out of the way of airborne chispies, but made sure his safety wire was tightly clipped to the back of his belt before leaning over the water to put his gaff to work.

There was an art to the gaffing, a dynamic synthesis of speed, skill, strength, courage, agility and hand-eye coordination that took years to master.   The hook at the end of the long pole had to be driven under the scales with a cephalad thrust at a point forward of the chispen's center of gravity.   Then the creature's momentum had to be adjusted—*never* countered—into a rising arc that would allow the gaff-handler to lever it out of the water and onto the deck of his scow.   The freezer man—Zaro in Albie's case—would take it from there, using hand hooks to slide the flopping fish onto the belt that would run it through the liquid nitrogen bath and into the insulated hold below.

Albie worked steadily, rhythmically, his eyes methodically picking out the shooting shapes, gauging speed and size.   The latter was especially important: too large a fish and the pole would either break or be torn from his hands; too small and it wasn't worth the time and effort.   The best size was in the neighborhood of fifty kilos—about the weight of a pubescent human.   The meat then had body and tenderness and brought the highest price.

Wings slashed, water splashed, droplets flashed through the air and caught in Albie's beard.   Time was short.   They had to pull in as many as they could before the inevitable happened.   Insert the hook, feel the pull, lever the pole, taste the spray as the winged beastie angrily flapped the air on its way to the deck, free the hook and go back for the next.   It was the first time all year Albie had truly felt alive.

Then it happened as it always happened: the furious battering opened a weak spot in the net and the school leaked free into the sea.   That, too, was part of the game.   After a moment of breath-catching, the men hauled in the remains of the net to pick up the leftovers, the chispies too battered and bloodied by their confused and frantic companions to swim after them.

"Look at that, will you?" the seated man said.   "They broke out and now they're heading back to the main body of the run!   How do you explain that?" The standing man said nothing and the seated one looked up at him.   "You used to work for Albie, didn't you?"

A nod in the dimness.   "Once.   Years ago.   That was before I connected with GelkCo."

"Why don't you pay him a visit?   Never know . . . he might come in handy."

"I might do that—if he'll speak to me."

"Oh?   He get mad when you quit?"

"Didn't quit.   The old boy fired me."

"Hello, Albie."

Albie looked up from where he sat on the sand in a circle of his men, each with a pile of tattered net on his lap.   The sun was lowering toward the land and the newcomer was silhouetted against it, his features in shadow.   But Albie recognized him.

"Vic?   That you, Vic?"

"Yeah, Albie, it's me.   Mind if I sit down?"

"Go ahead.   Sand's free."   Albie gave the younger man a careful inspection as he made himself comfortable.   Vic had been raised a beach rat but that was hard to tell now.   A tall man in his mid-thirties, he was sleek, slim, and dark with blue eyes and even features.   The one-piece suit he wore didn't belong on the beach.   His black hair was slicked back, exposing a right ear bereft of its upper third, a physical trait acquired during his last year on the chispen nets.   Restoration would have been no problem had he desired it, but apparently he preferred to flaunt the disfigurement as a badge of sorts.   It seemed to Albie that he had broken Vic in on the nets only a few days ago, and had sacked him only yesterday.   But it had been years . . . eleven of them.

He tossed Vic a length of twine.   "Here.   Make yourself useful.   Can I trust you to do it right?"

"You never let a man forget, do you?" Vic said through an uncertain smile.

"That's because *I* don't forget!"   Albie knew there was a sharp edge on his voice; he refused to blunt it with a smile of his own.

The other men glanced at each other, frowning.   Albie's mellow temperament was legend among the fishermen up and down the coast, yet here he was, glowering and suffusing the air with palpable tension.   Only Zaro knew what lay behind the animosity.

"Time for a break, boys," Zaro said.   "We'll down a couple of ales and finish up later."

Albie never allowed dull-witted men out on the nets with him: they took the hint and walked off.

"What brings you back?" he asked when they were alone.

"That."   Vic pointed toward the ship on the horizon.

Albie kept his eyes down, concentrating on repairing the net.   "Saw it this morning.   What's *GelkCo I* mean?"

"She's owned by the GelkCo Corporation."

"So they call it *GelkCo I*?   How imaginative."

Vic shrugged and began patching a small hole in the net before him, his expression registering surprise and pleasure with the realization that his hands still knew what to do.

"The Council of Advisors put GelkCo together so the planet could deal on the interstellar market as a corporation."

"Since when do you work for the C. of A.?"

"Since my fishing career came to an abrupt halt eleven years ago."   His eyes sought Albie's but couldn't find them.   "I went into civil service then.   Been on a research and development panel for the Council."

"Civil service, eh?"   Albie squinted against the reddening light.   "So now you get taxes put *into* your pay instead of taken out."

Vic was visibly stung by the remark.   "Not fair, Albie.   I earn my pay."

"And what's this corporation supposed to sell?" Albie said, ignoring the protest.

"Filet of chispen."

Albie smiled for the first time.   "Oh, really?   You mean they've still got chispies on their minds?"

"That's *all* they've got on their minds!   And since I spent a good number of years with the best chispen fisher there is, it seemed natural that I be put in charge of developing the chispen as a major export."

"And that ship's going to do it?"

"It has to!" Vic said emphatically.   "It must.   Everything else was tried before they came to me—"

"They came to me first."

"I know."   Vic could not suppress a smile.   "And your suggestions were recorded as not only obscene, but physically impossible as well!"

"That's because they really aren't interested in anything about those fish beyond the price per kilo."

"Perhaps you're right, Albie.   But that boat out there is unique and it's going to make you obsolete.   You won't get hurt financially, I know.   You could've retired years ago . . . and should have.   Your methods have seen their day.   That ship's going to bring this industry up to date."

"Obsolete!"   The word escaped behind a grunt of disgust.   Albie seriously doubted the C. of A.'s ability to render anything obsolete . . . except maybe efficiency and clear thinking. For the past few years he had been keeping a careful eye on the Council's abortive probes into the chispen industry, had watched with amusement as it tried every means imaginable to obtain a large supply of chispen filet short of actually going out and catching the fish.

The chispies, of course, refused to cooperate, persisting in migratory habits that strictly limited their availability. They spawned in the southern gulf during the winter and fattened themselves on the northern feeding shoals during the summer, and were too widely dispersed at those two locales to be caught in any significant numbers. Every spring they grouped and ran north but were too lean and fibrous from a winter of mating, fertilizing and hatching their eggs.

Only in the fall, after a full summer of feasting on the abundant bait fish and bottom weed indigenous to their feeding grounds, were they right for eating, and grouped enough to make it commercially feasible to go after them. But Gelk's Council of Advisors was convinced there existed an easier way to obtain the filet than casting nets on the water. It decided to raise chispen just like any other feed animal. But chispies are stubborn. They won't breed in captivity, nor will they feed in captivity. This held true not only for adult fish captured in the wild, but for eggs hatched and raised in captivity, and even for chispen clones.

The Council moved on to tissue cultures of the filet but the resultant meat was said to be nauseating.

It eventually became evident to even the most dunderheaded member of the Council that there weren't going to be any shortcuts here. The appeal of chispen filet was the culmination of myriad environmental factors: the semi-annual runs along the coast gave the meat body and texture; the temperature, water quality, and bottom weed found only on their traditional feeding shoals gave it the unique euphorogenic flavor that made it such a delicacy.

No, there was only one way to supply the discriminating palates of Occupied Space with filet of chispen, and that was to go out on the sea and catch them during the fall runs. They had to be pulled out of the sea and flash-frozen alive before an intestinal enzyme washed a foul odor into the bloodstream and ruined the meat. No shortcuts. No easy way out.

"I didn't come to gloat, Albie. And I mean you no ill will. In fact, I may be able to offer you a job."

"And how could a lowly old gaffer help out on a monstrosity like that?" He turned back to his net repair.

"By bringing fish into it."

Albie glanced up briefly, then down again. He said nothing.

"You can't fool me, Albie. Maybe all the rest, but not me. I used to watch you . . . used to see you talking to those fish, bringing them right into the net."

"You think I'm a psi or something?" The voice had laughter all around the edges.

"I *know* it! And what I saw on the tracking screen this morning proves it!"

"Crazy."

"No. You're a psi! Maybe you don't even know it, but you've got some sort of influence over those fish. You call them somehow and they come running. That's why you're the best.''

"You'll never understand, will you. It's—''

"But I do understand! You're a psi who talks to fish!''

Albie's dark lids eclipsed his eyes until only slim crescents of light gray remained.

"Then why,'' he said in a low voice, "did I have such a rotten season eleven years ago? Why did I have to fire the best first mate I ever had? If I'm a psi, why couldn't I call the chispies into the net that season? Why?''

Vic was silent, keeping his eyes focused on the dark ship off shore. As he waited for an answer, Albie was pulled pastward to the last time the two of them had spoken.

It had been Albie's worst season since he began playing the game. After an excellent start, the numbers of chispen flowing into the freezers had declined steadily through the fall until that one day at season's end when they sat in their boats and watched the final schools race by, free and out of reach.

That was the day Albie hauled in the net out there on the water and personally gave it a close inspection, actually cutting off samples of net twine and unraveling them. What he found within sent him into a rage.

The first mate, a young man named Vic who was wearing a bandage on his right ear, admitted to replacing the usual twine with fiber-wrapped wire. As Albie approached him in a menacing half-crouch, he explained quickly that he thought too many fish had been getting away. He figured the daily yield could be doubled if they reinforced the net with something stronger than plain twine. He knew Albie had only one hard and fast rule among his crew and that was to repair the net exclusively with the materials Albie provided—no exceptions. So Vic opted for stealth, intending to reveal his ploy at season's end when they were all richer from the extra fish they had caught.

Albie threw Vic into the sea that day and made him swim home. Then he cut the floats off the net and let it sink to the bottom. Since that day he had made a practice of being present whenever the net was repaired.

A long time passed before Albie started feeling like himself again. Vic had been in his crew for six years. Albie had taken him on as a nineteen-year-old boy and had watched him mature to a man on the nets. He was a natural. Raised along the coast and as much at home on the sea as he was on land, he was soon a consummate gaffer and quickly rose to be the youngest first mate Albie had ever had. He watched over Vic, worried about him, bled with him when a chispie wing took a piece of his ear, and seriously considered taking him in as a partner after a few more years. Childless after a lifelong marriage to the sea, Albie felt he had found a son in Vic.

And so it was with the anger of a parent betrayed by one of his own that Albie banished Vic from his boats. He had lived with the anguish of that day ever since.

"There's lots of things I can't explain about that season,'' Vic said. "But I still think you're a psi, and maybe you could help turn a big catch into an even bigger one. If you want to play coy, that's your business. But at least come out and see the boat. I had a lot to do with the design.''

"What's in this for you, Vic? Money?"

He nodded. "Lots of it. And a place on the Council of Advisors."

"That's if everything goes according to plan. What if it fails?"

"Then I'm through. But that's not a realistic concern. It's not going to be a question of failure or success, just a question of *how* successful." He turned to Albie. "Coming out tomorrow?"

Albie's curiosity was piqued. He was debating whether or not to let Zaro take charge of the catch tomorrow . . . he'd do an adequate job . . . and it was early in the season. . . . "When?"

"Mid-morning will be all right. The scanners have picked up a good-sized run up at the shoals. It's on its way down and should be here by midday."

"Expect me."

A hundred meters wide and at least three times as long: those were Albie's estimates. The ship was like nothing he had ever seen or imagined . . . a single huge empty container, forty-five or fifty meters deep, tapered at the forward end, and covered over with a heavy wire mesh. Albie and Vic stood in a tiny pod on the port rim that housed the control room and crew quarters.

"And this is supposed to make me obsolete?"

"Afraid so." Vic's nod was slow and deliberate. "She's been ready since spring. We've tested and retested—but without chispies. This'll be her christening, her first blooding." He pointed to the yellow streak creeping down the center of the scanning screen. "And that's going to do it."

Albie noticed a spur off the central streak that appeared to be moving toward a dot at the left edge of the screen.

"My, my!" he said with a dry smile. "Look at those chispies heading for my boats—even without me there to invite them in."

A puzzled expression flitted briefly across Vic's features, then he turned and opened the hatch to the outside.

"Let's go up front. They should be in sight now."

Under a high white sun in a cloudless sky, the two men trod the narrow catwalk forward along the port rim. They stopped at a small observation deck where the hull began to taper to a point. Ahead on the cobalt sea, a swath of angry white water, eighty meters wide, charged unswervingly toward the hollow ship. A good sized run—Albie had seen bigger, but this was certainly a huge load of fish.

"How many of those you figure on catching?"

"Most of them."

Albie's tone was dubious. "I'll believe that when I see it. But let's suppose you do catch most of them—you realize what'll happen to the price of filet when you dump that much on the market at once?"

"It will drop, of course," Vic replied. "But only temporarily, and never below a profitable level. Don't worry: the Council has it all programmed. The lower price will act to expand the market by inducing more people to take advantage of the bargain and try it. And once you've tried filet of chispen. . . ." He didn't bother to complete the thought.

"Got it all figured out, eh?"

"Down to the last minute detail. When this ship proves itself, we'll start construction on more. By next season there'll be a whole fleet lying in wait for the chispies."

"And what will that kind of harvesting do to them? You'll be thinning them out . . . maybe too much. That's not how the game's played, Vic. We could end up with no chispies at all some day."

"We'll only be taking the bigger ones."

"The little guys need those bigger ones for protection."

Vic held up a hand. "Wait and see. It's almost time." He signaled to the control pod. "Watch."

Water began to rush into the hold as the prow split along its seam and fanned open into a giant scooplike funnel; the aft panel split vertically down the middle and each half swung out to the rear. The ship, reduced now to a huge open tube with neither prow nor stern, began to sink.

Albie experienced an instant of alarm but refused to show it. All this was obviously part of the process. When the hull was immersed to two-thirds of its depth, the descent stopped.

Vic pointed aft. "There's a heavy metal grid back there to let the immature chispies through. But there'll be no escape for the big ones. In effect, what we're doing here is putting a huge, tear-proof net across the path of a major run, something no one's dared to do before. With the old methods, a run like this would make chowder out of anything that tried to stop it."

"How do you know they won't just go around you?"

"You know as well as I do, Albie, these big runs don't change course for anything. We'll sit here, half-sunk in the water, and they'll run right into the hold there; they'll get caught up against the aft grid, and before they can turn around, the prow will close up tight and they're ours. The mesh on top keeps them from flying out."

Albie noticed Vic visibly puffing with pride as he spoke, and couldn't resist one small puncture: "Looks to me like all you've got here is an oversized, motorized seining scoop."

Vic blinked, swallowed, then went on talking after a brief hesitation. "When they're locked in, we start to circulate water through the hold to keep them alive while we head for a plant up the coast where they'll be flash-frozen and processed."

"All you need is some cooperation from the fish."

Vic pointed ahead. "I don't think that'll be a problem. The run's coming right for us."

Albie looked from the bright anticipation in Vic's face to the ship sitting silent and open-mawed, to the onrushing horde of finned fury. He knew what was going to happen next but didn't have the heart to say it. Vic would have to learn for himself.

The stars were beginning to poke through the sky's growing blackness. Only a faint, fading glow on the western horizon remained to mark the sun's passing. None of the moons was rising yet.

With the waves washing over his feet, Albie stood and watched the autumn aurora begin to shimmer over the sea. The cool prevailing breeze carried smoke from his after-dinner pipe away toward the land. Darkness expanded slowly and was almost complete when he heard the voice.

"Why'd you do it, Albie?"

It wasn't necessary to turn around. He knew the voice, but had not anticipated the fury he sensed caged behind it.

"Didn't do a thing, Vic." He kept his eyes on the faint, wavering flashes of the aurora, his own voice calm.

"You diverted those fish!"

"That's what you'd like to believe, I'm sure, but that's not the way it is."

The run had been almost on top of them. The few strays that always travel in the lead had entered the hold and slammed into the grate at the other end. Then the run disappeared. The white water evaporated and the sea became quiet. In a panic, Vic had run back to the control pod where he learned from the scanner that the run had sounded to the bottom of the trench and was only now rising toward the surface . . . half a kilometer aft of the ship. Vic had said nothing, glaring only momentarily at Albie and then secluding himself in his quarters for the rest of the day.

"It's true!" Vic's voice was edging toward a scream. "I watched your lips! You were talking to those fish . . . telling them to dive!"

Albie swung around, alarmed by the slurred tones and growing hysteria in the younger man's voice. He could not make out Vic's features in the darkness, but could see the swaying outline of his body. He could also see what appeared to be a length of driftwood dangling from his right hand.

"How much've you had to drink, Vic?"

"Enough." The word was deformed by its extrusion through Vic's clenched teeth. "Enough to know I'm ruined and you're to blame."

"And what's the club for? Gonna break my head?"

"Maybe. If you don't agree to straighten out all the trouble you caused me today, I just might."

"And how do you expect me to do that?"

"By guiding the fish *into* the boat instead of under it."

"Can't do that, Vic." Albie readied himself for a dodge to one side or the other. The Vic he had known on the nets would never swing that club. But eleven years had passed . . . and this Vic was drunk. "Can't do it as I am now, and I sure as hell won't be able to do it any better with a broken head. Sorry."

There followed a long, tense, silent moment. Then two sounds came out of the darkness: one, a human cry—half sob, half scream of rage; followed by the grating thud of wood hurled against wet sand. Albie saw Vic's vague outline slump into a sitting position.

"Dammit, Albie! I trusted you! I brought you out there in good faith and you scuttled me!"

Albie stepped close to Vic and squatted down beside him. He put the bit of his pipe between his teeth. The bowl was cold but he didn't bother relighting it.

"It wasn't me, Vic.   It was the game.   That ship of yours breaks all the rules of the game."

" 'The game!' " Vic said, head down, bitterness compressing his voice.   "You've been talking about games since the day I met you.   This is no game, Albie!   This is my life . . . my future!"

"But it's a game to the chispies.   That's what most people don't understand about them.   That's why only a few of us are any good at catching them: those fish are playing a game with us."

Vic lifted his head.   "What do you take me for?"

"It's true.   Only a few of us have figured it out, and we don't talk it around. Had you stayed with me a few years longer, I might have told you if you hadn't figured it out for yourself by then.   Truth is, I'm no psi and I don't direct those fish into my net; they find their way in on their own.   If they get caught in my net, it's because they *want* to."

"You've been out on the nets too long, Albie.   Chispies can't think."

"I'm not saying they can think like you and me, but they're not just dumb hunks of filet traveling on blind instinct, either.   Maybe it only happens when they're packed tight and running, maybe they form some sort of hive-mind then that they don't have when they're spread out.   I don't know.   I don't have the words or knowledge to get across what I mean.   It's a gut feeling . . . I think they look on the net as a game, a challenge they'll accept only if we play by the rules and only if we give them a decent chance of winning."

He paused, waiting for another wisecrack from Vic, but none came.   He continued.   "They can gauge a net's strength.   Don't know how, but they do it. Maybe it's those few fish always traveling in the lead . . . if they find the net too strong, if there's no chance of them breaking out, they must send out some kind of warning and the rest of the run avoids it.   Sounds crazy, I know, but there's one inescapable fact I've learned to accept and apply, and it's made me the best: the weaker the net, the bigger the catch."

"So that's why you fired me when you found out I was repairing the nets with wire!"

"Exactly.   You were hunting for a shortcut with the chispies and there aren't any.   You made the net too strong, so they decided to play the game somewhere else.   I wound up with the worst season I ever had."

"And I wound up in the water and out of a job!"   Vic began to laugh, a humorless sound, unpleasant to hear.   "But why didn't you explain this then?"

"Why didn't you come to me when you wanted to experiment with my nets? Why didn't you go buy your own tear-proof net and try it out on your own time? I may have overreacted, but you went behind my back and betrayed my trust.   The entire crew went through pretty lean times until the next season because you broke the rules of the game!"

Vic laughed again.   "A game!   I must be drunker than I thought—it almost makes sense!"

"After forty years of hauling those winged devils out of the water, it's the only way I can make sense out of it."

"But they get caught and die, Albie!   How can that be a game for them?"

"Only a tiny portion of the run challenges me at a time, and only a small percentage of those go into the freezer.   The rest break free.   What seems like a suicide risk to us may be only a diversion to them.   Who knows what motivates them?   This is their planet, their sea, and the rules of the game are entirely up to them.   I'm just a player—one who figured out the game and became a winner."

"Then I'm a loser, I guess—the biggest damn loser ever to play."   He rose to his feet and faced out toward the running lights of the *GelkCo I* as it lay at anchor a league off shore.

"That you are," Albie said, rising beside him and trying to keep his tone as light as possible.   "You built the biggest, toughest damn net they've ever seen, one they'd never break out of . . . so they decided not to play."

Vic continued to stare out to sea, saying nothing.

"That's where you belong," Albie told him.   "You were born for the sea, like me.   You tried your hand with those stiff-legged land-roamers on the Council of Advisors and came up empty.   But you and me, we're not equipped to deal with their kind, Vic.   They change the rules as they go along, trying to get what they want by whatever means necessary.   They sucked you in, used you up, and now they're gonna toss you out.   So now's the time to get back on the water.   Get out there and play the game with the chispies.   They play hard and fast, but always by the same rules.   You can die out there, but not because they cheated."

Vic made no move, no sound.

"Vic?"

No reply.

Albie turned and walked up the dune alone.

"Albieeeeee!"

One of the dock hands came running along the jetty.   Albie had just pushed off and was following his crew into the early morning haze.   He idled his scow and waited for the man to get closer.

"Guy back at the boathouse wants to know if you need an extra hand today."

Albie held his breath.   "What's he look like?"

"I dunno," the dock hand said with a shrug.   "Tall, dark hair, a piece missing from his right—"

Albie smiled through his beard as he reversed the scow.   "Tell him to hurry . . . I haven't got all day!"

And out along the trench, the chispies moved in packs, running south and looking for sport along the way.

JAMES GUNN

Guilt

I.

*A*ll of us feel guilty. All of us have something to feel guilty about. The problem is that some of us don't feel guilty enough.—The 1996 Hearings on the Hardister Plan for Justice Reform.

Judge Meredith Nelson scanned the verdict on his bench one last time. He always tried to give the citizen the benefit of every doubt. "It is better," Sir William Blackstone wrote, "that ten guilty persons escape than one innocent suffer."

But there was no scrap of uncertainty in front of him. Intent read too high; restraint, too low. Regretfully, though with a faint thrill of power that he always felt and always tried to repress, he pushed the button on his bench marked "Execute."

II.

Guilt is the special form of anxiety experienced by humans-in-society, the warning tension of life principles violated, of conditions of human social existence transgressed, of socio-spiritual reality ignored or affronted, of God alienated, of self being destroyed—Edward V. Stein.

Patricia Williams stopped with the spoonful of mock-turtle soup almost to her lips, like Galatea turned back to stone by an angry god. Then her hand began to shake. The soup trembled from her spoon, splashing on her white blouse in ugly dark blotches like old blood, marring the spotless tablecloth. Her face was flushed. Shudders jarred her body.

Gary Crowder stared at the woman he loved. "Pat! What's the matter?"

The spoon dropped to the bowl. She let it go as if glad to be rid of the responsibility for holding it steady. "Nothing," she said.

In the elegant room at the top of the Harlem Hotel, with its understated color panels and its broad windows revealing the lights of the city slowly turning around them, the other diners stared at Patricia.   Gary wanted to take her tender body in his arms, wanted to calm the panic of her heart, wanted to shelter her from the knowing looks of those who were her inferiors in every way.   But that would only call more attention to her condition.

"Are you having an attack?" he asked.

But he knew what the matter was.   The others in the room knew what it was, too, and he could feel them draw back, as if Patricia had been stricken by the Plague and that by distancing themselves from her they could avoid contagion. But it was a blacker plague, a moral plague.   In the great judicial buildings that towered near the foot of the island, Patricia had been found not guilty enough.

Resentment surged through Gary, despite a lifetime of suppression—resentment at a system that would inflict such agony on an innocent like Patricia.   What criminal urges could she have?   What acts of hers need be restrained?

Somehow the system had failed.

III.

A fundamental inequity in our system of justice is that the law-abiding must pay for the entire cost of the police and judicial system, as well as the punishment of the convicted.   The ideal arrangement would be an automatic monitoring system and self-punishment—The 1996 Hearings on the Hardister Plan for Justice Reform.

Times had changed since Blackstone's day, Judge Nelson thought.   Then the criminal was punishable only after he had committed a crime; even then his guilt had to be proved by the testimony of uncertain and unreliable witnesses, and in most cases some residue of doubt remained.   No wonder Sir William had been concerned about the miscarriage of justice.   In his day—why, even as recently as the twentieth century—only one criminal in ten was ever caught and only one-tenth of those were ever brought to trial.

Today the city was free of crime.   The potential criminal was detected before he had committed his criminal act, and his guilt was increased to the point where he could not do it.

His father should have lived to see this day, his big, hearty, successful father, who had been a policeman back in the days when there still had been a need for men to stop crime or arrest criminals, his father who had died in the street facing a mob who had been throwing bottles and stones.

Nelson could not imagine living in a city where footpads lurked in every dark corner, where harlots brazenly walked the streets, where rapists waited for decent women, where thieves looted homes at will, where swindlers misused positions of trust, where bands of juvenile muggers tormented the old and the weak.

His wife and daughter could walk anywhere in the city, even at night.   It was a city without bars, and he would return to a home without locks.

Nelson pushed himself back from his bench and stood up. He felt pleased with himself, satisfied with his role in a world that handled antisocial problems so well.

IV.

If we are going to aim at the ideal system, we should try to detect the criminal before he commits his crime and stop him. We don't attempt anything like that now because we have no reliable means of detecting the intent to commit a crime and no effective means of stopping its commission. But it's our lack of ability rather than our ethics that holds us back—The 1996 Hearings on the Hardister Plan for Justice Reform.

Patricia was like a spastic, scarcely able to move without stumbling, but Gary helped her out of the sky-high restaurant, down the glass-enclosed elevator that Patricia had found so exciting on the way up, and into a taxi. All the way she had told him not to be angry, that what had happened was all right.

"I'm guilty," she kept saying. "I'm guilty."

But Gary knew it was only the guilt syndrome speaking. Every school child knew how it worked. The pituitary was ordering her adrenals to pour adrenaline into her blood stream. The adrenaline was increasing her heart action. It was taking blood from the skin and rerouting it to the brain and the muscles. It was increasing the blood-sugar level. If she had been in the jungle, her body would be ready for fight or flight.

It was the guilt syndrome, a warning that every time she thought about committing a crime she would feel like this again.

Gary told the taxi Patricia's address, enunciating clearly so that there would be no mistake. He didn't dare get into the taxi himself because his anger was running too high.

What had happened to Patricia was all wrong. She was not the kind of person who would even consider committing a crime; she was too good, too innocent for that. Gary knew it. He also knew that if he entered the taxi his anger might be reported to the Department of Justice.

No one was sure where the readings were taken. Everything else was revealed about the system but that. Inevitably, then, suspicion fell on every enclosed space that might conceal an encephalograph, a sphygmomanometer, a polygraph, or any of the more advanced devices that singly or in combination detected and analyzed emotional and mental states.

Detection might lie anywhere, in subways, elevators (had it been a mistake to use the elevator down from the restaurant?), telephone booths, even hair dryers, circumsenses, or door knobs. All of them, or none. Perhaps it was all done by light or air; maybe it came out of the sky like the finger of God.

Whatever it was, he couldn't take the chance that he might be stopped before he could correct the injustice that had been done to the girl he wanted to marry,

whom he wanted to make happy, whom he wanted to protect from fear and uncertainty.

The evening had started so hopefully.   After dinner in the most expensive place
he could afford he was going to tell her about his promotion to first supervisor.
Then could come the proposal.   And after that, he had day-dreamed, in his apartment or hers, the night-long ecstasy of excitation and fulfillment.   She could no
longer put him off—he did not resent it; it was by this he knew her innocence, her
desirability—she would no longer have a reason.

He knew her well enough to be sure she was thinking about the same thing,
though her dreams were spiced with the thrill of the forbidden.

V.

Guilt is the most important problem in the evolution of culture—Sigmund Freud.

Judge Nelson was only an average-sized man, just about six feet tall.   He was
much smaller than his big, blueclad father had been, but there was scarcely room
for him to stretch in the cubicle he occupied six hours a day, every other day.   It
was pleasant enough, with its soothing, color-varied walls, but not big.   It was
sufficient for the work he had to do; justice needed no larger sphere than this.

The little room held all he needed: a comfortable chair, the bench that gave him
the readings from the computer when he pressed the button marked CASE, and the
three buttons clustered beneath his right hand—EXECUTE, PROBATION, and DIS-
MISS—that symbolized the discretionary part of his work.

For this he bore the title of "Judge."   It was an honorable title, with a long
and noble tradition, and he would do nothing to diminish it.

Actually, the only button on his bench that looked at all used—part of the white,
incised lettering had been worn away—was the one marked "execute."   That
bothered him sometimes, but then he told himself that the computer put a case on
a judge's docket only when it was ready for action.   The system provided for
human judgment; no case could be decided merely by machine response.   Every
few days a case would appear—almost as if to test the alertness of the judge—in
which the readings seemed ambiguous or marginal.   The probation button sent
such cases back into memory for further investigation.   Seldom was there the kind
of clear error that called for dismissal.

But it had happened, and Nelson was determined to mete out justice.   He
remembered Reinhold Neibuhr's wisdom: "Man's capacity for justice makes democracy possible, but man's inclination to injustice makes democracy necessary."

Who knew what decisions were reached by the judges on the other shifts; some,
even, who occupied this room, whose fingers rested upon these buttons?   Certainly
Nelson didn't know.   He didn't want to know.   From casual conversations in the
judges' lounge, however, he had the feeling that he was more lenient—more careful
was how he thought of it—than some others.   Some, he thought, a bit scornfully
and perhaps unkindly, were mere button-pushers.

VI.

How can we punish a person for what he has not done, some of you ask?
The answer is simple: the prevention of crime is no more a punishment than the
discipline of a child to prevent harm to himself or others is cruelty.—The 1996
Hearings on the Hardister Plan for Justice Reform.

Gary looked toward the Tower of Justice, distant at the foot of the island but
clearly visible against the night sky.   It stabbed upward, tall, slender, bathed in
white light from base to spire.   Once he had thought it the symbol of justice
untouched by human passions, above the petty concerns of mortals; clean, unsullied,
humanity's finger straining like Adam's toward God.   Now it seemed more like
a straightened question mark, struggling to regain its crouch.

The Tower was a good ten kilometers away, and he had to traverse that distance
all on foot.   It would have been more sensible, he knew, to have gone home, to
have slept his anger away, and to have set about correcting the injustice to Patricia
tomorrow when he was calmer.   But he didn't care.   Perhaps tomorrow his courage
would leak away.   Tomorrow the Department of Justice might monitor his emotional condition and lay on him an inhibiting load of guilt.   If he waited he might
never act.

His sister Wylene, had she lived, would have been Patricia's age.   He squared
his shoulders, fanned the flames of his indignation, and set out down the island
across territory he had seldom traveled by foot.

VII.

If we could know with absolute certainty that a person intends to commit a crime
and will do it, given the opportunity, and if we could stop it, who among us
would say, "First let him break the law, first let him steal or rape or murder,
then we will punish him."?   The person who would let the crime occur would
be a monster.—The 1996 Hearings on the Hardister Plan for Justice Reform.

Judge Nelson turned toward the door of his courtroom as his fourth-shift replacement entered.   The man was dark, undersized, surly, and, as usual, ten
minutes late.   His name was Kassel, and Nelson knew no more about him.   Nelson
chose his friends as carefully as he performed his duties, and he had few friends
in the Department of Justice.   The work he did every other day was difficult
enough; he wanted to leave it all in the courtroom.

His position carried significant prestige.   Judges were supposed to be anonymous
servants of justice, but family knew what he did, and friends.   Nelson knew he
was admired by some, respected by others, perhaps feared by a few.   It was the
work he had chosen, that he had been selected for, and he accepted it and everything
that went along with it.

The biggest part of his job was the responsibility.   Every working day he affected people's lives; he considered the evidence, reached a decision, adjusted someone's guilt to the proper level. It was a weight he bore reluctantly but well; someone had to do it, and Nelson did it better than anyone.

Now he allowed himself a rare comment on someone else's performance. "You're late," he said to Kassel as he passed the man in the doorway.

"No matter," Kassel said, glancing back under heavy eyebrows. "I'll catch up quick and then do all the cases you had left over from your shift."

Nelson feared that Kassel was one of the button-pushers. "Not if you're thorough," he said mildly.

"Don't tell me how to do my job, Nelson!" Kassel said. "If you badmouth me I'll see that you get taken care of." He threw himself into the padded chair behind the bench.

"I've had less antisocial cases than yours among those that appear on my bench," Nelson said. It was as much a departure from his judicial reserve as he could allow himself.

As he started down the hall toward the judges' lounge, Kassel shouted after him, "That's it, Nelson! I'll show you who's antisocial."

VIII.

The troubles from which the world suffers at present can, in my opinion, very largely be traced to the manifold attempts to deal with the inner sense of guiltiness, and therefore any contribution that will illuminate this particular problem will be of the greatest value.—Ernest Jones.

At 110th Street, Gary decided to take a shortcut through Central Park. Once the decision would have been reckless, a bit later, foolhardy, and a few decades after that, suicidal. Now as he skirted Harlem Meer and The Loch he passed couples strolling hand-in-hand or arms about each other, old people on park benches talking about the past, joggers improving their physical condition, sportsmen tossing frisbees in the moonlight, wild animals ambling across the meadows between air-curtain walls.

He began to hear sounds of music as he neared the Reservoir. As he rounded the curve on its western side he came upon the musicians. They were dressed in makeshift uniforms, and they were playing a mournful, syncopated kind of music that made Gary think of death and grieving, of matters left undone that should have been done, of Wylene and, strangely, of Patricia.

As he tried to move past the group, a hand caught his shoulder and pulled him into the midst of the marchers. He found a clarinet in his hands and tried to give it back. "I can't play," he said.

"Play, brother!" a black face said.

"I'm in a hurry," Gary said.

"Nobody's in that much of a hurry," the other replied, as if they were the lyrics to the music the group was playing. "Play, brother!"

Reluctantly Gary put the mouthpiece to his lips and blew into it. To his surprise music came out, and not just any music but music that fit what everybody else was playing. It was a magic instrument he held that not only made magic music but magically made him feel as if he were making it.

For the moment he lost himself in the experience. He blew and blew, and the sad, guilty music came out, and the music the others made reinforced it, lifted it, made it part of something wonderful. He marched along to the slow beat, blowing music into the air, music that talked about death and sorrow and somehow, by making them into music, eased the pain of loss, made suffering into art.

IX.

Guilt is the process by which we socialize ourselves. Guilt is the unpleasant feeling we experience when we fail to live up to our ideals. Guilt is the internalized parent who says, "Thou should have, or thou should not have!" Without guilt we would still be savages.—The 1996 Hearings on the Hardister Plan for Justice Reform.

Judge Nelson sat in the judges' lounge, sipped his after-duty drink of espresso and brandy, and quoted Blackstone to Judge Thornhill. Thornhill was an older man of sufficient distinction and maturity that Nelson felt respect for him, perhaps even a bit of the awe that others felt for Nelson. After all, Thornhill had been a judge when Nelson was only a clerk—not much more than a computer jockey. He might have known Nelson's father.

Thornhill sipped his scotch on the rocks. "Of course Blackstone had it all wrong. Today the innocent suffer. The guilty do escape. Though, indeed, he meant it differently."

Nelson looked around the pleasantly darkened lounge, seeing shadowy figures here and there but not caring who they were, as if in his courtroom he saw too much and here he could turn off his vigilance. The quiet and anonymity gave reassurance that the city and its system of justice were running smoothly. "Perhaps we shouldn't stretch our comparisons too far," he ventured. "The innocent do not really suffer. Their guilt is enhanced. A bit of guilt never did anyone any harm."

"Or, to quote Hardister, 'All of us feel guilty. All of us have something to feel guilty about. The problem is that some of us don't feel guilty enough.' Have you ever seen one of them when it hits them?"

"When the button is pushed?"

"Yes."

"I suppose. It's hard to miss seeing that sort of thing once in a while if one is out in public at all."

"Not a happy sight, is it?"

"A little shock," Nelson said. "It must have some effect to serve as an effective notice. It soon wears off. And the citizen is better for it."

"Than without? I wish I could believe that."

"Than if he had been allowed to commit the crime that was welling up?"

"Oh, that," Thornhill said. "Of course. It just seems to me that there's a lot of it these days."

"More than there used to be?"

"By comparison with the amount of crime."

"But there isn't any crime," Nelson said.

"Exactly. Then why all the casework? Why all the citizens we observe getting notice?"

"Even if criminal impulses have been eliminated, we still find antisocial tendencies—"

"That isn't our job. Our job is to prevent crime, not to repress legitimate emotions, not to fine-tune society. How much honest dissent are we suppressing? How much variation in human response are we leveling?"

"I've always said," Nelson agreed, "that there are too many button-pushers."

"It's not that either." Thornhill drained his glass. "The cases come to us with little room for discretion. We're all button-pushers, when it comes to that. Sometimes I think our role is ornamental."

Nelson bristled a bit in spite of his respect for Thornhill. "It isn't as if guilt were bad. Actually we're in remarkably good shape as human history goes. No crime. No poverty. No human misery. Art is flourishing. . . ."

"Art is one of the few areas where emotions can be expressed safely, without fear of repression," Thornhill said gloomily. "Besides, art feeds on neurosis. We push things down in one place, and they spring up in another."

He put down his glass, got up slowly, and, nodding at Nelson, left the lounge. Nelson stared after the old man. He must be due for retirement soon, never having served as an appellate judge, much less a member of the Review Board. No wonder he sounded a little querulous.

X.

Out of guilt comes hope. Guilt holds up for us an ideal state that has not yet been realized; because of that ideal we are able to endure present inadequacies and the pain they cause. Excessive guilt is an overwhelming pain that makes even future bliss inadequate; insufficient guilt stems from an inability to imagine a better future.—The 1996 Hearings on the Hardister Plan for Justice Reform.

Columbus Circle was filled with an outdoor sculpture exhibition. Strange shapes fashioned out of rubber or plastic had been inflated to float in the air or bob along the ground; others changed their shapes or colors, and some emitted serpentine hisses, beastly groans, or half-human sighs. Even stranger-looking creations were fashioned out of plastic, extruded or shaped by flame or knife. A gigantic piece of ice was being carved by a woman wielding a blowtorch no bigger than a cigarette lighter into something grotesque but compelling.

Almost every piece of art moved Gary in ways that he could not explain.   They crouched.   They loomed.   They moved ponderously or swayed ominously.   They were the figures out of nightmares or the demons one pushes into the back of one's mind, out of sight, where no one will suspect their existence, where the omnipresent instruments of the Department of Justice can never find them.

Gary ducked and weaved his way through the exhibition trying not to think about the objects he was moving among or the feelings they inspired in him.   He was almost to the other side when he felt a strong hand on his arm.   He looked in annoyance into a stranger's cheerful, sweating face.   "Come along," the stranger said, "you're drafted."

"I'm busy," Gary said, and tried to pull away.

"Come along," the other said, undeterred.   "This is living sculpture.   Be part of it!"

Protesting, Gary was dragged to a spot where living men and women stood in unusual poses among white foam people.   All of them—meat creatures and foam things—were pointing in seeming horror at an empty platform; it was like a game of statue played in a wax museum.   Then, as the sculptor drew Gary through the group, the platform was empty no longer.   Gary was standing on it.

The sculptor pressed a white, foam figure into his arm and placed a knife in Gary's other hand.   Then Gary felt the hands of the sculptor on his body shaping him into position as if he were just some other kind of plastic material.

Gary looked around him, unable to understand what was happening.   The crowd that surrounded the platform was pointing at him.   The crowd was pointing at him!   He felt uneasy, disturbed, guilty.   It was like a nightmare.   He had nothing to feel guilty about.   He wanted to shout at them, "I haven't done anything!" But he choked it back and looked away, turned his eyes down.

The foam figure in his arms had been shaped into the form of a woman.   Her head was thrown back, her body was arched away from him, or perhaps from the threat of the knife in his hand.   He could see only her chin and the long sweep of her throat and the upthrust cones of her plastic breasts.

"Go on," someone said.   "Do it!"

Gary looked toward the voice.   There was a man where the voice had spoken; he was motioning with his hands.   Gary recognized him almost immediately.   The sculptor.

"It's all right," the sculptor said.   "It's art."

The real people and the plastic people were pointing.   He looked back and forth between them and the sculptor, and then down at the figure in his arms, dreading the knife, yet asking for it, begging for it.

"Do it!" the voice urged.   "It's art.   Not real.   No one can call you to account! It's all right to feel things!   You can do it and no one can demand justice!"

To be accused and to commit no crime.   It was like what had happened to Patricia, or Wylene.   Rage rose in Gary's throat.   Desire made his arm tremble. A sense of power surged through his body.   The world turned glittery.   He drove in the blade.   Again and again he struck, feeling the blade plunge through brief surface resistance and then slickly up to the hilt.

And the figure in his arms moved. He felt it move, and horror swept through his body, occupying all the places the feeling of power had existed. He held up his hand. It was shaking. The movement flipped red drops from the blade. The white bosom he held in his arm was red with something spurting through a multitude of cuts, and the body was moving, coming apart in his arms, crumbling, falling in bits of plastic onto the platform, and Gary turned and ran, dropping the knife, pushing his way through the pointing figures. . . .

XI.

Injustice is relatively easy to bear; what stings is justice.—Henry Mencken.

Judge Nelson was already halfway from the elevator to the great doors of the Tower of Justice, past the massive central figure of Justice covering her eyes with one hand while the other pressed a button on the bench in front of her, when a clerk clattered across the floor behind him. "Judge Nelson!" Nelson turned and waited until the young man caught up with him.

"Judge Nelson!" the clerk repeated breathlessly. "I'm glad I caught you. The Review Board wants to see you."

"Now?" Nelson asked.

"Yes, sir. Before you leave."

Nelson thought about the pleasant walk home he had been anticipating, the welcome from his wife, who always waited up for him no matter how late his shift, the moment he allowed himself to look down upon the face of his sleeping daughter, secure in her bed because of the work he did. And he shrugged and returned to the elevator with the blond-haired young man. The clerk seemed relieved and talkative now that his mission had been accomplished, and Nelson responded to his remarks absently, thinking it had not been so many years ago since he had been young and breathless like this clerk, wondering what challenges and fulfillments the future would bring.

It had brought satisfaction, though never moments as exciting as the promise when he had been named to the bench. Well, it was part of growing up to seek maturer gratifications and not to surrender to vain regrets or idle speculations, such as why the Review Board wanted to see him.

XII.

Guilt gives us ourselves, a sense of what we are as individuals measured against some social ideal; it gives us not only freedom but the possibility of transcending the self.—The 1996 Hearings on the Hardister Plan for Justice Reform.

Times Square was clean and uncluttered. All the tawdry little shops had been replaced by handicraft and art stores, with imaginative displays and bright little signs.   The garishness was gone.   There was advertising, of course—but tastefully and cleverly done, even though all the men looked a bit too worldly and the women looked wholesomely attractive but as if given the chance they would be naughty, a bit like Patricia when she was most appealing.

The theater had returned to Times Square; billboards were everywhere and marquees announced new productions and revivals of old favorites.   Even the streets— now cleared of tramps, pimps, and prostitutes—had been taken over by the players.

Gary found himself in the midst of a street production of "Oedipus Rex," and, to his dismay, cast in the title role.

The actors moved around him like electronic wraiths, yet they were as solid and real to Gary as his own flesh.   He felt the emotions and the words as if they had been imprinted on his brain, as indeed they were.   To an external observer, the action of the play would have seemed a blur, but it seemed to Gary as measured as a dream; each scene, each speech, seemed precisely paced, even though the key scenes stood out from the background like van Gogh objects outlined in black.

"There is a horrid thing hid in this land," Creon said, "eating us alive.   Cast out this thing, and all will be right again."

Gary-Oedipus replied, "For my own sake, I'll see this sin cast out.   Whoever killed Laius, let the same murderous hand find me too.   Caring who killed Laius is like caring who killed my own kin."

Tiresias, the blind seer, said to him, "You sought the killer of Laius.   I tell you he stands here.   Blind, who once had eyes, beggared, who once had riches, he shall make his way across the alien earth, staff groping before him, voices around him calling, 'Behold the brother-father of his own children, the seed, the sower, and the sown, shame to his mother's blood, and to his father, son, murderer, incest-worker.' "

Later he heard himself confess, "At Pytho I asked God if I were indeed the son of Polybus, king of Corinth, and was denied an answer; instead His voice gave other answers, things of terror and desolation, that I should know my mother's body and beget shameful creatures, and spill my father's blood."

When his wife, Jocasta, was introduced to the stranger from Corinth, he heard the leader of the Chorus say, "She is his wife and mother—of his children."

And at last, with guilt and grief raging through his body, he shouted, "Enough! Everything will come true.   I have seen too much misery to see more.   I am revealed in all my sinfulness—born in sin, married in sin, killed in sin."

He stabbed out his eyes and felt the pain as if it were his own and knew it as less than the pain he felt inside.

Leaving the scene it seemed to Gary as if he were blind, feeling his way with a staff, and he heard the Chorus say, "Look, citizens.   Here comes Gary Crowder, who answered the Sphinx's riddle and became the most powerful of men; good fortune loved him, and when he passed people turned to watch him.   Now he is miserable and low.   Citizens, beware, and do not count anyone happy or fortunate until the full story is told and death finds him without pain."

Suddenly Gary was free of the street theater, free of the electronic impulses that enslaved him to actions he had never taken, emotions he had not felt, and pain he had not earned. In actual time only a few minutes had passed. The Tower of Justice was not much farther now, and he moved on toward it, unpurged.

XIII.

Guilt creates God. Out of the family unit—mother, father, child—comes guilt; and out of guilt comes God, the ultimate parent, who sets for us the highest model, the impossible goals.—The 1996 Hearings on the Hardister Plan for Justice Reform.

The Board Room was at the top of the Tower, commanding a view of the city on all sides, like the eye of God. With compulsory smoke and fume suppression, the air was as clear as the moral climate, and the visitor could see from the Battery to the Bronx, from Queens to the Palisades. Nelson had been in the room twice before, when it was open for employee tours, but then it had been day and he had not been summoned.

The judges who made up the Review Board were all elderly. They had been elevated from the ranks of the appellate judges at the time other appellate judges were retiring. When one member of the Review Board died, or became too infirm to serve, the other two members elected a third. They were, after all, in the best position to judge. They had information on all judges and cases at their fingertips.

Literally it was true. They sat behind a long bench opposite the elevator door, their backs to the windows as if disdaining another reality than the one in front of them. Each section of the bench angled to follow the curve of the outer wall so that Nelson had to stand almost clasped within the arms of the bench looking from one judge to another.

To Nelson they all looked alike. They were alike in dignity and power, even though one was a woman, small, white-haired, and wrinkled, another was tall, thin, and black, with little silver curlicues in the black wool of his hair and beard, like turnings from a metal lathe, and the third was big and tanned and dark-haired. Nelson thought that the dark hair was a wig. They were named Barington, Stokes, and Fullenwider. Nelson knew them by their pictures. But there was something particularly familiar about Fullenwider.

Judge Stokes sat in the middle. "Judge Nelson?" he asked.

"Yes, sir."

"We have received complaints about your work."

"From the appellate division?" Nelson asked. He could not keep surprise from his voice.

"Not from the appellate division," Judge Barington said. Her voice was surprisingly big and strong. "Your judgments are seldom appealed."

"That in itself raises questions," Judge Stokes said. "Too few appeals suggests excessive leniency, just as too many suggests excessive severity."

"But what we are chiefly concerned about is the amount of your work, not the quality," Judge Barington said. "There have been complaints."

"By whom?" Nelson asked, though he thought he knew.

"That is irrelevant," Judge Stokes said.

Nelson wondered why Judge Fullenwider didn't say anything, and why he looked familiar.

"The evidence is available from the computer," Judge Stokes was saying. Nelson had missed something but perhaps it didn't matter; he couldn't believe he was standing here listening to his life being reduced to numbers. "You have the lowest case load of anyone in this jurisdiction. You are thirty per cent below the average."

Nelson struggled to remain calm, to behave the way a judge should behave. "Perhaps I'm more careful than the others," he said. In spite of his efforts, alarm was fluttering in his throat.

"If you don't handle your share of the cases, the work load increases for everyone else," Judge Barington said.

"A judge must make judgments," Nelson responded automatically, glad that he could pull these phrases out of past conversations, that he did not have to think. "That takes time."

"Nonsense!" Judge Stokes said. "The work isn't that difficult. 'All of us are guilty.' "

"Indecision can disqualify you from the exercise of your authority," Judge Barington said. "You can be removed by a vote of this Board if it finds you incapable of performing your duties."

"I know," Nelson said. It had come to this. "But surely there are more serious faults. I know some judges who no longer even have faith in what they're doing."

Judge Fullenwider spoke for the first time. "Who?"

Nelson hesitated, the puzzling familiarity still bothering him. "I don't know any names. One hears things. One puts things together."

Judge Fullenwider shrugged. "If there is disloyalty, if there is lack of faith, it will reveal itself. For now you are warned. Get your case load up to the average. You will not receive a second warning."

Now Nelson knew why Judge Fullenwider looked familiar. He looked the way he remembered his father. If he had been dressed in blue, with a cap on his head, the resemblance would have sent Nelson to his knees. Instead, he only nodded numbly and turned to the elevator.

On the way down to the lobby he thought, I'll have to be faster. I'll have to turn into a button-pusher like the others.

That made him feel worse. At least, he told himself, I didn't name anybody when they asked. But he knew he would have named Thornhill if his father—if Fullenwider has pressed him, and that was just as bad.

XIV.

Of all manifestations of power, restraint impresses men most.—Thucydides.

Gary Crowder was coming out of the appeal booth when Judge Nelson emerged from the elevator. Both looked shaken.

Gary stopped Nelson with a hand upraised in his path. "Are you a judge?"

Nelson frowned. The lobby was public territory but he cherished his anonymity, now more than ever, when his judgment, his professional conduct, had been questioned and his future was in the hands of others. "Yes," he said reluctantly.

Gary brought his hand forward to grasp Nelson's arm. "I've been trying to appeal a judgment," he said, "but they say I can't."

"They?" Nelson repeated. He was still thinking about the Review Board.

"The appeal booth there." Gary motioned with his free hand.

Nelson freed his arm with an impatient jerk of his shoulder and looked where Gary pointed. The glass-sided appeal booth, open and honest, was connected directly to the computer. It should accept an appeal automatically and refer it to the appellate court. "What did you say?" he asked, as something in the young man's babbling suddenly made sense.

"They said I couldn't appeal someone else's case," Gary repeated. "That's—"

"That's right," Nelson said, relieved of the need to act. He walked toward the door that opened into the night. Gary trotted along beside him, half-turned to look at Nelson's face. "It has to be your own case. Obviously we can't have people going around appealing anybody's case."

Gary looked ridiculous as he took a little hop to keep up. "But it's a girl!"

"Young women come under our jurisdiction, too," Nelson said with an irony that was wasted on the young man. The door opened for him, and he went out into the friendly night. Out there, where he had hoped to regain his composure and his confidence in himself, he was annoyed to discover that the young man was still with him.

"The way Patricia feels," Gary said, his voice high and tight—Nelson spotted it immediately as a symptom of adrenaline flow—"she can't appeal. Don't you see—she feels guilty? And she doesn't know what she's done."

"I assure you," Nelson said impatiently, "her case was considered carefully. The decision was justified. She had something to feel guilty about. 'All of us,' " he quoted, and felt compromised for having resorted to it, " 'have something to feel guilty about.' "

"But it's not fair," Gary said. "You don't know Wylene the way I do. You don't know how innocent she is, how pure and good. And now—"

"Wylene?" Nelson echoed.

"Did I say 'Wylene'?"

Nelson shrugged. "Wylene, Patricia. . . . I don't want to know her. The Department of Justice, in its wisdom, knows her far better than you do. You can believe that! Or not. It's immaterial to me and to the Department."

He turned away from the young man. As he turned he saw in front of him on the sidewalk the shadow of an upraised arm cast by the light from the doorway behind. It was an image out of every nightmare he ever had, and he waited for his father to strike. When the blow did not come, he turned and found the young man standing behind him, rigid, like a statue dedicated to anger.

Then the statue came to life like stone cracking. The upraised arm dropped to the young man's side, its crime unperformed.

"Young man," Nelson said, "are you all right?" But he knew what had happened. He summoned a taxi and helped the sick young man into the back seat. "Can you take care of yourself now?"

Gary nodded weakly. "I'm sorry," he said. "I shouldn't have—I'm sorry."

XV.

Guilt creates society. Without guilt society would have no ultimate power to persuade. Without society we would be barbarians—The 1966 Hearings on the Hardister Plan for Justice Reform.

In the morning Judge Nelson awoke with his heart pounding as if he had been running for many minutes. He was breathing rapidly. His muscles trembled. His hands were wet; his face was hot. He had the fading memory of a nightmare—no, not the memory but the feeling of inescapable terror, the need to flee and the inability to move.

He knew what it was. He'd had enough experience with it second-hand. Guilt. He never knew what it was for.

BARRY B. LONGYEAR

Proud Rider

Round-hoof'd, short-jointed, fetlocks shag ond long,
Broad breast, full eye, small head and nostril wide,
High crest, short ears, straight legs and passing strong,
Thin mane, thick tail, broad buttock, tender hide:
Look, what a horse should have he did not lack,
Save a proud rider on so proud a back.
                              —Shakespeare, *Venus and Adonis*

From the hills surrounding Miira, on the rutted road to Porse, four white stallions tossed their heads in unison and pranced in perfect step.   Bareback on the left lead horse, hands on hips, a glower on his face, a young boy in a brown jerkin turned his head toward the old man mounted on the left rear horse.   The old man held one hand on hip; the other held a pair of rude crutches.

"Father, we won't sell them, then.   But if we could rent them to Davvik the logger . . ."

"Silence!   No more of that!"

The boy looked forward, his glower deepening.   Noticing the hoof prints leading off the left side of the road into the sandy wastes of the desert, he pressed his left knee lightly against the horse's shoulder.   The horse and its companion wheeled left, followed by the old man's horse and its companion.   The boy turned and looked back at the mountains, crowded with great trees.   Davvik would pay four hundred movills a day for the horses.

"I know what you think, Jeda," the old man called.   "You would take them and make dray animals out of them.   Not while I live, Jeda.   Not while I live."

"Father . . ."

"Hold your tongue!"

The boy shrugged and let his horse find the path to the flats.   As the horses reached the hard sand, Jeda squeezed his knees together and his pair of mounts

615

stopped.   The old man nodded at his empty horse, and it stopped while he pulled alongside his son and called his horse to halt.

"I saw them move.   Both times I saw your knees move."

"What of it, Father?"   The boy spread his arms to encompass the desert and empty hills.   "Where is my audience?"

"No audience would sit still to watch such clumsiness."   The old man lifted his right leg up and over his mount's back.   "Help me down."

"Yes, Father."   Swinging his own leg over, the boy slid to the sand and walked to the left side of his father's horse.   He gripped his father around the waist; and the old man leaned his crutches against his horse, put both hands on his son's shoulders, and slid down.   With his crutches, the old man moved out onto the hard sand.

"The cord, Jeda."

The boy unwound a string from around his waist and handed one end to the old man.   Pulling the six-and-a-half meter cord tight, Jeda walked a circle around the old man, dragging his foot every few steps.   As the circle closed, he walked back toward the center, gathering up the string.   "What shall it be first, Father?"

"Dressage.   You need work on it."   The old man hobbled outside the ring, turned, and faced Jeda.   He watched as the four stallions pulled abreast of the ring and stood motionless.   Jeda, just as motionless, began putting the four animals through their drills.   He watched the boy closely but could detect none of the signals the boy made to the horses as they reared, wheeled, paraded, and pranced as a perfect team.   The boy needs no work on that, thought the old man; all he needs is an audience.   He's good, better than I was.   "Voltige, now Jeda!"

Jeda ran to the lead horse, leaped up and over it, falling in perfect position to jump the next stallion in line.   As the boy jumped the next horse and the next, his taut muscles standing out against his tanned skin, his father imagined the boy decked in the rider's silver-spangled tights, silver bows in the braided manes of the gleaming white stallions.   The old man had seen that once before, when he was only a boy himself, and his own father, mother, and uncle dazzled the crowd at the Great Ring in Tarzak.   Now, as the sun dipped into the horizon, Jeda began his tricks, balancing on one horse, tumbling off, then leaping to the next to balance on his hands.   He flipped from the horse's back only to land and pirouette on the next.   The old man watched Jeda's face and could tell the boy was no longer thinking of their argument.   Glowing in rapture, the boy and the stallions were one.

This is how it should always be, thought the old man.   But after a moment, he shook his head, knowing that it might never be.   Tonight the house would be quiet and sullen, until either Jeda or Zani, Jeda's mother, would begin the argument again.   The spell broken, the old man turned from the ring.

"Come, Jeda.   We go home."

Davvik turned to Zani, shrugged, and looked back at the old man, silently concentrating on his meal.   Jeda, seated on a cushion across the low table from Davvik, between Zani and the old man, shook his head and pushed the tung berries on his plate around with his finger.   Davvik leaned on the table.   "Hamid, you are unreasonable.   Look at Zani, your wife.   When will she get a new robe?"

The old man broke some cobit and dropped the two pieces of bread on his plate. "You sit at my table to insult my wife, Davvik?"

"It is not an insult, Hamid, but the truth.   Don't trust my words; look for yourself."

The old man lifted his eyes and turned to Zani.   Her robe, like Jeda's and his own, was many times patched and mended.   Her hair, still streaked with black, framed a tired face bowed in shame.   Hamid looked back at the logger.   "Miira is not a wealthy town, Davvik.   We are not the only family in patches."

"I have no patches, Hamid."   Davvik waved his hands about the room.   "No one in Miira, or anywhere on Momus for all that, need wear patches.   Not if they have any sense.   The new market centers are prospering, and my wood is bringing good prices.   Think what you could do with four hundred movills . . ."

Hamid slapped his hand on the table.   "They are liberty horses, Davvik!   They will not pull your sleds.   Never have their mouths felt a bit nor their backs a harness."   Hamid shook his head and turned back to his meal.   "What can a roustabout understand about liberty horses?"

Davvik clenched his fists and flushed red.   "And you, Great Hamid of the Miira riders, you understand, do you?"

"Yes."

"Then understand this, as well.   I am no roustabout; I am a logger—a businessman.   There are no more roustabouts, Hamid, because the circus is dead, gone, naught but a dream in an old man's brain!"

The old man pushed his plate from him, and peered through shaggy white brows at his wife and son.   Both seemed very concerned with their plates and eating utensils.   "Zani."

She looked up, not meeting his glance.   "Yes, Hamid?"

"Why have you invited this bastard son of a carnival geek to eat our bread?"

Davvik stood, his lips twitching with unspoken oaths.   Turning, he bowed toward Zani.   "I am sorry for you.   I tried, but it is no use."   He turned toward Jeda. "Boy, my offer of thirty-five coppers a day still holds.   I can use a good rider—"   He looked at Hamid.   "—to drive horses at useful work."   Bowing again, he turned from the room into the street.

Hamid turned back to his meal, but Zani clasped his arm with a fierce strength. He saw tears in her eyes.   "Old man, you asked me a question; now, you hear my answer!   I want my sons back.   That's why Davvik sat here tonight, and you shamed me.   Your son and I—we are ashamed!"

"Wife . . ."

"But whose wife will it be, Hamid?   Not yours, unless Jeda stays in this house and my three other sons come home!"   Hamid winced.   The old woman's threat was empty, but it hurt all the same.   He watched as she stood and walked into her room, pulling the curtain closed behind her.   The old man sighed and turned to look at his son.   His eyes cast down, Jeda sat holding his hands in his lap.

"And you, my son?"

Jeda shrugged one shoulder. "Am I a barker, Father, to find words when there is nothing to say?"

"You think I am wrong, then."

The boy looked up at nothing. "I don't know." He looked at Hamid, his hand on his breast. "Everything I feel agrees with you, Father." He dropped his hand shaking his head. "But everything I see agrees with Davvik. We aren't like the magicians or clowns; our act can't play the roadside fires. We need a ring."

"There are rings, Jeda. Here in Miira, the—"

"Father, to use the ring our act must draw coppers. When did the ring in Miira, or the Great Ring in Tarzak, last see riding?"

The old man shrugged. They both knew the answer. "There may be fairs, again. When I was a boy, the fairs had grand circuses."

"It has been a long time since you were a boy." Jeda placed his hand gently on the old man's arm. "Father, there will be no more fairs. The people of Momus trade differently now; there are stores, shops, markets."

"Then, why not a circus in itself? Ancient Earth had circuses that were on their own. Even the ship that put our ancestors on this planet made its way through the hundred quadrants bringing the circus to countless planets. They were wealthy."

"They had audiences, Father. Momus has been a show without an audience for almost two centuries. The people have turned to other things. We must eat."

The old man studied the boy. "You want to be a rider, don't you? You must; it is in our blood."

"Yes." Jeda withdrew his hand. "As did Micah, Taramun, and Desa, my brothers before me. But they wanted to marry, eat, provide for children. Is that wrong?"

"Bah!" The old man shook his head. "They are not riders. They are *teamsters*! They left this house." The old man made a fist, then dropped it in his lap. "They left this house. What about you, Jeda? Will you drive nags for Davvik?"

"Father, we cannot survive without an audience. The jungle acts, trapeze artists, dancing bears—where are they all now? An act like ours is not a circus; we must have many acts and an audience willing to pay to see them."

"Momus has people—"

"Father, they think they are circus people. They have already seen the show. Perhaps a circus every five or ten years to honor the old traditions, but they would not pay to keep a circus together between times. What do we do then?"

Hamid remembered the spark he had seen in the sky. "The soldiers, Jeda. There are many soldiers out there on the satellites."

Jeda shook his head. "They may not see us, Father. Great Allenby has decreed it. You know that."

"Allenby—a newsteller turned trickster!"

"The Great Ring made him our Statesman, Father. It is the law." Jeda stood and brushed the crumbs from his robe. "I must look to the horses."

Hamid nodded. "Jeda."

"Yes, Father?"

"Jeda, will you ride for Davvik?"

"I haven't decided."

The old man pulled himself to his feet with one of his crutches. "If you do, Jeda, you are welcome to remain here in my house."

Jeda nodded. "Thank you. I know it was difficult to say."

Hamid nodded and the boy went through the curtain into the street. Hobbling to the door, the old man looked after his son until he was swallowed by the dark. Listening, Hamid could make out Pinot on the other side of the fountain, singing to herself. No longer a singer, thought Hamid, but a cobit gatherer, selling roots instead of songs. His sons, no longer riders, but teamsters. And where, he thought, where are the lions, elephants, and bears? Where are those golden boys and girls who walked the highwire and flew above the sawdust from bar to bar? Where are the bands? The music and laughter gone, replaced by cheese making and pillow stuffing.

Hamid stepped through the door and looked up at the night sky. Even straining his eyes, he could not see them. "But *you* are there, and if I must move Heaven and Momus, I will have you as an audience for my son, the rider!"

In the swamps north of Arcadia, a great lizard exposed its belly to the sun and settled back in the ooze. After scraping a handful of bottom slime from below, the lizard smeared its warming belly, sighed, and dreamed of Mamoot's breadcakes. Mamoot's mother stuffed them with tung berries and coated them with thick crusts of salt. Opening one slitted eye, the lizard noted the position of the sun. Mamoot would not show at the edge of the swamp for two more hours. Seeing movement, the eye locked on a fat waterwasp and tracked it as it buzzed around closer and closer to the seemingly innocent lump of mud. Curling its tongue, the lizard tensed for the strike, then relaxed, letting its pink snake of a tongue flop from its mouth into the water. Fly away little morsel, thought the lizard. Mamoot would be angry if I spoiled my appetite.

"Stoop! Stoop!"

The lizard lifted its great head and turned in the direction of the call. It's Mamoot, thought the lizard. He is early, and I haven't finished my bath.

"Stoop! Come out here right now, you ugly moron!"

Rolling over, the lizard stood on its hind legs and began wading toward the noise.

"Stoop! Are you coming?"

"Oz, ahoot, oming!" answered the lizard.

"Coming now?"

"Oming ow!" The lizard shook its head and rolled up its tongue. Mamoot was angry already. There's no help for it but to hurry. Reaching the swampbush, the lizard pulled itself up on the spongy soil and shouldered through the underbrush.

"You better hurry, you smelly fat toad!"

The lizard pushed its way into the clearing and looked down to see Mamoot, hands on his hips, stumbing his foot in anger. Next to Mamoot was a larger version of the boy, holding some papers in one hand and his nose in the other. "Hake?"

The boy ran to the lizard and delivered a swift kick in a shin armored with thick, almost nerveless skin. "Look at you, you stinking lump! I'll give you cake, all right!
Go wash! I've brought my father to see you."

The lizard looked at the larger human with curiosity. The man pointed toward the clear watered lake, and made a show of holding his nose.

"Old."

The boy kicked the lizard again in the tail. "I don't care if it's cold, you foul-smelling slime snake! Get in there and wash!"

Imagining the icy lake water closing over its head, the lizard bent down at the shore and tested the water with its toe. A shiver ran from its toe throughout its mud-caked body. It turned back toward the boy and smiled. "Hake?"

The boy folded his arms. "You wash, Stoop! Right now!"

Stoop faced the boy, rose to its full height, and folded its arms. "Hake!"

The boy narrowed his eyes, trying to stare down the lidless lizard's gaze. After a few determined minutes of futility, the boy stamped his foot and turned to his father. "Show him, Father."

The man picked up a sack from the floor of the clearing and held it up for Stoop to see.

"Hake?"

"Yes," answered the man. "All the cake you can eat."

Stoop grinned and leaped into the water, hardly feeling the cold as it thought about the cake, a whole sack of cake. Its body clean, Stoop's head broke water as the lizard walked toward the shore. Mamoot stood on the shore soaking wet. "You, you *Stoop*, you! Look at me!"

The lizard left the water and grinned at the boy. "Hake?"

"Here, Stoop." The man held up a breadcake. "Come over here and get it."

Stoop lumbered over, took the cake from the man's hand, and sat on its hind legs to eat. Mamoot stormed over and stood next to his father. "Well, Father?"

The man looked at the papers, and then at Stoop. "It's big enough, all right. What can it do?"

"Stoop can do anything an elephant could do, and then some. I've trained him the same way you said Great Great Grandfather trained the elephants."

The man shook his head. "If we only could, Mamoot. Momus hasn't seen a great-beast act in over a century! And now, a circus." He handed one of the papers to the boy. "But look, Mamoot, we will need more than one."

Mamoot took the paper headlined **HAMID'S GREATER SHOWS. Now Organizing At The Great Ring In Tarzak. Auditions Daily.** Below the type, a parade of great Earth beasts was depicted, dressed in tassels with knobs of brass on the tips of their long white tusks. Each beast's nose curled around the tail of the beast in front of it. Mamoot held the paper out to Stoop, who took it with one hand while the other, claws extended, picked the tung-berry pits from between its teeth. The lizard shivered at the sight of the frightening Earth animals, but something stirred inside his green-armored hide at the sight of the colors, clowns, horses, and all the humans, all different sizes and shapes, stacked in tiers to be looked at while the fearsome beasts passed by.

"See the elephants, Stoop?" Mamoot jabbed the paper.

"Ssseee."

"That's our act, but we need more lizards. Smart ones; eleven more."

Stoop held the paper down so the boy could see, and poked the picture with a distended claw. "Phats ow?"

Mamoot shook his head. "No, they're all gone. The last elephant on Momus died before you were hatched."

Stoop nodded. "Or zards. Ow uch?"

"Four breadcakes a day for each lizard, but no deal unless we get eleven more."

Stoop rubbed its chin. "Ive."

"Four, and that's it!"

Stoop folded its arms and looked down its long snout at the boy. Friendship was one thing, but business was business. "Ive."

Mamoot fumed, stamped around, waved his arms, and ground his teeth. "All right! Five, you thief, but you better be back here in one hour with eleven more lizards, or no cakes for anybody!"

Stoop fell to his front legs and ran for the swamp, cutting a wide swath through the underbrush. As he hit the water, he heard Mamoot call. "Stoop!"

"Oz?" The lizard stopped in the water to listen.

"You tell 'em that everybody washes every day. You hear me?"

Stoop scratched his head and cursed himself for not holding out for six cakes. He shrugged, thinking of the spectacle of humans to be seen at the circus. In a moment, Stoop decided that the spectacle was compensation enough for the missing cake.

"You hear me, Stoop?"

"Oz," answered Stoop, "alla tie assshh." The lizard swam off in the muck, hoping to find eleven other lizards smart enough to learn to talk and perform, but not smart enough to figure out that they didn't really have to give Stoop one of their cakes every day in return for the job.

Tessia held the bar, waiting for her father, who was hanging from his knees with outstretched hands, to reach the top of his swing. As he came up, his body almost parallel with the grassy ground beneath, she pushed the bar from her. It swung down, drawing an arc through the empty air that reached its zenith at the moment her father reached the bottom of his swing, his body perpendicular to the ground. She saw herself releasing the bar, balled and somersaulting, and reaching her father, his back and arms arched to receive her, as he reached a point halfway through his outside swing. She would fall a long way, but the space was needed for the quintuple somersault. A slight breeze brushed her face, and she watched the leafy whips of the trees move. Catching the bar, she timed it and sent it back, empty.

"Good," called her father. "Wait for the perfect moment. Dead wind."

Tessia looked down, and the net as always seemed too small. But it had caught her every time she had tried the quintuple before. It was big enough. Kanta, her mother, stood beside the net, smiling. Tessia waved and looked back at the trees, which were still moving. This time I will make it, she thought, catching the bar and sending it back. In her heart, her pride at this knowledge met her pain. After she made the quintuple, the equipment would come down—the ropes, bars, stands, posts, and net sold for nothing; the family on the road as tumblers. But if I miss this time, the trapeze will stay up. We will be flyers for another day.

The wind died as the bar returned. "Wait for the next one," called her father. Tessia caught the bar and sent it back. As she pulled herself up to the high perch, she knew she could not fail on purpose. This was the moment. Kanta and Vedis both knew it; Tessia knew it. As the bar swung up, Tessia dove from the perch to meet it. Its cool weight in her hands, she used her own weight to increase the swing, heels over her head as she reached the top. As she descended, she swung her legs and body down, the gravity tugging at her cheeks.

"Ready!" Her father's voice came as if from a long distance away. As she reached the outside of her swing, using her arms to draw her shoulders well above the bar, a strange hush fell over the deserted glade. Her audience of insects, avians, and ground animals stopped to watch the golden girl in sequined blue drop down, down, swinging her legs forward. At the top of her swing, she left the bar, spinning—two, three, four, and—five! She didn't find her father's strong hands wrapped around her wrists anything remarkable. It was over. She had made the quintuple. Tears sprang to her eyes as she looked up into her father's beaming face.

"You did it, Tessia! You did it!" Vedis pulled her up and kissed her forehead.

"But it is the end, Father. Let me drop to the net."

Vedis released her at the bottom of his swing and she fell, landing in a sitting position. One bounce, then two, then she grasped the edge of the net and somersaulted over it. As she dropped to the ground, Kanta rushed to her, kissing and embracing her. Tessia hugged her mother, wishing the moment would never end. Opening her eyes, she saw an old cripple in rider's brown at the edge of the glade. Realizing that he had been seen, the old man raised a crutch in the air and waved it. "Hallo! I am Hamid of the Miira riders."

Kanta turned and looked. In seconds Vedis was down from the net standing next to his wife and daughter. "What is your business here, rider? We come here to be alone."

The old man hobbled closer and stopped next to the net. Looking at Tessia, he smiled. "I saw you, child; it was beautiful."

"Thank you, but you interrupt a moment dear to my family."

The old man looked at the three in turn, stopping on Tessia. "Child, I am here that the moment will never end."

Great Kamera leaned back from his table and clasped his hands over his large belly. The barker, in dusty red-and-purple robe, stood before him. "This thing you said in the street, barker. Repeat it."

The barker bowed deeply.   "Of course, Great Kamera, but there is a small matter . . ."

"You will be paid."

"Of course.   I never doubted—"

"Get on with it!"

"Yes, of course."   The barker grinned, exposing yellowing teeth.   "Great Kamera, I advertise auditions for the greatest show on Momus, a grand circus operated by the Great Hamid of the Miira riders."

"A rider?"

"Yes, Great Kamera.   Owner of the finest—"

"You tell me a rider will operate the shows?"

"Yes.   But as Great Kamera has undoubtedly learned through his many years, the first circus was started by a rider, Philip Astley. . . ."

"Barker, you presume to instruct me on the history of the circus?"

The barker bowed deeply.   "No, no, Great Kamera.   If I may repeat—"

"No!"   Kamera held up his hand.   "Not that.   What shows has he?"

"There will be Jeda, Hero and Great Emperor of all the horsemen, riding Hamid's own quartet of white stallions; there will be the Flying Javettes, featuring Tessia and the quintuple somersault; then, the Rhume Family and its Great Phant Lizards, featuring Mamoot and—"

"Barker.   Phant lizards?"

"A great-beast act, great Kamera, with fierce monsters whipped and driven from the swamps of Arcadia, tamed and trained by a small boy, who—"

"Go on.   What else?"

"The Great Riettas of the high wire will dazzle the crowds with its four-tiered pyramid.   Yarouze, the brave lion tamer, will put on a spectacle of daring—"

"Barker, I've never heard of any of these names.   Who are these people who pretend to bring a circus into being?"   Kamera rubbed his bald head and thought for a moment.   "In fact, I do not remember ever seeing a high-wire act before in my life.   Nor flyers, not even those lizards.   Is this some kind of joke?"

"Upon my life, Great Kamera.   The acts assemble now in the Great Ring."

"Koolis undoubtedly knows of this."

"Yes, of course.   The Master of the Great Ring has paid ten thousand movills for the privilege of exhibiting Hamid's Greater Shows."

"Koolis *paid* for the privilege, you say?"

"I arranged the contract myself."

Kamera rubbed his chin.   "Koolis parting with coppers can only mean he sees a greater amount returning."

"It is the truth, Great Kamera.   For his payment, Koolis will get a quarter of the gate."

"And, barker, I suppose Hamid, whoever he is, is looking for clowns, is he?"

"A circus is the proper setting for a clown, Great Kamera.   Do I not speak truly?"

Kamera nodded.   Years ago he had played a circus; a poor thing at one of the last fairs ever held.   It had been better; almost a spiritual experience.   "I make a good—no, an excellent living playing by myself here at the square in Tarzak. What would this Hamid pay if I condescended to lend my name and talents to his bill?''

The barker grinned and shook his head. ''The Great Kamera does not understand. Because you are master clown of Momus, Great Hamid will allow you billing for only one thousand movills.''

''I must *pay* to perform?''

''Yes.''

''That is nonsense! You said yourself, I am master clown of Momus!''

''True, true, Great Kamera.'' The barker rubbed his hands together. ''But, the star clown of Hamid's Greater Shows *will be* master clown of Momus.''

Kamera nodded. ''I see. Was Koolis swayed with similar logic?''

''Great Koolis also gets a quarter of the gate. You, Great Kamera, will get half of one percent for your coppers.''

''And Koolis gets twenty-five by paying ten?''

''Koolis also has the ring.''

''Hmmm.'' Kamera reached under his table and pulled a purse from beneath it, dropping the pouch in front of the barker. ''Before you lift those coppers, satisfy me on a point.''

''If I can, Great Kamera.''

''The circuses died on Momus for lack of an audience. Has this Hamid found an answer?''

The barker shrugged. ''Great Kamera, when I asked this same question of the Great Hamid, his answer was cryptic.''

''He does not depend on the soldiers, does he? Allenby will not allow them on the planet.''

''He only looked up, Great Kamera, and said 'an audience shall be provided.' ''

Koolis looked down at the old man sitting on the low stone wall surrounding the Great Ring. Hamid stared at the sawdust. The Master of the Ring looked at Jeda and Davvik, shrugged, and tried again. ''Hamid, I not only talked to Disus, but to Great Allenby himself. He will not be moved; the soldiers stay in the satellites.''

Hamid moved only his lips. ''Did Allenby see the parade?''

Koolis let out a sigh. ''It makes no difference.''

''If Allenby saw the parade, he could not deny the circus life.''

''Hamid, Allenby's concerns encompass the entire planet of Momus. The circus is not his entire world, as it is with us.''

''Us?''

Koolis looked offended. ''Yes, us.''

''If the circus dies, Koolis, you will still have the Great Ring. We will have nothing.''

Koolis spat in the sawdust. ''Hamid, you know nothing. I've beggared my family to give your circus a place to exist.''

''For a quarter of the gate.''

''Without an audience coming through that gate, it is twenty-five percent of nothing.'' Koolis slapped his hands against his legs. ''Without the soldiers, your circus—my ring—will be lost. It is my world, too, Hamid!''

The old man looked up and nodded. ''I owe you an apology, Koolis.'' He reached for his purse, then shrugged. ''But I owe many people for many things.''

Koolis smiled and sat next to the old rider, patting him on the knee. ''I'll put it on your account.''

Hamid looked from Koolis to his son. ''Well, Jeda, say it.''

Jeda lifted an arm, then lowered it. ''There are no coppers, Father. I see no other way.''

The old man turned to the logger. ''Well, Davvik, you get your way. The horses are yours.''

Davvik looked at his own feet, then shook his head. ''This is not what I want, Hamid. Believe me, I would rather you could keep them.'' He nodded his head at the great lizards being trained on the far side of the Ring, then up where roustabouts strung supports for the high wire and trapeze. ''But neither my wishes nor yours will feed your flyers or beasts.''

Hamid nodded. ''Take care of them, Davvik.''

Jeda walked to Hamid and placed a gentle hand on the old man's shoulder. ''I will be there, Father. I'll watch them.''

The old man looked up into his son's face. ''You go with Davvik?''

Jeda nodded. ''I'm a rider, and your circus has no horses.''

''I will pay him well, Hamid.'' Davvik put his arm around Jeda's shoulders. ''And if you can get your show going, I'll sell you back the horses.''

''Thank you, Davvik.''

The logger nodded, then turned to Jeda. ''We must go, then.''

''Goodbye, Father.''

Hamid put his hand over his son's, pressed it and nodded, his eyes closed. He felt the hand leave his shoulder and listened as the two left the Ring.

Koolis shook his head. ''After we sprinkle a few movills on our creditors, Davvik's coppers might keep us going another month—perhaps less. What then?''

''My mind is as empty as my purse, Koolis. . . .'' The old man looked up and saw a roustabout on the high-wire platform playing at stepping out on the wire. The man stumbled, but quickly caught the post behind the platform. Koolis stood and cupped his hands around his mouth.

''Break your neck, fool, and you pay your own funeral.''

Koolis turned to see Hamid hobbling off on his crutches. ''Hurry, Koolis; assemble the company. Hurry!''

Master Sergeant Levec scanned the indicators and adjusted a control with a feather touch. As the huge machine chewed through the blue-green sulphide vein, an extra drop of oil fell into the crushers dispersing a slight foam accumulation. ''You got to keep your eye on that, Balis. Too much foam can really gum up the works.''

''I apologize, Sergeant.'' Balis's hand left the control and reached for the purse beneath his lavender-and-white juggler's robe.

''Get back on that control!'' Levec shook his head as the juggler's hand sped back to the steering buttons. "Look, Balis, I thought we had a deal; you don't pay me every time you make a mistake. Just don't make it again."

"Yes, Sergeant. I got confused."

Levec caressed the cab frame he was using for support and patted it. "You'll get the hang of it. In another two weeks, the Montagnes will be back up in the satellites and you boys will be operating the pit."

Balis scanned the controls, indicators and progress track. "We are on the straight, Sergeant."

"Good. You can put it on automatic."

Balis flipped a switch, leaned back in his seat and sighed. "It seems so much to learn in two weeks."

"A little more involved than tossing around a few balls, eh Balis?" The juggler smiled, reached into his robe and produced four red spheres. Levec took them, sighed, and moved to the back of the cab for the additional headroom. A look of determination on his face, the sergeant made sure of his footing, fixed his eyes on the imaginary high point of the trajectory and began pitching the balls. His hands moved with a steady rhythm keeping no less than two balls in the air at once.

"Now, Sergeant, one hand!" Levec threw three complete cycles one-handed before he broke rhythm, dropping the balls. Balis laughed. "You'll get the hang of it."

Levec gathered up the balls and handed them to Balis. "Here."

"Keep them, Sergeant. I brought them for you."

Levec nodded. "Only to pay for your apologies, of course."

"Of course." Balis smiled. "I will miss you when the Montagnes return to the satellites."

Levec opened his utility bag and put the balls in it. Standing again, he nodded at the juggler. "Well, the Montagne must follow its orders." Levec slapped Balis on the shoulder. "But this does not mean we shall never see each other again. A detail will be down every few weeks to do maintenance."

"Still . . ."

"It's been a while. You better check the indicators." Levec turned and looked through the dusty sideport at the pit. A kilometer across and eight hundred meters deep at its lowest point, the pit resembled a great, stepped bowl. On each step a line of huge processors, connected by water, slurry, and power ducts, chewed their way around the bowl, widening it and producing copper, silver, iron, and arsenic for the satellite defense rings and orbiting bases of the military mission.

A movement in the pit caught his eye, and Levec reached to the console in front of Balis and slammed an orange panel. Power to the processors stopped. "Sergeant, what is it?"

"Something in the pit. Call it in." As Balis radioed pit control, Levec undogged the side door and stepped out on the catwalk. Far to his right, an enormous green animal was leaping down the steps of the pit. In a matter of seconds, it reached the bottom and began swimming the evil-smelling slurry pond. "Balis! Come out here and bring the monocular." As Balis came through the door, Levec took the monocular and focused on the animal in the pond. "Lookit that! Balis, I swear you can have my stripes if I've ever seen anything like that!"

Balis squinted against the sun. "It is one of the great lizards of Arcadia, Sergeant. I've never seen one out here on the desert so close to Kuumic."

"It's pulling something." Levec played the monocular back along the path the lizard had taken. "It looks like a cable or a rope. Look, at the top of the rim."

Balis took the monocular and focused on the rim. A crowd was gathered, watching the lizard. The other end of the rope appeared to be anchored to a high pole on the edge of the rim. Balis turned. On the opposite edge of the pit, another crowd was gathered. The lizard, having traversed the slurry pond, leaped up the steps to the left, still dragging the rope. As the animal disappeared over the opposite rim, the slack in the rope was taken up. Levec took the monocular and saw the rope being anchored to another high post. A figure climbed the post and stood on top, waving to the crowd. From where he stood, Levec could hear the cheers. The figure was handed a long, white pole. Balancing the pole across the rope, the figure began walking out over the pit. In moments the figure had only air between a swaying, narrow path and certain death. Levec switched to a higher powered lens and saw that the figure was a man; an old man. "Balis, who is that?"

"Sergeant, that is Great Tara of the high-wire Riettas. He is enough to make one's heart stop."

"He's so old." Balis watched Levec move and shift as the Montagne Sergeant walked the rope vicariously with the Great Tara. As he reached the center of the rope, the wind across the pit picked up and snatched at the old man's yellow robe. Levec held his breath as the old man sat down on the rope and leaned his pole into the wind. The wind gone, the old man did a backwards somersault on the rope, coming up to his feet again. He teetered for an instant, then resumed his walk above the pit. Lifetimes later, the Great Tara stood atop the anchor pole on the other side of the pit. At both ends of the rope a cheer went up, accompanied by signs, each one a letter, spelling **HAMID'S GREATER SHOWS—TARZAK**. Then the crowd was gone. Levec looked at Balis, confused. "They were all with that circus."

"Yes."

"But between Montagnes and trainees, there can't be more than twenty people here in the pit."

"True, Sergeant, but I heard that Tara put on a spectacle yesterday at the microwave relay station by climbing one of the guy wires supporting the broadcast antenna. There were only eight soldiers at the station."

Levec shook his head. "I don't know much about advertising, Balis, but it seems they're going about it the wrong way. Soldiers aren't even allowed planetside." Levec played the monocular along the rope, watching it sway in the wind. "But I sure wish I could see that show."

Balis smiled, entered the cab and pulled some flyers from his robe. In seconds he had them stuffed into Levec's utility bag.

Captain Bostany knew the perspiration running down her back was imaginary, but as she stood at strict attention before General Kahn, while he traced little circles on his command desk with a wicked-looking swagger stick, she swore her boots were filled to overflowing.

Kahn dropped the stick on his desk with a clatter, folded his hands and pursed his lips. "Let's try it one more time, Captain, shall we?"

"I . . . I await the general's pleasure."

Kahn pressed a panel on his desk causing the bulkhead behind him to part, disclosing an activated holographic command reader. "You know what this is I suppose?"

"Yessir."

Kahn smiled. "That will save some time. Captain, as you can see, the Ninth Quadrant Federation has enough hardware in orbit around Momus to destroy utterly any kind of force the Tenth Federation cares to send against us," the General held up a finger, "if, I repeat, if everything is functioning smoothly. With me?"

"Yessir."

Kahn picked up a sheaf of papers from his desk. "These are summary courts' records, Captain. As mission sociological officer, you will be interested to know that the Momus military mission has the worst petty disciplinary rate in the sector."

"Yessir."

"Captain, that includes the Quadrant bases around all three penal colonies!"

"Yessir."

"Captain, the men and women manning this mission are Montagnes, the most professionally disciplined soldiers in the Quadrant forces. This cannot go on. First, I want you to tell me why, then I want to know what you are going to do about it."

"Yessir. The positive soc—"

"So help me, Captain, if you start talking sociological parameters, biofeed responses, or negative poop loops again, I will eat your head off!"

"Well, General, it's a combination of things—that caused the disciplinary problems, that is. The analysis just completed. . . ."

"Skip that and get to what it is."

". . . ah, yessir. Well, sir, to be overly simplistic about it . . . ."

"Impossible."

". . . yessir. Well, sir, it's what we call acute environmental awareness."

"That's what you call it; what would I call it?"

"Cabin fever?"

"Go on."

"Well, sir, it's just that the isolation from the planet's surface is beginning to have neg— ah, well, sir, it's beginning to get to the troops."

"Now, Captain, we are at a point we could have reached an hour ago. Cabin fever, huh?"

"Yessir."

"I can think of maybe twenty military missions offhand that are similarly isolated for political reasons, environmental conditions, any number of reasons." The General waved the stack of papers. "None of them has this problem."

"Yessir, I mean, nossir. Everyone brought up on charges so far has undergone analysis to determine the soc— uh, to see if there is a common cause. Using that information, my department conducted additional surveys and found that the pattern extends to dependent families and civilian employees.''

''And?''

''Well, sir, it's probably a lot more complicated than it sounds. Doctor Graver, the chief of psych, says that it's probably symbolic for—''

''What is it, Captain?''

''Sir, uh . . . the personnel, they . . . want to go and see the circus.''

''Circus.''

''Yessir.''

Kahn studied an empty spot in the air until Captain Bostany had to break the silence or run screaming from the compartment. ''Sir, we traced the information about the circus to the crews operating the relay station, the open-pit mine operations . . . ''

''Momus doesn't even have a circus.''

Bostany reached into a folder and placed some papers in front of the General. ''We obtained these from the crews rotating from planetside.''

Kahn studied the flyers and shook his head. ''Captain, would you tell me why men, women, and children who have at their disposal a variety of the most sophisticated recreational facilities known to modern science, want to go see a circus?''

''Yessir,'' Bostany smiled and pulled a bound set of papers from her folder. ''I'm writing a paper on it.''

''Just *why*, Captain.''

''Yessir. Outside of actual sports activities, virtually all of our recreations are remote sensory. There is an unreality about them that leaves unfulfilled certain needs.''

''Unreality? Captain, have you ever used a fantasizer? You can climb the Matterhorn if you want, and even be frostbitten.''

''Yessir. But, before and after the experience, you know that the experience never was and that no challenge existed. Doctor Graver agrees with me that this phenomenon is actually a reach for reality.''

Kahn held up a flyer depicting a huge lizard in pink tights and tassels, holding a small, turban-wrapped boy high over its head with one hand. ''You call this reality?''

''That's what it seems to represent to the personnel.''

Kahn looked at the flyer and nodded. ''I guess it is, for Momus.'' He looked up. ''Your recommendation?''

''General, we have to let mission personnel get in some time planetside on a regular basis to see the circus, go backpacking, or just walk around and breathe fresh air.''

''You have another plan? Allenby would kill that one in a second, and you know why.''

''No other plan that is practical. Either get them planetside or replace the entire complement. We ran the sociological progressions, and visiting planetside on a rotating basis would have no adverse impact. The impact Lord Allenby fears happens only if the mission uses planetside bases.''

''Your department checked out the fortune teller's story, then?''

"Yessir; and her accuracy is uncanny, except for this.   Her recommendation was complete separation.   It's strange that she could be so accurate with one and miss so badly on the other.   But, she's hardly a computer."

Kahn snorted out a short laugh.   "Tayla the fortune teller has Allenby's ear; your computer doesn't."   Kahn reached for the communicator built into his desk. "Get me Ambassador Humphries."   He turned back to Bostany.   "Put together the best case you can, Captain.   You are about to meet the cashiered former Ambassador and present Statesman of Momus, Great Allenby, magician and news-teller."   Kahn shrugged.   "Part of that reality we're reaching for, I imagine."

While Captain Bostany explained her sociological progression tables, charts and diagrams, Allenby looked at the people seated on cushions around his table.   Am-bassador Humphries, as usual, scowled impatiently.   Seated next to the Ambas-sador, General Kahn remained properly impassive.   Across from Allenby, Hamid of the Miira riders looked at the center of the table, seeing nothing.   Next to Hamid, Tayla the fortune teller watched Bostany's performance through hooded eyes.   Bostany collected her papers and concluded: "Therefore, Lord Allenby, while the complete separation protects Momus from undesirable socio-impact, it is having an undesirable impact on the military mission.   As I have repeated, my department has determined that there will be no adverse impacts as a result of limited interaction between—"

"No!"   Tayla held up her hands, palms toward Allenby.   "I have seen what will be and what can be, Great Allenby.   I say that the soldiers must stay in the sky."

Allenby shrugged.   "Then, Ambassador Humphries, that is my answer.   The mission personnel remain off planet."

"Lord Allenby; be reasonable, man.   Captain Bostany is more than qualified to determine whether or not there will be problems from limited contact.   She has the command of the latest computerized investigation tools.   Against this, you would take the word of a spiritualist?"

"Humphries, from birth Tayla has been trained to absorb information, associate it, weigh probabilities, and project outcomes given a certain set of circumstances. There is nothing spiritual about it.   She couldn't tell you how she arrives at a particular conclusion, but I can tell you the conclusions are accurate.   I think the general can support what I say."

Kahn nodded.   "I saw Tayla observe our original occupation and defense plan of Momus, then point by point list the sociological results.   This has since been verified by Captain Bostany—that is, except the need for complete separation, as I think she has shown."

Allenby nodded at Bostany.   "Captain, I do not doubt your qualifications. However, a skilled fortune teller can do anything your computers can do, and a lot faster.   In addition, Tayla knows Momus.   There must be a factor, some seemingly unimportant fact, you failed to include.   Mission personnel will not come planetside."

"Great Allenby."   He turned to see Hamid looking at him through hazy blue eyes. The old rider's face was tired as death. "Great Allenby, I beg you. If the soldiers do not come down, the circus will die. We have been open now for only three nights, and already the tiers at the Great Ring are half-filled. The main attractions cannot continue without the soldiers."

"You have heard Tayla speak. Can I sacrifice the way of an entire planet's life for the sake of a few attractions?"

"I would ask Great Tayla a question." Hamid turned to the fortune teller. "Great Tayla, how is it that a few soldiers visiting my circus will destroy us when the ancestors of Momus, the old circus, traveled among worlds of strangers for many centuries?"

Tayla closed her eyes. "I see what I see."

Allenby stood. "Then, if there is nothing else?"

Hamid pulled himself along on his crutches until he stood in the light coming from the Great Ring. Still outside the spectators' entrance, he could not bring himself to enter. Moving to the side to stand alone in the dark, the old man listened to the music coming from within. He watched the pitifully few customers walking up and down the midway, peeking into the stalls and tents, reading the signs and listening to the barkers. The side attractions were falling off as well. But, thought Hamid, it is nothing to them. When the circus dies, they will play the squares and fires as before. But for us . . . He stood back in the entrance and for a moment watched Tessia and her parents high above the sawdust. He turned away. For us there will be no tomorrow. As a cheer erupted from the Ring, Hamid lifted his eyes to see a fortune teller's stall. Inside, a lone woman in the blue robe sat playing solitaire, unmindful of the noise and music. Hamid thought, shook his head, and thought again. It was so simple. Smacking his head, he hobbled off in the darkness.

"Great Tayla." Hamid nodded his head.

The old fortune teller squinted at him from her place at her table, then nodded. "Enter, Hamid. Be seated." The old man hobbled into the dark room, propped his crutches against the wall and lowered himself to the single cushion before Tayla's table. On the table, a single oil lamp illuminated the room. "What brings you?"

"It is your greatness that brings me."

She read the old man's eyes, disliking what she saw there. "Be clear, old rider."

Hamid nodded. "The captain fortune teller of the soldiers does not understand. I did not either."

"Understand?"

"Great Allenby spoke truly when he said you could do anything the captain's machines could do, and at greater speed." Hamid grinned. "But, our Statesman did not honor you enough."

"Get on with what you have come to say, Hamid."

"Great Tayla, you can do something the captain's machines cannot."

"Which is?"

"You can lie."

Tayla's face froze. "I told what I saw. All those soldiers and others here on Momus, they would absorb us. We, our way of life, would cease to be. It is the truth!"

Hamid nodded. "As much of it as is told. But the bases, all those soldiers, live up in the orbiting bases and stations. Our way of life is safe from them."

"No!" Tayla shook her head. "They must stay there; we can be safe only if they stay off Momus—all of them."

Hamid rubbed his chin. "Tayla, what did you see of the circus, if the soldiers only visited? You saw the circus born again, didn't you?"

Tayla closed her eyes. "I am tired, Hamid. Leave me."

"You saw it born again."

"Yes!" Tayla flinched at the loudness of her own voice. "Yes, but that only among other things . . ."

"You saw riders, high-wire walkers, flyers, great beast and jungle acts standing where they have not been for many years; center ring, main attractions . . ."

"Hamid, there is more."

"Yes, you saw more, Tayla. You saw fortune tellers tucked away in a little stall off the midway—sideshows, reading palms and leaves, telling the rubes what they would like to hear."

The old woman's eyes brimmed with tears. "Old man, Allenby will listen only to what I say."

"What if I took this to your daughter Salina? She is respected. What would her visions be? What if I took this to all the great fortune tellers on Momus? Allenby will not believe the captain, but would he believe ten, fifty, or a hundred fortune tellers?"

"They will see the same things I saw."

The old man shrugged. "Perhaps not. They are younger; perhaps they will be able to see beyond a vision of a sideshow."

Tayla laughed. "What can you tell me about what they would see, old rider?"

"I think they would see that fortune telling has changed since the days Momus was first settled. Riders, flyers, trainers, are the same as we were. But fortune telling has changed. It has grown. Great men and women of business come and sit before your table to hear the future and make their plans. You have outgrown the circus. I think they will see that."

The old woman frowned, then reached beneath her table and withdrew a clear glass sphere. She placed it on the table and adjusted the oil lamp. She sat for only a moment, staring deep within the glass, then closed her eyes and nodded. "I did not look beyond that vision. Understand my loyalty to the fortune tellers, Hamid. I saw this, and—"

"And lied!" Hamid gripped the edge of the table and pushed himself to his feet. He took his crutches, placed them under his arms and turned toward Tayla. "You will tell Allenby?"

Tayla looked into the old man's angry face.   "Yes, I will tell him."   Hamid hobbled toward the door.   "Hamid?"

He turned to face her.   "Yes?"

"I am ashamed.   But tonight in Great Allenby's quarters, I saw an old cripple prepared to destroy an entire people, just to put his son on a horse.   Is my shame any greater than his?"

Hamid looked at the old woman, then bowed his head.   "No, Great Tayla. You see better into my own heart than I do."

"It is my trade."

Hamid looked at her and smiled.   "Do I owe you for this visit?"

The old woman smiled and shook her head.   "No Hamid; I think we are even. Must you go?"

Hamid laughed.   "Yes.   I must see a man about a horse."

Allenby bid Koolis, Master of the Ring, goodbye and turned his attention to the tiers packed with Montagne soldiers, civilians and, best of all, hordes of excited, wide-eyed children.   The Ring stood brightly in the glow of eight searchlights General Kahn supplied to replace the rows of oil lamps, while from the bandstand, the musicians delivered a lusty march in preparation for the Great Parade.   Disus, Allenby's chief-of-staff, walked up and stood beside him next to the Ring.   "A marvelous spectacle, is it not?"

Allenby nodded.   "The man behind this, however, is the real marvel.   Koolis told me that Hamid began this without a movill in his purse; yet look at the acts he has assembled and the audience he has attracted."

Disus shrugged and waved an idle hand at the soldiers.   "If Hamid cannot go to the Montagne . . ."

"Don't finish that if you value your life.   See to our seats."   Grinning, Disus bowed and went off to negotiate for seating space.

Opposite the entrance, high on the last tier, an old man leaned on a crutch and surveyed the amphitheater.   Before the night's show, Koolis had stood before him shaking his head.   "Every last percentage of the gate has been exchanged for acts, food, materials, and supplies.   I keep the accounts, Hamid.   No matter the success; you will not find youself a movill richer."

"I have my reward, Koolis," he had said.

The Master of the Ring shrugged and shook his head.   "A high price to pay for sentiment, my friend."

"It is not sentiment."

"What then is your reward?   I do not understand."   Koolis left, shaking his head and fondling his fat purse.

As the Great Parade began, the old man leaned forward to see four brothers in silver-spangled tights mounted on four gleaming white stallions enter the Ring at the head of the parade.   Four brothers—whose sons and daughters will ride, and all their sons and daughters after them.

"Yes, Koolis," the old man whispered, "my fortune *is* made."